# DEPARTMENT 19
# ZERO HOUR

## WILL HILL

HarperCollins *Children's Books*

First published in hardback in Great Britain by HarperCollins *Children's Books* in 2014
This edition published by HarperCollins *Children's Books* in 2015
HarperCollins *Children's Books* is a division of HarperCollins*Publishers* Ltd,
HarperCollins*Publishers*, 1 London Bridge Street, London, SE1 9GF

Follow Will Hill on twitter
@willhillauthor

www.department19exists.com
www.facebook.com/department19exists

3

Copyright © Will Hill 2014

ISBN 978-00-0-750584-5

Will Hill asserts the moral right to be identified as the author of the work.

Typeset in Berylium by Palimpsest Book Production Limited, Falkirk, Stirlingshire
Printed and bound in England by Clays Ltd, St Ives plc

MIX
Paper from
responsible sources
FSC
www.fsc.org
FSC™ C007454

FSC™ is a non-profit international organisation established to promote
the responsible management of the world's forests. Products carrying the
FSC label are independently certified to assure consumers that they come
from forests that are managed to meet the social, economic and
ecological needs of present and future generations,
and other controlled sources.

Find out more about HarperCollins and the environment at
**www.harpercollins.co.uk/green**

For Jamie.

Thanks for changing my life. And sorry for everything I've done to you.

It would be easy to be clever

And tell the stones: Men hate to die

And have stopped dying now forever.

I think they would believe the lie.

**Robert Frost**


Surely there is some horrible doom hanging over us that every possible accident should thwart us in all we try to do.

**John Seward**

# MEMORANDUM

*From*: **Office of the Director of the Joint Intelligence Committee**

*Subject*: **Revised classifications of the British governmental departments**

*Security*: **TOP SECRET**

DEPARTMENT 1    Office of the Prime Minister

DEPARTMENT 2    Cabinet Office

DEPARTMENT 3    Home Office

DEPARTMENT 4    Foreign and Commonwealth Office

DEPARTMENT 5    Ministry of Defence

DEPARTMENT 6    British Army

DEPARTMENT 7    Royal Navy

DEPARTMENT 8    Her Majesty's Diplomatic Service

DEPARTMENT 9    Her Majesty's Treasury

DEPARTMENT 10   Department for Transport

DEPARTMENT 11   Attorney General's Office

DEPARTMENT 12   Ministry of Justice

DEPARTMENT 13   Military Intelligence, Section 5 (MI5)

DEPARTMENT 14   Secret Intelligence Service (SIS)

DEPARTMENT 15   Royal Air Force

DEPARTMENT 16   Northern Ireland Office

DEPARTMENT 17   Scotland Office

DEPARTMENT 18   Wales Office

**DEPARTMENT 19 CLASSIFIED**

DEPARTMENT 20   Territorial Police Forces

DEPARTMENT 21   Department of Health

DEPARTMENT 22   Government Communication Headquarters (GCHQ)

DEPARTMENT 23   Joint Intelligence Committee (JIC)

# PROLOGUE

Eight black-clad Operators made their way silently over the lip of the canyon, spacing themselves evenly out along the length of the ridge.

They bristled with weaponry, although not the kind they were used to carrying; they wore no stakes on their belts, no ultraviolet grenades or beam guns, no T-Bones. Instead, each Operator was carrying a suppressed SPAS-15 shotgun loaded with wireless taser cartridges that could immobilise a human being from four hundred and fifty metres.

Their target lay fifty metres below them: a wooden cabin built into the steep slope beside the dry riverbed that wound its way along the canyon floor. It was a small square building, with a white roof and a stone chimney emerging from its centre, and a wooden porch on its far side. The cabin was the last-known residence of an individual who was, as far as anyone was able to ascertain, unique: a vampire who had been cured of his condition and now went by the name of Adam.

The team had lifted off forty-five minutes earlier from Papoose Lake, the headquarters of National Security Division 9 that lay inside the military facility known throughout the world as Area 51. The flight time had been barely twenty minutes, but the team's orders had been to set down more than ten miles from the cabin, drive to within two, and hike the rest on foot. Adam was apparently no longer a vampire, and it was assumed that his supernatural senses had disappeared when he was cured, but General Allen, the NS9 Director, had no intention of leaving anything to chance.

The eight Operators had made their way silently through the barren rock and sand of the desert as the sun pounded down from overhead, the climate-control systems inside their black jumpsuits working overtime to keep them cool, until they arrived at the perimeter of the target zone and the squad's leader, Special Operator Tim Albertsson, had called in for final clearance to proceed. The response had arrived directly in his ear in the form of a single word.

"Go."

Albertsson led them down the canyon, moving silently at the centre of the wide spread. As they approached the cabin, his team spread out as if by remote control. The three Operators to Tim's right, and the three at the opposite end of the line, broke away and circled round the cabin. Two stopped on each side, facing the flat wooden walls with their shotguns raised, as the Operators who had been at the ends of the line met silently on the far side. Tim and the final member of the squad stopped five metres short of the rear of the cabin, forming the final edge of a perimeter of matt-black uniforms and steadily pointed weaponry.

Satellite reconnaissance had shown heat inside the cabin, but had been unable to positively identify its source. It was too diffuse: the product, it was suspected, of a wood-burning stove in the centre of the two rooms. Privately, Tim Albertsson believed they were going to find nothing in the cabin, and was highly sceptical of the intelligence that had been provided; a cured vampire, who had supposedly *been* cured in Nevada as part of a highly classified NS9 research project that nobody inside the Department was aware of, and whose existence and location had come from a source that General Allen would not discuss with anyone.

*There's so much wrong with this story,* thought Albertsson, as he made a final check of his squad's positions. *I'm not sure I buy any of it.*

Despite his reservations, Albertsson understood why his squad had been sent to the desert. If Adam was real, and *had* been cured, then he was quite simply one of the most important people in the world – perhaps *the* most important. What had been done to him might offer clues that led not only to victory over Dracula, but to the complete eradication of the vampire threat. The Director could hardly ignore such a possibility.

"Ready One," he said, speaking into the closed communications link that carried his voice directly into the ears of his squad. "Non-lethal only."

Seven Operators chorused their agreement back to him. Albertsson moved, stepping lightly on the balls of his feet, and approached the window in the rear wall of the cabin. John Brady, a third-year Operator who had come to NS9 from the Marines, shadowed him, keeping the distance between them constant. Albertsson reached the wall of the cabin and set his back against it, his shotgun raised to his shoulder. He took a deep breath, then darted his head out beyond the window frame and looked inside the cabin.

The main room doubled as both kitchen and living room; below the window was a metal sink, with a battered sofa sitting in the centre of the floor beyond it. To the right stood an antique chest of drawers, the top of which was patterned with angular lines of dust. To the left, a wood-burning stove vibrated gently as it coughed smoke up the chimney and out into the clear desert sky.

There was no sign of their target.

*As I expected,* thought Tim, cursing silently. *He's gone, whoever he is.*

"Bedroom," he said.

"Clear," came the immediate reply.

Tim stepped out and took a closer look through the window. There was nowhere the man could be hiding: no cupboards, no trapdoors. And as he scanned the small dwelling, he realised what the lines of dust on the dressing-table top were. They were the marks left by photo frames that hadn't been moved for a long time; the kind you only moved if it was necessary, like when you were leaving a place with no intention of ever coming back.

"Jameson," he said, addressing one of the Operators positioned along the cabin's front wall. "Move in. I want the place swept in five minutes so we can get the hell out of here."

"Roger," said Chris Jameson. As Albertsson and Brady made their way round the cabin to join up with the rest of the squad, Jameson pushed open the unlocked door and stepped inside. The last thing he would ever hear was a tiny click from beneath one of the floorboards, as his boot stepped heavily on to it.

Tim Albertsson rounded the corner of the wooden structure, and had a brief moment to marvel at the remarkable beauty of the snaking canyon before the cabin exploded with a vast, shuddering roar.

The wooden walls and roof blew up and out, splintering into a deadly cloud of flying wood as a huge orange fireball with a black heart bloomed up out of the ground. The sound hammered into

Albertsson's ears as heat blasted across the front of his uniform and the shockwave hurled him into the air. He tumbled, the horizon rotating wildly before him – desert, sky, desert, sky, desert, sky – until he crashed down to earth, his back and shoulders slamming against the hard-baked ground, and all he saw was grey.

When his vision cleared, he was looking up at a vast column of black smoke. His eyes were watering, his ears ringing, and he wondered, for a terrible moment, whether the blast had struck him deaf. Then he pushed himself up on to his elbows, and the howl of pain that burst from his mouth as his battered shoulders ground together reached his ears, and he knew it had not.

*Thank Christ*, he thought. *Oh Jesus, what the hell was that? It felt like a nuke going off.*

Gritting his teeth against the pain, Tim pushed himself up on to unsteady feet and surveyed the chaos before him. Four of his squad were lying on the desert floor, their eyes closed; each had been thrown at least ten metres by the explosion. John Brady was nearer, his face pale, his eyes wide and staring, his hands beating the ground rhythmically as he visibly tried not to go into shock. Tim lurched towards him, and saw what had happened to his friend.

Brady's legs were gone below the knees; all that remained were blackened stumps and shreds of uniform. Blood had splashed up his body and across the orange ground, but not in the quantities that Albertsson would have expected; the terrible wounds had been cauterised by the fire that had caused them.

Tim stared, his mind trying to come to terms with what he was seeing. Then he twisted the dial on his belt that controlled his helmet's comms system, praying as he did so that the technology hadn't been damaged in the blast. For several agonising seconds, there was only silence. Then a voice spoke into his ear.

"Code in."

"Albertsson, SO413," said Tim, his voice trembling.

"Go ahead."

"Operators down, emergency medical evac required, my location. At least one critical injury, double amputation below the knee. Severity of other injuries unclear."

"Despatching now. ETA thirteen minutes."

Albertsson cut the connection and dropped to the ground beside John Brady, unbuckling his belt as he did so; it came free with a series of thuds as the weapons and kit attached to it fell to the ground. Working as quickly as he could, Tim slung the belt under and around his friend's thigh then looped it round a splinter of the devastated cabin. He turned the piece of wood, tightening the belt round Brady's leg until his friend let out a scream of pain.

*Good sign,* he told himself.

He grabbed his knife from where it had fallen, sliced off the left sleeve of his uniform, and quickly repeated the process on the ruined right leg. When it was done, he staggered to his feet. Brady had passed out as Albertsson tightened the second tourniquet, but his pulse was regular, if dangerously weak. Across the steep canyon side, the remainder of his squad were drifting towards consciousness, letting out low groans and grunts that made their way directly into his ears. He counted again, knowing with dreadful certainty what he was going to find.

Himself. Brady. Four others.

Six Operators.

Two of his squad were missing.

Albertsson turned and faced the burning remains of the cabin; the heat emanating from it was overwhelming, and he was only able to take a few stumbling steps towards it before being driven back.

He stared into the inferno, searching for a way to dispute what his eyes and brain were telling him.

*If I can't see them, they're gone.*

A loud groan in his ear roused him from his thoughts, dragging him back from the edge of shock. He tore himself away from the blazing remnants of the cabin and began to attend to the members of his squad who *had* survived, patching wounds and splinting broken bones. He got Owen Meadows, the young Texan who had transferred from the Rangers only three months earlier, up on his feet, ordered him to keep an eye on John Brady, then redoubled his efforts, scrabbling back and forth across the steep, treacherous slope of the canyon.

Albertsson was pressing a square of gauze to a hole that had been gouged in Megan Irvin's forearm when the steady thud of helicopter rotors began to shake the desert floor. Tim jumped to his feet and saw the Black Hawk above the distant eastern horizon, flying fast and low towards their position. He was about to tell what was left of his squad to prepare themselves for evac, when Meadows shouted that Brady's heart had stopped.

"So what happened?" asked Julian Carpenter.

He was sitting on the narrow bed in his cell on Level H of the Loop, staring at an ashen Cal Holmwood. The Blacklight Interim Director had cut his connection with Bob Allen in Nevada only minutes earlier, and the shock of what his American counterpart had told him was written all over his face.

"Brady didn't make it," said Holmwood. "They got him on to the chopper back to Dreamland, but he arrested again and they couldn't restart his heart a second time. He was pronounced in the hangar at Papoose Lake. NS9 scrubbed the cabin, and found traces of Jameson and Denham, barely enough to fill a Petri dish. They were all but vaporised by the blast."

"What was it?" asked Julian. "What did Adam use?"

"Dynamite," said Holmwood. "Under the floorboards. God knows how much of it. They're trying to trace it, but they're not expecting much luck. You can buy dynamite in every builder's merchant in Nevada."

"And a pressure trigger by the door?"

Holmwood nodded. "You talked to him, Julian. Did he seem like the type of person who would do this?"

"No," said Julian. "Not at all. But desperation makes people do strange things, Cal."

"What do you mean?"

"I mean, he probably realised that once *I* knew he'd been cured, there were going to be people who would want to know how it happened. Maybe he didn't feel like spending any more time as a lab rat."

"But he talked to you," said Holmwood. "Voluntarily. He told you what happened to him, admitted he was cured, and let you leave. Why would he do that?"

"I don't know," said Julian. "He told me that the cure wasn't why I had come to see him, that I was there for some greater purpose. Maybe he thought that was more important."

"Your vision," said Cal. "What you saw in the cave."

Julian shrugged. "Maybe. Or maybe he knew there was no point in trying to pretend that he wasn't who I thought he was. Maybe he just wanted me gone as quickly as possible so he could run."

"We need to find him, Julian," said Holmwood. "It was already urgent, and now three NS9 Operators are dead. I need everything you know about Adam, everything he said to you, anything that might give Dreamland even the slightest clue about where he is. How long do you need?"

Julian looked at his old friend and saw fiery determination flickering in his eyes; despite the burden of leadership that had been thrust upon him, and the seemingly endless setbacks that Blacklight and its international counterparts had suffered, it was still there.

*God, he looks tired*, he thought. *How did it come to this? Henry gone, Cal in charge, and me in this cell, useless to everyone.*

"Julian?" said Cal. "I asked you how long you need to prepare a report on everything you know about Adam."

"I'm sorry, Cal," said Julian, shaking his head. "I'm afraid I can't do that."

# 7 DAYS TILL
# ZERO HOUR

# 1

# SAFETY MEASURES

Kate Randall put the folder down on the desk and closed her eyes.

She was sitting on a plastic chair inside her office in the Security Division, and had just finished reading through an Intelligence Division projection that had been commissioned two weeks earlier. Its cover was marked *Provisional Forecast of Losses and Damage in the Event of the Establishment of Supernatural (Type V) Social Dominance*, a typically dry title for a report whose true purpose could be summed up far more succinctly.

It was a prediction of exactly how bad things might get if Dracula came to power.

Kate had expected it to make grim reading, so much so that she had let the report sit on her desk for almost an entire day before summoning up the courage to open it. Now she wished she had left it longer; the numbers contained within the pale yellow pages were so awful, so terribly, dreadfully *huge*, that she could barely comprehend them.

She had been asked to present the findings at the next meeting of the Zero Hour Task Force, scheduled for the following morning, and she was already dreading the reaction they were going to elicit from her colleagues, who were struggling not only with the imminent arrival of Zero Hour itself, but with the seemingly endless list of other problems that had befallen the Department in recent months: the violent, treacherous defection of the Task Force's former member Richard Brennan, who had tried to kill both Kate and her boss, and who, it was presumed, was now at Dracula's side, telling him every plan they had made; the continued freedom of a number of the patients who had been turned and released from Broadmoor Hospital; and, most potentially devastating of all, the article the late Kevin McKenna had written under the influence of Albert Harker, an article that detailed the existence of both vampires and the men and women who policed them, and which was now out there, being read by an ever-increasing number of people.

"What do you make of it?"

The voice was familiar, but Kate still jumped in her seat. Standing by the door to her office, holding his own copy of the report, was Major Paul Turner, the Department's Security Officer and Kate's commanding officer. He was looking at her with a thin smile on his face.

"Jesus, Paul," she said, her heart racing in her chest. "Sneak up on me, why don't you? There are vamps who aren't as quiet as you."

"Sorry," said Turner, the smile testament to the fact that he wasn't. "Try not being so easy to sneak up on."

"I'll bear that in mind next time I'm sitting in my office in the middle of the day," said Kate, although a smile had now risen on to her face as well. "Can I help you with something?"

Turner waved his copy of the Intelligence Division report. "What do you make of it?" he repeated.

"It's horrifying," said Kate. "But I expected it to be. What about you?"

"It's worse than I thought," said Turner. "Not by much, but it's worse. And it's going to cause panic through the Department if it gets out. It has to stay Zero Hour only, at least for now."

"Agreed," said Kate. "No sense circulating the worst-case scenario."

Turner nodded, and threw his copy of the report down on to Kate's desk. She watched him run his hands through his hair, and marvelled at the evolution their relationship had undergone in recent months.

When she had first arrived at the Loop, her immediate response to the Security Officer had been the same as almost every other Operator's: outright terror. Turner was stern and cold, so much so that he often seemed more like some kind of military robot than an actual breathing, feeling human being. But then she had started dating his son, Shaun, who had been so different to his father that, were it not for their almost identical physical appearance, you would have doubted they were even related. Shaun had been passionate, and impulsive, and short-tempered, and loud, and full of life.

Until he died.

*Was murdered*, she reminded herself. *He didn't* die. *He was murdered by Valeri Rusmanov.*

In the aftermath of the loss of Shaun, Kate and his father had found themselves clinging to each other like shipwreck survivors to a barrel, desperately trying to keep alive the memory of the boy they had both loved. As a result, when Turner had needed a partner to run ISAT, the Internal Security Assessment Team that had been charged with investigating every serving Operator after the revelation that Richard Talbot, the original Director of the Lazarus Project, had spent his whole life in Valeri's service, Kate hadn't hesitated; she had walked into his office and volunteered.

Turner had asked her if she was sure, had warned her that

everyone was going to hate them for carrying out such an unsavoury task, but she had told him she was. He had been right; they *had* been hated for it, so much so that Richard Brennan had tried to kill them both to preserve the secret of his disloyalty. But they had persevered, and the experience, the siege mentality that they had adopted, had pushed them closer and closer together, until they spoke to each like equals, not as Major and Lieutenant.

"Any word from Valentin?" she asked.

"No," replied Turner. "Nothing."

Kate nodded. She knew the decision to let the youngest Rusmanov brother leave the Loop, with nothing more than a promise to find his former master and return, weighed heavily on the Security Officer. "Not yet, right?" she said.

"I hope so."

She got up from behind her desk and headed for the coffee machine that stood on one of the shelves that occupied an entire wall of her office. She filled two mugs, handed one to Turner, and took a long sip from the other.

"Tell me the truth," she said. "Do you really think he's coming back?"

"I have to," replied Turner.

She nodded again. "What's on your schedule for the rest of today?"

"I'm briefing Cal in ninety minutes," replied Turner. "Then Divisional assessments until four, and then I'm going home."

Kate frowned. Senior Blacklight personnel were allowed to live off base if they had families; it was how Jamie's dad had been able to hide what he really did for a living from Jamie and Marie for so long. She knew that Caroline Turner, who was Henry Seward's sister as well as the Security Officer's wife, was used to such domestic dysfunction, having been around Blacklight for most of her life. And Paul's devotion to her was abundantly clear; Kate did not think it would be an exaggeration to suggest that he couldn't live without her, especially after Shaun. But despite all that, she was still surprised to hear her commanding officer say that he was going home, with the Zero Hour countdown ticking and a Task Force meeting less than twenty-four hours away.

"How come?" she asked, then immediately blushed with embarrassment. "Sorry, sir, that's none of my business. Forgive me."

Turner smiled. "Nothing to forgive," he said. "We're having family for dinner. It's Shaun's birthday today."

An icy wave of shock crashed through Kate's system; she stared at the Security Officer, her mouth slightly open, her eyes wide and unblinking, her heart pulsing with thick, bitter waves of guilt.

*Oh God,* she thought. *How did I not know that? How did I forget?*

Her time with Shaun had been painfully brief, but still long enough to have the cautious getting-to-know-each-other conversations that only happen when you're starting to think you might be serious about someone; birthdays are only relevant if you think you might be around for the next one.

"Shit," she said, her voice trembling. "I totally forgot. You must think I'm an awful person."

Turner narrowed his eyes and fixed her with a look so full of reprimand that she almost physically backed away from it.

"I think nothing of the sort," he said, his voice low. "I know how much you and Shaun meant to each other. There's far too much going on around here for you to be expected to remember a single date, so I want you to stop being so hard on yourself. Is that clear?"

"I could come," said Kate, frantically. "I mean, if you wanted me to. I could come with you and—"

"No," said Turner. "You can't. If and when the world ever returns to normal, we'll see. But right now you have work to do."

"But..."

"That was an order, Lieutenant," said Turner, his voice calm and even. "Do I have to repeat it?"

Kate stared at him, her stomach churning with despair. "No, sir," she said. "That won't be necessary."

"Good," said Turner. "I'll pass your condolences on to Caroline, and make sure she understands that you aren't there because I wouldn't let you be, rather than because you refused to come."

"Thank you, sir," she said. "I'd really appreciate that."

Turner smiled, an expression that was so full of pain it took Kate's breath away.

"You're welcome," he said.

Kate sat at her desk for a long time after Paul Turner left her office.

Her mind was racing, struggling to process everything that was going on around her, trying to stop her being crushed into paralysis by the sheer scale of it all; Shaun, Paul, Zero Hour, Dracula, the Intelligence Division report. She looked at the folder lying on her desk and felt a sudden rush of hatred for its contents, for the warning it contained, in plain language and numbers; a warning that could not be rationalised away, or ignored.

*It's the end of the world*, she thought. *Unless we can stop it.*

# 2

# PLAYING ROUGH

Jamie Carpenter hurled himself to his right, crashing to the ground as the vampire's fist thundered through the air where his head had been a millisecond earlier. He rolled with the fall and sprang back to his feet, his momentum sending him sliding backwards across the tiled floor, his blue eyes locked on his attacker.

The vampire faced him. Her glowing gaze darkened from scarlet to a crimson that was almost black, her fangs gleamed in the fluorescent light of the bathroom, and a cruel smile rose on to her face.

"Fast," she said, nodding approvingly. "Not fast enough, though."

"We'll see," said Jamie. He was breathing hard, trying not to show it.

The vampire tilted her head to one side and growled, a low rumble full of menace. Jamie reached for the loop on his belt that held his metal stake, and found it empty. He cursed, inwardly; the attack had taken him by surprise, coming seemingly from nowhere, and his weapons were in his quarters, standing neatly in their moulded cabinet.

He was fighting for his life, and he was unarmed.

*Think*, he told himself. *Think, for God's sake.*

The vampire's smile widened, as though she could read his mind, could hear the panic steadily building inside him. He kept his gaze fixed on her, watching for the slightest movement, the tiniest tensing of muscle that might warn him her attack was coming, hoping there might be time for him to do something about it.

There wasn't.

The vampire moved in a blur of black and streaming red, her fist slamming into Jamie's chin with an impact that sent fireworks across his field of vision, constellations of red and white and yellow that spun and danced. A bolt of agony ripped through his head and he staggered backwards, his legs buckling, his arms reaching blindly for anything that might keep him upright, might keep him in the fight. His gloved hands closed on nothing, and he hit the ground in a tangled heap, his head pounding, his vision greying, his heart racing in his chest.

He scrambled backwards, trying to create separation, but was far too slow; the vampire landed on him knees first, pinning his arms to the floor, sending pain shooting through his shoulders and up the back of his neck. He bucked his hips, kicking his legs up and out, trying to shake her loose as she reached down and carefully, almost gently, took his face in her hands. Her eyes blazed red above him, and her fangs were huge and bright beneath lips that had curled into a wide smile. Jamie twisted and fought as she lowered her face towards him, trying to delay the inevitable, until he felt the warmth of her breath in his ear.

"Had enough?" she whispered, her voice a low growl.

Jamie threw his body into one final set of desperate contortions, but the vampire didn't move a millimetre. Finally, his face red with exertion and embarrassment, he nodded.

"Enough," he said.

The vampire kissed him softly on the cheek, then sat up, the glow in her eyes fading. She was still straddling his chest, but Jamie felt the pressure pinning him to the ground lessen. He flexed the muscles in his shoulders, felt them creak as they loosened, and looked up.

"Did you take it easy on me?" he asked. "Tell the truth."

Larissa Kinley held his gaze for a long moment, her smile fading, then dropped her eyes.

"Damn it, Larissa," said Jamie, trying to squirm out from beneath her. "I told you not to. What the hell is the point of this if you're not even trying?"

She frowned, and bore down again, holding him in place. "I *was* trying, Jamie," she said. "But are we training, or are you trying to get hurt? Because if it's the latter you can find someone else."

Jamie stared at her pale, beautiful face and felt his anger dissipate. He knew she was right; his girlfriend was rapidly becoming one of the most powerful vampires in the world, and could have ended their sparring session within the first few seconds had she wanted to. She could have broken every bone in his body, or simply killed him, without breaking a sweat, and, although it was galling to be so completely outmatched, it would be senseless for him to end up in the infirmary for no better reason than stubborn pride.

There was something else too; he knew that on some level, in a place inside herself that Jamie could never access, Larissa *wanted* to hurt him. Her vampire side was growing stronger and more powerful with each passing day, and, although he believed her when she claimed she had it under control, he knew exactly what that side of her wanted: to tear flesh and drink blood.

To kill.

"I'm sorry," he said, smiling up at her. "You're right."

Larissa smiled back at him. "Of course I am," she said. "As usual."

She arched her back and began to rise into the air, but he grabbed her thighs and pulled her back down. Her eyes flared, and Jamie felt a shiver pass through her; her vampire side was pushing for control, the animal part of her that he knew she regarded as almost a separate person. She let herself be brought back to the ground, then dipped her face towards his, a low growl emerging from her throat. The movement was so fast and fluid, like the strike of a cobra, that it took his breath away; he stared at her, utterly intoxicated by everything she was.

Her blazing eyes bored into him, her fangs gleaming centimetres from his face. He reached up, almost without realising he was doing so, and ran the tip of his index finger over one of the sharp white teeth, feeling its smooth hardness, the greasy sensation of the plasma that coated it. Larissa growled again, a guttural sound of pure lust in a moment that seemed to last forever. Then, all at once, the spell was broken.

The glowing light in her eyes flared black, then disappeared so quickly it was as though it had never been there at all; the pale brown eyes that she had been born with were suddenly staring down at him, wide and full of fear. Then she was moving, taking hold of his wrist and dragging him bodily across the bathroom. Jamie was pulled to his feet willingly, still reeling from the intensity of the moment that had so abruptly ended, which was for the best; Larissa was hauling him with such force that his shoulder would have dislocated if he had resisted. She shoved his hand into the sink, turned on the hot tap, and scrubbed at his fingers with liquid soap, her hands flying back and forth. Jamie let her scour his skin for several seconds, until he suddenly realised what she was doing.

"Hey," he said. "It's OK, Larissa. It's—"

She looked at him, and the expression on her face cut off his words like a guillotine. He watched in silence as she washed his hand again, then a third time, before towelling it dry and raising it to her face. She examined it carefully, searching, he knew, for any cut or scratch, no matter how small. Eventually she seemed satisfied and let go of his wrist.

"Bit of an overreaction, don't you think?" said Jamie.

"No," she said, staring at him with anger she was clearly trying to control. "I don't. I don't think there *is* such a thing as an overreaction when you're dealing with the most dangerous substance in the world."

"It's cool," said Jamie. "You didn't bite me. I'm fine."

"It is *not* cool. One drop of what's on my fangs is enough to turn you if it gets into your system. One tiny little drop."

"I know," said Jamie. "But remember where we are. Even if that did happen, they'd transfuse me in the infirmary before the turn even started. It's OK, Larissa, really it is."

She sighed. "I know, Jamie. I know you're careful and I know where we are. You just have to see this from my perspective. It's not much fun having something in your mouth that turns people into monsters."

Something about her choice of words struck Jamie as deliciously funny, and he let out a snort of laughter. He tried to hold it, not wanting her to think he wasn't taking what she said seriously, but failed; he started to laugh harder, casting apologetic glances at her between peals of hilarity. Larissa stared at him coldly, then gave in; her face curled into a smile that was, to Jamie's eyes at least, profoundly beautiful, and she started to laugh with him as he reached out and pulled her into his arms.

When their laughter had subsided, Larissa took a half-step back, and looked at her boyfriend. Her vampire side, the part of herself that she hated, but which she knew he found guiltily, maddeningly attractive, was gone, pushed back down to where it lurked, waiting impatiently for release. What remained was a teenage girl: awkward, conflicted, increasingly unsure of the world around her, and her place in it.

Almost a month had passed since she had challenged Cal Holmwood about the morality of what Blacklight and the other supernatural Departments actually did on a daily basis, had asked him to justify the murder of men and women who had, in the overwhelming majority of cases, never *asked* to be turned into vampires. The issue still gnawed at her insides, like an itch she was unable to scratch, but it was not the one that rose into her mind as she looked at her boyfriend. *That* was something else entirely; three words spoken by the Interim Director that she wished more than anything she had not overheard.

*Welcome back, Julian.*

Jamie's open, honest face was still flushed red from both laughter and the exertion of their sparring session, and Larissa felt her heart quicken. Part of it was love, or something very close to it, but part was a feeling of guilt so hot and caustic that it was very close to shame. She was almost certain that her boyfriend's father – the father he, and everyone else, thought was dead – was at that moment somewhere inside the Loop, most likely in one of the non-supernatural cells on Level H.

And she hadn't told Jamie about it.

She had lain awake most nights since her return from America, turning it over and over in her mind. The man to whom Cal Holmwood had said those three fateful words had been secretly imprisoned in the depths of the NS9 base in Nevada, and had been hooded and bound for their journey to the Loop, so she could not say with any certainty what he looked or sounded like. But it would be a remarkable coincidence if another man named Julian had received both the treatment he had been subjected to in America and the greeting from the Interim Director she had overheard.

*Back,* Cal said. *Welcome* back.

If she was right, if the man who had flown across the Atlantic in the *Mina II* with her really *was* Julian Carpenter, then the ramifications were almost unthinkable. He was dead, or at least believed to be. What would it do to the Department if he turned up, alive and well?

What would it do to Jamie?

And what would it mean for *her* if he found out she'd known and kept quiet?

"Do you ever think about it?" he asked, bringing her out of her thoughts and back into the bathroom. He was looking at her evenly, his eyes wide and clear.

"Think about what?" she asked, although she was sure she knew.

"What it would be like," said Jamie, "if we were both turned. We could live forever. Together."

Anger flared up inside Larissa. She forced it back down, refusing to give into it, to hate him for even suggesting such a repellent idea.

"No," she said, her voice barely more than a growl. "I don't ever think about that. And you shouldn't either."

"Why not?" asked Jamie.

"Because it's never going to happen."

"No. I mean, why haven't you ever thought about it?"

Larissa narrowed her eyes. "Are you actively trying to make me angry?"

"No," he said. "I'm genuinely not. It's a possibility, given what we do, and, since Zero Hour is only seven days away and we're no closer to stopping it now than when Dracula was resurrected, it's only going to become more likely. So why haven't you thought about it?"

*Stay calm*, she told herself. *It's not his fault. Stay calm.*

"If we survive what's coming," she said, her voice low and steady, "and if *this*, whatever it is that's between us, survives as well, I want to live. And I don't mean in some eternal freak show, Jamie; I mean a real, normal life. I want to grow up and I want to get old, with you. Why don't you get that?"

"I do," said Jamie. "But I don't know why *you* don't get how much easier it would make things. Your vampire side is the only thing that stops me panicking every time you're out there."

"I can handle myself," said Larissa, sharply. "I don't need you to worry about me."

"I know you don't," said Jamie. "Believe me, I know. I still do, though. Sorry."

Larissa looked at him. She knew that he trusted her, that he respected her abilities and her experience, and that his occasionally paternal attitude had everything to do with terror at the thought of losing her; she knew it came from a place of concern, not condescension.

It still pissed her off.

"Don't apologise," she said. "Just worry about yourself."

"I do," said Jamie. "All I'm saying is—"

"Jamie," she interrupted. "You can never ask me to turn you, OK?

Never, ever, ever. We're done if you do. So you have to promise me."

He stared at her for a moment that seemed to have no end, in which she tried to decipher his expression. There was affection and an openness to his features that suggested honesty, but there was disappointment too, bright and shining and obvious. The silence was full of unsaid things; it dragged on and out, until simultaneous beeps from their consoles broke the spell.

"OK," said Jamie. "I promise."

"Thank you," said Larissa, and lifted her console from her belt. The rectangular screen glowed white as the day's orders appeared in a single line of black text.

### G-21/PATROL_RESPOND/GRIDREF_B34_N51/1800

*Close to home,* she thought. *Good news.*

Larissa had been immediately placed in charge of a new Operational Squad when she returned from America. G-21 was comprised of herself, Jess Nelson, a Security Division Operator who had been moved on to the active roster, and Lieutenant Tom Gregg, one of the NS9 Operators she had brought back to the Loop with her. So far, their Operational performance had been flawless, and she had every intention of keeping it that way; Zero Hour loomed over everything, approaching as slowly and implacably as a tidal wave, but until it arrived, or was stopped, all Larissa and the rest of Blacklight could do was carry on doing their jobs, and doing them well.

What her screen showed was a routine operation: a section of the country that they would patrol and respond to any Echelon intercepts or Surveillance Division reports. It was the kind of mission that could turn into a series of pitched battles, or could involve six hours sitting bored in the back of a van, two outcomes that were highly appealing to the different sides of Larissa's increasingly split personality.

Jamie looked up from his console. "Training," he said. "Still. You?"

"Patrol Respond," she replied. "Nottinghamshire Lincolnshire border."

"Nice," said Jamie, and smiled. "I'll be in bed before you're even on your way back."

"I might come and wake you up," said Larissa, returning his smile with one of her own. "What do you think?"

"I think you should," said Jamie, then closed the space between them and pressed his lips to hers. She kissed him back instantly, feeling heat boil into her stomach and the corners of her eyes, then stopped before her vampire side was able to fully assert itself.

"Go," she growled. "Time to go to work."

"You too," said Jamie. "Stay alive."

"I'll try," said Larissa.

# 3

# QUESTIONS AND ANSWERS

Admiral Henry Seward swallowed a mouthful of lobster and tried not to let how wonderful it tasted show on his ravaged face.

His surroundings, and his view from the end of the grand dining table, had become so familiar that they had taken on the consistency of a nightmare, an endless purgatory from which there seemed to be no waking. He had lost count of his days spent imprisoned inside the château, and had long abandoned any belief in the possibility of rescue; all that remained, into which he poured the last of his remaining hope, were two things.

First, that he be strong enough to face his death with dignity when it finally came.

Second, that he might yet achieve some tiny victories in his last days and weeks. Refusing to acknowledge the splendour of the food and wine served to him each night was one such victory; it infuriated Dracula to see hospitality go unappreciated, although his own belief in appropriate behaviour prevented him from showing it. No matter

39

how choice the delicacy, how ethereal the wine, Seward responded with nothing more than perfunctory thanks. It was pathetic, if he was honest with himself, an act of stubbornness too small to be regarded as anything else. But in the position of impotence in which he found himself trapped, it was something, and something was better than nothing.

"Good?" enquired Dracula, from the opposite end of the table.

"Fine," said Seward, digging his fork into the gleaming white meat.

"In which case, I shall have the chef's fingers removed," said Dracula, his tone light and pleasant. "It is unacceptable for him to produce fare that is merely 'fine', and he has done so for several days now. Please accept my sincere apologies."

Seward felt a wide blade of despair slice through him.

*How long did you think it would take him to put an end to this?* he asked himself. *He sees you all too well.*

The chef in question was human, kidnapped from one of the finest restaurants in Paris during the first days of Dracula's occupation of the château. His disappearance had caused widespread speculation; on the rare occasions that Seward was able to see a television, usually in the vampire quarters in the cellars as he was being dragged back to his room after yet another session of torture, he had seen the man's face plastered all over the news. Opinion appeared evenly divided between the chef having committed suicide and having run off with one of his waitresses, a pretty Estonian girl who was also missing. The waitress, whose name was Ekaterina, was, in fact, standing beside the door of the dining room, her newly red eyes glowing, her expression one of professional neutrality; the vampire who had been sent to the French capital to acquire the chef had simply not been able to resist her.

"The food is excellent," said Seward, his voice low. "As it always is. As well you know."

Dracula smiled. "I have dined on delicacies you cannot conceive of, my dear Admiral. Of course I know. Just as I knew that, once your childish pretence had ceased to amuse me, it would not survive a threat to someone you consider innocent. You are so easily predicted, and so weak. So very, very weak."

Seward raised his fork to his mouth, chewed the piece of lobster, then spat it wetly on to the surface of the table. A tremor of anger rippled across Dracula's face, and Seward let a smile full of belligerence rise on to his own.

"Did you predict that?" he asked, his tone warm and polite, then swept an arm across the table. His plates, wine glass, water glass, and cutlery crashed to the floor in an explosion of noise and flying china. "Or that?"

Ekaterina's eyes widened with shock, but she didn't move; she had clearly learnt quickly that it was unwise to do anything inside the château without the express permission of its lord and master. Dracula half rose out of his chair, then paused; for a terrible moment, his eyes locked with Seward's, red spilling into their corners. Then the ancient vampire settled back into his seat and reached for his glass of wine.

"Tantrums are for children," he said, and took a long sip. "Such behaviour is beneath you, my friend."

"You threaten to torture an innocent man to make a point, then lecture *me* about behaviour?" asked Seward, his voice trembling.

"I made my threat only when *your* behaviour was becoming intolerable," said Dracula. "We can go back and forth on this matter all evening, if you wish?"

"It would be a waste of time," said Seward, his body shaking with impotent fury. "You cannot see the hypocrisy in everything you say and do, the vanity and the arrogance, so what the hell would be the point?"

Dracula's smile widened. "Perhaps you would prefer a bottle of warm milk to another glass of wine?"

Seward felt his face flood with reckless, furious heat. "I would prefer—"

His preference, which was about to include an extraordinarily graphic description of a coupling between Dracula's mother and a herd of wild horses, was cut off by a heavy knock on the dining-room door, an intervention that was probably for the best, at least as far as Seward's remaining well-being was concerned.

"Enter," said Dracula, setting his wine glass on the table and turning to the door with a look of profound disinterest on his narrow face. The door swung open and the large, instantly identifiable shape of Valeri Rusmanov stepped through it. The old vampire's eyes were glowing with faint crimson, and his face, as craggy and unforgiving as a mountainside, was set in a tight expression of displeasure.

"My lord," he said, glancing briefly in Seward's direction. "I am sorry to disturb you."

"And yet you have done so," said Dracula. "So be quick about the reason."

Valeri's eyes narrowed a fraction. Seward didn't think Dracula saw; the first vampire's treatment of his oldest ally was so casually dismissive that the Blacklight Director didn't really believe that he thought of him as an actual person, in possession of a mind of his own. But Seward saw it; he saw it very clearly.

"It is Mellor," said Valeri. "The vampire who came to us from California. You have seen him, my lord, he is tall, strongly built, with blond—"

"Must I listen to you describe him like some breathless teenager?" asked Dracula. "Tell me what this man has done."

"He took a boy from a village at the edge of the forest, my lord. Less than ten miles from here. The population of the village is barely a hundred, so the boy's disappearance has caused uproar."

Dracula looked down the table and rolled his eyes in a gesture of disarming familiarity.

*Like we're two old friends listening to how one of our kids screwed up*, thought Seward.

"What has been done?" asked Dracula.

"I have taken care of it, my lord," said Valeri. "I arranged the boy's body in the forest and made it appear as though he was killed by a boar. The villagers are out searching as I speak, and will doubtless find him shortly."

"You still have not provided a compelling reason for disturbing my dinner, Valeri," said Dracula. "I suggest you do so quickly."

There was a pause, also noted by Seward, and, when Valeri replied, his voice contained the faintest of tremors, as though he was working hard to keep his temper. "I wanted to know what you would have me do with Mellor, my lord. He knowingly broke one of the rules you set in place."

Dracula rolled his eyes again and reached for his wine. "Impale him," he said. "Place him on a pole in the courtyard as a warning to the others. It disappoints me that I should have to give you such obvious instruction, Valeri. Are you of any actual use to me, or do I keep you here for nothing more than nostalgia?"

Valeri didn't respond. Dracula took a long sip of his wine, then regarded his servant with narrowing eyes.

"Is there anything else?" he asked, his tone making it clear that it would be best for Valeri if there wasn't.

"No, my lord," replied the eldest Rusmanov, and turned towards the door, his face as impassive as ever.

"Valeri?" said Seward, politely, and felt adrenaline shudder through him as the old vampire turned to face him. Out of the corner of his eye, he saw Dracula set his glass down and lean back in his chair, an expression of curiosity on his face.

"You have something to say to me?" asked Valeri, his voice low and full of menace.

"I do," said Seward. "I was wondering why you let him speak to you like that?"

"I beg your pardon?"

"It's very simple," said Seward, smiling thinly. "Your master talks to you like a child, and treats you like the lowest of his servants. I just wondered why you let him."

Valeri's eyes narrowed. He took a half-step towards Seward, then glanced over at his master.

*Like a dog checking whether it's allowed to chase a ball,* thought Seward.

Dracula was still wearing the curious expression on his face as he met Valeri's gaze. Then he smiled, and turned to the waitress standing beside the door. "Leave us," he said, his tone even and pleasant.

"Yes, my lord," said Ekaterina, her eyes wide with obvious unease. She dipped a hurried half-curtsy and exited the dining room, closing the door behind her. Once she was gone, Dracula returned his attention to his oldest friend.

"Answer him, Valeri," he said. "And speak truthfully when you do."

Valeri fixed Seward with a look of utter contempt. "I have lived half a dozen lifetimes, Mr Seward, and in that time I have learnt what is important and what is not. Morality, decency, generosity, selflessness: all are vain and worth nothing. Only two things matter: honour and loyalty. I pledged loyalty to my lord when the world was a different place, pledged it to him for as long as I lived, and I still live. I would not dishonour myself by changing my mind now, like some fickle schoolgirl."

"What about love?" asked Seward. "You were married, Valeri, I know you were."

"Love is a lie," said Valeri, his eyes flaring. "It does nothing but weaken you."

"So you do not love your master?"

Valeri glanced over at Dracula, who was watching the exchange with the faintest hint of a smile on his face, and said nothing.

"You could kill him," said Seward, his voice low and urgent. "You could destroy him without breaking a sweat and it could be you who rules the world. Why the hell don't you?"

Dracula's smile disappeared. "Yes, Valeri," he said. "Why don't you?"

The eldest Rusmanov looked at his master, then back at Seward, his usually unreadable face full of a single clear emotion.

Fury.

And suddenly Seward understood. Despite his claims, Valeri's obedience owed nothing to loyalty, or honour. He was afraid of Dracula, *still* afraid, despite his master's weakness. And he was furious that Henry was provoking him towards having to admit that fear.

Long, pregnant seconds ticked by, in which nobody in the dining room moved. Then Valeri turned on his heels, strode through the door, and slammed it shut behind him, hard enough that the wood of the frame cracked along its entire length.

Seward leant forward and filled a glass from the neighbouring place setting with Château Angelus. He took a long sip, sat back in his chair, and smiled.

"It seems I touched a nerve," he said, pleasantly.

Dracula smiled widely. "Indeed it does, my dear Admiral," he said, reaching for his own glass. "And in the spirit of honest discourse, it seems only fair to inform you that, when we are finished with dinner, I am going to take out one of your eyes and eat it. I suggest you begin giving some thought to which one you will prefer to be without."

# 4

# THE NEEDS OF THE MANY

After stepping out of the lift on Level A Matt Browning took a moment to compose himself.

Before he rounded the corner and presented himself to the Security Division Operator stationed outside Cal Holmwood's quarters, he leant his back against the wall and took a slow series of deep breaths, his eyes closed, his hands at his sides, focusing entirely on the air flowing through his body. It was a ritual he used whenever he was summoned to speak to the Interim Director, one that had been required far more often than he would have liked over the previous ten days. Professor Robert Karlsson, the Director of the Lazarus Project, was in China on an information-sharing mission to PBS6, the People's Bureau of the Supernatural, and his absence, combined with Cal Holmwood's assertion that he had no time to deal with new people, had seen Matt become the project's de facto spokesman.

It was not just that talking to the Interim Director made him nervous, although he would be the first to admit that it did; it was the fact that he knew exactly what Holmwood was going to ask him, and exactly what his reply would have to be.

Matt took a final deep breath and stepped round the corner. The

Security Operator raised his MP7 by a few degrees and told him to identify himself.

"Browning, Matt, NS303, 83-C."

"Go ahead," said the Operator, and stepped aside.

"Cheers," said Matt, then immediately felt foolish for having done so. He walked down the short corridor and pushed open the heavy door at the end of it. Cal Holmwood, for once, was not seated behind his long desk; instead, he was sitting stiffly in one of two armchairs that stood round a now empty fireplace, a remnant, Matt assumed, of less formal, more opulent times. The Interim Director held a glass of water in one hand and gestured towards the second armchair with the other. Matt crossed the small room and took a seat.

"Drink?" asked Holmwood.

"No thank you, sir."

Holmwood narrowed his eyes. "Are you all right, Matt? You look like you're about to faint."

Matt swallowed. "I'm fine, sir."

"Are you sure?"

"Yes, sir. Honestly."

"All right," said Holmwood, regarding him carefully. "I have to update the Directors on the progress of Lazarus. What should I tell them?"

This was the moment Matt dreaded, the moment he *always* dreaded.

"Tell them there's nothing new to report, sir," he said, and felt embarrassment warm his cheeks. "I'm afraid that's the truth."

"That's what I told them last time," said Holmwood. "And the three times before that."

"Like I said, sir," said Matt, "it's the truth."

The Interim Director sighed deeply and set his glass down on a small table beside his chair. As he fixed his gaze on Matt's, he looked far older than his thirty-nine years.

"The finest minds on the planet," he said, his voice low and tired. "Cutting-edge equipment, an essentially unlimited budget, and you have nothing I can take to the others? No progress of any kind? None whatsoever?"

"I'm sorry, sir," repeated Matt. "We *are* making progress, every day, and everybody is working as hard as they can, harder than is healthy in most cases. But we're nowhere near a meaningful breakthrough."

"Why not?" asked Holmwood. "Layman's terms, Lieutenant."

Matt nodded. "Sir, the scale of what we're attempting is monumental. We're trying to map DNA that is at least sixty-five per cent unique in the entire natural world, reverse engineer a protein activation that *is* unique in the entire natural world, then synthesise a serum that will physically alter an individual on a genetic level. It's like being asked to make a century's worth of discovery in a fortnight, sir."

"Will we have a cure in the next decade?" asked Holmwood.

"I don't know, sir."

"Guess."

Matt wracked his brains, trying to settle on a number within a margin of error that didn't exist.

"It's possible, sir," he said. "Fifty-fifty chance."

"In five years?"

"Eighty-twenty against, sir."

Holmwood sat forward in his chair. "And what would you need to have a cure ready a year from now?"

Matt laughed: a short, sharp sound with no humour in it whatsoever.

"Honestly, sir?" he asked. "A miracle."

* * *

Matt's words rang in Cal's ears as the lift slowed to a halt on Level H.

He had moderated the bleakness of his report to the other Directors; he saw no sense in burdening them with the whole truth, especially when there was nothing any of them could do. But the reality was simple.

*The Lazarus Project needs a miracle.*

*We need a miracle.*

Holmwood was angry with himself for showing his disappointment in front of Matt; it was not fair to take bad news out on its bearer. He knew that the young Lieutenant spoke the truth, that the Lazarus Project team were working themselves into early graves in pursuit of a cure, and he was certain they would find one as quickly as it was humanly possible to do so.

But five years? A decade?

Part of him, a part he was now forced to accept had been almost hopelessly naive, had believed they would be administering vampire vaccines before the Zero Hour countdown was complete, vaccines that would render it irrelevant. Instead, he was forced to face a bleak reality. There was simply no chance of a cure arriving in time to stop Dracula's rise; all that was left to do was hope it was found before there was nobody left for it to help.

Inside the entrance to the non-supernatural containment facility, Holmwood nodded to the Security Operator, then walked quickly down the cell block. He tapped a nine-digit code into a wall panel beside a heavy metal door; it unlocked with a series of heavy thuds and the whir of spinning gears, and opened with a loud hiss. Cal took a deep breath, and pushed it.

Julian Carpenter looked up at him with eyes that were deep-set and sunken, pushed back by months spent alternating between darkness and fluorescent light. His face was covered by a thick beard, and his hair hung down across his forehead; his razor was long gone, one of the many privileges that had been removed following his refusal to cooperate over Adam. His cell was now almost bare; his own clothes were gone, replaced by a grey T-shirt and trousers, the personal effects he had carried with him on his long quest across America, including his only photos of his family, now stored in a locker behind the guard post. It had hurt Cal's heart to take them, but he had not hesitated; as far as he was concerned, Julian's refusal to cooperate was tantamount to treason, a selfish betrayal of everything he had once professed to hold dear.

"Cal," said Julian. He was sitting on the bed with his back against the wall, his arms wrapped round his knees. "What an unexpected pleasure."

"Julian," replied Holmwood, pushing the cell door shut behind him.

"Taking my stuff I can understand," said Julian. "But did you really have to put me on prison food? That was just cruel."

Cal fought back a smile; his old friend had not lost his ability to make him laugh in even the direst of circumstances, but he could not allow himself to be charmed. He needed to see the man curled up before him not as his friend, but as what he had become.

An uncooperative prisoner.

"Sorry," he said. "You can have regular food again whenever you want, as well as your things back. Just tell me what you know about Adam."

"Let me see my family," said Julian.

"You know I can't do that."

"Then we're both screwed, aren't we?"

Holmwood took a step into the cell, his hands balling into fists.

He was suddenly furious with his former colleague, at his stupid, reckless intransigence; he wanted to grab Julian and shake him until he saw sense.

"If you really cared about your family," he said, forcing his voice to remain steady, "you would tell me what you know. Adam might very well represent the only chance of finding a cure for Marie, and for reducing the threat your son faces every night. I don't think you give a shit about anyone apart from yourself, Julian. This is about you trying to assert your influence over a situation you must know you can't control."

Julian stared up at him and said nothing. His eyes, although sunken and red around the edges, still shone the same brilliant blue they always had.

*Jamie's eyes*, thought Cal. *One thing you gave him that's worth having.*

"I could have you tortured," he said. "It would give me no pleasure, but I could. There are things I could order that even you wouldn't be able to resist. Is that what you want?"

Julian didn't respond, or drop his gaze; his blue eyes remained fixed on his old friend.

"Say something, for Christ's sake!" shouted Cal. "What happened to the man I trusted with my life, Julian? Where the hell has he gone? I don't recognise this person you've become."

"What do you want me to say, Cal?" said Julian, softly. "Things change. I used to have a family, and a career, and friends, but all I have left is something you want. And I'll give it to you, Cal, gladly, if you give me one thing in return."

"I can't let you see your family, Julian," said Cal. "You know I can't. You'd be saying the same thing if you were me, and you damn well know it."

"Maybe so," said Julian. "But I'm not you. I'm just your prisoner."

"That's right," said Cal, his voice low and thick with anger. "You're a prisoner. And that's not all. You're a disgrace to the uniform you used to wear, to the uniform your son now wears, and to everything you once stood for."

Julian opened his mouth to speak, his eyes flashing with fury, but Cal steamrollered over him.

"I don't want to hear it, Julian. You have forty-eight hours to voluntarily tell me everything you know about Adam. After that, I will use every means available to compel you to do so, and I will personally ensure that you never see daylight again. So I suggest you think very hard about what you want your future to be."

# 5

# CHEWED UP AND SPAT OUT

## TELEORMAN FOREST, NEAR BUCHAREST, ROMANIA

The first thing the vampire felt as he awoke was the cold.

It surrounded him, pressing against his skin like razor blades; he was shivering before he even managed to open his eyes. The sky above him was black and blazing with stars; it hung low, looming down, inky and infinite.

The vampire pushed himself up on his elbows and looked unsteadily around. He was lying in a field, the grass hidden by a covering of deep white snow. A wooden fence ran round the edge, and at the south-eastern corner stood an electrical substation; the wires hummed in the freezing air, the electricity setting his teeth on edge. In the distance, across a dark expanse, pale orange light bloomed against the horizon. The vampire shut his eyes, attempting to gather himself.

For a terrible moment, he had no idea who he was; the searing cold seemed to have wiped his mind clear, leaving behind nothing but a vacuum. Where he was, and why, were unclear; the field and the substation were entirely unfamiliar. He squeezed his eyes shut more tightly, searching in vain if not for answers then for a clue, a single, solitary hint as to who he was and what he was doing in this snowy field. He only opened them again when a warm, pungent smell drifted into his nostrils, causing saliva to burst into his mouth in a torrent.

Beside him, lying in a patch of newly melted snow, was a freshly killed deer. It stared blankly at him, its mouth ringed with terrified foam. Hunger rumbled through the vampire, and he felt his fangs slide into place as heat spilled into his eyes. He lurched to his knees, his frozen limbs screaming in protest, then buried his face in the deer's throat, tearing at the soft flesh, digging for a vein or an artery. One split beneath his teeth and blood, still warm, spurted into his mouth; pleasure overwhelmed him and he threw back his head, his neck muscles standing out, his face coated with crimson. He rode out the wave of sensation, then clamped his mouth back over the pulsing vein and drank until he could drink no more.

When he was sated, the vampire rose to his feet. Steam was billowing from him in a thick cloud as the snow that had covered him melted, and his mind pulsed with the regained memory of himself. What he had been doing, the trail he had been following, returned to him in a nauseating rush, although why he had found himself lying in a field beside a dead deer still remained unclear. He pushed the sleeve of his coat back and looked at his watch. The time was irrelevant; the day was what mattered. There was a hole in his memory, and the vampire wanted to know exactly how deep it went. He read the small numbers in the date window and felt his lips curl into a thin smile.

It was two days later than he was expecting.

Somehow, somewhere, he had lost forty-eight hours.

The vampire dug his hands into the damp pockets of his coat and found a crumpled piece of paper in one of them. He pulled it out and unfolded it. Three words were scrawled on it, in a handwriting he didn't recognise.

### LEAVE ME ALONE

For several long seconds, he merely stared at it. Then understanding flooded through him, as he realised what the words meant, and who had written them. He stuffed the note back into his pocket and buttoned his coat with fingers that were still numb.

*I have to tell them*, he thought. *They need to know that I found him. That there's still a chance.*

The vampire known as Grey lifted himself easily off the ground, and flew steadily towards the distant light.

# 6 DAYS TILL
# ZERO HOUR

# 6

# HOME SWEET HOME

Valentin Rusmanov knew something was wrong the moment he touched down on the roof of his building.

His home, which was not so much a house as an entire block of Central Park West reconfigured into a vast mansion, was equipped with a remarkable array of security systems: laser grids, pressure pads, motion-sensor cameras, decibel monitors, thermal evaluators. The small electronic panel that was resting in the inside pocket of his suit jacket should have begun to beep as soon as he landed on the tiled terrace between the roof gardens and the glass dome that topped the building, giving him thirty seconds to disarm the system before his home was locked down.

Instead, there was nothing.

Valentin took the panel from his pocket and had his suspicions instantly confirmed. Where there should have been a pattern of green blocks representing the various zones of the alarm system, there were only two words of glowing red text.

59

Valentin narrowed his eyes and felt his fangs slide smoothly down from his gums. He floated quickly across the roof, noting the dead blooms of jasmine and nightshade that hung limply in their marble pots, and found what he was expecting: the ornate double doors that controlled access to the roof, smashed to splinters. Valentin let out a low growl, and floated silently through the hole where they had stood.

The staircase that led down from the roof opened on to one end of the corridor that ran the length of the top floor of the building, the floor which contained Valentin's private suite of rooms. In the more than a century since he had taken ownership of the building, tens of thousands of guests had danced and drank and laughed and killed in its many rooms, at party after debauched party. But at every single event, each one thrown with the ancient vampire's legendary style and generosity, there had been a single, non-negotiable rule.

Nobody went to the top floor.

Ever.

That rule had evidently been broken in his absence. The corridor's blood-red carpet was tracked with dirty footprints, and the pictures that had covered the long walls had been lifted from their hooks and smashed on the ground. Valentin surveyed the carnage, his heart accelerating in his chest. The corridor contained a mere fraction of his art collection, but had been home to several of his favourite pieces, including a Francis Bacon triptych that not even the most exhaustive record of the man's works had ever listed. He floated slowly forward, trying to control the rage that was building within him, and gripped the handle of the door to his study. He took a deep breath before turning it, steeling himself for what he was sure he was going to see.

The room had been destroyed.

Valentin's beautiful ornate desk, which had been carved from dark mahogany when the nineteenth century was still new, had been reduced to splinters and piled in the middle of the floor on top of a Persian rug that was now little more than lumps of coloured string. The shelves had been torn down from the walls, their contents smashed and scattered; next to the broken remnants of a pair of Chinese terracotta warriors lay the deflated corpses of three basketballs and the shattered glass of the tank they had floated in. His armchair had been shredded, its beautiful navy blue leather torn and hacked beyond repair, its stuffing spilling out like intestines. And spray-painted across the walls and ceiling, in a dozen different colours, was a single word.

## TRAITOR

For almost a minute, Valentin didn't move; he was frozen to the spot by the scale and frenzy of the invasion, his eyes wide, his face pale, the initial shock and outrage already evolving in the pit of his stomach into a boiling, howling fury beyond anything he could remember.

Something in the centre of what was left of his desk caught his eye: a narrow sliver of dark pink. Valentin forced his body into action, floated across the room, and picked it up with his long fingers. It was a Bliss cigarette, one of many that had sat in an ornate rosewood box on his desk, and had miraculously survived the ransacking. Valentin placed it between his lips, found a match, and lit it, dragging the smoke deeply into his lungs. The potent mixture of tobacco, heroin and human blood thundered into his system, and he felt an ethereal calm settle over him.

*You should have expected this*, he told himself. *Valeri was here the day before you left. You should have known there would be a price to be paid for what you did.*

Valentin finished the cigarette and ground it beneath the heel of his shoe. For the first time in as long as he could remember, he wasn't sure what he should do next. His first instinct was to bellow for Lamberton, the butler who had served him faultlessly for almost a century. But Lamberton was gone, his heart torn from his chest by Valentin's own hand, punishment for an act of stupidity that had threatened to blacken his master's name along with his own. It was a misjudgement that still made Valentin furious with disappointment; Lamberton's affection for his master had been exploited by the traitor Richard Brennan, and his determination not to trouble Valentin with the problem had left the ancient vampire with no choice but to destroy his oldest companion.

*I have not yet forgiven you*, he thought, as he floated back out into the corridor, *for what you made me do.*

Valentin felt a stab of pain in his heart as he looked at the priceless treasures that now lay in tatters; the accumulated wonders of a long life destroyed for reasons no grander than malice and spite. He flew slowly down the corridor towards the round atrium at the centre of the floor; there were identical spaces on each level of his home, the five above ground and the two below. All were flanked by two elevator shafts and opened on to the central staircase, the grand, sweeping column of marble and carved wood that Valentin thought of as the spine of the house.

He was greeted in the atrium by another deluge of spray-painted insults, and the twisted, broken remains of the Alexander Calder mobile that had hung from the ceiling since Valentin had liberated it from an SS Colonel fleeing for South America in 1945. The mobile's beautiful, delicate wings had been pulled down and torn apart, the broken shards strewn across the floor. Valentin stared at them, and realised he could not go downstairs; he knew what he would find, and the prospect of floating through the ruins of his life filled him with a despair so profound it was almost physical.

Then something drifted through the silent atrium, carried up from below on the faintest current of air, and his eyes flooded a dreadful crimson-black. It would have been undetectable to anyone without Valentin's supernatural senses, but to him it was as strong and clear as the beam of a lighthouse.

It was the scent of a vampire.

*Still here*, he thought, and felt his body physically tremble with anticipation. *Whoever did this. They're still here.*

The heat in Valentin's eyes built to an almost unbearable temperature. He floated in the air, letting the scent of the intruder fill his nostrils, tasting heat and blood and sweat. Then he swept silently forward, his jacket billowing out behind him, and descended the staircase like a bird of prey. He ignored the graffiti and destruction in the atria as he soared through them; his mind was burning solely with the prospect of vengeance. Within seconds, he was standing before the grand double doors that led into the ground-floor ballroom, the cavernous space where he had first encountered an agent of what would become known as Blacklight, where the chain of events that had led him to this moment had been set in slow, languorous motion.

Valentin took a deep breath, then threw open the doors. They hit the walls of the atrium with a noise like coffin lids slamming shut, the impact reverberating through the thick stone of the old building. He stepped into the ballroom and took a quick glance around the room; the grand chandelier, beneath which thousands of men and women had twirled and spun, lay shattered across the black and white marble floor. Tiles had been torn up and hurled throughout the room, sticking out of the walls and ceiling like splinters in skin. The long bar that ran the length of the far wall had been tipped over and smashed, its bottles and glasses now little more than a carpet of twinkling wreckage spreading out across the broken tiles. Then he saw the two figures standing at the edge of the floor, and the damage to the room was forgotten.

The vampires were embracing, frozen in the middle of what looked to Valentin's experienced eye like an amateurish waltz. The woman was wearing a long ballgown dripping with jewellery that he immediately recognised; it had been taken from the collection in his dressing room on the fifth floor. The man was wearing a tuxedo that had been crafted for Valentin by Coco Chanel in her apartment on Rue Cambon, as Europe breathed a sigh of relief at the end of the Great War. They stared at him with wide eyes, with the guilty half-smiles of people who have been caught doing something they are not supposed to.

"At last," said the man, finding his voice first. "The traitor returns. I'm surprised you have the nerve to show your—"

The last words the man ever spoke died in his throat as Valentin crossed the ballroom in a blur of navy blue and trailing red. The vampires, who had been happily desecrating his home for almost a month, didn't have time to blink before he was upon them.

Valentin closed a pale hand round the man's neck, crushed his windpipe as though it was tissue paper, and threw him across the cavernous room. The vampire crashed into the panelled wall, sending an explosion of blood and splintered wood into the air, then slid to the floor, clutching weakly at his neck as his face turned rapidly purple. The woman's eyes began to redden as her mouth yawned open, but before she could form a single syllable, Valentin shoved his hands through skin and muscle and took hold of her shoulder bones, his fingernails scraping across them like metal down a blackboard.

Blood gushed out across the backs of his hands, soaking the cuffs of his shirt, as the woman threw back her head and screamed in agony. Valentin lifted her into the air, blood raining down on to his face and neck, and spread his arms wide. The woman came apart with a sound like a roll of paper being torn in half, huge and wet. She fell to the ground in two pieces, her eyes wide with shock as her insides spilled out across the black and white tiles.

Valentin wiped blood from his own eyes and saw the woman's heart lying in the centre of the steaming mess. He stamped it flat, and what was left of the vampire burst with a series of pitiful bangs and thuds. Valentin had already turned away, and was bearing down on the other stricken male vampire like the angel of death, a bloodstained vision from the depths of some terrible nightmare.

The vampire raised a trembling hand in a futile plea for mercy. Valentin kicked it aside with such force that he heard the bones in the man's arm snap like cocktail sticks, then lowered himself over the vampire, his knees resting either side of the man's chest. Air whistled out of the vampire's ruined throat; he was incapable of forming words, but his eyes were wide and pleading.

Valentin didn't say a word; he began to punch the vampire in the face, over and over again, his arm rising and falling like a piston. Blood flew in the silent air of the ballroom, as the ancient vampire gave himself over entirely to the terrible, brutal beauty of revenge.

Sometime later his mind cleared.

What lay on the ground beneath Valentin was now little more than a bubbling mass of red and pink. His arm screamed with pain, and he found he could no longer raise it above his shoulder. He got slowly to his feet and stamped a foot through the vampire's chest, crushing the heart that was still flickering with life. There was a thump as what was left of the vampire's body burst, spraying the already soaked Valentin with yet more blood, but he barely noticed. The euphoria of vengeance was gone, and all that remained was the inevitable emptiness, the inescapable truth that one act cannot cancel out another.

He flew across the ballroom without a backward glance, then up the sweeping curves of the staircase and along the corridor until he was again standing in the middle of his study. He strode over to room's north wall, slid his fingers across a wooden panel that appeared identical to all the others until he found the tiny depression the invading vampires had missed, and pressed it firmly.

A motor whirred into life, and a large section of the wall slid out and to the side, revealing a vault with a round metal door that looked like it belonged on a submarine. Valentin placed a hand into a plastic slot and felt a needle break the skin of his index finger. A drop of blood fell into the chamber of a small centrifuge which spun into life, analysing the DNA contained in the crimson liquid. There was a long pause, then a black panel above the slot turned green and the door rumbled open. Valentin stepped through it and into the vault, a metal cube with an uncrackable safe at the rear and metal shelving on either side.

Two of the shelves were full of gold bars, gleaming under strip lights set into the ceiling. Below them were three shelves full of money: dollars, euros, pounds, yen and yuan, all wrapped tightly in clear plastic. On the opposite wall, clear plastic boxes contained bonds and share certificates, many of them more than a hundred years old.

Under the boxes lay three wooden racks full of wine bottles, and it was these that Valentin first turned his attention to. He reached out a blood-soaked hand, carefully lifted a bottle from the middle of the highest rack, and examined the label. The word *Petrus* was printed in ornate red lettering beneath a severe illustration of a bearded man and *1947* in simple black print. He had been saving the bottle, arguably the finest of the entire twentieth century, for an occasion that was special even by his own rarefied standards; he was now beginning to think that such an occasion might never arise.

Working incredibly carefully, Valentin applied an opener to the bottle's cork, until it gave way with a loud pop and an escape of air that was overpoweringly, almost impossibly fragrant as it entered his nostrils. He raised the bottle to his lips, took a delicate sip, and sighed deeply as a smile of glorious contentment appeared on his face. He took a second, longer drink, then put the bottle down and forced himself to focus.

Valentin lifted an elegant overnight bag from the bottom shelf, filled it with two stacks of each currency and two of the gold bars, and zipped it shut. He hoisted the bag on to his shoulder, picked up the bottle of Petrus, and took a long look around the vault; he knew there was every chance he would never see it again. Then he floated through the door, pushed it shut behind him, and flew out of his study, heading for the roof he had landed on less than fifteen minutes earlier.

\* \* \*

The ancient vampire looked out across the dark expanse of Central Park, swigging liberally from the priceless bottle of wine. His head was starting to feel agreeably fuzzy, and the lights of Manhattan that shimmered to the south were starting to ever so slightly blur.

*You could just go*, said a voice at the back of his head. It was the voice that had encouraged him to live exactly as he pleased for more than a century, to think of nobody but himself. *Fly south. Brazil, or Cuba. Let Blacklight deal with this.*

Valentin had stood in the grounds of the Loop barely three hours earlier, promising Paul Turner that he would find Valeri and Dracula, find them and deliver their location back to Blacklight, and he had meant it; he had leapt into the cold air of eastern England, burning with an alien desire to help prevent his former master plunging the world into darkness. But now, standing on the roof of his devastated home with the evening breeze fluttering against his skin, he found himself torn.

If the end was truly nigh, if the rise of Dracula was genuinely unavoidable, then the sensible thing to do would be to disappear into the dark corners of the world he knew so well and enjoy whatever time still remained. But something nagged at him, something that manifested as a stubborn reluctance to do so. Part of it was the invasion of his home, a cruel, petty violation that he had no doubt had been personally ordered by his brother. And another part was something that surprised him even as he realised it: a curious unwillingness to betray Paul Turner. The Blacklight Security Officer was hard, and had made absolutely no secret of his dislike and distrust of Valentin. But he was also honest, courageous, and utterly committed to both his mission and his men, qualities that the former General Rusmanov had once prized extremely highly, in the time when he had still been a man.

Valentin drained the bottle of Petrus and flipped it casually towards Central Park; it spiralled end over end, light reflecting off its dark green surface, until it disappeared into the gloom. Then he lifted the overnight bag, swung it over his shoulder, and stepped off the roof.

# 7

# POSITIVE MALE ROLE MODELS

Colonel Victor Frankenstein closed his eyes, hoping the billowing rush of gas would clear his mind.

The unnaturally long span of his life had contained many occasions that prompted him to consider the limits of the oath he had sworn to John Carpenter as the snow fell on Manhattan in the first hours of 1929. It appeared to be simplicity itself: protect the Carpenter family. But he had come to understand that there were *two* meanings to the promise he had made: protecting the Carpenters from the external dangers that seemed endlessly drawn to the family, and protecting them from themselves.

As far as the first interpretation was concerned, he had done his duty, and done it well. John had lived to be an old man, in no small part thanks to Frankenstein's interventions and watchful eye; even the recent revelation, that John had simultaneously struck a clandestine deal with Valentin Rusmanov in which Operator and vampire agreed not to pursue each other, did little to undermine the monster's sense of achievement.

He had similarly saved Julian Carpenter's life more times than he could remember; had stopped nails and fangs meant for his neck, had stood at his side as bullets and blades flew, and accompanied him safely back to the Loop night after long, dark night. And when the time came, he had done the same for Julian's son; he had gone to Lindisfarne, his ears ringing with rebuke, had stood with Jamie as he faced down Alexandru Rusmanov, and watched with great pride as the boy's quick thinking and bravery had ultimately won the day.

But the second interpretation? Protecting the Carpenters from themselves? On that count, he was not so sure.

Frankenstein had warned Julian in the aftermath of HUMMINGBIRD, the Priority Level 1 operation to Budapest that had seen Jamie's father destroy Ilyana, the wife of Alexandru Rusmanov, that repercussions for his actions were inevitable. But Julian, whom he had loved like a brother, and who possessed enormous capacities for kindness and loyalty, had also carried within himself an infuriating streak of arrogance. When Alexandru's revenge finally came, made possible by the traitor Thomas Morris, it had taken Julian by surprise. And although Frankenstein was one of only two people who really knew what happened the night that Julian died, he would always believe that he had failed to protect his friend from himself.

Now, barely more than two years later, he was already beginning to wonder if he wasn't failing Julian's son the same way. Jamie was similar to his father in so many ways: brave, headstrong, rebellious, loyal, utterly maddening, with a profound distaste for being told what to do, even when the advice was genuinely meant. He had seen for himself exactly how dangerous vampires were, yet was now in some kind of unnatural relationship with one of them, over the objections of both Frankenstein and his mother. He had also led an almost suicidally risky operation into the Parisian underworld to rescue the monster himself, which, although Frankenstein would always be grateful, had been remarkably ill-advised.

71

Finally, and worst of all, had been the bizarre relationship that Jamie had struck up with Valentin Rusmanov during the vampire's captivity in the Loop. Despite, or possibly *because* of, Frankenstein's explicit instruction that he not talk to Valentin under any circumstances, Jamie had become a regular visitor to the ancient vampire's cell. Frankenstein had gone down to the cell block and warned Valentin not to speak to Jamie again, making it clear that he, unlike some inside the Loop, would never trust a single poisonous word that emerged from the vampire's mouth.

Valentin's response had cut him to the bone; he had suggested that Frankenstein concern himself with why Jamie was going to a vampire for guidance, rather than to the monster who had sworn to protect him.

Frankenstein *had* wondered. And wondered.

And now he was on his way to talk to the one other person who might know.

The gas dissipated and the airlock's inner door swung open to reveal the long central corridor of Level H, the Loop's detention block. As he neared the last cell on the left, his footsteps echoing loudly in the still, silent space, he paused; he was momentarily overcome by an absurd urge to brush down his uniform and straighten his hair. He pushed it away, smiling to himself, and walked out in front of the cell.

Marie Carpenter looked up from a worn sofa and gasped; her eyes flared a deep, glowing red, and her face, which was every bit as beautiful as Julian had repeatedly described it, time and time again, curdled into a mask of revulsion. It was gone almost instantly, replaced by a warm, polite expression that he imagined would once have greeted visitors to the Carpenter family home, but it had been there; they both knew it.

For Frankenstein, it was nothing new; his appearance had been causing shock and dismay for well over a century and a half. But it still hurt.

"I'm so sorry," said Marie, getting to her feet and approaching the ultraviolet barrier that formed the front wall of her cell. Her face was colouring pink with embarrassment. "That was awful of me. I just... I wasn't expecting it to be you. Please forgive me."

Frankenstein forced a smile. "It's all right, Mrs Carpenter," he said. "At least you didn't scream." It was a small joke, but it managed to crack the ice, if not break it entirely.

"Call me Marie," said Jamie's mother, smiling back at him. "And do come in, please."

Frankenstein nodded and stepped through the purple barrier, feeling his skin tingle as he did so. He extended a hand, which Marie shook without hesitation.

"Victor Frankenstein," he said, more formally than he meant to.

"Marie Carpenter," replied Jamie's mother. "I saw you on Lindisfarne, but it's lovely to properly meet you. Although Jamie has told me so much about you that I feel like I know you already."

"Likewise," said Frankenstein. "He speaks about you with such love. His father did the same."

Marie winced, then quickly rallied. "I'm glad to hear that," she said. "I suspect you knew Julian far better than I ever really did."

Frankenstein shook his head. "I don't think so," he said. "The man who came home to you every night was the man he was. He only lied about what he did for a living."

"Quite a big lie, though, wouldn't you say?" said Marie, forcing a sad, narrow smile.

"Yes," said Frankenstein. "I would. I know he hated having to do it, if that's any consolation."

"It is," said Marie. "Not a lot, but it is. Henry Seward told me the same thing."

Silence settled over the cell, a silence in which the weight of the past hung palpably in the air. In the distance, Frankenstein heard the airlock door open.

"Anyway," said Marie, shaking her head and smiling more genuinely, "I stopped being angry with Julian a long time ago. And I'm sure you didn't come down here to talk about such gloomy matters?"

"No," said Frankenstein, relief at the change of subject clear in his voice. "I didn't come to talk about your husband. I came to talk about your son."

Marie's smile faded. "I thought as much," she said. "What has he done now?"

"He's not in any trouble," said Frankenstein, quickly. "I don't know what he's told you about me, or about—"

"He told me about the vow you made," interrupted Marie, her voice low. "To protect our family. He told me about that, Victor."

"I'm glad," said Frankenstein, feeling rare warmth spread through him. "I didn't know whether he would have."

Marie nodded. "He told me you knew Julian's father when he was young, which is hard for me to imagine. When Julian and I got married, he already seemed old. Jamie never even met him."

"I knew him very well," said Frankenstein. "And he would be very proud of his grandson, that much I can say for certain."

An expression of love, so fierce that it almost made Frankenstein take a step backwards, appeared on Marie's face.

"So he should be," she said, colour rising to her cheeks. "Jamie's a good boy, and his heart's in the right place. He means everything to me."

"And to me," said Frankenstein. "I have done my best to protect three generations of Carpenters, and Jamie is at least the equal of the men who went before him. I will protect him till the day I die, from anyone or anything that seeks to do him harm, and from himself, when necessary. But lately..."

"What?" asked Marie. Tears were standing in the corners of her eyes, the product of Frankenstein's obvious love for her son. "Go on, please."

"Lately, I've felt like I'm failing him," said Frankenstein, and grimaced; the words tasted bitter as he spoke them out loud. "I feel like I'm doing him more harm than good, that I'm hindering him rather than helping. I no longer know whether I'm keeping the promise I made."

Marie stared at him, her eyes wide and rimmed with tears. "Don't say that," she said. "Don't ever say that. I know you rescued him from Alexandru the night I was taken, and I know that you threatened to resign if he wasn't allowed to try and find me. I know you went to Lindisfarne even though Jamie had told you not to, when he had listened to the poison Thomas Morris put in his ear. So don't you ever say you're failing him. He and I would both be dead if it wasn't for you."

"Thank you," said Frankenstein, his voice a low rumble. "I didn't know how much you knew. It means a lot."

"Good," said Marie, firmly. "Because I meant it. I know what thinking you've failed feels like, believe me I do. I felt it every day for two years after Julian died, like I was putting the memory of a dead man above the son who needed me, but I didn't know how to stop myself. I look at the list of men he's tried to replace his father with, whether he knows he's doing it or not, and my heart aches for him. You, Henry Seward, Cal Holmwood, Paul Turner, even Valentin Rusmanov, for God's sake. It makes me feel like I'm still failing, because why would he try so hard unless I'm not enough for him?"

Marie's tears brimmed over and spilled down her cheeks. She made no attempt to hide them; they gleamed under the fluorescent light of the cell as they rolled towards her neck.

"Jamie knows you love him," said Frankenstein. "And he went through hell to get you back. He's a teenage boy in a world full of alpha males, men who are brave and wise and capable, who are everything any child would like their father to be. The tragedy is that his father *was* one of those men; he just never knew until it was too late. I think he's trying to understand the man Julian was, and is drawn to men who are like him. I don't think it's criticism of you, or rejection."

"I'm not so sure," said Marie. "He was so *angry* with me after Julian died. We were always at each other's throats. Sometimes it feels like he's trying to hurt me, even if he doesn't realise. Look at him now, with that Larissa creature. Even after what happened to me, to his father, and all the other people he's seen get hurt, he decides to go out with a vampire. Even though there are normal, *human* girls like Kate for him to be interested in. Why would he do such a thing?"

"I think it's called being a teenager," said Frankenstein, and smiled. "I never was one, so I can't speak from personal experience, but there seems to be nothing more boring to a teenager than what is good for them, and nothing more horrifying than parental approval."

Marie managed a small smile of her own. "I hope so," she said. "I hope that's what it is, I really do. Because I don't know what I'd do if—"

She stopped abruptly, tilted her head back, and gasped. Then her eyes flamed scarlet, and a furious expression twisted her features.

"Don't you know it's rude to eavesdrop?" she shouted, turning her head and staring out at the corridor. Frankenstein followed her gaze, and felt cold fingers dance up his misshapen spine as Jamie Carpenter stepped silently out in front of the cell.

"How long have you been standing there?" he managed.

Jamie shrugged. "Long enough."

"How dare you listen in on a private conversation?" said Marie, her eyes glowing fiercely. "Didn't I bring you up better than that?"

"A private conversation?" repeated Jamie, and grunted with laughter. "Is that what this is? Because it sounds to me like two people giving me a psych evaluation without even doing me the courtesy of letting me speak for myself. And trying to let my dad off the hook for being stupid enough to get himself killed."

"Jamie!" shrieked Marie. "How dare you speak to Victor and I like that?"

"Of all the people in the world," said Frankenstein, trying his hardest to keep his temper, to keep anger and the shame of being caught out of his voice, "surely *you* understand why he did what he did?"

"Why he didn't go to you when Tom Morris framed him?" asked Jamie. "Or to Henry Seward, or Cal Holmwood? Why he ended up lying dead on our drive instead of trusting his friends to help him when he was in trouble? I don't understand that, no."

"He was trying to protect you," said Frankenstein. "Both of you. If you can't see that, then—"

"Then what?" interrupted Jamie. "I know what he went through, I really do. I've seen it for myself, and I get why he had to lie to us about what he did for a living. I've honestly forgiven him for it. I was furious with him for leaving us for such a long time, but I'm not angry any more. I'm just disappointed."

"Don't you miss him, Jamie?" asked Marie. Scarlet fire still burned in her eyes, but her tone of voice had changed; it sounded horribly close to pleading.

Jamie met her gaze and shook his head. "The man I miss didn't exist, Mum. That was just a fiction, a version of himself he invented for me and you."

"Don't you dare say that," growled Frankenstein. "The man who raised you and loved you was real. He was my friend."

"Well, it doesn't matter now, does it?" said Jamie, turning to face his sworn protector. "Because he's dead."

Silence, icy cold and pregnant with recrimination, descended over the cell. Marie was staring at her son with obvious panic, clearly trying to understand how a simple conversation had turned so quickly into this poisonous stand-off. Frankenstein looked helplessly at her, feeling familiar pangs of shame begin to swirl in his stomach.

*You did this*, whispered a voice at the back of his mind. *You failed them both. You can't even protect them from each other.*

A loud beep finally broke the silence. Jamie pulled his console from his belt, thumbed the screen, and smiled.

"Well, how about that?" he said, his voice light and cheerful. "Another one of my desperate surrogate father figures wants to see me. I'd better not keep him waiting, in case he grounds me or takes my PlayStation away."

Jamie strolled through the barrier without a backward glance and disappeared down the corridor. Frankenstein was too shocked to speak; he simply could not convince his throat to form words. He looked at Marie Carpenter, and felt his heart lurch in his chest. She was staring in the direction her son had gone, the glow in her eyes slowly fading away to nothing. When she did find her voice, it was small and full of sadness.

"I don't think that went very well," she said.

# 8

# EYE IN THE SKY

*Click.*

"I'm bored, mate."

"Me too. Fag?"

*Click.*

"Just had one. Coffee?"

"Yeah, why not? I'll go."

"No bother, I'll get them."

*Click.*

"I offered first, mate. I'll be back in ten. Unless the queue is bad, which, you know, this time of day it might be. If it's bad, I might be half an hour."

"I won't hold my breath then."

"Probably for the best."

*Click.*

Justin Wallace grinned at his colleague, flicked him a casual V with the fingers of his right hand, then returned his attention to his screen as Simon let the door of the computer lab slam shut behind him. They had been cooped up in the small, airless room for almost a month, grinding through the project that was contributing a small amount towards their student debts, and any chance to step outside, even for a minute or two, was grabbed with both hands. They had prepared themselves for boring, perhaps even *very* boring, but neither of them had been ready for how interminably, soul-destroyingly tedious the job had actually turned out to be.

A small software start-up was preparing to launch the first iteration of their mapping software, and had employed Justin, Simon and two dozen other students around the country to select and collate the images that were required. They had bought several million from a company that provided photographs to many of the bigger, more established mapping services, taken once a second from a height of three hundred and ninety miles by a satellite called RapidEye 4 as it criss-crossed the globe in a series of orbits that had taken months to complete, and it was the job of Justin and Simon to wade through them all. Neither of them could see any reason why this new software would challenge the established companies in the sector, but the money was half-decent, if nothing else.

*Click.*

Justin was working his way through East Anglia, the swathe of flat farmland and forest that fitted snugly around the Wash, the large estuary that made it look as though some vast creature had taken a bite out of the eastern coastline of England. The satellite images came in sets of three, and Justin's job was simply to select the best one from each almost identical set and forward it to the compilers, where it would form one minuscule part of the giant high-definition map that was being constructed. He quickly examined three images of a nondescript patch of brown and green, selected one of them, and reached out to load the next set.

*Click.*

Justin frowned. The new images theoretically showed the same section of forest, an area of no notable interest thirty miles from the sea. But whereas the first showed the expected canopy of trees, the second and third were obscured by circles of bright purple light, slightly larger in the third image than the second. Justin pulled up his glitch folder from the toolbar at the bottom of his monitor, intending to select the first image for use and add the others to his error document, a running list of images that were over- or underexposed, or in some cases merely black squares where the image had failed to record. But something made him pause.

*They're different sizes,* he thought. *If they're errors, why are they different sizes?*

He reached out and loaded the next set of images. The first had been taken a second after the third image of the previous set, and the purple light was nowhere to be seen. But there *was* something in the corner of the photo; something that didn't look quite right. Justin dragged the image into his photo editor and magnified it, centring on the same area that was obscured in two of the previous set.

*What the hell?* he wondered, and leant in closer to the screen.

At 100x magnification, the canopy of trees appeared insubstantial, as though it had been superimposed over a second image. Beneath it, he could see a faint tracery of curving roads surrounding something long and straight, something that looked an awful lot like a—

"Who're you spying on?"

Justin clutched at his chest as he spun round in his chair. Simon was peering down at the screen, two steaming coffees in his hands and an expression of mild curiosity on his face.

"Jesus Christ," said Justin, his heart pounding in his chest. "Creep up on me, why don't you?"

"Sorry, mate," said Simon, without taking his eyes from the magnified image. "What have you got here? Glitch?"

"I don't know," said Justin, leaning back in his chair and rubbing his eyes. "I thought so, but it's weird. Tell me what you see."

Simon set the coffees down on the desk and leant in closer, a frown furrowing his brow. "Looks like there's something under the trees," he said, after a second or two. "Double exposure?"

"Probably," said Justin. "It's gone in the next image. But it follows directly on from these two." He reopened the images containing the purple circles.

Simon's frown deepened. "What the hell are they?"

"I don't know," said Justin. "It's like..."

Simon turned to look at him. "Spit it out, mate. It's like what?"

"Like there's something wrong with that bit of the forest," said Justin. He spoke slowly, trying not to let his mouth outrun the idea that was beginning to form in his mind. "Like something happened, whatever that purple light is, and it took a second or two to reset."

"Reset what?"

"I don't know," said Justin. "A shield, or some kind of camouflage. I don't know. But that looks like a runway to me, which means planes. There's no reason to hide an airport, no reason to even put an airport in the middle of a forest in the first place. So, if it's not an airport, what else has a runway?"

"An air-force base," said Simon.

"Right," said Justin. "Most of East Anglia is owned by the government. The RAF fought the Battle of Britain from about thirty miles south of where we're looking at, and Bomber Command flew from all over this bit of the country. This is British military heartland. So I don't know what it is. But I don't think it's a glitch."

"You're saying this is some secret RAF base?" asked Simon, his voice rising with excitement. "That's awesome, mate."

"I don't know," repeated Justin. "Maybe. But if so, what's that purple light?"

Simon became very still, and Justin realised with a rush of relief that the possibility blaring insistently in his mind had now occurred to his friend. It was so ludicrous that he had not wanted to say it out loud; instead, he had tried to make his colleague see it for himself. Simon grabbed the mouse and clicked open a new browser window; his fingers sped across the keyboard, finishing with a heavy thump on ENTER. A website burst on to the screen, a primary-coloured collection of images and text that assaulted the eyes.

## UKVAMPIRES.COM
## THE SITE THEY TRIED TO BAN!!!
## THE TRUTH THEY DON'T WANT YOU TO KNOW!!!

The main panel of the page was a long list of vampire stories, sightings, encounters, rumours and anecdotes. To the right was a black and white photo of a man looking to camera with a serious expression on his face, above two short lines of black text.

## KEVIN McKENNA
## NEVER FORGOTTEN

After his death, and the publication of the unauthorised copies of *The Globe* that now stood as his legacy, Kevin McKenna had been attacked by the tabloid press with such self-preserving viciousness that a pro-McKenna movement had formed almost immediately. The press accused him of being mentally ill, an attention-seeking fantasist, a dangerous criminal who had terrified an innocent public with a cruel practical joke, then killed himself rather than face the music, and a great many people, almost certainly the majority, were happy to accept that depiction.

But there were many who refused to believe what they were told, who had come to see McKenna as a hero, a man who had dared to speak truth to power and been murdered for doing so. These were the people who reprinted and reblogged his last words again and again, despite warnings and takedown notices. And there were more of them every day. In death, McKenna had become what he had never been in life: a touchstone, a rallying point.

A legend.

Beneath his photo were two prominent links, one in bright dripping red, the other in gleaming metallic silver.

### VAMPIRES – WHAT YOU NEED TO KNOW

### THE MEN IN BLACK – THE TRUTH BEHIND THE VISORS

Simon clicked the second link, filling the screen with a feverish list of alleged facts about the men in black, the classified anti-vampire branch of the military that Kevin McKenna had referred to in his final story as Blacklight. Simon scrolled down, and hovered the cursor over the penultimate line of text.

"There," he said, his voice low.

Justin leant forward and read.

THE MEN IN BLACK USE ULTRAVIOLET LIGHT TO
DESTROY VAMPIRES. THIS LIGHT APPEARS PURPLE
WHEN SEEN BY HUMAN EYES.

"Jesus," said Justin, his eyes locked on the screen. He took the
mouse from Simon's hand and clicked back to the images he had
so nearly dismissed as glitches. The purple circles filled the screen,
now seeming sinister, almost menacing.

"This is big," said Simon. "If we're right, then this is huge, mate.
It's the kind of thing we could get in real trouble for."

Justin rolled his eyes, trying to show his friend how ridiculous that
sounded. But in the centre of his chest, a cold sliver of fear had appeared.

*Will they be monitoring this?* he wondered. Can *they monitor this?*
*Do they know who I am?*

Trying to ignore the ice that had settled round his heart, he
copied the coordinates from the image header and opened a new
browser window. His fingers flew across the keys, bringing up the
website for the Land Registry, the government body responsible
for recording ownership of every square metre of the United
Kingdom. Justin pasted the coordinates into the search field at the
top of the page and watched as the results were returned almost
instantly.

REGISTERED TO: MINISTRY OF DEFENCE (UK)
TERRITORIAL LIST
ACQUIRED: 124.52
PREVIOUS REGISTRAR: LUX E TENEBRIS
FOUNDATION (REG. CHARITY 23494583)
NOTES: NONE

"MOD," breathed Simon, his eyes glued to the screen.

"Doesn't mean anything," said Justin, copying the number of the charity to his clipboard. "I told you they own most of East Anglia."

"I know, but..."

"Just hang on, all right. Let me do this."

Simon fell silent as Justin pasted the number into a search engine and hit ENTER. The results were minimal; the Lux E Tenebris Foundation was apparently concerned with architectural preservation, was indeed a listed charity, and had a registered address on Piccadilly in Central London. There was nothing else – no website, no contact information. Justin took the Piccadilly address back to the Land Registry and hit SEARCH.

"Holy shit," said Simon.

"Bingo," said Justin.

**REGISTERED TO:** LUX E TENEBRIS FOUNDATION (REG. CHARITY 23494583)
**ACQUIRED:** 5.7.24
**PREVIOUS REGISTRAR:** ESTATE OF ARTHUR HOLMWOOD, LORD GODALMING
**NOTES:** NONE

"Arthur Holmwood," said Simon. "He was in *Dracula*. Supposedly Bram Stoker knew him. McKenna named him in his article, mate. Said he was one of the founders of Blacklight."

"See the name of the charity?"

"*Light out of darkness*," translated Simon.

"Right. Fits, doesn't it?"

"Yeah," said Simon. "Makes sense, mate. If McKenna was right, and they've been keeping this whole thing a secret since the nineteenth century, then why wouldn't that be how they see it? Them in the light, the rest of us in the dark."

"Like kids," said Justin, his voice low. "Like children who can't think for ourselves. Who need *them* to look after us."

"Well, screw that," said Simon, and grinned at his friend. "Let's send this to a few people. Then we'll see how in control of everything they really are. Because, if *they're* real, then that means there's a good chance everything else McKenna wrote was true as well. Which means vampires, mate. Actual vampires, out there right now."

"It's all true," said Justin, tearing his gaze away from the screen and fixing Simon with a solemn expression. "I'm sure of it. It fits together too well to be anything else. Blacklight are real, just like Kevin McKenna said they were, before someone killed him. They're real, and we found them."

"Send it," said Simon. "The images, the links, the whole thing. Send it and let's see what happens."

Justin opened an email and began copying and pasting the images and URLs, feeling a trickle of excitement make its way up from his stomach, a trickle that felt like it was on the verge of exploding into a roaring torrent. When the attachments and links were in place, he wrote three words in the subject line.

### Check this out

Justin clicked on the RECIPIENTS field. "Who should I send it to?" he asked.

Simon smiled. "I think everyone in the PhD programme would be a good start."

"Every PhD candidate in the college?" asked Justin.

"In the university," said Simon. "The entire university."

Justin reached for the keyboard, then paused. "I'm logged in as me," he said. "They're going to know I sent it."

Simon shrugged. "Log out and send it from a public access account. But you did the searches from your login, so I reckon you're already screwed if someone decides to take a close look."

"Thanks," said Justin. "That's really reassuring."

"Just send it, you pussy," said Simon, and clapped his friend hard on the back. "Do you want to live forever?"

"That was the plan," said Justin, forcing a weak smile. He loaded an email group called CAM_EDU/PHD/ALL, took a deep breath, and clicked SEND.

"Done," he said, and exhaled loudly. "It's out there."

"Awesome," said Simon. "Now we wait."

"For what?" asked Justin.

Simon smiled. "For the shit to hit the fan, mate. That's what."

# 9

# BUSINESS AS USUAL

Jamie Carpenter paced back and forth in the lift as it rose steadily through the Loop, trying to convince himself not to be angry with his mother and Frankenstein.

*You know where it comes from. You know it's them worrying about you, wanting to protect you. You know it isn't as patronising as it sounded.*

He *did* know that, deep in his heart, and in his bones. But it did nothing to dampen the fire that was threatening to burst through him and burn everything in its path.

*Looking for a father figure to replace Dad. Such bullshit.*

Jamie had told the truth in his mother's cell; for a long time, he had been furious with his dad for leaving them, but had reached a place where he had been able to forgive him. He had never believed the stories that had been spread about Julian, about the plot he had supposedly been involved in, but there had clearly been *something* going on that he and his mother had been in the dark about. Now he knew what, he was able to understand, and forgive.

What still made him angry was the posthumous canonisation of his father; he was discussed in revered tones as some kind of superman, a legendary Operator, one of the great men of his generation. Which may all have been true – in fact, part of Jamie hoped it was – but did nothing to lessen his belief that his dad's death had been completely avoidable. The frame that Tom Morris had placed round him had clearly looked convincingly damning, but Jamie didn't believe that it could have withstood serious investigation, not with the resources the Department had at its disposal. If his dad had turned himself in to any of the men Jamie had suggested to Frankenstein, he was certain the truth would have been uncovered. Which might have meant that the whole chain of events that had seen his mother turned into a vampire and Frankenstein turned into a werewolf played out differently, or not at all.

Instead, Julian had run for home, attempting to deal with the threat on his own instead of asking for help, and had been killed by the very men who would have stood beside him if he had given them the chance. His behaviour had been reckless, and stupid, and entirely predictable; he had walked right into Tom Morris's trap, the opening move of a plot that would not be fully revealed until a dark night on Lindisfarne, more than two years later.

*He should be here now, helping me through this. Not dead because he was too stupid to trust the Department he gave his life to.*

Jamie had lied to his mum about one thing: he did miss his dad, terribly so at times. But the torture had not yet been devised that would have compelled him to admit so to anyone.

The lift doors slid open on Level A. He stepped out and set off on a walk he could have done blindfold; he had long since lost count of how many times he had been summoned to the same small suite of rooms, occupied first by Henry Seward and now by Cal Holmwood. As he strode down familiar corridors, he allowed himself a moment to dwell on the other thing he had overheard as he stood outside his mother's cell, the thing that had *really* made his blood boil.

*How dare they talk like that about Larissa? And Frankenstein claiming it's just some clichéd teenage rebellion? How dare he? How dare either of them?*

Jamie strode round the corner, nodded to the Security Operator, and pushed open the door to the Interim Director's quarters. Cal Holmwood looked up from behind the mountain range of files and folders that seemed to permanently cover the surface of his desk, and beckoned him forward.

"Jamie," he said. "Christ, get in here. Give me an excuse to stop all this bloody reading."

Jamie grinned, feeling his anger start to subside. "Aren't you enjoying life behind a desk, sir?"

"Watch it, Lieutenant," said Holmwood, but he was smiling as he spoke. "I've threatened to have you court-martialled more times than I can remember. Don't make me actually go through with it."

"Sorry, sir," said Jamie. He walked across the room and stood at ease in front of the Interim Director's desk. "You wanted to see me?"

"Yes," said Holmwood. "That's why I sent you a message telling you to come and see me. Was that too subtle for you?"

Jamie's smile widened. "Apparently so, sir."

"I'll use shorter words next time," said Holmwood. "I'm going to activate your squad today, if you tell me they're ready. That's why I wanted to see you."

"They're ready, sir," said Jamie, instantly. His stomach had already contracted into a tight ball of excitement at the thought of returning to the active roster, of being back out there helping the Department instead of stuck in the Playground watching Ellison and Qiang being run ragged by Terry, the fabled Blacklight instructor.

"Glad to hear it," said Holmwood, his smile fading ever so slightly. "What about you?"

Jamie frowned. "Me, sir?"

"A member of your last squad died, Jamie," said Holmwood. "It wasn't your fault, but it's the kind of thing that can stay with an Operator for a long time. I need to know that you've let what happened to John Morton go."

An image flashed into Jamie's mind, unbidden; Morton, dead, his face a mask of agony, his guts piled beneath him as he hung suspended in a room soaked with petrol. He pushed it away, back into the dark corner of his memory where it was stored, never to be entirely forgotten.

"I have, sir," said Jamie. "Morton was a good man, but he was a rookie who was a bad fit as an Operator. I tried to save him, and when I failed, I mourned him. Ellison did the same, and then we moved on, sir. Like we had to."

Holmwood stared, his pale green eyes fixed on Jamie's. "I hear what you're saying," he said. "And I have no doubt you mean it. But there's still—"

"I'm sorry, sir," interrupted Jamie. "But you'll recall that I tried to have John Morton removed from the active roster several times. He was an unhappy ending waiting to happen, sir."

The comment was a pointed one, and Jamie saw that its sharp edge had not been lost on the Interim Director; it had been Holmwood who had refused Jamie's initial request to deactivate Morton, and who had only grudgingly agreed after a civilian girl had died. His smile disappeared entirely and his eyes narrowed.

"Is there something you want to say to me, Lieutenant?" he asked.

"Yes, sir," Jamie replied. "Qiang Li has been a PBS6 Operator for three years, with a flawless record. He's nothing like John Morton, who was a man trying to prove he could handle something he couldn't. I'm fine, sir, Qiang is good, and Ellison is great, really she is. She's going to sit in your chair one day."

Holmwood grunted. "She's more than welcome to it," he said. "Tell her she can start tomorrow if she likes."

"I'm afraid I need her, sir," said Jamie, smiling at his commanding officer.

"Fair enough," said Holmwood. "So you're telling me I have nothing to worry about. Am I hearing you correctly?"

"Yes, sir," said Jamie. "I mean, there's still Zero Hour and Admiral Seward and the Broadmoor escapees and the regular vamps getting bolder every day because Kevin McKenna told the whole world they exist, but as far as my squad is concerned, you have nothing to worry about."

Holmwood burst out laughing, and Jamie joined in; sometimes there was nothing else to do but let the darkness be damned. Jamie would not have given good odds on himself, the Interim Director, or the building they were standing in, still existing in six months' time, let alone a year. But he was certain of one thing: that his friends and colleagues, and all the other men and women who wore the black uniform of the Department, would give everything they had, everything that they were, to hold back the tide as long as possible.

They would succeed, or they would die trying.

"I might as well not bother activating your squad," said Holmwood, grinning widely. "The three of you should probably just go on holiday instead."

"That's kind of you, sir," said Jamie. "I've always wanted to go to California."

"California's nice," said Holmwood. "But I was thinking more along the lines of grid reference 67-87?"

94

Jamie nodded. "Sounds lovely, sir."

"Good," said Holmwood. "Patrol Respond at 1800. I want a detailed performance evaluation of your new squad on my desk in the morning. And don't roll your eyes and tell me that it's just a Patrol Respond, because I know that, and I still want the report by 0900. Is that clear?"

"Yes, sir," said Jamie. "It's clear."

Holmwood sighed. "Good. Your new squad's designation is J-5. Go and tell Qiang and Ellison the news and leave me to my reading. If Dracula does take over the world, maybe he'll need a secretary. I'm starting to feel like that's mostly what this job is. Dismissed."

Jamie nodded and headed for the door. As he reached it, he paused, and turned back.

"Sir?" he said.

Holmwood looked up. "What is it, Jamie?"

"Does it ever feel pointless to you, sir?"

"Does *what* ever feel pointless to me?"

"What we do, sir," said Jamie. "Patrol Respond. Hunting down individual vamps when we know what's coming."

Holmwood shook his head firmly. "No," he said. "It doesn't ever feel like that to me and I'll tell you why. Because we save lives, Jamie, and saving lives is never pointless. Understood?"

Jamie nodded. "Yes, sir."

"Good," said Holmwood. "Now get out of here."


Cal Holmwood watched the door close and permitted himself a small smile.

There were a number of men and women within the Department whom it always heartened him to talk to; Paul Turner, perhaps surprisingly, was one of them, as were Angela Darcy, Patrick Williams and Victor Frankenstein. Jamie Carpenter, for all his flaws, was another; there was something irresistible about the young Lieutenant, a determination at his core that allowed Cal to believe, even just for a minute, that everything was going to be all right.

*It won't be,* he thought. *In all likelihood, everything is going to be very far from all right. But it's good to think otherwise, every now and again.*

Cal returned his attention to the reams of paper smothering his desk, and reopened a report containing the repair and upgrade schedule for the Loop's internal power supply; he had tried to get through it three times already, and was determined that this time he would at least make it past the first page. He was labouring through a seemingly endless paragraph when the terminal on his desk beeped, informing him that a message was waiting for him.

Cal signed into the server, opened his secure inbox and frowned.

The address the message had been sent from was not one he recognised. But more disconcerting by far was the subject line, which read FAO: HENRY SEWARD.

He double-clicked on the message, opening it. It contained only four words, and no signature.

### COME TO VALHALLA ASAP

# 10

# THE MYTH OF SISYPHUS, PART ONE

"I'm bored," said Ellison, for the fifth time in as many minutes.

"I heard you," said Jamie. "But short of magicking up a horde of vampires for you to stake, there really isn't very much I can do about it. So just sit tight."

"Yes, sir," said Ellison, smiling widely at her squad leader.

Qiang Li said nothing, but then he rarely did. The Chinese Operator Second Class simply nodded at his two squad mates and rechecked the magazine on his Glock.

Operational Squad J-5 had departed the Loop at 1800 hours, right on schedule. Their driver had headed west, guiding her powerful van to the border of grid reference 67-87, where Jamie ordered Ready One, the Operational state that permitted the use of force when necessary.

Patrol Responds were eight hours long, including an hour at either end for transportation; under ideal conditions, this meant six hours of sitting and waiting for something to happen, rather than eight. Conditions, both inside the Department and in the outside world, were currently far from ideal, however; it had been a long time since

Jamie had been on a Patrol Respond that hadn't turned hot within the first hour, often before the target grid had even been reached.

Operational Squad J-5 were now slowly approaching hour three.

"I'm bored," said Ellison, and this time Jamie ignored her.

In truth, he was bored too. He knew most Operators would kill for an evening as quiet as this one seemed to be proving, but he had been off the active roster for more than a month and was itching to get back to work.

After the inquest into Morton's death, which had taken two weeks and found no wrongdoing on the part of either himself or Ellison, Jamie had pleaded with Cal Holmwood to fill their squad with an Operator from the active roster, so that they could get straight back into the field. The Interim Director had refused point blank, and three days later Jamie had been disappointed to see that one of the newly arrived intake of Operators from PBS6 in Beijing had been assigned to fill his squad.

It wasn't that he didn't rate Qiang Li; on the contrary, the young man from Xinjiang Province had immediately impressed with his skill, temperament, and clear and obvious devotion to duty. Jamie's disappointment arose from his finally complete squad being sent for two long, soul-crushing weeks of training, to better acquaint themselves with one another. He had gone back to Cal Holmwood and tried to persuade him that this was an obvious waste of time and resources, but had got nowhere.

"All new squads are going through the same thing," Holmwood had said. "You need to stop expecting special treatment."

Jamie had protested, but had known it was an argument he wasn't going to win; instead, he had dedicated his time and energy to pushing his squad to their limits, so that when their day came they would be ready.

Now, at last, it was time; they were armed, equipped, willing and eager to destroy vampires. And their secure connection to the Surveillance Division, which would alert them instantly to any even potentially supernatural incident in their small corner of the country, was as silent as a church congregation on Sunday morning. Jamie stared accusingly at the van's fold-down screen, trying to will it into life; the green bar at the bottom, the one that showed the connection was active, glowed steadily, as though it was mocking him.

"This doing nothing is normal?" asked Qiang, slotting the magazine back into the butt of his Glock and replacing the pistol in its holster.

"No," said Jamie, a little too quickly. It sounded defensive, as though he was afraid his new squad mate was suggesting that being an Operator in PBS6 was more taxing than being one in Blacklight. "This is *not* normal. Especially not recently."

Qiang nodded. "Unlucky then," he said, and drew his pistol again.

*It's more than unlucky,* thought Jamie, his eyes still fixed on the screen. *It's bloody unheard of.*

One of the first things Frankenstein had told Jamie, during his earliest days in the Department, was that it was no use thinking in terms of a vampire society, some hidden community where every vampire knows each other and they all work together towards some dastardly goal. The reality was far more banal; there were vampires who were dedicated to violence and murder, just as there were vampires who abhorred such things; some vampires lived in Gothic castles, others in suburban houses and blocks of flats; some were predatory loners, while others were family men and women, their lives indistinguishable from the vast majority of the population, providing you excepted their need to drink blood. During her time with NS9, Larissa had talked to a vampire girl called Chloe in a Las Vegas nightclub; Chloe had never heard of Blacklight, or NS9, and believed that Dracula was nothing more than a character from old horror films.

Nonetheless, there was unquestionably *something* stirring up the vampire population. The news of Dracula's resurrection seemed to have reached even the most isolated of vampire ears and had caused an explosion of brazen activity; attacks had risen sharply, as had encounters between the public and the supernatural, and many of the incidents were punctuated with two words every Operator had come to truly hate.

## HE RISES

They were found sprayed on walls, daubed on front doors, and carved into the flesh of victims, their meaning abundantly clear: he's coming, and nothing can stop him.

The screen on the van's wall burst into life, hauling Jamie from his thoughts. He read the message as it scrolled on to the screen, his heart racing suddenly in his chest.

ECHELON INTERCEPT REF. 52312/6B
SOURCE. Emergency call (landline telephone 01572 232973)
TIME OF INTERCEPT. 20:53

TRANSCRIPT BEGINS.
OPERATOR: Emergency, which service do you require?
CALLER: Police.
OPERATOR: What is the nature of your emergency?

CALLER: There's a bunch of kids in the graveyard behind Our Sister of Grace in Oakham. My husband just walked our dog through there and they threw blood at him.

OPERATOR: Can you repeat that, please?

CALLER: They threw blood at him, the little sods. He's covered in it, all over the shirt I got him for Christmas.

OPERATOR: Is your husband injured?

CALLER: No, he's just shook up. Well, you would be, wouldn't you? Take the dog out and find a bunch of kids lighting candles and chucking blood about. Bring back national service, that's what I reckon. In my day we—

OPERATOR: The police are on their way, ma'am.

TRANSCRIPT ENDS.

INTERCEPT REFERENCE LOCATION. Our Sister of Grace Anglican Church, Oakham, Rutland. 52.6705°N, 0.7295°W

RISK ASSESSMENT. Priority Level 3

"Level 3?" groaned Ellison. "Jesus. Surveillance might as well have us getting cats out of trees."

"I thought you were bored," said Jamie.

"I am," she replied.

"Shut up then." He smiled at his squad mate, and pressed the button on the wall that connected the van's passengers to their driver. "Have you got the coordinates?"

"Yes, sir," replied the driver, her voice slightly metallic over the intercom.

"What's our ETA?"

"Eleven minutes, sir."

"All right then," said Jamie, strapping himself into his seat. "Let's go."

Their driver's estimate had been slightly optimistic; almost thirteen minutes had passed when the van pulled to a halt outside the gate of the graveyard that sprawled behind the small, neat church of Our Sister of Grace. Jamie activated the cameras on the left side of the vehicle and observed their destination on the van's screen.

The headstones and mausoleums beyond the gates were well tended, adorned with bright sprays of flowers and surrounded by neatly mown grass. Stone angels loomed over the path that ran through the middle of the cemetery, peering down from slanted roofs and the weathered crossbeams of crucifixes. Further away from the gates, the graveyard was less neat, less well kept; trees huddled together, their shadows intertwining beneath the light of a moon that was three-quarters full, and the paths winding between the headstones were wilder, more overgrown. In the distance, an orange glow flickered in the darkness.

"See it?" he asked.

"Uh-huh," said Ellison. "Looks pretty big, sir. Maybe we should call the fire brigade?"

Jamie smiled. "Feel free to stay in the van, Operator."

"No, sir," said Ellison, smiling back at him. "I wouldn't miss something this exciting for the world."

Qiang pulled his helmet on to his head and clicked its visor into place. He reached down and twisted a dial on his belt, setting his helmet's microphone to external.

"We go?" he asked.

"We go," said Jamie, pulling on his own helmet as Ellison did the same. "Ready One as soon as we're through the gate. Internal comms."

"Yes, sir," said Qiang.

"Yes, sir," said Ellison.

"All right," said Jamie. "We all know this is probably nothing, but we play the cards we're dealt. So do your jobs."

He pushed open the back of the van, leapt on to the tarmac, and held the door wide. Ellison and Qiang stepped down beside him, their black-clad shapes seeming to absorb the pale moonlight. Jamie swung the door shut and hammered twice on it with his gloved fist. The van pulled away, leaving them standing in the road; their driver would maintain a holding pattern until she was summoned to extract them.

Jamie stepped up on to the pavement and faced the graveyard. The wrought-iron gate loomed above him, a relic of a grander, more dignified era. It was standing slightly ajar. Jamie pushed it open, grimacing behind his visor as the metal gave out a shrill, echoing shriek, and stepped through it. His squad mates followed, their gloved hands dangling within reach of the weapons that hung from their belts, their faces hidden entirely by their purple visors.

The central thoroughfare of the graveyard was long and wide, curving gently to the right. Jamie led Operational Squad J-5 along it until they reached a narrower, more overgrown path that branched off to the left. He twisted a dial on his belt, switching his visor's filter to infrared. The fire stood out as a glowing ball of yellow and red in the centre of a landscape of black and dark blue; it was perhaps fifty metres away, straight ahead.

"Follow me," said Jamie, his voice sounding directly in the ears of his squad mates, but inaudible to anyone standing beside him.

"Yes, sir," chorused Ellison and Qiang.

Jamie twisted his visor back to normal and headed towards the flickering orange light. As he stepped carefully over tumbled headstones and fallen statues, he quickly saw that Ellison had been right; it really wasn't much of a fire. But someone in the graveyard had thrown blood at an old man doing nothing more provocative than taking his dog for a walk, and that was worth checking out, no matter whether his squad mates agreed or not.

The path turned sharply away to the left, setting off on a long curve that Jamie guessed took it back to the main gates. He stepped off it, enjoying the silence that came from grass underfoot, and picked his way between the graves. Thirty seconds later he stopped in the deep shadows of a towering sycamore, and took his first look at what they had been sent to investigate.

Four teenagers, wearing jet-black clothes and dark make-up around their eyes and lips, were sitting in a circle on top of a fallen gravestone. A pentagram had been marked on it with chalk, and a fire had been built beside it, from piled sticks and fallen tree branches. The teenagers were giggling and whispering to one another; Jamie saw open cans of cheap cider standing between them, alongside two plastic bottles full of dark red liquid.

*Probably got it at the butcher's,* he thought. *Just kids, playing vampires.*

Then he remembered that they were, at most, a year or two younger than him, and smiled behind his visor.

"This is nothing," he said. "I'm going to scare them and send them home. Circle round in case they try to run."

His squad mates voiced their assent. There was an almost inaudible rustle as they did as they were ordered.

In the clearing, the teenagers took hold of each other's hands, and one of them, a boy with neat blond hair above his heavily made-up face, began to speak in a deep tone of voice that he doubtless believed sounded ominous.

"Dark Lords of the Night, hear us. We bring fire and blood,

and we call to you in supplication, in the hope of your eternal favour. We call you, Lords, and we offer our souls to you, that we might see the everlasting night. Hear us, oh Lords, hear us, we beg."

*This is too perfect,* thought Jamie. He set his microphone to external, twisted the volume up to full, and stepped silently out of the shadows.

"Don't move," he bellowed. "Stay right where you are."

The screams that pierced the quiet of the graveyard were satisfyingly loud and high-pitched.

Two of the teenagers tipped backwards on to the grass, their eyes and mouths wide, and began to crawl frantically, digging at the dirt with their fingers, dragging themselves away from the dark shape that had roared at them with a voice like something from the depths of Hell. One slumped to the ground in a dead faint, her eyes rolling back in her head, her mouth hanging open, while the last, the blond boy who had spoken, leapt to his feet and fled, his face a wide, gasping picture of unadulterated terror.

He ran for the cover of the trees, his arms and legs pumping. As he reached them, Qiang stepped silently out from between the trunks, and the teenager skidded to the ground, screaming as he fell. He scrambled to his feet and backtracked, sobbing hysterically, searching desperately for a way out. A last-gasp break for the main path saw him confronted by the moving shadow of Ellison; at the sight of her the teenager screamed again, then slumped to his knees and threw back his head.

"Do it!" he howled. "Do it then, oh Dark Lords!"

Jamie grinned behind his visor. He had circled round the fire, cutting off the two crawling teenagers and herding them back as they cried and blubbered and insisted that they hadn't meant it, they had never thought it would work, they'd changed their minds, oh God, they'd changed their minds. Beside the fallen gravestone, the girl who had fainted was groaning as she slowly returned to consciousness.

"So you want to be vampires?" asked Jamie, his voice deafening and almost inhuman through his microphone's distortion filters.

"No!" screamed the girl. "No, we're sorry!"

The blond boy was still on his knees. "Yes!" he cried. "Ignore these weaklings! I want to be a vampire!"

Jamie walked silently across the clearing. Two of the teenagers whimpered and cowered away as he passed; he didn't so much as glance at them. He crouched down in front of the kneeling boy and twisted off his microphone's filters.

"No," he said, his voice now a normal tone and volume. "You don't."

The teenager frowned. "What are you?" he said. "You aren't what we summoned."

"You're right," said Jamie. "We're something else. Get off your knees and stand with your friends."

The boy got slowly to his feet, his face starting to colour pink. Jamie wasn't sure whether it was anger or embarrassment, although he suspected the teenager's friends would not let him forget 'Do it then, oh Dark Lords' in a hurry. He staggered across the clearing and hauled the girl who had fainted to her feet. She protested half-heartedly as he dragged her across to the others, and faced the three dark figures.

"What is this?" asked the teenager, a petulant tone creeping into his voice. "We didn't do anything wrong."

"What's your name?" asked Jamie.

"Why should I tell you that?" replied the boy.

"Because you'll be arrested if you don't," said Jamie. "And you'll spend at least one night somewhere much worse than a graveyard."

The teenager frowned. "I read Kevin McKenna's story," he said. "The one he wrote before you killed him. You're the ones he was talking about."

*We killed him?* thought Jamie. *That's new. I haven't heard that before.*

"Tell me your name," he said. "I'm not going to ask you again."

"You're murderers," said the boy, his voice high and indignant. "You kill people who haven't done anything wrong."

Jamie took a step forward. "Do you really want to be right about that?" he asked. "Think hard."

The boy swallowed. "Chris," he said. "My name is Chris Hollison."

"What about the rest of you?"

"Lauren Johnson."

"Wesley Chambers."

"Isabel Banks."

"Thank you," said Jamie. "So, Chris Hollison, you assaulted a member of the public. You call that not doing anything wrong?"

"You see?" hissed Lauren, digging her elbow into Chris's ribs. "I told you to leave the old man alone."

"Shut up," said Chris, the colour in his face darkening. "I'll handle this."

"No you won't," said Jamie. "You'll do what I tell you. Is that clear?"

"Yes," said Lauren, instantly. "We don't want any trouble."

Chris shot her a look of utter contempt, and Jamie suddenly understood the dynamic of the group of teenagers standing before him.

*Chris is the leader,* he thought. *He tells them what to do, and gets off on their obedience. And I bet he really doesn't like it when someone does it to him.*

"That's good," he said. "Luckily for you, the man you assaulted doesn't want to give a statement, so no charges are going to be brought. But I'm afraid you have a much bigger problem. You've seen the three of us."

Wesley and Isabel looked at each with wide-eyed expressions of panic, and Jamie felt his heart soften.

*These aren't bad kids*, he thought. *They don't really want to be vampires. They just went along with something and now they regret it. Maybe next time they'll tell their friend to piss off.*

"Why is that a problem?" asked Chris. His eyes had narrowed and he was looking coldly at Jamie.

"Because you can never tell anyone what happened here," said Jamie. "Ever. And I need to be sure I believe you before I can let you go."

"We won't tell anyone," said Lauren, quickly. "Will we?" She looked round at the others, who responded with huge, exaggerated nods.

"I might," said Chris. "Given that I can't see how you're going to stop me. You *are* the ones McKenna wrote about, aren't you? The vampire police."

"Don't worry about who we are," said Jamie. "Worry about what will happen if you don't do what I tell you."

Chris narrowed his eyes even further, then smiled smugly. "You can't threaten us," he said. "You're the police. Our parents pay your salaries."

Jamie took a step towards the teenager and let his gloved hands move fractionally towards his belt. Chris glanced down; his smile faltered as he saw the array of weaponry that was now within reach.

"Tell me the truth," said Jamie. "Do I look like a policeman to you?"

Chris didn't respond, but nor did he step back.

Jamie pulled his console from his belt, logged into the population database, and entered the names the teenagers had given. The results appeared, showing four matches: all between fifteen and seventeen years of age, all living within a mile of the graveyard. He patched them across to the Department's civilian control programme and tapped ENTER. A new window appeared, containing an abridged version of the Official Secrets Act, and the first of the names alphabetically.

"Isabel Banks," he said, and held out the console. "Sign this."

The girl walked forward, until Chris Hollison called for her to wait. She turned back, her face pale with worry.

"What is it?" she asked.

"Are you going to just sign something without even knowing what it is?" asked Chris. "What does it feel like to be so stupid? Describe it to me."

Jamie felt familiar anger race through him, and told himself to stay calm. There had been boys like Chris Hollison at every school he had attended: bullies, who got what they wanted by intimidation, who gave the impression of being smarter and cooler than everyone else, even though they always turned out to be full of shit.

*And cowards,* thought Jamie. *They're always cowards when someone comes along who's scarier than them.*

They were the boys who had targeted him after his dad had died, sensing isolation and weakness; the boys, he knew, who had made his friend Matt's life a misery.

*Maybe this won't be a complete waste of time,* thought Jamie.

"Watch your mouth, Mr Hollison," he said. "It's an amended version of the Official Secrets Act. It states that you will never discuss or in any way acknowledge your interaction with the three of us. Sign it, Isabel."

She cast a final look at Chris, then shuffled forward and scraped her finger across the console's screen.

Jamie loaded the second page. "Wesley Chambers."

Wesley walked forward and signed. He did so without hesitation, although Jamie noted that he didn't meet Chris Hollison's eye as he walked back to stand beside Isabel.

"Chris Hollison."

The blond teenager shook his head. "I'm not signing that."

"Yes you are," said Jamie. "The only question is whether you do so voluntarily."

"You can't make me," said Chris, his tone more petulant than ever. "And even if you could, you can't check whether I obey it. So what's the point?"

"As I speak," said Jamie, "a monitoring grid is being put in place. Before you even get home, we'll be watching and listening. Phone calls, emails, internet activity, conversations with your friends and parents and brothers and sisters. We can listen to you through your mobile phones, even when they're switched off. And, for a period of time that is entirely up to me, you're going to be followed. You'll never see them, but you should get used to knowing that you're being watched. There's nowhere you can go that we can't follow, and nothing you can say that we can't hear. So you *are* going to sign, Mr Hollison, and then you're going to keep your mouth shut. Because, if you don't, you're going to find yourself in a small room with no windows while your parents wonder why you never came home from school. Am I making myself clear?"

The four teenagers stared at him with open horror.

"That's bullshit," said Chris, his voice quavering. "You can't do that."

"I already have," said Jamie. "Sign."

Hollison walked slowly forward, his face like thunder, and scrawled his name on the screen. He stayed for a moment longer than the others, staring belligerently into the opaque purple of Jamie's visor, then stepped back.

"Lauren Johnson," said Jamie.

The girl signed, then hurried back to her friends. Jamie placed the console on his belt, and looked at the teenagers.

"What happens now?" asked Wesley.

"You go home," said Jamie. "You don't say anything about this to anyone, and you go on with your lives."

Three of the teenagers sighed heavily, as though they had been holding their breath during the entire process. Smiles rose on their faces, and they looked at each other with obvious relief.

Chris Hollison didn't sigh, or smile. He was still staring at Jamie, his face full of anger.

*You don't know how this happened, do you?* thought Jamie. *How you got put in your place in front of everyone. You're trying to think of some way to save face.*

He was almost certainly correct. But as Chris Hollison opened his mouth, a deep growl emerged from the undergrowth behind him. A frown creased the teenager's forehead. Then he was flung forward as something leapt on to his back, driving him screaming to his knees.

# 11

# NORTH OF THE BORDER

## THIRTY MINUTES EARLIER

The helicopter swept north, its running lights dark, its heavy shape little more than a shadow above the landscape.

The armour-plated hold could carry twenty-four fully equipped Operators, but was occupied by only two. Paul Turner and Kate Randall sat facing each other, their helmets beside them, their weapons and kit checked and ready, even though Cal Holmwood had assured them they would not be needed.

The Interim Director had summoned them to his quarters and shown them the message he had been sent as the first Operational squads were heading out of the Loop. Kate, who knew about Valhalla from Jamie's and Larissa's descriptions of the place, was delighted when Holmwood ordered them to follow it up; it had long been somewhere she wanted to see.

Paul Turner, on the other hand, did not appreciate being summoned anywhere by anonymous message, and clearly did not believe that Cal should be jumping simply because someone inside Valhalla told him to. But the Scottish commune, which was one of the oldest vampire colonies in Britain, was home to men and women who had always treated Blacklight as allies rather than enemies, and it was Cal's belief that they would not have made contact unless it was important.

"Four minutes," said their pilot, his voice rattling out of speakers set into the walls of the hold.

Kate felt excitement ripple through her as the helicopter began to descend. Despite Cal Holmwood's assurances, safety could never be one hundred per cent guaranteed in any situation that involved vampires, especially a large number of them in one place, and her nerve endings were starting to twitch. Opposite her, Paul Turner wore the expression of a man who wants to get an annoying job out of the way and focus on more important matters.

As they sank steadily towards the southern end of Glen Shiel, Kate peered out at the landscape rushing past below. In daylight, it would have been spectacular: the jutting peaks, twisting green valleys and sparkling lochs of western Scotland. At night it was dark and foreboding, a vista of shadows upon shadows, that slid together to create a canvas of black that stretched to the horizon. The helicopter banked left, avoiding a sheer wall of rock that rose seemingly from nowhere to their right and affording Kate a fleeting glimpse of the entire valley. At the northern end was light, a yellow and white glow studded with what looked like red and blue and green.

*That must be it*, she thought. *Valhalla.*

Cal Holmwood had given them a brief history of the community before they left his quarters, but Kate had already heard most of it from her friends. It had been founded in the 1960s by the vampire known as Grey, who had intended it as a place where vampires could live peacefully, away from the temptations and dangers of the normal world. It welcomed anyone, as long as they were prepared to work: gardening, building, tending the herd of cattle that supplied the residents with blood.

There was a single rule: no resident of Valhalla was permitted to harm another human being, on pain of expulsion. This had been considered sacrosanct, the central ethos on which the community was founded; it had also, as far as the founder himself was concerned, been a lie. Each year Grey had left Valhalla for several weeks, to refresh himself; it was a pilgrimage of sorts, a chance to reacquaint himself with the outside world. The reality was that Valhalla's founder had used his time away to murder young girls and drink their blood.

His fellow residents would likely never have known had Larissa Kinley not failed to die when Grey sank his fangs into her neck. She had led Jamie and Frankenstein to Valhalla the previous year, under the pretence of searching for Marie Carpenter, and confronted the old vampire about his crimes. Grey had confessed, and gone into voluntary exile from the place he had founded, promising to seek penance for the things he had done and the harm he had caused.

*Blood*, thought Kate. *That's what it always comes down to, despite the best intentions. Blood and death.*

The helicopter spun into a hover, scattering dust and earth in an expanding circle, and lowered itself towards the ground. Kate turned away from the window and looked at her commanding officer.

"Helmet?" she asked.

"Carry it," said Turner. "Don't put it on unless I tell you to."

"Yes, sir."

The helicopter touched down with a squeal of rubber. Paul Turner was already moving, unbuckling himself and sliding open the heavy door. Cold air rushed into the helicopter, sending a shiver down Kate's spine as she unfastened her harness. Then her boss was reaching back into the hold and extending a gloved hand towards her; she took it and let him help her down to the ground, picking up her

helmet as she did so. The two Operators crouched and ran clear of
the punishing downdraught from the rotor blades that whirred above
them. With a roar of engines, their pilot hauled the helicopter into
the air and guided it away down the valley. Kate watched it go, then
turned to look at the remote place it had delivered them to.

A crystal-clear river gleamed before her, frothing over rocks and
gullies as it made its way south. A large wooden wheel had been
positioned in the current, and was revolving steadily in the darkness.
Behind her, a metal arch had been erected, and covered in creeping
vines and sprays of wild flowers. Pale wooden branches were fixed
to the top of the arch, arranged to form eight letters.

## VALHALLA

"Come on," said Turner, and walked towards it. "Let's get this done."

Kate followed, trying to keep from smiling as her eyes adjusted
to the darkness and the small community came into view. There
was one road, a rutted dirt track that ran in a straight line from the
arch to the base of the hill that rose up in the distance. Wooden
houses stood on either side of the road, sometimes three or four
deep. Kate guessed there were fifty or sixty, many of which looked
new: whitewashed walls and bare wooden frames, gardens still in
their infancy, light blazing in many of their windows.

Some of the older homes were little more than wooden cubes
with a window in the centre of each wall, while others were far
larger and more luxurious, built of brick and stone, with tiled roofs,
wooden porches and neatly tended gardens. Flower beds and row
after row of vegetables filled the spaces between the houses and ran
beyond them in long straight lines.

At the foot of the hill, the road widened into a clearing then branched away briefly to the right and left. More houses had been set into the gentle lower slopes, including the grandest building in the community, a two-storey wooden ranch house with a long porch that looked across the river and down the glen. In front of the house, Kate could see a number of men and women had gathered; they stood in small groups in the cold night air.

"Let me do the talking," said Turner.

"Not a problem, sir," said Kate.

They walked up the sloping track with multicoloured light bulbs shining in long strings above their heads; they lent the place an oddly whimsical feel, like the memory of a fairground. As they reached the clearing, a man stepped forward to meet them; he was tall, wearing an elegant dark blue suit over a lemon-yellow shirt, and his face wore a frown of open suspicion.

"Where is Admiral Seward?" he asked.

"Not here," replied Kate's boss. "I'm Major Turner. This is Lieutenant Randall."

"That doesn't answer my question," said the vampire, and Kate saw a glimmer of red appear in the corners of his eyes.

"It's the only answer you're going to get," said Turner. "We can return to the Loop, if it's unsatisfactory?"

The vampire bared his teeth, and growled. "I sent a message on what has always been a secure line to the Director of Blacklight," he said. "If it has been compromised, I need to know."

Turner stared at the vampire. "Admiral Seward is no longer in active charge of the Department," he said, eventually. "Cal Holmwood is now Interim Director. *He* received your message and *he* sent us here."

"What happened to Henry?" asked a woman standing in the crowd. "Is he all right?"

Turner narrowed his eyes. "*Don't you know?*"

"Why would we?" said the vampire who had spoken first. "Living here is a rejection of the rest of the world. We get little in the way of gossip."

"He was taken," said Turner. "Valeri Rusmanov attacked the Loop and took Admiral Seward. To Dracula, we assume."

A chorus of gasps rose from the crowd. One of the vampires crossed himself and bowed his head.

"You'd heard about *that*, though?" said Kate, drawing a sideways look from her boss. "You knew Dracula was rising?"

"Some things are too big to hide from entirely," said the vampire who appeared to be in charge. "News of his rise has even reached us here. I am Lawrence, and we are sorry for your loss. You are both welcome here."

"Thank you," said Turner. "Although I would appreciate it if someone would tell us exactly why we *are* here."

Lawrence tilted his head to one side, then nodded. "It's Grey," he said. "He returned last night, but is refusing to speak to us. All he will say is that he needs to talk to Henry Seward."

"Returned from where?" asked Turner.

Lawrence shook his head. "I have no idea. He's been gone for more than six months. He swore penance before he left, for the crimes he had committed, so I assume he believes he has completed it. But I don't know."

"Perhaps he'll talk to us," said Turner.

Lawrence shrugged. "Perhaps. Although you're not Henry Seward."

"No," said Turner, breaking into a smile that instantly made Kate uneasy. "I'm not. For one thing, I lack his patience. Will you take us to him or not?"

**117**

For long seconds, Lawrence didn't respond. Then he grunted, a low noise that Kate suspected was a laugh, and nodded. "I'll take you," he said.

"Fantastic," said Turner. "Lead the way."

The front door of the ranch house opened on to a living room covered in dust.

The remnants of abandoned spiderwebs hung from the corners of the ceiling, and the thickly covered floorboards were tracked with footprints that criss-crossed the wide space. Lawrence would go no further than the doorstep; he pointed towards a door at the back of the room.

"Through there," he said. "If he'll see you. You know the way out when you're done."

Turner nodded, then strode across the room and knocked heavily on the door. Kate glanced over at Lawrence as he did so, but the vampire's expression was unreadable. No response came from beyond the plain wooden door. Turner waited a second or two, then pushed it open, revealing only darkness, and stepped through it. Kate crossed the room and followed, letting the door swing shut behind her.

"You are not Henry Seward," said a voice from within the darkness that caused Kate to gasp. The sound was remarkable, an otherworldly rumble of bass that took her breath away.

"Well spotted," said Paul Turner.

A lamp flickered into life, revealing the room and its occupant. It was a study, its every surface piled high with books and papers, all buried beneath a thick coat of dust. Before a large, smeared window that looked on to the hill that rose behind Valhalla stood a desk, behind which sat a man who appeared to be in his late sixties or even early seventies; large, broad-shouldered, with a face that was

118

tanned and deeply lined, and a sweeping mane of grey hair that extended well below his collar. He regarded them with mild suspicion.

"Henry would not come?"

Turner sighed; he was clearly tired of explaining himself. "Admiral Seward is a captive of Dracula, Mr Grey. Cal Holmwood is now Interim Director, and he sent us. I am Major Turner and this is Lieutenant Randall."

Grey's face creased with a momentary grimace of pain. "Got him, did they?" he said. "That's a shame. Are you looking for him?"

"Of course," said Turner.

"And I hope you find him," said Grey, fixing his wide, expressive eyes on the Security Officer. "He was a good man."

"He still is," said Kate.

The old vampire transferred his gaze to her, and nodded. "You are right, of course," he said. "My apologies. If I had been faster, then maybe..." He trailed off, then forced a smile. "Although perhaps all is not yet lost."

"What do you mean?" asked Turner. "Do you have information?"

"About Henry?" said Grey. "I'm afraid not. But I *do* have information, and that is not all. I have hope, Major Turner, for all of us. Would you like some?"

"Yes," said Turner. "I would."

"Good," said Grey. "Then I will accompany the two of you to the Loop. Holmwood and the rest of your colleagues will want to hear what I have to say."

Turner narrowed his eyes. "Whatever you have to say, you can say to us now."

"No," said Grey. "I risked my life for this information, and I will deliver it to the Blacklight Director personally."

There was a long pause full of tension. Turner stared at Grey, who stared right back, a thin smile on his face.

"Fine," said Turner, eventually, and turned to Kate. "Go down to the river and call for extraction, then let the Loop know to expect three passengers in the helicopter when we arrive."

"Yes, sir," said Kate, and headed for the door.

"Surely it would be easier for me to meet you there?" said Grey.

Turner shook his head. "Absolutely not," he said. "The defence grid would likely burn you alive, and, even if it didn't, I can't authorise a civilian arrival at the Loop. You come in the helicopter with an explosive charge strapped to your chest, or you don't come. Your choice."

Grey shrugged. "It means little to me either way, Major. I will accompany you, if that is what's required."

"It is," said Turner. "I'm choosing to trust you, so I hope your information is worth it. It had better help us find Dracula."

The vampire who was supposedly the oldest in Great Britain got to his feet, and smiled. "It will do more than help you *find* him, Major Turner," he said. "It will help you *destroy* him, once and for all."

# 12

# THE MYTH OF SISYPHUS, PART TWO

Lauren and Isabel screamed again. Jamie, who had frozen for a millisecond or two, bellowed, "Go!" and ran forward, Ellison and Qiang close behind him.

Chris Hollison was screaming and thrashing beneath something dark and growling, and, as Jamie arrived and reached for it with his gloved hands, his first thought was that it was a dog, or even some hugely overgrown fox; it smelt of rot and filth, and the noises rising from it were entirely animal.

He took hold of it and pulled, but it was strong, whatever it was; it bucked and growled and clung to Chris Hollison, who was wearing an expression of almost uncomprehending terror. Qiang appeared at Jamie's side, seized the creature, and the two of them hauled for all they were worth. There was a suspended moment, in which everything was frozen: the teenager on the ground, the creature atop him, the two Operators trying to pull it loose.

Then, like a cork popping from a champagne bottle, the creature lost its grip. Jamie and Qiang stumbled backwards with it in their arms, then threw it against one of the crumbling headstones. There was a crunch, and it slumped to the ground.

"Jesus Christ," said Jamie, not taking his eyes from the fallen creature. "Check him."

"On it, sir," said Ellison, kneeling beside the staring, gibbering Chris Hollison.

Qiang stepped up next to Jamie, drew his torch, and turned it on. The bright white beam illuminated the shape lying at the base of the headstone, giving them their first clear look at it.

It was an old man.

His eyes glowed weakly, more pink than red, and his beard, which reached his chest, was matted grey. He was wearing a blazer that hung open to reveal an emaciated torso, and skin that was mired with grime and dirt. His trousers had once been blue jeans, but were now an indeterminate brownish-green, and his feet were bare, the nails at the ends of his toes curled and yellow like a bird's talons.

Behind Jamie, Lauren and Isabel had stopped screaming, but were still sobbing and repeating, "Oh my God!" over and over. Wesley sounded like he was struggling to breathe, and Chris Hollison was still on the ground beside Ellison, making noises that didn't sound completely human.

"Is he bitten?" asked Jamie.

"No," said Ellison. "He's fine."

"Shame," said Jamie, then chastised himself silently for such a thought.

"What was that?" shouted Lauren. "Seriously, what the hell was it?"

Jamie stepped aside and turned to face her. "That is what you were trying to summon," he said. "Still think it was a good idea?"

Lauren shook her head, her wide eyes fixed on the old man.

Jamie stared at her for a long moment, then nodded. He turned to face the vampire, twisting his comms back to internal and drawing his stake.

"I've got this," he said, and took a step towards the old man.

The vampire leapt forward with a speed that took Jamie completely by surprise, crashing into his legs with the force of a runaway car, sending bolts of agony through his body and knocking him sprawling to the ground. Jamie heard Lauren and Isabel scream yet again, and twisted on the ground, bringing his head round to see what the hell was happening.

The old man shambled across the clearing, his eyes now blazing crimson, a thick growl rising from deep within him. Ellison raised her T-Bone and fired it with a bang of exploding gas; the vampire ducked his head, and the metal projectile tore through the air above him and rocketed away into the darkness.

Qiang backed away from the onrushing vampire, drawing his Glock from his belt. He brought it up, but the old man was upon him before he could pull the trigger, swinging a skinny arm that crashed into the Chinese Operator's chest. Qiang was thrown up and back, his limbs flailing as he flew over gravestones and bushes and hit the ground, hard. His head missed the thick edge of one of the graves by millimetres, making Jamie wince behind his visor; even with his helmet protecting him, Qiang would have been in a lot of trouble if he had connected with the sharp stone corner.

Jamie scrambled to his feet and ran forward, the four teenagers forgotten. He drew his MP7 and aimed it at the fleeing vampire, but Ellison beat him to it. She stepped across him, aimed her Glock with steady hands, and squeezed its trigger three times. The gunshots were deafeningly loud in the still air of the graveyard; they echoed against the stone and wood and, in the distance, Jamie heard shrieks of fear. Then three bursts of red bloomed from the back of the old vampire; he tumbled to the ground and lay still.

"Nice shot," said Jamie, trying not to let his relief appear in his voice.

"Thanks," said Ellison. "I didn't see that coming, sir. Not from him."

Jamie shook his head. "Me neither," he said. "Never underestimate a vamp, whatever they look like. We got lucky."

Qiang emerged from behind the gravestone his head had so narrowly missed, moving slightly unsteadily.

"Are you OK?" asked Jamie.

"I am fine, sir," said Qiang. "My apologies."

"Nothing to apologise for," said Jamie. "Take care of it."

Qiang nodded, drew his stake, and set off towards the writhing vampire. Jamie turned to face the teenagers, who had huddled together at the foot of one of the larger graves, their faces white with panic, and turned his microphone back to external.

"On your feet," he said. "You're going to watch what being a vampire really means. And I don't think you're..." He trailed off, as something burst into his mind.

Isabel, Lauren and Wesley were looking up at him with clear and obvious terror.

There was no sign of Chris Hollison.

"Shit," said Jamie. "Where's your friend? Tell me."

Wesley shook his head, his eyes never leaving Jamie's visor. "I don't know," he said, honestly.

Jamie looked around. The graveyard was dark, and full of places to hide, and he lambasted himself for having taken his eyes off the insolent teenager.

"I'm thermal," said Ellison, her voice appearing directly into his ear. "No sign of him."

There was a wet thud in the distance as Qiang staked the old vampire, but Jamie barely heard it; he was scanning the dark graveyard, concern rising in his chest as he desperately tried to tell himself it wasn't a problem.

*He signed the Act. He won't say anything.*

But he didn't believe that, not for a single second. Keeping their mouth shut was not something that came naturally to boys like Chris Hollison.

"Shit," he repeated, under his breath. "Shit. Goddamnit, *shit.*"

"What do you want me to do, sir?" asked Ellison.

"Talk to Surveillance," said Jamie. "Arrange for police to go to his house and put the fear of God into him."

"Yes, sir," said Ellison.

"It is done," said Qiang, appearing beside his squad mates.

"Good," said Jamie. He stared down at the three frightened teenagers. "We're done here," he said. "Don't forget this happened, but remember what I told you, and what you signed. Try and put it behind you."

The teenagers didn't respond; they looked silently up at him, their faces pale. Jamie could see them shaking in the light of the fire, shivering as though they were cold, the skin on their arms raised in gooseflesh. He twisted the dial on his belt and established a connection with their driver.

"Ready for extraction from insertion point," he said. "ASAP, please."

From the shadowy doorway of a looming stone mausoleum, Chris Hollison watched the three black figures walk through the gates of the graveyard and climb into the back of a waiting van.

His heart was thumping in his chest, his legs felt like jelly, but the hands that held his mobile phone were steady; its screen glowed in the darkness, REC flashing in red letters in its upper right corner. As the van pulled away, Chris tapped the screen with his thumb. Two words appeared: SAVE and DISCARD. He pressed SAVE, put the phone in his pocket, then set off for home at a run, his friends forgotten, his mind focused entirely on getting to his bedroom and uploading the footage he had just taken.

*Nobody's going to believe that just happened,* he thought. *Until they see it.*

Operational Squad J-5's journey home was quiet; the three Operators sitting in the back of the van had barely spoken by the time their driver guided the vehicle through the containment tunnel and on to the wide grounds of the Loop.

The remainder of the Patrol Respond had passed without incident. Jamie had seriously considered abandoning the operation after they left the graveyard, but had decided against it, for three reasons: if Chris Hollison turned out to be a problem, then it was his problem; his squad needed to gain experience of working together quickly; and they still had four hours before they were due to return to base. But as it turned out, he might just as well have followed his first instinct; the connection to the Surveillance Division had stayed stubbornly silent.

The atmosphere in the van wasn't unpleasant, not exactly; it was more the quiet introspection that came from being reminded, as if it was ever possible to truly forget, that their work carried the constant prospect of injury and death. Qiang had not been seriously hurt when the old man attacked him, and the teenagers had survived their encounter with a vampire, the one that they had apparently been so keen to have, without any physical damage. Nonetheless, Jamie was already analysing his role in the incident in the graveyard, turning it endlessly over and over. It wasn't just that Chris Hollison had got away; in the chaos of combat, particularly combat that involved civilians, such a situation was always a possibility. What *was* bothering him was the realisation he had let personal feelings affect his actions, at least in part, and he was already beginning to feel the dull heat of embarrassment in his stomach as he thought about what he had done.

*Unprofessional. Bad example. Poor leader.*

Technically, Jamie had followed protocol; when an incident involved non-supernatural civilians, they were to sign the Official Secrets Act, be made aware of the consequences of breaking it, and then sent on their way. This, if the raw facts were all that were considered, was what had happened.

What he had *really* done was abuse his authority, along with the power granted by his appearance and anonymity; he had used his position to punish a boy who reminded him of those who had made his and Matt's lives so miserable. Chris Hollison had been a prick, no doubt about it: a loudmouth, know-it-all bully. But had he really deserved to be told that he was going to be watched and followed wherever he went, that his phone was going to be tapped? Had he deserved to be scared and humiliated in front of his friends?

*No*, thought Jamie. *He didn't deserve that. None of them did.*

Operators were not perfect, nor were they robots, and Jamie would be the first to admit that he was not always able to remove his personality, and its many flaws, from the work that he did. He had learnt to live with such failings. But this felt like he had crossed some kind of line, like he had done exactly what he had always hated seeing done to others; used his power to terrorise those weaker than himself. Looking back on it, he could see that he had handled it badly. With hindsight, he knew that he had let himself down. But at the time? As he watched the smug face of Chris Hollison change when he realised that he wasn't in control of a situation, maybe for the first time? When he had seen the impotent rage fill the teenager's face? *That* had felt good. Great, even. And that was what was worrying Jamie now.

*This isn't some way for you to settle old scores,* he told himself. *This is the light, what's left of it, standing against the darkness. This is the most important thing in the world, and you have to be better than that. Your squad mates* need *you to be better than that.*

The van rolled into the Loop's hangar and pulled to a halt in one of the bays along the right-hand wall. Jamie and his squad mates unclipped themselves from their harnesses and got up from their seats, stretching their arms and rotating their necks. It was just after two in the morning, relatively early by the nocturnal standards of Blacklight, but Jamie was tired; the operation had drained him. He pushed open the door, stepped down on to the concrete, and waited for his squad mates to join him. They came quickly, exiting the vehicle and standing at sharp attention in front of him. Ellison's blond hair waved gently in the night breeze, while Qiang looked for all the world as though he'd just stepped out of the pages of a magazine; he didn't have so much as a hair out of place.

"Good work," said Jamie. "That wasn't the mission any of us were expecting, not one that anybody is going to tell stories about, but it was what it was, and there's one less vampire in the world than before we went out. So consider that a good night's work, and I'll see you both tomorrow when our orders come through. Until then, dismissed."

"Thank you, sir," said Qiang. He nodded, *almost* smiled, then turned on his heels and walked quickly towards the double doors that led into the rest of the Loop.

Ellison stayed where she was. She ran a hand through her hair, then pulled off her gloves and smiled at Jamie.

"Strange one," she said.

"No kidding," said Jamie, and grinned. "I don't think Qiang was particularly impressed that he ended up getting flattened by some vampire pensioner. We're going to have to up our game tomorrow."

Ellison laughed. "Don't worry," she said. "Qiang is a tiny bit in awe of you, so you're fine."

"I seriously doubt that."

"It's true," said Ellison. "He told me."

"Really?" said Jamie. "I wasn't sure he talked. What did he say?"

"That it's an honour for him to work alongside a descendant of the Blacklight founders," said Ellison. "And that he hopes to do a good job. I think he's feeling the pressure of representing PBS6."

"He's got nothing to worry about," said Jamie.

"That's what I told him," said Ellison. "Goodnight, sir."

She turned and strolled away across the hangar. Jamie watched her go, his mind mostly full of the incident with Chris Hollison, the report he had to write for the Interim Director, and whether or not his girlfriend was back from her operation, but still able to commit a small part of its processing power to admiration for his squad mate.

*I got lucky with Ellison,* he thought. *Very lucky.*

He walked across the hangar, pulling his console from his belt. He was about to start typing a message to Larissa when the plastic rectangle vibrated in his hands. The screen changed, displaying the new message icon. Jamie thumbed it open, and grimaced as he read the short line of text Cal Holmwood had sent him.

**MY QUARTERS. NOW.**

# 13

# THE GREY AREA

"What the hell did you think you were playing at?" shouted Cal Holmwood. His face was bright red, and he was gripping the edge of his desk with such force that his knuckles had turned white. Beside him, Paul Turner stood silently, his face as impassive as ever. "How could you be so utterly stupid?"

Jamie winced. "I'm sorry, sir," he said, forcing himself to maintain eye contact with the Interim Director. "I lost control, sir."

"Lost control?" bellowed Holmwood, his face darkening to an alarming purple. "You were filmed by a civilian. You're on the bloody *news*, you stupid boy."

Jamie's eyes widened. "I'm what, sir?"

"Take a look for yourself," shouted Holmwood. "Christ, I should put you in a cell for this. I've had the bloody Chief of the General Staff on the phone, telling me the Prime Minister wants you court-martialled. I've got bloody politicians trying to tell me how to do my job, all thanks to you."

The Interim Director hammered a series of commands into the terminal on his desk. The screen on the opposite wall of the room bloomed into life and Jamie turned towards it, panic creeping up his spine.

*The news? The Prime Minster? A court martial? Jesus, what the hell is all this?*

Holmwood opened a list of civilian broadcast channels, scrolled down to BBC NEWS 24, and hit ENTER. A rectangular window filled with a live feed of the news network, and Jamie gasped.

Playing in the centre of the screen was camera-phone footage of the Our Sister of Grace cemetery, where he and his squad had been barely five hours earlier. As he watched, the old vampire, a growling, shambling shape, sent Qiang spinning through the air, before the dark figure of Ellison fired her pistol, bringing him down. Jamie saw himself standing beside her, his MP7 in his hands, his purple visor turned towards the camera.

The footage was horribly, awfully clear.

"Shit," he whispered.

Below the video, which appeared to be playing on a loop, the red and white news ticker scrolled relentlessly from right to left.

MOD DENIES EXISTENCE OF SECRET ANTI-VAMPIRE ORGANISATION | APPEARANCE OF ALLEGED MEMBERS MATCHES DESCRIPTION OF THE LATE KEVIN MCKENNA | CAMBRIDGE EMAIL FORWARDED MORE THAN FIFTY THOUSAND TIMES

"How did this happen, Lieutenant?" asked Holmwood. "How did you manage to screw up a simple Patrol Respond so badly?"

"I don't know, sir," said Jamie, his panicked mind racing with worst-case scenarios. "It was a routine Echelon intercept, four kids lighting fires and splashing blood around, trying to summon vampires. I warned them off and made them sign the OSA, but we were attacked by a vamp. One of them disappeared in the confusion, sir."

"You didn't look for him?" asked Turner.

"Of course we did," said Jamie. "There was no sign of him. But he'd signed the OSA, so I ordered a police visit to his house and carried on with the operation. I had no idea he was filming us."

"Well, he was," said Holmwood, and pointed.

Jamie followed the Interim Director's finger and felt his heart stop in his chest. On the wide screen, standing outside a large detached house with a man and woman who looked like the dictionary definition of suburban middle class, was Chris Hollison. He was wearing a smart blue shirt and his blond hair was neatly combed as he looked into the camera, EXCLUSIVE scrolling rapidly below him. At the bottom of the screen, the rest of the day's headlines cycled past in turn; one item caught Jamie's eye, even as horror at the sight of Chris Hollison flooded through him.

BREAK-IN AT BUCHAREST MUSEUM – AUTHORITIES REFUSE TO CONFIRM MOTIVE WAS THEFT

"Joining us now," said the newsreader, "is the young man who shot the footage that we're bringing to you exclusively tonight. Chris Hollison, can you hear me?"

There was a tiny delay, then the teenager nodded. "I can hear you," he said.

"Chris, can you tell us how you came by these remarkable images?"

"Certainly," said Hollison. "Some friends of mine and I were hanging out in the cemetery at Our Sister of Grace after school, but we lost track of time, so when we tried to go home the gates had been locked. We were going to climb the fence when the three people you can see in the video appeared and started threatening us."

"Threatening you?" asked the newsreader.

Hollison nodded. "They claimed we had assaulted somebody, which was ridiculous. I asked who, and they wouldn't tell me. Then one of them, the leader, pointed a gun at me and said we had to sign the Official Secrets Act."

"I'm sorry?"

Hollison shook his head. "I know it sounds crazy," he said. "It sounded crazy to me at the time. So I told my friends not to sign it, because we hadn't done anything wrong and I know my rights, you know?"

"Right," said the newsreader. "Did you get a look at the man who threatened you?"

"I don't know if they were men or women," said Hollison. "All three of their faces were covered by visors, like the ones riot police wear. Except these were purple."

"Purple?"

"Purple," said Hollison, firmly. "Like McKenna said."

There was a pause. "You're referring of course to the late Kevin McKenna, who published an editorial in which he claimed not only that vampires existed, but that the British government maintained a secret organisation that policed them. Do you believe that's who you encountered tonight?"

"Yes," said Hollison. "I think everything Kevin McKenna wrote was true. I watched them murder a man in cold blood, they threatened to bug my parents' phones and emails, and told me and my friends that we were going to be followed and watched for the rest of our lives to make sure we never told anybody what we saw. But you don't have to take my word for it. You can just watch the video."

"Chris Hollison, thank you very much," said the newsreader. "We're going to have more on this story throughout the night—"

Cal Holmwood muted the screen and looked at Jamie, his eyes full of disappointment.

"That's not what happened, sir," said Jamie, his insides burning with fury at the way Chris Hollison had spun the evening's events. "We didn't murder anyone. We destroyed a vampire that had just *attacked* him, for God's sake. And everything I said to him followed protocol."

*That's not strictly true, is it?* whispered a voice in the back of his head, but he pushed it away.

"It doesn't matter, Lieutenant," said Turner, his voice as smooth and cold as ice. "What you just heard is the narrative that is being picked up by every newspaper and television station in the world. We cannot defend you without confirming that Kevin McKenna was telling the truth."

"But the footage doesn't show anything," said Jamie, aware that his voice was rising with emotion. "There's nothing that confirms vampires are real, or that anything he said was true."

"It doesn't matter," repeated Turner.

There was a heavy moment of silence, in which Jamie's outrage disappeared and was replaced by an awful, creeping dread.

*This is really bad*, he told himself. *This is so much worse than I realised.*

"Do you have anything to say for yourself, Lieutenant?" asked Cal Holmwood, the colour in his face at last beginning to fade.

"Only that losing Chris Hollison was my mistake," Jamie said. "I want it clear that it was no fault of Ellison or Qiang. And that I'm sorry, sir."

"I've heard that from you before, Lieutenant Carpenter," said Holmwood. "I'm starting to get tired of it."

Jamie didn't respond.

"You will remain on the active roster, but only because I can't afford to bench you," continued Holmwood. "When all this is over, when we reach Zero Hour and whatever comes after it, you can expect to be asked to revisit your actions of today. Do I need to tell you how incredibly disappointed I am?"

Jamie shook his head, as a lump rose into his throat and settled there. "No, sir."

"Fine. Then you may consider yourself dismissed. Get out of my sight."

"Thank you, sir," said Jamie, his voice little more than a croak. He turned away, noting the unchanged expression on Paul Turner's face as he did so, and walked stiffly towards the door. When he rounded the corner of the main Level A corridor, he sagged against the grey wall, his hands on his knees, his eyes squeezed tightly shut.

*Well done, you stupid, stupid boy. What if he means it this time? What if he court-martials you? You bloody deserve it.*

Jamie couldn't breathe. His chest felt like it was being constricted in a vice as he fought back the cyclone of rage and shame that was boiling inside him.

*How many times has Paul Turner tried to warn you? How many times has he told you that you can't just do whatever you want and expect to get away with it? How many times has he tried to save you from yourself?*

"Shut up," he whispered, dragging air into his lungs. "Shut up, just shut up."

He knew, deep down, how tolerant Cal Holmwood, and Henry Seward before him, had been with him, how far they'd indulged him. But rather than being grateful, rather than learning from his mistakes and moving on, what had he done? Convinced himself he was invincible, that he would never receive anything more than a slap on the wrist. He had abused their faith in him, their trust, and this was where it had got him: on the verge of tears outside the Interim Director's quarters, with his Blacklight career hanging by a thread.

Jamie lurched down the corridor towards the lift. As he pushed the call button, he said a silent prayer, asking a God he didn't believe in to ensure that the lift was empty when it arrived, and waited.

The doors slid open with Jamie holding his breath in front of them. Mercifully, the metal box was empty.

*Thank you.*

He stepped inside, thumbed the button marked H, and leant against the wall as the lift began its descent.

When it slowed to a halt, Jamie was through the doors before they were even halfway open, walking unsteadily into the airlock that sealed the detention block. Gas billowed around him, the light turned green, and he was moving again, his footsteps echoing loudly, his gaze fixed on the last cell on the left.

With the last of his composure, Jamie walked out in front of the ultraviolet barrier that formed the fourth wall of his mother's cell. She looked up at once, and the expression of concern on her face was enough to send him over the edge; he staggered through the barrier, his face collapsing into a mask of misery and shame, and began to cry. Marie Carpenter flew up off the sofa she had been lying on and wrapped her son in a hug that lifted him off his feet, but which felt to Jamie like the gentlest embrace in human history.

"What's the matter?" she asked, her voice low and soothing. "Are you all right? Is someone hurt?"

"I did something stupid, Mum," said Jamie, between sobs. "Something really stupid, and I'm in trouble."

# 5 DAYS TILL
# ZERO HOUR

# 14

# WHICH DO YOU WANT FIRST?

Jamie Carpenter took a seat at the far end of the long Ops Room table and found that he couldn't meet Cal Holmwood's eye.

*Yesterday was yesterday,* he told himself, as he studied the surface of the desk. *Nothing you can do about it now. You just have to get on with today.*

He had stayed with his mother for a long time the previous night. When his tears had stopped, he had been instantly ashamed of himself; it was appalling, a Blacklight Operator crying to his mum when something went wrong, and he had said so. His mother, who was a strong contender for the most patient person he had ever known, whose natural instinct, with the sad exception of Larissa, was to see the very best in everyone, had lost her temper with him for maybe only the seventh or eighth time in his life. Her eyes had flared red, and she had told him that he needed to stop thinking that he could handle whatever the world threw at him.

"You're still just a boy," she said. "You do a man's job, and Holmwood and all the others treat you like one because that's what they need you to be, but you're *not* a man yet. I'm so proud of you, of all the things you've done, and if you tell me you're ashamed of yourself again I'm going to get very cross with you. Do you hear me, Jamie?"

He had told her that he did, and she had hugged him so tightly that for a moment he couldn't breathe. When she let him go, they had talked for almost an hour, about nothing in particular, the way they used to before the darkness had infiltrated their lives.

"Zero Hour Task Force called to order," said the Interim Director. "All members present."

Jamie knew that membership of the Task Force was a privilege, and it was one he didn't take lightly; the group had been set up explicitly to deal with the prospect of the return of Dracula to his full, ungodly strength, and to develop and implement a strategy to try and prevent such an unthinkable horror. But while membership was a source of great pride, it was also an endlessly gruelling responsibility.

Zero Hour, the Intelligence Division estimate of the point at which Dracula would regain his full power, was now less than a week away, and they were no closer to either locating the ancient monster or devising any way of stopping him if the date came and went. Everyone inside the Loop knew what was coming, but only the men and women of the Zero Hour Task Force really, truly understood; they were privy to details that were classified from everyone else.

*Sometimes I wonder if it would be better not to know,* thought Jamie. *Perhaps ignorance would be bliss.*

Out of the corner of his eye, he saw Larissa looking at him, her eyes narrowed. He had not messaged her the previous night, as he had promised to; by the time he'd left his mother's cell, grateful for, but unconvinced by, her insistence that everything would be all right, he had been completely drained, capable of nothing more than heading to his quarters and falling into a shallow, dreamless sleep.

He looked at his girlfriend. She tipped her head to one side and widened her eyes, the question in the movement clear.

*Are you all right?*

Jamie gave his head a single shake, and forced the thinnest of smiles as Paul Turner stood up and joined Holmwood at the head of the table.

"Good morning," he said, his voice as flat and empty as ever. "As per the agenda, Lieutenant Randall will now brief you on the findings of the Intelligence Division report that Security commissioned, and which will be sent to you all later today. I warn you now, it does not make for comfortable reading."

*There's a surprise*, thought Jamie.

"Thank you, sir," said Kate, getting to her feet as Holmwood and Turner took their seats. She seemed calm, at least as far as Jamie could tell; her face was pale, her hands steady, her eyes clear and focused. "The report is entitled *Provisional Forecast of Losses and Damage in the Event of the Establishment of Supernatural (Type V) Social Dominance*. I don't think I need to explain what that means to anyone here?"

There was a moment of silence, before she continued. "Good. The report is based on a number of models and simulations, and attempts to allow for possible variations in Dracula's actions if he is allowed to complete his rise, what his motivations and ambitions may be, and their effect on the wider vampire populace. All variables are addressed in depth in the full report, so as a result the figures I'm going to give you now should be treated as best estimates. The situation we are facing is entirely unprecedented, and is too fluid to be modelled with any great degree of certainty.

That said, I have some headline numbers that you should take on board. It goes without saying that these are fully Zero Hour classified, and not to be shared or discussed with anyone outside this room."

Kate looked around, checking for any dissent or lack of understanding.

"All right," she said. "The Intelligence Division projects, based on an amalgamation of the various models, that the unchecked rise of Dracula will result in the deaths of between twenty-five and thirty million people within twelve months."

There was a sharp intake of breath around the table.

"Christ," said Patrick Williams, his voice low.

Kate nodded. "I know," she said. "Trust me, I do. The second projection is harder to quantify, as it deals with the potential spread of vampirism. The evidence provided by Valentin Rusmanov under interrogation confirms that prior to his death, Dracula operated a strict policy of allowing no new vampires to be turned. However, we cannot assume that this will remain the case, or how possible enforcement of such a rule would be. Given that, Intelligence projects a rise in global vampire numbers of almost twelve hundred per cent in the two years following Zero Hour, at a cost of approximately eighty million human lives."

Jamie fought back the urge to laugh. The number was so ridiculous, so impossibly huge, that it was incomprehensible.

*Eighty million people. All dead, if we don't stop him.*

"I should reiterate," said Paul Turner, "that these are just numbers, for now at least."

The air in the Ops Room seemed suddenly cold; it was as though Kate's words had sucked the vitality out of it. Jamie stared at the tight, pale face of his friend; she returned his gaze as the rest of the Zero Hour Task Force sat in silence, struggling to digest what they had just been told.

"The report makes a final prediction," said Kate, her calm tone eerily similar to Paul Turner's. "It suggests that if Dracula is allowed to rise unchecked, and the second projection proves accurate, vampires will outnumber humans within eight years of Zero Hour. That they will be the dominant species on the planet in less than a decade."

She sat down, not meeting anyone's eye. There was stunned silence around the table, full of palpable horror.

*Nobody thought it would be that bad,* thought Jamie. *Not in a million years. My God.*

Cal Holmwood got slowly to his feet. His face was ashen.

"Thank you, Lieutenant Randall," he said. "Copies of the report will be sent to you all later on today. Read it, understand it, but be aware that as of right now, it changes nothing. Our goals and priorities remain as before. The purpose of this Task Force has always been to stop Dracula from rising, and this should do nothing but sharpen our focus and strengthen our resolve. If we fail, people will die. That is the responsibility we bear, and now we know the numbers. But if we do our job, then maybe numbers are what they will stay. I don't want anyone to be disheartened, or demoralised. We know the stakes now, nothing more. We know precisely why we cannot allow ourselves to fail."

Jamie felt the icy horror crawling within him recede, just a little.

*He still believes we can stop this,* he thought. *If he does, then I have to.*

"All right," Cal said. "I'm sure many of you have little stomach left for bad news, but I'm afraid the reality is what it is. Major Turner?"

Paul Turner stood up again and cast his empty gaze across the men and women of the Task Force. "Thank you, sir," he said. "Operators, please direct your attention to the screen."

Jamie watched as the wall screen at the head of the Ops Room flickered into life. Turner tapped rapidly on his console, first opening a window then expanding it to fill the screen. It showed an area of forest beside a straight road, in the centre of which burned a large campfire. Beyond the flickering orange flames, he made out half a dozen tents, with smoky silhouettes wandering between them. At the side of the road, facing a camera they presumably had no idea was watching them, a dozen men and women stood in a neat line, drinking from steaming travel mugs and holding a series of brightly painted signs and placards. What was printed on them was clear, and Jamie's heart sank as he read.

## BLACKLIGHT = FASCISTS

## VAMPIRES ARE PEOPLE TOO

## THE MILITARY ARE
## THE REAL BLOODSUCKERS

"What you are looking at," said Paul Turner, "is public land beyond the border of the Loop, approximately seven hundred metres outside the authorisation gate. This is live footage."

"Outside the border of the *Loop*?" said Patrick Williams. "This is a classified facility, for God's sake. No one knows it exists."

"No longer true," said Turner. "Yesterday an email was sent from a Cambridge University laboratory. It contained a series of digital images, and quickly went viral. The Surveillance Division estimates that in the last sixteen hours it has been forwarded more than ninety thousand times and posted to social media sites on almost half a million occasions. It is already impossible to stop the spread of the images and the information attached to them."

"What are the images?" asked Jack Williams, his face as pale as a ghost's. "For Christ's sake, spit it out."

The Security Officer turned his head and fixed Jamie's friend with a look that would have sent most men scuttling under the table to hide. Jack didn't flinch; he returned the stare with a cold, determined one of his own.

"The images, Lieutenant Williams," said Turner, "were taken by a commercial imaging satellite four months ago, to be used for GPS mapping. They show the detonation of the ultraviolet bombs that ended Valeri Rusmanov's attack on the Loop."

"Jesus," said Angela Darcy. "The coordinates."

Turner nodded. "The sender of the email, who if I have my way will spend the rest of his life in prison, was clearly aware of the story that Kevin McKenna published before he was killed by Albert Harker. Whoever they are, they traced the ownership of the land in the images through the Land Registry, and included the record in the email. It shows the purchase of the land, *this* land, that we are sitting at the centre of, by the Ministry of Defence from a charitable organisation called the Lux E Tenebris Foundation. That organisation had Jonathan Harker, Albert Holmwood, John Seward and Abraham Van Helsing as its original board of directors."

"Shit," said Jack Williams.

Turner nodded. "For those of you who have not seen the news this morning, last night, an Operational Squad conducting a Patrol Respond was secretly filmed by a civilian using a mobile phone. Before you all start shouting at once, which squad was involved is not important, and will remain classified information. And all things considered, the footage *could* have been worse. It does not conclusively prove the existence of the supernatural, nor does it reveal explicit detail about this Department. But when placed alongside an email showing ultraviolet detonations at this location, a location *linked to the men named in Bram Stoker's novel*, the case against us starts to become compelling."

"We're caught, aren't we?" said Angela, softly. "They know we're here."

"Yes," said Turner. "And video surveillance suggests they are not happy."

"This is outrageous," said Jack Williams. "What the hell do they think they're doing?"

"Is it allowed?" asked Angela. "The protesting, I mean. They can do this?"

Larissa frowned. "Yes, it's allowed," she said. "They're on public land. And I suspect they *think* they're protesting the killing of vampires."

"I can see that," snapped Jack. "Why, though? I bet none of them has ever seen a vamp."

"Most of the people who marched against the Iraq war had never met an Iraqi," said Larissa.

"You think this is the same as that?" asked Jack, his face reddening. "Really? Those people waving signs are the people we risk our lives every night to protect. I can't believe this."

*She knew*, whispered a voice in the back of Jamie's head. He was staring up at the screen, his stomach churning. *Larissa saw this coming a long time ago, how what Blacklight does would be perceived. She knew it would look like murder.*

"We've encountered civilians twice this week who didn't seem surprised to see us," said Patrick Williams. "They'd read McKenna's work, and they believed it."

146

The Security Officer nodded. "The tide is turning," he said. "Those who believe aren't being laughed at any more, and there are more of them every day. The first protesters arrived overnight, and eight more have joined them in the last three hours. We have every reason to expect that rate to increase as the day goes on."

"There's nothing we can do about the phone footage," said Andrew Jarvis, the Zero Hour representative of the Surveillance Division. "It's everywhere. Unbelievably stupid for one of our own to get caught like that, but not fatal, as Major Turner said. The MOD is maintaining a refusal to comment, and it's holding for now. As far as the email goes, no newspaper is going to run it, not yet at least. But I'm afraid there's nothing more we can do. We're issuing takedowns as fast as we can, but we can't make either story go away, not completely. Eventually, we're going to reach a tipping point, and it's going to be open season on us when we do."

"Everyone in this room understands that Surveillance is doing all that can be done," said Holmwood. "In the short term, the SOP remains the same, especially where civilians are concerned. It may need revising as this information continues to spread, but you will be advised of any changes as and when. As I said, our focus, our priority, remains the same. And it is in relation to Dracula that I am finally able to bring you something that is at least *close* to good news."

Jamie sat forward in his seat, his curiosity piqued; by the Interim Director's standards, this almost qualified as hyperbole.

Holmwood pulled his radio from his belt and spoke into the microphone. "Bring him in."

Jamie felt excitement flutter in his stomach.

*Valentin*, he told himself. *It has to be. Valentin's back.*

But he was wrong.

The Ops Room door opened and a Security Division Operator stepped through it, leading a dark figure by the arm. Larissa instantly hissed, a loud, threatening noise, and Jamie glanced at his girlfriend; her eyes had turned the colour of molten lava, and her face was twisted with bright, shining hatred. He frowned, taken aback by her response to the new arrival.

Then realisation struck him like a bolt of lightning.

"Grey," he said, out loud.

The old vampire raised his head and peered out from beneath a mane of almost-white hair. His gaze came to rest on Jamie, and a smile rose on to his lined face.

"Mr Carpenter," he said, causing several of the Task Force to gasp at the booming rumble of his voice. "It's good to see you again. And Miss Kinley, of course, and Colonel Frankenstein. Where is Mr Morris?"

"Dead," growled Frankenstein. "In Hell, with any luck."

Grey's face fell. "Oh," he said. "I'm sorry. I have not been keeping up with current events."

"Operators," said Cal Holmwood. "This is Mr Grey, the founder of the Valhalla commune in Scotland. He has information that I believe you will want to hear."

"Quite so," said Grey, forcing levity back into his voice. "Quite so, Mr Holmwood. And I thank you for the opportunity to relay my information in person. Who I am is not strictly relevant to what I am about to tell you, but suffice it to say that I have been a vampire for a long time, and I have no wish to see Dracula rise."

"Right," growled Larissa. "It might interfere with you murdering teenage girls."

Grey grimaced. "I highly doubt that it would," he said. "But

I cannot blame you for your anger. I do not expect your forgiveness."

"What?" asked Jack Williams, frowning deeply and looking around the room. "Can someone please tell me what is going on here?"

"*He* turned me," said Larissa, without taking her smouldering eyes from the old vampire. "Valhalla is supposed to be a place for vampires to live in peace, but every year for God knows how long he's been going out into the world and feeding and killing. The rest of Valhalla threw him out last year when they found out."

Every pair of eyes in the room settled on Grey.

"Everything she says is the truth," said the old vampire. "I was cast out, and rightly so. I have been on a journey, in the hope that I might find some way to atone for the things I have done. That journey is why I am here with you now."

"Tell us what you know," said Paul Turner. "Out with it."

Grey nodded. "There are legends," he said. "When you live a life as long as mine, you hear a great many of them, and you realise that the vast majority are of no substance whatsoever, passed down for nothing more than entertainment. But occasionally one takes root, and endures. You are no doubt aware that the circumstances of Dracula's own turning have never been known, that how he became the first of my kind remains a mystery. And in truth, the details do not matter. What *does* matter is a legend that tells of that time, and suggests a way to defeat him."

Grey paused, smiling.

"*And?*" said Turner, eventually.

"The legend states," said Grey, "that the first victim of Dracula holds the key to his destruction."

Silence descended over the Ops Room.

"Valeri?" said Jamie, frowning. "Valeri is the key to destroying Dracula?"

"How does that help us?" asked Frankenstein. "Valeri has been loyal to his master for more than four centuries."

Grey's smile widened. "Valeri may not have been Dracula's first victim," he said.

There was a clamour of voices, until Grey raised his hand and continued. "For decades, even centuries, rumours have persisted of another vampire, a victim who pre-dates Valeri, perhaps only by as much as a day or two. The *first* victim, a man Dracula fed on after his turn was complete, and who would be almost as old, almost as powerful as the first vampire himself."

"We need to find out if he's still alive," said Jack Williams, his eyes wide. "We need to go and—"

"No need," said Grey. "I have already found him."

This time, after several seconds of stunned silence, it was Angela Darcy who found her voice first.

"I'm sorry?" she said. "You *found* him?"

Grey nodded. "I found him. He's still alive."

"Where?" asked Paul Turner.

"In Romania," said Grey, turning to face the Security Officer. "The legend of Vlad Tepes, the Wallachian prince who became Dracula, ends in 1476 when his army was routed near Bucharest and his final reign came to an end. I followed the legend back, to a place called the Teleorman Forest, where Vlad allegedly fled when the battle was lost. There, in villages and farms, I was told stories of a man who lived in the forest, who had lived there forever. The tales had been passed down through the generations, but nobody I talked to believed they were fiction. There are places in the forest that they will not go, places that children are forbidden from even approaching. They do not believe that what lives in the forest means them harm, but they know to leave it alone.

"I doubted their stories, but at the heart of the forest, something came for me, something old and incredibly powerful. Two days later, two days I have no memory of, I awoke at the edge of the forest with a freshly slaughtered deer at my side and this in my pocket."

Grey held out a hand, and the Operator who had escorted him into the Ops Room handed him a plastic evidence bag. The old vampire held it up; sealed inside was a piece of paper marked with three words in heavy capital letters.

## LEAVE ME ALONE

"At which point, I must confess, my nerve failed me," said Grey. "I returned home, and attempted to make contact with Henry Seward. I am deeply sorry for his loss."

Larissa grunted with laughter, a harsh sound without any humour in it. Jamie glanced at her; the red in her eyes still blazed fiercely, and he could see the tips of her fangs below her upper lip. He fought back thoughts that had no place in the Ops Room and returned his gaze to Grey.

"So you found him," he said. "And the legend claims he can stop Dracula, if he is who you think he is. But how, exactly? You said 'the first victim of Dracula holds the key to his destruction', but what does that actually *mean*? That only he can kill him, like some kind of prophecy? Or that he can show us some weakness we can use? Or there's something in his blood or... what?"

"I have no idea," said Grey. "I have told you everything I know, the legend, and the location."

"So we need to go to Romania," said Jack Williams.

"I would say so," said Grey. "But before you get too excited, before you all saddle up and head for the forest, I must make sure that you truly understand, for the sake of my conscience. It is an old place, dark and forgotten. What lives there, what I encountered, was a force of nature, nothing less. It shook the ground and the trees. I flatter myself more powerful than most creatures that walk the earth, and I am grateful to have escaped with my life. The fact that I did shows that he is capable of mercy. But if you search him out, which I have no doubt you will, it would not be wise to expect it."

"Noted," said Cal Holmwood. "Thank you, Mr Grey. You will be escorted back to Valhalla."

"You're welcome, Mr Holmwood," said Grey, nodding towards the Interim Director. "Good luck to you all."

The old vampire walked out of the Ops Room, his security escort close behind him. When the door swung shut, Cal Holmwood faced the Zero Hour Task Force.

"I have spoken to the other Directors," he said. "We are in the process of assembling a multinational team to investigate the information you have just heard, an operation that will be Priority Level 1 and Zero Hour classified. It will likely be extremely dangerous, given Grey's description of the power of the first victim, and its objectives will be uncertain, given how little information we have to work with. But it represents a chance, no matter how small, that things can still be turned back in our favour."

"I volunteer, sir," said Jamie, his heart pounding at the prospect of such an immediate chance to make up for his mistakes in the graveyard.

"So do I," said Larissa.

Holmwood shook his head. "Inclusion in the team will be by selection only. If anyone from Blacklight *is* selected, they will be notified by 0900 tomorrow. Today's orders will be posted as usual, and I expect them carried out to the best of your abilities. Is there anything else?"

"What about Brennan, sir?" asked Jack Williams, instantly.

Holmwood looked over at his Security Officer. "Paul?"

Turner nodded. "Richard Brennan was ID'd disembarking a cross-channel ferry at Calais," he said. "Local police were informed, and we despatched a Security team, but he was gone."

"How the hell did he get *on* the ferry?" asked Jack. "I thought we had the borders locked down?"

"You know as well as I do that there's no such thing as a sealed border, Lieutenant," said Turner. "Brennan removed his chip, so we have been reliant on mugshots and known aliases and border-control awareness. Don't you think an experienced Operator would be able to get through that, if he was determined? Couldn't you, if you had to?"

"Jesus," said Jack. "So that's it then? If Brennan's gone, Valentin Rusmanov is our only shot at finding Dracula before Zero Hour."

Turner shook his head. "It's a lead," he said. "We know that Brennan sailed from England to France, and given that he set off a bomb in the Loop and wrote HE RISES before he fled, we can make a reasonable assumption about where he's going."

"To Dracula," said Angela Darcy.

"Precisely," said Turner. "Which means we know that Dracula is not in this country, and is likely somewhere on the continental land mass."

"Great," said Jack. "That narrows it down."

Turner narrowed his eyes. "I said it was a lead, Lieutenant. I didn't say it was a good one, but we work with what we have. Would you rather I'd kept the information to myself?" He stared coldly at Jamie's friend until Jack dropped his gaze.

"All right then," said Holmwood, frowning briefly at his Security Officer. "Be careful out there, and remember what you've heard this morning, particularly with regard to civilians. It's not just the vampires who are hostile now. Dismissed."

# 15

# BY A THREAD

Henry Seward raised his wine glass to his lips with a trembling hand, trying to ignore the pain that boiled in the hole where his left eye had been. He had not tried to resist as it was plucked from its socket, not even when Dracula had swallowed the glistening orb like it was a delicious petit four, for a simple reason.

There was no fight left in him.

He believed, deep down in the part of himself that still remembered the world beyond the stone walls of the château, that he had resisted as hard as he could, for as long as he could. He knew this was where his life would end, this old building full of monsters, at the whim of perhaps the only true demon to have ever walked the earth, and had made peace with it. He could endure no more pain, no more humiliation, no more days and weeks of sickening impotence.

All he could do was pray for it to end.

"How's the wine?" asked Dracula.

Seward focused his remaining eye on the vampire sitting at the distant opposite end of the table.

"It's good," he said. "What is it?"

Dracula smiled. "It's a 1941 Haut-Brion. Valeri rescued it from the cellar of Hermann Goering at the end of what I understand was known as the Second World War. A conflict I would dearly love to have seen."

"I'm sure you would have enjoyed it," said Seward, and refilled his wine glass.

"As am I, my dear Admiral. Valeri has told me much, both about that war and the one that preceded it. I must confess that, even as a military man, I cannot conceive of a war so vast that it drew in the entire world, much less two of them barely twenty years apart. Humanity's appetite for death and destruction clearly did not diminish during the years I lay dormant."

Seward laughed, despite the flare of pain in his head. "No," he said. "It most certainly did not. Advances in technology allowed us to kill each other with ever greater ease, and we used them with huge enthusiasm. We industrialised murder."

Dracula's smile widened. "A fine turn of phrase," he said. "That is exactly what Valeri described. Death dealt by explosives that fell from the sky, or were fired halfway around the globe on rockets. Gas, and poison, and bombs that destroyed whole cities. Undoubtedly effective, but impersonal, and possibly *too* easy. There was a time when you had to watch the light leave the eyes of the man you killed, had to feel his warm blood douse your sword hand. It took true resolve. What resolve is needed to press a button and wait for an explosion in some distant land?"

"Don't worry," said Seward. "The machete and the knife are still popular in much of the world. Torture too."

"So much has changed," said Dracula. "There is much that I confess I do not yet understand. But at their core, it seems people remain the same. In the end, it always comes down to spilled blood."

Seward drained his glass, and set it unsteadily back down on the table. The wine took the edge off the pain that filled his body, reducing it to a dull, persistent throb. It never truly left him; it was there when he woke up in the morning, and, when he managed to fall asleep at night, it infiltrated his dreams.

"And me?" he asked. "What death do you have planned for me?"

"You would talk about such an unpleasant matter?" asked Dracula.

"Not with any great enthusiasm," said Seward, the ghost of a smile flickering across his face. "But I would rather know than not. I am hoping for an officer's death, with honour. With dignity. But I can't convince myself that will be the case."

"No," said Dracula, his tone gentle, almost apologetic. "I'm afraid it will not."

Seward's heart sank in his chest. He had expected it, but expectation did not lessen the pain that came with the extinguishing of his last flickering flame of hope. His stomach churned, and he felt tears rise in the corners of his eyes.

"What then?" he asked. "Impalement?"

Dracula rolled his eyes. "You really should not believe everything you read. My enemies were impaled as warnings to their comrades, to break their morale and their spirit. I do not think such a thing would prove effective against your Blacklight colleagues."

"No," said Seward, his voice momentarily full of fierce conviction. "It wouldn't."

Dracula sat back in his chair. "What good can come of this, my dear Admiral?"

"I don't like surprises," said Seward.

"I really recommend that you do not know."

"Tell me," said Seward.

"Are you sure? Some things cannot be un-known."

"Tell me."

Dracula took a long sip of his wine, and told him.

Seward stared with his remaining eye, grey sweeping into his vision from all sides. His stomach revolved and he realised, with helpless certainty, that he was going to vomit.

His mouth yawned open, and the contents of his stomach, including the pale pink slivers of veal he had eaten only minutes earlier, were ejected on to the white tablecloth and delicate porcelain plate that would shortly have held his dessert. His head swam, and he fought for breath as his gag reflex triggered over and over, forcing air and saliva up and down his gullet, until he began to cough and splutter like a drowning man.

Grey rushed towards him, full of swirling pinpoints of red and white and yellow. Then it gave way to black, and he knew no more.

Dracula smiled as he watched Henry Seward lose consciousness.

The Blacklight Director's eye rolled back in his head as he pitched left and slid to the floor with a heavy crash, sending his chair flying; it clattered against the wall and lay as still as its former occupant. The ancient vampire waited, watching for any sign of a swift recovery, then picked up the silver bell that sat on the table and gave it a sharp ring. Before the peals had faded away, the door to the dining room swung open and one of Valeri's vampires appeared, a look of barely restrained eagerness on his pale face.

"My lord," he said. "How may I assist you?"

"My guest has taken an unfortunate turn," said Dracula, motioning in the direction of Henry Seward's prone form. "Take him back to his quarters and ensure that he is comfortable. Then send Valeri to me. I would speak with him."

"At once, my lord," said the vampire, bowing deeply. He flew down the dining room, lifted the Blacklight Director easily into his arms, and headed back towards the door, carrying his load carefully.

*Pathetic*, thought Dracula, as he watched the vampire depart. *So desperate to please, so weak and furtive and eager.*

The first vampire finished his final slice of veal, savouring meat so rare it ran with blood. A second vampire, the girl named Ekaterina, cleared the table, including Seward's foul mess, with silent precision, before returning with a beautifully delicate almond tart and a small bowl of crème fraîche. He was enjoying the last sweet mouthful when a knock on the door echoed through the dining room.

"Come," he said, setting his napkin on the table and lifting his wine.

The door opened and Valeri stepped through it, his heavy footsteps instantly annoying to Dracula's ears.

*You could fly round the world without stopping for breath*, he thought, as his oldest friend approached, *yet you cannot spare me your infernal clatter?*

"You sent for me, my lord," said Valeri.

"I did," replied Dracula, and took a long sip of his wine. It was good for Valeri to be made to wait; the years in which his master had lain in the ground had given birth to a streak of independence that he was steadily crushing out of his old General. When he was ready, he put the glass down.

"Have you acquired the item I asked you for?" he said.

"I have, my lord," replied Valeri.

Dracula frowned. "And you did not think to bring it to me?"

"It arrived less than an hour ago, my lord. I did not wish to interrupt your dinner."

*Clever*, thought Dracula. *I cannot reprimand him when I have instructed him so often not to do so.*

"So be it," he said. "Get it now."

For a long moment, long enough to be dangerously close to insubordinate, Valeri didn't respond. Then he bowed his head, said, "Of course, my lord," and exited the dining room.

*Damn Seward and his needling*, thought Dracula. *There is still a spark in him that has not yet been snuffed out.*

The door opened again and Valeri strode back into the dining room, holding a long wooden crate under one arm. He set it down on the centre of the long table, and stepped respectfully back. Dracula got to his feet, not allowing his excitement to show on his face, and walked round to face the box.

"The theft has made the news, my lord," said Valeri, as the first vampire twisted open a pair of heavy padlocks. "But my man was careful. There is nothing to lead anyone here."

The final lock fell away. Carefully, almost reverentially, Dracula lifted the lid of the wooden box, and smiled the wide, happy smile of a child.

# 16

# THE MAN YOU WANT TO BE

Cal Holmwood leant against the wall of the lift as it descended, trying to process the Zero Hour Task Force meeting that had just ended. It had been nothing short of revelatory, even by the standards of the highly classified group.

He had seen a copy of the Intelligence Division report in advance, but hearing the numbers spoken aloud so bluntly by Kate Randall, and seeing the expressions they elicited on the faces of men and women who were no strangers to death, had been sobering.

*I'm glad Kate spoke first,* he thought. *At least Grey gave them some semblance of hope.*

There was much that was unreliable about Grey and the information that he had provided, and under circumstances, Holmwood would never have sanctioned an operation based on such flimsy intelligence. But these were not normal circumstances, and a vampire that was almost as old as Dracula himself could be immensely useful. If he could be persuaded to join them, it would go a long way towards levelling the playing field.

*Valeri. Valentin. Dracula. The first victim.*

*Two on their side, two on ours.*

Holmwood had relayed Grey's information to the other Directors in a conference video call that had started after midnight and lasted well into the early hours of the morning. By the end of the call, after a refreshingly minor amount of bickering and squabbling, they had agreed to send a small, multinational team into the Teleorman Forest to search for the first victim, if he existed. Holmwood had insisted that at least one Blacklight Operator take part in the mission, given that his Department had provided the intelligence. This had been agreed, as had Bob Allen's suggestion that Larissa Kinley be placed on the team, regardless of her affiliation; she was, they all knew, the only Operator from any Department who had even the slightest chance of being able to stand up to a vampire as powerful as Grey had described.

That accounted for two spots on a squad that it had been decided should number six. After a debate that approached, but never quite reached, the status of heated, it was agreed that the other four places would be occupied by Operators from Germany, Russia, America and South Africa.

All that remained was the question of who would *lead* the mission.

Russia and Germany argued at length over exactly whose jurisdiction Romania fell under, until Bob Allen suggested that one of his Operators act as squad leader, a suggestion clearly designed to circumnavigate the infighting among the European Departments, that was agreed to before either the SPC or the FTB were able to form the first syllables of their objections. Allen left the call to go and brief the Operator he had in mind for squad leader, and each of the affected Directors promised that they would make their selections by 2200 GMT.

Which was in about fifteen hours.

The doors slid open on Level H and Cal made his way quickly round to the human detention block he had visited so often in recent weeks. He had come to hate it; the uniform grey walls and floors and ceilings, the rows of heavy cell doors, and, above all, the bitter, selfish creature that had replaced one of the men he had loved most in the world, whom he was on his way to see for what would likely be the final time.

Holmwood paused for a moment outside the door of the cell, preparing himself for a conversation he would never have chosen to have, but would not shy away from now that his hand had been forced. He reached out, keyed his override code into the panel on the wall, waited for the heavy locks to disengage, then pushed the door open.

Julian Carpenter looked up from his usual position, seated on the bed with his back to the wall, his arms wrapped round knees that were drawn up to his chest. His expression momentarily weakened Holmwood's resolve; there was misery there, possibly even despair, but also clear and obvious affection.

"Cal," said Julian. "Time for the last rites?"

"Julian," said Holmwood, pulling the door closed behind him. "You know it doesn't have to be like this."

Julian shrugged, and looked down at the bed.

"I gave you forty-eight hours," said Cal, fighting to keep his voice calm and steady. "Time's up. This is your last chance to do what's right, Julian, and I'm begging you to take it. Because after this I wash my hands of you."

Julian looked up, his eyes flashing. "I can't, Cal," he said, his voice suddenly thick with emotion. "You know I can't. It will leave me with nothing. I want to see my wife and son."

"You already have nothing," said Cal. "You're in no position to bargain. Why can't I make you see that?"

Julian stared into his eyes, and said nothing. Anger burst through

Holmwood, furious frustration at his old friend's refusal to see sense, to spare him this horrible duty.

"Your son," he said, his voice low and dangerous. "The one you claim to care about so much, just volunteered to take part in a mission to look for the second most dangerous vampire in the world. And he didn't do it for himself, for glory, or ego. He did it because it may be the only way of stopping Dracula for good, and he didn't even hesitate. That's what he's like, Julian. He's brave, and he's impetuous, and he makes stupid mistakes and sometimes he makes me so angry I want to strangle him, but he genuinely cares about other people more than himself, rather than just saying he does. You would be so proud of him, but you're never going to get the chance to be, because the same stubbornness that got you in this mess in the first place is going to stop you doing what you know is right. What you know could help save lives, but you don't care about that, do you? You only care about yourself, about getting what *you* want. Your son wouldn't even recognise the man you've become, Julian. He'd be ashamed of you."

Julian flinched. "My wife—"

"You want to talk about Marie? When this facility was attacked by Valeri and his bloody army of vamps, your wife fought them with her bare hands. Nobody told her to, she'd received no training whatsoever, and she was beside herself with worry about Jamie. But she put that aside, and she did what needed doing. And you know what? I don't really think you give a damn about your family, any more than you do about anyone else. So this is it, Julian. This is the end of the road for you and me. I'm done with you."

Holmwood marched across the cell and hammered three times on the door. He heard footsteps immediately, as the Security Operator exited the guard post and headed down the corridor.

"1961," said Julian, his voice little more than a whisper.

Cal froze, then turned slowly back to look at his old friend.

"What did you say?" he asked.

Julian's eyes were still fixed on the green blanket he was sitting on; they were ringed red, sickly bright against the ghostly pale of his face. "Adam," he said. "He was turned in 1961."

The locks behind Holmwood clunked and whirred. The door swung open to reveal the Security Operator, his hand resting on the butt of his Glock.

"Everything all right, sir?" he asked.

"Fine," said Holmwood, without taking his eyes from the huddled shape on the bed. "Wait out there. Close the door."

The Operator nodded, and did as he was told. As the locks re-engaged, Holmwood took a deep breath.

"Go on," he said, his voice low. "Go on, Julian."

Jamie's father raised his head. "He told me he was turned in 1961, Cal. He was twenty, so he must have been born in 1940, or maybe '41. He was raised in California, in Bakersfield, but I don't know whether that's where he was born. After he was turned, he moved to New York, and drifted into the same circles as Alexandru and Valentin Rusmanov. He met a girl at one of Valentin's parties, at his house on the Upper West Side. Emily, her name was. She was twenty and newly turned, so maybe a year younger than him biologically, two at the most. I don't know where she was from, Adam never told me, but somewhere in the Midwest. Her dad was a Methodist preacher. They left New York and got married, then moved to San Francisco. She disappeared after they'd been together twenty years, so probably 1985, maybe 1986. Adam went bad for a while, fell in with a gang of vamps in the Tenderloin, and got picked up by NS9 in a flophouse he was sharing with them. Then he spent however long in Nevada, being experimented on, until he was cured."

Holmwood felt cautious excitement begin to spread through him. "What was his name, Julian?" he asked, his voice almost hoarse. "What was his real name?"

"I don't know it, Cal," said Julian. "I'm sorry, that's all I know. You have to believe me."

And with that, he lowered his head to his folded arms, and began to cry.

# 17

# RETRACED STEPS

*THE BLACK SEA COAST*
*ROMANIA*
*SIX HOURS LATER*

Valentin Rusmanov stared up at the dacha in which he had spent the long summer months of his childhood and tried to work out what exactly he was feeling.

Behind him, below the barren headland that marked the edge of the estate, the waves crashed against the cliffs, sending up great sprays of salt water that filled his nostrils with their acidic scent. The storm was starting to blow, whipping the water into foaming peaks and sending wind howling through the trees that filled the grounds of the grand summer house. The port of Constanța, less than three miles across the bay, was barely visible as the roiling thunderclouds closed in.

Valentin had skirted their edges as he made his final approach, the rain lashing his face and steaming up from the boiling red of his eyes. The clouds appeared to rise endlessly, so high that even his supernatural eyes could not see their end. He was soaked to the skin, his clothes clinging to his cold flesh, but he barely noticed as he looked up at the dacha.

Despite himself, there was nostalgia. His youth, although dysfunctional and full of horrors that no child should have witnessed, had nonetheless been luxurious to the point of debauched; neither he, nor his brothers, had ever wanted for anything. He could see himself and Alexandru sprinting down the slope towards the promontory where Valeri's chapel now stood, hands clasped together, hair flying out behind them, their faces pink with exertion and mouths wide with laughter that had still been full of innocence.

The memory was over five hundred years old, but it felt like it had happened only yesterday. It went directly to the part of himself he would have never admitted existed, the part that missed his brothers and the lives they had once led; lives that had been plunged into endless darkness at the whim of their former master, when he had first become more than a man.

Alongside the nostalgia was anger, an emotion that was never far from the surface, despite Valentin's gleaming, charming façade. Anger at his remaining brother for the violation that had been visited on his home in New York, and for his willingness to unleash Hell on earth for no better reason than blighted, desperate loyalty to a man who had spent more than a century as a pile of buried ash.

And anger at himself, for not destroying his brother when he had the chance, before Valeri had been able to provide the distraction of tearing out Larissa Kinley's throat.

Despite the driving rain, and the electricity that was rapidly gathering in the air around him, Valentin could isolate nine distinct vampire scents emanating from the dacha above him, nine individual combinations of blood and sweat and pheromones. He would have expected them to have been aware of his presence by now, but was happy to discover that their senses were clearly far duller than his own; the element of surprise would make things even easier.

Far worse than the smell of the vampires, however, was the odour drifting from the chapel behind him: a foul stink of rot and decay, so thick he could almost taste it. He looked up at the house, indulging himself in his memories, then turned his back on it and flew slowly towards the edge of the cliffs.

The stench intensified as soon as Valentin opened the chapel door, causing his throat to tighten and his stomach to churn. He felt his fangs slide into place and the heat in the corners of his eyes rise; the smell was so bad, so *wrong*, that his vampire side had leapt forward, asserting control. It was death and pain, agony and fear, helplessness and violated despair.

The chapel looked as it had since Valeri had built it in the early 1900s, when the two brothers had been on better terms. Two rows of wooden pews faced a plain stone altar and a stained-glass depiction of the crucifixion grotesque in the detail of its violence, but faded by more than a century of wind and salt. Valentin made his way round the altar and down the spiral stone staircase behind it, the smell thickening around him. He knew what he was going to find beneath the chapel; the only question was just how bad it would be.

The bottom of the stone pit, in which Valentin assumed his brother's long-held dream of reviving their former master had been realised, was covered in a thin crust of dried blood. Beside the bottom step of the staircase stood an empty glass tube, the number *31* printed on its side beneath an accumulation of dust. Valentin barely noticed it; his attention was fixed on the dreadful tableau that surrounded the pit.

Suspended from a series of ropes and pulleys were the corpses of five naked women. Their backs were arched, their wrists and ankles bound, the skin that still remained mottled black and covered with thick patches of sprouting mould. They had been gagged when they died, but the material had long since fallen to the floor, revealing wide screams of eternal agony. Their torsos were misshapen, twisted and swollen as their organs had settled and begun to decompose, and their throats still bore the marks of their murders, wide cuts that ran from ear to ear.

The smell was eye-watering: old blood and rotten flesh and the remnants of the potent, acrid gases that had escaped the stricken women's bodies. Their eyes were gone, and they stared at him with empty sockets full of reproach. Beetles shuffled across the green and black skin, and white bone gleamed where their foreheads had been, the skin chewed away by rats that had climbed up the women's hair.

*Here*, thought Valentin. *In this place. This is where the end began.*

He stared down into the pit, then growled and spat on the dried blood. Then he turned away from the women whose unwilling sacrifices had birthed a monster back into the world, and flew up the stone staircase without a backward glance. He swept through the chapel, giving momentary thought to tearing it down with his bare hands, and thundered back out into the storm. The rain had worsened, and he accelerated as he flew up the sloping grounds towards the dacha, determined to do what he needed to do and leave this old place behind. He reached out for the ornate brass handle on the front door, then paused as a memory from his childhood rooted him to the spot.

*The exact year was lost to him, although he believed he had been either eight or nine, young and scrawny and trailing after his brothers as though they were gods.*

*The sun had been blazing down from a perfect blue sky; he could remember the feeling on his skin so clearly, the warm prickle that was not uncomfortable, but that warned him he was about to burn. Alexandru* and Valeri had run off into the woods that backed on to the house, delighting in his inability to keep up with them; he had tried, his heart pounding in his chest, his limbs pumping for all they were worth, but they had eventually disappeared into the distance. He had returned to the house on the verge of tears, forcing himself not to give in to them; his father had made it clear on numerous occasions that Rusmanov men did not cry.

Valentin had heaved open the heavy front door, intending to seek out the comforting words and arms of Ivana, the governess to whom he was far closer than either of his parents. She would most likely be in the kitchen, overseeing the preparation of dinner.

As the door swung silently on well oiled hinges, he heard a noise he didn't recognise. It sounded like the panting of Sasha, the Labrador he had been given for his birthday when he was very young, only louder and deeper. He wandered into the grand entrance hall, and was about to call out for Ivana when something stopped him, a strange sense that he had stumbled upon a secret.

Instead, he followed the sound towards his father's study, at the north-east corner of the house. The door was slightly ajar, and the grunting and growling was louder than ever as he stood outside, his feet rooted to the spot. Curiosity was coursing through him, threatening to overwhelm him, but his father's study was a private, sacred space, and the punishment for entering it without permission was likely to be both severe and protracted. Valentin stood listening to the strange noises, desperate to know what was making them, until a solution suddenly occurred to him. He inched towards the door, soft on the balls of his feet, and leant forward until his eye was level with the gap between it and its frame, and looked down at the floor; his feet were still safely three inches outside the limit of his father's study. He lifted his eyes, and looked into the room.

Alexei Rusmanov was leaning over the wide desk that stood at the rear of the room, his hands gripping the edges of the wooden surface, his eyes closed, the noises that Valentin had followed emerging from between his gritted teeth as his narrow body rocked back and forth. Beneath him was Anya, the maid who had joined their household the previous winter when she turned sixteen, the fourth member of her family to serve the Rusmanovs. Her black skirt was crumpled around her hips, and one of her legs was sticking straight up in the air, her stocking rolled down and gathered at her knee. She was staring up at the ceiling, her face expressionless, her arms lying on the desk at her sides.

Valentin stared. He was instantly certain that this, whatever it was, was something he was not supposed to be seeing, but he was unable to tear himself away. His mother had gone into Constanţa with her sisters and their summer guests, as they did most days; perhaps this was simply what happened when his father was alone in the house.

Perhaps it was normal.

He was pondering this possibility when his father suddenly raised his head, opened his eyes, and stared directly at him.

"Who's there?" bellowed Alexei Rusmanov, leaping up from the desk and hauling his trousers closed. "Valeri? Is that you, boy?"

Anya rolled over on the desk and looked towards the door, her cheeks flushing with shame. She scrambled to her feet, pushing her skirt down and smoothing her clothes back into place. Valentin watched, utterly unable to move.

Caught, he thought, frantically. I'm caught.

"Out!" bellowed Alexei, pointing at Anya as he strode round his desk. Her eyes widened momentarily, then she fled, scurrying out through the door that connected the study to the servants' passageways that ran behind the wood-panelled walls of the dacha. Alexei didn't give her so much as a glance; he stormed across the room, kicked the door open, and grabbed his youngest son by the back of his neck. Valentin's paralysis broke, and he yelled and squirmed as his father dragged him into the study and slammed the door shut.

"You little rat!" shouted Alexei, throwing his son to the floor. "You dare to spy on me?"

Valentin fought to find his voice. "I wasn't spying, Papa," he managed, his voice choked with tears. "I wasn't, truly I wasn't. I heard noises, Papa, and I followed them. I'm sorry. I'm sorry."

Alexei stared down at him with hot fury dancing in his eyes, his hands already undoing the belt that would be the instrument of Valentin's punishment. Then the anger disappeared, and his father reached a hand down to him. Valentin took it, and let himself be hauled roughly up on to unsteady legs.

"It's not your fault," said Alexei. "You are a curious creature, Valentin, and you always have been. The error is mine."

"I'm sorry," repeated Valentin.

"Don't be," said his father. "There is no need. There are things every boy should know, in time. Normally, they come later, but you have always been unwilling to wait for anything. So perhaps it is time."

Valentin had no idea what his father was talking about, but he nodded eagerly; being talked to was infinitely preferable to being beaten.

"Men and women," said Alexei. "They are not the same. You understand this, yes?"

"Yes, Papa."

"Good. They are different, because what God intends for them is different. Men are hard creatures, because God wants us to fight, and kill, and defeat our enemies. Women are soft, because God wants them to keep their men happy, to provide for them, and care for them. Do you see?"

Valentin nodded.

"When the world was much younger than it is now, the men would hunt animals for food while the women waited at home, ready to clean and cook them. When the men returned, discussing the hunt with their women was forbidden. Can you tell me why?"

Valentin nodded eagerly. "Because it was not their business."

Alexei smiled, an expression full of warmth and pride. "You are so clever, my son," he said. "That is exactly why. It was not their business. What the men had done would upset the women, and it was better for them not to know. Because what the men did was for the good of everyone. Do you understand?"

"Yes, Papa."

"So you understand why your mother does not need to know what you saw in this room. It would upset her, and you would not want to upset her, would you?"

Valentin frowned. "Of course not, Papa."

"That is because you are a good boy, Valentin. And why we are both so proud of you."

"Thank you, Papa."

Alexei knelt down and beckoned his son forward. He went willingly, and let himself be enveloped in his father's arms.

Valentin left the study full of love. The Rusmanov patriarch was hard, and often cold, but his youngest boy never doubted his love for his sons; it would only be much later, in the fullness of adulthood, that he would realise how poisonous and damaging that love had truly been.

He made his way quickly out on to the grounds, searching for any sign of his brothers. The sun hung in the sky above Constanţa to the east, and the grass and trees shimmered in its gentle glow as motes of dust swirled in the light. It was never silent outside the dacha; the forest rustled constantly with movement, and the waves crashing at the base of the cliffs were always audible. But there was a stillness, a peace, to the place; it heartened Valentin, and he set about his search with a wide smile on his young, handsome face.

As he rounded the north-east corner of the sprawling house, he heard voices coming from the stable block that stood at the edge of the forest. Valentin quickened his step, so much so that he was almost running when he reached the door and pulled it open.

His heart sank, just a little; at the far end of the building, watching with obvious impatience as one of the staff shoed his favourite horse, stood Valeri. Valentin had hoped it had been Alexandru he had heard; they could have gone for a ride through the forest, or out along the cliff path. Valeri could, on increasingly rare occasions, still be persuaded to do such things with his youngest brother, but they were now invariably accompanied by a grim expression of duty and an insistence on silence throughout.

"What is it?" shouted Valeri, staring at him with a stern expression on his face. "What do you want?"

Valentin stood up straight and walked down the stable block. "A word in private, brother," he said.

Valeri cursed, ordered the blacksmith to hurry, and strode down the stables, his greatcoat billowing out behind him. "Speak then," he said, as he arrived at his brother's side. "What is so important?"

Valentin took a deep breath, then told his brother what he had seen in their father's study. His voice was lowered, but he could not hide his excitement at the prospect of approaching the status of equality with the rest of the Rusmanov men; he had known the time would eventually come when his youth no longer counted against him, and he was hopeful that the moment had finally arrived.

Valeri listened in silence as he finished his tale, then smiled thinly and shook his head. "Is that it?" he asked. "Father has taken every maid and governess that has ever set foot in our house, yet you come running in here to tell me what I already know like some gossiping scullery maid?"

Embarrassed heat rose into Valentin's cheeks.

"And now you're blushing *like a scullery maid*," said Valeri, smiling cruelly.

Valentin looked down at the dirt floor of the stables; he could no longer meet his brother's eye. Then a hand shot out and took hold of his arm, squeezing it hard.

"Say it," said Valeri.

"Say... what?" gasped Valentin, through the pain.

"Say, 'I'm a scullery maid.'"

"No," said Valentin. "I won't—"

Valeri squeezed again and twisted, his fingers digging into the soft flesh of Valentin's arm. "Say it," he said, his voice low and full of menace.

Tears welled up in the corners of Valentin's eyes. "No," he managed again. "You can't—"

Valeri twisted harder.

The pain was awful; it burned and pulsed, and Valentin wondered almost absently whether his brother would actually break his arm out of nothing more than spite. He pulled and pushed, trying to loosen the grip, but couldn't; it was like trying to break free from a statue. Shame and frustration roared through him as the pain increased. He wanted to scream that it wasn't fair, that Valeri was bigger than him, but he knew such a protest would only encourage his brother; it was a complaint completely unbefitting a Rusmanov. Anger, at himself and at his stupid, hateful brother, boiled up through him, filling him with fire, scorching everything in its path, and, acting on nothing more than furious instinct, Valentin did something he had never done before.

He balled his free hand into a fist, reared back, and punched his older brother square in the face.

Valeri's eyes flew open, and he released his brother's arm. Then his expression of surprise turned to one of clear, terrible delight.

The momentary rush of euphoria that had filled Valentin as the punch connected evaporated, and he ran for the stable door, his heart pounding in his chest, his brother thundering after him. He made it through the door and, as the dacha's grounds opened up before him, believed for a single, glorious moment that he might escape. Then Valeri crashed into him, wrapping thick arms round his legs and driving him to the ground.

Valentin started to cry, bitter tears of pure frustration, and hated himself for them. Pain and fear mingled into panic, but beneath it something deeper and more primal thrashed and howled: the sickening horror of helplessness. He screamed for mercy as Valeri dragged him back into the stables by his ankles, flipped him up and over, and rammed his head into the horse trough.

The water was freezing; it sprayed up his nose and poured down his throat, and he began to cough underwater. His eyes were open, but he could see nothing as pressure began to build in his chest; he bucked and thrashed, whipping his head back and forth as the cold began to numb it. And in some distant corner of his mind he understood that Valeri wasn't going to let him go, that he was going to drown him in the horse trough.

Red and grey spots circled at the edges of his vision as he began to suffocate, his lungs screaming for air, his body weakening with each passing second. As he went limp, when all he could see was grey and all he could feel was pain, he was jerked upwards, his brother's hand in his hair, and thrown down to the hay-covered floor.

He lay there for a long time, coughing and sobbing and dragging air into his trembling body. When he was finally able to move, he curled himself into a ball, unable to face his brother; shame filled every fibre of his being, every bit as hot and sharp as the physical pain in his chest.

"Look at me," said Valeri, softly.

He shook his head, his eyes fixed on the floor.

"Look at me, brother."

Valentin slowly turned his head, and looked. His brother was standing

*over him, regarding him with an expression that could easily have been
mistaken for affection by someone who did not know Valeri Rusmanov.*

*"Next time you hit someone," he said, "be brave. Men don't run, brother.
Men stand and fight."*

*Amen to that*, thought Valentin, and turned the handle.

The door slid open with a long, juddering screech, and Valentin
instantly heard movement from within the depths of the house. He
walked calmly into the centre of the entrance hall, which had always
been immaculate in his father's day; now dust coated the floor and
the furniture, and several of the wooden wall panels were broken
and scratched. He ran his hands through his hair, pushing it back
from his forehead and sending a torrent of rainwater cascading down
his neck, and waited for whoever was lurking in the dacha to show
themselves.

For a long moment, there was only silence. Then Valentin heard
footsteps thud across the floor from the direction of the kitchen,
and a vampire in his mid-twenties strolled casually out of the
corridor.

"About time, Pete," said the man. "Seriously, how long does it
take to..."

His voice trailed off as he saw the smiling figure of Valentin
standing before him. He stopped dead in his tracks, his eyes widening
and flickering red in the corners, and opened his mouth as the
ancient vampire moved.

Valentin crossed the space between them in a blur and took the
vampire by the throat, cutting off whatever sound he had been about
to make. He lifted the man into the air, carried him backwards as
though he weighed nothing, and slammed him into the wall with
an impact that shook the entire house. The vampire's eyes flared

open with shock and pain, his fists beating futilely at the hand that was holding him.

The youngest Rusmanov slid the man down the wall until his scrabbling feet touched the floor, then hammered his right leg out in two devastating kicks. The vampire's legs broke mid-shin with a pair of sickening crunches; the colour disappeared from his face as though it had been sucked out and, as the hand around his throat released him and let him slump to the floor, he let out a piercing howl of agony.

Valentin stepped back, leaving the stricken vampire screaming and clutching at his shattered legs, and took a deep breath. Throughout the house he could hear the rattle of footsteps and a cacophony of frightened shouts and growls. He isolated the separate sounds, and nodded to himself as the noise grew louder.

*Eight more of them. As I thought.*

He kept moving until his back was almost against the front door, a position from where he could not be surrounded. It was unquestionably overcautious, as Valentin doubted that the vampires making their way through his family's house were capable of causing him a problem from whichever direction they attacked, but he saw no need to complicate matters; he had no desire to be inside the dacha any longer than necessary.

The wide entrance hall was suddenly full of movement and noise as vampires spilled into it from the corridors on either side. They crowded round their fallen friend, shouting and shrieking and asking him what had happened, failing entirely to notice the stranger standing in the shadows. The vampire with the broken legs was alternately screaming and gritting his teeth against the pain, but was nodding his head in the direction of the door, trying in vain to warn his friends. In the end, Valentin spared him further effort.

**179**

"Ladies and gentlemen," said Valentin, his voice loud and pleasantly warm. "Please may I have your attention?"

The eight vampires turned as one, their eyes flooding red, their fangs sliding into place, guttural growls and high-pitched hisses rising from their throats. Valentin smiled as he took a closer look at them; they were a ragtag bunch of five women and three men, the youngest barely out of her teens, the oldest a man who looked as though his vampire side was the only thing allowing him to walk unaided. At the centre of the group, a woman who appeared to be in her late forties pulled herself together slightly quicker than the others, and it was to her that Valentin turned his attention.

"I'm prepared to overlook the fact that you are trespassing in property that belongs to my family,' he said. "Providing you answer me one simple little question. Where is my brother?"

The woman spat on the floor as the rest of the vampires howled with derision. "You have no authority here, traitor," she said. "This house belongs to Valeri, and we are here at his command. Here, waiting for you."

Valentin smiled. "Tell me your name."

"My name is Genevieve," hissed the woman. "*Yours* is traitor."

Valentin's smile widened. "Indeed. Valeri is part of my family, to my eternal shame and regret, so I believe you'll find my statement was quite accurate. But let's not dwell on that. You say you are here at my brother's command?"

The vampires growled their agreement.

"And you," continued Valentin, directing his gaze squarely at Genevieve. "You are in love with him, are you not?"

Her eyes widened, and her cheeks coloured a red that was visible even through the scarlet glow radiating from her eyes. "I don't... I refuse to..."

"There is no sense denying that which is obvious," said Valentin. "It was clear from the way you said his name. So my brother sent the nine of you here to stand guard, in case I made an appearance. Then what? You are expected to kill me?"

"Correct," said Genevieve, her voice low and thick. "You must pay for your treachery."

"And what then?" asked Valentin. "What promises did he make, if you were successful in destroying me? I imagine *you* were assured a place in his bed, but I fail to see what could have motivated the rest of you to accept such an assignment. Money, perhaps? Power? Fear?"

More growls rose from the cluster of vampires, although they were less full-throated than before, and Valentin believed he could hear uncertainty in at least one or two of them. Genevieve, who was clearly their leader, whether self-elected or otherwise, seemed to sense it too.

"He mocks us!" she shrieked. "He belittles our faith in our master!"

"You are wrong," said Valentin, his voice low and gentle. "I am not mocking you. I am trying to help you. If you attack me, you will all die. And, whether you want to believe it or not, Valeri is fully aware of that outcome. You are not his favourites, his advance guard, or his trusted lieutenants. You are cannon fodder, nothing more. But if you tell me where he is, I will spare you, as it is clear that you have been misled."

"We will tell you nothing," said Genevieve.

"Last chance," said Valentin, certain that it would not be taken. The woman was obviously devoted to his older brother; her fervour was going to carry the rest of the vampires with her, to their doom.

"For you," snarled Genevieve, and leapt forward, her eyes blazing, her face twisted with hate.

Valentin moved with a speed that defied reality and met her in mid-air. His hand shot out and crunched through her sternum as though it was made of balsa wood. A shocked grunt burst from Genevieve's mouth as his fingers found her heart and tore it from her chest; her eyes widened momentarily, before she exploded in a thunderclap of crimson blood that soaked Valentin from head to toe. He landed gracefully on the wooden floor, threw the remains of the heart aside, and barrelled into the remaining vampires like a tornado descending on an unsuspecting town.

Two of them, a man and a woman in their twenties, instantly tried to run, their nerve clearly having failed them, but Valentin caught them before they reached the corridor and drove their skulls together with a sickening crunch. They fell to the ground, their heads grotesquely misshapen, their eyes rolling wildly.

He turned back towards the remainder of the terrified, panicking vampires, and found a punch heading towards him; it would have decapitated any normal human being, but to Valentin it appeared to be moving at a snail's pace. He slid to his left, gripped the elbow of the swinging arm, and pulled it out at the shoulder. The former owner of the arm, a hugely obese vampire in his fifties, stared dumbly at the disembodied limb for a second, as blood spurted from his shoulder. Then he threw back his head and screamed, a guttural howl of agony.

Valentin changed his grip on the severed arm, took hold of it by the wrist, and swung it like a baseball bat. The ragged stump connected solidly with the vampire's chin, sending him flying across the hall and into the wood-panelled wall head first. He slid to the ground, his eyes rolling, his limbs jerking and spasming. Valentin was already moving, throwing the arm aside and sweeping towards the four remaining vampires, who were now wearing expressions of dreadful despair.

*I warned them,* thought Valentin. *I gave them all the chance to walk away unharmed. This is their choice.*

Two of the vampires swung punches, but they might as well have been trying to connect with a column of smoke; by the time the intended blows reached their target, Valentin was simply no longer there. There was just enough time for surprise to register on their furrowing brows before Valentin pulled out their throats with two casual swings of his arms. Twin geysers of blood gushed into the air as the vampires sank to their knees, their eyes full of terrible confusion.

Valentin ignored the overpowering aroma of freshly spilled blood, and faced the last two vampires: a woman who looked barely old enough to vote, and a man who would have appeared far more at home behind a desk in an accountancy firm. They seemed frozen where they stood, but when he took a step towards them, the girl grabbed the man, flung him towards Valentin, and bolted for the front door.

Valentin took a millisecond to admire the purity of her survival instinct, then reached out and caught the thrown vampire by the hair. The man wore a beatific look on his face, as though he had concluded that what was happening to him simply could not be real. The expression didn't change, even when Valentin gripped his neck with his free hand and tore his head off with a sound like an opening zip and a high-pressure jet of blood. Valentin spun fluidly, and threw the head with all his supernatural strength. It struck the fleeing vampire girl in the lower back, and Valentin heard the distinctive crack as her spine broke. The girl's limbs went instantly limp, her legs tangled beneath her, and she crashed to the ground, her eyes wide and uncomprehending.

Valentin did a slow turn, surveying the carnage. The entire

altercation had lasted no more than fifteen seconds, and he had not come close to being injured himself, but he felt no satisfaction as he looked around at the devastated vampires; they had been put in harm's way by his brother, in blissful ignorance of the true danger they might face. All he felt was pity, and the ever-present anger towards Valeri, a ceaseless rage that churned slowly in the pit of his stomach.

The ancient vampire walked across the entrance hall and tore out one of the ornamental balusters that held up the banisters of the wide staircase; it came free easily, a heavy piece of wood with a sharp, jagged end. Moving quickly, Valentin plunged it in and out of the chests of the ruined vampires; they burst in a series of crimson splashes, coating the wooden floor and walls of the hall red. When it was done, he dropped the baluster and turned to face the vampire whose legs he had broken, whose scream of pain had drawn his friends to the killing floor. The man stared up at him with abject terror, his eyes wide and full of tears.

"Please..." he whispered. "Please... don't..."

Valentin walked across the hall, his shoes leaving deep tracks in the pooling blood, then crouched down and stared into the stricken vampire's eyes. "What's your name?" he asked.

"Jackson," managed the vampire. "My legs... Oh God... it hurts..."

"They'll heal," said Valentin.

Jackson grimaced. "My... friends..."

"Dead," said Valentin. "As I warned them they would be. You heard me warn them, didn't you, Mr Jackson?"

The vampire nodded his head, ever so slowly. "My... legs..." he repeated. "Broken..."

Valentin narrowed his eyes. "How long have you been a vampire, Mr Jackson?"

"Six... months."

"My word. You are little more than an infant. Your legs can be healed, Mr Jackson, with enough blood. They're badly broken, I'm sorry to say, so you may need rather a lot, but luckily for you there's plenty of it around. I would suggest you move quickly, though, before it begins to dry."

"I can't..." said Jackson. "My... friends..."

"Your friends are all dead," said Valentin, sharply. "Would you care to join them?"

"No..." said Jackson, the tears spilling from his eyes and running down his cheeks. "Please don't..."

"Then tell me where my brother is."

"I don't know," sobbed Jackson. "You have to believe me. Genevieve knew... but she never... I never..."

Valentin narrowed his eyes, then glanced over at the splash of blood that was all that remained of the woman who had attacked him. Anger surged through him, alongside a thick wave of frustration; somewhere in the rapidly spreading puddle of blood had been the information he needed, and now it was gone.

*Stupid,* he told himself. *Reckless and stupid. That was a child's error.*

He swallowed down the bitter cocktail of emotions, and turned his attention back to the crying vampire.

"I'm not going to kill you, Mr Jackson," he said, and smiled. "Congratulations."

Jackson frowned through his tears. "Why not?" he asked, his voice a hoarse whisper.

"Because you're going to help me," said Valentin. "I don't think you'll go to Valeri, not in light of your failure to kill me. But I'm sure you will not be able to resist telling the exciting tale of how you faced Valentin Rusmanov and survived, and I have no doubt that it will eventually reach my brother's ears, which is why you get to live. I want him to know that I am looking for him. I want him to know that I am coming."

Jackson began to cry harder than ever. "Thank you," he whispered. "Thank you..."

"You're welcome," said Valentin, his face twisting with contempt. "Although permit me to give you two pieces of advice. Firstly, make better choices regarding the company you keep. And secondly, the next time you face death, try to do so with more dignity than you have shown today."

Valentin stood up and strode across the entrance hall. As he gripped the front door handle for what he dearly hoped was the final time, a heavy thud and a shriek of pain sounded behind him. He glanced back over his shoulder, and allowed himself a brief smile at what he saw.

Jackson had tipped himself on to his front, and was lapping up the blood of his friends like a dog, his face a mask of shame and humiliation. Valentin watched him for several long seconds, then stepped out into the rain, pulling the dacha's door shut behind him.

# 18

# IF AT FIRST...

"Goddamnit!" shouted Matt Browning, then instantly blushed a deep red as the rest of the Lazarus Project turned to look at him.

"Are you OK?" asked Natalia Lenski from the desk beside his, her voice low.

"Yeah," said Matt, and sighed deeply. "Sorry, everyone."

His colleagues gave him a series of shrugs and shaken heads that made it clear he shouldn't worry about it. He smiled, and turned to face Natalia as the low hum that usually filled the lab returned to its normal volume.

"It's the sample we took from Larissa," he said. "It has parts of the same evolved structure that we've seen in Valentin and Dracula, but I can't make them coalesce. There's something happening there, something that predisposes her to greater strength and speed than normal vamps, but I can't figure it out."

"You cannot expect to figure out the processes of an alien DNA structure using incomplete evidence and such a small sample size," said Natalia, smiling gently. "I think you are too hard on yourself."

The colour in Matt's face, which had been starting to recede, flared deep pink. "Thanks," he said. "I know you're right, it's just—"

"It's just that you want to prove the theory that Mr Holmwood gave your name to," finished Natalia. "I understand. But you should not worry. The theory is correct, in every case we have analysed. *Why* it is correct can wait."

Matt stared at his colleague.

*My friend*, he reminded himself. *She's my friend. Or maybe...*

He didn't allow himself to finish the thought; it was too full of possibilities, both good and bad. Instead, he focused on what Natalia had said; he knew, deep down, that she was right.

Matt was more proud of the Browning Theory than he had been of anything in his entire life. He hadn't named it, and had been crippled with embarrassment when Cal Holmwood had done so, at least at first. Now, although he would never have admitted it to anyone, he liked the sound of it. It was incomplete, as his current frustrations attested; the precise scientific reasons for why it worked were still unknown, and that fact, he knew, would frustrate him terribly until they became clear. But the central tenet of the theory was uncontested; that there was a proportional relationship between the age of a vampire and the subsequent power of the people they turned. Human beings turned by older vampires were likely to become more powerful, and see their supernatural abilities increase at a far faster rate.

What they *did* know was that something happened within the contagious vampire virus, inside the revolutionary DNA that coated their fangs; it clearly evolved as its vampire host aged, becoming more potent, making it able to pass on greater power when it was introduced into a new human system.

It shouldn't work; there was nothing in the history of biology that was even remotely similar. Evolution within a species took place when two sets of DNA were combined during conception, creating mutations in the pattern from which the offspring was grown. There were no records of any other DNA strand evolving independently, and no other example of a virus that could not only change the DNA of the host it infected, but also essentially reboot the host's system, making physical changes take instant effect.

Vampirism, and the transformation it induced, was unique in the entire natural world.

There had long been an assumption that age was related to power; it was why the Rusmanov brothers, and Grey and other old vampires, were so disproportionately strong, having acquired strength and experience over the long years of their lives. But the Browning Theory explained why Larissa Kinley, Marie Carpenter, and the escapees from Broadmoor Hospital were so far ahead of most vampires that Blacklight encountered: because Grey, Alexandru Rusmanov, and Dracula – by proxy – had turned them.

The connection now seemed obvious, but it had taken Matt to realise it first, then prove it. The Browning Theory had deepened Blacklight's understanding of vampires, including the ones that were currently arrayed against them, had allowed the Department's Operators to be appropriately careful as they hunted down the Broadmoor victims, unquestionably saving lives, and, even more recently, had given birth to a project so highly classified that only Cal Holmwood, Professor Karlsson, and Matt himself were even aware of its existence.

*Don't even think about PROMETHEUS,* he told himself. *Not now.*

"I need some fresh air," said Matt. "Let's go for a walk."

Natalia frowned. "Now?"

"Yes," he said, and got up from his chair. "Right now."

The two teenagers walked across the long runway of the Loop and on to the wide fields beyond. They walked side by side, so close that their hands had brushed together on several occasions, causing a feverish debate to take place within Matt's head.

*Should I hold her hand? Am I supposed to hold her hand? Does she want me to hold her hand?*

They carried on in silence, heading for the perimeter of the Loop. Beyond the inner fence, the laser grid twinkled red as wide beams of ultraviolet light filled the exclusion zone between the outer fence and the treeline. Matt stopped at the edge of the grass, feeling heat from the lasers on his face and electricity in his teeth.

"It is strange," said Natalia. "From so close, it is difficult to tell whether this is meant to keep people out or in."

A shiver raced up Matt's spine as he stared out into the thick green and brown of the forest.

*I know what you mean,* he thought, as he turned to face Natalia.

The girl standing in front of him was a genius. There was nothing hyperbolic in such a description; she was an honest-to-goodness, curve-disrupting genius, with an IQ that had never been accurately measured.

She had been identified as a person of interest by the Russian Security Services when she was barely ten, and had been recruited into the SPC from the University of Leningrad when she was eighteen. Almost immediately, she had been sent to a foreign country, where she knew absolutely nobody, to work on the most important scientific project in the history of humanity. And the Lazarus Project was lucky to have her; she was staggeringly intelligent and highly capable, one of the very foremost minds of her generation.

She was also, Matt had concluded, the most beautiful thing he had ever seen.

Her face, slender and soft-featured and remarkably pale, still bore the last remnants of the injuries she had sustained when the bomb Lamberton had placed in Kate's quarters had detonated right in front of her. The room's heavy door had saved her life, shielding her from the worst of the blast, but she had broken a number of small bones, and been sliced to ribbons by flying wood and metal.

The sun slid behind a cloud, as though keen to afford them privacy. Natalia was looking at Matt with an expression that seemed to be mostly nervousness, but Matt could see affection too; he was certain that he could.

God, he hoped he could.

*Stay calm,* he told himself. *Take it easy.*

"Matt?" she asked, her voice low and soft. "Are you OK?"

"I'm fine," he said, and smiled. "I was just thinking how little I know about you. We sit two metres apart for sixteen hours every day, but all I really know is your name and where you went to university."

"That is all you know?" she asked, her eyes fixed on his.

Matt felt heat rise into his face. "Tell me something," he said, quickly. "Something I don't know about you."

She stared at him for a long moment full of crackling tension. "When the FSB came to take me from my home," she said, eventually, "the men of my village thought I was a criminal. They did not understand me, and they did not like that I was cleverer than them. They thought I was some kind of... what is the word... something unnatural?"

"A freak," said Matt, softly.

Natalia's mouth curled into a small, sad smile. "Yes," she said. "A freak. They thought I was a freak. The FSB came and they told my mother and father that I was valuable, that I should be making a contribution to my country. My mother did not want me to leave,

**191**

and started to cry. My father asked how much money they were going to give him for me."

"Jesus," whispered Matt.

"One of the men was a Colonel named Gregorovich," said Natalia. "When I was at university in Leningrad, it was him who stayed in touch with me, who made sure I was OK. He told my father that he did not deserve to have such a child, and that I would be better off away from them. My father got very angry, and tried to stop them from taking me, but one of the FSB men hit him in the stomach with his gun, and he fell to the floor. They took me out of the house, with my father on the ground and my mother screaming, and most of the village had gathered outside to watch. Some of them were shouting things, and one of them spat on me as I was taken to the car. Gregorovich took out his gun and shot the man in the chest, and left him bleeding in the road. I got into the car with them and we left. I have not seen my family since."

Matt stared at her, his eyes wide.

Natalia blushed deeply. "Was that not what you meant by something you didn't know?" she asked.

"No," he said, shaking his head. "That definitely qualifies. I just... I can't believe that happened to you. It's awful."

Natalia nodded. "It was," she said. "But it was a long time ago. And now I am here."

Matt took a half-step towards her, his arms stiffly at his sides. He was suddenly incredibly aware of them, and found himself wondering what people usually did with their arms and their hands, what *he* usually did with his; nothing felt comfortable, or natural. Natalia took a small step of her own, eyes wide, lips slightly apart, her small body seeming to tremble slightly in the cool of the shade.

Matt swallowed hard. They were so close that he could have

reached out and touched her, which was exactly what he was trying to will himself to do when the console on his belt let out a loud beep.

For a second, the world seemed to pause. Matt's hands were centimetres away from his body; they had stopped en route to a destination that he was not remotely sure of. Natalia's eyes were wide and fixed unblinkingly on his. Then the spell was broken, and Matt was fumbling for his console as Natalia blinked and shook her head, as though trying to clear it.

He thumbed the screen, his heart pounding at the possibility of what might have been about to happen, and looked at the message that appeared.

FROM: Holmwood, Interim Director Cal (NS303, 34-D)
TO: Browning, Lieutenant Matt (NS303, 83-C)
Come and see me ASAP. Lazarus business.

"Is everything OK?" asked Natalia. Her voice was low, and it sounded like she was out of breath.

Matt looked up from the console; pale pink had risen into the skin of her face, and the moment, so pregnant with promise, was gone. He held out the console; she took it from his hands and read the message.

"We should go," she said, handing the plastic rectangle back to him. "You must not keep him waiting, and I should get back to the lab."

*To hell with that,* thought Matt.

"Come with me," he said.

"To see the Director?"

"Yes."

Natalia frowned. "He did not ask for me."

"I don't care," said Matt. "It's to do with Lazarus, so why shouldn't you be there too? The Professor is in China and I'm no more senior than anybody else."

"I don't know," said Natalia. "Are you sure?"

"No," said Matt, and grinned widely. "But you're coming with me. And I don't care whether Cal likes it or not."

"She can't go in," said the Security Operator stationed outside the Interim Director's quarters. "She's not on my schedule."

Natalia tugged at Matt's arm. "This is stupid," she said. "I will just go."

"You don't have to go anywhere," said Matt. He smiled at her, then turned back to face the Operator. "You have me on your schedule, right?"

"Correct."

"You know the Interim Director ordered me to come and see him as soon as possible?"

"Right again."

"Great," said Matt. "So you know it's probably important?"

The Operator shrugged.

"I'll take that as a yes," said Matt. "But I'm afraid I'm not going in there without my colleague. So you're going to have to explain to Colonel Holmwood why his urgent message went unanswered. I'm sure he won't blame you."

The Operator narrowed his eyes. Matt could see him turning the situation over in his mind, trying to find the solution that carried the lowest possible likelihood of trouble for himself. After a long pause, which Matt waited silently through with a pleasant smile on his face, the man spoke.

"I have to call this in," he said. "Stay where you are."

"Of course," said Matt, glancing over at Natalia. "We aren't going anywhere."

The Operator moved away from them, pulling his radio from his belt, and holding it to the side of his face.

"Matt!" hissed Natalia. "What are you doing?"

"Don't worry," he replied. "It's fine. Cal trusts me."

Natalia frowned. "This is not like you," she said. "I hope you are not doing this for me?"

Matt smiled. He wanted to explain that he wasn't doing it *for* her, but rather *because* of her; that when he was with her, he felt as though he could do anything.

"Don't worry," he repeated.

Down the corridor, the Security Operator nodded, then placed the radio back on his belt. He strode towards them with a face like thunder, and jerked a gloved thumb in the direction of the door.

"You can go in," he said. "Both of you."

"Thanks very much," said Matt, and turned to Natalia. "After you."

She gave him a long, careful look, before giving in to a small smile that warmed his heart, and walking down the corridor towards the Interim Director's quarters. Matt nodded politely at the Security Operator, then followed her.

*I'm going to pay for that,* he thought, as he stepped round Natalia. *One way or another. But right now I couldn't care less.*

He had pushed the heavy door open no more than a few centimetres before Cal Holmwood's voice boomed through the gap.

"What the hell do you think you're playing at, Browning? Get in here, both of you."

Natalia looked at him with wide, nervous eyes. Matt placed a hand on her shoulder, feeling a vast cloud of butterflies descend into his stomach as he did so, and mouthed, "Trust me." Then he pushed the door all the way open, and stepped through it.

Cal Holmwood was seated behind his desk, his face pink with obvious anger. Matt crossed the room, wondering momentarily whether he had misjudged the situation, had read too much into the Interim Director's friendly manner towards him during their Lazarus update meetings, and had actually managed to do nothing more than get both of them into completely unnecessary trouble.

"I asked for *you*, Lieutenant," said Holmwood. "If I had wanted Miss Lenski to accompany you, I would have sent her an order as well."

"Yes, sir," said Matt. "I wouldn't have brought her, but your message said it was Lazarus business, and with the Professor away, I thought it would be good to have her here. I'm sorry if I was wrong, sir."

"You're not wrong, Lieutenant," said Holmwood, the colour in his face gradually calming. "Insubordinate, and bloody infuriating at times, but not wrong. Have you been taking lessons from Lieutenant Carpenter?"

Matt frowned. "Jamie? What's he done?"

"Something stupid," said Holmwood. "And classified, although I'm sure that won't stop him from telling you about it. Breaking fundamental rules seems to be a hobby of his lately."

"OK, sir," said Matt. He didn't have the slightest idea what the Interim Director was talking about, but he resolved to go and find Jamie as soon as they were finished here.

"To be honest," said Holmwood, nodding at Natalia, "it's probably for the best that she's here. I need someone to relay what I'm about to tell you back to Lazarus, and you're going to be prepping for departure."

Matt frowned again. "Departure, sir?"

Holmwood nodded. "We have new intelligence regarding the vampire who was allegedly cured by Christopher Reynolds, when the treacherous bastard was working for our friends in Nevada. The cured vampire known as Adam. NS9 are launching a mission tomorrow in the hopes of locating him and securing his cooperation. General Allen has requested a technical observer from the Lazarus Project to go with his team, and with Karlsson away, I'm sending you. You are to extract tissue and blood samples for circulation to the rest of the Departments, then bring Adam back here for examination by Lazarus. You told me you needed a miracle, Lieutenant Browning. I may just have found you one."

Matt stared at the Interim Director, his heart pounding in his chest, his mind racing with possibilities.

*The DNA of a cured vampire. Holy shit. Holy shit. An endpoint we can work back from. A process we can reverse engineer. Holy shit.*

"That is remarkable," said Natalia, her eyes wide. "Such a subject could allow for a big leap forward."

Holmwood nodded. "I certainly hope so, Miss Lenski. If they can find him, that is, and if he agrees to help."

"Why wouldn't he help?" asked Matt.

"Hopefully, he will," said Holmwood. "But given that he fled his last-known location, and left behind an IED that killed three NS9 Operators, I'm taking nothing for granted, and neither are the Yanks. They're going after him fully armed and Ready One. Go with them, find him, and bring him in."

*An IED?* thought Matt. *When was that? That didn't come up in any of the reports.*

"OK, sir," he said. "When do I leave?"

"You depart on the *Mina II* at 0700 tomorrow," said Holmwood. "You're going to arrive in the middle of the night, so get some sleep when you arrive. The NS9 briefing will be on your console within the hour, so read it, study it, and be in the hangar at 0630. Miss Lenski, you will communicate this development to your colleagues downstairs. Clear?"

"Yes, sir," said Natalia. She glanced over at Matt, and he felt warmth rush through him as he saw the obvious pride on her face.

"Lieutenant Browning?" asked Holmwood.

"Yes, sir," he replied. "I'll be ready, sir. Thank you."

"All right then," said the Interim Director. "Dismissed."

Matt nodded and headed for the door, Natalia beside him. As he reached out to take hold of the handle, Cal Holmwood called his name.

"Yes, sir?" he asked, turning back.

"Next time I tell you to come and see me, you come on your own. Is that clear?"

"Yes, sir," said Matt. "I'm sorry, sir."

"My capacity for indulging you and your friends is not infinite, Lieutenant," said Holmwood. "And neither is my patience. Now get out."

# 19

# NO REGRETS

As the Zero Hour Task Force meeting disbanded, Larissa saw Kate nod at her, then jerk her head in the direction of the Ops Room door. She looked around at Jamie, saw him deep in conversation with Jack Williams, and felt a stab of frustration. She was extremely worried about her boyfriend; the look of defeat on his face as he shook his head at her had sent a chill up her spine. But she knew that Jamie would not appreciate her interrupting his conversation to ask him why he had seemed on the verge of tears, so she turned back to her friend and nodded. Kate smiled and headed for the door, carefully making her way through the black-clad mass of her colleagues. Larissa waited for a second or two, then followed.

Kate was waiting in the corridor, a wide smile on her face. Larissa felt a similar expression rise on to her face as she let the door swing shut, despite her concern for Jamie; there had always been something irresistible about her friend.

"Hey," said Kate.

"Hey yourself," she said, and pulled her into a tight hug. Kate didn't struggle in the embrace, not that doing so would have done her any good; Larissa was now far, far stronger than any human, and if she decided to hug someone, they were going to be hugged whether they liked it or not.

"OK?" asked Kate, frowning.

"Fine," said Larissa. She released her grip and stepped back. "You?"

"I'm all right," said Kate. "Are you sure *you* are? You're acting like you haven't seen me in months."

"It feels like that," said Larissa. "Sometimes."

The mixture of amusement and concern on Kate's face warmed her heart. Her relationship with Jamie was endlessly complicated, without even taking into account whatever was going on with him now; her relationship with Matt was compromised, if only slightly, by the fact that she had once almost killed him, even though she hadn't meant to. But her relationship with Kate? That was something she could understand, that appeared impervious to the shifting sands their lives were now all built on. Larissa was absolutely certain that if they had met in the real world, away from all the madness and darkness that now surrounded them on a daily basis, they would still have been friends. They were compatible, in that easy, impossible-to-define way that separates friends from acquaintances.

"Let's get something to eat," suggested Kate. "I skipped breakfast."

Larissa hesitated.

"Don't worry about it," said Kate. "It's cool if you don't want to; you don't have to think of an excuse."

Larissa shook her head. "It's not that, not at all. I *do* want to. But I need to talk to Jamie first. There's something going on with him."

"When is there ever not?" said Kate, smiling. "But you're going to be here for a long time if you're waiting for him to come out."

Larissa frowned. "What are you talking about?"

"He came out twenty seconds after you," said Kate, and pointed down the corridor towards a pair of double doors. "He went into the hangar."

"Are you serious?"

Kate nodded.

"Hang on for a minute," said Larissa, then turned and rocketed along the corridor, heat rising in the corners of her eyes. She slammed through the double doors and scanned for her boyfriend. There was no sign of him, but she could smell him; the familiar scent was faint but unmistakable, confirmation that Kate's eyes had not deceived her.

· Larissa flew to the hangar doors and floated at the edge of the shade, centimetres away from the sunlight that would cause her to burst into flames. She couldn't see Jamie anywhere, even with her supernatural eyesight. She stared for a long moment, then flew back the way she had come, descending to the ground in front of Kate, who looked at her with narrowed eyes.

"Everything all right?"

"I'm not sure," said Larissa. "I don't think so. But if he doesn't want my help he can deal with it on his own." She smiled. "Right now, I'm starving."

The two girls found a table in the corner of the canteen on Level G and took their seats. Kate had a bowl of fresh fruit, some yoghurt, and a mug of steaming black coffee. Larissa, whose supernaturally enhanced metabolism made putting on weight all but impossible, had filled her own plate with bagels, bacon, scrambled eggs, fried tomatoes, and mushrooms. She attacked her breakfast as Kate filled her in on developments in the Security Division.

"... the ISAT thing is still there, you know? I don't think either Paul or I are ever going to truly be rid of it. Everyone kind of grudgingly accepts that it needed doing, and everyone feels better now it's done, but it's going to take them all a long time to forget what is was like sitting in that chair while we asked them whether they were a traitor or not. And it's all still messy, with Shaun and working with his dad every day, but it's OK. It's getting easier."

"Good," said Larissa, through a mouthful of eggs. "That's good."

"What about you?" asked Kate, tipping yoghurt on to her fruit. "How much of your head is still in Nevada?"

Larissa grinned. "Funny. Really funny."

"Sorry," said Kate, smiling. "I just think it's sort of amusing that you think we don't know you wish you were still there. You're not as good at hiding things as you think you are."

*Oh, really?* thought Larissa. *You'd be surprised, my friend. Very surprised.*

"I miss it," she said. "I'm not going to pretend I don't. I miss the open spaces, and people that didn't look at me like I was something too dangerous to turn their back on. But when I was there I missed you and Jamie and Matt. So what does that tell you?"

"That you haven't found somewhere you can be truly happy yet?"

Larissa shrugged. "Maybe. The grass is always greener, right?"

"So they say," said Kate. "But you and Jamie are good? Everything's OK?"

Larissa considered the question for a second or two. *Were* they all right? If Kate had asked Jamie, she suspected that he would have already said yes, everything was cool. But she wasn't quite so sure; the conversation about what it would be like if they were both vampires had shaken her, and refused to leave her mind, and her concern over whatever was wrong with him now had been joined by anger that he had disappeared after the Zero Hour meeting without talking to her. And on top of those problems, worse by far than either of them, was the secret she carried with her every minute, the secret that grew heavier with each day that passed without sharing it with her boyfriend.

"I think so," she said, eventually. "I hope so, at least. It's hard, me being what I am and him being normal. It makes things weird, and even though he swears he can handle it, I never quite believe him. Is that bad?"

Kate smiled. "No," she said. "I think that's fine."

She nodded. "It's not just that, though. The America thing is always there too." She paused for a second. "General Allen tried to persuade me to stay, did you know that?"

Kate shook her head.

"Well, he did," said Larissa. "He said he could get Cal Holmwood to agree to a transfer."

"What did you say?"

"I asked him if Jamie would be able to come too. Allen said he'd like nothing more, but that there was no chance in hell."

"Descendant of the founders and all that," said Kate.

"Right," said Larissa. "But here's the awful thing. I almost said yes anyway."

"But you didn't."

"I wanted to, though."

"But you *didn't*. And if that doesn't tell you how you feel about Jamie, and where your loyalties really lie, I don't know what will."

Larissa looked at her friend and felt something shift inside her. "There's something else, Kate," she said. "Something I overheard, that I wasn't supposed to. Something I think Jamie would want to know, but I'm just—"

"Don't even think about it," interrupted Kate, her eyes flashing with sudden anger. "If you're keeping some secret from Jamie, I don't want to know anything about it. We said we wouldn't do this, Larissa, the four of us, and I for one meant it."

"I know," said Larissa. "No more secrets, I remember. But this is something—"

"Didn't you hear me?" asked Kate. "I said I don't want to know. You want my advice? Tell your boyfriend whatever it is. Secrets get out eventually, we both know that, so just tell him now. It'll be better in the long run."

*Will it?* wondered Larissa. *I'm really not sure about that.*

"OK," she said. "I'm sorry for bringing it up. Let's talk about something else."

Kate smiled. "No problem," she said. "Let's talk about Zero Hour. That should cheer us up."

The two girls burst out laughing, drawing curious looks from the surrounding tables. Zero Hour hung over the Department like the sword of Damocles, ever-present and seemingly unstoppable. Each Operator had been forced to find their own way of dealing with it; some had withdrawn to the point of mutism, others had taken to training obsessively in the Playground and the simulators. Kate, Larissa was pleased to see, had clearly decided that making fun of the situation was the best approach.

"Right," she said. "The end of the world is always good for a laugh."

Kate nodded, her laughter subsiding. "That's the thing, you see. That's what I can't get my head around, why the numbers I just read out make no sense. *It's the end of the world.* I mean, not like if an asteroid hit the planet and everything died, but the end of the world we recognise. The one we understand."

"Unless we've got it all wrong," said Larissa. "And Dracula is just planning to keep his head down and not bother anyone."

Kate laughed again, but her good humour was clearly gone. "Do you think that's likely?"

"No," said Larissa.

"Me neither," said Kate. "I think it's all going to burn unless we stop him. I just don't know whether I believe we still can."

Larissa nodded. That was the fear that lurked at the back of her mind, at the back, she suspected, of every Operator's: that it was already too late to stop what was coming, that the digital display in the Ops Room ticking relentlessly down to Zero Hour was little more than an affectation, and all their planning and preparation would turn out to be nothing more than futile gestures against a darkness that was implacable.

"I have to," she said. "Otherwise what's the point? We might as well just hang up our uniforms and spend our last days on a beach somewhere."

"Don't tempt me," said Kate, smiling widely.

"Who's tempting?" said Larissa. "I could fly us both to Mustique in about two hours. Just say the word."

"I think Cal might have something to say about that," said Kate. "Court martial, in all likelihood."

Larissa sighed extravagantly. "You're probably right. Maybe next year, if there is one."

The two Operators finished their breakfast in a silence full of warmth and camaraderie. When the plates and bowls were clear and the mugs were empty, Larissa sat back in her chair and looked at her friend.

"Serious question," she said. "What chance do you give us when Zero Hour arrives? One in ten? Twenty? Worse?"

Kate shrugged. "I don't know," she said. "I wouldn't say the odds were good. I'd say they were far *from* good, if I'm honest."

"Me too," said Larissa. "But here's the weird thing. I wouldn't change where we are, and what we're doing, for anything. I've thought about this a lot, about the different ways my life could have gone, so I can say it with absolute certainty. Right here, right now, I wouldn't change a thing."

"Me neither," said Kate, instantly. "Despite everything with my dad, and Shaun, there's nowhere I would rather be than here. Sometimes I think it would be nice to be lying in a warm bed somewhere out there, with no idea of the darkness all around me. And it probably would be. But you know what? I'd rather know what's coming, and have the chance to at least try and do something about it. Even if we fail, and Dracula rises and the world burns and eighty million people really do die, I'd rather be able to tell myself that I tried."

Larissa grinned.

"Amen to that," she said. "A-bloody-men."

# 4 DAYS TILL
# ZERO HOUR

# 20

# THE CHOSEN FEW

Jamie Carpenter was pulled out of a dream about his father by the loud beep of his console.

He reached for the plastic rectangle and stabbed blindly at its screen with his finger, hoping to hit the exact section that would dismiss the message causing the ungodly noise. He missed, and when the beep rang out again he forced open his eyes and hammered the screen so hard it almost cracked.

In the dream, he and his dad had been standing in the living room of their old house in Brenchley. The window was broken, and the coffee table was smashed, and Jamie knew it was the night his dad had died, the night that Alexandru Rusmanov had come for them. His mother wasn't there; in reality, she had been standing against the wall opposite the window, her hands clutching her face, her eyes wide with terror. But in the dream, it was just the two of them. His father had been saying something, something that Jamie couldn't understand, although he had been sure it was important. His console had woken him before he could ask his dad to repeat it.

Jamie pressed the heels of his palms hard against his eyes and squeezed them shut, the remnants of the dream still floating at the edges of his barely awake mind. Then he swung himself out of bed and started to fill the coffee machine.

*No more bullshit*, he told himself. *No more self-pity. Just get on with it.*

The smell of boiling coffee began to fill his small quarters, bitter and enticing. Jamie waited for it to finish, studiously ignoring the message waiting on his console; he doubted it was a summons to a court martial, but it was still unlikely to be good news, whatever it was. It was far too early for it to contain his squad's orders for the day, which meant it was something unusual, although that was a word that had no real meaning inside the Loop.

The previous day had been a strong contender for the worst he'd endured since joining Blacklight, which was saying something. After the Zero Hour Task Force meeting, he had slipped away through the hangar and out on to the Loop's grounds, avoiding anyone who might want to talk to him, including Larissa. He knew it had been cowardly, but he had simply been unable to face the prospect of explaining to his girlfriend exactly how badly he had screwed up, so he had gone where he knew she couldn't follow: out into the bright late-morning sun.

He had wandered the grounds for a long time, lost in his thoughts. As he made his way back to the hangar, he had seen Matt and Natalia walking across the runway together, and had ducked behind one of the supply sheds. Matt was his best friend, but he could no more face him than he could Larissa.

Jamie had spent the rest of the day locked in his quarters, ignoring messages from Matt and Larissa and Kate, increasingly urgent demands that he answer them and tell them what was going on. By the time 1800 rolled around, he had rarely been so relieved to head out on a Patrol Respond.

It had gone better than their first, although that wasn't difficult. Qiang and Ellison had been sympathetic and reassuring, insisting that the incident with Chris Hollison could have happened to anyone, that it was a miracle it had never happened previously. Jamie had appreciated their concern, told them so, then ordered them to focus on the operation at hand.

Eight hours later they had returned to the Loop, tired but satisfied with their night's work: three dead vamps, a civilian couple rescued from a home invasion that had been on the verge of turning extremely unpleasant, and no injuries or failures of protocol. He had dismissed his squad mates, and fled for the privacy and security of his bed.

*Enough hiding*, he thought. *I'm done with that.*

Jamie poured a mug of coffee and took a sip. The liquid burned his lips, but he didn't care; the caffeine was what he needed, the energy to get dressed and go out there and do his job. When the mug was empty, he sat down on his bed and opened the message that had woken him up.

### NS303-67-J/OP_EXT_L1/LIVE_BRIEFING/OR/1500

### ATTACHED: PRELIMINARY BRIEFING.
### LOCATION: ROMANIA.
### TARGET: THE FIRST VICTIM OF DRACULA.

*That can't be right*, thought Jamie, incredulous. *There has to be some mistake.*

He was still staring at the screen two minutes later, trying to make sense of the orders he had been sent, when a heavy knock shook the door of his quarters. He jumped, then threw the console down on his bed and went to the door. The locks had barely slid clear of their housings before it was thrown open and Larissa stormed into the room. She stared at him with eyes that glowed the colour of fire.

"You're not dead then," she said, her voice low and full of barely contained anger. "I was starting to wonder."

Jamie recoiled from the fury boiling out of his girlfriend, and raised his hands in placation. "I'm sorry," he said. "About yesterday, I really am. I just needed—"

"Eight messages, Jamie," said Larissa, her voice little more than a growl. "I sent you eight messages, and I know Matt and Kate sent you at least that many again. I waited for you outside the Ops Room, after you didn't message me when you said you would, and you ran away, where you knew I couldn't follow you. I tried to find you all afternoon, and you hid from me. Then you went out on patrol without a single word, and you couldn't even be bothered to let me know you were home safely. Do you really, honestly think that qualifies as reasonable behaviour?"

"No," said Jamie. "I don't. It was selfish and cowardly and I have no excuse. I'm sorry, Larissa."

The fire in her eyes faded, ever so slightly. "What's going on, Jamie?" she asked. "And don't say nothing, because I'm going to punch you if you do. Tell me the truth. I want to help."

"I screwed something up," he said. "And I couldn't face you, or Matt, or anyone else. I'm sorry I avoided you, I really am, I should have told you what had happened, but I just couldn't. I needed a few hours to get my head together. I really am sorry."

"How badly did you screw up?" asked Larissa.

"Really, really badly," said Jamie, forcing a tiny smile. "Or at least I thought I did. But then I got sent this." He held out his console.

She took it, read the orders, then looked at him with blazing eyes and a wide smile full of pride, as she pulled her own console from her belt and showed him the screen. Identical orders glowed on it, plain black text on the white background.

"You too?" he said. "Both of us?"

Larissa nodded, then wrapped him in a tight hug and rose effortlessly into the air, spinning him elegantly in the small space of his quarters.

"Amazing!" she shouted. "That's completely amazing. I'm so proud of you."

Jamie grinned as he dangled in her grip. "Put me down, for God's sake," he said. "It's just an operation."

Larissa lowered him back to his bed and floated above him, her eyes glowing.

"It's not *just* an operation, Jamie," she said. "It might be *the* most important operation the Department has ever ordered. And we get to go."

"I know," said Jamie. "I don't get it either."

Larissa frowned. "What don't you get?"

Jamie forced a smile. "I get why you're going. You're the most powerful Operator in the world, and if I'm going after a vampire who might be almost as strong as Dracula, I'm putting you on my team, every time. But I don't get why I'm going too."

Larissa's eyes flared with clear annoyance. "You're one of the best Operators in this Department, Jamie," she said. "Holmwood knows how good you are, and he trusts you. Why are you doubting yourself all of a sudden?"

"Because it was my squad Cal was talking about in the Zero Hour meeting," he said. "The Operator who got filmed and ended up on the news. That was me."

He quickly filled her in on the fiasco that his new squad's

**213**

inaugural Patrol Respond had become, sparing her the worst of the dressing down he had received from the Interim Director and the extent of the crying he had done on his mother's shoulder. She listened, the glow in her eyes fading to reveal an expression of sympathy.

When he was finished, she narrowed her eyes. "It's not that bad," she said.

"Cal seemed to think otherwise," said Jamie. "So did Paul Turner."

"I'm sure they did," said Larissa. "But after McKenna and the email, how long did they really think we'd be able to stay a secret? I'm sure they're pissed off at you, but they have to understand that it was inevitable. It's not your fault."

Jamie felt his heart swell at her faith in him, biased and almost blind though it was. "It *was* my fault," he said. "*I* lost Chris Hollison. I was taking something that wasn't his fault out on him, and it backfired."

"And that was stupid," said Larissa. "And I seriously doubt you need me to tell you so. But talking about a court martial? That's bullshit, Jamie, and you know it."

"Maybe," he said. "And I'm hoping it won't come to that, I really am. But you can see why getting these orders was a bit of a surprise, given that it's less that thirty-six hours since Cal *was* talking about it, whether he was completely serious or not."

"Maybe he's better at letting things go than you are," said Larissa. "Maybe he's big enough to put the mission ahead of personal anger."

Jamie frowned; an unsettling though had just occurred to him.

"You didn't do anything, did you?" he asked.

"Like what?"

"Like saying you'd only go if I got to go as well."

Larissa smiled. "No, Jamie," she said. "Cal doesn't tend to discuss

214

Operational personnel with me. I found out five minutes ago, same as you. I promise."

"So what the hell is going on?" said Jamie. He was suddenly feeling incredibly frustrated, as though the ground had been pulled out from under him in the Interim Director's quarters two nights earlier, then pulled out from under him again this morning.

"Why does there have to be anything going on?" asked Larissa. "There's a Priority Level 1 operation, we both got selected for it, and the briefing is in nine hours in the Ops Room. That's all you need to be thinking about."

"I suppose so," said Jamie, his expression brightening. Regardless of whatever was going on behind the scenes – and he was sure there *was* something, despite what Larissa thought – this was a mission he was thrilled to be part of, especially in light of Larissa's orders; it would have killed him to watch her leave without him, bound for the birthplace of vampires, looking for a way to end Dracula once and for all.

"Good," said Larissa, and smiled at him. "I have to take care of some stuff, but I could meet you back here after lunch? We'd have an hour or so before the briefing. Unless you're planning to hide from me again?"

The look on her face told Jamie everything he needed to know about how she was suggesting they fill that hour. He smiled back at her, heat rising from his stomach and into his chest.

"No more hiding," he said. "I promise. And that sounds like a plan to me."

Larissa closed the door to Jamie's quarters behind her and flew steadily down the Level B corridor towards the lift at the end. As she did so, she pulled her console from her belt and opened the second message Cal Holmwood had sent her, the one that had arrived immediately after the orders that had been sent to both her and Jamie.

FROM: Holmwood, Cal (NS303, 34-D)
TO: Kinley, Larissa (NS303, 77-J)
Come and see me ASAP.

She let herself float in the air as the lift ascended, enjoying the sensation, her mind turning the message over and over. She had told Jamie the truth; she had played no part in his selection for the mission to Romania, and had only found out that she was to be involved when the order had appeared on her console. And being summoned to see the Interim Director was not an unusual occurrence, especially not with Zero Hour so close. But something about the message made her uneasy, something that she could not quite put her finger on.

When the lift opened its doors on Level A, she slid back to the ground, feeling familiar disappointment at having to do so, and strode down the corridor towards Cal Holmwood's quarters. The Security Operator stationed in the short corridor outside waved her through without bothering to check his schedule; she was an unmistakable figure inside the Loop, recognised and whispered about by everyone. She walked past the Operator without casting so much as a glance in his direction, and pushed open the door.

Cal Holmwood looked up from his desk as she entered the room, and smiled.

"Lieutenant Kinley," he said. "Come in."

"Thank you, sir," said Larissa. "You wanted to see me?"

"I did," said Holmwood, pushing aside a teetering pile of paper as Larissa stopped in front of his desk. "I assume you saw your orders?"

She nodded. "I did, sir. Thank you for having so much faith in me."

Holmwood smiled. "I have complete faith in you," he said. "But in this case, it wasn't my call. The mission to Romania is being briefed and led by NS9, and they selected its personnel."

Larissa frowned. "Why are NS9 in charge? Why not us or the SPC?"

"That's between me and the other Directors, Lieutenant," said Holmwood. "Although, if you were to suggest that it was easier to let NS9 lead it than it was to get the European Departments to agree, you might not be a million miles away from the truth."

Larissa smiled. "So that's why Jamie's going."

Holmwood's smile disappeared. "Yes," he said. "You are no doubt aware of Lieutenant Carpenter's behaviour two nights ago?"

"He told me, sir."

"Of course he did," said Holmwood. "So it won't surprise you to know that if I had my way, he wouldn't be going anywhere near this operation?"

"No, sir," said Larissa. "That doesn't surprise me."

"Good," said Holmwood. "Unfortunately, his name is on the NS9 selection list and I can't stop them taking him without removing him from the active roster. And for some reason, even now, I find myself unwilling to take that step. Do you think I should?"

*You're asking me if I think you should bench my boyfriend?* thought Larissa, her eyes widening. *Jesus.*

"No, sir," she said. "Whatever mistakes Jamie may have made, he'll do the Department proud in Romania. And I think you know that, sir."

Holmwood shrugged, and allowed the smallest of smiles to creep on to his face. "Maybe," he said. "I hope so, for all our sakes. But I didn't ask you here to talk about your boyfriend, Larissa. A situation has arisen that requires you to make a decision."

*Great. I'm sure this is going to be straightforward.*

"What situation, sir?"

"Are you aware of the supposed existence of a vampire who was cured of the condition?" said Holmwood.

"I heard rumours, sir," said Larissa. "When I was in Nevada. They called him Adam."

Holmwood nodded. "What I'm about to tell you is classified *above* Zero Hour. Is that clear?"

*More secrets,* she thought. *Awesome.*

"Yes, sir."

"Intelligence has come to light that appears to confirm that Adam is real. Or was, at least. It suggests he was cured at NS9, as part of a black project that ran in the 1990s under the supervision of Christopher Reynolds, also known as Richard Talbot."

"The first Director of the Lazarus Project? The one Jamie killed?"

"The same," said Holmwood. "The project was investigating the possibility of weaponising the vampire virus, in response to rumours that the SPC were attempting to do the same. The reality was that Reynolds was working for Valeri Rusmanov, attempting to cure the weaknesses of vampires without removing their strengths. According to our source, he succeeded with Adam."

"Your source being the man who came back from Nevada on the *Mina II* with me?" asked Larissa.

Holmwood shook his head. "The source is not important, Lieutenant. And I have told you before that you are not to speak of him."

"I'm sorry, sir," she said. "So Adam was cured? Like, genuinely cured?"

"Apparently," said Holmwood. "It was a failure from Reynolds' perspective, as Adam was cured of the condition entirely. He was released with the other test subjects when NS9 discovered that the SPC rumours were false, and shut the programme down. Reynolds had destroyed all the records and disappeared, so nobody knew what had really been going on in his lab, never mind what had happened to Adam. He slipped right through their fingers."

"Jesus," said Larissa, her face pale. "General Allen must be furious."

"That would be rather an understatement," said Holmwood, and smiled. "Anyway. Acting on this new intelligence, NS9 is sending a team to locate Adam and bring him in, and I don't think I need to tell you just how far a workable cure might tip the odds in our favour when Zero Hour gets here."

"No, sir," said Larissa, although it wasn't the potential military applications of such a discovery that had risen instantly into her mind; she was thinking of Marie Carpenter, and of herself.

"Lieutenant Browning is departing for Nevada in thirty minutes," said the Interim Director. "I have received an official request from General Allen for you to accompany him, and take part in the operation to find Adam and bring him in, a request that precedes your selection for Romania. Both operations are Priority Level 1, both are vital to the strategic aims of this Department, and you, not to put too fine a point on it, are by some distance the most powerful Operator any of the Departments have. As a result, I am leaving the choice up to you: Nevada or Romania."

"Surely the first victim is more important?" said Larissa. "If what Grey said is true, and only he can stop Dracula?"

"Perhaps," said Holmwood. "Or perhaps not. The very idea of the first victim is based on little more than legends and rumours, an old vampire prophecy that may turn out to be entirely meaningless. Whereas, if Adam truly was cured, he represents a tangible, scientific path that Lazarus can follow, a path that could shorten their work by a decade. But I also know how much you enjoyed your time in Nevada, so it's up to you. Bob Allen will be happy either way."

Larissa stared at the Interim Director, her heart surging with a wave of rare pride. She knew how much Bob Allen respected her, how sad he had been when the time had come for her to leave, but it was still heartening to know that she was apparently the first choice for two operations that could define the future not just of NS9 and Blacklight, but of all the Departments. She was also surprised to realise how much it meant to her to hear Cal Holmwood refer to her as the most powerful Operator in the world; it represented a huge improvement on how she believed she was normally perceived inside the Loop, as something dangerous and unnatural.

As a freak.

But although her heart was momentarily full of pride, her mind was racing with doubt. She *did* miss the desert, and she had loved the vast majority of her time at NS9. But it had ended badly; she had broken promises and been forced to disappear without even saying goodbye to the people who had become her friends, the sad, shameful result of a situation she had badly, wantonly misjudged.

A situation that would be waiting for her if she went back, more poisonous and destructive than ever.

*I can't see them,* she thought. *Danny, and Kara, and Kelly, and Aaron. I'd be too ashamed.*

Then the voice she hated, the one she had come to think of as the voice of her vampire side, cruel and vicious and violent, whispered in the back of her head.

*Don't pretend this is about them*, it said, in a tone as slick as oil. *Admit the truth to yourself, even if you can't admit it to anybody else.*

*Admit that you can't face Tim Albertsson.*

Larissa felt her throat tighten, her stomach start to churn; she growled, involuntarily.

"Are you all right, Lieutenant?" asked Holmwood.

"I'm fine, sir," she managed. "I'm sorry. I'll go to Romania, sir. The potential for trouble there seems far greater, so I think I'll be more useful."

"Only if the first victim does actually turn out to exist," said Holmwood. "But either way, I'm sure NS9 can handle Adam."

"Yes, sir," said Larissa, trying not to let the relief show on her face. "I think so too."

"Fine," said Holmwood, and nodded. "I'll then see you and Lieutenant Carpenter in the Ops Room at 1500. Until then, dismissed."

Larissa walked quickly out of the room, strode past the Security Operator, and waited until she was in the lift and making the short journey back down to Level B before she exhaled a huge breath, one it felt like she had been holding for hours. She lowered her head, taking air in and letting it slowly drift back out, feeling the panic that had risen in her in Cal Holmwood's quarters begin to recede.

*I can't see him*, she thought. *I'm sorry if that's selfish, if I should go to Nevada and help them look for Adam. But I can't see Tim.*

*I just can't.*

# 21

# HOMELAND SECURITY

Kate walked into her office in the Security Division to find Paul Turner already waiting for her, his expression characteristically neutral.

She groaned, inwardly; her commanding officer's presence only ever meant trouble, and she had been hoping for at least enough time to drink a second cup of coffee and sort through her schedule before the first crisis of the day presented itself.

*No such luck,* she thought. *I don't know why I'm even surprised.*

"Morning, sir," she said, with as much cheerfulness as she could muster. "Everything all right?"

Turner smiled. "Is it ever?" he asked.

Kate rolled her eyes. "You're a beacon of hope and happiness, sir. Anyone ever tell you that?"

"Not that I recall."

"Funny, that," said Kate. "So what's going on? How are our guests?"

The encampment that had sprung up in the forest had been the topic on every Operator's lips for the past day and a half. She knew that the Security Officer would have preferred to keep it Zero Hour classified, but to do so was simply not feasible; at least a dozen Operational Squads had passed the protesters overnight, on their way to and from their Patrol Respond grids. From the conversations Kate had overheard, in the canteen and corridors of the Loop, opinion appeared evenly split between a conviction that the right to protest was one of the fundamental freedoms that Blacklight helped to protect and a belief that the camp should be cleared and its ungrateful, trouble-making occupants thrown in jail. Kate leant instinctively towards the first viewpoint, although a small, vicious bit of her that she was not proud of thought the second option sounded like a damn good idea.

"Enjoying their fifteen minutes of fame," said Turner. "They're the front page of every newspaper, and the first article in every TV bulletin. Well, alongside Chris Hollison's footage of our own celebrity Operator."

Kate nodded. The video of the graveyard had been playing on the BBC News Channel barely an hour earlier, as she ran on a treadmill on Level F.

"I saw it, sir," she said.

"As did most of the country," said Turner. "Or so it seems, at least."

"And you're still not going to tell me who it was?"

"You don't need to know," said Turner.

"Fine," said Kate. "So what are we going to do about it, sir?"

"Nothing," said Turner, emphatically. "For now, at least. The MOD will continue to deny our existence and the existence of vampires. But you and I both know that's not going to wash for much longer. Soon, perhaps even very soon, someone is going to find a vampire who is happy to stand in front of a camera, and then it's game over. And we can't move the protesters. They're on public property and they aren't breaking any laws, even though their protests are nothing more than an ignorant nuisance."

Kate watched the Security Officer closely as he spoke. There seemed to be genuine hurt in the corners of his eyes, in the downward turn of his mouth, as though the protesters offended him, rather than annoyed him.

"Anyway," he continued, "we're watching them, and if any of them sets a toe on government land they'll be in a cell before they even know what happened. For now, you and I, and this Division, have bigger things to worry about."

Kate frowned. "Like what, sir?"

Turner picked up a pile of folders from beside him on Kate's desk.

"Most of these are from the Surveillance," he said. "A few from Intelligence. All are from the last thirty-six hours, since the Cambridge email went viral." He opened the first one. "Four teenagers wearing what was described to the police as 'Goth clothing' were assaulted in Leeds by at least twelve men, possibly as many as fifteen. Three of the victims were hospitalised, one with suspected brain damage. The men who were arrested claimed they thought the teenagers were vampires, so they were protecting themselves. *Protecting themselves*, Kate. By stamping on an innocent teenager's head because he was wearing black clothes and make-up. This was last night, on a well-lit street in the centre of the city."

"Jesus," said Kate, her stomach churning at the thought of such vicious, unprovoked violence. "That's awful."

"I know," said Turner, and opened the second file. "Petrol was poured through the letterbox of a house in Stockport in the early hours of this morning, then set on fire with matches. The occupants of the house were mercifully not at home, and two suspects were arrested after a neighbour called the police. They confessed to arson and attempted murder, and said they had done it because, and I quote, 'There were always lights on in that house after dark, and you never saw anyone coming or going, so we reckoned they must be vampires.' The man and woman in question both work from home, and admit to being night owls. They're being treated for shock in Stepping Hill Hospital."

He set the file aside and picked up another. "A man broke his wife's jaw and nose because she allegedly attempted to bite him." Another file. "Two national supermarkets have sold out of garlic, and regional stores are reporting shortages. Churches have been overwhelmed with requests to bless crucifixes and provide holy water. Halal butchers are being harassed about the blood they drain from animals." Yet another. "On two separate occasions, more than a hundred miles apart, police were called to disturbances in graveyards and found them being patrolled by men and women calling themselves Operators and carrying wooden stakes. *Two different* places, for God's sake."

Glacial cold had spread slowly through Kate as she listened to the Security Officer. She had seen the best that humanity had to offer during her time in Blacklight, moments of remarkable bravery and integrity, but had also seen men and women at their worst, scared and desperate and lost.

"I had no idea it was so bad out there," she said.

"Things fall apart quickly," said Turner. "Once something like this gathers momentum, all we can do is try to minimise the damage. People are scared, and confused, and they're lashing out. It's only a matter of time until someone is killed."

"And they're blaming us," said Kate, softly. "For keeping the vamps secret."

Turner nodded. "It's only to be expected," he said. "People don't like being kept in the dark, even when it's for the best. They don't care how many lives we've saved over the years and decades, or how many monsters we've destroyed. All it takes is for them to hear the word 'secret' and they throw tantrums like children. Like babies."

Kate shook her head. "I'm not so sure, sir," she said. "People being outraged because they didn't know about us is one thing, and it's plainly ridiculous. It's no different than the government denying for decades that MI5 existed, or pretending that GCHQ wasn't sharing civilian data with the NSA. I think most people accept that their government can't keep them safe and be completely transparent at the same time. But being outraged because we hid the existence of vampires is something else, and I have some sympathy."

Turner narrowed his eyes. "Really?"

"Yes, sir. Vamps have been a danger to human beings for more than a century, but we never informed the public, never told them how to protect themselves. We made the decision not to. We managed it on their behalf, and we kept the incidents down, but the ones that did take place, the ones that we couldn't stop, were massacres, like the one I saw happen to the people I grew up with. None of whom had the slightest idea what was happening, or what they were supposed to do about it. They died terrified and screaming, surrounded by monsters that they had been told didn't exist, told so their entire lives. Maybe one or two of them might have survived if vamps had been common knowledge."

"What's your point, Lieutenant?" asked Turner. His eyes were still narrowed. "Where are you going with this?"

"My point is that I think outrage is a reasonable response to what the public is only now just starting to find out," said Kate. "But not for the reasons they think. As you said, it's not going to be long until some vamp gives an interview or goes on TV and the public realise that they aren't all monsters, not all sadists and murderers, that most of them are just normal people who live similar lives to them. And when they do, there's going to be a wave of outrage that makes the people in the forest with their signs look like the mildest inconvenience."

"Explain," said Turner, although Kate could see from his expression that he already knew where she was headed.

"Members of this Department have destroyed thousands of vampires over the years, sir, probably tens of thousands. Men and women who were killed *just because they were vampires*, not because of anything they'd actually done, any crimes they'd actually committed. No charges, no trials, just a T-Bone stake through the heart and some carefully worded lies for their families. And we're still doing it, sir, every night when the squads go out on Patrol Respond. It's a necessary evil, and I have no doubt that we've saved at least as many lives as we've ended, but none of that is going to matter. This is what Larissa warned us about when she came back from NS9, sir. To the public, this is going to look like mass murder, pure and simple."

Turner put the files he was holding back on to the desk. He closed his eyes and rubbed his temples and forehead with his fingers, then opened them and smiled gently at Kate.

"You agree with her, don't you?" he said, his voice low. "You think Larissa's right."

"I don't know," said Kate. "I think there's truth in what she says, but then I think about Alexandru and Valeri Rusmanov, and all the other monsters I've seen with my own eyes, and I don't know. I don't think destroy on sight is the right SOP, but I don't have a better solution either. I think a vampire prison would be too difficult to hide, not to mention incredibly dangerous, and, until Lazarus finds a cure, I can't think of any other alternatives. But it troubles me, if that's what you're asking. It does."

Turner nodded.

"Don't you ever have doubts, sir?" she asked.

"No," said Turner, instantly. "I was ordered to do the things I've done for Blacklight and I never hesitated, never asked why. Maybe I should have, but I didn't, and it's too late for me to start now. I've waded through blood for this Department, Kate. I've seen things I wouldn't wish on my worst enemy, and I've done things that will never truly leave me, not if I live for another century. So I have to believe they meant something. I have to believe I did them for good, no matter how hard they were."

"What would you do?" asked Kate, her voice low. "If you couldn't believe that any more?"

Turner looked at her, his face paler than ever, the translucent pallor of a ghost.

"I'd put my pistol in my mouth," he said.

Kate frowned. "Don't even joke about that."

"I'm not."

Silence settled uneasily on Kate's office. She stared at the Security Officer, attempting to gauge whether he was serious, whether he meant what he said. She had never known him to lie, and she was trying her hardest not to let the awful image of him with a gun in his mouth take root in her mind.

"So what do we do?" she said, eventually, trying to keep her tone light. "Practically, I mean, about what's going on out there. What's the plan?"

Turner shrugged. "There isn't much we can do," he said. "The police are dealing with the incidents as they happen, and Surveillance is modelling new filters for Echelon to try and make sure we only send squads to genuine supernatural incidents. But there are going to be a lot of false and incomplete reports over the coming days, and we're going to see a lot of time and energy wasted. We'll continue to deal with it all as best we can, and cross our fingers."

"And in the longer term?" asked Kate. "How long can we carry on without coming clean, without admitting who we are and what we do?"

"I don't know," said Turner. "Every journalist in the country is going to be digging now, so it's going to get out eventually, maybe even quickly. Without official confirmation from the MOD, it will all be conjecture, no matter how convincing a case they manage to make, and we need to keep it that way, at least until Zero Hour. After that, maybe none of this will matter."

"Maybe not," said Kate. "I doubt it, though. This is pretty much the biggest story in history. I don't think it's going to just go away, no matter what Dracula does."

"It will go away when people start dying," said Turner, his grey eyes empty. "Especially in the numbers you read out yesterday. But let's hope it doesn't come to that."

# 22

# YOUR DEAD BODY

"Did you find him?" asked Julian Carpenter, as Cal Holmwood pushed open the door of his cell. "Did you find Adam?"

"Hello to you too, Julian," said Cal. "NS9 are working on it. That's all I can say."

Julian nodded. "I told you everything I know, Cal. You believe me, don't you?"

"I said I believed you," said Cal. "I meant it."

He watched carefully as his old friend nodded again. He had reinstated Julian's privileges after he had finally, belatedly cooperated; as a result, his face was clean-shaven, and the photos of Marie and Jamie had been returned to pride of place on the small shelf above his bed. But there was something in Julian's demeanour that made him uneasy; it was an eagerness that almost felt like desperation.

Cal had hated having to threaten him, in particular having to use the man's family as the stick with which to beat him, even though he had never wavered in his conviction that it was the right thing to do. And part of him genuinely hoped, however naively, that his old friend might still manage to make a new life for himself, out there in the real world. But now, as he looked at Julian's gaunt face and sunken, staring eyes, he was not so sure.

"I'm releasing you, Julian," he said. "As I promised you I would, under the conditions I've explained previously. I need to know where you intend to go. We need to make amendments to it before you're taken there, wherever it is."

"Amendments?" asked Julian.

Holmwood sighed. "Don't play innocent, Julian. Cameras, microphones, recorders, motion sensors. You have to disappear."

"Don't worry," said Julian. "I'm good at that."

Holmwood managed a half-smile. "So where to?"

"Do you remember my mother's cottage, near Caister-on-Sea?" asked Julian. "You came for the weekend once, when Jamie was little. It had a red door and a walnut tree in the middle of the garden."

"I remember. You and I went fishing off the sea wall."

"That's right," said Julian. "When we got home, Marie had made lemon cake. It was my favourite and she'd made it as a surprise."

"I said I remember," said Cal, gently.

Julian nodded. "I'd like to go there," he said. "To that cottage. I can't go back to Brenchley. There are too many memories."

"Fine," said Cal. "I'll make the arrangements. And for what it's worth, Julian, I think it's a good decision. I think a bit of peace and quiet might do you good. I'll aim to have you moved—"

"Don't do this," said Julian, his eyes suddenly fixed on the Interim Director's. "I did what you wanted, Cal. Please don't do this to me."

Cal felt pain stab at his heart. The look on his old friend's face threatened to undo him; it was helplessness, awful and humiliating.

"I told you, Julian," he said. "This is the only option."

"I could still be useful, though," said Julian, his voice a hoarse whisper. "I'm still me, Cal, still the man you knew. You could reinstate me and I could help. I could still do something..."

"No," said Cal, as his friend's words trailed off. "You can't. I'm sorry."

"This is it then?" asked Julian. His eyes were red-rimmed and full of tears. "This is how it ends for you and me?"

"It's not the end of anything," said Cal, trying to ignore the lump that had taken up residence in his throat. "It's a new beginning for you, a new life. When this is over... I don't know, maybe we can talk again. But for now, this is all I can do for you. I hope you can see that."

Julian nodded, and dropped his eyes to his bed.

"There's something you can do for me, though," said Cal. "As one friend to another, completely off the record. A last favour, if you will."

Julian looked up, resignation written all over his face. "What is it?"

Cal smiled. "The night you died," he said. "You can tell me how the hell you did it. I've been trying to work it out for months."

A smile rose on to Julian's face; it was thin, but it was a smile nonetheless.

"Off the record?" he asked.

"Of course," said Cal.

"You'd better sit down."

He did as he was told, pulling the plastic chair over from beside the door and settling into it.

"Come closer," said Julian.

Cal narrowed his eyes, but leant forward.

"Closer."

His eyes narrowed even further, but he humoured his old friend.

"You will never, ever know," whispered Julian, his smile widening into a grin that contained no humour whatsoever.

Cal sat bolt upright. "What?"

Julian shook his head. "You can stop me seeing my family. That's fine. You can put me under house arrest, like some naughty kid. That's fine too. But you can't take everything from me, Cal. I won't let you."

"I was at your funeral," said Cal, his face darkening with anger. "I saw the medical report on your body. Your *dead* body."

"I know."

"Tell me how you did it," he said. "That's an order."

Julian shrugged. "I'm not an Operator any more. You've made that very clear. So you don't get to give me orders."

"Did Frankenstein help you? There's no way you pulled it off on your own, and he was your closest friend. He was the only person who knew you had Jamie chipped when he was a baby. Did he help you do it, Julian? Tell me."

"Why don't you ask him?" said Julian.

"I will."

"You should. Let me know what he says."

Cal stared at his old friend for a long moment, then sighed. "This is petty, Julian."

"I know."

"Does it really give you that much satisfaction to know something I don't?"

"Some," said Julian. "It amuses me to think of you trying to work it out."

Cal rolled his eyes, then got up and pushed the chair back across the cell with his foot. "For the record," he said, "it's not house arrest. It's precautionary surveillance."

"Semantics."

"You're still alive," said Cal. "It could be a lot worse."

"Right," said Julian.

The Interim Director opened the cell door. "Someone will come and collect you tomorrow," he said.

"I'll be here," said Julian. Then he looked up, worry ghosting across his face. "The mission you told me about, Cal. The one Jamie volunteered for. Is he going?"

"He's going."

"Will he be coming back?"

Cal looked at his old friend, saw the desperation in his eyes, and realised that, on this one subject, he couldn't lie to him.

"I don't know," he said. "I hope so."

# 23

## BROAD HORIZONS

Matt Browning's first thought upon entering the *Mina II* was disappointment that it had no windows.

He had walked up the ramp and into the belly of the supersonic plane with butterflies swirling in his stomach. Part of it was the pressure he put on himself to do well at whatever was asked of him, a weight he had been carrying on his shoulders his whole life. This mission was no different, even though his role was only that of observer. Another part, far greater than his almost constant nervousness and need to please, was excitement. Matt had never been on a plane, nor left the country of his birth; family holidays in the Browning household had been week-long trips to Blackpool and Skegness. Now he was going all the way to *America*, and would be doing so in a plane that aviation enthusiasts would have gladly given one of their kidneys for the chance to look at, never mind fly in.

He had been accompanied into the *Mina II*'s hold by two members of the Science Division and a Security Operator. These men were the plane's permanent crew, who oversaw her smooth running and protected her from prying eyes wherever she went in the world. As the pilot throttled up the huge engines, and the plane began to gather speed along the Loop's long runway, Matt had gripped the arms of his seat and looked over at his travelling companions; veterans of supersonic travel, all three were already fast asleep.

As the wide, angular jet climbed steeply into the sky and accelerated west, Matt's disappointment had been mollified by a pair of wide high-definition screens that lowered from the ceiling. One allowed the *Mina II*'s occupants to watch a vast selection of live satellite television channels. The second, brilliantly, was a continuous feed from a camera positioned in the plane's belly, pointing directly downwards. By the time the screens lowered and hummed into life, they were already high over the Irish Sea and still accelerating; the screen showed a wide expanse of grey-blue water, punctuated by the white lines of rolling waves.

Now, as they neared their destination, the screen was showing a landscape that was as alien to Matt as the surface of the moon. Desert stretched out in every direction, an impossibly wide vista of orange and red studded with the occasional oasis of washed-out green. Roads and trails tracked through the barren landscape, straight lines of grey and twisting loops and whirls of pale brown, and every now and then Matt's eyes were drawn to tiny clusters of white and grey, desert settlements of such isolation that he could not imagine any rational human choosing to live in them.

As the *Mina II* began to descend, its headlong blast across the Atlantic and the majority of the North American continent almost complete, her pilot banked her south, dipping the angular port wing to almost ninety degrees. The camera swung upwards and, in the distance, for a fleeting second, Matt saw an incongruous huddle of vast, gleaming buildings surrounded by wide urban sprawl.

"Ever been to Vegas?"

Matt looked round, and found the Security Operator smiling at him.

"No," he said. "I'd love to, though."

"You should," said the Operator, shutting his eyes again as he spoke. "At least once. Do it before you're too old."

Matt stared at the distant city. Larissa had told him and Jamie and Kate stories about Las Vegas when she got back from her time at NS9, and not just about Chloe, the vampire girl who seemed to have profoundly changed her view of the world in which Blacklight existed; she had told them about the casinos, about vast floors of green-felted tables and flashing, rattling machines, about bars and restaurants that never closed, about roads that were eight lanes wide. Now he had briefly seen it for himself, from inside a plane that the public didn't know existed.

He smiled as the *Mina II* levelled out and descended rapidly towards the ground. It was rare that he found himself with time to actually think about what his life had become, to marvel at how crazy, how dangerous, how remarkably weird it really was.

The plane touched down with a squeal of tyres and a roar that shook his bones. He was pressed back in his seat as the jet screamed along the runway, until the engines slowly began to wind down, and his companions unclipped themselves from their safety harnesses and began to gather their possessions. Matt did likewise, his stomach churning with sudden excitement. He felt the plane turn left, then roll to a complete stop; a second later the wide ramp at the rear of the hold rumbled into life, dropping steadily down and out towards the ground.

Heat beyond anything Matt had felt before swirled into the enclosed space. It felt as though the air was made of burning sandpaper, and the light that blazed into the hold was so bright it hurt his eyes.

"Welcome to Nevada," said one of the Science Division Operators, and smiled. "Try not to get melanoma."

Matt forced a smile in return and got up from his seat. He walked down the ramp on slightly unsteady legs, shielding his eyes with his hand, and stepped on to the soil of another country for the first time in his life. Before him, blindingly white and seemingly endless, was an enormous salt flat, the remains, he knew, of the long-dry Groom Lake. The runway they had landed on sliced across it and stretched away into the shimmering distance; he followed it until it disappeared, and saw a low collection of hangars and buildings nestling between two low ranges of mountains that rose to the east and west.

*Area 51*, he thought. *I'm standing in the middle of Area 51. My God, the things people would do to swap places with me now, even just for a minute.*

A black SUV was making its way towards them, kicking up a huge cloud of dust, partially obscuring a squat truck with huge wheels that was following it. Matt waited beside the two Science Division Operators and the *Mina II*'s flight crew, who had shut down the engines and disembarked. The Security Operator remained inside the hold; he would stay with the plane until she took off, even though she would be parked in a hangar belonging to Blacklight's closest ally.

"Why didn't we land at Papoose Lake?" asked Matt, squinting against the sun.

"Nowhere to put her under the mountain," said one of the Science Operators. "Picking up and dropping off, we go right to NS9's front door. But if we're staying overnight we land here."

Matt nodded, feeling sweat beginning to form on his forehead and beneath his arms. By the time the black SUV pulled up in front of them, he was already very, very hot, despite the climate-controlling fabric of his uniform.

The woman who got out of the vehicle was tall, dressed in similar all-black, and looked somewhat severe, at least to Matt's eyes; she was in her late thirties, her face tanned and remarkably rectangular, as though straight lines and right angles had been all that were available when it was designed. Her dark hair was tied back in a short ponytail, and the expression on her face was one of studied professionalism.

"Good morning," she said, staring directly at Matt. "I'm Captain Lindsey Hawkins, Groom Lake Security Detachment." She looked at the two Science Division Operators and smiled. "Lieutenant Teller, Lieutenant Greenaway. Nice to have you back with us."

"Thank you, Captain," said one of the men. Matt had not asked any names, so didn't know whether it was Teller or Greenaway who spoke; he belatedly wondered if that had been rude of him.

Hawkins nodded, and turned her attention to the flight crew. "Major Grant, Lieutenant Phillips. The four of you are in the same accommodation block as usual."

"The one next to the bowling alley?" asked the man who Matt assumed was Major Grant, by virtue of his more advanced years; the man standing beside him, who was presumably Lieutenant Phillips, looked barely old enough to have started shaving.

Hawkins smiled. "You got it," she said. "I hope you brought your wallet."

Grant smiled. "I left it at the Loop," he said. "I thought that would be safer."

"Now why don't I believe that?" asked Hawkins. "A jeep'll be out to get the four of you in about five minutes. You good here till then? I have to take our VIP straight round the mountain."

*She's talking about me*, realised Matt. *VIP. I'm a VIP.*

"Sure," said either Teller or Greenaway. "We'll just hang out here in the shade." He looked round, at the squat truck that was preparing to tow the *Mina II* towards the long row of hangars by a thick cable attached to her landing gear, and widened his eyes theatrically. "Oh, hang on..."

"Don't be a baby," said Hawkins. "It's not even hot yet."

"That's demonstrably not true," replied the Science Operator, smiling widely. "Go on, get out of here. We'll be fine here on the burning tarmac."

"All right," said Hawkins, and pulled open the rear door of the SUV. "I'll see you all this evening. I'll be the one rolling strikes and taking your money. Lieutenant Browning, if you're ready?"

"Thanks," said Matt, and climbed up into the vehicle. The air-conditioned interior was glorious, the tan leather seat soft and comfortable. As Hawkins climbed behind the wheel and pressed her foot on to the accelerator, he was already fighting the urge to close his eyes.

"So you're Blacklight?" said Hawkins, glancing at him through the rear-view mirror as they sped across the salt flat. "You look a little young, if you don't mind me saying?"

*Of course not*, thought Matt. *Why would I mind that?*

"I'm seventeen," he said.

"Jesus," said Hawkins, smiling into the mirror. "I've got two nephews older than you. You must be shit-hot at something."

Matt met her eyes. "I'm just here as an observer."

"Right," said Hawkins. "And I just work at a regular air base like I tell my mom."

Matt smiled. "You're not NS9 then?"

"No," said Hawkins, accelerating as they left the lake bed and joined a tarmac road that ran round the base of the mountain rising up to the left of the car. "I'm Air Force, technically. I got recruited into Intelligence six years ago, and stationed out here a year later."

"You must have seen some stuff."

Hawkins laughed. "You've no idea. Vampires aren't the only things in the universe that we don't want anyone to know about."

"Really?" said Matt, his mind suddenly full of possibilities. "Like what?"

"Classified," said Hawkins, her smile wide. "Sorry."

The road wound between the mountain and a chunk of fallen rock the size of an office building. For a moment, all Matt could see were walls of grey, until they emerged from the pass and a hangar appeared through the SUV's windscreen: a huge semi-circular opening hacked out of a sheer wall of rock. Hawkins drove into it and brought the SUV to a halt.

"Here you are," she said. "Good luck with your observing."

"Thanks," said Matt. He grabbed his bag, opened the door, and stepped out into Dreamland, the headquarters of National Security Division 9. The SUV turned in a tight circle and disappeared, leaving him standing in the middle of the hangar on his own. He looked round at the rows of jeeps and vans, at the thick glass that enclosed an armoury, at the guard posts that stood at the edges of the wide entrance.

*It's the same as the Loop,* he thought. *Exactly the same. I wonder which one came first?*

"Lieutenant Browning?"

Matt turned towards the voice and saw a young woman in a black Operator's uniform approaching him. She was short and thin, with a pretty face and chopped black hair, and was smiling widely as she stopped in front of him.

"I'm Matt Browning," he said. "Reporting as requested."

"I'm Kara Porter," she replied. "I'm to take you to the Director, but we can swing by your quarters and drop your stuff off first if you want?"

Matt shook his head. "No need," he said. "I'm ready."

Kara nodded. "Follow me," she said, and set off across the hangar. Matt followed her, trying not to look at everything around him with the open mouth of a tourist.

*The number plates on the vans are different. Her uniform is a fractionally different shade of black to mine. The sunlight is brighter than I've ever seen it.*

"It's great to meet you, Matt," said Kara, as she led him through a pair of double doors in the corner of the hangar and into a grey corridor identical to the one that ran through the centre of the Loop's Level 0. "Larissa talked about you all the time."

"You knew Larissa when she was here?" he asked.

"Everyone knew her," said Kara, smiling. "She was kind of hard to miss. But we were friends, her and me and a few others. We were devastated when she left."

*So was she,* thought Matt.

"That's cool," he said. "She's awesome. And she loved it here."

Kara's smiled faltered, momentarily. "That's good to hear," she said. "We loved having her. It was a shame how it ended, but I don't blame her. Will you tell her that for me, when you get home?"

Matt frowned. "How it ended?"

"Didn't she tell you?" asked Kara, her eyes narrowing.

"Tell me what?"

"Things just got... well, they got kind of messy. There was some weirdness between her and Tim Albertsson, one of our Special Operators, and it all sort of unravelled."

242

Matt stared, unable to keep the shock from his face. Kara noticed it, and her eyes widened as she realised what he was thinking.

"Jesus," she said. "Nothing *happened* between her and Tim. I know Jamie Carpenter is your friend, and Larissa loves him, she really does. She couldn't wait to get back to him. She even asked our Director whether he could transfer Jamie out here."

*Did she?* thought Matt. *Something else she must have forgotten to mention.*

"So what was the weirdness between them?" he asked. "What happened?"

"Shit, I shouldn't have even brought this up," said Kara, the dark skin of her cheeks flushing. "I just assumed you knew. This is for Larissa to tell you, not me."

"Larissa's not here," said Matt. "So you're going to have to."

"It was just a *thing*," said Kara. "Tim had a crush on Larissa and she didn't really notice until it had got seriously big. So it got weird and awkward, because they were friends and they worked together, and Larissa blamed herself for not noticing sooner and shutting it down, and then Tim tried to kiss her and she warned him—"

"Hold on," interrupted Matt. "He tried to kiss her? When everyone knew she was with Jamie?"

"Yeah," said Kara. "Like I said, Tim *really* liked her. It was kind of pathetic, to tell you the truth. We tried to talk him out of it, but he wouldn't listen, and it ended up with Larissa basically threatening to kick his ass if he tried anything else. And then Larissa got called home early, right in the middle of the whole Tim thing, so she went and she left us here."

"I don't understand," said Matt.

"Larissa's mission was—"

"To bring new Operators back to Blacklight," said Matt. "I know."

"Right," said Kara. "So early on, when she'd only been here for a week or so, Tim asked her if she'd pick him to go back with her. His family are European and he's obsessed with Blacklight, all the history and everything. Larissa said she would, and that she'd take me and three of our friends as well, if we wanted to go. She had to take six, and I don't know who the other one would have been. Anna Frost, if I had to guess. Anyway, we said yes, because everyone wants to see the Loop, right? The founders and the Fallen Gallery and that stuff. So she was happy, because I think what she wanted were some people at the Loop who she knew were on her side, you know, and we were happy, and Tim was *delighted*."

*People who were on her side at the Loop?* thought Matt, with an inward grimace. *What about me and Jamie and Kate? Don't we count?*

"I bet he was," said Matt, as they stopped outside a grey metal door.

"Right," said Kara. "But then she got called home and didn't take us with her. And that was so obviously because of Tim, and I guess she felt that if she wasn't taking *him* then she couldn't take the rest of us. So she picked six totally different names and disappeared on that plane of yours. She didn't even say goodbye."

"Jesus," said Matt. "You weren't kidding when you said it was a mess, were you? I didn't have a clue about any of that. She never mentioned it at all."

Kara shrugged, and forced a small smile. "Can't blame her, I suppose," she said. "Although she could have at least told us that she'd changed her mind. We would have understood, and that way we could have actually said goodbye to her. But what's done is done. I'm sure I'll see her again."

"Probably," said Matt. "It's a small world."

*Although I hope it's not small enough for me to ever run into Tim Albertsson. There are a few things I'd like to say to him if I did.*

"Here we are then," said Kara. "General Allen is expecting you."

"OK," said Matt. "It was nice to meet you."

Kara smiled. "You too, Matt," she said. "I'm sorry if I told you anything you didn't want to hear."

"It's all right," said Matt. "I'm glad Larissa has people here that care about her. She deserves it."

Kara nodded and walked quickly away down the corridor. Matt watched her go, then turned to the door. On the wall beside it was a grey intercom box with a black button at the bottom. Matt pressed it, heard a long buzzing sound, and waited.

"Yes?" said a voice.

"Lieutenant Browning, sir."

"Matt!" shouted the voice. "Welcome, son! Come on in."

The metal door unlocked. Matt pushed it open, and stepped into General Allen's quarters.

The main room was structurally similar to the one five thousand miles away that was occupied by Cal Holmwood, but while that space was grey and functional, General Allen's quarters felt immediately warm and welcoming. A wide desk stood to one side, in front of walls panelled with dark wood. The screen opposite was in the same place as in Holmwood's room, but was surrounded on both sides by a sprawling collection of photographs and flags and pennants and scarves in black and gold, the colours of the West Point football team. The occupant of the room was rounding the desk and making his way towards Matt, a smile on his face, his hand extended.

"Lieutenant Browning," said General Allen. "Pleasure to meet you, son."

"Thank you, sir," said Matt, taking hold of the offered hand. The grip that closed round his fingers felt like a vice, and he tried not to wince as his arm was pumped up and down.

"Larissa told me all about you," said Allen. "It's great to put a face to the stories."

"Thank you, sir," repeated Matt. He was already beginning to wonder whether he could live up to the version of himself that Larissa had clearly enthused about during her time in Nevada.

"Come and sit down," said Allen, releasing Matt's hand and motioning towards a pair of sofas. "Drink?"

"Water, sir?" said Matt.

"Coming right up," said Allen, and strolled towards a fridge at the rear of the room.

Matt lowered himself on to one of the sofas and watched his host as he extracted a bottle of water and a can of Diet Coke; the NS9 Director was huge, as tall and broad as a wrestler, with the deep tan and weathered face of someone who has spent many years in the desert. Allen strode back across the quarters and smiled widely as he handed the bottle over; Matt could feel an almost supernatural warmth emanating from him, an invisible wave of overpowering charisma.

"How was the flight?" asked the Director, flopping down into the other sofa and opening his drink.

"Short, sir," said Matt, and took a long sip of his water. He was feeling slightly overwhelmed; on his own, far from home, and surrounded by people who seemed so different to those he had left behind.

"Of course," said Allen. "She's a hell of a plane."

"Yes, sir."

"You know why you're here, right?" asked Allen. "Cal briefed you?"

Matt nodded. "Yes, sir. I'm to act as an observer to the team you're sending to locate Adam."

"That's it," said Allen. "The operation is code-named GARDEN OF EDEN. Our Intelligence Division is working on the information we received from Cal Holmwood, and expects to have a target location by the time the team departs."

"So where are we going, sir?" asked Matt. "If we don't have an actual location?"

"San Francisco," said Allen. "The intelligence we have suggests it as the most likely place that Adam would return to. We've commandeered a laboratory on the USF campus. That's where you're going to take Adam when you find him, so you can do what you need to do before you bring him back here. Is that all clear?"

"Yes, sir," said Matt, his stomach suddenly full of nerves. "Absolutely."

"Are you sure, son?"

"I'm a scientist, sir," said Matt. "I'm not an Operator."

Allen smiled. "Cal wouldn't have sent you here if he didn't think you could handle it," he said, his voice deep and warm. "I asked for a member of the Lazarus Project to go with my team and he sent me you. On a personal level, I'm glad he did, because I've wanted to meet you for a long time, but he didn't have to. He chose you."

Unfamiliar pride spread through Matt's chest and he smiled. "That's good to know, sir," he said. "Thank you."

"You're welcome, Lieutenant," said the Director. "GARDEN

OF EDEN departs at 1800, with the briefing to be carried out in flight. Until then, have a look round, get some sleep, make yourself at home. Be back here ready to go fifteen minutes before departure."

"I will, sir," said Matt, his stomach churning. "I'll be ready."

# 24

# THE SPIRIT OF COOPERATION

"Operators," said Cal Holmwood, staring down from behind the lectern at the front of the Ops Room. "This is DARKWOODS, a multinational operation under the command authority of NS9. I trust I don't need to make either of you aware of the Priority Level we're dealing with here?"

"No, sir," said Jamie, and glanced over at Larissa as she echoed him. The colour in her face had faded, thankfully; they had dressed hurriedly before making their way up from Level B, and she had been worried it might not do so quickly enough.

"Good," said Holmwood. "The two of you were selected by NS9 to represent our Department on this operation. In addition to the squad leader Nevada are sending, there will be three Operators joining you in Germany. Please don't bother asking me who they are, because I don't know. You're scheduled to depart for the FTB in ninety minutes, so let's not waste any more time than is necessary. Direct your attention to the screen behind me."

Jamie looked up at the flat wall screen as Holmwood stepped out from behind the lectern, his insides cold with disappointment.

*So that's why I'm going,* he thought. *Not because Cal forgave me for what happened in the graveyard, but because it wasn't his decision to make. If it had been, there's not a chance in hell I'd be going. I can see it all over his face.*

The screen came to life, displaying satellite imagery of a vast expanse of forest, a seemingly endless landscape of green and brown. Grid references and topographical survey data appeared in boxes at the left of the screen, as the name of the operation glowed in white letters at the top.

*Darkwoods,* thought Jamie. *Seems about right, looking at that. Jesus.*

"This," said Holmwood, "is the Teleorman Forest in central Romania, not far from Bucharest. It is approximately twelve hundred square miles in size, and has existed relatively unchanged for more than a thousand years." The Interim Director tapped a series of keys and a yellow dot appeared at the edge of the forest, near a small village. "This is where Grey woke up after his search for the first victim ended." He tapped the console again and a red ring appeared.

"This has been selected as your primary search area, based on Grey's recollections, which are incomplete and contradictory at best. It encompasses almost a hundred square miles. Satellite and thermographic imaging has proven inconclusive, meaning we have absolutely no idea what's in there. You should consider it a starting point, not a definitive range. Is that clear?"

"Yes, sir," said Larissa.

Holmwood nodded, and turned his gaze on Jamie.

"Yes, sir," he said.

"Good," said the Interim Director. "I'm no fan of hyperbole, and I don't normally pay much attention to prophecies and legends. But I do believe in telling it like it is. We all know what the potential implications of this operation are, as well as the high possibility of disappointment. Grey's testimony is far from reliable, and we have no way of assessing the theory of the first victim without putting him in a lab, *if* he even exists. But if there is any truth to the story, any truth whatsoever, then this will be remembered as one of the most important missions in the history of this, or any other, Department. If the first victim is real, he will be more than four centuries old, and most likely almost as powerful as Dracula himself. I'm certain that I don't need to explain why that would make him a potentially game-changing asset. So if he's real, you find him, and you bring him back here, by whatever means necessary."

"What if he doesn't want to come, sir?" asked Jamie.

"I don't suggest you give him that option," said Holmwood. "Now listen to me, both of you. From a tactical standpoint, you and the rest of your team are going to be searching for a vampire who is believed to be one of the oldest in the world, and whose disposition and motives are entirely unknown. Disregard Dracula, and the legend, and everything else, and you're still looking at an operation that has the potential to be extremely dangerous, and I want you to treat it accordingly. Regardless of certain incidents that have taken place in the last forty-eight hours, I have no desire to see either of you return to the Loop in a box. So be careful over there. Very careful."

"We will, sir," said Jamie, looking across at Larissa. She returned his gaze, red flickering in the deepest corners of her eyes.

"I believe you," said Holmwood. His face, which had been tight with professionalism as he spoke, softened, and he looked at the two young Operators with clear affection. "Don't make me regret doing so. You'll be briefed again when you arrive in Germany, and everything we have has been forwarded to your consoles. Study it, take it all in, and be in the hangar at 1630. It goes without saying that the existence of this Operation, as well as your roles in it, is Zero Hour classified. Please take that to mean don't tell anyone under any circumstances, not don't tell anyone apart from your friends if you feel like it." He fixed his gaze firmly on Jamie, and it took all of his resolve not to look away. "All right. Good luck to you. Dismissed."

"Thank you, sir," said Larissa, standing up.

Jamie did likewise, nodded to the Interim Director, and followed his girlfriend out of the Ops Room. He had barely shut the door behind him before Larissa pressed herself against him and threw her arms round his shoulders.

"Take it easy," he said.

"I told you," said Larissa. "Even if it was NS9 who chose you for the mission, you could hear how highly Cal rates you."

"All he said was that he doesn't want either of us to die," said Jamie. "I'm not sure that's a particularly glowing endorsement."

Larissa released her grip on him and narrowed her eyes. "This is a big deal, Jamie," she said. "Maybe the biggest deal of all time, and you and I get to go, together. You need to get excited."

Jamie forced a smile. "I am," he said, although he wasn't. What he *was* feeling was a knot of nervousness twisting in his stomach; the mission was his opportunity to redeem himself, to show that he could be trusted, and he was terrified of screwing it up.

"Do you know anyone who's been to the FTB?" asked Larissa.

Jamie nodded. "Dominique's been a few times. Angela's been, and Cal and Major Turner, obviously."

Larissa grinned. "And us, in a few hours," she said. "We need to go through the intelligence before we get ready to go."

"OK," said Jamie. "One of the briefing rooms will be empty."

Larissa's eyes flashed as she shook her head. "My room," she said, and smiled, wickedly.

The helicopter touched down with a heavy thud and Larissa felt a burst of excitement crackle through her.

The flight from the Loop to Complex 17, the headquarters of the German Office of the Supernatural that was universally referred to as the *Schwartzhaus*, had been frustratingly long; it had taken almost an hour to cover the three hundred and fifty miles between East Anglia and the outskirts of Dortmund, a distance that Larissa could have travelled on her own in barely half the time. As a result, she had spent the journey impatiently fiddling with the weapons and equipment on her belt, and reading and re-reading the intelligence summary on her console. It contained little more than the information Cal Holmwood had given them in the Ops Room, but it helped to alleviate her frustration, at least momentarily.

"All right," said Jamie, as the helicopter throttled down. "Let's go and say hello."

Larissa unclipped her safety harness, slung her bag over her shoulder, and floated across to the wide door that filled one side of the helicopter's hold. She twisted its handle and slid it open, breathing in the cool evening air that swirled into her nostrils as Jamie leapt down on to the tarmac. She floated down beside him and took her first look at the *Schwartzhaus*.

Her first thought was how different it looked to both the Loop and Dreamland, which were largely identical in design, despite the NS9 facility having been built beneath a mountain.

The *Schwartzhaus* was something else.

Instead of a central structure with a hangar built into one side of it, the FTB base was a ring of eight single-storey buildings with wide, empty spaces between them. In the distance, on the other side of the buildings where she could also make out the long lights of a runway, stood a row of large rectangular shapes, which Larissa assumed were the hangars and vehicle maintenance depots. A road led from where the helicopter had landed towards the nearest building of the ring, which had a large number five printed on its side. A door stood open in the centre of the wall, from which a dark figure was emerging.

"Different," said Jamie, pointing away from the buildings.

Larissa followed his gesture and saw what he was referring to. Where the Loop was surrounded by forest and Dreamland by empty desert, beyond the distant security towers of the *Schwartzhaus* she could see the rising silhouettes of industrial buildings and hear the steady hum of traffic.

*Hidden in plain sight*, she thought. *Not like us.*

Behind her, the helicopter's engines built back up to a crescendo of noise. She flew forward, Jamie crouching and running beside her as the rotors began to scream, churning the air and pushing it against their backs. The helicopter lumbered into the air and thudded away to the south-west as Larissa stopped halfway along the road that led to Building Five. The FTB Operator, a small, neat woman with her hair tied back in a ponytail, stepped forward with her hand extended.

"*Guten Abend*," said the woman, as Larissa took her hand and shook it. "I am Krista Gottlieb, the Security Supervisor for Complex 17. You are most welcome."

"Thank you," said Larissa. "It's good to be here."

Gottlieb smiled, then shook Jamie's hand. "Please follow me," she said. "The others are waiting."

"We're the last ones here?" asked Jamie.

"That is correct," said Gottlieb. "Please, follow me."

The Security Supervisor turned and strode towards the square building. Larissa glanced over at Jamie as they followed; her boyfriend's face was creased with a deep frown.

*Stay calm,* she silently told him. *Being last doesn't mean anything. It doesn't make us look bad.*

Larissa knew that Jamie was still preoccupied with the mistake he had made in the graveyard, and terrified of going back to Blacklight without his reputation fully rehabilitated; she just hoped his obvious tension didn't create the very situation he was trying to avoid.

The two Operators followed Gottlieb into Building Five, and found themselves standing in a square room containing nothing apart from a pair of metal lift doors and a small button set into the wall. The Security Supervisor pressed it, and the three of them waited in a silence that was not entirely comfortable; tension was radiating out of Jamie in waves that were almost visible.

"Are these buildings all the same?" asked Larissa, trying to break the silence.

"Yes," said Gottlieb. "They are all controlled from below, and access from more than one cannot be granted at the same time. If the base is attacked, they can work as bottlenecks."

"Makes sense," said Larissa. She glanced at Jamie, who didn't appear to be listening. "Makes it harder for an attacking force to get inside in large numbers."

"Exactly," said Gottlieb. "It has never happened here, thankfully. But we must always be ready, especially now."

Larissa nodded.

*Lucky,* she thought. *I've seen what can happen. Seen it* ____ *____*

The attack on the Loop was seared into the memor____ who had been involved, and she was no exceptio____ screams had filled the air, blood had sprayed and run across the tarmac, and she had felt the flesh burned away from her own bones by an explosion of ultraviolet light that had been visible from space.

The lift doors slid open and they stepped inside. Gottlieb pressed a button marked B and, when the doors opened again, they revealed a long corridor painted a pale blue that seemed far less oppressive than the grey that covered every surface inside the Loop. The Security Supervisor led them along it and stopped outside a pair of frosted glass doors.

"In here," she said. "The best of luck to you all."

"Thank you," said Larissa, and looked pointedly at Jamie.

"Cheers," he managed, then lowered his eyes back to the floor.

Gottlieb nodded, then walked away down the corridor. Larissa waited until she disappeared round a distant corner, then turned on her boyfriend.

"Snap out of this shit," she said, feeling heat behind her eyes. "Do you hear me, Jamie? Right now."

He recoiled. "What are you talking about?"

"If you go looking for the second most powerful vampire that's ever lived wound up this tight, you're going to get yourself or somebody else killed," said Larissa. "Holmwood and Turner aren't here, and we are. So you need to let go of all the shit that's happened over the last couple of days, get your head clear, and focus on what we're here to do. Everything else can wait."

Jamie's eyes narrowed, then widened to their usual dimensions.

"You're right," he said, his voice low. "I'm sorry. I've got this, I promise."

"All right," said Larissa, and smiled as relief flooded through her. "I believe you."

She turned back to the frosted doors. Stencilled on the glass was the word *Geschäftstätigkeit*. She cast a final, reassuring glance in Jamie's direction, then turned the handle and pushed the door open.

The room fell silent as Larissa and Jamie entered it; the three Operators gathered at a round table in the middle of the room looked up and took stock of the new arrivals. They were two men and a woman, their expressions somewhere between friendly and cautious, their eyes clear and focused.

"Hey," said Larissa, forcing a smile. "I'm Larissa Kinley. Good to meet you all."

"Jamie Carpenter," said Jamie, from beside her.

The silence was broken by a chorus of greetings and the scraping of chair legs on linoleum as the Operators got to their feet and made their way towards Larissa and Jamie, smiles on their faces, hands outstretched.

"Good to meet you both," said a tall, blond-haired man with a deep tan and wide shoulders. "Kristian Van Orel. Military Detachment Alpha, South Africa. I heard we had a vampire and a Blacklight descendant on the team, but I wasn't sure if I believed the rumours. I'm glad they turned out to be right."

Larissa's smiled widened, partly as an involuntary result of the charm radiating out of Kristian Van Orel's pores and partly because of the grin that had risen on to the face of her boyfriend. Jamie stepped forward and shook the South African's hand, as the woman who had been sitting next to him offered her own to Larissa.

"Greta Engel, FTB," said the woman. "It is an honour to meet you. I have heard many stories."

"Thank you," she said, shaking the German Operator's hand. "It's good to be here."

The FTB Operator looked to be in her late twenties, tall and narrow, with brown hair that brushed her shoulders. Her green eyes gleamed under the fluorescent glare of the overhead lights, and she stood easily in the well-balanced, relaxed stance that Larissa had come to recognise as characteristic of Operators, regardless of which Department they were from.

Engel moved over to say hello to Jamie, and Larissa found herself looking into the hard face of the third and final occupant of the room. The man's skin was pale, his jaw almost perfectly square, his grey eyes piercing below a scalp that was closely shaved. His body was thickly muscled, its lines and contours clear through the black material of his uniform. He looked Larissa up and down, then nodded.

"Arkady Petrov," he said. "SPC."

Larissa frowned. "Petrov?" she said. "Were you related to—"

"Yuri was my uncle," said Petrov.

"Shit," said Larissa. "I'm sorry for your loss."

Petrov nodded again. "Thank you," he said. "I am looking forward to working with you." Then he was gone, greeting Jamie with the same gruff manner, and leaving Larissa wondering what he must have been through in the last few months.

Yuri Petrov had been the SPC Director before Aleksandr Ovechkin, and a legend in the supernatural community; a former member of the Spetsnaz, he had spent more than a decade in the KGB, including its bloody, paranoid transformation into the post-Soviet FSB, before moving to the SPC and rising to its head.

He had been murdered by Valeri Rusmanov and his followers on the night that Dracula was resurrected, murdered inside the vault in which the first vampire's ashes had been kept for almost a century, having fought to his very last breath. It had been Petrov who had warned Henry Seward that access to vault 31, arguably the most highly classified secret in any of the Departments, had been compromised, information that had led to the discovery of Thomas Morris's treachery against Blacklight. He had deserved far, far better than what had been done to him; he had been tortured and torn to pieces, his disembodied head placed on the pillar that had held Dracula's ashes to greet the rescue party that Seward and Paul Turner had led.

*So much death,* she thought to herself. *General Petrov and Shaun Turner and Thomas Morris and all the others. So much misery and grief.*

Engel and Van Orel had circled back to the table in the centre of the room. Larissa pulled out a chair and joined them, leaving Jamie talking to Petrov.

"The Security Supervisor told us we were the last to arrive," she said. "Are we missing someone?"

Van Orel shook his head. "Our squad leader is in with the FTB Director. He should be back any minute."

"He got in this morning," said Engel. "He was the first to arrive. He's very enthusiastic, very... *American,* but I think we are in good hands."

"Great," said Larissa. "I worked with most of the senior NS9 Operators. They're good people."

Behind her, the door opened again. Larissa turned to see who would be leading them into Romania and felt her heart stop in her chest, the blood freeze in her veins.

"Lieutenant Kinley," said Tim Albertsson, smiling widely as he walked to the front of the room. "Lieutenant Carpenter. Welcome to Germany."

# 25

# AN UNLIKELY SOURCE

### SAN SEBASTIÁN, NORTHERN SPAIN

Valentin Rusmanov leant back in his chair and confessed something to himself that he would never have admitted to anyone else.

He had absolutely no idea what to do next.

The promise he had made to Paul Turner as they faced the bloody proof of Richard Brennan's betrayal, that he could find his brother and his former master and bring their locations back to Blacklight, seemed destined to be broken. Valeri had amassed a huge portfolio of property over the decades and centuries, and Valentin had visited every location that he was aware of: the cabin in the Swiss mountains, the apartments in Rome and Zurich, the vast estates in Colorado, Moscow Oblast and New South Wales, the islands in the Grenadines and Philippines.

All to no avail.

Several of them had contained cadres of Valeri loyalists, fanatics similar to those he had found standing guard in the dacha in Romania. Valentin had unleashed tortures and torments that he had not applied for hundreds of years, inflicting agonies that no human or vampire could withstand, but found himself no closer to his goal.

The vampires he had tortured had received their orders third or fourth hand, via a series of intermediaries who had disappeared back into the darkness. Only Genevieve, if the vampire known as Jackson was to be believed, had been in possession of first-hand information, and Valentin had killed her. Since her death, he had found a wall of silence around his brother's location, one that he was increasingly sure was impenetrable.

A waiter placed Valentin's Americano down on the glass top of the table and backed discreetly away. He took a long sip of the wonderfully bitter drink, settled back in his chair, and tried to push away the memory of what he had told Paul Turner before he left the Loop.

*I said I could find Valeri and Dracula, if he let me. But I was wrong. They're hiding and I have no idea where they are.*

He had travelled to San Sebastián as a last resort. The beautiful Basque port had been Ana Rusmanov's favourite place in the world, and Valentin had hoped that his brother's relentless, all-consuming love for his dead wife might have influenced his choice of hiding place. But after three days of futile searching, he had reached two conclusions: firstly, that Valeri's desperate obedience to his master had evidently trumped his nostalgic devotion to Ana, and secondly, that the eldest Rusmanov had clearly kept his cards far closer to his chest than Valentin had realised.

*They're somewhere I don't know, somewhere Valeri never told me about. Which means they could be anywhere in the world. Which means this is impossible.*

He took another sip of his drink, deep in thought. Around him, the narrow cobbled streets of San Sebastián's Parte Vieja thronged with life as tourists moved in slow clusters of camera lenses and baseball caps around the Basilica of Saint Mary of the Chorus and the shops and restaurants that catered to their every need. Young men and women, many of them clearly too young to drink, spilled in and out of the bars and the bodegas, laughing and drinking and shouting. Valentin, who had taken the study of humanity to the level of a fine art, was so engrossed in their charming, awkward interactions that he didn't notice the smell of the vampire until it was standing beside him.

"I thought you were your brother," said a lilting, childlike voice. "I'm really pleased you're not."

Valentin's eyes flared involuntarily red, and his heart leapt in his chest.

*Good Lord,* he thought. *Unforgivable, to be crept up on so easily. Absolutely unforgivable.*

He turned his head and found himself looking up at an uneven mountain of a man, with a small head and a pale, empty face. The vampire was peering down at him with an expression of enormous nervousness.

"Anderson," said Valentin, his voice smooth and friendly, his equilibrium instantly recovered. "What an unexpected pleasure. If you are here to fight, may I suggest we repair to a more discreet location? I don't think your master will appreciate us appearing on the evening news."

"Fight?" said Anderson, his brow creasing with confusion. "Why would we fight?"

Valentin narrowed his eyes. "You are not here on my brother's orders?"

Anderson gave his head a long, slow shake. "I thought you were him," he said. "I thought you'd come looking for me. I thought you were going to make me go back."

"Back where?"

"*There*," said Anderson, as though it was the most obvious thing in the world. "Back to him."

"You know where my brother is?"

"Of course I do."

"Where is he?" asked Valentin, trying to keep the eagerness from his voice.

Anderson frowned. "I'm not supposed to tell anyone."

"You can tell me, Anderson. Valeri and I are family."

"But I saw the two of you fighting. And he calls you a traitor now."

"Brothers fight," said Valentin. "And they say unkind things about each other. But blood is always what matters in the end."

Anderson nodded. "It's sad when families fall out with each other. It's a shame."

"It is," said Valentin. "Will you tell me where my brother is, Anderson? So I can go and put things right with him."

"I don't know," said Anderson. The vampire's face was screwed up with the physical effort of trying to decide what to do. As the colour in it began to rise alarmingly, Valentin decided to try a different approach.

"You are no longer associating with my brother?" he asked. "Is that right?"

Anderson nodded, his face unfolding with relief at being asked a question he knew how to answer. "I wanted to go, so I asked him if I could go, but he told me I had to stay, because I'd be no good without him and it was dangerous for me to be out in the world on my own. But he was never very nice to me, not like Alexandru was, so I left anyway. Now I live in a little house not far from here, with a cow and some pigs and two dogs, and when I smelt your scent yesterday I was afraid, because I thought he'd found me. So I decided to be brave, and come and see what you wanted. But you're not Valeri."

"No," said Valentin. "I am not. When did you leave, Anderson?"

"After the fight at Blacklight."

"Because my brother didn't treat you well?"

"Yes," said Anderson, his voice low. "But not just that. Because of the other one too."

"Dracula?"

Anderson winced. "I don't like to hear his name. I won't say it."

"Why not?"

"Because he scares me. People think I'm stupid, but I know enough. I know what will happen when he's better and it makes me sad. I like the world as it is."

Valentin smiled. "So do I, Anderson. So do I." He gestured towards the empty chair opposite his own. "Why don't you sit down and join me?"

Anderson hesitated, his big, empty face incapable of pretence, then lowered himself into the chair, its wicker sides creaking appreciably as the waiter instantly appeared beside them. Valentin ordered a second Americano, and, after a long moment's consideration, Anderson asked for a cup of coffee with an umbrella in it. He looked nervously at Valentin as the waiter scurried away, clearly unsure whether he had done the right thing, and the ancient vampire fought back a smile. Anderson, who had committed countless murders and inflicted innumerable tortures on the orders of the two elder Rusmanovs, possessed a gentle simplicity that felt strangely like innocence, and Valentin wondered whether the misshapen vampire would hurt a fly without someone to tell him to do so.

He doubted it.

"So my brothers and I all smell the same?" he asked.

Anderson flinched, clearly fearing rebuke, his eyes widening, his face twisting with worry. Then he saw the warm smile on Valentin's face and broke into one of his own, a happy, sunny expression of relief.

"Not now," he said. "But from a distance, yes. I knew it was one of you, but I couldn't tell which one. For a moment, I thought... I thought..."

"You thought I might be Alexandru," said Valentin, gently.

Anderson nodded, and looked down at the table. The waiter reappeared, and there was silence as he unloaded their drinks from his small tray. When he departed, clutching a handful of euros, Anderson raised his head, and Valentin saw tears in the huge vampire's eyes.

"Do you miss him?" asked Valentin. "Alexandru?"

"I do," said Anderson, his voice strained and unsteady. "I loved him."

"So did I," said Valentin. "For a long time, I loved him very much."

"He loved you too," said Anderson. "He didn't like Valeri, but he talked about you often. He missed you."

"I felt the same," said Valentin. "It was hard, though. The vampire who died was not the man I missed."

"I don't understand," said Anderson. "He was your brother."

"He was," said Valentin. "But he wasn't the same, by the end. Do you understand what I mean?"

For a long moment, Anderson's face went blank, as though the power to it had been cut. Then one of the saddest smiles Valentin had ever seen rose slowly on to it.

"I do," he said. "He went bad. After Ilyana, he went bad."

*Alexandru went bad long before that,* thought Valentin. *Decades, maybe centuries even. But you're right, that was the final straw. That was when the last part of the man he had been died.*

"That's right," he said. "You stayed with him, though. You were loyal."

Anderson's smile broadened, becoming something that was close to beautiful. "I was," he said. "To the very end. I was there when he died, when the boy killed him."

"Jamie Carpenter," said Valentin.

Anderson nodded. "He pulled a cross down on Alexandru, and his friends hurt us. One of them hurt me, but I escaped."

"And Valeri took you in?"

"Yes. He told me it was what Alexandru wanted. He said they had talked about it."

*You poor creature,* thought Valentin. *Passed from one master to the next, like a slave.*

He took a sip of his Americano. "But you didn't like being with him?"

Anderson shook his head. "He wasn't nice to me. Not like Alexandru. Alexandru treated me well."

*Alexandru tortured you and tormented you and made you do awful things in his name,* thought Valentin. *He was a sadistic, abusive bully, but you loved him, and that's what you remember.*

"You did the right thing, Anderson," he said. "By leaving, I mean. Valeri is a shadow of the man Alexandru was, and you were right not to let him tell you what to do."

Anderson nodded. "I know," he said. "I was so scared, but I did it. I have a farm, south of here, where I live now. I have a cow and two dogs and—"

"And some pigs?" interrupted Valentin, smiling gently at the vampire.

"That's right," said Anderson, his face a mask of happiness. "There are seven of them. I could show you, if you wanted? It's not far."

"I'd love to see them," said Valentin. "But I'm afraid I can't go now. I have to see my brother, as I said."

Anderson's face fell, but he nodded. "Maybe some other time?" he said, in a small voice.

"Definitely," said Valentin. "As soon as I'm done with Valeri. If you tell me where he is, I can go and see him tonight and get it over with."

Anderson frowned, but this time the block that Valeri had placed in his head failed to hold. "He's at his château," he said, slowly. "With his master. That's where they are."

"His château?" asked Valentin.

"Château Dauncy," said Anderson. "That's what it's called. It's north of here, in France. Near Bordeaux."

"Thank you, Anderson," said Valentin. "You've done the right thing."

The vampire smiled, then drank his coffee in one long slug. He put the cup, tiny in his huge hands, like a child's toy, back on the table and got slowly to his feet.

"I should go home," he said. "Thank you very much for the drink. If you wanted to come and see me sometime, that would be nice."

"It would," said Valentin. "And I will. I promise."

Anderson looked at him for a long moment. "I don't think you will," he said, eventually. "But that's all right. It was kind of you to say it."

"I'm a man of my word, Anderson," said Valentin. "If I say I'll do something, I do it. You can trust me."

Anderson nodded, but said nothing.

"All right," said Valentin. "Goodbye then, Anderson. Look after yourself, and your cow and your dogs and your pigs. If the worst happens, if the one whose name you don't like to say does rise, you keep your head down. And be careful."

"I will," said Anderson. "It was nice to see you, Valentin. You aren't as scary as I remember."

Valentin laughed, a warm sound that floated out across the crowded street. "I'll take that as a compliment," he said. "For what it's worth, I suspect you are probably right."

Anderson nodded a final time, then disappeared into the crowd and was gone.

Valentin sipped his drink and lit a Bliss cigarette from the silver case resting on the glass tabletop. A voice was whispering at the back of his mind that what he had just done, manipulated Anderson's simple, honest emotions by pretending to care about him, made him no better than either of his brothers, but he silenced it. There was too much at stake for such soft thinking, and too little time left. The best thing Anderson could do was get himself as far away as possible from any vampire involved in what was coming, and stay there.

*In any case,* he rationalised to himself, *Anderson said quite plainly that he does not want Dracula to rise, and his distaste for Valeri was all too clear. He and I are on the same side.*

Valentin let the effects of the Bliss-infused smoke roll through him, marvelling at the remarkable turn of events that had just taken place. After weeks of bloody, frustrating searching, the information that he had started to believe he would never acquire had fallen into his lap because, on some basic, elemental level, he and his brothers shared a common scent, a smell that had blazed like a beacon to

Anderson, and given rise to a fearful curiosity that had got the better of him.

*It's about time we made a breakthrough,* he thought, draining the last of his drink. *Blacklight has been fighting with everything it has just to stand still. Maybe this is the moment the tide turns.*

Valentin ground out his cigarette and looked at the mass of people flowing in every direction in front of his table, men and women laughing and stumbling through their small lives without the slightest idea of the Hell that awaited them if a conflict they could never know was taking place ended with the wrong side victorious. He envied them their lack of vision, their willingness to embrace the small and the mediocre, their ability to be satisfied inside their cages, their endless, unjustifiable optimism.

Their humanity.

*Château Dauncy,* he thought, getting to his feet and pulling his coat round him. *Near Bordeaux. That shouldn't be too hard to find.*

# 26

# INTO THE WILD

## TELEORMAN FOREST, NEAR BUCHAREST, ROMANIA

"Well," said Tim Albertsson, looking round at the members of
the DARKWOODS team and trying to force a smile, "I guess the
message is pretty clear."

Jamie Carpenter didn't respond; his gaze was locked on the wide
tree in front of them. Nailed to its trunk was a wolf, its stomach
sliced open and pinned back, exposing its insides. Maggots crawled
across its organs and gathered in a squirming pile where the animal's
blood had pooled at the base of the tree.

"Right," said Van Orel, his face pale. "Don't go any further."

"Subtle," said Engel, her voice little more than a whisper.

The six Operators were standing at the very edge of the Teleorman
Forest, at the perimeter of their target area. The helicopter that had
carried them the short distance from the *Schwartzhaus* had set down
in the same field where Grey had woken up barely three days earlier,
confused and hungry and missing forty-eight hours. The desecrated
tree stood at the northern edge of the field, to one side of a path
that led into the forest, its disembowelled warning strung up for all
to see.

Jamie stared at the wolf, his stomach slowly revolving, icy cold creeping through him.

*We're in the right place,* he thought. *Something knows we're here. And whatever it is, it doesn't want to be disturbed.*

To the east, the glow of electric lights lit the night sky a pale orange. Before them, the forest stretched out for what seemed like forever, towering rows of trees that quickly became indistinct from each other, such was the darkness between their trunks and the absence of light from above. To the west, a small village sat at the foot of a low hill; pinpricks of electric light shone from windows, and smoke drifted into the air from a handful of chimneys.

"What's the plan?" said Larissa.

Tim Albertsson tore his gaze away from the wolf and faced his squad. "All right," he said. "Larissa, I want aerial reconnaissance of the area. Satellite results have been inconclusive, so I want you to tell us what's in there, OK?"

"OK," said Larissa, her voice low and cold. "Sir."

Jamie looked at his girlfriend. There was a narrowness to her eyes and a set to her jaw that he recognised all too well; it meant that someone, usually him, was in trouble. But she wasn't looking at him; she was looking at their squad leader. Tim Albertsson returned her stare, the faintest hint of a smile on his tanned, handsome face, until Larissa made a noise that could easily have been either a grunt of laughter or a growl of anger, and shot up into the sky, disappearing instantly from view. Albertsson craned his neck in the direction she had disappeared, then smiled at the rest of them.

"Good," he said. "Jamie, Kristian, I want you in that village. Find out what they know about the forest, and don't let them say nothing. They live twenty metres away from it. Arkady, Greta, the three of us are going to set up camp. We're going in at first light tomorrow, so tonight is likely to be the last rest any of us gets for a while. Is that all clear?"

Jamie frowned. "How is Larissa going to come with us if we go in at dawn, sir?"

"Carefully," said Albertsson, and smiled. "There's going to be heavy shade beneath the trees and she'll be fine as long as her skin is covered. She went out during the day in Nevada plenty of times."

*Did she?* wondered Jamie.

"Did you work with her when she was there?" he asked.

Albertsson's smile widened. "Very closely," he said.

"Really?" said Jamie. "She's never mentioned you."

Albertsson shrugged. "That doesn't surprise me."

Jamie didn't respond; he stared at the American, his gaze steady.

"Any other questions, Lieutenant?" asked Albertsson. "You have orders in hand."

Jamie let him wait for a long second or two. "No, sir," he said, eventually, and turned to Van Orel. "You ready?"

The South African wore a slight frown on his face, but he nodded. "Let's do it," he said.

Jamie unclipped his MP7 and T-Bone, and set the weapons down on a tarpaulin sheet Engel had spread over the snow-covered ground. He flipped the visor of his helmet down, then checked his Glock as Van Orel followed his lead.

*I don't want to scare anyone,* he thought. *And I don't think there are going to be any vamps in this village. But I'm not going anywhere unarmed. Not tonight.*

Jamie marched off across the field with Van Orel beside him and his mind racing with suspicion. If anyone had asked him whether he trusted Larissa, he would have instantly told them that he did, and would have been telling the truth. But there were things that nagged at him, that caught in the back of his mind and stayed there.

The elephant in the room, the one they'd agreed to never discuss again, was the wild goose chase she had led him and Frankenstein on when his mother was being held captive by Alexandru Rusmanov: a desperate, headlong trip to Valhalla that Larissa had claimed would help them find Marie Carpenter, but which had in reality been solely about settling a personal score with Grey, the vampire who had turned her.

It had been selfish, and duplicitous, and could easily have put Jamie's mother in harm's way; that it hadn't had been due only to a combination of luck and deduction. Larissa had apologised for it, time and time again, and he had accepted her explanation; that she had been scared for her life and desperately trying to prove herself useful so she didn't receive a T-Bone stake to the heart. He knew it was an unending source of guilt for his girlfriend, and he had forgiven her, genuinely so, a long time ago.

Jamie had no doubt that she was still keeping things from him, despite the promise that the two of them and Kate and Matt had made to each other in the aftermath of the death of Alexandru and the loss of Dracula's ashes, when they had become so inundated by lies and secrets that it had started to feel as though they might drown. They had pulled themselves clear before it was too late, and sworn to tell each other the truth, no matter what.

*No more secrets,* he remembered. *That's what we told each other.*

But keeping their pact had proved harder than even Jamie, who had a cynical streak a mile wide, had expected; secrets piled up so quickly inside Blacklight, a complex web of things that you were allowed to tell certain people but not others, that it was completely impossible to maintain absolute transparency.

He had known for a while that Larissa hadn't told him everything about the time she had spent at NS9. There were clear holes in her account of the trip she had taken to Las Vegas, about her interaction with Chloe, the vampire girl she met beside a nightclub pool, and about what she had done in the desert; she had definitely not told him that she was able to go out during daylight if her skin was fully covered. But the one aspect of her time in Nevada he had been *sure* that his girlfriend had been straight with him about was her friends. Her face lit up whenever she talked about them, which was often, and he felt like he already knew Kara, Danny, Kelly and Aaron, despite never having met them.

But in the many hours Larissa had spent talking about NS9, she had never mentioned Tim Albertsson, not even once.

Jamie was certain of it.

An almost-full moon hung above his head as they reached the edge of the field, its silver light illuminating little, such was the darkness at the edge of the forest. Even with the night-vision filters of his helmet turned up to full, Jamie found the murkiness that surrounded him and Van Orel unsettling. But as they reached the low stone wall that enclosed the field, it was immediately clear that there were creatures that lived at the edges of the Teleorman Forest who appeared not to mind it.

Standing in the centre of the small, neat village were almost a dozen men and women, shotguns and axes in their hands, expressions of obvious distrust on their faces.

"I have to say," said Van Orel, over the comms connection that linked the two Operators, "this place is not going to win any awards for friendliness."

Jamie smiled behind his visor. "No kidding," he said. "Do you want to take the lead on this?"

"No thanks," said Van Orel. "I'm very happy to play backup."

"Kind of you," said Jamie, and winced as the South African laughed directly into his ear.

*All right then,* he thought. *Let's get this over with.*

He stepped up and over the wall, his boots thudding on to the ground on the other side. Van Orel followed him as Jamie raised his visor, felt a momentary surge of panic as he remembered his carelessness in the graveyard, and flipped it back down.

"Watch them closely," he said into his microphone. "Cameras, phones. We don't need to end up on the news."

"Got it," said Van Orel.

Jamie lifted the visor again and approached the villagers, trying to summon a friendly expression on to his face.

"Hello," he said. "Do any of you speak English?"

There was no response from the villagers; they merely stared at him, their breath clouding in the cold air, their weapons hanging at their sides. Then a man stepped forward, and regarded the two Operators with eyes that were little more than dark slits.

Jamie swallowed hard. The villager towered over him by at least half a metre; his muscle-clad torso was covered by a woollen coat that was stretched tight across his chest and biceps, above tree-trunk legs wearing blue jeans and a pair of heavy black boots. The dark eyes peered down at Jamie from either side of a flat, squashed nose that sat above a thick black beard covering the man's cheeks, chin and neck.

"I speak English," said the man, his voice a low rumble.

Jamie nodded. "Great," he said, his mouth dry. "My name is Jamie. I'm a Lieutenant in the British Army. I'd like to ask you some—"

"You are lying," growled the man. "You are not army."

Jamie frowned. "Excuse me?"

"You are vampire police," said the man. "You think that we are all backward out here, away from your cities, but we know what you are. You are the Blacklight."

"Christ," whispered Van Orel, whose visor and microphone were still in place. "So much for below the radar."

"How do you know that word?" asked Jamie.

"I read it, vampire policeman," said the villager. "Are you surprised that I can read?"

Jamie could feel his annoyance at the man's attitude threatening to boil into anger. He had said nothing to cause any offence, and the aggression seemed unwarranted.

"No," he said. "I'm not surprised you can read. What is your name?"

"Florin," said the man.

"And what's this village called?"

"You could not pronounce it," said Florin. Behind him, one of the other villagers laughed.

"Easy," said Van Orel, his voice low and urgent in Jamie's ear. "Take it easy, man."

"You're probably right," said Jamie, forcing a small smile. "I probably couldn't. Do you mind if I ask you a few questions?"

Florin shrugged.

"Thank you," said Jamie. "We're looking for someone who lives in the forest, someone who has lived there for a long time. Do you know who I'm talking about?"

Florin's eyes narrowed even further. "Nobody lives in the forest."

"Are you sure?" asked Jamie. "We have other information."

"I am sure, policeman," said Florin. "The forest is a place of death. A cursed place. What is in there does not live."

"So there is something?"

"You saw the wolf," said Florin. "It was not there yesterday."

"So it was put there for us?"

"I am not saying anything," said Florin. "You leave now."

"One more question," said Jamie.

Florin shook his head. "No more."

"Come on," said Van Orel.

Jamie knew he should follow his squad mate's advice, but was reluctant to do so; it galled him to slink away when he was told to, like a schoolboy sent out of the classroom by a teacher. But he also had no desire to aggravate the situation until it turned physical; there would be little to be gained from violence, on either side.

"Fine," he said. "We'll go. Thank you for your time."

Florin said nothing. Behind him, the rest of the villagers began to disperse, but the huge man didn't move; his eyes stayed fixed on Jamie's own. Jamie met the dark gaze for a long moment, then turned back towards the wall. Van Orel was already on the other side, waiting for him. Jamie was about to climb over the pale stone and join his squad mate when the villager's voice rumbled again, and he turned back.

"Do not go into the forest," said Florin. "If you value your lives, and your minds, you will not go in. It is old, and full of darkness. We stay at the edges, and we do not enter it unless we must. If you go in with your uniforms and your weapons, then I fear that all that awaits you will be sorrow. So leave, while you still can."

"You know what's in there, don't you?" said Jamie, his voice low. "Is it a vampire? A very old vampire?"

"It is death," said Florin. "Cold, and patient, and empty. We will not speak again." And with that, the huge villager turned and strode away without a backward glance.

Jamie watched until the man's towering shape disappeared into the gloom, then turned to face Van Orel. The South African had flipped up his visor and had an incredulous expression on his face.

"Mate," he said. "Where the hell are we? I mean, seriously."

Jamie smiled. "Not a clue," he said. "Let's head back. Maybe Larissa will find something."

"So you and Larissa," said Van Orel, as the two Operators fell back into step beside each other. "That's a thing, right?"

Jamie nodded. "It's a thing."

"That's cool," said Van Orel. "She seems awesome."

"She is."

Van Orel smiled. "She's sort of terrifying too. Or is that just me?"

"Trust me," Jamie said, and grinned widely. "It's not just you."

Floating in the darkness above the thick canopy of trees, Larissa tried to hold back the desperation that was threatening to crash through her like a tidal wave.

She loved hearing Jamie say she was awesome, and didn't mind him agreeing with Van Orel that she was terrifying; her vampire side, lurking as always in the back of her mind, took it as a great compliment. And she knew it was wrong to eavesdrop, to use her supernatural abilities to listen to people who didn't know they were being listened to, but as far as she was concerned, the current situation justified it.

She had floated above the camp for several minutes, listening to Tim talk about her to Jamie with a familiarity that made her blood run cold. She didn't know whether her boyfriend already suspected that something was going on, that there was a history he wasn't aware of, but it would only be a matter of time if Tim continued to be so deliberately suggestive. At some point, Jamie, whose temper could be dangerously short on occasions, would demand to know exactly what Tim was implying, and even though Larissa knew she had technically done nothing wrong – she had pushed Tim away when he kissed her in Mexico, had warned him not to try it again in Las Vegas – it was going to be hard convincing Jamie of that when she had carefully cut Tim out of every story she had told about her time in Nevada. He trusted her, she was sure of that, but she would not be able to blame him if he was unable to believe her.

*If* Tim kept talking, that was. If she couldn't find a way to shut him up.

When the American Special Operator had walked into the Ops Room of the *Schwartzhaus*, Larissa had almost laughed out loud at the bitter irony of the situation. She had – selfishly, she knew – turned down the mission to search for Adam precisely because she had wanted to avoid ever seeing Tim Albertsson again.

Now he was not only on the same operation as her *and* the boyfriend she had kept his existence a secret from, but was in charge of it.

*Worse*, she thought, as she floated in the cool air above the forest. *So much worse. So unfair.*

But even as the thought entered her head, she knew it was nothing more than self-pity. Tim Albertsson being chosen to lead DARKWOODS was unquestionably unlucky, but the situation she was now trying to find a way out of was entirely of her own making. If she had been honest with Jamie when she got back from Nevada, if she had told him about Tim and his feelings for her and explained straight away that nothing had happened, then things would be very different; they would be able to present a united front to Tim, both of them aware of his apparent determination to cause trouble, and ready to repel his comments and smiles and glances.

She wouldn't be feeling panic squirm in her stomach, panic that was bordering on despair.

She wouldn't be trying to work out, for the umpteenth time, exactly *why* she had decided not to tell Jamie about Tim.

She wouldn't be wracking her brains for ways to keep two members of a squad of six away from each other.

She wouldn't be worrying about herself instead of focusing on one of the most important missions in the history of Blacklight, the very thing she had chastised Jamie for after they landed in Germany.

Larissa took a deep breath and sank rapidly to the ground, arriving at the small area that would serve as their camp at exactly the same moment as Jamie and Van Orel. She had no intention of allowing Jamie and Tim to talk to each other without her there again, if she could possibly help it. The Special Operator looked up at the sudden return of half of his squad, and smiled.

"Larissa," he said. "Report."

"Nothing to tell," she replied. "I can't see anything through the trees. There are no breaks, no clearings, and the whole forest is thick with jasmine and nightshade, so I can't smell anything either. If he is in there, we're going to have to search for him on the ground."

"I thought as much," said Albertsson. "But good work anyway. How was the village, you two?"

"Friendly," said Van Orel.

"Really?"

"No," said Jamie. "Not in the slightest. One of the villagers spoke English, and he told us not to go into the forest. As far as they're concerned, the only thing in there is death."

"Nice," said Engel. "I can't wait."

"What about the wolf?" asked Petrov.

"Apparently it wasn't there yesterday," said Jamie.

"So it was put there for us," said Albertsson. "Whoever is in there knew we were coming."

"It looks that way, sir," said Jamie.

Larissa looked round at her squad mates. The night air was bitterly cold and the atmosphere in the camp reflected it; during the briefing and their journey to this dark corner of Romania, the squad had been loud and lively, full of the usual bragging and mutual sizing up that occurred whenever Operators who didn't know each other were thrown together. Now there was a palpable air of unease. Their location was every bit as remote as the briefing had described, and Larissa, who alone had seen the sprawling forest from above, seriously doubted whether it was going to be possible to call for help if something went wrong once they were inside it.

"All right," said Albertsson. "We all knew how this was going to go. So we're going to take it like any other operation, slowly and carefully, watching each other's backs every step of the way. Each of you is the best there is, which is why I asked for you. I have complete faith in you all. So get some rest now, and when the sun comes up we do our jobs. Arkady, Jamie, get the shelter up. Greta, Kristian, build us a fire. Larissa, come sit with me. I want a detailed report of what you saw from above."

Larissa's stomach churned. "I told you what I saw, sir," she said. "I think it's a better use of my time if I help get the camp up and running."

Tim Albertsson smiled. "By all means, Lieutenant. Do what you think is best."

Larissa stared at the Special Operator, fighting back both the heat in her eyes and the desire to wipe Tim's smile off his face with her fist. She nodded, almost imperceptibly, and turned away to find Jamie watching her steadily, his eyes narrowed.

*This is impossible*, she thought, as she floated over to her boyfriend and started unpacking the squad's gear. *This is absolutely impossible. What the hell am I going to do?*

# 27

# ON THE TRAIL

## SAN FRANCISCO, CALIFORNIA, USA

Matt Browning pressed his hands against the flat of the leather seat as the SUV turned the corner at Potrero Avenue and Twenty-First Street and hoped none of his fellow passengers noticed the deep breaths he was taking.

It didn't matter how many times in the last eight hours he had been reminded that his role was merely that of an observer; he was still wearing a Glock 17 in a shoulder holster beneath his hoodie in an unfamiliar city alongside men and women he didn't know, looking for a man nobody was certain had ever actually existed.

To Matt, whose life was rooted in the measurable and explainable, it was more than slightly unnerving.

The three NS9 Operators sitting in the back of the SUV with him were also in plain clothes. The sun was sinking steadily towards the horizon, beyond the wharfs and beaches and the great red span of the Golden Gate Bridge, but was still stubbornly bright, which meant there was no cover of darkness to hide the all-black uniforms the Operators were used to. It forced them to go as civilians, and Matt found it disconcerting – it was rare for him to *see* sunlight, let alone take part in a daytime operation.

Far less disconcerting had been his discovery that one of the Operators he would be accompanying to San Francisco was Danny Lawrence, whom Larissa had spoken about with great fondness. She had often said that he looked like a farmer, and Matt had been amused to see that she was exactly right; Danny was tall and broad, with a loud voice and an equally loud personality that had immediately put Matt at his ease. Danny had greeted him with a wide smile and immediately asked him how Larissa was; it had warmed Matt's heart to see the obvious affection in the American's face as he did so.

"She's well," he replied.

"Glad to hear it," said Danny. "Tell her we miss her."

Matt had promised he would, then followed Danny on to a helicopter that rumbled to a halt outside the wide hangar doors. They had been in the air for ninety seconds when Major Simmons demanded their attention.

The squad leader was a tall, broad man in his forties, whose demeanour could not have been more different to Danny's; his forehead was creased into a permanent frown and a thick black moustache bristled above a mouth which appeared to deal only in expletive-splattered growls. He was apparently notorious within NS9 for being a hard, borderline vicious taskmaster, but he was also held in enormous esteem; the Operational success rating of squads under his command was second to none, and his record was full of incidents of exceptional, almost foolhardy bravery.

"Listen up," he said. "This is GARDEN OF EDEN. You know where we're going and you know why. What you may *not* know is that Intelligence has actually pulled its thumb out of its ass and come up with something useful for a change. Andrews?"

Simmons turned to the Operator sitting beside him, a woman in her twenties named Abby Andrews. She regarded the Major with a look of obvious distaste, then faced the rest of the squad and cleared her throat.

"The intelligence that Major Simmons is referring to," she said, "suggests that our Operational target, the allegedly cured vampire known as Adam, was born in Bakersfield, California, in either 1940 or 1941. There were one thousand, two hundred and thirty-four boys born in Bakersfield County in those two years, including twenty-seven named Adam. Working on the assumption that Adam is not the target's real name, we assessed the list in its entirety and found registered death certificates for seven hundred and twenty-one of the men on the list, leaving a potential pool of five hundred and thirteen. This was cross-referenced against marriage records, as the intelligence provided to my division claimed that the target married a woman named Emily, born at a similar time somewhere in the Midwest. This search returned two possible results, one of which was flagged as promising. John Allen Bell, born February 3rd 1940 in Bakersfield, California, married Emily Sarah Anderson, born September 9th 1941 in Wichita, Kansas, in Portland, Oregon on April 23rd 1965.

"We checked property records and found a series of leases in San Francisco throughout the 1970s and 80s, along with a record from the mid-nineteenth century that showed the purchase of a tract of land near Caliente, California, by an Alfred Bell, John Bell's great-grandfather. This land matches the coordinates of the cabin where our source claims to have met with the target, and where three NS9 Operators were killed last month. Finally, we found an agreement dated 21st March 1963 for the purchase of 3338

Twenty-First Street in San Francisco, California, in the name of Emily Bell. The property remains in her name, and is now the primary geographical target of this operation."

For a long moment, there was silence. It was Helen Landsman, the fifth member of the squad, who eventually broke it.

"So if Adam was ever actually real," she said, slowly, "and you've managed to find him, you've got the right Emily, and for some reason he's gone back to a house she bought some fifty years ago, then this op should be plain sailing."

"I've told you what I know," said Andrews. "I can hold your hand when we get there, if you like?"

Landsman smiled. "That won't be necessary. But thanks."

"Any time," said Andrews.

"All right, enough," said Major Simmons. "We've got a location and a target, and that'll do for now. Now shut up, all of you. I don't want to hear another word until we're on the ground."

"Fifteen blocks," said Major Simmons. "Get your shit together."

Danny looked round at Matt and rolled his eyes. Matt did his best not to laugh; he did not think Simmons would appreciate it in the slightest.

"So Larissa and Jamie," said Danny, his voice low. "It's a real thing, right?"

"Really?" whispered Matt. "You want to talk about this now?"

"Why not?" said Danny. "Fifteen blocks might take an hour in this city."

"Yes," Matt said. "It's a real thing. Despite what Tim Albertsson might have thought."

Danny frowned. "You know about all that? What did Larissa say?"

"Nothing," said Matt. "She's never mentioned him. Kara told me, when I got here this morning."

"Jesus," said Danny, and smiled. "That must have been quite a welcome."

"It was. Not really what I was expecting."

"Tim was such a dick about her," said Danny. "We tried to get him to see sense, did Kara tell you that?"

"She did," replied Matt. "It didn't sound like he wanted to hear it."

Danny shook his head. "He really didn't. And so he freaked her out and we all got screwed because of it."

"I heard."

"He's a friend of yours, right?" said Danny. "Jamie Carpenter?"

Matt considered this for a moment, long enough for the beginnings of a frown to emerge on Danny's face. On one hand, he regarded Jamie as his best friend, the best he'd ever had; they had been through so much together, a lifetime's worth of victories and defeats in barely more than six months. On the other, he wondered how much he really knew Jamie, if at all.

He had repeatedly tried to get hold of his best friend the previous day, had sent him messages and knocked several times on the door to his quarters, but to no avail. He had wanted to tell him about the mission he was now on, but more than that, he had wanted to know if his friend was all right; there had clearly been something going on with him, and Matt had wanted to see whether there was any way he could help. He had got nothing back, though; not so much as a message saying that Jamie was fine.

"Matt?" asked Danny, a small smile on his face. "It wasn't meant to be a trick question."

"Sorry," said Matt. "Supersonic jet lag. Not a lot of fun. Yes, Jamie's a good friend of mine."

Danny nodded. "A descendant of the founders," he said. "Pretty cool."

"You'd never know it," said Matt. "He's proud of what his family did, but he doesn't think it makes him special, or anything like that. And even if he did, Larissa and Kate would slap it out of him."

Danny laughed. "I can believe that of Larissa," he said. "Really, really easily. Kate's the girl who helped run your ISAT, right? I heard that was rough."

Matt shook his head. "You have no idea," he said. "One of our own Operators tried to kill her over it, and I don't think the rest of them have forgiven her yet."

"That's bullshit," said Danny. "It needed doing. It *clearly* needed doing, given what happened."

"People didn't like having their loyalty questioned," said Matt. "Even the ones with nothing to hide."

Danny nodded. "We've still got it all to look forward to," he said. "Our ISAT starts up in three days. I hope the team doesn't get the same treatment your friend did."

"What was that, Lawrence?" shouted Major Simmons.

"ISAT, sir," said Danny.

"What the hell is ISAT?" demanded the squad leader.

"Internal Security Assessment Team," said Danny. "A friend of mine in Security told me they're starting up at the end of the week. Background checks, polygraphs for every serving member of the Department. It's a rat hunt, sir."

"Nobody tells me a damn thing around here," growled Simmons.

"Can't be too careful, sir," said Danny. "Right?"

There was no response.

\* \* \*

Twenty minutes later the Operational Squad climbed out of the SUV and stretched their arms and shoulders. Matt watched them, trying to suppress a smile; they were doing their best to look inconspicuous, in their T-shirts and jeans and trainers, but he could still see pistol grips sticking out above belts and tasers sitting in pockets. He had no doubt the illusion would be good enough, however; he had come to understand that there was a general reluctance among the wider populace to look for the abnormal or the out of place, for anything that might disrupt the tiny corner of the world they had carved out for themselves.

*They don't see because they don't want to,* he thought. *Because it's easier not to. That's why we were able to stay a secret for so long, to lie to them about the vamps for so many years. Because they didn't want to know.*

Matt stretched his neck, closing his eyes as the muscles tensed then relaxed. When he opened them again, Major Simmons was pointing at him. "You stay in the car," he said.

Matt frowned. "Sir?"

"Simple enough concept," said Simmons. "We find the target, you stay here and wait for us to bring him back."

"Those aren't my orders, sir," said Matt.

"They are now," said Simmons. "I just gave them to you."

"I'm supposed to accompany you in the search for Adam, sir."

"And I'm telling you that isn't an option," said Simmons, his face colouring as his temper began to fail him. "You're not an Operator, and I don't need you getting under everyone's feet. Am I making myself clear?"

"Yes, sir," said Matt, trying not to let the nerves fluttering in his stomach appear in his voice. "So perhaps *I'm* not being clear. The Interim Director of Blacklight ordered me to accompany you on this operation as a representative of the Lazarus Project, at the request of General Allen, and I don't believe that what he intended was for me to wait in the car. Maybe you should call him and get clarification?"

Simmons stared at him for a long moment, then grunted and turned back to Landsman, who was looking at Matt with a mixture of surprise and admiration on her face. He could feel his heart pounding in his chest, the horrible weight of the pistol under his armpit, the tremble in his legs that he prayed wasn't visible; he forced himself to move, to turn away from his squad mates and take a look at where they were.

The block of Twenty-First Street they were standing on rose at a steep angle from the east and plateaued as it approached Dolores Street to the west. It was a clearly affluent residential road, the homes tall and narrow with garages beneath them and sets of steps that led up to their front doors. Trees grew out of the pavements and, apart from the distant, steady hum of car engines, the street was quiet. Their black SUV pulled away, heading slowly down the hill as Major Simmons ordered the squad to gather round him. Matt watched the car make a left at the end of the block, feeling a strange sense of loss as it disappeared from view, then did as he was told.

"Operators," said Simmons, his voice low, his icy gaze momentarily settling on Matt. "This is our primary target. 3338 Twenty-First Street. I don't think anyone here is dumb enough to think that we're going to knock on the door and have Adam come quietly, but this is where we start. Lawrence, you're going to the front door. Andrews, I want you in the yard behind the house in case he runs. Landsman, take position at the eastern end of the block, I'll take the west. Browning, you stay here and watch the street. Move out."

Simmons jogged away up the hill, as Landsman headed down towards the junction with Guerrero. Andrews crossed the street and disappeared down the narrow gap between 3338 and its neighbour, leaving Matt and Danny alone on the pavement. Danny nodded, flashed a brief smile in his direction, then walked across the road towards the target location as though he didn't have a care in the world, just a man out for a stroll in the late afternoon sun.

Matt walked down the block and leant against the trunk of an acacia tree that had sprouted up through a square of cracked paving slabs. From the cool of the shade, he watched as Danny climbed the steps and knocked lightly on the front door of the narrow house; he heard the series of thuds clearly through the flesh-coloured speaker nestling in his ear. Taped to his left wrist was a tiny microphone, through which he could communicate with the rest of the squad, although the thought of actually speaking into it made him feel faintly ridiculous, like a Secret Service agent in a film.

As predicted, there was no response to Danny's knock.

"Try again," said Major Simmons, his voice low and deep in Matt's ear.

From across the street, he saw Danny nod, then knock on the door a second time, harder.

Again, nothing happened.

There was a long, pregnant pause, until Simmons spoke again. "Crack it."

"Yes, sir," murmured Danny, and slipped something short and narrow out of one of his pockets. He leant against the door, shielding what he was doing from anyone who might have been watching, then turned the door handle and slipped inside the house. Matt watched, a shiver of excitement rushing up his spine.

"House is clear," said Danny, in a low voice. "Downstairs is empty, but there's food in the kitchen. There's a suitcase and clothes in the upstairs bedroom. Nothing else sir."

"Anything with a name on it?" asked Simmons.

"Not yet," said Danny. "Let me finish my sweep."

Matt's heart sank. The food implied that *someone* was living in the house, and the suitcase of clothes was encouraging; a man on the run would presumably want to be ready to leave at a moment's notice, and would likely not have wasted time on home comforts. But without confirmation that they had the right person, and with no new information to go on, all they would be able to do would be stake out the house and wait for whoever lived there to return.

Movement caught the corner of Matt's eye, and he looked up. A woman in her late twenties was emerging from 3340, navigating a pushchair through the door before turning round and pulling it carefully down the steep steps that led to the pavement.

Matt looked back at the house that was their target location. There was no sign of Danny, the other members of the squad, or anybody else. He took a deep breath and stepped out of the shade of the acacia. As he crossed the road, he summoned up his friendliest, most non-threatening smile, and met the woman as she reached the bottom of the steps.

"Hello," he said. "Can I ask you a question?"

The woman spun round, her eyes widening with surprise, then narrowing with immediate distrust. "What do you want?" she asked, manoeuvring herself between him and the pushchair. "I have to be somewhere in five minutes. My friend is expecting me."

*Jesus,* thought Matt. *She's scared of me. Is this what happens when you have kids? Are you just scared of everyone?*

"I'm sorry," he said. "I don't mean to bother you, and it won't take a minute. I just wanted to ask you about your neighbour. The man who lives in 3338?"

The woman frowned. "You mean Johnny?"

*John Bell*, thought Matt. *Bingo.*

"That's him," he said.

"Are you a cop? What's he done?"

"No," said Matt, raising his hands in what he hoped was a placatory gesture. "Nobody's in any trouble. I just need to talk to him. Do you know where he is?"

"Why would I?" asked the woman. "I stay out of other people's business."

"Of course," said Matt. "Does he have a job that you know about? Or any friends he might have mentioned?"

The woman's eyes narrowed even further. "Are you sure you're not a cop?"

"I'm not a cop."

The woman looked him in the eye for a long moment. "I've only talked to him a couple of times," she said. "I said hello when he moved in, and then we walked to the store together last week. He told me he works at SafetyNet, on Balboa."

"What's SafetyNet?" asked Matt.

"It's a charity," said the woman. "A suicide helpline. I have to go."

She walked rapidly away down Twenty-First Street, casting suspicious glances back over her shoulder every few seconds until she turned on to Guerrero and out of sight.

"Browning?" asked Major Simmons. "Are you talking to someone?"

Matt raised his wrist to his mouth. "I was, sir," he replied. "A neighbour. She told me someone called Johnny lives at 3338 and works at a charity called SafetyNet."

"That tallies, sir," said Andrews. "Our source claims that Adam's wife killed herself. Apparently, she couldn't handle the idea of living forever."

"Shit," said Simmons. "All Operators, regroup on Browning's

position. Andrews, get on the line to Dreamland and get me an address for this SafetyNet. We're moving."

Matt put his hands back in his pockets and watched as Danny exited 3338 and jogged over to him, a smile on his face.

"Good work," he said, clapping him hard on the shoulder. "If you'd stayed in the car, we'd have missed her. Now we've got a lead."

Matt grinned. He knew that being the lone member of the squad still on the street when the woman emerged from 3340 had been nothing more than luck, but he was proud of himself for having stood up to Major Simmons, and for forcing himself to talk to her. Such action did not come naturally to him; under normal circumstances, talking to strangers filled him with an unease that bordered on panic.

Landsman and Simmons converged on Matt and Danny at the same moment, having made their way back from the ends of the block. Simmons nodded brusquely in Matt's direction, a gesture he was sure qualified as high praise from the Major, as Andrews emerged from the space between the houses and walked quickly across the road to join them.

"6350 Balboa," she said. "Ten minutes, maybe fifteen."

"Is he there?" asked Simmons.

Andrews shook her head. "I don't know," she said. "Intelligence is on it, sir."

"Of course they are," said Simmons. "Get the car, Lawrence. Let's go find out for ourselves."

# 28

# DEEP COVER, PART ONE

## KOLA PENINSULA, RUSSIA

The man no longer knew how long he'd been walking.

He believed it could still be measured in hours, but he was far from sure; it could have been days, or even weeks. The cold made clear thinking impossible, made thoughts drift apart and float away, as insubstantial as smoke, and it took all his remaining strength to focus on the two things that still mattered: his destination, and a deep, primal urge to keep moving.

He raised a foot clad in a heavy waterproof boot, dragging it free of snow that reached almost to his waist, pushed it forward with all his strength, and watched it disappear back into the white powder. Inside a huge sealskin coat, sweat poured down his body, pooling at the crooks of his elbows and the small of his back. His breath came in shallow rasps behind the mask and goggles that were keeping frostbite from the skin of his face.

The man took another step, then another, and another, then flopped down into the snow on his back, fighting to catch his breath; air billowed from his mouth and rose in a cloud so thick it seemed almost solid.

Four steps. Three metres closer.

With a gloved hand, he pushed back the sleeve of his jacket, exposing a GPS locator fastened round his wrist. He checked the red numbers that glowed on its screen for the hundredth time, and let them settle over him as he gazed up into a beautiful, darkening purple sky.

*One point one five miles north-east,* he told himself. *Another mile. Just one more mile.*

The man had made his way to Russia by a long, circuitous route, doubling back on himself time and again even as his brain screamed at him to hurry, to get moving. In Munich, he had destroyed everything he owned, burning his clothes and documents in a brazier that he paid a homeless man twenty euros for permission to use, having retrieved a completely new identity from a locker in the train station, a locker he had filled five years earlier, during a supposed holiday to Bavaria.

Getting to Munich had not been difficult; a combination of regional French trains, boarded at stations that had no CCTV cameras, and thumbed lifts from the endless stream of cars and lorries trundling north. Crossing the Channel had been easily the most dangerous part of his journey so far; he knew that he was being hunted, that the clandestine machinery of the British Intelligence Services had rumbled into life in pursuit of him, and he knew from long experience that the first thing to happen would be the circulation of his photograph, name and description to every airport and port in the country.

He had lain low in Dover for several weeks, in a safe house he had procured for exactly this eventuality, waiting for the worst of the heat to die down. When he could wait no longer, he had boarded a ferry for Calais with a fake passport in one pocket and a cyanide pill in the other. His orders were absolutely clear on this point: *Do not, under any circumstances, allow yourself to be taken alive.*

From Munich, he had made his way north, travelling at night, avoiding contact with anyone other than the kindly souls who pulled over to the side of the road and offered to take him closer to his destination. He skirted round the edge of the Czech Republic, even though it was a longer route. He had no desire to cross more national borders than was absolutely necessary; they represented by far the likeliest point of capture, even the sleepy backwoods crossings of eastern Europe. He crossed into Poland at Görlitz in the late afternoon, trying not to visibly hold his breath as his passport was scrutinised. It was fine work, the best that money could buy, but it was not flawless, as no forged document ever is.

The border guard had examined the passport, held on to it for a moment that seemed to last forever, then grunted and handed it back.

From Wrocław, the man caught a dilapidated but surprisingly comfortable train north-east into Belarus, sleeping in short bursts with the straps of his bag wound tightly round his wrist and ankle to deter potential thieves. In Orsha, he bought gloves, goggles, as much thermal clothing as he could wear, the sealskin coat, and found a farmer who agreed to take him to the Russian border, but would go no further. The man didn't try to persuade him; instead, he offered the farmer two hundred euros for the shotgun that was lying in the back seat of his truck, a deal to which he readily agreed.

A mile from the edge of Belarus, the man slung the gun over his shoulder and hiked east into the deep forest.

The trees were tall and packed tightly together, the darkness between them absolute. There was no way for the man to see whether anyone was pursuing him, so he pressed ahead, his breath hot behind the mask, the shotgun resting in his shivering hands. For long, silent hours, he hiked through falling snow, until, as dawn began to break in front of him, he crossed the border into Russia.

Frozen to the bone, barely able to keep putting one foot in front of the other, the man had stumbled on to a farm as the sun climbed overhead, and paid the hard, taciturn woman who owned it to drive him into Smolensk. From there he caught a sleeper train to St Petersburg and boarded a second train north.

The train was full of Russian soldiers and sailors, carrying order slips in their gloved hands as they headed for postings at Murmansk and Polyarny. They eyed the man with outright suspicion, but none went so far as to ask him what his business was in the Arctic heartland of the Russian military. The man kept his gaze trained out of the window, watching snow slowly obliterate the landscape, until ice coated the glass and he could see nothing but his own fractured reflection.

*One more mile,* he told himself. *One step at a time. Get up.*

The man allowed himself ten seconds' more rest, then forced himself back to his feet. The warehouse in Orsha had sold snowshoes, and he could no longer remember why he had decided not to buy a pair; they were bulky, and unwieldy to carry, but would have been invaluable in the situation he now found himself. Without them, each step was a Herculean challenge, a draining, energy-sapping nightmare. For the hundredth time, he cursed his own stupidity, hauled a foot out of the deep, sucking snow, and shoved it forward.

Time passed.

He had no sense of it any more; the darkness of the polar winter was seemingly infinite, the landscape unchanging. The red numbers on his GPS, ticking down with agonising slowness, were the only evidence that he was making progress, that his lurching, laboured steps were carrying him towards his destination.

*Nine hundred and seventy-one metres.*

*Nine hundred and sixty-seven metres.*

*Nine hundred and fifty-five metres.*

He was close now; he could hear the thunder as ice-breakers made their way up the Murmansk Fjord in the distance, could smell the churning water on the air. He forced himself not to run, not to expend what little energy he had left in a burst that would leave him panting and breathless and still short of his destination. Instead, he focused on the slow metronomic motion of his steps: one foot, then the other, then the other.

An unknowable amount of time later, in which the man's sense of himself had begun to disappear along with his perception of time, and he had become nothing more than pain and sweat and harsh, loud breath, he saw something ahead of him. He was part snow-blind, part delirious with desire for rest, and at first he assumed that it was nothing more than a cruel trick played by his reeling mind. But as he trudged forward, he began to believe, despite himself, that it was real; something regular and even, glimpsed through the tightly packed tree trunks and the great untouched ridges and valleys of snow.

Something with straight lines and edges.

*A fence,* he thought. *It's a fence. I'm almost there.*

The man pressed forward, his eyes fixed on the interlocking diamonds of wire that sparkled in the light of the moon that had risen overhead, bright and almost full. The fence was high, topped with snow-heavy coils of razor wire, and the man knew that he was now almost certainly being watched from some distant bunker; he was well inside the perimeter that would be monitored by the men and women who populated his destination. It didn't matter, though; he *wanted* them to see him.

He wanted them to know he was coming.

The man accelerated; he knew it was foolish, but he simply could not stop himself. What lay beyond the fence was the reason he had travelled so far, and it was finally in sight. The snow flew up around his churning legs as he panted behind his mask, his lungs working overtime, his muscles screaming at him, but his heart was suddenly full of joy.

*I made it,* he thought. *I really made it. I'm home.*

A low growl rumbled through the freezing air, vibrating the man's bones and stopping him dead in his tracks. His nerves, dulled for so long by cold and monotony, were suddenly humming, as adrenaline coursed through his system. The man forced himself still, fighting back the chemical urge to run, and listened to the darkness of the forest.

Somewhere to his left, a branch snapped. Then the growl came again, longer and louder, and fear gripped at the man's heart.

*Not now. Not when I'm so close. Please not now.*

He pulled his torch from his pocket and flicked it on. The beam illuminated almost nothing, a triangle perhaps three metres long and two metres wide. Beyond it, darkness crowded in, thick and malevolent. He risked a look at the fence; it had been so close, almost within reach, but now the distance between him and it seemed like miles. The man turned slowly, trying to keep the torch beam steady, searching for the source of the growl, wishing for ignorance, wishing he didn't know what was making it.

He swung the torch, shuffling his feet round in the knee-deep snow, then stopped. In front of him, reflecting the light of his torch, was a pair of huge brown eyes. The man swallowed, his mouth dry, his limbs trembling with fear.

As he swung the shotgun slowly off his shoulder, a dark section of the forest beyond the eyes moved.

# 29

# EVERYTHING IS A CHOICE

## SAN FRANCISCO, CALIFORNIA, USA

For the second time in less than an hour, Matt Browning found himself standing outside a building on his own.

SafetyNet was based inside a wide office building made of steel and glass; the charity's logo was one of half a dozen designs attached to the wall beside the front door on small brass plates. Matt was standing in the parking lot beside it, having been stationed there with orders to make sure that nobody fitting their target's description emerged. Given that the description comprised of little more than *male, in his forties, medium height with a deep tan*, Matt had already resolved to stop and question any man that came through the front door.

Major Simmons had given the squad their orders as they pulled up outside the building, having navigated their way through the gridlocked maze of one-way streets that comprised the centre of San Francisco. Simmons himself would wait in the lobby, Andrews would position herself at the back of the building, and Lawrence and Landsman would go up to the offices of SafetyNet to look for Adam, or John Bell, as it appeared he was once again going by. Nobody was to draw a weapon unless it was absolutely necessary, or to identify themselves in any way, to anyone. The ideal scenario was that they would find John Bell sitting behind a desk, from where he would come quietly, with the minimum of fuss. Matt doubted that any member of the squad genuinely believed it would be so straightforward, but he saw no harm in hoping.

*Everything doesn't always have to go wrong*, he thought. *Surely?*

Through his earpiece, he heard Danny Lawrence's voice as he introduced himself to someone who presumably worked for SafetyNet.

"I'm looking for an employee of yours," said Danny. "John Bell?"

"You a cop?" asked a male voice. "What's he done?"

Matt smiled to himself in the parking lot; it seemed as though everyone in San Francisco automatically assumed the worst when questioned.

"Nothing," said Danny, his voice light and friendly. "I have a message for him, that's all. It needs to be delivered in person."

"Johnny's working," said the man, and Matt felt tension surge into his stomach. "He's taking calls. I'm not going to interrupt him if he's talking to someone."

"Of course not," said Danny. "We'll wait here, and you can send him out when he's finished with his call."

"I suppose so," said the man. He sounded unconvinced, but Matt was sure he would do as Danny said; the young Operator was relentlessly charming, and had a natural, easy-going authority about him. His mind raced with the confirmation that John Bell was not only real, but was sitting inside the building in front of him.

"Great," said Danny. "We'll be here."

"All right," said the man.

A few seconds later Danny spoke into his microphone. "Everyone catch all that?"

"Two minutes, Lawrence," growled Simmons. "If he's not standing in front of you in two minutes, you go in there and drag him out. Is that clear?"

"Yes, sir," said Danny.

Matt shifted his weight from one foot to the other, back and forth, excitement bubbling through him. He was suddenly aware that the moment when he would need to do his job was imminent; if Danny and Landsman brought Adam out, they would head directly to the laboratory on the University of San Francisco campus that had been commandeered, where Matt would be expected to step to the fore.

He would need to take blood, label up the samples to be sent back to Nevada and England, and complete a provisional DNA analysis as quickly as possible. His excitement at the thought of stepping back into a world he understood was tempered by the prospect that he had been trying to ignore ever since he boarded the *Mina II*: that there would be nothing of any use in Adam's blood, that the cure would have left no genetic trace for Lazarus to work from. Matt didn't want to believe it, but he had to allow for the possibility; if he didn't, the potential for disappointment was enormous.

The office building sat silently in front of him. Matt stared at it, wondering why nothing was happening; a minute had to have passed already, if not the two that Simmons had given as a deadline.

*Come on*, he thought. *He's just one man. How hard can this be?*

Then he remembered the photos he had looked through on the *Mina II* as it soared towards Nevada, high-resolution images taken in the aftermath of NS9's ill-fated visit to Adam's former cabin.

An enormous pillar of grey-black smoke rising from the orange floor of the Californian desert.

The crater where the cabin had stood, where two NS9 Operators had been almost completely atomised.

John Brady dead on a stretcher, his legs gone below the knees.

Matt raised his eyes to the third floor of the office building, looking for any sign of movement through the tall glass windows. The excitement that had briefly filled him was gone, replaced with a deep sense of unease.

*Definitely more than two minutes. Way more. What's going on in there?*

His attention was so focused on the third floor that he almost didn't notice the dark silhouette of a man appear on the roof of the building, five storeys above the parking lot. Matt craned his neck, wondering for a moment whether his eyes were playing tricks on him in the fading light of the early evening, and watched as the figure ran towards the edge of the roof and leapt off it. He sailed through the space between the building and its neighbour and landed on the lower roof with a rattling thud and a shout of pain loud enough that Matt heard it clearly, even from street level.

The sound broke his paralysis. He raised his wrist to his mouth and shouted into his microphone.

"There's someone on the roof!" he yelled. "He jumped to the next building."

A burst of static howled through his head, and he squeezed his eyes shut against the pain.

"Come in," he said. "Come in, anyone, come in."

There was a hissing crackle, then Major Simmons' voice came through, sounding as distant as a radio transmission from the moon.

"Browning? Come in?"

"On the roof, sir," Matt shouted. "Bell's on the roof."

A second burst of static filled his ears, followed by the Major's garbled voice.

"Give... pursue... reinforcements."

Matt bellowed with frustration. There was no sign of anyone in the lobby, where Major Simmons should have been, no sign of movement anywhere in the building. Through his earpiece he heard what sounded like running footsteps, and looked up at the roof again. The figure had reached the edge of the next building; as Matt watched, he hurled himself on to the adjoining roof and disappeared. From somewhere high above, he heard the thump of a closing door.

*Do something. Make a decision, for God's sake. Do something.*

Matt swore loudly, then took off along Balboa as fast as his legs would carry him. His hair rippled back from his face as his feet pounded the pavement, his arms pumping up and down. He didn't risk so much as a look over his shoulder to see whether any of his squad mates had appeared; his attention was focused entirely on the building in front of him. It was a red-brick cube, tall and wide, with an unmarked pair of double doors standing at the back of a small parking lot. Matt raced across the tarmac and reached for the handle. As his fingers touched the smooth metal, the door burst open with a loud bang and slammed into his face.

The impact broke his nose, sending a firework display of red and white light across his vision. His legs gave way beneath him and he crumpled to the ground, his mouth open, pain thundering through his head. He hit the tarmac on his back; blood poured down his throat, hot and metallic, as a groan emerged involuntarily from his mouth. Something passed above him, followed by the sound of running footsteps. The noise clattered into his skull, slicing through the thick fog of pain, and he forced himself to sit up, blood spilling from his nose and splattering on to the tarmac, startlingly red.

Matt raised his head and saw a man sprinting across Balboa, heading for Third Avenue. He staggered in the same direction until he reached the pavement, and looked down the street towards SafetyNet, hoping to see Danny and the others coming to his aid.

There was no sign of them.

"Hey, man."

Matt spun round, his heart pounding, and found himself looking into the wide-eyed, earnest face of a teenager clutching a skateboard under his arm.

"Man, are you all right?" he asked. "You're, like, covered in blood, dude."

Matt frowned, then shoved past the kid without answering and broke into a shambling run. Behind him the teenager shouted, 'Hey!', then muttered 'asshole' under his breath. Matt ignored him; he urged his shaking legs forward, and was rewarded as he turned the corner on to Third Avenue.

The running man was still in sight, barely a block ahead.

Matt took a deep breath and ran down the street, gritting his teeth against the pain that radiated from his broken nose every time his feet thudded on to the pavement.

The man had reached Anza and was hopping impatiently from one foot to the other, waiting to cross the road; a long orange and white bus was slowly making its way across the junction with Third. Matt ran down the sloping street, grateful for the contours that made San Francisco so distinctive. He was closing on the man, could see brown hair reaching down to the collar of a yellow T-shirt, jeans that were fluttering above battered Converse. He was barely ten metres away when the man darted out behind the bus and sprinted across the road, sparking a furious cacophony of car horns and shouts of angry surprise.

Matt redoubled his efforts. He had never been any good at sport, preferring to spend his time curled up with a book or leaning over a keyboard, but he had regrettably extensive experience of running away from people; as a result, he was light on his feet, and possessed unexpected reserves of stamina.

*This is weird,* he thought, as he neared the wide lanes of Anza. *I've never been the one doing the chasing before.*

The thought made him grin, despite the hot ball in his chest that was threatening to turn into a stitch. He glanced to his left as he approached the road and saw that it was empty. The far lanes, the ones running west, were hidden by the bus that had now stopped; he was just going to have to hope for the best.

Matt belted out into the road without slowing and looked to his right as he passed the wide rear of the bus. Anything coming at speed was going to hit him; there would simply be no avoiding it.

The road was clear.

At the junction of Second Avenue, a block to the east, Matt saw lines of traffic held on a red light and breathed a sigh of relief. Then he refocused his attention on his target; the man was running for his life towards the wide, bustling expanse of Geary, a block to the north.

*Not going to catch him,* thought Matt. *He's too fast.*

He tried to dismiss the thought as a relic of the old version of Matt Browning, the version who had only ever doubted himself, had always believed that he would fail, but realised it wasn't his subconscious trying to sabotage him.

It was simple fact.

The man was sprinting with everything he had, his feet flying across the pavement. And slowly but surely, the gap between them was widening.

*If he gets across Geary, I'm going to lose him.*

Matt reached deep into his reserves of strength and demanded everything his tiring legs had left. They responded; the gap began to close, but not fast enough, nowhere near fast enough, and he realised with sudden clarity what he was going to have to do. He reached beneath his arm and drew the Glock that he had tried to refuse in the Dreamland hangar, insisting that he wouldn't need it.

He pushed himself for ten more steps, then skidded to a halt and raised the gun. What he was about to do was madness, he knew; he was a mediocre shot at the best of times, when his chest wasn't heaving and his legs didn't feel like jelly. But if he was going to do it, it had to be now; the block was deserted, apart from himself and the running man.

Geary, on the other hand, would not be, and Matt knew he could not discharge a firearm on a busy San Francisco street, no matter how urgent the operation. He would probably not get into trouble for doing so, such was the air of panic that was permeating the supernatural Departments, but he would simply not be able to live with himself if he hit some innocent bystander.

If he was going to shoot, he had to shoot now.

The man was twenty metres from the junction as Matt sighted down the pistol's barrel and squeezed the trigger. He was aiming for the legs, hoping to bring him down without killing him, but as the gun bucked in his hand and the deafening metallic bang removed the sound from his ears and replaced it with a high, screaming whine, he saw that he had missed. A cloud of dust burst from the wall of a building five metres behind the target. Matt swore and aimed again. He took a deep breath, held it, then pulled the trigger a second time.

An explosion of concrete burst up behind the man's sprinting feet; his legs twisted, collided with each other, and sent him into the air in a graceless spiral of flailing limbs. He crashed to the ground with a thud, and began to crawl.

Matt wasted no time on pity; he ran down the street, the Glock swinging in his hand. As he closed the distance, the man lurched to his feet and turned towards him. His face was incredibly pale, his eyes wide and staring, his mouth tight with pain as blood poured from a dozen small holes in his legs. Matt stopped and levelled his pistol.

"Don't move," he said.

The man took half an unsteady step backwards.

"I said don't move," said Matt. "I'm not here to hurt you. But I need you to stay where you are."

"You're with them," said the man.

Matt nodded. "I'm with them," he said. "And you're John Bell. Or should I call you Adam?"

The man's face wrinkled with disgust. "Don't call me that," he said. "My name is John."

*Thank God,* thought Matt.

"Listen to me, John," he said. "I know what happened to you, and I'm sorry. You can believe me or not, but I really am. And I'm not here to make you go through that again, I promise. I'm here because you might be able to save millions of lives."

"I can't," said John Bell. "I can't do anything."

He took another step backwards, on to the corner of Third and Geary.

"Please stop moving," said Matt, taking two quick steps forward, the Glock trembling in his hands. "I really don't want to shoot you."

"I can't," repeated John Bell. "I can't go back there. Do you understand that?"

"I do," said Matt. "Honestly, I do. This isn't about that, you have my word on it. No one is going to hurt you again. I know you talked to someone in the desert, someone who was looking for answers. You want to help, John, I know you do. That's what working at SafetyNet is, right? A way for you to make amends?"

Bell's face crumpled, as tears brimmed in his eyes.

"I thought I could do something," he said. "I thought that maybe I could help. That I could be free. But I can't, can I?"

"You can," said Matt, his voice almost a shout of desperation. "Yes you can, John. I need to examine you and take some of your blood. That's all, I swear. After that, you can come back here, back to work, back to your life. I promise you."

Bell glanced over his shoulder, then produced a heartbreakingly gentle smile. "You believe that, don't you?" he said. "You really think they'll let me go when you're done with me."

"Yes," said Matt. "I do. Please, just come with me."

The man glanced over his shoulder again.

"I can't," he said. "I'm sorry."

John Bell turned, far faster than Matt was expecting, and shambled out into the road as fast as his damaged legs would carry him. Matt screamed for him to stop, and was tightening his finger on the pistol's trigger when the truck that Bell had seen rumbling along Geary ploughed into him.

There was a thunderclap of blood and a deafening squeal of brakes as Bell was sent flying into the evening air, then disappeared beneath the truck's wheels.

# 30

## DEEP COVER, PART TWO

### KOLA PENINSULA, RUSSIA

The bear rose up on its hind legs as it lumbered forward, and even as terror crashed through him, a tiny part of the man's brain was able to marvel at its sheer size. Its head was almost three metres above the snow, its legs as thick as tree trunks, its coat a deep, dark brown soaked with melted snow. It peered down at him, breath billowing in white clouds from its open mouth, then roared, a terrible, earth-shattering sound that drove the man back half a step.

The bear instantly came forward, closing the distance between them to less than five metres as the man raised the shotgun, suddenly so small in his hands, to his shoulder. His breath was coming in sharp bursts – in, out, in, out, in, out – and the gun barrel was shaking in the night air.

*It isn't even going to get through his coat*, thought the man. *Not unless it's point-blank.*

He risked the quickest of glances over his shoulder towards the fence, then checked the GPS locator on his wrist, not taking his eyes off the bear for more than a millisecond each time.

*Eighty-seven metres.*

*So close. I was so close.*

Moving incredibly slowly, the man slid to his right until his back was facing the fence; his gaze remained locked on the huge brown eyes, which were regarding him with what looked like curiosity. Carefully, he raised a foot and placed it back down behind him, keeping the shotgun aimed at the animal's head. A low growl rumbled from the bear's throat, but it didn't move.

The man took another step backwards, then another, opening the gap between himself and the animal. Growling steadily, the bear watched as he backed away, and for a moment, the man allowed himself to entertain the prospect that he might still reach his destination in one piece.

Then the bear lumbered forward and roared again, spit flying from its mouth in thick ribbons. It pawed the snow-covered ground, its eyes narrowing and fixing directly on the man. He took another step backwards, but the bear had clearly decided not to let him go; it loped towards him, its huge body swinging from side to side, its mouth hanging open to reveal rows of teeth the size of shot glasses.

The man raised the shotgun and pulled the trigger. The blast was deafening; it echoed through the dark forest like a clap of thunder, causing the man to grimace with pain as the sound reached his ears.

The effect on the bear, however, was far more pronounced.

The huge animal's eyes widened, then it turned tail and disappeared into the forest so quickly that the man momentarily wondered whether he had hallucinated the entire encounter. Then he saw the footprints the bear had left in the snow, footprints as wide as dinner plates, and laughter burst from his mouth, a cackle of triumph that was dangerously close to hysterical.

*Not today, bear,* he thought. *Not now. Not today.*

In the distance, the man heard an alarm begin to wail, a steady rise and fall that filled him with delight. He turned awkwardly in the deep snow and looked at the destination he had doubted he would ever reach.

*They'll be coming. The shot will bring them and they'll take me home.*

The man lurched towards the fence, wondering what would come first, searching torch beams or the voices of the Operators that carried them. He waded through the snow, the fence drawing closer with each laboured step, his eyes fixed dead ahead, his heart thumping in his chest.

He smelt the bear a moment before the attack came: a thick animal scent, full of wildness and primal hunger. He tried to turn, bringing up the gun as he did so, but was far, far too slow.

The bear's huge paw crashed into the side of his head like a sledgehammer, sending him flying through the air. The power of the blow was devastating; the man's limbs went limp as he spun like a rag doll, his eyes rolling uncontrollably in their sockets. The shotgun spilled from his hand and he thudded to the ground beside it. The snow broke his fall, but slid inside his clothes, pressing against his skin like daggers made of ice. A sound left the man's mouth, a guttural noise that his reeling mind didn't recognise as human; it sounded like the howl of a dying animal.

His mind was thick and full of fog, and his eyelids seemed to weigh several tons. He fought to keep them open, to resist the urge to let himself slip down into the sweet darkness of unconsciousness.

Using every last ounce of strength he had left, the man raised his head. The bear was nowhere to be seen, although he knew it was there, watching from the darkness, waiting to move in and finish him off. He hauled himself up to a sitting position, then rolled towards the shotgun, reaching for it with grasping fingers. The movement sent a bolt of pure agony stabbing into the side of his head, and he screamed, a high-pitched noise that sounded distant and disconnected. He flung back the sealskin hood and grabbed at his left ear, trying to squeeze out the pain that was tearing through him as his vision greyed. Nausea boiled up through him, and he resisted the urge to vomit as he coughed and spluttered and tasted acid in his mouth.

When the pain finally subsided and his vision cleared, the man scanned the clearing again.

Dark shadows. Gleaming snow.

No bear.

Carefully, he took his hand away from his ear and looked at it; the glove was soaked through with blood. The man's eyes widened, and he raised his hands to his left ear and clapped, softly.

Nothing.

He clapped again, harder, then harder still.

Nothing.

*I can't hear,* he thought, panic rising through him. *I can't hear out of that ear.*

*Deaf.*

Trying not to move his head, fighting back rising waves of panic, the man picked up the shotgun. Through his remaining good ear, he could hear shouted voices in the distance.

*Not close enough,* he thought, with sudden, awful resignation. *By the time they get here, there'll be nothing left but a smear of blood.*

The man raised the gun to his shoulder and climbed to his feet. The effort required was superhuman, but he found it from somewhere, from the primal place where everything that doesn't matter is stripped away, leaving two fundamental opposites.

Live.

Or die.

He tried to slow his breathing, focusing on nothing but himself, the gun and the bear. His vision narrowed to a small window beyond the end of the shotgun's barrel. His finger rested on the trigger, holding it steady at a quarter pull. He heard his heart thumping in his chest, could feel adrenaline coursing through him.

*Come on,* he screamed inside his head. *Come on. Come on.*

For a long moment, there was silence.

Then, with a guttural growl and the thunder of galloping paws, the bear burst from the trees to his right. Its eyes were narrowed with the prospect of the kill, its mouth open joyfully wide, its teeth huge and sharp. The giant paws, tipped with thick, tearing claws, propelled it across the ground at a speed that made no sense for so large an animal.

The man twisted against the snow, the gun swinging with him, and was face to face with the bear as it thundered into him, its huge weight driving him flat on his back. It bore down, its damp, rotten smell filling his nostrils, its breath a fetid fog that rolled across his face, its roar like rolling thunder in his surviving ear, and he felt something awful as it raked at his stomach with its paws, something profoundly wrong. A single coherent thought filled his mind, as blood that could only be his own began to spray in the freezing air.

*Take. You. With. Me.*

The shotgun moved slowly, as though he were trying to drag it through quicksand. The bear roared again, then lunged, its huge maw snapping down towards his throat. With the last of his strength, the man pushed the shotgun up and out, and the bear's teeth closed on the barrel with a metallic crunch. Two of them shattered with a noise like breaking plates, and the roar changed, as pain and confusion burst through the animal.

Then the man pulled the trigger.

The shot was muffled by the dense bone and thick fur of the animal's head, but it reverberated up the man's arm, hammering his shoulder back against the snow. The back of the bear's head exploded in a steaming geyser, ragged chunks of skull and brain carried upwards on an eruption of blood. Then, as its huge brown eyes rolled back white, the bear slumped to the ground beside the man, blood pumping out of the hole where the top of its head had been, and lay still.

For a long, empty moment, the man didn't move.

The blood-drenched shotgun shook in his hands, as steam rose from both him and the bear in delicate plumes of white. He could taste the animal's blood on his lips and in the back of his throat, coppery and horribly warm. His mind was frozen, the ability for coherent thought swept away by the sheer, blinding horror of what had befallen him, of what fate had cruelly placed in his path when he had been so close to home.

Operating on pure instinct, he craned his head forward, looked down at his stomach, and didn't recognise what he saw. Where there should have been thick white sealskin, there was only red and purple, a quivering, bubbling mass that gleamed horribly in the moonlight. He let his head fall back against the snow and closed his eyes.

The man felt no pain, just a relentless, sucking tiredness, stronger than he had ever known. He gave himself over to it and sank into gentle oblivion.

*Darkness.*
*Warm.*
*Empty.*
*Darkness.*

*Then noise.*
*Distant.*
*Voices.*
*Shouting.*

The man opened his eyes and found himself looking at a white ceiling.

It was moving, the square tiles sliding past at speed. Floating above him was a chaos of tubes and bags, suspended on a shiny metal frame. Beyond them, a doctor wearing a white coat and a surgical mask stared ahead, his eyes wide and staring.

The man opened his mouth to speak, but no sound came out. He tried again, licking his cracked lips, and managed a gargling noise, like the sound of a newborn baby. The doctor looked down.

"Lie still, yes?" he said. "Do not try to move."

The man made no response.

"You have been badly injured," said the doctor. "We are taking you to surgery. Do you understand what I am saying to you?"

The man tried to nod, but couldn't. He concentrated, and managed to twist his mouth into the distant approximation of a smile.

"Good," said the doctor. "What is your name? Can you tell me your name?"

"Brennan," whispered the man, the words little more than croaks. "Richard... Brennan. *Safeguard.*"

Then his eyes rolled back in his head, as his heart stopped beating.

# 31

# A HUNDRED SMALL PIECES
# OF BONE

## SAN FRANCISCO, CALIFORNIA, USA

The truck skewed as it braked, its trailer fishtailing through a cloud of tyre smoke and dust, before coming to a juddering halt. Matt stared at it, frozen with horror, until screams began to ring out along Geary, breaking his paralysis.

*Oh God. Oh God oh God oh God. Oh God.*

He staggered along the side of the truck's cab, his hand over his mouth to keep out the swirling dust, until he reached the pool of red spreading steadily from beneath the third pair of wheels. He could hear shouted voices behind him, and at least half a dozen people making emergency calls, but he ignored them all; he got down on his hands and knees, his limbs shaking violently, and peered under the truck, dreadfully certain of what he was going to see.

John Bell was lying on the tarmac, staring up at the underside of the truck with wide, dead eyes. He was coated in blood, his arms and legs twisted and broken, but the look on his face was one of unmistakable relief, of glorious escape. Matt reached under the truck, taking care to avoid the smoking rubber of the tyres, and gently pressed his fingers against Bell's neck.

Nothing.

Matt let out a rasping sob, then pushed himself backwards, wiping his fingers furiously on his jeans. He lurched back to his feet, then cried out as a hand dropped on his shoulder and spun him round.

"Hey," said a man in a white T-shirt, his eyes wide. "Hey, you saw that, right? He jumped right out in front of me. There wasn't nothing I could do. You saw, right?"

Matt nodded, trying to slow his racing heart. "Yeah," he said. "I saw."

"You'll tell the cops? When they get here, you'll tell them he ran out?"

"I'll tell them."

The man nodded. He seemed to be on the verge of shock, and Matt couldn't blame him. Behind the man, a small crowd had gathered on the pavement, all of them staring at the rapidly spreading pool of blood with a mixture of disgust and excitement on their faces. He was suddenly furious with them; wanted to point his gun at them and make them understand that it was a person lying dead beneath the truck, not some grisly piece of street theatre. John Bell had been as real as any of them, every bit as scared and confused and lost, and now he was dead, and he was never coming back.

Out of the corner of his eye, he saw Danny Lawrence and Hannah Landsman running down Third Street towards him, their guns drawn. He took a step away from the truck driver and waved them over. They arrived beside him, and as Hannah took charge of the situation, ordering the driver and the rest of the gawking onlookers to get back, Danny took hold of Matt's arm.

"Are you all right?" he said, his voice low. "Jesus, Matt, what the hell were you thinking?"

Matt frowned, then shoved the hand away. "What was *I* thinking?" he asked, his voice thick with sudden anger. "Where the hell were *you*? I told you all what was happening."

"Bell knew," said Danny. "He knew, or he was just more paranoid than we were expecting, it doesn't matter which. He told a colleague he was going to the bathroom, so we were down on the second-floor landing waiting outside the door while he must have been making his way to the roof. When your message came through, Simmons and Andrews came in to find us, but we had to go back up and come down, and we didn't know which direction you'd gone. I'm sorry, Matt."

"It's all right," he said. "It's over, in any case."

"Where is he?" asked Danny.

Matt pointed at the thick puddle of dark red.

Danny grimaced. "Christ," he said.

"He killed himself," said Matt, his voice low and empty. "He thought I wanted to take him back to another lab. I told him I didn't, but he wouldn't believe me. He ran out in front of that truck."

"What a mess," said Danny, his eyes still staring at the spilled blood. "Jesus, what a God-awful mess. Are you sure you're OK?"

"I'm fine," said Matt. "I need my bag. It's still in the car."

"What for?" asked Danny.

"To do my job."

Understanding dawned on the American Operator's face. He raised his wrist to his mouth and ordered their driver to bring the black SUV to the corner of Third and Geary. It arrived less than a minute later, at the same time as the rest of their squad and a fleet of police cars and ambulances, lights blazing, sirens howling.

"Don't worry about them," said Danny. "Do what you need to do."

Matt nodded, then walked across to the SUV. Behind him, he could hear Major Simmons informing the police that they would be allowed to examine the scene when his men were finished, and not a single minute earlier. The discussion had escalated to a shouted argument by the time Matt had retrieved his bag from the back seat of the car and returned to the tarmac beside the body of John Bell; he ignored it, focusing only on what was within his control.

From his bag he took plastic vials and Petri dishes with screw tops, along with a plastic pouch of medical instruments. As the argument on the pavement reached a deafening crescendo, culminating in Major Simmons informing the policeman that he would be committing career suicide if he said another goddamn word, Matt knelt down and crawled underneath the truck.

Working quickly, he spooned John Bell's blood into the vials, grimacing as he did so. When they were filled and sealed, he took a large pair of tweezers, lifted a dozen quivering bits of torn flesh into the Petri dishes, and screwed them shut. It felt wrong, taking from the man only what he needed and leaving the rest of him lying broken in the road, but there was nothing Matt could do for him; the man had gone beyond help. Matt wormed his way further under the truck, until he was beside John Bell's head. The wheels were so tall that once he was in the cavity between them he could sit upright; he did so, and removed a heavy syringe from his bag.

*You can do this,* he told himself.

Carefully, he prised the man's head from the tarmac. It came free with a horrible tearing sound, leaving a thick patch of hair glued to the ground with blood.

Matt's stomach churned as he slowly pushed the head forward. Beneath the blood-soaked skin, the skull felt like a broken eggshell; like a hundred small pieces of bone moving beneath his fingers. He took a deep breath and pushed the syringe into the back of John Bell's neck, where it met his shoulders. There was an audible crack as the thick needle pierced the spinal column, a crack that caused Matt to retch, violently. He coughed, spat out the saliva that had flooded his mouth, and drew the plunger back. Spinal fluid, thin and clear, spurted into the chamber of the syringe. Matt pulled until it was half full, then withdrew the needle and placed it in his bag with the vials and dishes and instruments. He took a couple of long, shallow breaths, then crawled back out from under the truck.

At the corner of the block, Simmons, Landsman and Andrews were squared up to the emergency services. Everyone seemed to be shouting at once, either at each other or into radios and phones, trying to establish exactly who was in charge of the gruesome scene that had played out on a busy San Francisco street as the evening drew in. Danny Lawrence was standing on his own on the pavement; Matt emerged, he reached down a hand and pulled him to his feet.

"Get everything you need?" he asked.

Matt nodded.

"Good," said Danny, and forced a thin smile. "We're getting out of here. I'm going to take you to the lab at USF and you can get on with your work. That sound OK?"

Matt frowned. "What about the others?"

"I'll send the car back," said Danny. "Don't worry about them. What's in your bag is the priority."

"Are you sure?" asked Matt.

"I'm positive," said Danny. "They'll be fine. Local cops, paramedics, nothing they can't handle. Come on."

Matt followed Danny to the SUV. Behind him, someone shouted that they better not dare leave, because nobody was going anywhere until someone came up with some damn answers, but he ignored the voice; he was tired, and his heart hurt.

Matt settled on to the back seat of the car as Danny climbed into the front and told their driver to go. The car pulled away from the kerb and accelerated, quickly leaving behind the chaos that Matt, at least in part, had caused. He tried to process it all, to begin to rationalise what had happened and his role in it, but couldn't; his mind was too full of horror.

As the car headed north, Matt clutched his bag tightly and closed his eyes. He wondered whether he would ever be able to forget the sight of John Bell spinning through the evening air, his face wearing an expression of victory as his lifeblood sprayed out of him.

He doubted it.

# 3 DAYS TILL
# ZERO HOUR

# 32

# THE CENTRE CANNOT HOLD

The wail of the Loop's general alarm tore through the base, thumping into Kate Randall's head and jerking her out of a dream in which she could fly.

She sat bolt upright and forced her gummy eyes open, grimacing at the deafening noise. The digital clock glowed steadily on her bedside table: 05:13.

*Quarter past five in the morning*, she thought. *Brilliant. Absolutely brilliant.*

Kate swung her legs out of bed, staggered across her quarters, and dragged her uniform down from its hook on the back of the door. She had managed to get one leg into the black jumpsuit when the alarm cut out, leaving behind a high ringing echo. A second later her boss's voice filled the Loop, emerging from the speakers that nestled in the upper corners of every room in the base.

"Attention," said Paul Turner. "Security Division, report at once to your Code Blue stations."

*Code Blue*, thought Kate, as she hauled her uniform past her hips and over her shoulders. *Perimeter breach.*

She zipped herself up, and was splashing cold water on to her face in an attempt to wake herself up when her console beeped.

She fumbled for it with clumsy hands and thumbed its screen into life.

FROM: Turner, Major Paul (NS303, 36-A)
TO: Randall, Lieutenant Kate (NS303, 78-J)
Meet me in the hangar ASAP.

Kate opened the door to her quarters and stepped out into the corridor. Several of her neighbours were standing in their doorways, their faces screwed up with tiredness and concern. A few raised their eyes enquiringly as she passed, but she merely shrugged and kept walking.

On Level 0, Kate exited the lift and saw Operators from her Division had taken up their stations outside the double doors that led into the hangar. She nodded at them, showed them the message from the Security Officer, and they stepped aside.

The hangar was never entirely silent, especially not in the early hours of the morning when Operational Squads were returning from Patrol Responses. But it *was* quiet as she walked towards Paul Turner, her boots clicking loudly on the concrete floor. Her commanding officer was standing beside one of the black SUVs that were parked against the long, curving wall, his face as expressionless as ever. He nodded curtly as she stopped before him.

"Morning," he said.

Kate smiled. "Good morning, sir. Sleep well?"

Turner's lips curled fractionally at the edges. "Absolutely," he said. "For about an hour. You?"

"The same," said Kate. "What's going on, sir?"

"Perimeter breach at sector 7G," said Turner. "Our Operators on the fence have contained it, but I need to check it out. You're coming with me."

Kate nodded. "Yes, sir. What was the source of the breach?"

"You'll see," said Turner, and opened the SUV's passenger door. "Get in."

Kate did as she was told. Turner climbed behind the wheel, guided the vehicle out of the hangar, then accelerated along the long road that bisected the wide circular grounds of the base.

Up close, the perimeter of the Loop was a blinding array of light and movement. On the other side of the inner fence and the manned guard posts, an impenetrable grid of lasers moved as if of their own accord, a halting dance of bright red beams. Beyond the outer fence, which stood more than six metres tall and was topped with coils of vicious-looking razor wire, was the exclusion zone, a fifteen-metre border that ran between the fence and the surrounding forest. The exclusion zone was monitored by a myriad of hidden cameras and sensors, and illuminated by the purple beams of hundreds of ultraviolet lights, rendering it impassable to vampires.

*Unless they fly over it*, thought Kate. *The radar blanket is supposed to catch them if they do, but it didn't seem to help when Valeri arrived with his army.*

In truth, Kate had harboured concerns about the perimeter since before she had joined the Security Division; she was sure that it acted as a compelling deterrent, but she did not believe it was capable of actually preventing a vampire, or vampires, from gaining access to the base. Major Turner had agreed with her, somewhat to her surprise, but had refused her permission to research ways to improve the system.

"There's no way we can wall off the entire sky," he had said. "You saw what Valeri did here, and to the SPC in Polyarny. Better to assume that they'll get in if they're determined, and concentrate on what happens then."

A thick concrete fence post passed the car's window, with 7A printed on it in large black letters. Ahead of them, Kate could see a patch of darkness, where the red and purple lights were not shining.

*7G*, she thought.

Turner slowed the car, its bright headlights picking out a pair of Operators standing by the darkened section of fence, and brought it to a halt beside them. Kate climbed out and looked at sector 7G, but the darkness was total; she could see nothing.

"Lights," said Turner.

"Yes, sir," replied one of the Operators, and tapped the console in his hand.

There was a hum of electricity, then the maintenance lights that topped the inner fence rumbled to life and sector 7G was illuminated pale yellow.

Kate gasped.

Tangled in the razor wire at the top of the outer fence was the body of a man. Twisted beneath him was a piece of carpet, and he was gripping a flag tightly in his dead hand. It had unfurled and was fluttering against the metal mesh; it read **THE SUPERNATURAL ARE NOT MONSTERS**. The man's eyes stared emptily up at the sky, his mouth open in an eternal scream of pain. His body was covered in blood from where the razor wire had torn at his skin; it had stained the metal links of the fence and pooled on the ground below. Kate followed the crimson streak downwards, her stomach churning, and saw the second body.

The second man had made it over the outer fence and was lying on his back in the space usually occupied by the laser array. One of his legs was visibly broken, snapped horribly at mid-thigh, but that was not the worst that had befallen the dead man, not what made Kate suddenly fear she was going to be sick. His body and face were criss-crossed with terrible burns, lines of seared black skin that ran in merciless straight lines; one of them had cut across his left hand, leaving nothing more than a charred stump, while another had burned away his lips, revealing yellowing teeth. The man was lying in a pool of crimson, his ruined face turned towards the inner fence. With slowly dawning horror, Kate saw that the man's eyes had been burned out of his skull; the empty sockets stared at her, red and raw.

"Jesus," she said, her voice low and trembling, then turned to the Security Officer standing impassively beside her. "What the hell happened here?"

Turner looked at her. "You tell me," he said. "It seems pretty clear."

Kate took a deep breath and returned her gaze to the two corpses. She tried to look at the gruesome scene dispassionately, to concentrate on narrative rather than spilled blood and pain, and quickly saw that the Security Officer was right; it was horribly clear what had happened.

"The two of them somehow got past the sensors and the cameras and to the edge of the exclusion zone," she said. "They were hurrying, because they must have known they would be seen when they crossed it, so they climbed the fence and used that carpet to try and get over the razor wire. One made it, but he fell and broke his leg, so he couldn't get out of the way of the lasers. They burned him to death, or the shock killed him, I don't know. The other man saw what happened, and tried to get over the fence to help, but slipped off the carpet. The razor wire tangled him and cut his throat. Does that sound about right?"

"It does to me," said Turner, then addressed the Operator who had turned on the lights. "Is that what happened?"

"Yes, sir," he replied. "I killed the power when the man fell, but the lasers take ten seconds to shut down. I was in attendance ninety seconds later, but they were both already dead, sir."

"You went in and checked?" asked Turner.

"Yes, sir," said the Operator. "There's a maintenance break right there." He pointed, and Kate followed his gesture. Set into the concrete pillar with 7G printed on it was a metal door, its handle flush with the surface.

*I never knew that,* thought Kate. *Never knew there was a way beyond the fence. Although of course there would have to be.*

"How did they get so close without tripping any of the sensors?" asked Turner.

"Luck?" said the Operator. "They've been spreading out through the forest since they arrived, walking and shouting and singing. The police have been in there a dozen times to turn them back."

"I'm aware of that," said Turner, his eyes narrowing slightly. "Given that I'm the Security Officer. I was specifically asking about these two."

The Operator nodded. "I'm sorry, sir. I don't know how they got through the sensors."

"Find out," said Turner. "If they've mapped them, move them. But first, get the bodies out of there. I want them examined in the infirmary, then released to their families. I'll have the security-camera footage leaked to the media."

Kate frowned. "Sir?"

"They won't run it," said Turner. "But it'll be on the internet within an hour. I want everyone to see what happens to people

**332**

who try to break in here. Maybe it will dissuade anyone else from being so stupid."

*That's clever,* thought Kate. *Cold, but very clever.*

"I need a ladder, sir," said the Operator.

"I'm sorry?" said Turner.

"I need a ladder to get the body down from the wire."

"And?" said Turner. "Do you want me to build one for you? Call the hangar and have an engine brought out, for God's sake."

The Operator took the radio from his belt and spoke rapidly into it. Kate watched him for a second, then turned to the Security Officer.

"From the protest camp?" she said, gesturing towards the bodies.

"I would expect so," said Turner. "Bloody stupid way to get yourself killed, but I suppose you have to admire it."

"Really?" asked Kate.

Turner shrugged. "They risked their lives for something they believed was worthwhile. Does that remind you of anyone we know?"

Kate smiled, and nodded. She watched the Security Division Operators let themselves through the access door and into the space between the fences as behind her, from the direction of the hangar, she heard the rumble of an approaching engine. The Operators unrolled a black plastic bag and laid it on the ground beside the man whose burns had shocked her so badly; she looked away as they lifted his lifeless body on to it and began to zip it shut.

"This is going to happen again, isn't it?" she said, her voice low.

"I'm sorry?" said Turner.

"Maybe not this exact thing," said Kate. "But something like it. Then something else will happen, and something else after that. It's going to get out of hand."

Turner nodded. "It's already getting out of hand," he said. "I don't know how much longer we can control the situation." He pulled his console from his belt, unlocked it with his thumb, and held it out to Kate.

She took it from his gloved fingers and looked at the screen. Filling it were thumbnails of the pages of two police reports. She tapped the first image as Paul Turner continued to speak.

"Intelligence received those overnight," he said. "Three civilian deaths, all involving the suspicion of vampirism. Two teenagers, both identifying as Goth, beaten to death in a park in Guildford yesterday evening. One of the attackers was a schoolmate of the deceased, another a neighbour."

Kate felt cold creep through her. On the screen of the console, school photographs of the murdered teenagers stared at her with heavily made-up eyes.

"Paul Whates," she said. "Amy Underwood. They were the same age as me, sir. Both of them."

"I know," said Turner.

"Someone killed them because they like to dye their hair and wear eyeliner?"

"Someone killed them because they thought they were vampires," said Turner. "I honestly don't know if that's better or worse."

"There's no better here, sir," said Kate, tearing her gaze away from the photos to look her commanding officer in the eye. "There are only degrees of worse."

Turner nodded. "I agree," he said. "People are scared, and they're starting to turn on each other. And there's nothing we can do that's going to make any difference, apart from coming up with a cure or killing every vampire on the planet. Do you see either of those things happening quickly enough?"

"No," said Kate, her heart heavy in her chest. "I don't."

"Neither do I," said Turner. "I'd love nothing more than to be wrong, for your friend Matt and the rest of Lazarus to make this all go away, or for the Romania team to bring us something back we can destroy Dracula with. But I'm not holding my breath on either count."

Kate frowned, as something slotted together in her mind. The team that was to search for the first victim had been despatched the previous evening, and she had not seen Jamie since the Zero Hour meeting the morning before that, had not seen Larissa since their breakfast shortly afterwards, and had not laid eyes on Matt for days, possibly weeks.

*Probably just coincidence,* she thought. *But if not...*

"Sir," she said. "Do you know where my friends are?"

Turner narrowed his eyes. "Which ones in particular?" he asked.

"Matt," she said. "And Larissa, and Jamie."

"Yes," said Turner. "I know where they are."

"Are you going to tell me?"

The Security Officer's eyes narrowed even further, and Kate braced herself to be told no. Then Turner sighed, and shook his head as a tiny smile appeared on his face.

"I shouldn't," he said. "It's all classified above Zero Hour. But I trust you. And that's not a mistake on my part, right?"

"No," said Kate, instantly. "You can trust me, sir."

Turner nodded. "Jamie and Larissa were selected by NS9 to be part of DARKWOODS," he said. "Which is the mission to search for the first victim, acting on Grey's intelligence. They're in Romania as we speak. And Matt is in America, the Lazarus Project observer on GARDEN OF EDEN, an operation designed to locate the man known as Adam, a vampire who was allegedly cured. And before you ask, I have no updates on how any of them are doing. That's all the information I have."

"Thank you, sir," said Kate.

Her heart was swelling with pride at the thought of what her friends were doing, of how *vital* the two operations were to the future not just of Blacklight, but of everything.

*I'm not even surprised,* she thought. *Somehow they always end up at the centre of everything.*

"So what do we do, sir?" she asked.

Turner glanced towards the hangar. A bright red fire engine from the Loop's emergency services fleet was approaching, metal ladders gleaming on its roof. He waved his arm until the driver steered the red truck towards them, then turned back to Kate.

"Right now?" he said. "We do what we can, and hope it's enough. That's all we can do."

# 33

# BY DAWN'S EARLY LIGHT

The sky to the east was a glorious deep purple, the colour of a week-old bruise, as Jamie Carpenter opened his eyes.

The sun had not yet crawled above the horizon and it was bitterly cold, even inside his sleeping bag. The tarpaulin and plastic shelter had kept out the snow that had fallen relentlessly through the night, but not the whistling, creeping wind; it had worked its way into every warm corner, icy-cold fingers that searched and pried.

Jamie sat up, keeping the sleeping bag wrapped tightly round him, and shivered. Dawn was still half an hour away, maybe slightly less, and he felt physically exhausted, like his limbs were full of concrete and his head was made of glass. His mind felt slow, as though it needed shutting down and rebooting, and he tried to remember when he had last had more than four hours of uninterrupted sleep. He rubbed his upper arms with his hands, trying to will life back into them, and looked around the camp.

Tim Albertsson was asleep on his back beneath the edge of the shelter, one hand tucked behind his head. He looked a picture of

337

contentment, as though he was sleeping under the finest duvet in the most luxurious hotel room in the world, rather than in a snowy field at the edge of the Teleorman Forest. There was the hint of a smile on the American's tanned, handsome face, and the expression caused Jamie a momentary burst of anger.

*He's even smug when he's asleep*, he thought.

Jamie knew he was prone to making snap judgements, a quality that was not one of his best, and had caused him trouble in the past. He had taken an instant liking to Thomas Morris, who had turned out not only to have been working to betray Blacklight from within, but to have been involved in the death of Jamie's father. Conversely, he had initially disliked Frankenstein and *loathed* Henry Seward, two men for whom he had come to have the utmost respect.

As a result, he would never have claimed to be the most reliable judge of character, and he was hoping that this would prove to be the case with Tim Albertsson; that the fault lay with him and that, in time, he would come to see the American's finer qualities, would be able to respect him as an Operator even if he never came to like him as a person.

Jamie genuinely hoped so, because he currently felt very differently.

Right now, he hated Tim Albertsson.

Absolutely hated him.

It wasn't just that there was obviously something between the American and Larissa that he wasn't being told, although that was certainly reason enough. It was the way Albertsson talked, and walked, just the fundamental way he *was*; he reminded Jamie of the bullies who had swaggered round the playgrounds of the many schools he had attended after his dad had died, absolutely certain of their superiority to those around them, full of unwarranted, unjustifiable arrogance.

*Come back to me when you've faced down Alexandru Rusmanov and lived to tell the tale,* he thought. *Then you can act like a big shot as much as you want.*

Next to Albertsson, Arkady Petrov lay asleep on his side, his shaven scalp protruding from the thick green sleeping bag, his breathing light and steady. Jamie was sure that the cold, which he found utterly debilitating, posed no problem at all for Petrov, who had been raised in the biting teeth of the Russian winter and whose home base lay inside the Arctic Circle.

In the centre of the camp lay the sleeping forms of Van Orel and Engel. They had – involuntarily, he presumed – huddled together during the night, and were spooning like a couple on their honeymoon. Jamie smiled, wondering how embarrassed the two Operators would be when they awoke.

In the latest of the snap judgements that he was trying to stop himself making, he had decided that he liked Kristian Van Orel; liked him a lot. The South African was funny and self-deprecating, and seemed disinterested in the importance of age or experience. As far as Jamie, who worried endlessly about both of those issues, was concerned, it was a significant point in his favour.

At the southern edge of the shelter, where the snow that covered the rest of the field was piled steep and high, an empty sleeping bag lay crumpled on the groundsheet. Jamie stared at it, then dragged his protesting body out into the cold and went to find his girlfriend.

Snow crunched beneath his boots as he ducked under the corner of the shelter and stood up, stretching his aching arms towards the sky. His head was beginning to clear, and he allowed himself a moment to marvel at the vista of purple and orange that filled the sky to the east.

"Morning."

Jamie smiled at the sound of Larissa's voice, and turned towards it. His girlfriend was perched on a tree branch at the edge of the dark forest, high above the camp. She looked even paler than usual, but her eyes glowed momentarily red at the sight of him, and a smile rose slowly on to her face.

"Morning," he replied, picking his way carefully up the slope towards her. "I thought your watch finished two hours ago?"

"It did," she said. "I didn't see the point of waking anyone else."

"So you could get some sleep?" he suggested.

Larissa shrugged. "I'm not tired."

Jamie reached the wide trunk of the tree, depressingly aware that his feet were already numb, even through his boots, and looked up at her. "Are you coming down?" he asked.

Larissa didn't answer. Jamie was about to repeat the question when she pushed herself off the branch, floated gracefully down to the snow-covered ground, and closed his mouth with her own, the kiss passionate, almost violent. His eyes widened with surprise, then closed as he felt heat in his stomach, felt Larissa press herself against him. He gave himself over to the kiss, luxuriating in something that was warm and soft rather than cold and hard, then forced himself to break it and step back.

"Are you all right?" he asked.

Larissa narrowed her eyes, the red in their corners pulsing. "I can't kiss my boyfriend?"

Jamie shook his head. "You can," he said. "You most definitely can. But maybe when we're not in the middle of a Priority Level 1 operation?"

**340**

Larissa looked at him, her expression unreadable. Jamie stared back; the kiss had been so urgent, so aggressive, almost like she'd been trying to prove something with it. As he looked at her, he realised he could wait no longer to find out what she was hiding from him.

"What happened in Nevada, Larissa?" he asked. "With you and Tim. And please don't say nothing."

"Nothing," she said.

"I don't believe you," he said. "I'm sorry. I just don't."

Larissa's eyes flared momentarily, before a look of profound sadness crossed her face. "It's not what you think," she said, softly. "I understand if you don't believe that, and I don't blame you, but it's the truth. Nothing happened between me and Tim, absolutely nothing. He was someone I thought was a friend, but he turned out not to be. I should have told you everything when I got back to the Loop, and I will, I promise I will. But this isn't the time or the place."

"You never mentioned him," said Jamie. "Not even once. But he talks like you were best mates, and he keeps smirking at me, like he knows something I don't."

"I know he does," said Larissa. "I'm sorry. All I can say is that it isn't what you think. Please try and trust me."

Jamie stared at her, searching within himself for the strength, and the patience, to do as she asked. "OK," he said, eventually. "I'll try."

They stood in silence for a long moment, the freezing air whistling around them, the eastern sky lightening.

"Do you reckon Kate and Matt are still asleep?" he asked, eventually.

Larissa smiled. "Kate will be at her desk in Security by now," she said. "You know she will. And Matt should be having dinner, with any luck."

Jamie frowned. "What are you talking about?"

"Nevada is ten hours behind us."

"What does that have to do with Matt?" asked Jamie.

It was Larissa's turn to frown. "Matt's in Nevada," she said, slowly. "Helping NS9 look for Adam. Didn't he tell you?"

"I haven't seen him for a couple of days," said Jamie. "When did he leave?"

"Yesterday morning," said Larissa. "And whose fault is it that you haven't seen him? I know he tried to find you the day before yesterday, when you spent the whole day feeling sorry for yourself."

"Shit," said Jamie. "He probably wanted to tell me about it."

Larissa nodded. "I'm sure he did."

Jamie grimaced.

*I can't do anything about it now,* he told himself. *I'll apologise to Matt when we get home.*

"We should wake the others," he said.

"Why?" asked Larissa, her voice suddenly low and urgent. "We could just go in there right now, you and me. We don't need the rest of them. I can protect us."

"We can't do that, Larissa."

"Why not?"

"You know why not," he said. "Because we've got orders to follow."

Larissa hissed loudly, and Jamie took an involuntary step back. "Orders?" she growled. "Since when do you give a shit about orders? You've disobeyed more than you've followed, and you've been right more times than not. Trust yourself, Jamie. Trust me. We can do this."

"Do what?" asked a voice.

Jamie spun round and saw Tim Albertsson standing at the edge of the shelter, regarding them with a wide, easy smile. Behind him, he heard a low growl emerge from Larissa's throat.

*What the hell is going on here?* he wondered. *I mean, seriously.*

"Nothing," he said. "We were just about to wake the rest of you."

Tim nodded, his smile growing even wider. "Glad to hear it," he said. "It's nearly dawn, and we need to be in the forest before your girlfriend bursts into flames, don't we? Come on, Engel's making coffee."

The American ducked back under the shelter. Jamie turned to Larissa, and recoiled; her fangs were clearly visible, her eyes blazing red, and she was staring at the spot where Albertsson had been standing with open, roaring fury.

"Larissa," he said. She gave no indication of having heard. "*Larissa,*" he said again, and grabbed her arm.

She turned on him with the speed of a striking cobra, her fingers closing round his hand, a terrible hiss bursting from between her bared teeth. Jamie stared, frozen with shock, until she blinked and let go of his arm, and the person in front of him was once again the girl he loved.

"I'm sorry," she said. "Did I hurt you?"

Jamie shook his head. "I'm fine," he managed. "Are you OK?"

"No," said Larissa. "I'm not."

"And what about Albertsson?" he asked.

"What do you mean?"

"I mean that I've seen you look at people like that before," said Jamie. "It normally doesn't end well. For them, at least."

Larissa shrugged, and smiled a thin, unpleasant smile. "I don't know what you're talking about," she said. "But if you're saying

**343**

that Tim should be careful, I agree with you. This forest seems like a dangerous place."

"We have been here before," said Arkady Petrov.

Larissa looked round at her squad mates and sighed. The Russian was right; she recognised the clearing they were standing in, the sprays of early wildflowers and low bushes that rose around the bases of the huge tree trunks, the mingled mixture of fragrances that filled the air.

"No we haven't," said Tim Albertsson, stabbing at a topographical survey map with a gloved finger. "We're here, see. *That's* where we made camp, *that's* where we came in, *this* is where we are. We're going in the right direction."

"We are going in circles," said Petrov, his voice flat and even.

"What are you saying?" said Albertsson, rounding angrily on the Russian Operator. "That I don't know how to read a map?"

Petrov said nothing; he merely stared at Albertsson with his dark grey eyes.

"Arkady is right," said Larissa. "We've been here before. We must have got turned around somewhere."

"How could you possibly know that?" asked Albertsson.

Larissa shrugged. "I know."

Albertsson rolled his eyes. "Well, isn't that awesome? No, thanks for that, seriously. *You just know.* That's really helpful."

"Hey!" said Jamie, his eyes flashing with anger. "It's not her fault we're lost."

"Are you taking your girlfriend's side, Lieutenant Carpenter?" asked Tim. "What a colossal surprise. I'm sure nobody saw that coming."

"I don't give a shit what you saw coming," said Jamie, his face colouring a dark red. "She's right, Arkady is right, and you *know* they're right. You just don't want to admit it."

"Thank you for your input, Lieutenant," said Albertsson. "I'll be sure to give it the consideration it deserves." The American stalked away from the rest of the squad, flattened the map against one of the tree trunks, and began to trace a route on it with his finger, muttering angrily to himself.

Larissa glanced at Jamie, whose gaze was still fixed on Albertsson's back, and then looked at the rest of the squad. Petrov was leaning against one of the trees, rolling a cigarette with practised ease. Van Orel was looking at Jamie with a small smile, its narrow curve full of what Larissa believed was support, and Engel was standing off to one side, her face impassive. It was already clear that the German Operator was hating every second of DARKWOODS; her dismay at the behaviour of her squad mates was obvious.

*And perfectly justified,* thought Larissa. *This is going bad.*

She took a deep breath as she waited for Tim to order them to move out again. She had told nobody, not even Jamie, but her head was swimming; it was as though the forest had been designed to overwhelm her, to nullify her supernatural abilities. The smells that rose from the ground as they made their way deeper and deeper into the dark trees grew stronger and more intense; spring wildflowers that gave off sweet, complicated scents, mushrooms and fauna that smelt of rot and decay, the thick stench of animal blood and waste. And beneath it all buzzed a constant, maddening drone, a relentless, painful rattle that burrowed into her ears, making clear thinking difficult, and causing her to wonder if there was something wrong with her. She had asked Jamie if he could hear it, and he had looked at her with a frown.

"Hear what?" he had asked.

345

Larissa hadn't replied.

*This is going bad,* she thought again, as Tim Albertsson folded the map and strode back towards his squad.

*It's going bad fast.*

In truth, things had started badly and got worse.

The squad had been ill-tempered from the moment she and Jamie had returned to camp, fractious and anxious and seemingly spoiling to pick fights with one another. They had taken down their shelter in near silence, before stepping past the disembowelled wolf and into the forest. The discovery that the snow that covered the field had largely failed to penetrate the thick canopy of trees briefly lifted spirits; searching their target area would have taken weeks if they'd been forced to wade through waist-deep snow. But barely a minute had passed when Van Orel, whom Albertsson had ordered to take point, stopped abruptly.

"Jesus Christ," he breathed.

His squad mates gathered behind him, then froze in their tracks as they saw what had made him halt.

In front of them was a gallery of dead animals.

Wolves had been pinned to half a dozen trees, their grey fur soaked with blood, their innards spilled. Between them, two of the widest trunks were decorated with the corpses of red deer, their mouths coated with foam, their eyes bulging; Larissa stared at them, marvelling at the strength it must have taken to lift the heavy bodies and drive wooden stakes through thick muscle and old, heavy bark.

Two wild boars had been butchered and arranged on the floor of the forest, surrounded by bushes that were full of flayed squirrels, badgers, foxes and rats, the small corpses hung in neat, gruesome rows.

*Designed,* thought Larissa, and shivered. *Arranged, especially for us.*

"What the hell?" whispered Albertsson.

She turned to look at their squad leader, and saw his eyes widened with fear. Then Tim noticed her looking and collected himself; he stepped forward, his eyes narrowing as he pulled off a glove and dipped a finger in the blood of the nearest wolf.

"Still warm," he said.

"It was done while we were asleep," said Engel, saying out loud what everyone was thinking. "Asleep fifty metres away."

Larissa felt her vampire side straining, begging for release. She felt familiar heat in the corners of her eyes, felt the itch in the roof of her mouth as her fangs began to move.

"This is a final warning," said Petrov. "Last chance to turn back."

"To hell with that," said Albertsson, although Larissa didn't think the tone of his voice matched the determination of his words. "We're not going back till we find what we came here to find. Let's move out."

# 34

# LET THE PAST REST

Cal Holmwood stood in the hangar of the Loop, a splitting headache pounding through his skull, and waited for his friend to be brought out.

After the general alarm had ceased its ungodly screeching, he had received a message from Paul Turner explaining what had happened out on the perimeter and assuring him that the situation was under control. Cal didn't doubt it; he had more faith in his Security Officer than in any other member of the Department, himself included. But despite that faith, he had not been able to persuade his tired, aching body to return to sleep. Instead, he had lain awake for almost an hour, staring alternately at the dark ceiling of his bedroom and the glowing numbers of the digital clock on his bedside table, until he had admitted defeat, showered, dressed, and trudged out to his desk.

The mountain of files and folders that was piled precariously on its surface was nothing less than an Everest of red tape. At the summit was a new report from the Surveillance Division, which he lifted down and opened.

REPORT 7542/B
SUBMITTED: 0342

BY: MAJOR ALEXANDER PIERCE/NS303, 41-F
FAO: INTERIM DIRECTOR CALEB HOLMWOOD/
NS303, 34-D
SECURITY: PRIORITY LEVEL 1, DIRECTOR EYES ONLY

SUBJECT: APPLICATION OF SECURITY
SURVEILLANCE MEASURES TO CIVILIAN PROPERTY,
AS PER SURVEILLANCE DIVISION ORDER N426/9

BEGINS.

Surveillance installation completed as follows:
– Voice-activated recording installed across property and
grounds.
– Location tracker/voice-activated recording devices installed
on both (2) vehicles currently at the property.
– Motion-activated camera coverage of property and grounds.
– All telecommunication lines breached and automatic recorders
installed.
– Thermal ground sensors installed.
– Mobile telecommunications monitoring grid installed over
property.
– Keychecks and keylogs installed on laptop computer within
the property. Spyware installed for future user network
migration.
– Remote thermal-monitoring net installed, covering property
and grounds.
All systems checked and functioning.

ENDS.

Cal had repeatedly made it clear to Julian that if he was to eventually be released it would be under strict surveillance. He had not spelt out just how intrusive it would be, but he felt no guilt; Julian knew exactly how this game was played and as far as Cal was concerned, he was already bending over backwards for his old friend.

*Nobody else would have had any chance of ever leaving their cell,* he thought, as the double doors at the rear of the hangar swung open. *And maybe he shouldn't either. But I made a promise.*

Three figures emerged, walking rapidly across the concrete floor towards him. Two were Security Division Operators, in full uniform with MP7s resting in their gloved hands. Between them, dressed in a shirt and jeans, and with a black hood over his head, was Julian Carpenter.

The scuffed leather bag he had carried with him across the Atlantic was hung over his shoulder, and his uncuffed hands swung at his sides. Cal had told the Security Operators not to restrain the prisoner unless he resisted, which he had not considered was likely. The two men had no idea who they were escorting; they had been ordered to pass the hood through the cell's food slot and wait until the prisoner knocked on the door twice before they opened it. Julian had been told to do so once the hood was in place, and had been specifically ordered not to say a single word to either of the Security Operators. As a precaution, Cal had selected two men who had not joined the Department until after Julian's supposed death; to them, he was nothing more than a name from the past, whose voice would be unfamiliar if Cal's old friend decided to defy his orders.

The Operators and their prisoner stopped in front of him. "Reporting as ordered, sir," said one.

Cal nodded. "Very good," he said. "Get the transport ready."

The Operators chorused, 'Yes, sir,' and made their way across the hangar towards the line of black SUVs. Cal waited until they were out of earshot, then clasped his friend's shoulder.

"Are you all right, Julian?" he asked.

The hooded figure nodded. "I'm great, Cal. Why wouldn't I be?"

Holmwood smiled. "Show me your arm," he said.

Julian pushed up his left sleeve and presented his arm for inspection. The skin below the elbow was wrapped with a thin bandage, which Cal carefully unravelled. Beneath it was a short incision, sealed shut by a row of neat black stitching. One of the Department's surgeons had been sent to Julian's cell the previous evening, using the same protocols of hood and silence, to implant the final condition of his release: a new locator chip inserted into the thick muscle of his forearm.

"Clean work," said Cal. "Hope it didn't hurt too much."

Julian laughed. "I've had worse."

"Are you ready to go?"

"Is there any point in me trying to talk you out of this?"

"No," said Cal.

"Then I'm ready."

The Interim Director took his friend's hands in his own and squeezed them tightly. "Don't do anything stupid, Julian," he said, his voice low. "Please don't. Just keep your head down. When this is all over, we'll talk again, I promise. But for now, just think about Jamie and Marie. OK?"

Julian tightened his grip on Cal's hands, then broke the hold.

"I will be," he said. "Believe me, I will. Goodbye, Cal."

"Goodbye," said Holmwood. He walked across the hangar, then paused at the double doors and watched as the Security Operators helped Julian into the back of one of the SUVs. As it pulled out on to the grounds of the Loop, Cal fought back a profound sense

351

of loss, a mingled wave of sadness and guilt that threatened suddenly to sweep through him. He took a deep breath, then pushed open the doors and strode towards the lift at the end of the Level 0 corridor.

*One conversation I wasn't looking forward to done*, he thought, as he stepped into the lift and pressed the button marked B. *One to go.*

The moment of silence after he knocked on the door was so long that Cal began to believe that Frankenstein wasn't there.

If that proved to be the case, a large part of him would be relieved. The old monster had just about emerged from the dark period following his rescue from Paris, a period in which he had become a virtual recluse, but he still spent more time alone than Cal thought was healthy, even though he understood the reason.

It was the same reason that Larissa Kinley had jumped at the chance to escape to Nevada, that kept Marie Carpenter inside her cell despite the Interim Director's repeated offers to relax the conditions of her detention.

It was shame, pure and simple.

Frankenstein was ashamed of what he had become.

Not a reanimated patchwork of dead parts and pieces; *that* reality, the monster had long since come to terms with. What he was ashamed of was what he had been turned into on the island of Lindisfarne by a bite that dripped poison, before his long fall, and the loss of all that he was. A lycanthrope.

A werewolf.

The Interim Director was about to pull the console from his belt and search for Frankenstein's locator chip when an unmistakable voice rumbled through the door.

352

"Wait."

Cal did as he was told, until the locks disengaged and the door swung open. The monster filled the doorway, towering over him by half a metre, his eyes narrow, his thick black hair tousled and falling across his high forehead.

"Cal," grunted Frankenstein. "What do you want at this ungodly hour?"

"I need to talk to you, Victor. Can I come in?"

Frankenstein shrugged, and stepped aside. Cal walked into the neat, sparse room.

"Coffee?" asked Frankenstein, closing the door behind them.

"No thanks," said Cal.

"I'm going to make some."

"That's fine."

Frankenstein filled a kettle that looked tiny in his oversized hands and spooned coffee into a mug. As the kettle began to boil, the monster regarded him with a curious expression.

"So what's going on, Cal?"

"Something miraculous, Victor," replied Holmwood. "One of our oldest friends has come back to life. But you already knew that, didn't you?"

Frankenstein frowned. Then, slowly, a thin smile spread across his face. "So it is Julian you're keeping downstairs," he said. "I thought as much."

"Why?" asked Cal. "What made you think that?"

Frankenstein shrugged. "A prisoner that only you are allowed access to," he said. "A man who flew in from Nevada barely two months before new intelligence came to light about a cured vampire. Wasn't hard to connect the dots."

Cal stared at the monster. He had been expecting denial, or

refusal to comment, but Frankenstein's admission that he knew Julian was alive had been startlingly forthcoming.

"You knew," he said. "All along, you knew he wasn't dead, and you never told me. You let me grieve for him. Why?"

Frankenstein frowned again. "You know why."

"Your oath to the Carpenters takes precedence over your loyalty to the Department?"

"I've never made any secret of that. The two have rarely been at odds, but this, unfortunately, was one of the times when they were."

"It was a court-martial offence," said Holmwood. "Or *offences*, I should say. Aiding and abetting a fugitive, lying to the Director of the Department, conspiracy, God knows what else."

"I understand that," said Frankenstein. He poured boiling water into his mug and stirred his coffee.

"Did you help him fake his death?" asked Cal. "I know you kept him updated on Jamie and Marie once he was gone, but did you actually help him escape?"

"What do you think, Cal?" asked Frankenstein, and took a long sip of his coffee.

"I think you were on the team that went to bring him in when his arrest warrant was issued," said Holmwood. "And I remember you insisting that be the case. So I think you did, yes. I think you and Julian cooked something up between you and you helped him escape, even though he was wanted for treason."

"Did you ever really think he was a traitor?" asked Frankenstein, his voice low. "Whatever the evidence, whatever Thomas Morris hung round his neck, did you ever actually *believe* that he could do something like that?"

"No," said Cal, his voice rising with anger. "He was my friend too, Victor. Don't try and make it seem like you were the only one who stood by him. I loved him too."

"If you loved him," said Frankenstein, "then you should have no problem understanding what I did."

There was a long moment of silence.

Ever since Cal had received the video call from Bob Allen informing him that Julian Carpenter had just driven in from the Nevada desert and surrendered, he had been surprised by the emotion that filled him most often when he thought about the situation his old friend had created. It wasn't relief that he was still alive, or excitement, or sympathy for Jamie and Marie; it was *anger*, hot and bright and burning at the very limit of his self-control.

He was furious that Julian had not trusted him, and Henry Seward, and Paul Turner, and the rest of his friends and colleagues, to stand with him when he needed them. No matter how compelling the evidence against him had appeared at the time, Cal was unshakeable in his belief that they would have looked beyond it and found a way to help him.

But instead he had run, leaving a cowardly trail of devastation behind him: a family damaged almost beyond repair; a crack in the Department from which had spread the awful, whispering tendrils of betrayal and paranoia; and a yawning hole in the lives of the men and women who had known him. And if Frankenstein had been in on it, if the monster, whose instincts and judgement were usually so sound, had actually helped Julian do something so utterly stupid and reckless, then that only made it worse.

"You swore to protect the Carpenters," he said. "You didn't consider that the best way to do that might have been to bring Julian in?"

355

"The second most powerful vampire in the world had sworn vengeance against him," said Frankenstein. "A vampire who would never stop, would never tire of waiting for his revenge, and would not have thought twice about butchering Jamie and Marie for the sheer joy of doing so."

"We could have protected him," said Cal.

"Could you?" asked the monster. "I watched Valeri bring an army in here and murder half the active roster, barely three months ago. And compared to Alexandru, Valeri is a model of restraint. Julian believed that if the world thought he was dead, his family would be safe."

"He was wrong," said Holmwood.

"I'm fully aware of that now, Cal," said Frankenstein, his voice a low rumble. "But I didn't know at the time, and neither did Julian, so what was done was done. I'm sorry if you're upset, or annoyed, or if you feel betrayed. I'm afraid there was no time to worry about anyone else."

Cal sighed. He had not expected an apology, he would, in fact, have been astonished to receive one, but he had nonetheless been expecting *something* that at least resembled contrition.

"How did you do it?" he asked. "How did you fake Julian's death?"

Frankenstein narrowed his eyes, then smiled. "He wouldn't tell you, would he?" he said. "You asked him and he wouldn't tell you."

"No," said Cal. "He wouldn't tell me."

Frankenstein grunted with laughter. "He always was a law unto himself. But you can't really think I'm going to tell you when it's clear he doesn't want you to know?"

"I thought you might be more reasonable than him."

"Then I'm sorry to disappoint you."

Cal scowled, feeling his frustration intensify. "You're impossible," he said. "Both of you. You always have been."

"At least I'm consistent," said Frankenstein, "if nothing else. Was there something more?"

"I'm sorry?"

"You said you wanted to tell me something. Was it just that Julian is alive?"

"No," said Cal. "It wasn't just that. I came down here to tell you that he has been released."

Frankenstein's smile disappeared. "Released?"

"Under strict surveillance," said Cal. "He was taken out of the Loop this morning."

"Where to?"

Cal shook his head. "I'm not going to tell you that, Victor. All you need to know is that he's been released and is under strict orders not to attempt to contact anyone within the Department, under any circumstances. Including Marie and Jamie."

Frankenstein grunted with laughter. "You've known Julian almost as long as I have," he said. "Do you honestly think he's going to follow that order?"

"Of course not," said Cal. "I'm not an idiot, Victor. But it was that or locking him up for the rest of his life, and I couldn't do that to him. I probably should have, but I just couldn't. My conscience weighs heavy enough as it is."

"You did the right thing," said Frankenstein.

"I really don't care whether you think so or not," said Cal. "But thanks."

"You're welcome," said Frankenstein. "So why are you telling me this, Cal? You're obviously driving at something, so just spit it out."

Cal nodded. "There's no way Julian can get access to his family," he said. "Not unless someone inside the Department helps him. So I need to know, right now, about any procedures the two of you established for staying in touch, any back channels you used to use, or anything else that I should be aware of."

"There's nothing," said Frankenstein.

"Are you telling me the truth, Victor?"

"Will you believe me if I say yes?" said Frankenstein. "You're going to have to decide for yourself."

"If he tries to contact you," said Holmwood, "I'm trusting that you'll do the right thing and tell me. I understand the oath you swore, and I've always respected it, but Jamie is the priority, not Julian. Is that clear?"

"He won't try to come through me," said Frankenstein. "He'll know that's what you'll be expecting. But if he does, I'll tell you. I promise you that much."

"Thank you, Victor," said Cal. "I believe you. And I hope it goes without saying that Jamie doesn't need to know about any of this?"

Frankenstein smiled. "What do you take me for, Cal? An idiot? He'd burn this whole place to the ground, with you and me inside it."

Cal nodded, a smile of his own rising on his face. The monster was right; if Jamie found out that two of the men he trusted the most, in whose hands he regularly placed his life, had been concealing the fact that his father was still alive from him, the explosion would be audible from miles away.

His console beeped into life on his belt. Cal tilted the plastic rectangle and saw NEW MESSAGE glowing on the screen. He tapped OPEN, saw who it was from, and quickly closed it.

"I have to go," he said.

He was about to turn towards the door when he noticed that Frankenstein had slid a hand beneath the collar of his shirt and was scratching slowly at his skin. Cal flushed with embarrassment, and considered pretending he hadn't seen, but it was too late; the monster was regarding him with narrowed eyes.

"I'm sorry, Victor," he said. "I didn't mean to stare."

Frankenstein's gaze remained unchanged for several long seconds. Then his eyes widened to their normal misshapen sizes, and the faintest flicker of a smile curved his grey-green lips.

"Don't worry about it," said the monster. "It feels like my skin is on fire. I never felt anything like it before I was bitten."

"How long?" asked Holmwood.

"The night after tomorrow," said Frankenstein. "I can feel it, Cal. I know how that must sound, but it's the truth. I can feel it coming, feel it pulling at me. I'll go into a cell this afternoon."

Cal grimaced. He hated the requirement that his old friend spend three days of every month locked in a concrete box, but he also understood that it was absolutely necessary from a security perspective. He had visited Level H during the last full moon and the noise coming from Frankenstein's cell had been astonishing: a cacophony of howls that chilled the blood and growling roars that shook the thick walls.

"Are you getting any closer to controlling it?" asked Cal.

Frankenstein gave him a long look.

"No."

The monster pushed the door closed behind the Interim Director and pressed the button that engaged the locks; they slid loudly into place.

He stood still for a long moment, his palms flat on the surface of the door, his head slightly lowered, his mind churning. Then he strode back across his quarters and began to make another cup of coffee. As he waited for the water to boil, he tried to push away the guilt that was building in his stomach, like clouds gathering before a storm.

Frankenstein had taken no pleasure in lying to Holmwood; he had always respected the Interim Director, and that respect had grown with the job Cal had done since Henry Seward had been lost, and leadership of Blacklight had been thrust unceremoniously upon him. But some things went deeper than professional respect, things that were older, and more important.

As the kettle began to bubble again, the monster crouched down in front of his locker. It contained only a small fraction of the possessions he had accumulated over the course of his long life; there were storage units and apartments groaning at the seams in a number of cities around the world, so many that he no longer had a remotely accurate idea of what any of them contained. The locker held the mementoes that meant the most to him, objects he would never have shown to anyone, never dreamt of explaining their importance. There were photographs, letters, three small framed drawings, a thick woollen scarf with the letters HBC sewn into it, a pair of binoculars, a linen bag containing twelve piano keys, a first edition of *Frankenstein* signed by Mary Shelley, a programme from the 1853 premiere of *La Traviata* at Teatro La Fenice, a rusted metal can with chemical symbols printed on it, six small squares of coloured glass, a thick bundle of postcards bound with twine, and a black radio handset.

He lifted the radio out carefully, almost reverently, and let his thumb rest against its power button. In all likelihood, the batteries would be flat; it had been more than two and a half years since the handset had been turned on. He didn't know whether it would still be tuned to the frequency that had been agreed, but it wouldn't matter; he knew it by heart.

For long seconds that stretched into minutes, Frankenstein wrestled with an overwhelming desire to turn the radio on, just for a little while. He knew with absolute certainty that Julian would try to reach him via the method they had agreed many years before; all he would have to do would be press the power button, and wait.

# 35

# A HARD DAY'S NIGHT

Matt Browning watched the numbers at the bottom of the screen tick past midnight, sighed deeply, and pushed himself back from the keyboard. The chair wheels squeaked across the floor of the laboratory as he closed his eyes and tried to slow his racing mind, to force it into neutral, even just for a moment.

*Two more minutes*, he thought. *One hundred and twenty seconds. Then we'll know.*

He had been working solidly for six hours, stopping only to get another Diet Coke from the dispensing machine or to pace impatiently back and forth while the university's computer network processed a new run of data. It was not an unusual workload, certainly not by the standards of the Lazarus Project, where he would regularly look up from his screen to discover that ten or twelve hours had passed, apparently in the blink of an eye.

It was, however, almost unbearably stressful.

The Lazarus Project had a specific goal, but no fixed deliverables, no benchmarks or timeline checkpoints. As a result, it was largely impossible to end each day with any reliable sense of what contribution you had made. Everyone simply worked as hard as they could, for as long as they could, then came back the next morning and did so again.

What he was doing now, on the other hand, was a contained project that was objectively straightforward, involving a clear series of steps and processes, a fixed timeframe, and a group of people who had no idea what he was doing approaching him with infuriating regularity and asking why it was taking so long.

*I'm sorry!* he wanted to yell. *I'll just rush the most important specimen collection of all time, one that can never, ever be done again if I screw it up. Is that what you want?*

He knew it wasn't; his squad mates were simply desperate to see whether the operation had been a success, as he was himself. Major Simmons had only arrived at the laboratory with Landsman an hour earlier, having spent the evening dealing with the chaos that had been unleashed at the corner of Geary and Third; from what Matt had overheard, it had eventually taken a call from an office inside the Pentagon to placate the Chief of the SFPD and the city controller, so vast had been their outrage. At the same time, an NS9 containment squad had been flown up from Nevada, and was currently in the process of formally informing the dozens of eyewitnesses that they had in fact *not* seen what had happened in front of their eyes, and making them sign official documents that said so.

Danny Lawrence had driven Matt straight to the lab, leaving the carnage of John Bell's final act behind them, and he had immediately got to work. The required tasks were not difficult; by Lazarus standards they were, in fact, almost insultingly easy. But their potential implications were so huge that he had found his hands shaking even as he removed the specimens from his bag.

*Stay calm,* he had told himself. *You know you can do this. And Cal wouldn't have sent you if he didn't think so too.*

Working slowly and carefully, Matt had isolated eight samples of blood and eight small pieces of John Bell's body. Each sliver of pale flesh was placed into a plastic dish, sealed, and put into a refrigerator to await transportation back to Nevada, where two of them would remain. Four would be returning with him to the Loop, and the other two were backups, redundancies in case anything befell the primary samples. As they cooled in the refrigerator, Matt had turned his attention to his most important task, even though it involved little more than pressing a series of buttons.

First, he placed drops of Bell's blood on to a pair of slides and fed them into a gene sequencer; the machine would use an enzyme to copy the DNA within the blood millions of times, providing a far larger sample with which to work. That enlarged sample was then sent to Dreamland, where the NS9 supercomputer array would break the whole into manageable chunks and create a hugely simplified map of the genetic code within. It was no substitute for the comprehensive microanalysis that would be carried out back at the Lazarus labs, but it would hopefully provide early indications of exactly what they were dealing with; if there was anything clearly out of the ordinary inside John Bell's DNA, it would be revealed.

Second, Matt fed a pair of plastic slides into a desktop machine that looked like a laser printer and was unimaginatively called a blood analyser. The slides contained minute squares of photographic film, soaked with a series of different chemicals; when Matt inserted a drop of John Bell's blood through a tube in the top of the machine, it would be spread out and passed across the slides, causing a series of reactions and providing results for a battery of standard tests.

Again, the sample blood would be subjected to every single conceivable test once he got it back to the Loop, but this blunt analysis would highlight anything that was obviously unusual. It was, however, maddeningly slow, at least in comparison to the equivalent machines at Dreamland and at the Loop; the machine, a model which had been superseded by faster, more powerful evolutions, would take two hundred and forty minutes to deliver a result.

Matt had now been waiting for two hundred and thirty-eight.

*Two minutes.*

*Two minutes to go.*

He was trying his hardest not to get his hopes up. There were absolutely no guarantees that the process that had cured John Bell of vampirism would have left any permanent evidence within his blood cells and, even if it had, there were no guarantees that it would be recognisable for what it was, especially after such a rudimentary series of tests. But still...

*One minute.*

Matt's respect for what Jamie and Larissa did every night was boundless; he admired the bravery required to go out into the darkness searching for monsters, and he knew the world became a fractionally safer place with each vampire they destroyed. But he had come to believe that the wider battle for the future of humanity was not going to be decided at the end of a stake; it was going to be won, if it was won at all, in a laboratory.

Victory would come when a process existed that could undo the genetic changes that had been imposed on vampires; when they could be cured, rather than destroyed.

The blood analyser beeped three times, announcing that it was done.

Matt took a deep breath, and rolled himself back to the desk. The computer screen in front of him was grey, its rainbow cursor spinning endlessly. He waited, resisting the urge to scream with impatience, until the screen shifted to a white background. Diagrams and graphs and long columns of black text filled it, but he was only interested in the lines of red at the top.

UNIDENTIFIED ABNORMALITY PRESENT IN SAMPLE. SEE SECTION 5 FOR DETAIL. FURTHER TESTING RECOMMENDED.

Matt stared at the words, trying not to burst into tears as a great wave of relief crashed through him.

*There's something there*, he thought. *Something in the blood.*

"Holy shit," said Danny Lawrence.

Matt jumped and spun round in his chair; the NS9 Operator was standing behind him, staring at the screen with obvious wonder.

"Jesus, Danny!" said Matt, his heart thumping in his chest.

"Sorry, man," said Danny, and clapped Matt on the shoulder, his eyes still fixed on the screen. "This is real, right? This isn't a simulation? This is John Bell's actual blood?"

"It's real," said Matt, and pointed at the box labelled Section 5. It was full of long chains of chemical formulas and symbols. "This is it, right here. *This* is what we were looking for. Something that was in Bell's blood that shouldn't have been, that the computer doesn't recognise."

"What is it?" asked Danny.

Matt shook his head. "I don't know," he said. "Not yet. Those first three lines are enzymes, protein-based at a guess, and some of the rest of it looks like catalytic RNA. But I won't know what it is or what it does until I get the samples back to the Loop and start unpicking them."

"Is it a cure, though?" asked Danny, his voice full of hope. "Did we find it?"

"I don't know," repeated Matt. He saw his colleague's face fall and quickly continued. "I'm not saying that it definitely *isn't*, I just can't say for certain that it is. But if I had to guess, I'd say that what we're looking at is a result of what was done to him. It may be a functioning cure that we just have to extract, or it may be some by-product of the process that we have to take as a starting point and reverse engineer. But either way it's monumental. It's huge."

"I need to tell the others," said Danny, his face now covered with a wide smile. "They're going to want to see this."

"Go get them," said Matt, returning the smile with a weary one of his own. "I'll wait here."

Danny nodded, and marched away towards the laboratory doors. The rest of the squad were waiting for news in the building's cafeteria, at the other end of a long corridor.

As he waited for them to arrive, Matt remotely accessed the Blacklight server, logged into it, and clicked COMPOSE on the toolbar at the top of the messaging client. He dragged the results from the blood analyser into the empty message as an attachment, then tabbed to the window that displayed the progress of the provisional DNA analysis; the Dreamland computers were grinding through the process, but were still almost thirteen hours away from providing their first results. NS9 would send those results to the Lazarus Project as soon as the analysis was complete, by which time Matt hoped he would be back at his desk, beginning in-depth investigation of the anomaly that the blood analyser had identified.

Matt addressed the message to Professor Karlsson and clicked SEND. He wanted to send them the actual data, rather than just the results page, so they could get to work in his absence, but restrained himself; he would send it as soon as they were back in Nevada, from a server he was sure he could trust. When SENT appeared on his screen, Matt pulled his console from his bag and typed a message to Natalia Lenski, telling her that he would be bringing physical samples of the cured vampire with him to the Loop as soon as was humanly possible. It was past eight o'clock in the morning in England, so he wasn't worried about the possibility of having woken her up; she would most likely have been at her desk for at least an hour already.

A reply arrived almost instantaneously. Matt thumbed it open.

FROM: Lenski, Natalia (NS304, 11-L)
TO: Browning, Lieutenant Matthew (NS303, 83-C)
Well done. Am so proud of you.

Matt grinned as heat bloomed in his chest. His fingers flew across the console's screen.

FROM: Browning, Lieutenant Matthew (NS303, 83-C)
TO: Lenski, Natalia (NS304, 11-L)
Thanks :) I'll be home soon...

The laboratory door flew open and Matt found himself surrounded by his squad mates; they shouted excitedly, and clapped him on the back, and jostled and cheered and celebrated. Major Simmons stood apart from them, watching the commotion with the ghost of a smile on his hard face.

"I didn't do anything," protested Matt, grinning widely. "I really didn't. We just found the right man."

The NS9 Operators were not interested in such modesty, false or otherwise; they congratulated him over and over, until his back hurt from endless gloved blows and his arm ached from being pumped up and down. When calm finally began to descend once more over the lab, he looked around at his squad mates.

"We should go," he said. "I need to get the samples back to Nevada."

Major Simmons nodded, and stepped forward. "All right," he said. "You heard him. Pack up everything, and I do mean everything. I want it to look like we were never here. Browning, are you still plugged in to anything?"

"The DNA analysis is running at Dreamland," said Matt. "But there's no way to access it once I cut the connection."

Simmons nodded again. "Good," he said. "We'll take the computer you've been using with us. I want nothing left to chance."

"Yes, sir," said Matt.

"All right," said Simmons. "Then get to it, all of you."

The men and women scattered across the laboratory, gathering up their equipment, removing empty cans and used mugs, wiping down surfaces and eradicating footprints, as Matt turned his attention back to his screen. He killed the external connections, erased the cache, the IP record and the keylogs from the laboratory server, then shut down and disconnected the computer itself. It went into his bag along with the samples, which he removed from the refrigerator and placed into a vacuum bag that closed with a loud hiss of escaping air. He sealed the bag, wrapped it in three thick layers of protective foam, then took a last look round the lab for anything he might have forgotten.

Major Simmons walked over to him. "All set?" he asked.

"Set," replied Matt. "Ready to go, sir."

"Good," said Simmons, then drew his pistol and pointed it at Matt's head. "Nobody move a damn muscle."

# 36

# THE OLD AND THE FORGOTTEN

*TELEORMAN FOREST, ROMANIA*

Jamie watched Larissa glide easily round a shaft of sunlight, and smiled despite himself.

The light was pale yellow, thick with dust, and fell to the ground from a tiny gap in the canopy overhead as straight and true as a laser beam. The rest of the forest was thick with shadow, dark and cold and gloomy, but the look on Jamie's girlfriend's face, as she skirted within millimetres of the light before swooping away, was a reminder that it was still morning; despite the darkness surrounding them, Larissa was clearly relishing the opportunity to fly during the day.

After the tension within the squad had threatened to boil over as they stood in the clearing for what only Tim Albertsson refused to admit was the second time, a palpably dangerous moment in which it had taken every ounce of Jamie's self-control not to break the stock of his MP7 over the American's smug, stupid face, they had finally started to make progress. The going was slow, torturously so, but they were now deep in the perpetual twilight of the forest and moving forward. But part of the reason he was so pleased to see the momentary bloom of happiness on Larissa's face as she evaded the beam of light was because his girlfriend was acting more and more strangely with each hour that passed.

Her eyes were constantly flaring red, and her movement was both incessant and increasingly erratic; she would dart away in one direction, then swoop so low that her outstretched fingers brushed the ground, before disappearing up into the darkness near the tops of the trees, all without a word to anyone. When he asked her what was going on, she just shook her head and muttered about the smell, and the noise. Jamie, who knew his senses were painfully dull in comparison to hers, could detect only the earthy aroma of the forest, and could hear nothing out of the ordinary. Telling her this had not helped, however; she had given him a withering look of disappointment, and floated back into the air.

Since the grotesque arrangement of corpses, Jamie had seen no signs of animal life at all among the trees. On several occasions he had heard the faint snap of a branch, or caught the low bushes and shrubs moving in the corners of his eyes, as though something had disturbed them, but he had *seen* nothing; it had begun to feel like they were the only living things in the forest.

*Apart from the man we're looking for,* he told himself. *Obviously.*

Jamie was a country boy at heart; he had grown up in Kent, the south-eastern county known as the garden of England, and had spent a great many weekends of his childhood stomping through woods with a stick in his hand and his father at his side. Those distant places, copses of oaks and sycamores full of foxes and squirrels and birds, bore no resemblance to where he now found himself; the Teleorman Forest felt like an entirely different world, and not a welcoming one.

"Stop right there."

Jamie looked up, startled out of his memories. It was Larissa's voice, raised and urgent, a command not a request. He looked along the path the squad were steadily beating through the thick underbrush and saw her floating in the air ahead of them, her hand out, her eyes fixed on the forest floor. Van Orel, who was on point, did as he was told, stopping where he stood.

The rest of the squad followed suit.

Jamie glanced around, and felt a shiver run up his spine. He had become acutely aware, as they made their way deeper and deeper into the forest, of exactly how isolated they were becoming, of just how far away help would be if something went wrong in this old place.

"What is it?" shouted Albertsson. "What's going on?"

Larissa didn't respond. Without taking her eyes from a patch of ground beneath where she had stopped, she flew to her left and pulled a thick branch from the trunk of one of the trees. She glided back to her previous position, held out her gloved hand, and dropped the branch.

The chunk of wood hit the ground with a deafening clang of metal that echoed through the forest, making Jamie jump and causing his hand to fly to the handle of his pistol. An explosion of splinters drifted through the cool, gloomy air, before silence and stillness took over again.

"Come forward," said Larissa. "Very slowly."

Jamie moved up tentatively with the rest of the squad, his heart pounding in his chest. Larissa pivoted in the air until she was upside down, then reached down with her long arms and tore out several handfuls of shrubs, now coated in wood dust.

"Oh Jesus," said Engel.

Lying on the newly exposed patch of forest floor was a metal bear trap. Its teeth were clamped round the remains of the branch that Larissa had dropped, and were rusty and caked in dirt. The trap looked old, but still vicious; the teeth formed a silver-brown grin around the shattered branch, like that of some ancient shark.

"Nobody move," said Albertsson, his voice low. "Stay right where you are. Larissa, can you check if there are more of them?"

Larissa nodded, and flew slowly away in the direction the squad had been heading. Jamie stared down at the trap, his stomach a tightly clenched ball, wondering what would have happened if Van Orel had stepped into it. It had been less than two metres in front of the South African when Jamie's girlfriend had ordered them to stop.

*It would have taken his leg off,* he thought, and felt his head swim.

"A bear trap," said the South African, his voice little more than a whisper. "It didn't even occur to me to be looking. Are there even bears in Romania?"

Engel nodded. "Lots of them," she said, her eyes fixed on the trap. "Did you even read the briefing on this place? Second largest European population after Russia. Bears, and wolves, and wild boars, and God knows what else."

"In which case," said Albertsson, "where the hell are they all? I haven't seen anything move since we left camp. Have any of you?"

"No," said Petrov. "I have seen nothing that was not dead."

His comment hung in the air. Bears and wolves were apex predators, and yet there was no sign of them in a place that should have been their natural home.

"Maybe because there's something worse than them here," said Jamie, giving voice to the thought that had taken root in all of their minds.

Albertsson shot him a look that Jamie was sure was meant to be dismissive, but which contained far too much uncertainty to be convincing. He returned the look with an even stare, until the American Operator looked away.

From somewhere up ahead there came a second clang of metal, closely followed by a third. Jamie tried to slow his heart, his eyes fixed on the gloom into which his girlfriend had disappeared. For a long, empty moment, nothing moved or made a sound. Then Larissa flew slowly out of the darkness, her face pale.

"Two more," she said. "That's all I could see, but I'm not guaranteeing that's all there is. I suggest you all tread very carefully."

Albertsson nodded. "You heard her," he said. "I want everybody looking at their feet as we move. This is no place for a medical evac."

The members of the DARKWOODS squad nodded, and Van Orel led them onwards again, even slower than before. The trap had spooked them all; that much was obvious to Jamie as he carefully followed the path flattened by his squad mates, suddenly grateful for his place at the rear of their column. If there were more traps in their path, three pairs of feet would reach them before his.

Albertsson may have been stating the obvious, but he was also right; this would be no place to have to deal with an injured Operator. It had gone unspoken, but every member of the squad was fully aware that the possibility of any kind of conventional evacuation was now remote; their consoles and radios had all lost signal within thirty seconds of entering the forest, leaving them no means of contacting the outside world. If something happened to one of them, their best chance of survival was going to be to hold tightly to Larissa's waist and hope she could fly them both to help in time.

*And that would mean losing our most valuable weapon,* thought Jamie. *The only one of us who has the slightest chance of standing up to him when we find him.*

Although he was sure it wasn't a conviction that all his squad mates shared, Jamie had absolutely no doubt they would find the first victim. He didn't know long it would take, what state they would be in, or what was going to happen when they found him, but he was certain that they would. And what was more, he had begun to believe that the first victim *wanted* to be found, regardless of how that sounded. The tableau of dead animals had appeared to be a warning to come no further, but if whatever lived at the heart of the forest *really* wanted to be left alone, it could very clearly have murdered them all as they slept.

*I think he's intrigued,* he thought. *He could have killed Grey, and he could have killed us, but he didn't. I think he wants to know why we're here, and what we want.*

The thought was strangely comforting. Jamie was not remotely convinced that he or any of his squad mates were going to make it out of the forest alive, but he was increasingly sure they were going to *reach* their target, if nothing else; what happened then would be in the hands of fate.

Ahead of him, the squad were debating the bear traps. Engel believed they had been put there to deter humans, which she saw as proof that they were going in the right direction. Van Orel and Albertsson agreed with her, while Petrov remained his usual silent self. Jamie disagreed; the traps had not been placed on any discernible path, or hidden in such a way as to make it likely that a human being might stumble into them. And Florin, the villager that he and Van Orel had spoken to the previous evening, had made it clear that anything beyond the very outskirts of the forest had been treated as off-limits to the local population, for several generations at least.

*They were for animals,* he thought. *Not for us. I'm sure of it. Maybe the first victim laid them, or maybe not. But I don't think it means we're going the right way. I don't think it necessarily means anything.*

"Jamie!" shouted Tim Albertsson.

He looked up and saw the Special Operator standing with his hands on his hips.

"Yes, sir?" he replied.

"Take point," said Albertsson. "It's your turn."

Jamie smiled, as murderous thoughts raced through his mind. "Yes, sir," he said.

He walked up the short column of Operators, past Petrov and Engel, past the gently smirking Albertsson, and past Van Orel, whose mouth twitched with a tiny smile of sympathy. Jamie stepped to the front of the line and began to walk, taking great care with each step. Ahead and above him, Larissa flew slowly back and forth, scanning the upcoming terrain. She glanced down as he led the squad deeper into the forest, and gave him a fierce smile that warmed his heart.

*She doesn't look like that at you, Tim,* he thought. *Whatever happened in Nevada, whatever the two of you aren't telling me, she doesn't smile at you like that.*

Jamie quickened his step, trying as far as possible to keep to a straight line, to stay on the heading that Tim Albertsson had chosen. He had absolutely zero faith in the American's directions, but nor did he have any better ideas of his own. And if nothing else, the next time they arrived at a clearing or an obstacle they had already encountered, it would give him great satisfaction to be able to say that he had simply been doing as he was told.

As Jamie trudged forward through the permanent gloom, his squad mates fell quiet, and the silence beneath the towering canopy crowded in, unnatural and unnerving. The forest should have been alive with noise, home to a cacophony of chirping and buzzing and the scuttling of the hundreds and thousands of animals that should have been living on its floor and in its trees and undergrowth.

But there was nothing.

It was as still and silent as a mausoleum.

*Dead*, Jamie thought, and shivered. *It's dead in here.*

Jamie had been on point for almost two hours when they found it.

He had led them through mile after mile of endless, indistinguishable forest, stepping carefully round deadfalls and over thick patches of brush, the kind that could easily be hiding two rows of metal teeth, hungrily awaiting a carelessly placed foot.

Nothing was different. Nothing changed.

Tim Albertsson continued to stubbornly insist they were going in the right direction, but Jamie and the rest of the squad knew full well that he was only saying so for his own benefit; the NS9 Special Operator's map had long since ceased to correspond to the terrain they were walking through, and their GPS locators had lost signal at the same time as their consoles and radios.

Jamie stepped carefully across a narrow stream, the meandering water as devoid of life as the rest of the Teleorman Forest, and was waiting for the rest of the squad to join him when Larissa whispered his name in his ear, startling him. His girlfriend was capable of moving with utter silence, a trait that, while regularly useful, never ceased to be unnerving.

"Christ," he said, turning to face her. "You nearly gave me a heart attack. What the—"

"There's something up ahead," she said, her face pale, the corners of her eyes glowing red. "Something bad."

Jamie froze. "What is it?" he asked.

Larissa shook her head. "I don't know. It's the air, something about the way it feels. Like it's wrong."

"All right," he said. "Is it safe?"

"I don't know," she replied. "I think so. It feels old, like it's been used up. But I don't know."

"What's going on?" asked Tim Albertsson. He had crossed the stream and was frowning at them.

"Something ahead," said Larissa. "Sir."

Albertsson narrowed his eyes. "Alive?"

"No," said Larissa. "I don't think so. Not any more, sir."

"Let's see it then," said Albertsson. He pushed between them and strode forward. Larissa shook her head and leapt back into the air, leaving Jamie to take a moment to ensure his temper was at least largely under control before following his squad leader.

It had once been a stone circle, that much was still clear.

The remains of the stones themselves were visible, peering out from beneath the moss and weeds that had claimed them over time. Jamie couldn't tell how tall they had been, or whether they had been inscribed or carved or arranged; they were now little more than twelve mounds of grey and green. They were not, however, what was occupying the minds of the six Operators.

The space between them was a wide, perfect circle of dark brown earth, devoid of even the tiniest sign of life; not so much as a single green shoot or animal track spoilt the flat surface. Around its perimeter, the forest continued, climbing up and away in every direction.

But inside the circle there was nothing.

Beyond the stones and the return of the dark green gloom stood a tight ring of trees. Jamie stared up at the narrow, seemingly even spaces between their trunks, at the point high overhead where their uppermost branches almost met, and thought they might be some variety of oak; it was difficult for him to be sure, as every one of the trees was dead.

Their trunks were twisted and gnarled, spindly columns of black and grey that jutted up towards the sky. They looked as though they had been burned, but if so, the fire had been remarkably localised; there were no other dead trees visible beyond the ring of oaks, no smaller trees younger than their neighbours.

Larissa stood beside Jamie, the expression on her face tight and uneasy, as Tim and the others turned slowly at the centre of the circle, taking it in.

"It smells wrong," she said, her voice low. "This whole place. There's something that I almost recognise, something I know I should be able to identify, and then something else, something *deeper*. I don't like it, Jamie."

Jamie nodded in agreement; he didn't like this place either. A circle of stones was unsettling enough, even though they now lay in ruins. He had paid attention in history in the days when he had still gone to school, and he understood what stone circles had once meant: solstices and seasons and rituals.

Sacrifices.

Blood.

The empty patch of ground was somehow worse, however; it seemed unnatural, almost artificial, as though it shouldn't exist. But he was standing in the middle of it.

"It doesn't make any sense," said Tim Albertsson. "What the hell is this? What was done here?"

Petrov shook his head. "Nothing good," he said.

*Damn right,* thought Jamie. *Larissa's right, this place is bad. You can feel it.*

"There's nothing here," said Van Orel. "Let's keep moving, eh?"

Albertsson nodded, with apparent reluctance; he seemed momentarily unwilling to leave the circle with its mysteries unsolved. But after a second or two, he nodded again, more firmly, and stepped off the bare earth.

"Let's move," he said. "Petrov, you're on point."

The Russian nodded, and strode across to join the Special Operator on the green of the forest floor, Engel and Van Orel close behind him. Jamie was about to do likewise when Larissa growled at his side.

"What is it?" he asked, although he didn't want to know. He didn't want to be standing in the circle any more; he didn't like the feel of the soft earth beneath his boots, the dead oaks crowding over him, their branches like skeletal fingers.

"I knew I recognised it," said Larissa. "I was trying to place something less normal. I can't believe it took me so long." She crouched down, scooped up a handful of the brown earth with her gloved hand, and held it beneath her nose. "Salt," she said, shaking her head. "This whole place smells of salt."

"Salt?" said Jamie. "Why salt?"

"People salted the earth where bad things happened," said Engel, from beyond the edge of the circle. Her eyes were wide. "So nothing could ever grow again. It was done to places that were considered unholy."

Fingers of ice danced their way up Jamie's spine.

"Let's get out of here," he said, trying to force calm that he didn't feel into his voice.

He walked across the circle, hoping his legs were not visibly trembling. Larissa dropped the earth, brushed her glove clean against the thigh of her uniform with a look of disgust on her face, then floated into the air and joined the rest of the squad.

Jamie was suddenly incredibly aware that he was the only Operator still standing inside the stone circle, and it took all the composure he had left not to break into a run. His mind played cruel games with him as he walked; it showed him the earth rising into a huge brown hand that pulled him down, showed the oaks closing in on him, creating an impenetrable wall of dead wood that trapped him forever in this old, *deep* place.

He was two metres from the edge of the circle when something hissed loudly from the base of the tree in front of him.

Jamie stopped dead, as still as a statue.

"What the hell was that?" asked Van Orel, his hand going instantly to the butt of his Glock.

Larissa growled, her eyes reddening as she looked at her boyfriend.

"Get away from the tree," said Jamie, his voice low and tight. "All of you. Now."

The squad members frowned, but Jamie's voice was full of the authority of conviction, and they did as he said; they backed away from the old tree in both directions, moving round the edge of the circle, until they could see what Jamie could see.

The snake slithered up out of a wide hole at the base of the tree and down on to the bare earth without making a sound. Its body was dark brown, covered in looping patterns of black. Its triangular head swept left and right above the ground, as though it was searching for something. Then its black eyes locked on Jamie, and it hissed again.

"Oh Jesus," said Engel.

"Shut up," said Jamie, his voice low.

"That doesn't belong—"

"Shut up," growled Jamie, his gaze fixed on the snake.

Its head hung motionless above the ground, but the rest of it was still coiling out of the tree, seemingly without end; two metres, then three, possibly even four. It hissed again, its mouth yawning open, its forked tongue darting out, its fangs clearly visible.

Jamie's heart pounded in his chest; he was forcing himself not to panic, to breathe, to think, for God's sake, *think*. He knew absolutely nothing about snakes; he had never needed to know anything about them, or given any thought to the idea that a day might come when he would. All he could think to do was stay still, and not turn his back on it.

"Don't move," said Larissa. "I'm coming to get you."

Jamie nodded. Out of the corner of his eye, he saw his girlfriend rise silently into the air and circle round behind him. The snake flicked its head in her direction, then slid silently forward over the salted ground, closing the distance between them to barely a metre, hissing steadily.

*Striking distance*, thought Jamie.

Larissa floated down behind him. He could hear her breathing, deep and steady, and a second later he felt hands slide under his armpits.

"On three," she whispered. "One."

The snake arched its back, raising its head further off the ground. "Two."

It hissed, louder than ever, its long body vibrating.

"Three!"

Larissa hurtled up and back, hauling Jamie into the air. For a terrible moment, her gloved hands slipped across the smooth material of his uniform, and he felt sure she was going to drop him. Then she tightened her grip, her fingers digging roughly into the soft flesh beneath his arms, and he cried out in pain.

The snake struck, its head turned to the side, its mouth wide and full of fangs. The razor-sharp points closed where his legs had been, on nothing. The snake heaved itself forward, its mouth opening again, but Jamie was beyond its reach as Larissa carried him out of the circle and set him down beside the rest of the squad. The six Operators watched the furious, thrashing snake, their eyes wide with shock.

"Grass snakes," said Engel, her voice low. "Small vipers. They're all that should be here."

"Jesus Christ," said Van Orel. "I've seen boomslangs and Cape cobras. I even saw a green mamba once. But I've never seen anything like that. Never."

"Me neither," said Albertsson, quietly. "We had rattlers where I grew up, but they stayed out of your way. That thing went straight for you."

"I know," said Jamie, feeling his heart slowly begin to decelerate. "I saw."

In the centre of the circle, the snake had ceased to thrash. It had stopped hissing, but its head was low to the ground and darting in every direction, as though searching for new prey. After a minute or so, it began to slide back into the hole it had emerged from, its body gliding across the ground with an eerie lack of sound.

Jamie watched it disappear, then turned to Larissa, who was staring at the circle of newly churned-up earth with a look of profound unease on her face.

"Thank you," he said, and kissed her delicately on the cheek.

Larissa smiled. "For what?"

"For saving me," said Jamie.

Larissa's smile widened. "It's what I do," she said.

Petrov took point as the squad moved out again, heading further into the forest. Jamie watched Larissa rise back into the air, trying not to think about what would have happened to him if she had not been there to lift him from harm's way; it was too chilling a prospect to allow himself to dwell upon.

And at the northern edge of the circle they left behind, long covered by dirt and moss, long stripped of the power it had possessed, lay a stone which had once existed in both this place and another, a cruel garden of statues and stars and evil that spanned dimensions.

It was the stone altar upon which the long, bloody chain of events that had eventually led the six Operators into the darkness of the forest had been set into motion, but it was now old, and forgotten.

# 37

# DOWN THE RABBIT HOLE

*SAN FRANCISCO, CALIFORNIA, USA*
*EIGHT HOURS AGO*

Major Simmons moved, looping an arm round Matt's neck from behind and pressing the Glock hard against his temple. Instantly, acting on pure instinct, the rest of the Operators drew their pistols and pointed them at their commanding officer.

"Everybody back away," said Simmons. "Slowly. Browning, put your gun on the desk."

"Sir?" said Andrews, her voice full of incredulity as she sighted down the barrel of her Glock. "What the hell are—"

"Shut up," said Simmons. "You just shut the hell up." He jabbed the gun against Matt's head. "Don't make me ask you again, Browning."

Matt was frozen stiff by shock and fear. The Major's arm was pressed tight against his throat, constricting it, preventing him from breathing, from forcing his body to move, to do as he was told before his head was blown off.

"Now!" bellowed Simmons, his breath hot in Matt's ear. Matt took a shallow, rattling breath, swallowed hard, and drew the pistol from where it still hung beneath his armpit. He lowered it to the desk with a shaking hand.

"Major," said Danny, his voice low, his pistol steady. "Put the gun down. Put it down now."

Simmons grunted with what might have been laughter. "I don't think so, Lieutenant. You think you can take me out without hitting the lab rat, then by all means take your shot."

Danny took a step forward, but didn't fire. Matt looked frantically round the laboratory and saw the silent Glocks of Andrews and Landsman gleaming dully beneath the fluorescent lights. His mind was racing, thundering with panicked questions, full of the terrible spectre of Professor Richard Talbot, whose gun-filled embrace had felt identical to the one he now found himself in.

*What the hell is this? What the hell is going on? How can this be happening again?*

"All right," said Simmons. "Browning, you and I are going to walk out of here, nice and slowly, and get in the car. I see any of the rest of you, I see so much as a shadow in the rear-view mirror, and I'll blow his head off. I assume that's clear?"

"It's not going to happen, sir," said Danny, shaking his head and taking another step forward.

"Yes it is," said Simmons. "Unless you want his death on your conscience. Browning, pick up your bag."

"Don't do it, Matt," said Danny. "Don't you move, OK?"

Simmons rammed the barrel of the Glock against the side of Matt's head again. He cried out, in pain and fear, but tried to focus on Danny, who Larissa had always said was a good man, a decent man, someone you could trust.

"Last chance, Browning," growled Simmons.

"Put the gun down, sir," said Andrews, her voice high and

unsteady. "This isn't you. Whatever's going on, we can fix it. Just put the gun down."

"You don't know anything," said Simmons. "Not a damn thing. Browning, I'm going to give you to the count of three to pick that bag up, and then I'm going to shoot you in the head. One."

Matt looked pleadingly at Danny, desperate for the Operator to tell him what to do. He had no doubt that Major Simmons meant what he said; at the count of three, he would kill him, and to hell with the consequences.

"Two."

"Damn it, sir!" shouted Danny, his eyes narrowing with fury. "Stop this!"

The arm round Matt's throat tightened, telling him everything he needed to know. He felt Simmons take a breath, preparing to speak the final number of his countdown, and his nerve failed him; he reached out and picked up the bag that contained the reason they had come to San Francisco, the samples that in all likelihood represented their only real chance of survival.

"Good boy," said Simmons. "Keep doing exactly what I tell you and you might just get out of this in one piece. The rest of you, stay right where you are. Browning and I are leaving now, and whether you believe it or not, I really would prefer not to kill any of you."

The Major pushed him towards the laboratory's main doors, keeping Matt between himself and the rest of the squad and their pistols. Matt went without resistance, his mind attempting to process what was happening, searching desperately for a way to stop it, trying to will himself to think like Jamie or Larissa.

*If he gets us out of the lab, then I'm on my own,* he thought. *Danny and the others would have taken their shot by now if they were going to.*

*But if Simmons is telling the truth, and we're going to the car, then at some point he's going to have to move the gun. Maybe there'll be a chance to do something.*

Simmons backed up against the laboratory door and kicked it open. Matt locked eyes with Danny as he was dragged backwards through them. Then the door swung shut, and he was on his own.

Matt was hauled roughly along corridor after corridor, Major Simmons' pistol removed from his temple and now pressed hard between his shoulder blades. He stumbled and staggered, his limbs threatening to tangle with sheer panic, but managed to stay upright until they reached the door he and Danny Lawrence had walked through seven hours earlier, when his head and heart had been full of optimism.

"Keep moving," hissed Simmons. "Through the door."

Matt pushed it open and felt cold night air whistle across his face, sending a shiver through him. Beyond the door was the Biology Department parking lot; the black SUV that had ferried them back and forth across the city was the only vehicle in sight. Simmons manhandled him towards it, then released his grip.

"Passenger seat," he said. "Don't get any ideas."

Matt shook his head, and walked unsteadily round the back of the car. Simmons kept his pistol trained on him every step of the way, then drew a fob from his pocket and unlocked the car. Matt pulled the passenger handle and felt his heart sink as the door opened with a heavy *thunk*. Simmons opened the door on the other side of the car, and pointed the pistol at him as he clambered up into his seat and fastened his safety belt, the bag of samples on his lap, his legs shaking beneath it. Simmons climbed into the car, settled behind the steering wheel, and started the engine.

"Where are we going?" asked Matt, his voice low and shaky.

"Shut up," said Simmons, as he put the car into gear. "You don't need to know."

Matt looked desperately up into the rear-view mirror, hoping to see Danny and the rest of the squad burst out of the building, guns blazing.

Nothing.

Simmons revved the SUV's powerful engine, then swung it across the parking lot. Its headlights picked out the low walls and green lawns of the university campus, and a single lane of road. It wound down to the main gate and out on to the streets of San Francisco.

*This is madness,* thought Matt. *We're both chipped. They can track us wherever we go.*

A simple way for Simmons to get round that particular problem formed in his mind, unbidden, and he felt his gorge rise. His stomach was a tight knot of fear, but his brain was still screaming for him to do something, *anything,* to not just let himself be a victim yet again.

The SUV accelerated down the road, the wind howling as it gathered speed. Simmons' face was expressionless, his attention fixed on the road ahead. A long shallow bend was all that stood between them and the open gate, which was flanked by high brick walls and a small security post. Matt stared, feeling his hope dwindle as they headed towards it.

Then an idea struck him.

He looked into the mirror and saw the empty parking lot disappearing behind them.

He looked over at Simmons, who was gripping the steering wheel with both hands, including the one holding the Glock.

He looked at the Major's unfastened seat belt.

Then he moved.

Matt swung the bag as hard as he could, slamming it into the Major's face and pressing it against him. Simmons bellowed with fury and grabbed at the bag, trying to push it away. The Glock fired involuntarily with a bang that was deafening agony in the confined space, punching a neat hole in the car roof. Matt felt gloved fingers take hold of his and bend them back, but he continued to push against the bag with all his strength. The gun fired again, and again, the muzzle flashes blinding, the noise unbearable as the windscreen glass broke. Matt screamed in pain and fury, swung his left leg over the SUV's central console, and stamped his boot down on Simmons' foot, pressing the accelerator to the floor.

The engine screamed and the big car leapt forward, its wheels thumping over the high kerb at the edge of the road and churning grass beneath them. Simmons pounded at Matt's hands; he heard one of his fingers break, and a millisecond later felt the pain gallop up his arm as Simmons finally dragged the bag clear of his face. He swung the pistol towards Matt as he grabbed hold of the steering wheel with his free hand, a look of indescribable rage on his crimson face. Then he looked through the windscreen, and his eyes widened as the headlights illuminated a wide expanse of dark red bricks.

Simmons slammed his free foot on the brake, but Matt bore down on the accelerator with all his strength, a scream of fury emanating from his mouth as he grabbed the Major's Glock and pushed it upwards. The SUV thundered across the grass, throwing up a great cloud of dirt and dust, and smashed into the wall head-on.

There was an explosion of noise as the front of the car disintegrated with a grinding scream, the remains of the windscreen exploded, and the air bags deployed with a cacophony of deafening bangs. Matt was hurled forward against his seat belt with an impact that would have made him scream if all the air hadn't rushed out of him with a sound like a bursting balloon. His head whipped forward, sending electric fire up the back of his skull and across his shoulders, and thumped against the air bag. He tried to lift it, but the pain was sickening: a deep, squirming agony that felt like it was radiating from his very bones. He gritted his teeth, pushed his howling muscles into action, and screamed against the air bag as his head finally came up, as slowly as a breaching submarine.

The driver's seat beside him was empty.

His bag was lying in the driver's footwell, beneath the steadily deflating air bag, with the Glock beside it. But there was no sign of Major Simmons.

Matt raised his head, trying to move his whole upper body rather than just his damaged, protesting neck, and looked through the windscreen. All that remained was a jagged ring of safety glass clinging to the frame; the rest had been blown out into the night. He reached down to release his seat belt and cried out in pain again as the bones of his broken finger ground together. He lifted it up before his face and felt his stomach revolve; the finger was snapped at its midpoint at a forty-five-degree angle, pointing crazily away in a wholly different direction to the other three.

He took a deep breath, released his seat belt with his good hand, and turned ever so slowly towards the door. He pulled the handle, his dazed brain wondering almost absently whether crashed cars really blew up like they did in the films his dad had loved to watch, and felt relief flood through him when the door opened with a high-pitched screech of metal.

Matt climbed slowly down on to the grass and carefully ran his functioning hand over the back of his neck. He could feel nothing out of place, no protrusions or hollows that shouldn't have been there; the knowledge did nothing to lessen the pain, but it provided some small comfort. He leant carefully back into the car, picked up the Glock with a trembling hand, and staggered round the rear of the SUV. From behind, the car looked undamaged: its lights shone red in the darkness; its rear window was intact; its metallic black paint shimmered in the glow of a street light.

On the other side of the car, he found Major Simmons.

He was lying on the grass beside what was left of the front of the vehicle, staring up at the night sky with empty eyes. His head was flattened on one side, his neck twisted at an unnatural angle, his face covered in a thick layer of dark red blood. Matt approached slowly, unwilling to take anything for granted, despite the clearly catastrophic nature of the Major's injuries, and prodded the man's ribs with the toe of his boot. The body rocked to one side, then settled back on to the grass.

Matt let out a loud, involuntary sob, a sound that was part relief and part vicious triumph. Then, immediately, came guilt, sharp and hot.

*I killed him*, he thought. *Oh Jesus. I actually killed him.*

A cold voice spoke inside him, one he hadn't heard before, and which sounded an awful lot like Jamie's.

*You did what you had to do*, it said. *What you needed to do.*

Then to Matt's utter horror, Major Simmons blinked, and made a rattling, gurgling sound that would haunt his nightmares.

He dropped to his knees beside the stricken man. "Don't move," he said. "Stay still. I'll get help."

Simmons took a wet, rasping breath. "Too late," he said, the words little more than slurred grunts. "Too... late."

"Just hold on," said Matt. "I'll fetch the others."

A pool of blood was spreading rapidly out from beneath the

Major's head. His eyes rolled, then fixed momentarily in place. "*Safeguard*," he wheezed.

Then he died.

Matt stood up on unsteady legs, his mind close to being overwhelmed by horror, and looked at the ruined bonnet of the car. It had concertinaed as it ploughed into the wall, folding up and in on itself so that its front wheels, buckled and shredded, had come to rest above the ground. The wall had bulged outwards, showering the devastated car with red dust, but had stayed standing. A patch of dripping crimson marked the spot where Simmons had collided with it after he had been thrown through the windscreen.

Matt crouched carefully, put the Glock on the ground, and pulled Major Simmons' radio from its loop on his belt. He keyed open the line and raised the handset slowly to the side of his head.

"Danny?" he said, his voice trembling. "Are you there? Over."

"Matt?" said Danny, instantly. "Where are you? What's happening?"

"Simmons is dead," said Matt, sounding on the verge of tears. "I'm by the main gate. Can you come? Please?"

"There in thirty seconds," said Danny.

Matt dropped the radio and leant back against the side of the car. He closed his eyes, feeling the adrenaline that had galvanised him into action ebb away; as it did so, the true scale of the agony in his neck presented itself and gleefully joined forces with the pain blooming from his broken finger. Matt lowered his head, his eyes still closed, his knees weak, and breathed slowly in and out until he heard the distant drumbeat of running footsteps. He opened his eyes, and forced a smile as Danny Lawrence sprinted across the grass towards him.

"Jesus Christ, Matt," said Danny, skidding to a halt and surveying the remains of the SUV with wide eyes. "Are you OK? What the hell happened?"

"We crashed," said Matt. "Simmons wasn't wearing his seat belt, so I stood on his foot."

"You did what?"

Matt took a deep breath. "On the accelerator..."

"You crashed on purpose?" asked Danny.

Matt tried to nod, but the motion sent a wave of nausea through him. "That's right," he managed.

Andrews and Landsman appeared, their pistols in their hands.

"Jesus," said Andrews, frowning at the ruined vehicle. "Are you all right, Matt?"

"No," grunted Matt, forcing a tiny, watery smile. "My finger is broken, and my neck is messed up." He pointed at Simmons' body. "What was this, Danny? What happened to him?"

The Operator shook his head. "I don't know," he said. "I called it in as soon as the two of you left the lab. We were waiting for instructions when you radioed. Did he say anything?"

"One word," said Matt. "Safeguard."

"Safeguard?" asked Danny. "What the hell is Safeguard?"

# 38

# COLD WAR ECHOES

Cal Holmwood turned into the short corridor that led to his quarters, anxious to read the message that had arrived on his console at the end of his conversation with Frankenstein, and found himself confronted with the familiar sight of the Security Officer waiting outside his door.

"Paul," he said, and smiled at his friend as he unlocked the door. "What tales of happiness and reasons for optimism have you got for me this morning?"

Major Turner smiled. "Two deaths by misadventure," he said. "Three murders. How's that?"

"You're just a ray of sunshine, aren't you?" said Holmwood, and pushed open the door. "After you."

The Security Officer stepped past him and into the room. As he did so, Holmwood momentarily considered slamming the door shut, running up to the hangar, stealing one of the helicopters and heading for the horizon, leaving the Loop and everything it contained far behind. Instead, he took a deep breath, and followed his colleague.

"Two accidental deaths," said Cal, settling into the chair behind his desk. "Please tell me you're talking about the incident at the perimeter? Not two more since then?"

Turner stationed himself in front of the desk and nodded. "Yes, sir," he said. "The two men have been identified as Mark Potter, aged twenty-one, from Winchester, and Scott Marshall, aged thirty, from Durham. Both had their wallets in their pockets, along with a number of stickers and leaflets, and the phone number of a solicitor in Peterborough."

"They were expecting to be caught," said Cal. "Not die."

Turner nodded again. "Yes, sir. This wasn't martyrdom, it was civil disobedience that went wrong."

"Very wrong," said Cal. There was no malice in his voice, just weariness; two more deaths seemed almost insignificant when set against the tide of blood and violence that surrounded the Department. When he first set foot in the Loop as a starry-eyed twenty-one-year-old, he would never have believed that he could be capable of regarding the loss of two human lives with such dispassion, but it was now the reality he found himself in. If he dwelt on them all, they would paralyse him.

"Agreed," said Turner. "They didn't deserve to die like that."

"They didn't deserve to die at all," said Cal. "They were protesting, for God's sake, and they climbed a fence they shouldn't have."

"Yes, sir," said Turner.

Cal rubbed his eyes and nodded. "All right," he said. "It's done, in any case. Where are we in terms of clean-up?"

"The bodies are about to be released to the coroner," said Turner. "Police are informing the families and will be releasing the names to the media. I ordered the security-camera footage leaked, and surveillance confirms it's already appearing online."

"Smart," said Cal. "What's the fallout going to be like?"

"The deaths are going to be front-page news," said Turner.

"So we can expect the protest encampment to grow in response. People are going to believe we killed these men, and since I assume we won't be making any statement to the contrary, it will quickly become accepted as the truth. I'm going to recommend an immediate doubling of the perimeter patrols, with your permission."

"That's fine," said Cal. "Whatever you need to do."

"Thank you, sir," said Turner. "The three murders were vampire-related. Mistaken identity. I've sent you the files, but there's nothing we need to do."

"All right," said Cal. "Anything else?"

"No, sir," said Turner. "That's all. Have we heard anything from Romania?"

Cal shook his head. "Nothing," he said. "No contact since they entered the forest this morning. We've got satellites overhead, and FTB reconnaissance flights, but the target area is impenetrable."

"What about Adam?" asked Turner.

"I got a report from Lieutenant Browning five minutes ago," said Holmwood.

"What does it say?"

"I don't know," said Cal. "I haven't had a chance to read it yet. Hang on."

He opened his desktop terminal and logged in, his fingers tapping rapidly on the keyboard. There was a low hum as the wide screen on the wall opposite the desk shimmered into life. At its centre was the Blacklight crest and motto, the Latin phrase that had been a favourite of Abraham Van Helsing.

*Lux E Tenebris.*

Paul Turner turned towards the screen as Cal opened the report that had arrived in his inbox. It comprised eighteen lines of simple black text; the Interim Director and the Security Officer read them together, their eyes fixed on the screen.

REPORT 7545/C
SUBMITTED: 0245
BY: LIEUTENANT MATTHEW BROWNING/NS303, 83-C
FAO: INTERIM DIRECTOR CALEB HOLMWOOD/ NS303, 34-D
SECURITY: ZERO HOUR CLASSIFIED

SUBJECT: OPERATION GARDEN OF EDEN

BEGINS.

Am currently en route back to Nevada. ETA 0425 local time.

The subject previously known as ADAM, since identified as John Bell, was located by our squad at his place of employment, a charity in central San Francisco. I pursued him as he attempted to flee, confronted him, and was able to confirm his identity before he took his own life.

I have isolated flesh and blood samples, and run provisional tests. These tests show an unidentified abnormality in John Bell's blood. Provisional DNA analysis should be available within approximately twelve hours, and thorough investigation can begin as soon as I am able to return to the Loop with the physical samples.

ADDITIONAL/PERSONAL: After my initial research was complete, Major Richard Simmons put his gun to my head and took me hostage, for reasons that are as yet unknown. He was killed while attempting to escape, and I sustained a neck injury in the same incident. Major Simmons spoke the word SAFEGUARD before he died, but NS9 have so far found no mention of it in their databases.

ENDS.

"Jesus Christ," said Holmwood, his voice low. "I know Rich Simmons."

"Me too, sir," said Turner. "I've been on operations with him. More than once."

"Does Safeguard mean anything to you?" asked Holmwood.

"No," said Turner.

"I don't like this, Paul."

"Nor do I, sir. They stopped Simmons, though, whatever it meant. And Browning seems to have done us proud."

Holmwood nodded. "An unidentified abnormality," he said. "What the hell does that mean? Has he found a cure or hasn't he?"

"I think it means he doesn't know," said Turner. "And that he's being very careful not to get carried away. But he thinks they've found *something*, Cal. That much is obvious."

Cal stared at Matt Browning's report, his mind racing. He wanted to believe the young Lieutenant had found something that might qualify as good news on a day that already seemed destined to be long and full of the opposite; wanted to believe it so much that his heart was pounding with something worryingly close to longing.

*An unidentified abnormality,* he thought. *It needs identifying, quickly.*

"All right," he said. "I want Browning home today. The *Mina II* is still in Nevada, right?"

"No, sir," said Turner. "I sent her to Beijing this morning. Professor Karlsson is finished at PBS6 and asked for extraction."

"Damn it," said Cal. "What's his ETA?"

"Ten hours from now, sir."

"I want the *Mina* checked and refuelled and sent to Dreamland as soon as she lands," said Cal. "The *minute* she lands. Is that clear?"

"Yes, sir," said Turner. "I could have an RAF transport chartered within the hour if you don't want to wait?"

Cal shook his head. "It's a twenty-eight-hour round trip to Nevada, allowing for time on the ground. Sending *Mina* will still be quicker, even if we have to wait ten hours until she gets here."

Turner nodded. "I'll take care of it."

"Good," said Cal. "Thank you. Dismissed."

Turner nodded and strode towards the door. He had almost reached it when the Interim Director spoke again.

"Paul," said Cal, his voice low. The Security Officer stopped, and turned back. "What are the chances of this actually being anything? Whatever it is that Browning has found?"

"I don't know, sir," said Turner. "I imagine we'll find out soon enough."

"I want to believe he's on to something," said Cal. "But I don't want to get my hopes up. Do you know what I mean?"

"Yes, sir," said Turner. "I do."

There was a long moment of silence, broken by Holmwood's console vibrating loudly into life on the surface of his desk. The Interim Director picked up the plastic rectangle, read the newly arrived message, and swore heartily.

"Aleksandr wants me to call him," said Holmwood. "It's urgent, apparently."

Turner nodded. "I'll leave you alone."

"No, stay," said Holmwood. "I'm probably going to be telling you about it as soon as we're done. You might as well hear it from the horse's mouth."

"If you're sure?" asked Turner.

"I am. Sit down."

The Security Officer walked over to one of the pair of armchairs that stood below the wall screen and did as he was told. Cal closed Matt Browning's report, opened a live video connection, and brought up his contacts list. He scrolled down until he reached the name of his Russian counterpart, and clicked CALL. A square window opened and was filled instantly with the lined, heavyset face of Aleksandr Ovechkin. The SPC Director smiled thinly as the secure connection was established, but he looked tired, and even paler than usual.

Holmwood's heart sank.

*Christ. This doesn't look like it's going to be good, whatever it is. Brilliant.*

"Aleksandr," he said. "It's good to see you."

"You too, old friend," said Ovechkin. "You are well?"

Holmwood laughed. "As well as can be expected. You?"

The SPC Director shook his head. "I am not so good, Cal. Not so good at all. This is a very difficult call for me."

A chill ran up Holmwood's spine. He glanced over at Paul Turner; the Security Officer was watching the screen with an unreadable expression on his face.

"Well, spit it out," said Cal, forcing a smile he hoped would come across as reassuring. "We've known each other too long for any bullshit, Aleksandr."

Ovechkin nodded. "That is why I asked you to call me personally, my friend. I would not have you hear this from anyone else."

Holmwood's smile disappeared. "Hear what? Out with it now, Aleksandr. You're starting to make me nervous."

"I am sorry," said Ovechkin. "I have to tell you that Richard Brennan is dead. He died yesterday, here in Polyarny."

For long seconds, silence filled the room. As was so often the case, it was the Security Officer who regained his composure first.

"Colonel Ovechkin," he said. "This is Paul Turner. Are you saying that the SPC has successfully eliminated Richard Brennan?"

"No, Major Turner," said the SPC Director. "That is not what I am saying. It is more complicated than that."

"So what *are* you saying?" asked Holmwood, his tone sharp. "My patience is starting to wear thin, Aleksandr."

"I will tell you everything," said Ovechkin. "But as I do, I would ask you to keep what you said moments ago in your mind, about how long you and I have known each other. And I would ask you to afford the same courtesy to my predecessor."

*Yuri?* wondered Holmwood. *What the hell has he got to do with this?*

General Yuri Petrov, the uncle of one of the men who was at that moment marching into the darkness of the Teleorman Forest, had been a legend in the classified community to which Cal had devoted his life, and his loss had been deeply felt. Henry Seward had often referred to Petrov as the hardest man he had ever known, and Cal had never seen anything to cast doubt on his friend's claim.

"I'll do that, Aleksandr," he said. "Now, please. Tell me."

"Yesterday evening our Surveillance Division picked up a man hiking through the forest that surrounds this facility," said Ovechkin. "It is not uncommon for hunters and trappers to approach our physical borders, although most have sense enough to turn back before they get too close. We monitored the man, whose route appeared likely to lead him on to restricted land, and prepared a team to intercept him if he didn't change course."

"Let me guess," said Holmwood. "He didn't?"

Ovechkin shook his head. "He did not. The team was despatched, but before they reached the man there were two gunshots, and the heat signature we were monitoring became confused. When my men arrived, they found him lying beside a brown bear, which he had managed to kill with a point-blank shot to the head. The man had sustained terrible injuries, but he was still breathing when he was brought into the base. My medical staff were unable to save him, but he regained consciousness on his way to surgery, and told one of the doctors that his name was Richard Brennan."

"Jesus," said Holmwood. A hundred questions were jostling for priority in his mind. "What the hell was he—"

The SPC Director held up his hand. "There is more, Cal. Let me finish, then ask your questions."

Holmwood stared at the screen for a long moment, then nodded.

"Thank you," said Ovechkin. "We checked his DNA against the sample that your Science Division provided, and confirmed that he was who he claimed to be. My intention was to inform you of his death last night, but there was something else in the report I received from my medical staff. As well as his name, Brennan also said a single word, in Russian. *Safeguard.* I ordered a search of our network for all references to such a word. Hidden deep in our Research Division files, accessible only by the Director and a former member of this Department by the name of Yevgeny Demidov, we found the records of a project. A project codenamed Safeguard."

Cal glanced over at Paul Turner again; the Security Officer was gripping the arms of his chair so tightly that his knuckles had turned white.

"I remember Demidov," said Holmwood. "He's dead."

"He died seven years ago," said Ovechkin. "A cardiac arrest in his sleep. He was a disgusting slob, a disgrace to our Department. He is not missed."

"What was Safeguard?" asked Turner. "What was he doing?"

"It was a black project," said Ovechkin. "Classified above Top Secret. I had no idea it existed until yesterday, and there is nothing to suggest that Yuri Petrov was aware of it either. But the records show it ran for almost twenty years."

"You can give me the detailed history later, Aleksandr," said Holmwood. "Just tell us what it was."

The SPC Director sighed deeply. "Spies," he said. "Demidov was making spies. And Richard Brennan was one of them."

# 39

## STAY BURIED

### TELEORMAN FOREST, ROMANIA

As Arkady Petrov led them deeper and deeper into the forest, Jamie found himself wondering how such a place could still exist.

The generally accepted wisdom seemed to be that the world was smaller than it had ever been, that there was nowhere left to explore, no dark corners into which to shine a light; the North and South Poles reached so often they had become tourist destinations, Everest scaled time and again, the deepest reaches of the Amazon braved, the great wildernesses of Siberia and Canada mapped. Satellites, GPS, camera phones, the internet: all had combined to increase knowledge and reduce mystery.

*But then again*, thought Jamie, *we kept vampires a secret for more than a century. So who knows what else is still out there?*

The Teleorman Forest was large, although not in comparison to the great Russian steppes or the seemingly endless frozen wilds of Alaska. But the facts were indisputable: all their equipment, the modern technology that connected them to the outside world and which Jamie was only now truly realising they had come to rely on so heavily, had failed barely thirty minutes after they had stepped into its trees.

There were no signals, no radio, no satellite contact.

They were on their own.

Cut off from the chain of command, the tension within the squad was rising with every minute that passed. It seemed clear to Jamie that Tim Albertsson was struggling with the pressure of leading the operation; without surveillance, without the ability to contact his superiors in Nevada for clarification, mistakes that were made would be his and his alone. Jamie almost felt sorry for the American; Operators throughout the Departments were trained to function as parts of a whole, to adhere to mission objectives and patrol grids and Operational parameters. Initiative was encouraged, of course, and self-sufficiency was drummed into every man and woman who underwent training. But theory was one thing; being forcibly separated from a support structure that you had come to take for granted was quite another.

The rest of the squad were all dealing with the isolation in their own way. Petrov had become even more stoical, if that was possible; his hard, pale face was entirely expressionless, and he spoke only when he had something directly related to the operation to say. Engel seemed to be shrinking before Jamie's eyes; her jovial manner seemed ever more forced as she withdrew into herself, as though it was an act that she herself no longer believed. Van Orel had gone the opposite way; he had become louder and more manic as they made their way through the unchanging landscape of green and brown, rattling out a stream of jokes and anecdotes so relentless that Tim Albertsson had eventually ordered him to shut up. And it was obvious to Jamie that Larissa, her already apparent frustration amplified by the sudden unreliability of her supernatural senses, was fighting a pitched internal battle with her vampire side.

He knew the signs all too well. She was flying constantly and erratically, responding to comments with frowns and rolled eyes and grunts that were close to growls, and regularly soaring away through the trees, separating herself quite intentionally from her squad mates. Jamie knew that her vampire side was hardest to resist when she felt uneasy or threatened; the combination of the strange properties of the forest, the operation itself, and whatever was between her and Tim Albertsson, was clearly causing her to feel both.

*I can wait until we get out of here*, Jamie thought. *Because there's no sense in making this situation even worse. But then one of them is going to tell me what's going on, whether they want to or not.*

He swallowed down a deep yawn of exhaustion. The incident with the snake had left him drained; the adrenaline that had flooded his system as he stared at the reptile's black eyes had long since worn off, and evening was drawing in. The constant gloom was deepening into a darkness that would soon be absolute, and although it was currently going unsaid, he was sure his squad mates were far from pleased at the prospect of making camp among the trees.

The squad had gradually spaced out as they continued their seemingly endless march; there were now a hundred metres or so between Petrov on point and Jamie at the rear. As a result, the Russian's voice sounded small and distant when he called for them to stop.

"All stop," relayed Tim Albertsson. He was currently third in line, behind Engel and ahead of Van Orel. "What is it, Petrov?"

"You will want to see this," said the Russian.

"What is it?" repeated Tim.

"I do not know," said Petrov.

*Great*, thought Jamie, as he jogged up to where the SPC Operator was standing. *What today has really lacked is something weird and inexplicable.*

He joined his squad mates as they gathered round Petrov. Larissa had floated to the ground and was looking at the Russian with obvious impatience, her eyes flickering red.

"So?" said Albertsson. "What's going on?"

They were standing in a small clearing, no more than five metres in diameter. A huge tree, its trunk as wide as a car, stood at its northern edge, and the floor was covered by the tangle of shrubs and bushes that made travelling through the forest such hard going.

Petrov looked at Albertsson, then raised his foot and brought it down on the ground, hard. A loud bang echoed through the trees as his boot connected with something solid, making Jamie jump.

"What the hell?" asked Van Orel.

Petrov shrugged. "Wood."

"Get some light in here," said Albertsson, drawing his torch from his belt. Jamie and the rest of the squad followed suit as Petrov stepped aside. The torch beams revealed a worn patch of grass, through which the outlines of wooden boards could be clearly seen. "Find the edges," said their squad leader, spreading his hands through the grass.

Jamie crouched down and ran his hands over the ground. He could feel the smoothness of the wood beneath his gloved fingers; it felt strange in this overgrown place. He found an edge and began to rip at the foliage, exposing a straight line in the dirt.

"Here," he said.

Van Orel quickly found a corner, half buried by a low bush sprouting between his feet. Engel had found the opposite one, and was brushing torn grass away from it as Albertsson and Petrov worked an edge. Larissa cleared the final corner, her eyes glowing in the last of the fading light.

"OK," said Engel, as the shape was revealed.

It was a wooden square, two metres long on each side. Moss and grass covered most of its surface, and the wood that was visible was stained dark by years of dirt; it looked as though it had been lying there for a great many years.

Jamie got to his feet and stepped back. His squad mates did likewise, their eyes trained on the strange discovery. Eventually, it was Van Orel who said what they were all thinking.

"What's underneath it?"

Larissa leant down and took hold of one of the edges with a gloved hand. She lifted it with no discernible effort, sending up clouds of dirt and dust as the wood separated from the forest floor, creaking and screaming as it came loose. It was huge, a solid block almost fifteen centimetres thick, but Larissa handled it like a feather. She raised it to shoulder height with one hand, in what Jamie was sure was a deliberate demonstration of her supernatural strength, then tossed it aside. It crashed to the floor, and lay still.

The squad stepped forward. A pitch-black hole stared up at them, its edges square and neat.

"Lieutenant Kinley," said Tim Albertsson, his gaze fixed on the empty space. "How would you feel about finding out how deep this goes?"

Larissa nodded, stepped effortlessly into the air, pirouetted, and disappeared into the hole.

"There's a floor," she shouted, instantly. "And a tunnel heading north. Wooden boards. Five metres down."

"Is there a ladder?" asked Albertsson.

"No," said Larissa. "You'll have to rope down. I'm going to see where this goes."

"Stay where you are," shouted Albertsson. "Is that clear?"

Silence.

"Yes, sir," said Larissa, eventually, her voice dripping with sarcastic obedience. "Perfectly clear, sir."

Albertsson grinned, then turned to the rest of his squad. "Petrov," he said. "Fix a rope. You, Engel, Van Orel, you're coming down with me. Carpenter, you're staying up here."

Jamie frowned. "Are you serious?" he said.

Albertsson squared up to him. "I'd have thought that was obvious, Lieutenant. Did you think I was joking?"

"You don't want to know what I think," said Jamie, his eyes locked on the American, familiar angry heat spilling into his stomach.

Albertsson smiled. "You're right," he said. "I genuinely couldn't care less. Someone has to stay up here and keep watch while the rest of us are underground. I've chosen *you* to be that person. Are you refusing a direct order?"

Jamie stared at him, fighting the overwhelming urge to sink his thumbs into the Special Operator's windpipe. "No," he growled. "Sir."

"Good," said Albertsson. His smile widened, as though they were suddenly the best of friends. "I'm so glad. Thank you."

"Rope is ready," said Petrov.

Jamie looked over at him. The Russian Operator was staring at Tim Albertsson with what appeared to be his usual neutral expression, but Jamie could see the tiniest downward curl at the corners of the man's mouth.

*Looks like I'm not the only one who can see that you're a dick, Tim.*

"All right," said Albertsson. "Van Orel, you go first. Engel, second, I'll follow you. Petrov, you bring up the rear. And if anything happens up here, don't rely on comms, Carpenter. You shout your head off, OK?"

Jamie nodded, then watched as his squad mates lowered themselves one by one into the hole and disappeared. He stared at the black square for a long moment, trying to work out whether he wanted to burst into tears at the petty, frustrating unfairness of Tim's behaviour or throw his head back and let the rage that was bubbling inside him out in a primal scream.

*Or throw a grenade down there after them,* he thought, then pushed the idea away, disgusted at himself for even having allowed it to cross his mind.

Larissa watched her squad mates descend the rope hand over hand, wrestling with the urge to break Tim Albertsson's neck as soon as his feet touched the wooden floor of the tunnel.

She had heard the conversation between him and Jamie, heard Tim single out her boyfriend to be left behind, and she could feel her vampire side raging with the desire to commit violence; she took a series of slow, deep breaths as Van Orel landed with a thud, followed by the rest of their squad.

Larissa had obeyed Tim's instruction not to explore, but the immediate surroundings were already clear to her supernatural eyes. The tunnel was long and straight, with wooden boards for a floor and packed earth for its walls and roof, held in place by thick struts and beams that looked like tree trunks. It reminded her of photos of the battlefields of World War One, where long tunnels had been dug to place mines beneath enemy positions.

*This could be just as old,* she realised, as Petrov dropped on to the boards. *At least. Maybe older.*

Her four squad mates drew their torches again and shone them down the tunnel towards her. The light was blinding and she narrowed her eyes, a guttural warning growl rising from her throat. The torch beams were instantly lowered, and as she waited for her vision to clear, her squad mates made their way towards her.

"Shit," said Van Orel. "Sorry, Larissa."

"It's fine," she said. "This way."

Tim Albertsson stepped forward. "Larissa, you take point," he said. "I want to know if there's anything down here."

Larissa reached out, grabbed a handful of the American's uniform, and pulled him close enough that she could feel the heat rising from the skin of his face.

"You're pathetic," she whispered, her voice so low that only he could hear it.

She released him, and flew away down the tunnel before he had time to respond. There was a moment's silence, before heavy footsteps followed her.

After a length of time that felt unknowable, but was likely no more than two or three minutes, Larissa saw something in the distance. The tunnel was perfectly straight, long and wide, built deep and solidly, and her vision was the only one of her supernatural senses that she still fully trusted. She could smell nothing but damp earth, and her head was fuller than ever with the incessant noise that had been plaguing her since they first set foot inside the forest.

"Something up ahead," she said.

"Hostile?" asked Tim Albertsson.

"I don't think so," said Larissa. "It looks like light. Electric light."

"Down here?" said Engel.

"That's what it looks like," said Larissa.

"Ready One," said Albertsson.

Larissa fought back the urge to laugh; given the target they had been sent to Romania to search for, permission to use force seemed somewhat redundant. Instead, she quickened her speed, flying steadily towards the distant glow. When she got within fifty metres of it, she saw that she had only been partly right. Bright white electric light was indeed radiating from a bulb hanging from the roof, but it was contained within something far stranger than she could have expected.

Filling the height and width of the tunnel was a wall. Its lower half was made of bricks that had been painted white, its upper half of glass. In its centre was a metal door, which, were it not shut, would lead into a space Larissa and her squad mates could see through the panes of glass.

It looked like a control room.

Two large metal cabinets stood to one side, their shelves packed with server boards and panels that flashed relentlessly with red and blue lights. Opposite them, a simple desk contained a computer and two racks of complicated-looking machinery. The computer's screen was dark, although an amber light glowed on its side.

"This is crazy," said Van Orel. "What the hell is this?"

Larissa shook her head. "I don't know," she said.

The room was roughly three metres wide. On its far wall, an identical door stood open, leading into a tunnel that appeared to be a continuation of the one they were standing in.

"Can we get in?" asked Albertsson.

"I can open the door," said Larissa. "But whoever built this place is going to know as soon as I do. Look." She pointed to two plastic boxes that sat in the upper corners of the room; red light blinked steadily from lenses at their centres.

"Alarms," said Petrov.

"Alarms," said Larissa. "The door is probably rigged too."

"This doesn't make any sense," said Albertsson, staring through the glass. "Who builds an IT office under the goddamn forest? And what the hell are those machines doing?"

"I think the bigger question," said Van Orel, pointing to the door on the other side of the room, "is where does that tunnel go?"

"I don't know," repeated Larissa. "But I think we'd find the man we're looking for at the end of it."

"The first victim?" said Engel. "You think *he* built this?"

"Who else?" asked Larissa. "We know that nobody else comes here. And where we came down didn't look much like an entrance to me, or at least not one that's been used in the last fifty years. It looked like an exit. Or an escape route, more likely."

"Escape from what?" asked Albertsson.

"How should I know?" said Larissa.

"I would like to know what those machines are," said Petrov.

*You and me both*, thought Larissa. Although she had a strong suspicion, one that she wasn't prepared to share with her squad mates.

Not yet, at least.

"All right," said Albertsson. "If we can't go through without alerting him to our presence, we head back."

"He's already alerted to our presence," said Larissa. "Obviously. You saw the dead animals, we all did. We should just go through."

"No," said Albertsson. "We have no idea where that tunnel goes, or whether there are more of them. We'd be like rats in a maze. We're going back to the surface."

Larissa looked at him. "But if we just—"

"That's an order," said Tim Albertsson, his voice like ice.

"Fine," said Larissa. "*Sir.*"

Jamie watched Van Orel prod at their fire with a branch, and pulled his sleeping bag more tightly round his shoulders. It had been cold in the forest by day, the dense canopy preventing all but the occasional shaft of warming sunlight from reaching the ground.

By night, it was absolutely freezing.

He had listened with what he hoped had seemed like professional calm as his squad mates described what they had found in the tunnel, had looked with apparent interest at their photos of the strange white room and its unidentified machines, and listened to their theories about exactly what it might be. Inside, he had been burning with outrage. It felt like his worst days at school, in the months after his father had died; as if he was on the edge of everything, that things were happening, but he wasn't allowed to be a part of them.

Larissa was clearly desperate to talk to him alone, most likely to express her solidarity over Tim's blatantly personal decision to leave him outside the entrance to the tunnel, but the opportunity had so far failed to present itself. The DARKWOODS squad had regrouped and struck out along what they hoped was the same path taken by the underground tunnel; Tim was working on Larissa's assumption that there was something at the other end, even if none of them knew what it might be.

But night had fallen, bringing with it a darkness that was quickly total, and they had walked for barely fifteen minutes before Tim

Albertsson ordered them to stop and make camp. They had pitched their shelter, built a fire that produced little warmth, and eaten; now they were resting, the exertions of the day clinging heavily to their bones and muscles, and talking in the awkward way of groups of people who feel they ought to get to know one another.

"Your toughest operation," said Engel. "The very worst you've been on."

"Easy," said Van Orel.

"Really?" asked Petrov. "For me it is not easy."

"Vamps attacked a tourist shark boat called the *Quint* in False Bay," said Van Orel. "Just off the coast of Cape Town. The boat's operator called the coastguard when it didn't come back in and they couldn't hail it, and we intercepted a message from another boat saying they'd seen the *Quint* adrift as the sun went down. Blood in the water, two figures on the deck, one of them seemed to have glowing eyes. You know the drill."

The members of the squad nodded in unison; they knew it all too well.

"So my squad got the op," continued Van Orel. "The coastguard took us out to the *Quint*, which looked deserted. We boarded her, and in the cabin we found these two vamps in a blood coma. Have you ever seen that? Where a vamp has drunk so much that it's overwhelmed them? It looks like an overdose. Anyway. We found the captain dead in the cabin next to them, so we staked the vamps and searched the rest of the boat. No sign of anyone. Then I saw this little camcorder attached to the TV, so I pressed PLAY."

Van Orel looked round at his squad mates, who were hanging on his every word.

"They'd been feeding on the tourists, bleeding them, then

throwing them over the side for the sharks. You've never seen anything like it, or at least I hope you haven't. The blood in the water, the froth, the Great Whites breaching and spinning and biting. There had been twelve people on board the *Quint* that day, not counting the captain. All were gone."

"Jesus," said Larissa, her voice low.

Van Orel nodded. "I've had *harder* operations, much harder. I mean, when it came down to it, this was two vamps who were so out of it they barely knew we were there. But it stays with me like none of the others. It was sport, nothing more. Twelve people murdered and used as shark bait for the sake of a home movie."

"*Scheisse*," said Engel, her voice barely more than a whisper. "What about you, Jamie?"

He felt eyes settle on him; his short Blacklight career was already the stuff of legend. Only Tim Albertsson looked disinterested.

"There are two," he said. "I can't choose between them. The first I ever went on, which wasn't even actually an authorised operation. To get my mother back from Alexandru Rusmanov."

There was a series of nods; the story of how a teenage boy with barely any training destroyed the second-oldest vampire in the world had swept through the supernatural Departments like a hurricane.

"The second was Paris," he said. "Colonel Frankenstein was being held by an old vampire called Dante, who called himself the king of Paris, and I took a team to rescue him. Dante ran a theatre, a vampire theatre, where they tortured and murdered humans on stage every night for entertainment. We destroyed him and every other vamp in the place, and we got Frankenstein out, even after his lycanthropy took hold of him. I'm still not sure how we managed it, to be honest."

"Were you there, Larissa?" asked Van Orel.

She shook her head. "No," she said. "Not on that one."

Jamie watched her closely, searching her face for signs of anger. The decision not to take either her or Kate Randall to Paris with him had been one of the hardest he had ever had to make, and he had genuinely worried that it might represent the end of him and Larissa before whatever was between them even had a chance to get off the ground. And Larissa *had* been furious, although she had accepted his almost desperate desire not to see her in danger while he was trying to focus on rescuing Frankenstein.

Accepted it, but not agreed with it. Not in the slightest.

"Why not?" asked Tim Albertsson, smiling narrowly.

Larissa shrugged. "It was Jamie's call," she said. "You'll have to ask him."

"Jamie?" asked the American.

"Do I have to explain my decisions to you?" he asked.

Albertsson held his hands up in mock surrender. "I'm just asking," he said, his tone light. "We're all friends here, right?"

"Right," said Jamie. "Sure we are."

Engel frowned deeply, then turned to Tim. "What about you?" she asked.

"Hard to pick one for me too," said Albertsson. "I led the squad that searched for Adam, the supposedly cured vampire, and lost three men in the process. Did you hear about that?"

The Operators nodded; word of the disastrous mission in the Californian desert had got around, despite its classified status.

"The toughest, though?" continued Albertsson. "That would have to be Mexico, after Valeri's vamps broke the jails. The leadership of a cartel in Nuevo Laredo were in the Florence Supermax when it was cracked, and were all turned. They went home, murdered everyone who had taken their places while they were inside, and took everything back over. We went in to get them before they got too settled." He looked over at Larissa and smiled. "Didn't we?"

The vampire shifted uneasily as attention swung her way. "We did," she said. "I was attached to Tim's squad for the operation."

"And we were glad to have her," said Tim. "We entered the house and did a sweep, but they were waiting under the floor for us in the basement. We engaged them, and destroyed what we thought was all of them, but there was no sign of their leader, a General called Garcia Rejon. He ambushed us, blasted a hole in Larissa, and fled. I ordered everyone to hold, but she went after him anyway."

"It didn't really register that I'd been shot," said Larissa, quietly.

"Right," said Albertsson. "I got the rest of my squad together and we climbed up through the hole Rejon had made to escape, and all the time there's shrieking and screaming outside. By the time we got there, all that was left of him was a streak of blood across the lawn."

"That doesn't sound that bad," said Jamie. "It sounds like Larissa did most of the work."

"She did," said Albertsson, and smiled widely. "What makes it the toughest op I've been on was what happened in Rejon's garden, after the fighting was over. When it was just Larissa and me left."

Ice crept up Jamie's spine. He looked over at Larissa and flinched; her face had turned so pale it was almost translucent, and she was staring at Albertsson not with anger, but with eyes full of pleading.

"What happened?" asked Engel.

Albertsson looked around, savouring the attention. "Nothing," he said. "That was the problem."

Silence descended, thick and awkward and full of unasked questions. Jamie felt the rage he had been trying to control since the squad first stepped into the forest roar through him; it took every iota of his willpower to hold it at bay. Larissa had dropped her eyes and was staring into the fire, shock written across her face. The rest of the squad were looking uneasily at one another, unsure how to respond to Albertsson's story, the point of which had simultaneously been ambiguous and utterly obvious.

"Petrov?" asked Engel, trying for a light, cheerful tone, but getting nowhere near it. "What about you?"

The Russian gave her a long look, then shook his head.

"No more talk," said Albertsson. "Get some rest. Tomorrow's going to be our day, I can feel it."

Within a minute, Van Orel, Petrov, Engel and Albertsson were asleep; a symphony of deep breathing and gentle snoring rose into the freezing night air. Jamie had closed his eyes, but was wide awake, his head spinning, his stomach churning with anger and bitter, frustrated confusion. As a result, he was the only member of the squad who heard Larissa shake Tim Albertsson awake and whisper that they needed to talk, urgently. He lay as still as a corpse in his sleeping bag, his heart pounding, scarcely able to believe what he had heard.

"Sure," said Tim. "It's well overdue. Let's talk."

"Keep your voice down," whispered Larissa. "Not here. Let's take a walk."

"Fine," whispered Tim.

There was a shuffling noise, which Jamie assumed was Albertsson extricating himself from his sleeping bag. Then he heard the soft crunching of icy grass and tiny twigs as his girlfriend and the American Special Operator stole away into the night.

*　　*　　*

Larissa walked beside Tim Albertsson, ordering herself to stay calm.

In the years since she had been turned, years in which she had seen some of the very worst that humanity had to offer, she had come to think of herself as extremely difficult to shock, if not borderline impossible. Nonetheless, she was utterly astonished by Tim's behaviour; the American was acting like a petty, jealous schoolboy, rather than a man in charge of one of the most important operations that had ever been ordered.

She had spent a great deal of time since she left Nevada wondering what would happen if she met Tim again; the prospect had always been a real one, given the insular nature of what they did. She had allowed for the possibility that he might be angry with her, might even hate her for what she had done, for the promise she had broken. But she had not been prepared for his sheer vindictiveness; as far as she could see, he was quite deliberately attempting to ruin her relationship with Jamie, and humiliate her into the bargain.

Jamie had instantly noticed Tim's apparent agenda against him, his sly digs and provocative comments, and Larissa had promised to tell him the truth when the operation was over. It had placated him – or at least, she hoped it had – but had made her absolutely furious; she had never intended to tell him *anything* about Tim, had made that decision as she sat in the *Mina II* on her way back from Nevada. But at this point, it would actually be something of a relief to do so; she knew Jamie well enough to know that what he was imagining in his head would be far worse than the actual reality.

But beyond the impact of Tim's behaviour on herself, and Jamie, she was genuinely concerned about his continuing ability to lead the operation; he seemed to be so obsessed with what had happened, or rather *hadn't happened*, between them that she was not at all sure he was thinking clearly. And that was dangerous, for everyone.

After five silent minutes, they arrived in a small clearing. Larissa turned to face the Special Operator, red flooding into her eyes as she felt her self-control threatening to desert her.

"What the hell is wrong with you?" she said, her voice little more than a growl. "Do you think this is clever, what you're doing? Are you having fun?"

Albertsson looked incredulously at her, then laughed and shook his head. "That's great," he said. "Play the victim, why don't you? Again."

"What are you talking about?"

"Drag your head out of your ass, Larissa," said Tim, his voice filling with anger. "How do you think it looked when you left Nevada the way you did? Danny and Kara and the others, they all thought they were going to Blacklight with you when you went. So did I, as a matter of fact, because you promised. You said the actual words to our faces. And then you just left, without bothering to tell us that you'd changed your mind, without even saying goodbye. What do you think that did to my relationships with them, Larissa? They blame *me* for you leaving and not taking them with you. They think I did something to scare you away."

"You did," hissed Larissa. "You kissed me. And in Vegas you told me you wanted to, even after I'd warned you not to do it again. How was I supposed to take you back to the Loop with me after that? How would I have been able to sit in briefings and meetings every day with you and Jamie, after you'd made it very clear that you can't take no for an answer? You're an idiot if you can't see that."

"The Director asked me why you didn't take me," said Tim, his face colouring crimson. "He knows something happened. You damaged my career, Larissa, and you turned my friends against me.

So am I just supposed to let you off the hook for that? Act like it never happened?"

Larissa rolled her eyes. "Oh please," she said, her voice dripping with contempt. "If your career is so damaged, then why did General Allen put you in charge of this operation? And if the others think less of you now, well, I'm sorry, but that's really not my problem. I *did* leave because of you, and I didn't take them because of you, even though it broke my heart not to. You don't think I would be happier at Blacklight if they were there with me? You don't think I wish it had all ended differently? Believe me, I do. So you don't just get to make me out to be the bad guy and pretend that you didn't do anything, because this, *all of this*, is your fault. You selfish prick."

Albertsson stared at her, his eyes narrow. "Maybe I should just tell Jamie," he said. "About Mexico and Vegas. Just get it all out in the open and let him decide for himself. He's a grown man, and secrets are never good."

Larissa was moving before she knew she was going to, her eyes blazing crimson. She closed a gloved hand round Tim's neck, lifted him into the air, and hurtled across the clearing, a guttural roar rising from her throat. She slammed him against a wide tree trunk and held him there, five metres above the ground.

"You will not say one word to Jamie about this," she growled. "Not now, not ever. Do you understand me?"

Albertsson glanced down at the ground, then grinned widely. "I'm not afraid of you, Larissa," he said.

She moved her face in closer to his, her breath clouding the freezing air, her fangs huge and razor-sharp. "You should be," she said, and released her grip. Albertsson's eyes widened, and he cried out as he slid down the tree trunk and hit the ground, hard.

Larissa didn't wait to see him get up; she rocketed away through the dark forest, her mind pounding with the desire to get away from everything, and everyone.

Including herself.

# 40

# SAFEGUARD

"I'm sorry," said Cal Holmwood. "You're going to have to run that by me again. I don't think I heard you right the first time."

"I think you did, Cal," said Colonel Ovechkin.

"No," said Holmwood, shaking his head and smiling wildly at his Russian counterpart. "I can't have. Because what I *thought* I heard you say was that one of my Operators, a man who actively tried to kill my Security Officer and one of my best young Lieutenants, was a spy for your Department. But that can't be what you said, surely? It just can't be."

The Blacklight Director's voice had risen steadily as he spoke; he was shouting as he said the final words. The SPC Director looked back at him, his expression a mixture of embarrassment and anger; he was clearly not used to being spoken to in such a way, regardless of the circumstances.

"That *is* what I said," said Ovechkin. "And I have already told you that this is also news to me, Cal. I would appreciate it if you keep your temper under control."

Holmwood stared at the screen, temporarily struck dumb with outrage.

*My temper?* he screamed inside his head. *You're telling me you had a spy in my Department and you're worried about my temper? HOW DARE YOU?*

Mercifully, before he managed to speak, to say something that he would almost certainly later regret, Paul Turner stepped in.

"The Director's temper is hardly the issue here, Colonel," said the Security Officer. "Please can you tell us exactly what it is you have discovered?"

Ovechkin stared at Cal Holmwood for a long moment, then switched his attention to Turner. "Of course, Major," he said, each word sounding as though it caused him physical pain. "The records that we have found show that in the early 1980s Demidov was charged by our Director at the time, a man by the name of Zellev who I do not think either of you ever met, to compile intelligence reports on the other supernatural Departments. These were standard strategic documents: strengths, weaknesses, equipment, command structures, etc. Very similar, I have no doubt, to the files that you kept on us."

"I'm sure you're right," said Turner. "The Cold War is not a period that any of us should look back on with pride."

"On that point, you and I are in complete agreement, Major Turner," said Ovechkin, his face twisting momentarily into a hard, narrow smile. "It is much better now that we are all friends."

"Indeed," said Turner. "Go on."

Ovechkin nodded, and continued. "After the intelligence reports had been completed, Demidov made a proposal to Zellev, a proposal that appears to have been known only to the two of them. It related to advances in techniques of psychological conditioning, and centred on Demidov's belief that a combination of psychotropic drugs and hypnotic suggestion could implant instructions within a human being so deeply that they would follow them without question. The proposal was a request for permission to explore his theory, which was granted."

"Who were the test subjects?" asked Turner.

"Political prisoners," said Ovechkin. "Enemies of the state. The experiments were carried out in the gulags of Siberia and Chukotka, under Demidov's supervision. After less than two years, he reported to Zellev that the techniques had been perfected."

"What happened to the subjects of his experiments?"

"There are no records of them, Major Turner," said Ovechkin. "I'm sure you are capable of drawing the same conclusion from that as I have."

*No shit*, thought Holmwood. *Experimented on like rats, used up, disposed of.*

"I am," said Turner. "Unfortunately."

Ovechkin nodded. "Demidov's report outlined the idea for Safeguard. It was hypothetical at the time, as only the most cordial of relationships existed between us and the other Departments, but Demidov claimed that, if he was given access to foreign Operators, he could condition them to provide us with intelligence without compromising themselves in the process. When we began to re-engage more fully with the supernatural community in 1992, Demidov asked for permission to revive the project. Zellev gave it."

"Jesus Christ," said Holmwood. "I can't believe this, Aleksandr. I can't believe the SPC would sanction such a project, no matter who the Director was."

"I can imagine," said Ovechkin, his thin smile returning. "Just like I find it hard to believe that NS9 would attempt to weaponise the vampire virus, or that Blacklight would conduct operations inside SPC territory and deny having done so. It is all very hard to believe. But that was the world."

"If these were sleeper spies," said Turner, dragging the conversation back on track, "why did Brennan plant bombs designed to kill myself and Lieutenant Randall?"

"The Safeguards were programmed to avoid detection at all costs," said Ovechkin. "I would speculate that Brennan was concerned that the investigation you and Lieutenant Randall were conducting was likely to lead to his discovery, so he attempted to halt it. It appears that when his attempt failed, he ran."

"And came home," said Holmwood, his voice thick with anger. "Right?"

Ovechkin didn't respond.

Silence settled uneasily over the Blacklight Director's quarters, full of dark corners and half-truths, of history far from fully buried. Eventually, it was Paul Turner who spoke.

"Do you know how Demidov got to Brennan?"

"Yes," said Ovechkin. "The Safeguard records are extremely comprehensive. Brennan attended a strategy symposium here in Polyarny."

"When?" asked Turner.

"Nine years ago."

"So what the hell actually happened?" asked Holmwood. "Demidov had him dragged out of his bed, hypnotised, pumped full of drugs and sent home? Why wouldn't Brennan have resisted? Or reported it when he got back here?"

"The techniques appear to have been extremely sophisticated," replied Ovechkin. "Subjects were left with no awareness of anything unusual, as the process itself was deleted from their memories. When the technique was correctly applied, the new instructions would appear to be things the subject had *always known*. They would know they were spies, but as far as they knew they always had been, and had *chosen* to be. They would have no understanding that anything had changed."

"Victims," said Turner.

"I'm sorry, Major?"

"You keep referring to them as subjects," said the Security Officer. "Let's call them what they were. Victims of an appalling, unjustifiable violation."

"Of course you are correct," said Ovechkin. "Although I do not think that terminology is of the highest importance at this point."

"No," said Holmwood. "So let's get down to what is. How many of these Safeguards did your predecessors send into my Department, Aleksandr?"

"Six," said Ovechkin. "I am sorry, Cal."

For a seemingly endless moment, Holmwood didn't respond; he couldn't think straight, couldn't collect the thoughts that were rushing through the filters in his mind.

*Six. Six of our Operators, reporting our every move to the SPC. For how many years? And why the hell didn't ISAT pick the rest of them up?*

He glanced over at Paul Turner. The Security Officer's face was paler than ever, and the Interim Director guessed that he was asking himself the same questions.

"Who?" managed Holmwood. "Tell me their names."

"I have a list, as well as every report they ever submitted. I am sending it all to you now, as a gesture of the friendship between our Departments that we greatly value, especially during these troubled times. I do not know whether it will make you feel better or worse, but I can tell you that the other five names on the list are all deceased. Brennan was the last."

Holmwood considered this, but all he felt was numb. He had devoted the vast majority of his adult life to Blacklight, and had spent most of those years as a dyed-in-the-wool true believer, as a proud soldier of the forces for good. Now that view of the world, which had once been so clear, so sharp and solid, was mired in endless shades of grey. The very fabric of what his Department and its equivalents did felt as though it was unravelling; lie piled upon lie, secret upon secret, horror upon horror. If they somehow managed to prevent the rise of Dracula, he was no longer sure that there remained a future for Blacklight, or for NS9, the SPC, or any of the others. There had been so much blood, so much death, and the cracks were finally beginning to show.

*We're no longer the good guys,* he thought, with a sadness that stabbed at his heart. *Maybe we were once, but those days are gone. Now we're the lesser of two evils.*

*And that's all.*

Matt Browning's report appeared in his mind, and he winced. "It wasn't just us, was it?" he said.

"I am sorry?" said Aleksandr.

"It wasn't only Blacklight that Demidov and Zellev infiltrated. Major Simmons of NS9 took one of my Lieutenants hostage this morning, at gunpoint. He tried to leave a live operation with him and a set of specimens that might prove vital to the work of the Lazarus Project, but my Operator managed to kill him. *Safeguard* was his last word. This was barely eight hours ago."

"That is... regrettable," said Ovechkin.

*Why?* wondered Holmwood. *Because Matt Browning almost died, or because you're going to have to explain all this to Bob Allen?*

"I'm assuming his intention was to take the specimens to Russia?" said Turner.

"I do not know," said Ovechkin. "We are still analysing Demidov's preliminary data. Our conclusion is that the Safeguards were intended as observers, rather than saboteurs. But there is much we do not yet understand."

"It's quite a coincidence," said Turner. "Brennan goes rogue to avoid detection, then Simmons tries to steal invaluable information, and they die within twenty-four hours of each other."

"Our investigation is ongoing," said Ovechkin, his face pale. "As I told you."

"What about everywhere else?" asked Holmwood. "Not just NS9, but the FTB, PBS6, all the other Departments. How many of their Operators did you send back to them as traitors?"

Ovechkin flinched. It was a tiny gesture, but Holmwood saw it; a momentary flicker of pain, or shame, or both.

"Many," he said. "A great many, over the years."

"Are they all dead as well?"

"Many of them are," said Ovechkin. "But no. Not all of them."

"Christ," said Holmwood. "This is going to cause chaos."

"Maybe not," said Turner. "If the Departments can get to them before they realise they've been identified, maybe they can be removed."

"Maybe," said Ovechkin. "Although, as you said, Major Turner, the timing of Major Simmons' actions does seem highly coincidental. Unless he perceived some threat to his cover that we are not aware of."

"Tell the rest of the Departments to exercise extreme caution when you inform them, Aleksandr," said Holmwood. "The Safeguards are clearly prepared to use force to evade capture."

"The data suggests that was an element of their programming," said Ovechkin.

"What Brennan did was more than just using force," said Turner. "It was a carefully planned strategy. He manipulated Valentin Rusmanov's servant into planting the bombs that were meant for myself and Lieutenant Randall, then wrote HE RISES where he left the tracking chip he'd cut out of his own arm. There's no other way to view his behaviour than as a calculated attempt to make it appear he betrayed us to Dracula, knowing full well that's the assumption we'd be likely to make."

"But he didn't," said Holmwood, his voice low. "He was working for our friends."

*Which means we've lost our best lead to Dracula's location,* he thought. *All our hopes now lie with Valentin. God help us.*

"I am sorry, Cal," said Ovechkin. "There are only so many different ways I can say so."

"Fine," said Holmwood. He gave his head a quick shake, trying to clear some of the fog that had settled into it. "Send through everything you have on our Department, and don't make the mistake of assuming this matter is closed. But there are other calls you need to make right now, Aleksandr, and if I were you I'd put Bob Allen at the top of your list. One of his men just held a gun to a Blacklight Operator's head and I'm pretty sure he's going to be keen to know why. Let's speak again when the rest of the Departments are up to speed."

"Agreed," said Ovechkin. "I wish this had not happened, Cal. I hope you can believe me."

"I believe you," replied Holmwood. "Start putting it right."

# 41

# THE PRODIGAL SON

### SOUTH-WESTERN FRANCE

Valentin Rusmanov floated in the cold night air, the smell of the sprawling pine forest below him filling his nostrils. His eyes glowed steadily in the darkness as he stared at his target: the squat, distant shape of Château Dauncy.

As he had suspected, finding it had not been difficult.

After saying goodbye to Anderson in San Sebastián the previous evening, he had walked down on to the dark, deserted beach and risen silently into the air, disappearing instantly from view. Using cold, damp banks of low-lying cloud as cover, Valentin had accelerated north-east, soaring and gliding over rising thermals and between shifting areas of pressure, the air fluttering his jacket like wings, his travel bag hanging below him like a bomb about to be released from its housing, until the illuminated spread of Bordeaux appeared and he dropped unnoticed into its maze of dark streets.

He took a room in a grand, slightly faded hotel on the northern bank of the Garonne that he was sure he had stayed in before, paying for two nights even though he only intended to stay for one. It was one of the annoyances of being a vampire, as hotel checkout times were invariably long before the sun went down, and thus impossible for the supernatural to accommodate.

Valentin, whose personal wealth was so vast as to be essentially incalculable, didn't notice such things, however; he merely handed over an emerald-green card embossed with the name of a bank in Zurich that the vast majority of the world's very richest men and women had never heard of, took a map of the Gironde from a shelf beside the reception desk, and retired to his room. There, he unfolded the map on the bed, and immediately found what he was looking for: Château Dauncy, twenty miles to the south-west, in the middle of a pine forest that spread almost all the way to the Atlantic coast.

*I probably flew over it on my way here*, thought Valentin, and allowed himself a small smile.

He ordered oysters and *magret de canard* from room service, opened one of the bottles he had filled with the blood of a boy he had turned in Rome, and lay back on the bed.

*Tomorrow*, he thought. *Tomorrow I will keep the promise I made.*

Now that time had come.

Even from a distance of ten miles or more, Valentin's supernaturally sharp eyes could pick out the bright squares of the château's windows, could hear snatches of conversation as they floated on air that felt thick and full of electricity. As if on cue, a clap of thunder rolled in the distance, reverberating in his ears and through his bones. Lightning flashed to the north, and it began to rain; a light drizzle of cold, salt-edged water that quickly became first a steady downpour, then a hammering torrent. Thunder boomed again, closer this time, and Valentin smiled as the wind picked up speed and water fell from the heavens.

He had considered flying straight back to Blacklight with the information he had gleaned from Anderson, but had quickly decided against it; he could not be entirely certain the intelligence was accurate without visiting the château himself. He didn't believe for a moment that Anderson would intentionally lie to him, as he was certain that deception was beyond his abilities. It was, however, quite possible that the huge, child-like vampire was wrong.

*When I see them*, he thought, *that's when I'll know. When I see Dracula and my brother with my own eyes.*

Valentin took a deep breath and flew slowly towards the château, a dark shadow passing silently above the vast, churning forest.

In the study on the top floor of Château Dauncy, Dracula's eyes flared a deep, oily crimson; he threw his head back, the scent of the past filling his nostrils, his body trembling with sensation.

Valeri rose instantly from his chair and flew to his master's side. "My lord," he said, his voice full of concern. "What is it?"

Dracula slowly brought his head level, his eyes blazing, and the eldest Rusmanov frowned as a thin smile broke across the face of his master.

"Your brother," said the first vampire, rolling the words round his mouth as though they tasted delicious. "He is coming."

Valeri's frown deepened. He took a deep breath, inhaling the mingled scents of the château and the forest, and narrowed his eyes. "Are you sure, my lord?"

"You cannot smell his treacherous stench?" asked Dracula.

"No, my lord. I cannot."

"I can," said Dracula, his smile widening into a grin. "It seems my power has finally overtaken yours, my old friend. Perhaps order is finally returning to the world."

"Perhaps so, my lord," said Valeri, trying not to let the rebuke register on his weathered face. "Where is my brother?"

Dracula rose to his feet and crossed to his desk. The wooden box containing the item that Valeri had dutifully acquired stood on top, its lid open. The first vampire lifted it out, smiled, then fastened it to his belt and flew across the study. Valeri followed his master as he pulled open the door to the balcony and floated through it. Wind and rain gusted into the room, and a shiver ran up Valeri's spine; he told himself it was the cold air of the storm, but wasn't able to entirely convince himself. There was a nagging voice in the back of his head, a voice that sounded maddeningly like Henry Seward's, that insisted it was something else.

Fear.

Not of Dracula, or what his rise was going to mean for a world that Valeri had long held in contempt; fear over what role there would be for him in the new world, if his master no longer needed him to provide comfort and counsel.

*Where will that leave you?* the voice asked. *What will you do then?*

"Out there," said Dracula, pointing at the dark expanse of the forest. "Above the trees. He is almost here."

"I will deal with him, my lord," said Valeri.

Dracula shook his head, sending rainwater spraying from his long hair. "I asked you to do so some time ago, Valeri. You failed. I will handle this myself."

"Of course, my lord," said Valeri, shame burning in his chest. "What would you have me do?"

"Gather everyone and meet me in the courtyard," said Dracula, returning his gaze to the roiling horizon. "Bring our guest too."

"My lord," said Valeri. "Surely there is no need to—"

Dracula's hand closed round his neck and the rest of his suggestion died in his throat. The first vampire's face was suddenly twisted fury, his eyes flaming with blackened red, a thunderous growl rising from deep within him; he lifted Valeri effortlessly into the air and drove him backwards against the stone wall of the balcony with terrible, almost casual force. Valeri felt the skin on the back of his head split like tissue paper, felt warm blood cascade down his neck as pain arrived in the centre of his skull, sharp and huge.

"Need?" growled Dracula. His face was mere millimetres from Valeri's, steam rising in clouds from where rainwater was running into the heat of his eyes. "You speak to me of need? There is no *need* for you to concern yourself with anything other than doing exactly what I tell you, when I tell you. Your usefulness is at an end, Valeri. I no longer need *you*. Is that clear?"

Valeri's eyes widened with shock as the air in his lungs ran out. He forced a tiny nod, the motion sending nauseating pain through his head, and felt his master's grip loosen, enough for a whistling current of air to make its way down his throat.

"Will you do as I have ordered?" asked Dracula, his swirling eyes turning Valeri's stomach. "Now, and always? Or have we reached the end of our association? Think hard, old friend, before you answer."

"I... will..." managed Valeri, and, all at once, the pressure on his neck was gone. He slid to the wet ground, his hands going to his damaged throat as he sucked in air that felt like cold fire. He raised his head, his heart thumping with dreadful misery, and saw Dracula extending a hand down towards him. There was a long, pregnant moment, second after second that thrummed with tension, until Valeri took his master's hand, as both vampires had known, deep down, that he would, and allowed himself to be pulled to his feet.

"You are a proud man, Valeri," said Dracula. "You always have been. Pride is a virtue, but it bruises easily. It scars. If you and I are to continue on our path together, swallow down your pride, and do it now. I cannot have you with me unless I can rely entirely on your obedience. Do you understand?"

"I do," said Valeri, his voice cold and dead. "*My lord.*"

The first vampire narrowed his eyes and stared at him. Long seconds passed, during which Valeri knew his fate was being decided, and in which he realised, to his own surprise, that he cared little about the decision.

*I gave you my life,* he thought, his heart a ball of ice in his chest. *Both my lives. You live now only because of me. And this is how you repay me.*

Then something occurred to him, a thought that sickened him to his very core.

*Valentin was right.*

A smile rose on to Dracula's narrow face. "Good," he said, and clapped Valeri hard on the shoulder. "Then let us say no more about this unpleasantness. Rouse your comrades and bring our guest to the courtyard. I will meet you there."

The first vampire turned and leapt gracefully over the wall of the balcony, from almost exactly the same spot where Henry Seward had made an ill-fated escape attempt.

*Can it only have been a month since then?* wondered Valeri. *It seems so very much longer.*

He stared at the empty balcony, then flew back through the study and down the wide staircase of the château, to carry out the orders he had been given.

As Dracula descended slowly to the cobbled surface of the courtyard, he gave serious consideration, not for the first time, to killing Valeri Rusmanov.

To do so would give him no pleasure; his old friend was the first human being he had ever turned, and he had rarely regretted the decision. Valeri's long service had been solid, if sometimes lacking the imagination and appetite for improvisation that distinguished the truly great servants, qualities that had always been far more evident in the youngest Rusmanov, the man who was now approaching in the darkness. But regardless of Valeri's limitations, the truth, that he would never have spoken out loud, was that Dracula would always be grateful for the diligent quest that had restored him to life, a quest that had taken over a century to achieve. He was simply no longer sure that it should be enough to guarantee Valeri's continuing survival.

The eldest Rusmanov had undoubtedly proved useful during the long, maddening months of Dracula's recuperation, but the first vampire was beginning to believe that it had given him an inflated sense of his own value; he could not permit *anyone* to consider himself irreplaceable, or anything that came close to approaching his equal. Everyone, human and vampire, was his subordinate, and that was how it must stay.

Valeri had seen him at his very worst: as weak as a baby, and just as unable to feed and care for himself. And although nobody else in the château had been granted access to him during those first terrible weeks, Dracula sensed that the perception of him among the gaggle of Rusmanov acolytes who filled the cellars was of a sick man, a vampire far below the height of his powers. Now that was clearly no longer the case, it was possible a demonstration was in order; a restatement of the hierarchy, an illustration of the punishment awaiting even the slightest instance of subordination or presumption.

And nothing would send a greater message, to both the vampires in the château, and the ones in the wider world who were awaiting news, than if he pulled his oldest friend's beating heart from his chest and drank its blood in front of everyone.

But as the courtyard rose up to meet him, Dracula again ruled it out, at least for now. Fear had always been his weapon of choice, the cornerstone upon which his new authority would be built, but fear was unreliable; it prompted the subservient to make decisions based purely on self-interest, in the hope of their continued survival. This could be powerful, when wielded carefully, and Dracula was a veteran of such bloody work. It could not, however, replace the comfort that came from true, selfless loyalty. Providing the lesson he had just been forced to teach Valeri had been truly taken in – which was something he knew he was going to have to keep a careful eye on – then his oldest companion could be relied upon to make decisions based only on what was best for his master, with his own profit, even his own life, a secondary consideration. This was something more valuable even than fear; it was adoration.

It was love.

Valentin Rusmanov's breath froze in his chest.

*So it's true,* he thought. *Part of me didn't want to believe it, even now, but it's really true. He is risen.*

He had swooped down into the tightly packed mass of pine trees half a mile from the low stone wall that marked the edge of Château Dauncy's grounds, and made his way towards it, floating above the increasingly sodden ground. Light glowed from what seemed like a hundred windows, and warm yellow lit the courtyard beyond the wall; the grand old building looked as though it was preparing to host some official function, rather than hiding the most dangerous creature in the world.

When he reached the edge of the forest, where the tall trees gave way to row after row of low vines, Valentin paused. His dark suit blended into the shadows as his supernatural eyes scanned the château for any sign of his brother or his former master; he had realised he could smell them both when he was still halfway across the forest, but he had not turned back, even as his heart sank in his chest and a chill crept up his spine.

Until he saw them, he would not believe.

Rain lashed down in sheets, sliding in diagonal lines across the old stone walls, battering out a drumbeat on the cobbles of the courtyard. Valentin watched from the treeline, concentrating on preventing his eyes from glowing involuntarily red; he did not want to give his position away to any watching guards. He scanned the outbuildings, the sheds and huts that had presumably once been used to tend the vines, the low eastern and western wings, then focused on the courtyard before the towering wooden doors, and gasped.

To one side of the door, a man stared down at him from empty eye sockets. The point of the wooden pole he had been impaled on emerged from his mouth, encrusted with blood. The man's long, soaking wet hair whipped back and forth in the strengthening wind, sliding across his naked shoulders and chest. His arms were broken, his wrists and ankles bound. Blood had poured in enormous quantities down the man's legs and pooled on the cobbled ground into which the pole had been sunk.

Valentin stared at the stricken man, and tried to remember the last time he had seen someone impaled. It had been more than five centuries earlier, in the last weeks of Dracula's final reign as Prince of Wallachia, when Valentin had first made peace with the prospect of his own death; there had seemed little chance that he, or his brothers or their master, would survive the battle that was coming. Dracula had been raging, accusing his court of betrayal and sedition, ordering torture and death with furious abandon; new heads appeared on spikes each day, fresh bodies twisting on poles on the castle walls, as blood ran in rivers through the streets.

Then the impaled man coughed around the pole that had been forced through his body, a wet explosion of phlegm and blood and gathered rainwater that splattered the stake, and it took all Valentin's strength not to cry out in shock. The man's body spasmed, rattling against the wooden pole, then was still. Valentin looked closer and saw bloody fangs emerging from the man's mouth, scraping against the wood, and his stomach churned.

*A vampire*, he realised. *Impaled alive and left up there in endless agony. The birds have had his eyes, but he still lives. Dear God.*

He wondered what the man had done to deserve his fate, although long experience told him that the crime, whatever it was, was unlikely to have justified such terrible punishment. Then movement caught his eye, near the long, slanted roof of the building.

A dark silhouette leapt casually over the uppermost wall and descended gracefully towards the ground, its jacket billowing in the wind, the telltale red glow visible in its eyes, even through the driving rain. It touched down on the cobblestones of the courtyard, and stepped forward into the yellow glow of the lights.

Dracula's face was exactly as Valentin remembered it: pale and narrow, a tight covering of skin over sharp bones. The chin was pointed, jutting out beneath a mouth that was thin, the lips barely visible, even when curled into a smile, as they were now. A jet-black moustache sat beneath a steep nose, either side of which boiled the red-black eyes of madness, of terrible, unholy power. Valentin stared at them across the rows of vines and felt himself drawn in, experiencing a strong, almost overpowering urge to rush forward and throw himself at Dracula's feet, to prostrate himself and beg forgiveness for his disloyalty. He blinked furiously, shook his head, and looked back at his former master.

The first vampire was staring directly at him. His long black hair was rippling in the wind, and his smile had widened into a grin that chilled Valentin's blood. He was wearing a dark blue suit, now soaked black by rain, and hanging from his belt was a sword so large its tip almost scraped the ground.

"Valentin!" shouted Dracula, his voice warm and friendly. "Come out and let us see one another. It has been far too long, old friend."

For a long moment, Valentin did nothing. He briefly considered fleeing, as fast as he was able; he had seen his former master with his own eyes, which meant the promise he had made to Paul Turner was fulfilled. But fleeing was not in Valentin's nature.

He took a deep breath, and floated out of the trees.

"Dracula," he said, his voice steady. "It has indeed been many years. How are you?"

The first vampire narrowed his eyes. "Dracula?" he said. "Would you not call me lord? Or master?"

"I would call you by your name," said Valentin. "As I am no longer in your service."

"That saddens me, Valentin," replied Dracula. "Your long second life, which you have chosen to fill with baubles and indulgence, you owe to me. Have you forgotten?"

"I have not forgotten," said Valentin. "But nor would I have you pretend that you turned me out of altruism, or for any reason other than it suited you to do so. So I say I owe you nothing."

"I disagree," said Dracula, his grin disappearing.

"And that saddens *me*," said Valentin. "But it changes nothing."

The two vampires stared at each other across the vineyard. Valentin hung in the cold air, the rain lashing against his face, his every muscle screaming at him to turn and run. Dracula had also risen off the ground as he spoke, and was floating easily above the cobbled stones of the courtyard.

"I see your sword has found its way back to you," said Valentin.

Dracula glanced down at the heavy blade hanging from his belt and smiled. "It was found while I slept," he said. "A museum in Bucharest was kind enough to look after it for me."

"That was certainly good of them," said Valentin.

For a long moment, there was no sound other than the steady percussion of rain on the ground. The air was thick with the strange, bittersweet taste of nostalgia, of something that felt – to Valentin, at least – almost like camaraderie.

"I will make you this offer only once, Valentin," said Dracula. "Renounce this foolish rebellion and take your place at my side. Your sins can yet be forgiven."

"And I will give you my answer only once," said Valentin. "Never."

"You disappoint me," said Dracula. "And your capacity for treachery astonishes even me. You would truly stand with the enemies of your family, against your own blood?"

Valentin grunted with laughter. "You are no family of mine. And neither is Valeri. I am flattered to see you so desperate for me to join you, although if my brother is the best that you have been able to recruit, I must confess I am not surprised. But I will remain where I have always been, Dracula. On my own side."

The first vampire opened his mouth to answer, but a rush of movement cut him off before he formed his first syllable. Vampires, at least a hundred and fifty of them, maybe more, flooded into the courtyard: men and women, young and old, of every conceivable shape and size. They ran and flew and shambled through the rain, growls and high-pitched hisses emerging from their throats, their glowing eyes all fixed firmly on Valentin. As a show of strength, it was pitiful, as Dracula would well know; if he had presented Valentin with a thousand vampires, or five thousand, it would have been very different, which suggested his former master had other motives for filling the courtyard with his followers.

*He's not trying to impress me*, realised Valentin. *It's the other way round. He wants them to see their enemy.*

A chill ran up his spine.

*It's really coming. It's coming and I don't know if I can stop it.*

*War.*

The vampires twitched and snarled across the soaked cobblestones of the courtyard. Dracula floated easily in the air in front of them, regarding Valentin with an expression that seemed almost sorrowful.

"Last chance, old friend," said the first vampire. "Join me, and we will forget this insubordination. Otherwise go, and enjoy what time you have left."

Valentin narrowed his eyes. "You would let me go? Even though I know your location?"

"It matters not," said Dracula. "Fly to your friends in black and tell them where I am. Bring them here, if you would. They will be welcome, and they will see that it is already too late."

*I don't believe that*, thought Valentin. *I can't.*

There was a sudden commotion in the courtyard, and the low roar of hissing and growling intensified as someone made their way through the vampire ranks. The crowd slowly parted, spitting and clawing instinctively at one another as they moved, to reveal Valeri Rusmanov striding across the wet cobblestones. Valentin's eyes darkened to a glowing crimson, as hatred rushed into his stomach and began to churn, as hot and bitter as acid. Then they widened in shock, as he saw what his older brother was dragging along behind him.

Henry Seward looked like he had been run over by a train. His body was pitifully thin, his skin loose on his bones, his hair white, his face ravaged by pain and suffering. One of his eyes was missing, leaving a raw red crater, while the other swivelled manically in its socket, seeing everything and nothing. Valeri hauled him forward by his upper arm like a father dragging a disobedient child home to be disciplined, and pushed him out before the crowd of vampires. Seward staggered unsteadily, his feet sliding across the wet stones, looking as though the wind might blow him over at any second, but righted himself. His remaining eye focused, and he stared out at the dark vineyard.

"Valentin?" he called, his voice little more than a croak. "Are you there?"

Dracula nodded at his prisoner, giving him a wide, condescending smile. "He's there, my dear Admiral," said the first vampire. "He can hear you. Do you have something you would say to him?"

Seward nodded, his face a miserable mask of defeat. Valentin stared helplessly across the rows of vines, his heart aching at what the Director of Blacklight had been reduced to. Then Seward's face changed; the pain left it, his swollen, broken mouth twisted into a snarl of belligerence, and the voice that emerged from it was a voice that had commanded men, that had inspired trust and demanded obedience.

"Run!" bellowed Henry Seward. "Bring everyone and kill them all! Kill them all, Valentin! Kill them—"

Dracula raised a pale hand. Valeri wrapped his arm round the prisoner's throat, cutting off his furious exhortations, and pressed it there until Seward went limp. Then he released his hold, letting the unconscious Blacklight Director drop heavily to the ground. Seward's head hit the concrete, and Valentin smelt the blood before he saw it squirt out across the cobblestones and mix with the rain.

"You heard your new master," shouted Dracula, smiling widely. "Run along, Valentin. Run along."

Valentin took a final look at his brother and his former master, then rocketed into the air without a backward glance. His heart pounded in his chest as he flew north-west, towards the distant speck of land that was England and the men and women to whom he was bringing news that was both good and awfully, terribly bad. As he accelerated, the wind rising around him to a shrieking howl of resistance, the rain soaking him to the skin, Henry Seward's words echoed in his head.

*Kill them all. Kill them all. Kill them all.*

# 2 DAYS TILL
# ZERO HOUR

# 42

# THE LOCKED ROOM

## TELEORMAN FOREST, ROMANIA

Jamie Carpenter awoke shivering from sleep that appeared to have utterly failed to refresh him. His head felt fuzzy, his thoughts slow and laboured; the pale gloom of the forest morning hurt his eyes, and his back cracked and creaked as he sat up and looked over to where Larissa had arranged her sleeping bag.

His girlfriend was wrapped in the thick green material, her chest rising and falling steadily. On the other side of the camp, he could see the sleeping shape of Tim Albertsson in the deep shadow cast by one of the thousands of towering trees.

*They came back then,* he thought, bitterly. *That's something, at least.*

It had taken Jamie a long time to get to sleep after Larissa and the American had left the camp together; his mind had been racing with horrible possibilities, his imagination torturing him with images of Tim and his girlfriend kissing, of them writhing on the forest floor, their uniforms cast aside, the glow from her eyes illuminating them both. Eventually, sheer exhaustion had overwhelmed him, and he had fallen into a rough approximation of sleep, full of bad dreams.

Jamie stretched his arms above his head, feeling the muscles in his shoulders protest, and relished the morning silence. The absence of sound in a place that should have been full of life remained unsettling, but right now, as he sat shivering inside his sleeping bag in the slowly paling dawn, it was a relief.

"Morning," said Van Orel, sitting up and rubbing his eyes.

*Of course*, thought Jamie, and smiled. *Of course you'd choose this second to wake up.*

"Morning," he said. "Sleep well?"

Van Orel shrugged. "I slept," he said. "Technically, at least. You?"

"The same."

The South African rotated his head, sending an alarmingly loud series of cracks echoing through the campsite, then spat a thick wad of phlegm on to the remains of the fire.

"Up and at it, sir," he said, in the direction of Albertsson. "Today's our day, right?"

There was no response from the Special Operator.

Beside Van Orel, Engel raised her head, took a look around, and groaned. "We're still here," she said. "I thought it was a nightmare."

"We are here," said Petrov, sitting up and squinting at her through narrowed eyes. "It is real."

"Thank you, Arkady," said Engel, and smiled at him. "For a moment there, I wasn't sure."

"I'll tell you what *I'm* sure of," said Van Orel, getting unsteadily to his feet, and rubbing furiously at his limbs. "Our squad leader seems to have decided that one of the perks of leadership is a lie-in whenever he wants one."

"Why do you all hate quiet so much?" asked Larissa, her voice emerging from somewhere deep inside her sleeping bag.

Engel and Jamie laughed, and even Petrov couldn't resist cracking a thin smile.

"Come on, sir," said Van Orel, staggering across the camp to where Tim Albertsson was lying. "If we have to be awake, then so do you. Only fair." He prodded the Special Operator with the toe of his boot. "Rise and shine."

Albertsson didn't move.

The South African frowned, and pushed again, harder. Albertsson rolled over, his sleeping bag flopping open.

"Oh shit," said Van Orel.

There was something in the South African's voice that instantly cleared Jamie's mind, as though he had just drunk a double espresso or stepped into a cold shower. He got to his feet and crossed the camp, stepping over the remains of the fire as Petrov and Engel moved as well, unzipping their sleeping bags and pushing themselves up on unsteady legs.

"What is it?" he asked, as he arrived beside Van Orel, and looked down.

The breath froze in his lungs.

Tim Albertsson gazed up at them with blank, staring eyes on which the morning dew had collected, giving them the impression of being full of tears. His face was ghostly white, his lips purple, his forehead as smooth as a baby's. One side of his neck was a ragged mass of pale pink flesh and milky-white bone. Jamie stared at it, uncomprehending, as the rest of the squad arrived.

Nobody screamed.

Whenever he thought back to this moment, which would prove to be often, it would be one of the two things Jamie would always remember: the silence, as Tim Albertsson's death sank slowly into each of them, and the first response any of them actually made.

Without a word, Petrov pulled his ultraviolet beam gun from his belt, flicked it on, and shone purple light directly into Tim Albertsson's face. Engel cried out, slapped the Russian's hand aside, and rounded on him.

"What on earth are you doing?" she demanded.

Petrov frowned. "Being sure," he said. "That is a vampire bite."

"You don't know that," said Engel, her eyes blazing. "I told you that bears live in this forest, and wolves, and wild boar. It could have been any of them."

"Then why did we hear nothing?" asked Petrov. "And where is the blood?"

Engel blinked, then knelt down and pressed her fingers against the undamaged side of the Special Operator's neck. After a long, empty moment, she closed his eyes, sending water spilling down the sides of his head.

"Look at his skin," said Van Orel, his voice low. "He's been bled white."

"It must have been so strong," said Engel, her gaze locked on Albertsson's face. "To make no sound, to stop him from making any. All while we were sleeping next to him."

"I didn't do it," said Larissa.

Every member of the squad turned slowly towards her, Jamie included. She was standing apart from them, her feet centimetres above the ground, her eyes flickering red in their corners.

"Nobody said you did," said Van Orel.

"I know," said Larissa. "But some of you were thinking it, or starting to, at least. Because it makes sense. But I didn't kill him."

"Hey," said Jamie, frowning at her. "Nobody's accusing you of anything, Larissa. This isn't helping."

She looked over at him, her expression neutral, then gave him a curt nod.

"So what the hell is this?" asked Van Orel, his voice unsteady. "Is it *him*? Is it another warning?"

Petrov shrugged. "We still do not even know if the first victim is real," he said. "Larissa is the only vampire we have seen in this forest."

Jamie winced, and turned towards his girlfriend, trying to silently convey with his eyes how much he needed her to stay calm, to stay rational while they worked this out. But if she noticed, she clearly decided not to take his advice on board.

"That's right," she said, staring at Petrov with narrow, glowing eyes. "I am. And Tim and I have been arguing since this operation began, to say nothing of how he was treating Jamie."

"Larissa," said Jamie, his heart pounding. "Don't—"

"Shut up," she interrupted. "Say whatever you have to say, Arkady. Let's get it out in the open."

Petrov returned her gaze, then shrugged. "I am not saying anything."

The five remaining members of the DARKWOODS squad looked at each other, the tension between them so thick it was almost palpable. Jamie was staring at Petrov; even though his insides were crawling with horror at the sight of Tim Albertsson's pale, empty face, he was furious at the Russian's obvious implication, and with his own mind for having immediately turned to what he had seen while the majority of his squad mates were asleep.

*No,* he told himself. *Don't even think that, no matter what was between her and Albertsson. You need to get on her side, right now. She needs you.*

But he couldn't forget the way Tim had behaved throughout the previous day, how embarrassingly obvious the tension between him and Larissa had become, and what the American had said when Jamie's girlfriend woke him up and told him they needed to talk.

*He said it was overdue,* he thought. *Like it's been brewing since Larissa was in Nevada, at least.*

"What now?" asked Van Orel. "Just what the hell do we do now?"

"We go on," said Larissa.

"Just like that?" asked Van Orel, and let out a laugh that Jamie thought sounded worryingly close to hysterical. "Just carry on like nothing happened? Like our squad leader wasn't bled dry while we were asleep two metres away?"

"Get a hold of yourself," said Larissa, her eyes flashing red.

"Get a hold of myself?" said Van Orel, his eyes wide. "Something came in here while we were asleep and tore out Tim's throat and drank his blood until he was empty. And none of us heard a thing, not a bloody thing. What's to stop it coming back tonight, huh? What if it's just going to pick us off, one at a time, until there's nobody left? What if—"

"That is enough," said Petrov, his voice loud and firm. "It does no good to think like that."

"I can't help it!" shouted Van Orel. "I don't want to die in this bloody forest!"

"I will not tell you again," said Petrov. "That is enough."

Van Orel stared at the Russian Operator, then lowered his eyes.

"We have to keep going," said Larissa. "I know you're scared, and that's OK. I'm scared too. But we can't report this, because we have no comms. We can't ask for guidance, or new orders, for the same reason. So what do you want us to do? Go back to the landing site and say that we abandoned the Priority 1 operation that was entrusted to us because we couldn't do our jobs without Tim to tell us how?"

"For God's sake, Larissa," said Engel, looking at the vampire girl with wide, wet eyes. "Have some humanity. Please."

Larissa shrugged. "Think whatever you want," she said. "On operations, people die. Particularly on Priority 1s. If this is the first time any of you have been through this, then I'm sorry, I truly am. But it's the risk we all signed up for, Tim included. So I say we do what we were sent here to do."

"I agree," said Petrov.

Van Orel rounded on him. "You do?"

"Yes," said Petrov, his grey eyes narrow. "I do."

"So do I," said Jamie. "This is a terrible thing, obviously it is, but I'm not going back to the Loop with my tail between my legs to tell my Director I couldn't cope when things went wrong. And I'm sorry to say this, because I know how self-serving it's going to sound, but Tim wouldn't want me to. If one of us had been killed, he would have carried on. You know he would."

"Tim was squad leader," said Engel, fiercely. "He had the authority to make that decision. Who put you in charge?"

Jamie shook his head. "Nobody," he said. "But it's an important point. We need a new squad leader."

"That's not what I meant and you know it," shouted Engel.

"Nevertheless," said Larissa, "Jamie's right."

"So I suppose your vote is for him then?" asked Van Orel.

"My vote goes to Arkady," said Jamie, before Larissa had time to respond.

Petrov tilted his head to one side and looked at him, but said nothing.

"OK," said Van Orel, looking enormously relieved. "Arkady, sure. OK. I can get behind that."

"So can I," said Larissa. "Engel?"

"Jesus Christ," replied the German Operator. She appeared on the verge of tears. "His body is barely cold, for God's sake. What are we going to do with him? Leave him here and hope we find him on our way back, *if* we even get out of here alive?"

"We carry him," said Petrov. "We make a frame and we carry him in his sleeping bag."

"So you'll do it?" asked Van Orel. "You'll be squad leader?"

Petrov nodded. "I will do it," he said. "If that is what is wanted."

"It is," said Larissa.

"Fine," said Petrov. "We continue. Kinley, Engel, make a frame. Van Orel, Carpenter, take down the camp. Ten minutes."

"Yes, sir," replied the squad, as one.

Jamie immediately saw that Engel and Van Orel, who had both seemed on the verge of losing it, were calmer for having been given orders to follow. He was about to start folding down the shelter when Petrov spoke again.

"First," he said, "we will have a moment of silence for Special Operator Albertsson."

Out of the corner of his eye, Jamie saw a momentary grimace cross his girlfriend's face, before she dropped her gaze respectfully to the ground. He did likewise, focusing on the patch of dirt between his feet, doubt and darkness crowding his mind.

As he had finally drifted to sleep in the early hours of the morning, with his girlfriend and his squad leader still somewhere else, Jamie had momentarily wondered whether it was possible for this operation to get any worse. Now, in the cold gloom of the morning with a dead body lying on the ground before him, his squad mates brimming with paranoia and uncertainty, and a dark hole in his heart where his faith in Larissa should have been, he had his answer.

Things could always get worse.

# 43

## LYING DOWN

### CAISTER-ON-SEA, NORFOLK, ENGLAND

Julian Carpenter stubbed out his cigarette, then ran the half-full packet under a tap and threw it in the bin along with his lighter and an overflowing ashtray.

He had quit smoking when Marie had announced she was pregnant with Jamie, and had never fallen off the wagon, not even in the long, desperate months when he criss-crossed America in search of Adam. But the previous morning, after the Blacklight SUV had driven away and left him standing outside a cottage he had not seen with his own eyes for almost five years, he had walked the two miles to the village shop and bought two bottles of vodka and three packets of Marlboros.

The rest of the day had passed in a blur of sobbing and drunken, violent recrimination, the vast majority of it aimed inward. He was angry with Cal Holmwood, and with Bob Allen, but he was *furious* with himself for the way he had handled things, for the blind panic that had overwhelmed him after what he had seen in the California desert – the terrible, nightmarish vision of his son as a vampire – and had driven him voluntarily into captivity; first in Nevada, and then at the Loop, where his family had been an agonisingly short distance away, completely oblivious to his presence. He had eventually passed out on the sofa in the cottage's living room, his heart heavy in his chest, his throat raw, his mind awash with despair.

*It's worth it,* was the last thing he could remember thinking before he lost consciousness. *It's all worth it, as long as Jamie's OK. As long as he's safe.*

He had awoken as the sun dragged itself lazily over the horizon, and had staggered outside to watch light spill slowly across the Broads. His head was pounding, his stomach churning with acid, and he sat in the garden and drank coffee and smoked as dawn broke. Fear was pulsing through his body, the fear that this was his life now, this aimless, endless nothing. He started to cry again, and wondered how long he would be able to cope with this new reality, how long he would be able to resist placing the shotgun that was kept on top of the bookcase in the dining room under his chin and...

*No,* he thought. *Not that. Never that.*

Julian watched sunlight creep across the garden his mother had once kept so pristine that it barely looked real, but which was now an overgrown tangle of weeds and climbing vines; the light was watery yellow, and moved languidly, as though it saw no reason to hurry. It reached his bare feet, rolled up his legs and arms and chest until it washed slowly over his face. He closed his eyes, letting its warmth revive him, allowing the feel of the sun on his skin to fill him with something other than anger, and made a decision.

*This is not how this ends. You're not going down like this. Not without a fight.*

He forced himself up on to legs that felt like jelly and staggered back into the cottage. There was one thing he knew, even through the fog clouding his mind, one thing of which he was certain: the only way he could even *try* to help keep his son safe was by again becoming the man he had once been.

The man who died.

Showered, dressed, and with the sodden cigarettes dissolving in the bin, Julian compiled a mental checklist of what he needed.

First, and most importantly, was the ability to move without being tracked by Blacklight. He had examined the cottage and its grounds the previous morning, as he was making a start on the first bottle of vodka, and had seen immediately that working around the surveillance net that had been put in place would be impossible; it was as tight as any he had ever seen. He was going to have to think creatively, and decide his movements based on how they would appear on the screens in the Surveillance Division, which meant removing the tracker on the underside of the car parked beside the cottage was out; the moment it stopped transmitting, or one of the many cameras showed that the car was gone but the tracker wasn't, Cal would send a team to take him back in. But a solution would have to be found; there were places he needed to go, one in particular, that he didn't want Blacklight to know about.

Julian placed a tea towel, his mother's carving knife, and the last of the vodka on the table, and sat down. He forced himself to breathe, trying to keep his heartrate slow and steady, then rolled up the sleeve of his shirt and surveyed the bandage that encircled his forearm. He had no idea what advances had been made to the locator chips during his time away from Blacklight; in his day, it had been possible to remove them without damaging the small metal units, or triggering any kind of alarm.

There were no guarantees that was still the case.

*This might be over before it even starts,* he thought.

Slowly, he unwrapped the bandage. Beneath it, the incision that had been made by one of the Blacklight doctors was still red, the stitches black and ugly. Julian reached for the vodka and realised with embarrassment that his hand was shaking; he gripped the glass bottle tightly, and tipped its contents over his forearm.

The pain as the alcohol hit the wound was enormous, like dipping his arm into a box of white-hot razor blades. Julian threw his head back, his teeth gritted, the cords of muscle in his neck standing out, and waited for it to pass. It did so slowly, shifting gradually from searing agony to a low, hot throbbing. Julian took a long, deep breath, put the vodka bottle down, and picked up the carving knife.

Working as carefully as possible, he ran the sharp tip of the knife along the length of the incision, slicing open the black stitches. They split with a snapping noise that seemed horribly loud, and with each one that gave way, the wound peeled further open. The pain intensified, and he started to sweat from his forehead as his stomach churned with nausea. Then, finally, the last of the stitches was gone; he wiped his brow with the back of a trembling hand and examined the wound.

It was a slender oval of bright red and angry pink. Julian slid the point of the knife into it, keeping the sharp edge away from the raw flesh, and gently pressed the flat of the blade against one side of the wound, widening it. At the bottom of the shallow incision, no more than a centimetre below the surface of his arm, he could see the dull grey metal of the locator chip. Skin had already begun to heal over it, brand new and pale, and he realised with sinking resignation that he would have to cut through it to get the chip out.

Julian withdrew the knife, poured vodka over it, and tried to steady his hand; the sharp point of the blade was shaking dangerously. He worked the knife slowly back into the wound, clenching his jaw as vodka touched raw flesh, sending brief flashes of agony through his arm. He steadied the blade at one end of the chip, above the translucent layer of new skin. He took a deep breath, then pressed the point against it, and cut.

The pain was unreal, a thunderbolt of agony that erupted out of his forearm and charged into his head, sending him dizzy. The chip disappeared from view as blood welled up in the wound, covering the knife and spilling out on to the kitchen table. Julian shook his head, trying not to pass out from the pain, and pushed the knife forward. Something tore with a sound that seemed deafening inside his head, and he screamed at the ceiling, his face bright white, his eyes squeezed together as his vision began to grey.

*Faint,* he thought, distantly. *I'm going to faint.*

As his head started to swim, Julian let go of the knife and swung his fist up as hard as he could manage. It slammed into his ear, sending a jarring lightning bolt of pain through his head. His vision cleared instantly, and his reeling mind tried to focus again on the task at hand. He gripped the handle of the knife, and using what felt like the last of his resolve, dug the tip of the blade under the smooth side of the chip, slicing through flesh as he struggled for purchase. Blood spurted out of the wound in a glistening red arc and pattered down on to the table.

*What if you cut a muscle?* his mind asked, almost absently. *Or an artery?*

Julian pushed the thought away and bent the knife blade backwards with what little strength he had left. For long, awful seconds, nothing happened. Then, with a final burst of pain, the locator chip came loose; it was carried out of his arm on a fresh wave of blood and splashed on to the wooden table.

Euphoria flooded through him, momentarily overwhelming the pain in his arm and his concern at the amount of blood that was soaking into the table; the metal chip was proof that he was *not* helpless, that his misfortunes had not beaten him all the way down. But it was gone as quickly as it arrived, as Julian surveyed the carnage he had wrought on himself.

He simply could not bring himself to tip vodka into the wound again, so he pressed it together as firmly as he dared, sealed it shut with strips of stationery tape, and tightly rewrapped the bandage. Blood seeped through it almost instantly, but didn't spread too far, and he sighed with relief. Infection was a genuine concern, but he would deal with it as and when.

Julian picked up the chip, tied it securely to a rubber band, and put it round the wrist of the arm he had just performed impromptu surgery on. It was vital that it appear to Blacklight as though nothing had changed, so he would need to carry the locator with him most of the time. But now it could be taken off if the situation required, and that gave him an advantage over the men and women who were watching him, no matter how small.

*OK*, he thought. *What's next?*

The answer came without him even having to think about it.

It was time to go home.

Julian drove to Norwich in silence.

The elderly dark green Mercedes that had belonged to his mother had been extremely reluctant to start, but perseverance and a colourful range of shouted insults had eventually seen the engine splutter into life. The car handled like a tank, and seemed to be drinking petrol at an alarming rate, but its leather seats were soft and comfortable, and the big engine had lost little of its power; it devoured picturesque mile after picturesque mile, until Julian turned off the main road and into a trading estate at the edge of the city.

In an electronics shop the size of an aircraft hangar, he bought a torch and the best radio handset he could find. It was a sleek black device, capable of transmitting across a wide frequency spectrum, with an encryption filter that made it impossible for anyone to monitor any conversation he might use it for, and a fingerprint sensor that locked its control panel. He paid cash at the till, stowed the radio under the passenger seat of the Mercedes, and headed back east.

On the outskirts of Great Yarmouth, he found what he was looking for: a second-hand car dealership with a neon sign in the shape of a deck of cards over its entrance next to the words FULL HOUSE CARS. Julian parked in the car park of a vast twenty-four-hour supermarket on the other side of the road, took his chip off his wrist and put it in the glove compartment, and headed towards the car dealership. It looked as though its best days, assuming there had actually been any, were long behind it, which Julian hoped would make it the kind of establishment willing to deal in cash and forget names and faces.

He was right. Twenty minutes later he was driving his mother's Mercedes towards the seafront with the owner of FULL HOUSE CARS, a vastly overweight man by the name of Bobby, with a bald head and a goatee, following behind in the decade-old Ford Focus Julian had just bought with a small bundle of fifty-pound notes.

Outside a chain hotel overlooking the sea, Julian took the keys to the Ford and sent Bobby on his way. He left the Mercedes in the hotel car park, then walked round to a long outdoor seating area that faced the flat grey expanse of the North Sea. He took a seat at one of the picnic tables, then carefully removed the locator chip from his wrist and taped it to the underside of the bench, pressing it firmly between two of the wooden boards. Then he strolled as casually as he was able to his new Ford, and climbed behind the wheel.

If Blacklight was closely monitoring him, and he was convinced it would be, for at least the first few days of his release, they would see that he had left his mother's cottage, driven to a retail park outside Norwich, then to a supermarket in Great Yarmouth, and was now stationary outside a hotel on the seafront, with his car parked in the same establishment. If they were watching *incredibly* closely, they might have noticed that he hadn't appeared to get out of the car at the supermarket, and if they had him on continuous surveillance, they would eventually become suspicious when he didn't move from the picnic table; if nothing else, he would need to go to the bathroom at some point.

*Three hours there*, he thought, as he turned the Ford's key. *Half an hour to get what I need. Three hours back.*

It was a clear risk; his destination would undoubtedly have been flagged in whatever fake profile Cal Holmwood had given the Surveillance Division, and the potential for discovery was far higher than he would have liked. But there was simply nothing he could do about it; he had taken what precautions he could, and now he would simply have to hope that his luck held.

*I'm due some good fortune*, he thought, and smiled as he put the car into gear. *Surely I must be.*

Two hours and forty minutes later Julian Carpenter turned the Ford into the driveway of the house he had once shared with his family.

He left it in front of the garage, the same place he had always parked his silver Mercedes when he got home at night. Marie and Jamie had believed he had been returning from a long day spent behind a desk at the Ministry of Defence facility at Manston, sixty miles to the east, which was partly true; he *had* driven back from Manston each evening, but only after a helicopter had ferried him there from the Loop.

It had been easier to keep his real life a secret in those final years, when he had been spending more and more time devising strategy with Henry Seward and less and less on operations. As a younger man, he had been required to spend so many nights out of the house that Marie had once accused him of having an affair, a charge he had infuriated her by laughing at. He hadn't been able to help it; he had wanted to tell her how much easier keeping another woman secret would have been than the truth.

It had been a crazy way to live, he saw that now. He should have resigned his commission when he married Marie, or when Jamie was born at the latest, but he had been unwilling to give up the part of his life that gave him purpose, and pride, and excitement. He had not neglected his family; he had been as attentive and loving a husband and father as had been humanly possible, and had regularly pushed Blacklight's goodwill to the limit in the process. In the subsequent years, he had often wondered whether his increasing prioritisation of his family over the Department had made it easier for his colleagues to believe that he was capable of betraying them, when Thomas Morris's trap slammed shut on him.

Julian got out of the car and looked around in the cool light of the mid-afternoon. He had driven past the house without slowing, checking to see whether it was occupied; if it was, his task would be that much harder. But it had been obvious, even as he sped past, that it was empty; the windows of the living room and the quartered pane of glass in the front door were boarded up, and a heavy padlock hung from the garage door. The oak tree at the bottom of the garden, from the branches of which Alexandru Rusmanov and his acolytes had been watching the last time he stood on this driveway, had grown even fuller; it cast shadow over more than half the lawn, which was now a patchwork of weeds and fallen leaves. A squirrel stared at him from a low branch, a nut in its mouth; it didn't seem surprised to see him, or scared of him. Julian looked at the tree for a long time, cold fingers dancing up his spine, then turned towards the house.

And froze as he realised where he was standing.

*This is where I died,* he thought, looking down at the gravel of the drive. *Right here. This is where my life ended.*

There was a stain beneath his feet, long faded. Julian stared at it, his heart pounding, until he forced himself to tear his gaze away, and walked unsteadily along the front of the house. Red letters had been sprayed across the boards that covered the living room's picture window, forming a single word that made him grimace as he read it.

## TRAITOR

Julian had seen the press reports of the cover story that had been put up after his death, a horribly detailed fabrication that claimed he had been caught in a plot to sell national-security secrets to a Somalian Islamist group. He had not taken the blackening of his name personally, as he would have done exactly the same thing in Henry Seward's position. But he had hated the thought of what the stories must have done to Marie and Jamie; believing they were the family of a traitor would have been heartbreaking for them and, as the graffiti attested, would not have made them popular.

He tried to put such thoughts out of his mind; torturing himself with the details of how he had hurt his family would not do him, or them, any good. He turned his back on the hateful graffiti and walked round the side of the house, heading for the back garden. The gate was shut and bolted, but the lock had never been strong, and two heavy kicks sent it tumbling. Julian paused for a second, waiting to see whether the noise had alerted any of his neighbours, if indeed the same people still occupied the houses whose roofs were visible above the trees to the right and left.

Silence.

Julian stepped through the gate, and on to the crazy-paving path that had led between two expanses of immaculate lawn in the days when Marie had tended to it. Now it was as overgrown as the front garden, the path looking like some old trail through deep jungle. He made his way along it, taking care not to turn an ankle on one of the uneven slabs of stone, treading down weeds and bending long grass as he passed. At the top of the garden, on a wide patch of bare earth, stood the shed he had built in the first weeks after they had bought the house, when all their belongings had been in storage and Marie and Jamie had still been living with his mother in the cottage that was now once again his home; it was the shed he had driven more than a hundred and fifty miles for.

He had always padlocked the door, but not for the reasons that his family and neighbours believed; the shed had contained valuable tools and expensive garden equipment, but they were not what he had been securing.

Now it was standing ajar.

Julian pulled it open and stepped inside. The shelves on either side of the shed were empty, and they and the floor were covered in a thick layer of dust; his footsteps sent a cloud of it blooming into the air, making him cough as he crouched down and started pulling up the floorboards.

They came easily; they had never been firmly fixed, either to each other or to the ground beneath them, despite how they had appeared. Julian lifted them one at a time and leant them against the wall. When the task was finished, he stepped back and looked at what had lain beneath them for more than fifteen years, unbeknownst to anyone.

The hatch appeared to be intact.

Julian had been confident that it would, despite the length of time that had elapsed. It was made of thick lead, like the rest of the bomb shelter he had installed below the garden; just one of the many secrets he had kept from his family. There was a keypad set into its smooth surface, which was the only thing that gave him cause for concern. If its batteries had failed, there would be no way to open the hatch from the outside.

*Which is exactly the point, of course*, he thought wryly to himself. *Wouldn't that be a kick in the teeth?*

He brushed away a fine layer of dirt, held his breath, and pressed the keypad's power button. For a horribly long moment, nothing happened. Then, as the tension began to become unbearable, green light flickered beneath the small rectangle and illuminated the numbered keys.

Julian released his breath in a low rush and typed in a nine-digit code. The word OPEN appeared on the screen above the keypad, and from beneath the ground came the muffled sounds of heavy locks disengaging. He gripped the handle and, with a rush of stale air and a rattle of loose dirt and gravel, heaved the hatch up and back. Below him, electric lights flickered into life, illuminating a stainless-steel ladder. Julian took a last look behind him, and climbed down.

It was like stepping back in time. The man who had sold him the shelter had rhapsodised to Julian about the thickness of the walls, the blast that they could withstand, and the levels of radiation they could keep out. He had listened politely, even though it had been clear to him that the man was still living in a time when Soviet missiles might have fallen from the sky at any moment; Julian had no intention of explaining what he was actually going to use the shelter for.

There were two shelves of canned and dried food and a large plastic barrel of distilled water, in case the occasion *had* ever arisen when he needed to spend a prolonged period of time beneath his garden. But the shelter's true purpose rested silently on large metal racks standing either side of the ladder he had just climbed down.

One held MP5 submachine guns, Glock 17 pistols, a pair of American M4 carbines, and boxes of ammunition. A T-Bone gleamed on the top shelf of the other, above rows of regular and ultraviolet grenades, three UV beam guns, a pair of canvas holdalls, and a folded Blacklight uniform. The pungent scent of gun oil hung thickly in the air, a smell that reminded Julian so powerfully of the Loop that it brought tears to his eyes. He blinked them away, and got to work.

In a pale purple hotel room overlooking the sea, Julian set a steaming mug of instant coffee down on the table, briefly regretted destroying his remaining cigarettes, then pushed the thought away.

He had driven back from Brenchley to Great Yarmouth as quickly as he had dared, which, given that the car boot was full to the brim of extremely restricted weaponry, had not been all that fast.

He had retrieved his locator chip from beneath the picnic-table bench, half expecting a squad of Operators to swoop down on him as he did so, ready to bundle him into a van and take him back to his cell. He had transferred the bags from the Ford into his mother's Mercedes, then walked into the hotel and booked a room.

He didn't want to spend the night in Great Yarmouth; he wanted to be back at his mother's cottage, checking his weapons and equipment and considering his next move. But he forced himself to look at the situation from an external perspective; as far as Blacklight knew, he had been sitting on the bench outside the hotel for almost seven hours. If they thought he had been drinking throughout, which would be a perfectly reasonable assumption given the circumstances and the location, then it would not do to arouse their suspicions by being seen to drive home. The sensible thing to do would be wait until the morning.

*Twelve more hours,* he told himself. *That's nothing. Not after two and a half years.*

Julian took another sip of his coffee. He had ordered a sandwich from room service, and he examined the new radio he had bought as he waited for it to arrive. He had installed and charged the battery, and turned the handset on, watching the colour screen bloom into life. Now his fingers moved quickly across the keypad, tuning the handset to a frequency that he and his oldest, closest friend had agreed upon, when they had been younger and the world had seemed much less dark.

There was a crackle as the radio tuned, then silence. Julian had expected nothing else, but he still felt a momentary pang of disappointment as the reality of his exile was hammered home once again. The day had felt good, like he had made progress on a solvable problem; the silence made him wonder, not for the first time, whether there was any point in even trying to change his situation, or whether he should simply do as he had been ordered, and keep his head down.

Julian considered this as he drained his coffee, then raised the radio and broke the explicit promise he had made to Cal Holmwood.

"Come in, Victor," he said. "Victor, do you copy? Come in."

# 44

# THE WALL

"I'm not crazy, right?" asked Van Orel. "Tell me you're all seeing this too?"

"Yeah," said Jamie, his voice low. "I see it."

"Me too," said Larissa.

"And you can see what it is?" asked Van Orel.

"Yes," said Petrov. "It is a wall."

After taking down their camp, the DARKWOODS squad had continued to pick their way through the trees, across streams and impassable deadfalls, heading deeper and deeper into the forest.

There had been little conversation. Arkady Petrov led them silently onwards, Larissa floating at his shoulder, Jamie bringing up the rear of the reduced column. In front of him, Engel and Van Orel carried the body of Tim Albertsson between them on a makeshift stretcher, wrapped in his sleeping bag. The death of the American had soured the atmosphere within the squad from professionally neutral to outright poisonous; the air was thick with suspicion and paranoia.

It had also, as far as Jamie was concerned, brought out the worst in two of his squad mates.

The decapitation of their chain of command had revealed a hitherto unseen streak of panic in Kristian Van Orel. The South African's relief at the election of Petrov as squad leader had been almost desperate, and had placated him momentarily. But now, as the forest swallowed them, he was muttering almost constantly to himself; from what Jamie overheard, he appeared to be saying goodbye to his family, an act of fatalism that worried him deeply. And Greta Engel's palpable horror at the death of Albertsson had quickly evolved from concern over the treatment of his body into obvious suspicion of Larissa; she was glancing up at his girlfriend every few seconds, clearly unable to help herself.

It was making Jamie, who could see the entire squad from his position, increasingly nervous; he knew how sharp Larissa's supernatural senses were, and there was no chance she was unaware of Engel's scrutiny. If the German couldn't at least manage to make her suspicions less obvious, a confrontation was simply inevitable; he was sure it was already taking a great deal of Larissa's resolve to resist bringing the situation to a head right now. In the event of such a confrontation, he was not remotely concerned for the safety of his girlfriend; if a physical altercation took place between her and Engel, the result would not be in any doubt whatsoever.

*That* was what scared him.

Jamie knew there was a struggle taking place inside Larissa, a struggle whose outcome was far from certain. Her vampire side was never far from the surface, and the situation that the squad found themselves in was almost tailor-made to bring it out; the isolation, the constant tension, the effect the forest was having on her senses, the tunnel and its strange control room. If she came to believe that she was genuinely being suspected of murder by at least one, maybe more, of her heavily armed squad mates, it would not be long until her vampire side asserted itself entirely; it was at its most persuasive, its most powerful, when she felt threatened.

It was also the reason why Jamie couldn't be absolutely certain that she hadn't killed Tim Albertsson.

He wanted to believe her, and he hated himself for not being entirely able to do so. But the facts as he saw them were straightforward: there had been something between Larissa and Albertsson, something she had never told him about, but which had made the American openly hostile towards him. For almost thirty-six hours, Jamie had thought about little else, which he acknowledged was an awful thing to admit during a Priority 1 operation. With painful thoroughness, his mind had worked its way through every possible scenario.

Had they kissed? Had they slept together? Had they had an affair in Nevada? Was it still going on?

If so, was that why Albertsson had selected him for the operation? To rub his nose in it, to flaunt how stupid, how naive they thought he was? In which case, it would make sense that Larissa wouldn't want him to find out, and would be angry with Tim if she thought he was on the verge of giving the game away.

Would that have been enough to make her kill him?

*It's possible*, he told himself. *If he refused to stop, and she felt threatened, then it's definitely possible. You know it is.*

As if on cue, Larissa looked back at him from her position above the squad, and smiled. Jamie returned it as best he could until she turned away, then let the expression fade from his face. He had no idea what to do about the concerns wheeling through his head; all he could think to do was watch, and wait, and hope that if things went wrong, he could stop them before too much blood was spilled.

"I can see something!" shouted Larissa from overhead. "Up ahead. Something big."

"What is it?" called Petrov.

The wall – the Russian was right, that was exactly what it was – curved away to the east and west. It was a seemingly endless row of trees, their towering trunks pressed against each other without the smallest gap between them, their tops mingling into the distant canopy. The squad stood at the vast wooden barrier's base, staring up at it.

"There's no way this is naturally occurring," said Van Orel, his voice low. "Someone planted them like this."

"How long would it take for them to grow so big?" asked Engel.

Petrov shook his head. "Many years," he said. "Perhaps hundreds."

*Centuries*, thought Jamie, and shivered. *The patience required to do something like this, the sheer bloody-minded resolve. I can't begin to imagine it.*

Petrov looked up at Larissa. "Can you look for a way through?"

The vampire nodded, and flew rapidly away to the east, her supernaturally sharp eyes examining the wall closely.

"I don't like it," said Van Orel. "Looks like it's meant to hold King bloody Kong."

"Not necessarily," said Jamie, his voice low. "If the whole wall curves like this section does, then it's a circle. What if *he's* inside, and the wall is to keep everyone else *out*?"

"That is good sense," said Petrov. "Everything has been designed to keep people away. The dead animals, the traps, and I am certain the machines in the tunnel as well. Perhaps this is some final barrier."

"It's a bloody big one," said Van Orel.

"He really doesn't want to be found, does he?" said Engel. "I wonder why?"

"Why don't we go and ask him?" said Larissa.

The whole squad jumped. Jamie felt his heart accelerate in his chest as he spun round to see his girlfriend hovering five metres away; her return had been absolutely silent.

"Jesus Christ!" shouted Van Orel. "What the hell are you playing at, sneaking up on us like that?"

Larissa rolled her eyes, the tiniest of smiles curling the corners of her mouth. "There's an entrance," she said. "Follow me."

The squad followed the vampire round the base of the wall as she fluttered impatiently above them. Jamie stared up at the towering wooden barrier as they walked, his mind struggling to fully comprehend it. He understood the incredibly long lives that vampires were capable of living, objectively at least; he and Larissa had talked about it at length, and he believed he was sympathetic to the problems it caused even if, deep down, a part of him that his girlfriend hated could not quite get over the idea that it sounded brilliant. The wall was the hypothetical made physical; a structure that had taken an incredible amount of time to grow, and had been planned by someone who had known they would be around to see it complete. It was time measured not in hours and days and weeks, but in decades and centuries.

In generations.

"Here," shouted Larissa, and swooped down to the ground. "Right here."

The four Operators stopped and looked where she was pointing. At the point where two of the huge tree trunks met, a rectangular hole had been cut. It was barely wide enough for a human being, but its straight edges were clear evidence that it was deliberate. As was the fact that it would have been very hard to see without Larissa's supernatural eyesight; shrubs and bushes blocked it almost entirely from view, no doubt by design.

"I saw at least two more of them," said Larissa, her eyes glowing red with excitement. "This was the closest."

"OK," said Petrov, and drew his T-Bone. "We go through."

Jamie's heart was thudding in his chest like it was about to explode. Five pairs of eyes were fixed on the hole between the trees, on the entrance it clearly was. Five chests rose and fell, the sound of breathing the only noise in the silent, empty forest, until Petrov stepped forward, turned himself sideways, and slid through the opening.

For long seconds, there was only silence, pregnant with tension. Then the Russian's voice echoed back to them through the hole; it sounded low and thick, as though it had suddenly been filled with emotion.

"It is OK."

Larissa moved instantly; she let out a low growl, and disappeared through the entrance. Van Orel grinned, as though he had suddenly, belatedly become aware of how truly strange the situation they found themselves in was, and followed her. Jamie stood aside so that Engel could go next, then took a deep breath, and squeezed through the narrow opening.

# 45

# JOURNEY'S END

## TELEORMAN FOREST, ROMANIA

Jamie's first thought was that it reminded him of the Loop.

On the other side of the wall of trees was a vast circle of neatly tended grass, across which ran two stone paths that formed a cross at the middle. The forest canopy hung overhead, as thick and impenetrable as ever, but with a number of remarkable modifications. Square holes had been made in it at wide intervals, forming three long concentric rings; sunlight blazed down through them in neat shafts, hitting the ground on a beautiful arrangement of gardens and vegetable patches.

Beyond the shimmering edges of the light, the ground was covered with the same dull grass as the rest of the forest. But where the sunbeams touched down, great blooms of flowers sprang up, high and colourful, sending intoxicating scents into the air; roses, chrysanthemums, lilies, orchids, and countless others that Jamie didn't recognise. To the left of where the squad were standing, rows of vegetables were bathed in sunlight, their green stalks lush and full.

"My God," said Jamie, his eyes wide, his voice low. "This is incredible."

Larissa appeared at his side, her mouth hanging open with apparent disbelief. "This is his place," she said, softly. "He *made* this, Jamie. He built it so he could be safe outside, but things would still grow. Can you imagine even thinking of such an idea?"

Jamie shook his head.

*No*, he thought. *I can't. I just can't. This is crazy.*

"Building," said Petrov, and pointed towards the centre of the circle. "Ready One. Carpenter, take point."

Jamie nodded and drew his T-Bone, his eyes still fixed on the streaming beams of sunlight. It felt like being inside a cathedral, like being in the presence of something glorious; where the rest of the forest was full of gloomy darkness, this felt like a place of peace, of tranquillity. He led his squad mates across the grass and on to the nearest stone path; the contrast between the perpetual twilight and the pillars of light was blinding, but when he squinted he could make out an angular shape ahead of them.

"What is it, Larissa?" he said, his feet thudding on stone.

"Looks like a cabin," she said, narrowing her glowing eyes.

"Is he here? Can you smell him?"

Larissa shook her head. "The air's so full," she said. "The flowers, the trees, it's overwhelming. But he's here. I'm sure of it."

Jamie nodded, and quickened his pace. He led the squad past a pair of glorious flower beds, over which bees and butterflies were fluttering lazily, and fought back the urge to laugh; the place felt unreal, like it shouldn't exist. It made no sense that it should be here, but he was walking towards the centre of it.

"This is so bloody *weird*," said Van Orel from behind him, his voice full of confused wonder. "I keep expecting to wake up."

Jamie grinned, and glanced over at Larissa. She smiled back at him, her eyes dancing red, and he felt a strange feeling spread suddenly through him; it was a dizzying, swirling happiness, completely inappropriate for a Priority Level 1 operation, but utterly insistent.

It felt close to euphoria.

The squad walked through the innermost ring of light with Jamie's attention still fixed on his girlfriend; he guessed that the awe he and the rest of the squad were feeling inside the walled circle paled into insignificance next to the wonder that must be filling her mind. Once they were past it, Jamie's vision cleared, and he saw that Larissa had been right; before them was a log cabin, built long and low with pale wood that stood out in the gloom. Smoke spiralled from a stone chimney, and a door stood in the centre of the wall they were approaching.

"Hold," said Petrov, when they were fifty metres away. "Kinley, you will be in the air. Carpenter, you will stay on point, I will follow you. Van Orel left, Engel right. Nobody will do anything without my go. Is that clear?"

"Clear," chorused his squad mates.

Jamie felt a familiar cold settle into him as Larissa rose silently into the air, the sensation of the world around him sharpening and slowing down that always took place when violence moved from possible to likely. He welcomed it; more than that, he trusted it. He raised his T-Bone behind him as Petrov moved up to his shoulder and Engel and Van Orel slid silently away to the left and right. Jamie took a deep breath, and was about to take a first careful step towards the cabin when its door swung open, and a man with a wide smile on his bearded face strolled out and looked at them.

The five members of the DARKWOODS squad froze where they stood.

The first victim – for that was who the man surely was – was tall and appeared to be in his mid-thirties, although they all knew that his true age was far, far greater. He was dressed in blue jeans and a checked shirt, and wore heavy, scuffed leather boots on his feet. His hair was roughly chopped, and his black beard was full and thick. Jamie looked more closely, his heart thundering in his chest, his skin covered in gooseflesh, and saw that the man's eyes were green with a dancing flicker of red in their corners, full of life and warmth.

"Good morning," he said. "My name is Gregor. I presume you are looking for me?"

# 46

# OUT OF THE BAG

Paul Turner drained his fourth cup of coffee and waited for Kate Randall to knock on the door of his office. It was 10.29am, and the young Lieutenant was always scrupulously punctual; it was one of the many things he liked about her.

The Security Officer had slept better than he had expected. He had stayed with Cal Holmwood for more than an hour after the Director had ended his video call, talking through the ramifications of the SPC Director's revelation. Aleksandr Ovechkin had assured them that the project known as Safeguard was dead, that Richard Brennan had been the last Blacklight Operator to fall victim to it, and neither Turner nor Holmwood had doubted the truth of what they had been told; the SPC regime was very different than it had been in the Soviet era.

And the truth was, they *had* to take Ovechkin's word for it; ISAT was complete and had found no other persons of interest within the Department. If there *were* still spies inside the Loop, and the Safeguard programming was deep enough that ISAT had not exposed it, there was very little they could do.

Turner was still debating whether to tell Kate about Safeguard. There was no obligation for him to do so; despite her Zero Hour clearance, she was merely a Lieutenant, and objectively speaking, a highly inexperienced one at that. But she had become far more important to him than her rank suggested, and even though they were his stock in trade, he didn't like keeping secrets from her.

His watch ticked over to 10.30. Ten seconds later there was a knock on the door to his office.

Turner smiled. "Come in," he called.

The door opened and Kate stepped through it. She nodded respectfully as she closed it behind her, then crossed the room and stood in front of his desk.

"Good morning, sir," she said.

"Morning," he replied. "Sleep well?"

Kate grinned. This had become an ongoing joke between the two of them, as the honest answer was almost always, 'Badly, if at all.'

"Great," she said. "You?"

"Like a baby. Sit down."

Kate settled herself into a chair and rested her clipboard on her knees. It contained the overnight reports from the Surveillance, Security and Intelligence Divisions, and rarely offered anything in the way of good news.

"Report," he said.

"More vampire-related violence against civilians, sir," said Kate. "No deaths, which is something, I suppose, but a dozen assaults, GBH, ABH, two attempted murders. It's getting worse, just like you said it would."

Turner nodded. The situation outside the Loop was absolutely precarious. Despite the continuing absence of any official statement regarding the supernatural, belief was spreading rapidly, bringing fear and paranoia with it. The Surveillance Division had all but abandoned their efforts to get Kevin McKenna's editorial taken down from the internet; it was moving far faster than they could keep up with.

Those who believed, including the men and women responsible for what were becoming nightly attacks on anyone who aroused their suspicions, were still the minority, but Turner was not sure how long that would remain the case. He was starting to believe they were on the brink of a major social collapse, a panic that would cost hundreds, if not thousands, of lives.

The reports coming in from the other Departments confirmed that the problems were not confined to the UK. It was a small world now, smaller than ever before, and the same fear that was rippling through Blacklight's island jurisdiction was taking root in every corner of the globe. NS9 had already advised the Pentagon to prepare for the possibility of deploying the National Guard to maintain order, and had told the White House not to discount the option of declaring martial law. Russia, Brazil, Germany and South Africa had all taken similar steps. China, where access to the internet was censored and monitored, was coping better; its vast rural population was easier to keep uninformed, and the government was already in possession of highly efficient machinery to crack down on any disorder. Despite that, the reports coming out of Beijing were not devoid of concern; PBS6 was clearly not taking the situation lightly.

*It's a powder keg,* Turner thought. *The whole planet. All that remains to be seen is where the spark comes from.*

"All right," he said. "We're deploying the active roster at maximum capacity, and we've instructed the police to expect an increase in violent crime. Unless the situation changes, there's not much more we can do right now."

Kate nodded. "Yes, sir."

Turner looked at his young Lieutenant for a long moment.

"I have to tell you something," he said, eventually. "Something that happened yesterday."

Kate leant forward in her chair. "OK," she said. "Tell me."

Turner was about to do so when his console beeped into life. He picked it up off his desk and thumbed it open to reveal a message from the Director of the Surveillance Division.

FROM: Griffiths, Major Alison (NS302, 41-D)
TO: Turner, Major Paul (NS303, 36-A)
TV Channel 3. PRIORITY LEVEL 1.

Turner frowned, and passed the console to Kate. She read the message as he tapped keys on his desktop terminal, turning on the screen that hung on the wall of his office and tuning it to Channel 3.

The screen showed the familiar primary-coloured set of *Coffee Break*, a hugely popular news and chat show that ran for ninety minutes every weekday morning. Two large sofas were arranged round a wide coffee table that was usually covered with newspapers, magazines and coffee mugs, but was empty except for a glass bottle of dark red liquid. A huge picture window behind the sofas normally provided a sweeping view of the Thames, but was covered by a heavy black curtain, creating a deep gloom on the set. Turner frowned, then looked at the three figures sitting on the sofas.

On the left, in their usual places, were Patrick and Helen, the presenters of *Coffee Break*. Patrick was in his early fifties, handsome, hugely charming, with a wide smile and white hair; he had been a children's television presenter before switching channels and conquering light entertainment, and Turner remembered watching him interview pop stars and introduce cartoons on Saturday mornings two and a half decades earlier.

Helen was barely half Patrick's age, a pretty blond who had once been an underwear model, but had quickly made the transition into TV, presenting a series of talent shows and appearing as a guest on innumerable comedy quizzes. There had been a number of unkind columns written when she got the job on *Coffee Break*, by pundits who dismissed her as eye candy, reliant entirely on her looks and the figure that had once seen her in great demand as a model. But she had surprised her critics with an intelligence they had not expected, and an absolute inability to suffer fools; the internet was full of clips of her losing her temper with guests who had attempted to justify viewpoints that were stupid, or ignorant, or both. The almost palpable chemistry between her and Patrick only added to what was a slick, highly entertaining ninety minutes of television.

On the sofa opposite the presenters sat a man in his early twenties, wearing blue jeans and a black T-shirt, his legs stretched out and crossed at the ankle. He was looking at Patrick and Helen and smiling as though he didn't have a care in the world, as though he spent all of his mornings on a live television show that a quarter of the country was watching.

Turner realised what he was looking at a millisecond before a pink banner appeared at the bottom of the screen, containing five terrible, devastating words.

### EXCLUSIVE: I AM A VAMPIRE

He grabbed the phone on his desk, searched its memory for Alison Griffiths' name, and held it to his ear. "Put this on every screen in the base," he said, when the Surveillance Director answered. "Right now." He slammed the phone down, then grabbed his radio and twisted its dial to the setting that broadcast his voice through the entire Loop. "Attention," he said. "This is the Security Officer. Please direct your attention to the nearest screen."

"Oh shit," said Kate, her eyes wide. "Is this live?"

Turner nodded. "It's happening now," he said. "Give me my console, Kate."

Kate looked down, a frown on her face, then held the plastic rectangle out towards him; she had clearly forgotten she had it. Turner took it from her and typed a message to the Director of the Intelligence Division, ordering him to alert the civilian authorities, knowing it was redundant even as his fingers tapped the screen; there was nothing they could do to stop what was about to happen.

"Welcome back to *Coffee Break*," said Patrick, looking sombrely into the camera. "For those of you who are just joining us—"

"Where have you been?" interjected Helen.

"Right," said Patrick, casting a smile in her direction before returning his gaze to his audience. "But if you *are* just tuning in, Helen and I are joined this morning by Gideon, who is here today because he claims – and I can't quite believe that I'm about to say this – that he's a vampire. A real, blood-drinking, living-forever, supernatural vampire. Isn't that right, Gideon?"

The man on the sofa nodded. "That's right."

"At his request, we've blacked out all the windows, so I apologise if you can't see us quite as well as normal," continued Patrick. "What would happen if we hadn't covered them?"

Gideon smiled. "I would catch fire," he said. "And your cleaners would have a very messy sofa to deal with."

"You would catch fire?" said Helen, sitting forward. "You would actually burst into flames?"

"Yes," said Gideon. "The fire is purple, which is something to

490

do with how ultraviolet light reacts with my cells. It burns very hot and very fast."

"I assume it would be very painful?" said Patrick.

"It hurts," said Gideon. "I can promise you that."

"And you would die?" asked Helen.

Gideon shook his head. "Not necessarily," he said. "We're very hard to kill. But if I didn't put out the flames, I'd burn down to a pile of ash."

"But you wouldn't be dead?" asked Patrick. He was now sitting forward as well, enthralled by what their guest was saying.

"I could still be revived," said Gideon. "Even from ash. With enough blood, I could be myself again in an hour or two."

"How is that possible?" asked Helen.

Gideon shrugged. "I'm no biologist," he said. "Ask Blacklight. I'm sure they understand the science better than I do."

Paul Turner felt his insides turn to water.

*That's it,* he said. *No amount of denials are going to work, not this time. It's out there.*

"Blacklight," said Helen. "That's the organisation Kevin McKenna wrote about, in the editorial that has become a phenomenon on the internet. The organisation he described as the vampire police."

Gideon nodded. "They're more like the vampire SAS," he said. "They're soldiers, highly equipped and resourced. They have the authority to destroy vampires where they stand. No trials, no judges. Just execution."

"So McKenna was right?" said Patrick. "In what he wrote?"

"Everything Kevin McKenna wrote was the truth," said Gideon. "Why else would they have killed him?"

Turner reached for his radio, his hand seeming to move in slow motion, and keyed it to the Security Division frequency.

"Squads nine through twelve report immediately to the hangar," he said. "Maintain readiness and wait for orders. Out."

"Jesus," said Kate, her voice low. "This is bad, Paul. This is really bad."

Turner didn't respond; his attention was already focused back on the screen.

"So," said Patrick, "how does somebody become a vampire? Can you tell us?"

"Again, I'm no expert on the science," said Gideon, uncrossing his legs and sitting forward. "But you have to be bitten. There's something in the bite that changes you. You can't be turned by sharing toilet seats."

Patrick and Helen both burst out laughing, and Turner felt anger boil into his stomach.

*You idiots,* he thought. *You irresponsible, reckless idiots. You have no idea what you're doing.*

"So what happened to you, Gideon?" asked Helen. "I'm sorry if that's too personal."

Gideon smiled. "Not at all, Helen," he said. "It's fine. I was bitten by a man I met at a party, almost twenty years ago. We were... well, you don't need to know the details. But he bit my neck. I didn't think anything of it at the time."

"Twenty years ago?" asked Patrick, incredulous. "How old are you, if you don't mind me asking?"

"I've been alive for forty-four years," said Gideon.

"That's unbelievable," said Helen. "You don't look a day older than twenty-one."

"The ageing process slows down when you're turned," said Gideon. "It doesn't stop, so if any of your viewers think vampires live forever, then I'm afraid they're wrong. But it does slow down. A lot."

"I think most of my friends are going to be pleading for someone to bite them," said Helen, grinning widely.

Patrick burst out laughing, and Gideon flashed a warm smile in her direction.

"I can imagine," he said. "But I wouldn't recommend it. I don't think they'd want it if they knew what it's really like."

"Right," said Patrick, a serious expression appearing again on his face. "So what is it like? I mean, day to day?"

Gideon shrugged. "I can't go in the sun," he said. "And I have to feed. Apart from that, I can live a normal life. And there are benefits, of course."

"When you say feed," said Helen, "do you mean drink blood?"

Gideon looked her square in the eyes. "That's right," he said.

"You've brought some with you this morning," said Patrick. "That's what's in that bottle, right?"

"Right," said Gideon. "That's lamb's blood. I have a butcher who keeps it for me."

"So it doesn't have to be human?" asked Patrick.

Gideon shook his head. "No," he said. "It doesn't. Although there are vampires who won't drink anything else."

"Why not?" asked Helen, her face growing pale.

"Because it tastes better," said Gideon. "I'm sorry, but that's the truth. A *lot* better."

"And what happens if you don't feed?" asked Patrick, his voice low.

"The hunger takes you," said Gideon. "Imagine the hungriest you've ever been in your life, multiply it by a thousand, and that's what the hunger feels like. If you resist it for too long, it will drive you crazy. And I mean that literally."

"Has that happened?" asked Helen. She was as white as a ghost now, her eyes wide. "I mean, to anyone you know?"

"Not first hand," said Gideon. "But I've heard stories. Some vampires think they're doing the right thing by refusing to feed. But the hunger breaks them, and they feed anyway. There's no stopping it."

"That's horrible," said Helen, her voice tiny.

"I completely agree," said Gideon.

"This has stopped being fun, hasn't it?" growled Kate. "Now that he's talking about blood and crazy people. You *idiots*."

Affection for his young Lieutenant filled Paul Turner as the phone on his desk began to ring, Major Griffiths' name glowing on its screen. He glanced fondly at her as he picked it up.

"Go ahead," he said.

"Social media has gone completely off the charts," said the Surveillance Director. "Almost ten thousand mentions a minute and increasing rapidly. 999 is jammed, and every TV news channel in the country has cut in live to follow this. And it's not just here, Paul. This is going out all over the world."

"Talk to Intelligence for me," said Turner. "Make sure the police understand that there are going to be riots when this is done. And alert the other Departments, if they aren't already watching. They need to know what's happening."

"Yes, sir," said Griffiths.

"Thank you," said Turner. He hung up the phone and looked back at the screen.

"So," said Patrick. There seemed to be an uneasy atmosphere on the *Coffee Break* set, a tension that had not been there when the interview began. "You said there were benefits to being a vampire, apart from ageing less quickly. What are they?"

Gideon grinned. "I can fly," he said. "I'm stronger than any normal human in the world, faster too. And it's very, very hard to kill me."

"*You can fly?*" said Helen, her face a mask of incredulity. "Are you really telling us that?"

Gideon didn't answer. Instead, he leant back on the sofa and slowly, almost casually, floated up into the air. From beyond the small set the cameras were focusing on, a chorus of shouts and screams rang out. Gideon came to a halt a metre above the sofa and hovered, smiling at Helen.

"My God," she whispered. Her eyes were huge, her face translucent.

"This is real," said Patrick, his voice thick with fear. "I want everyone watching this to know that there are no wires being used, no camera tricks. What you are seeing is really happening, right in front of us."

Gideon spun slowly upwards, until he was standing on thin air. Then there was a blur of movement, and he was sitting between Helen and Patrick on their sofa; he had crossed the set faster than the cameras could follow. Helen screamed and jumped to her feet, as Patrick scrambled away, his eyes wide and full of terror.

"I'm sorry," said Gideon, his smile shrinking. "I didn't think you would believe me unless I showed you. I didn't mean to frighten you."

Helen didn't look as though she believed him; she had retreated towards the curtain that covered the windows, her entire body visibly shaking, her hands covering her mouth, her huge eyes fixed on the vampire. Patrick was breathing deeply and rapidly; as Turner watched, he made a visible effort to calm himself, and turned back towards Gideon.

"I'm sorry for our reaction," he said, his voice audibly trembling. "You have to understand, that was quite a shock."

"It's OK," said Gideon. "I understand completely. Do you mind standing up for a moment?"

495

Patrick nodded and got to his feet. Gideon did likewise, then took hold of the long sofa and lifted it into the air as though it weighed no more than a feather. He held it easily at shoulder-height for several seconds, a small smile on his face, then carefully put it down.

"That's incredible," whispered Patrick, his voice hoarse. "It's impossible."

Gideon stepped at normal speed over the coffee table and settled back on to the guest sofa. "No," he said. "It's not."

Very, very slowly, Helen sat back down next to Patrick. She perched on the edge of the sofa, as though readying herself to flee, and looked with obvious fear at her co-presenter.

"There was something else that Kevin McKenna wrote in his article," said Patrick. "He said vampires have red eyes."

Gideon nodded.

"But your eyes are green. They're the same colour as mine."

"Our eyes aren't *always* red," said Gideon. "It's mostly an involuntary reaction, if we're threatened, or angry, or if we smell blood. But it can be controlled."

"Can you show us?" asked Patrick.

"Yes," said Gideon, then turned to Helen. "But I should warn you in advance, it can be quite unsettling."

"It's OK," said Helen, her pale cheeks colouring pink with embarrassment. "I'm fine now, honestly. It was just a shock when you flew. Oh God, I can't believe I just said that. You *flew*."

Gideon smiled sympathetically. "Are you sure?" he asked.

She nodded.

"All right then," said Gideon. "Don't say I didn't warn you."

The camera zoomed in on his pale, handsome face as glowing pink slowly began to drip into the corners of his eyes. It deepened to scarlet as the whites disappeared, then blazing to crimson as the irises were swallowed up. The light reflected on the skin of his face, turning it red, and glowed so fiercely that the camera was forced to zoom out to keep Gideon in focus; the supernatural light bloomed around his head like an aura.

The shot switched to Patrick and Helen on the other sofa, their mouths hanging open, their eyes comically wide. Then Helen's hands leapt back over her mouth.

"Oh my God," she cried, from behind her fingers.

The shot cut back to Gideon, who was regarding the presenters with his terrible, glowing gaze. But it was not his eyes that had caused Helen to cry out; the vampire had opened his mouth in a wide grin, and clearly visible below the straight line of his upper teeth, bright white and wetly gleaming, was a pair of long, pointed fangs.

"I don't understand," asked Patrick. "How has it been possible to keep people like you a secret? How didn't we know about you until now?"

Gideon smiled. The red in his eyes disappeared and his fangs rose back into his gums. "Because the government has gone to great lengths to keep it that way," he said. "If I'm walking down a street at night and a member of Blacklight sees me, they will kill me, and the same goes for the rest of my kind. So most vampires choose to keep their heads down. It has never been in our interests for the public to know we're real."

"Have you put yourself in danger by coming here today?" asked Helen.

"I would imagine so," said Gideon, and shrugged. "But it was time to end all this secrecy. McKenna's article started the process, and Blacklight couldn't put the cat back in the bag. People started to wake up. And now they know."

Helen nodded sympathetically.

"I want to thank you for spending time with us, Gideon," said Patrick. "I know you're in a hurry to leave, and I think we can all understand why, given what you've told us. But I think it's no exaggeration to say that we have seen the world as we know it changed this morning. So thank you for your honesty, and your bravery."

"You're very welcome," said Gideon, and smiled.

"One last thing," said Patrick. "What advice would you give our viewers if they encounter a vampire?"

"Make sure they don't," said Gideon. "That's the best advice I can give them. Because not all vampires are like me. Some of them are monsters, and you might not know until it's too late."

# 47

# BE CAREFUL WHAT
# YOU WISH FOR

## *TELEORMAN FOREST, ROMANIA*

"I knew someone would come," said Gregor. "After I let the old vampire live. Are you here to kill me?"

Arkady Petrov shook his head. "No," he said. "We are not here for that."

"You are Blacklight," said Gregor. "Is that not the reason you exist?"

Petrov frowned. "I am not Blacklight," he said. "But you know of them?"

Gregor shrugged. "This forest is still part of the world," he said. "I hear many things. And I have been listening to you talk to each other since your helicopter set down in the field beyond the trees. So I ask you again: are you here to kill me?"

"No," said Petrov. "That is the truth."

"I am very glad to hear it," said Gregor.

*Of course you are,* thought Jamie. *You don't want to have to kill five Operators. Because you know that then the Departments would send a hundred.*

"You are the man we are looking for?" asked Petrov. "The one they call the first victim?"

"Do they call me that?" asked Gregor, and laughed. "I did not know."

"But you are him?" pressed Petrov.

"I have come to understand that I was the first man to be bitten by the vampire who became known as Dracula," said Gregor, his eyes momentarily shimmering red.

"Can you tell us what happened to you?" asked Engel.

Gregor frowned. "Why should I do that?"

"It would be helpful for us," said the German Operator.

"Would it?" asked Gregor. "I cannot see how. I was bitten, but I did not die. When I awoke, I was different. I presume this is a process you are all familiar with."

Engel tried again. "There is a belief that something out of the ordinary happened to you."

"Who believes that to be true?"

"There is a prophecy—"

Gregor boomed with laughter, cutting her off. "Prophecies are for fools," he said. "Stories to tell around campfires. Are you saying that you, men and women of science and technology, have sought me out because of some whispered legend?"

Jamie frowned. "Why else would we be here?" he asked.

Gregor faced him. "To ask me to fight," he said. "On your side in the war that is coming. Is that not the case?"

"Yes," said Larissa, her eyes glowing at the corners. "That's right. What do you say?"

"Shut up, Larissa," said Petrov.

Gregor's welcoming expression disappeared, replaced by narrowed eyes and a set of the jaw that turned Jamie's insides to water. The

**500**

old vampire turned slowly towards Petrov. "Do not speak to her like that in my presence," he said, his voice the slow ice of a glacier. "I will not have it."

Petrov stared at the first victim, their gazes locked together. There was silence, sudden and thick with the possibility of violence, until Larissa spoke. "It's all right," she said. "He's our squad leader. It's OK."

Gregor narrowed his eyes even further, until they were little more than glowing crimson slits. Then he opened them, and the smile returned to his face as he nodded at Larissa. "Forgive me," he said. "I do not like men who behave uncivilly towards women, and my temper has always been a weakness."

*You and me both,* thought Jamie, and smiled.

"What happened to the man you carry?" asked Gregor, and nodded towards the wooden stretcher that held the body of Tim Albertsson.

"I think you know," said Larissa, her eyes darkening.

"As I said," said Gregor, his smile widening. "Men who threaten women make me angry."

Jamie's eyes widened with sudden understanding.

Larissa had been telling the truth; she didn't kill Albertsson.

The first victim did.

Relief swept through him, closely followed by guilt at his failure to entirely trust his girlfriend's innocence.

*What did Albertsson do to her, though?* he wondered. *What made the first victim kill him? What threat did Tim make?*

The thought made his skin itch with anger, and he found himself momentarily, viciously glad that the American was dead. He immediately pushed the feeling away, demanding better of himself, ordering himself to stay calm, and returned his attention to Gregor.

But to his left, it became instantly clear that Van Orel had reached the same conclusion as him.

"*You* killed him," said the South African, his voice low and full of outrage. "While he slept. Like a coward."

Gregor's eyes narrowed again, and darkened to a pulsing crimson. "Careful," he said. "Be very careful."

"Why?" asked Van Orel, his voice rising. "In case you kill me too? In case you kill us all? You know damn well we couldn't stop you, so do it if you're going to. Bloody well get it over with."

Petrov shot a furious glance at Van Orel, its unspoken message abundantly clear.

*Shut the hell up. Control yourself.*

"Is that what you want?" asked Gregor, softly. "To die?"

Van Orel laughed. It was an ugly noise, high and rasping; it sounded like something inside him was on the verge of breaking. Jamie stared helplessly, then saw movement in the corner of his eye, and felt his heart stop in his chest.

Engel had raised her T-Bone and was pointing it directly at the first victim's heart.

"You killed him," she said. "And for what? *Because he was uncivil?* Ridiculous."

"Do not point your gun at me," said Gregor.

Jamie gasped. The first victim's voice had lowered to a depth and bass that shook the ground beneath his feet. Engel trembled visibly, but did not lower her weapon.

"Why not?" she asked, her voice unsteady. "You are a murderer, and I do not face murderers unarmed."

There was a blur, and then the first victim was standing in front of Engel, his hand gripping the barrel of her T-Bone, his eyes blazing. She shrieked as he jerked the weapon out of her hands and hurled it towards the distant wall of trees, where it disappeared into the gloom.

"I told you," he growled, leaning his face in close to hers, "not to point your gun at me. You are in my home." Then there was a second blur, and the vampire was again standing on the porch of his cabin, his gentle smile restored.

Petrov turned and glared at his squad with eyes full of warning. "The next one of you who talks," he said, "I will shoot myself. Is that clear?"

Engel looked at her squad leader, her eyes wide and full of shock. She opened her mouth to say something, or possibly simply to burst into tears, but Petrov raised a single gloved finger in her direction. The German Operator stared at it, then closed her mouth, her face a mask of misery. Jamie watched the silent exchange, then returned his attention to Gregor, who appeared to be waiting politely for them to conclude their business. Petrov pointed his finger at each of his squad mates in turn, before turning back towards the cabin.

"You built this place," he said.

"I did," said Gregor. "It took many years, but time is not something I have lacked."

"You do not like visitors," said Petrov. "The wall. The traps. The dead animals."

"You are most perceptive," said Gregor. "And you are correct. I have taken steps to ensure my isolation. The people of this corner of the world are superstitious fools, and fear keeps them away. The forest is itself a natural shield, as satellites and planes find it hard to see beneath the green. And the wall stands before anyone with the determination to make it this far. You, my friends, are only the second people ever to find their way here."

"There's more, though," said Larissa, ignoring the glare that Petrov gave her. "Isn't there? My vampire senses don't work here, not properly. Some of it is the forest itself, the darkness, the plants and trees. But I think some of it is deliberate. I think some of it has to do with your underground room."

Gregor smiled. "You found the tunnel?"

"We did," said Larissa. "What are the machines that are down there?"

"Communications disruptors," said Gregor. "Signal blockers and scramblers. A white-noise generator. One or two other things."

Larissa's eyes flared. "A white-noise generator?" she growled. "So that's why I haven't been able to hear properly. I thought I was going crazy."

"I am sorry," said Gregor. "I'm afraid that is exactly why I installed it. To discourage other vampires, like yourself."

"Yet you let Grey live," said Petrov, trying to regain control of the exchange. "The old vampire you mentioned. Why? You must have known others would come."

"It would have been easier to kill him," said Gregor. "Far easier. But the truth is, I did not want to. I am not a fan of death."

"You killed Albertsson," said Engel. The words sounded like sobs.

"I occasionally make an exception," said Gregor.

"And you didn't really care whether anyone else came," said Jamie. "We could have brought a thousand men in here and it wouldn't matter. You know we can't make you do anything you don't want to."

Gregor shrugged. "You are correct, of course," he said. "Although such a prospect gives me no satisfaction. In my experience, little good comes from the use of violence."

Jamie looked up at the old vampire, and realised something with sudden certainty. He smiled. "You're not going to help us," he said. "Are you?"

Petrov fixed him with eyes like daggers, but he ignored his squad leader; he kept his gaze fixed on the first victim.

Gregor shook his head. "No," he said. "I am not going to help you."

"Why not?" cried Engel. "You happily kill a man for some minor offence, yet you won't help us destroy the greatest evil that has ever walked the earth? What possible reason could you have for refusing?"

"Why would I feel compelled to explain myself to you?" said Gregor. "You and your friends will fight Dracula, and I am sure you will fight well. I wish you success. But it is not my fight."

"You're a coward," said Jamie, his voice low and full of anger. "That's all you are. A bloody coward."

Gregor turned to face him, a tiny smile of incredulity on his face. "What did you say?" he asked.

"You heard me," said Jamie. "You know how powerful Dracula is, and you have more reason to hate him than anyone else on earth. If he isn't stopped, if he's allowed to rise to his full strength, then thousands of people will die, maybe millions. But you don't care about them, do you? You only care about this prison you've made for yourself."

"I admire your passion, my friend," said Gregor, his voice suddenly low and dripping with danger. "I genuinely do. But I would advise you to think carefully before you speak again. I have made my feelings on rudeness clear."

Jamie grunted with laughter. "Right," he said. "You made it clear that you have no problem killing a man for insulting a woman, and equally clear that you won't help us prevent a global genocide. So what am I supposed to make of that? Tell me."

Gregor's eyes churned with crimson. He growled, a low sound that rumbled through the forest floor.

"Lieutenant Carpenter," said Petrov, his voice sounding eerily similar to Paul Turner at his angriest. "You will not say another word. Not a single one. Is that absolutely clear to you?"

Jamie faced the Russian, fury and bitter frustration roaring through him, searching for release. Engel and Van Orel were staring at him with wide, fearful eyes, Larissa with a fierce smile full of clear and obvious pride. He bit his tongue, hard, and tasted warm, coppery blood in his mouth.

Then he nodded.

"I am asking you to reconsider," said Petrov, turning instantly back to face Gregor. "You have made this place your home, and perhaps you think that nothing can touch you here. Perhaps you are even correct. But if Dracula rises, he will burn everything to ash. Can you be certain that you will be spared?"

The first victim sighed deeply. "I made a decision a long time ago," he said. "An amount of time that you cannot imagine, that is only numbers to you. And that decision was to withdraw from the world that you inhabit. I watched everyone I loved grow old and die, even the ones who drove me away when it became clear what I had become. Wars have come and gone, some of them on my doorstep, and I have stayed here. Genocides have scarred humanity, time and again, and I have stayed here. Because, when you have lived a life measured in centuries, it is hard to care about petty squabbles. So I will not fight. Not for you or anyone else."

Petrov didn't respond.

"What if you didn't have to?" said Larissa, suddenly.

"I am sorry?" said Gregor.

"Fight," said Larissa. "What if you didn't have to fight?"

The first victim narrowed his eyes. "Go on," he said.

Larissa stepped forward, the eyes of Petrov and her squad mates following her closely. "We know more about vampires now than we ever have," she said. "There's a theory, named after a friend of mine, which I believe. It explains why some of our kind are stronger than others."

Gregor said nothing, but gave an almost imperceptible nod of his head.

"Old vampires make more powerful vampires," continued Larissa. "Something happens as we age, an evolution that alters the liquid that coats our fangs. I was turned by the vampire you met, who is believed to be the oldest in Britain. As a result, I am faster and stronger than most, even though it's barely three years since I was turned."

"Make your point," said Gregor.

"Any human being turned by you would become an incredibly powerful vampire," said Larissa. "Not instantly, but very quickly. Maybe even strong enough to fight Dracula, especially if there were more than one of them. All we would need would be samples of your blood and the plasma on your fangs. That might be enough. You could stay here, away from everything, and still have saved the world."

"Maybe so," said the first victim. "But I'm afraid my answer remains the same."

"You animal!" shouted Engel, her voice high and wavering. "You cruel man!"

"What if I took them from you?" growled Larissa, ignoring her squad mate.

Gregor smiled gently. "You could not," he said. "And you know you could not. Please do not try."

"I feel sorry for you," said Jamie. "I really do."

The first victim turned towards him, his eyes darkening. "I have warned you once already," he said, his voice a thunderous rumble. "Do not make me do so again."

"What does it matter?" said Jamie, smiling narrowly. "If you don't help us, Dracula wins. And if Dracula wins we all die. So pardon me for not giving a shit about your warning."

Gregor growled, but said nothing. His narrow, glowing eyes had settled firmly on Jamie, who swallowed hard, trying not to let his fear show in his face or voice.

"You won't fight," he said. "Fine. If you don't want to risk your life, you don't think what's coming is worth that, that's up to you. No problem. But to refuse to give us even the slightest chance of an advantage, even though it would cost you nothing? That is cowardice. That is *bullshit.*"

Gregor tilted his head to one side. "You are truly not afraid?" he said.

"I'm afraid," said Jamie. "I'm terrified. But not of you."

"You truly would do anything to stop Dracula? To prevent his rise?"

"Yes," said Jamie.

"No matter the cost?"

"Yes."

The first victim smiled. "I believe you," he said. "You have the insolence and stupidity of youth, and you would do well to learn to respect your elders. But I believe you mean what you say. And I cannot pretend not to sympathise with your cause, even though I will not allow you to milk me like some beast of burden. But I will help you." He paused, looking directly at Jamie. "I will give you what you want."

Jamie took a deep breath. At the back of his mind, a possibility was forming, cold and dreadful. But on some level he realised he had always been aware of it, even as the orders for the operation appeared on his console screen.

He had always known that it might come to this.

Then the first victim moved, at a speed that was impossible to follow with human eyes, and an arm, impossibly strong, as immovable as a tree trunk, looped round his neck, pushing his chin up and back.

Jamie's eyes widened.

Time slowed, thickening to something viscous as the figures in the clearing waded through it.

He saw Larissa's mouth fall open in a silent scream.

Saw Petrov turn and raise his T-Bone.

Saw Van Orel take an unsteady, stumbling step backwards, his eyes wide, and, at the same moment, the reality of exactly what was about to happen crashed into Jamie.

He felt a body that seemed to be carved out of stone press itself against his back, and a single hot breath in his ear.

*I don't want this,* he suddenly thought. *I thought I did, but oh God, I don't want this. Somebody help me, please. Please.*

Then he felt a pain so sharp it was almost sweet as the first victim's fangs slid through his skin and into his neck.

# 48

# NIGHT FALLS

*TELEORMAN FOREST, ROMANIA*

Larissa was already moving as a scream burst from her open mouth, her eyes billowing with red-black fire, her fangs erupting from her gums.

From some vast distance, she heard her squad mates cry out in shock and fear, but the sounds barely registered; her gaze was locked on her boyfriend, his feet helplessly kicking the air as the first victim lifted him off the ground, blood squirting down his neck from the holes the ancient vampire's fangs had made.

*God no. Oh please, please no. Not him. Not this. Oh please.*

She thundered towards him, her scream mutating into a terrible howl of fury, her hands curled into claws, her mind pounding with hate, her vampire side in complete control. She reached out, ready to sink her nails into the first victim's eyes, to rip him to pieces with her bare hands, to rend and tear and kill.

At the last possible millisecond, Gregor moved with a speed that seemed to defy reality, even when seen through Larissa's supernatural eyes. His face wore an expression of apparently genuine surprise as he held Jamie out of her reach with one hand and swung the other in a tight, compact arc. It hit her in the chest with the force of an exploding bomb.

The impact was beyond anything she had ever known, the power behind it far greater than that of even Valeri Rusmanov. It sent her rocketing up and back, towards the distant wall of trees, and, as she flew helplessly through the air, her eyes rolling, her limbs shocked limp, a single thought filled her reeling mind.

*He pulled that punch. That wasn't even close to what he's capable of.*

Jamie felt his body start to shake uncontrollably as he hung in the first victim's grip.

The pain in his neck had disappeared as quickly as it had arrived, but had been replaced by something worse: an unscratchable itch that was spreading through his body, hot and sharp and hungry. It felt like a million tiny ants had hatched in his bloodstream and were now marching through his veins, slashing and tearing at his insides, breathing fire and spitting poison.

His eyes rolled in their sockets, his hands clenched and unclenched, and his tongue felt too big for his mouth, huge and thick and alien. His legs spasmed in the cool forest air, drumming ineffectually against the vampire's chest and stomach.

He tried to form a coherent thought, to force his mind into motion; he thought that he had heard Larissa scream, thought he had heard her cry and then fall silent, and he tried to focus on her, tried to use the image of his girlfriend to drag himself free of the quicksand that was pulling him down.

Then, through the nausea that was tightening its grip on him, he heard someone – he thought it might have been Arkady Petrov – shout 'Go!'

\* \* \*

Kristian Van Orel was, quite simply, more scared than he had ever been in his life.

He had been frightened by the dead animals that had welcomed them the previous morning, by the forest itself, huge and dark and unnaturally empty, by the brutal murder of Tim Albertsson that had taken place mere metres from where he had been sleeping with a head full of nightmares, and now by the ancient vampire who had bitten his squad mate. But despite the terror coursing through him, years of training took over when he heard the shouted command of his squad leader, and he threw himself into action.

Van Orel had watched as Larissa was sent flying, so instead of rushing the first victim, closing the space and playing into the hands of the vampire's enormous strength, he took three quick steps backwards, drawing his MP7 as he did so. He raised it to his shoulder and squeezed the trigger, sending a volley of bullets in Gregor's direction. The ancient vampire was still holding Jamie Carpenter in one hand, but his wide back was between Van Orel and his squad mate, so he had aimed directly at it.

The bullets thudded home, sending plumes of scarlet blood into the air from holes punched in the first victim's flesh. Gregor whirled round, his face contorting with fury, then threw back his head and bellowed in pain. The noise was unearthly, and Van Orel took another step backwards, this one involuntary. Out of the corner of his eye, he saw Petrov and Engel circling away from him, trying to surround the ancient vampire. Van Orel sighted down the barrel of his gun, intending to force the first victim back towards his colleagues, but before he could tighten his finger on the trigger a second time, the vampire leapt towards him in a blur of impossible speed.

Something hammered into his wrist, numbing it instantly. The

512

MP7 flew from his grip, sailing away into the distance. Van Orel had a millisecond to register that his gloved hand was pointing ninety degrees in the wrong direction before pain rushed into him like water from a breaking dam, and he screamed.

Gregor appeared before him, as though materialising from thin air, grabbed him by his collar, pushed him backwards until he was suspended above the ground at almost forty-five degrees, then stamped a foot down on his right leg. There was a horrible sound, like the branch of a tree snapping, before agony so huge it was incomprehensible swept through Van Orel's body, and he vomited as he floated to the ground, his eyes rolling back in his head, his mind overwhelmed.

Arkady Petrov saw bone tear through the black fabric covering Van Orel's lower leg, saw his squad mate scream and collapse to the ground, and allowed for a possibility that had only previously occurred to him in the abstract.

*I might be about to die. Right now, right here in this place.*

Over the course of his career, Petrov had seen many friends and colleagues die, including the uncle he had loved like a father, the man who had first introduced him to the twilight world of the SPC. He had found himself in situations where the odds of survival had seemed slim, been caught in ambushes and traps, the victim of bad intelligence or changing circumstances. But he had never found himself in a situation that, deep down, he didn't believe he could handle, that his intelligence and skills and experience couldn't get him out of.

Now, with his squad in tatters around him, Petrov's unshakeable faith in himself cracked for the first time. Gregor was remarkably, almost unbelievably, powerful, and he was not at all sure that the vampire could be defeated, at least not by him. But as he drew his T-Bone he made a promise to himself.

*Die like Yuri did. No surrender. To the last.*

The first victim was standing over Van Orel, Jamie Carpenter dangling from his fist like a toy, and looking down at the South African with a curious look on his bearded face; the palpable fury that had momentarily appeared as bullets crunched into his back had given way to what looked like sadness, or possibly even disappointment. Beyond the vampire, Engel was staring wide-eyed at the stricken Van Orel, the sudden, violent collapse of the situation written across her face. Petrov forced himself to ignore her; he took a deep breath, aimed his T-Bone at the vampire's armpit, and fired.

There was a rush of exploding gas as the metal stake rocketed towards its target; he waited for the crunch of shattering bone, for the sight of blood in the cool morning air. Instead, there was a ripple of movement, followed by the awful sight of Gregor gazing coldly at him, the metal stake held easily in his hand. Petrov stared, frozen to the spot, unable to comprehend what the vampire had done. Then the first victim flicked his wrist, as casually as if he was swatting a fly. The stake tore through the air with a loud hum, and crashed into Petrov's helmet.

The hardened structure held, saving the Russian's life.

The armoured plating cracked in a wide, jagged fissure, but the metal stake didn't reach the fragile skull beneath; it rebounded up into the air, spinning wildly. Petrov's knees gave way beneath him and he slumped to the ground; it had felt like being hit in the head with a sledgehammer.

He fought for breath, trying to hold on to consciousness, if for no other reason than to face death head-on, as his uncle had done.

Through a field of vision that was mostly grey, he saw the first victim carry Jamie forward and pluck the metal projectile out of the air a second time. Gregor turned, raising the hand that held the stake like a man about to throw a javelin, and faced Greta Engel.

Engel stared at the gleaming stake in the vampire's hand and felt the last of her courage leave her.

"Don't," she said, and dropped her MP7 to the grass. "Please don't."

The first victim growled, and took two long strides towards her.

"Why are you fighting me?" he asked, his voice like thunder. "You asked for my help."

Engel didn't respond; she simply stared at the bearded, handsome face of the ancient vampire, and hoped that he would make her death quick. They were utterly, completely outmatched by his power, but there appeared to be little viciousness in him, and she clung to the faint hope that he might yet show mercy.

"Answer me!" he shouted. "Have I not been generous?"

To Engel's right, there came the sound of crunching grass. She risked a glance in that direction, and felt fresh terror burst through her at what she saw.

Larissa Kinley was walking towards them, her eyes glowing the colour of molten steel. One of her hands was pressed tightly against her chest, where the first victim had struck her, and she was moving slowly, the effort of each step etched clearly on her face. But she *was* moving, her gaze locked on the old vampire.

Gregor growled again, swinging the limp form of Engel's squad mate towards Larissa. Jamie was unconscious, but the blood running down his neck had slowed to a trickle, and she could see his chest rising and falling steadily.

"Don't come any closer," said the first victim, and placed his free hand round Jamie's neck. "I'll kill him if you do."

Larissa stopped. Her face was twisted with hatred, the hand hanging at her side clenching and unclenching, but she did as she was told. Engel stared at her for a long moment, wracked by an overwhelming sense of helplessness, a desperate desire to be somewhere, anywhere other than this hidden corner of the world.

"I have done what was asked," said Gregor, nodding towards Jamie's unconscious form. "Why do you fight me?"

Larissa spat a thick wad of blood on to the grass. Engel grimaced; the liquid was almost black, and she suspected it had risen up from somewhere deep inside the vampire's body.

Somewhere vital.

"Give him to me," said Larissa, her voice trembling. "While there's still time. Give him to me and we'll leave."

Gregor frowned. "Time for what?" he asked. "To stop the turn?"

Larissa didn't answer.

"This is what he wanted," said Gregor, speaking slowly, as though addressing a child. "Surely you see that? This is what he was asking for. What *you* were asking for."

"I asked for your *help*," said Larissa. "I didn't want him turned."

The first victim's face softened. "You love him."

"Yes," growled Larissa. "I do."

"I loved a woman," said Gregor. "Centuries ago. I loved her with all my heart, and then I watched her get old, and sick, and at the end I watched her die. I would not wish that on anyone, no matter how you may feel now. You are so young, and you cannot truly know what it means to watch someone wither and shrink, to see the light leave their eyes. It will be harder than you can possibly imagine."

"I don't care," shouted Larissa, her voice high and unsteady. "I don't want this miserable half-life for him. I *want* to watch him change and grow and get old. I want him to *live*."

Gregor smiled, gently. "But this is what *he* wanted," he said. "No matter the cost, I said, and he agreed. Do you not trust him to know his own mind? Or perhaps he truly cares more about other people than he does his own happiness. I wonder if you could say the same?"

Despite the agony that was radiating through her body, Larissa felt new pain stab at her heart as the ancient vampire spoke.

*It doesn't matter what Jamie wanted!* insisted her vampire side. *Who cares? He doesn't know what this is like, not really. He thinks it means you fly and punch things and never get old. You know better.*

But it *did* matter what Jamie wanted; if she gave herself the authority to overrule his decision, where would that leave them? Not only would she be rejecting the only help the first victim appeared willing to give them, but she would also be betraying Jamie's trust, overturning the huge, selfless gesture he had made, and making it count for nothing.

*He'll never forgive me*, she thought. *Never.*

"You have nothing to say?" asked Gregor. "So be it. I will let you decide. I know you are fast, and if you clean his blood within the hour, perhaps the turn will not take." He carefully laid Jamie's unconscious body on the grass, and stepped back. "I leave it up to you."

Larissa hissed involuntarily. Her vampire side was screaming that this was some kind of trap, but she didn't believe that was the case; she thought it was something far neater, and far worse.

*He's giving me the chance to do the right thing*, she thought. *The selfless thing. So that if I don't, I'll have no excuses. It will be because I chose not to.*

She took a half-step towards her boyfriend. "The others," she said. "My squad mates."

"I will take them out of here," said Gregor. "Send your colleagues to where you made camp when you first arrived. Your friends will be waiting there."

Larissa wasted no more time. She had no way of knowing with any certainty whether she could trust the first victim, but there was literally no time to lose; she would simply have to take him at his word and hope that he was telling the truth. Without taking her eyes from Gregor's face, Larissa lowered the visor of her helmet and fastened it in place, taking care that every millimetre of her skin was covered. When it was secure, she walked slowly forward and picked Jamie up from the ground.

Then she leapt into the air, flew up through one of the wide beams of sunlight, and disappeared into the pale blue sky above.

# 49

# SIDE EFFECTS

## GREAT YARMOUTH, ENGLAND

Julian Carpenter screamed as he lurched up in his bed, clutching at his chest. He looked around at the dimly lit hotel room, his heart racing, his skin covered in a film of sweat, his arms shivering in the gloom. He felt sick, his stomach churning, his head thick and heavy, as terror pulsed through him.

*Jesus,* he thought. *Oh Jesus Christ. That was so bad.*

Julian pushed the covers off his lower body and staggered into the bathroom. He poured himself a glass of water, drank it, poured a second, and carried it to the window on the eastern side of the room. He pushed the curtains back and looked out at the flat grey expanse of the sea, feeling his heart begin to slow, and drained his glass again.

There was a tattered armchair beneath the window and he flopped down into it, still only half awake, feeling the last dregs of the dream pulling at him. As it faded, nausea hit him, and he doubled over, squeezing his eyes shut.

*Infection,* he thought. *Poison.*

When the nausea had abated, at least slightly, Julian unwrapped the bandage on his forearm and winced at what he saw. The skin around the incision he had opened up the previous day was red, and felt hot to the touch; thin tendrils of dark pink were making their way up his arm towards his elbow and down towards his wrist. Carefully, he rewrapped the wound, and wondered idly where he was going to get antibiotics from; the small doctor's surgery in the village near his mother's cottage would require him to register, to show proof of identity and address, items that he no longer possessed. He guessed he would have to go to Norwich, to the hospital or one of the walk-in centres, where he could get a prescription with a fake name that would go unchallenged.

*Add that to the list,* he thought. *Like I don't have anything else to worry about.*

Julian got up, and was relieved to find that his legs felt capable of supporting him. He crossed the small room and switched on a tiny kettle that sat on a tray beside instant tea and coffee and shrink-wrapped biscuits. As he waited for it to boil, he allowed himself to tentatively think back to the dream that he had woken from, the one that had made him scream in his sleep.

He had been in the house in Brenchley, looking for something. He couldn't remember what, but it hadn't mattered; he had been possessed of the dream-need to find it, whatever it was, and had been searching through the sideboard in the living room when he heard the front door open behind him.

"Marie?" he shouted, because in the dream he had forgotten that his wife was a vampire, locked away in the bowels of the Loop.

There was no response from the hallway.

"Jamie?" shouted Julian. "Is that you?"

Silence.

He got up and walked across the living room, aware that it was now packed with the same round tables and plastic chairs that filled the Ops Room. He picked his way through them, rested his fingers on the handle of the door that led into the hallway, and he realised he was scared.

This house was where he had been his happiest, and should have felt safe. But he had died on the gravel drive outside, and it now felt alien and hostile. Dread squirmed through him, and he wondered briefly whether he should open the door. But dreams have an insistence, are capable of reducing a person to a mere passenger inside a story over which they have no control. His hand turned involuntarily, and the door opened with a click that sent a shiver up his spine.

The hallway was empty.

The dread did not leave him as he stepped through the door. There was no entrance to the kitchen to his right, as there should have been, and the front doors to his left filled a towering stone arch that looked as though it belonged in a castle, or an old château. But he recognised the carpet beneath his feet, the umbrella stand, the side table and its telephone, the pale green of the walls, the wooden staircase leading up to the first floor.

Julian stood in the half-familiar house, his stomach knotted with fear he couldn't have explained, his arms and back crawling with gooseflesh. Then a voice floated down the stairs, and he found himself fighting back tears.

It was Marie's voice, high and soft as she sang Jamie's favourite lullaby, the one that had always persuaded him to sleep, when everything else had failed. The words, so achingly full of the past, were carried on the air and brought a lump to Julian's throat.

*Rock-a-bye baby, on the treetop,*
*When the wind blows, the cradle will rock.*

Beneath the words, Julian heard a gurgling sound, the happy almost-laughter of his infant son. He wanted to rush up the stairs, throw open the door of the nursery, and sweep his family into his arms.

But he couldn't move. He was rooted to the spot, and could do nothing but listen.

*When the bough breaks, the cradle will fall,*
*And down will come baby, cradle and all.*

Tears spilled from his eyes and ran down his cheeks. He couldn't breathe, couldn't force air into his chest; it felt like his heart had swollen to a size that meant there was no room inside him for anything else. He listened as his wife began the lullaby again, wondering how long the dream would allow him to enjoy this gift, this precious moment his subconscious had conjured for him.

*Drip.*

Something landed on his shoulder, just hard enough to make a sound.

*Drip. Drip drip.*

Julian turned his head. It moved at the contrary speed of dreams, always too fast or far too slow. On the shoulder of his jacket, the grey morning coat he had worn when he married Marie, and which he hadn't even realised he was wearing, four drops of red were merging together. His head began to lift, and for a millisecond or two, Julian fought it to a standstill; he didn't want to look up.

He didn't want to see.

Pain raced up the back of his head and his muscles overcame his authority. His head rose up and back, and he looked, unable to shut his eyes.

Spreadeagled on the ceiling was his son.

Jamie stared down at him with eyes that glowed the colour of lava. Fangs, impossibly huge, protruded from his mouth, bright white and dripping with poison. The lower half of his face was soaked in blood, and his mouth was twisted into a grotesque smile, an animal smile.

"Too late," growled Jamie, blood spilling from his mouth and falling on to Julian's face. "Too late, Dad."

The kettle boiled with a rattle of plastic and a plume of steam. Julian tipped hot water and coffee granules into a mug and stirred it quickly. The dream was already fading, the details melting away, leaving behind a profound sense of unease that seemed to go all the way to his bones. He carried the coffee across to the chair and looked out again at the sea.

*I'll drink this, then I'll get moving,* he told himself. *Lots to do.*

On the seafront, a teenager dragged a protesting dog against the wind. The sea crashed in dirty grey-white waves against the beach, leaving silt and seaweed behind. Julian watched, waiting for the uneasiness to pass, aware that it seemed reluctant to do so.

*Ridiculous,* he told himself. *Snap out of it, Julian, for God's sake. It was just a dream.*

# 50

# NO TIME TO LOSE

Larissa touched down on the concrete floor of the hangar, gasping in pain, her mouth full of her own blood, her unconscious boyfriend in her arms. Two of the Department's doctors ran towards her, pushing a stretcher between them, but she snarled at them to get out of the way, hoisted Jamie up, and flew towards the double doors that led into the rest of the Loop.

Her flight from Romania had been almost an hour of constant agony. She was sure the first victim's punch had broken something inside her, something fundamental; it hurt to breathe, let alone move, and she was coughing up blood at an alarming rate. She had radioed the Loop as she crossed the North Sea, explained what had happened, and ordered them to have a transfusion ready when she arrived. But there had been a second reason for her call; she wanted the Surveillance Division to track her approach, as she had started to seriously doubt that she was going to make it home. Jamie was a dead weight in her arms, and she found herself unable to fly at anything like her usual speed; by the time she crossed the foaming grey breakers where the sea met the east coast of England, it was taking all of her strength to simply stay in the air.

She was not worried for herself; as horribly painful as her injuries were, she knew they were nothing that a litre or two of blood would not fix. But she was terrified for Jamie; if she fell from the sky, and nobody came to find them, the chance to stop his turning might disappear forever. And despite Gregor's words, despite the guilt and shame that filled her, as bitter and sharp as the physical pain radiating from her chest, she simply could not let that happen.

The doors slammed against the walls as she pushed through them and headed for the lift at the end of the Level 0 corridor. Halfway there, her strength finally failed her, and she stumbled to the ground. She growled, the light in her eyes glowing weakly, and tried to push herself back into the air.

Nothing happened.

She tried again, feeling tears of frustration welling up inside her, and again.

Nothing.

Larissa let out a great sob of pain and misery, and staggered slowly towards the distant metal doors. Each step was agony; the pain had spread from her chest to fill every part of her, from her shoulders and legs to the tips of her gloved fingers. Jamie moaned in her arms, his face contorting at whatever nightmare was running through his unconscious mind, and she redoubled her efforts.

*One step at a time*, she told herself. *One foot, then the other.*

She walked forward, as halting and unsteady as a ventriloquist's dummy. When she finally reached the lift, she pressed the button marked C and slumped against the metal wall, letting Jamie's feet down to the floor and leaning him upright against her, giving her screaming, protesting muscles a tiny moment of relief. Then the lift slid to a halt, and as the doors opened to reveal the long central corridor of Level C, she realised she could go no further on her own. She twisted the dial on her belt that controlled her helmet's microphone, raised the volume to full, and screamed for help.

Doors the length of the corridor instantly swung open, concerned faces peering out from behind them. An Operator Larissa didn't recognise strode through the door nearest the lift with an expression of annoyance on his face, took one look at her and the unconscious figure in her arms, and raced to help.

"Is he breathing?" asked the Operator, as he arrived in the lift. "What happened?"

"Bitten," she managed. "He was bitten. Infirmary."

The Operator's eyes widened. Then he pulled Jamie from her grasp, threw him over his shoulders, and took off down the corridor without another word. Larissa followed him, slowly; without her boyfriend to carry, she was just about able to walk unaided. By the time she pushed her way through the double infirmary doors, the Operator and one of the Blacklight doctors had deposited Jamie on the narrow bed nearest the entrance. His chest was rising and falling, but his skin was horribly pale, and the puncture holes in his neck had turned an ugly, virulent red.

Larissa staggered across to the bed. The Operator glanced at her, a concerned expression on his face, but she ignored him; instead, she watched the doctor run into one of the supply cupboards and emerge with a rail full of plastic bags of blood. Her stomach rumbled at the sight of the red liquid, but she forced the hunger away; for now, at least, his need was greater than her own. The doctor started hooking the bags on to a drip stand beside Jamie's bed, his gaze fixed on her.

"How long?" he asked.

Larissa flinched. "What?"

"Since he was bitten," said the doctor. "How long?"

"An hour," said Larissa. "Seventy minutes at most."

"All right," said the doctor, clipping the first blood bag to an IV tube. "Then we've got a chance." He broke open a plastic bubble, pulled out a sterile needle, and connected it to the bottom of the tube. As Larissa watched, her heart thumping in her chest, he took a pair of scissors and started cutting open the sleeve of Jamie's uniform.

*Please*, she thought. *Please let this work. Let me have been fast enough.*

Behind her, the infirmary doors swung open again. Then hands took hold of her shoulders, and she cried out as she spun round, her eyes filling with red, a growl rising from her throat.

Kate Randall was looking at her with a look of such compassion that Larissa felt her heart tremble in her chest. Standing behind her friend were Paul Turner and Cal Holmwood, their faces grave.

"Larissa," said Kate. "Jesus. I heard your message. Is he OK?"

She tried to form the words of an answer, but found it an impossible task. She had time to shake her head before Kate wrapped her arms round her and pulled her tight against her chest. She just about managed not to cry in front of two of the most senior members of the Department, but for a long moment, as she let her head rest on Kate's shoulder, she simply couldn't breathe; the weight of everything that had happened had settled on to her shattered chest, crushing the air out of her.

"Operator," said Paul Turner, his voice low. "Did Lieutenant Kinley give a report?"

"No, sir," said the man who had carried Jamie down the corridor. "She shouted for help and I found them in the lift. She told me he was bitten."

"How long ago?" asked Cal Holmwood.

"An hour," said the doctor. "That's what she told me."

"You're transfusing him?" asked Turner.

"I was about to," said the doctor.

"Don't," said Turner. "Not yet."

Anger surged through Larissa's exhausted body. She pushed Kate roughly away; her friend stumbled backwards, frowning with confusion.

"What are you talking about?" asked Larissa, her eyes flaring as she fixed them on the Security Officer. "He needs to be transfused now."

"Who bit him?" asked Turner.

"What the hell does that have to do with anything?" she asked.

"I asked you a question," said Turner. "Who bit Lieutenant Carpenter?"

"The first victim bit him!" she shouted. "We found him, he refused to help, then he changed his mind and bit Jamie. Does that answer your question? Is there anything else you want to waste time asking me right now? Or can we get on with transfusing him before it's too late?"

"It's not that simple, Larissa," said Holmwood. "I think you know it isn't."

"The Browning Theory," said Turner.

"Right," said Holmwood. "This could make Carpenter more powerful than the Rusmanovs."

Turner nodded. "Maybe powerful enough to stand up to Dracula."

Larissa stared incredulously at the two men. "It *is* that simple," she shouted. "You save him or you let him turn. It couldn't be *more* simple." She turned to the doctor. "Do it."

The doctor grimaced, and looked at Paul Turner. The Security Officer didn't move so much as a muscle.

Larissa felt her vampire side rise up, bringing with it reserves of strength she didn't know she possessed. "Do it," she repeated, her eyes blazing crimson. "Right now. Or I'll make you."

"Stand down, Lieutenant," said Turner, staring at her with his maddeningly empty eyes. "Don't do something you'll regret."

"Please, Larissa," said Kate, her voice small. "Just take it easy."

Larissa laughed, a grunt of utter disbelief. "I don't understand any of you," she said. "You're his colleagues. You're supposed to be his friends. And you would rob him of everything that makes him human so you can use him as a weapon. How can you live with yourselves?"

"Larissa," said Holmwood, a pained expression on his face. "You need to understand—"

"No," she interrupted. "I don't need to understand anything. *You* need to understand that this transfusion is going to happen, and that I will kill anyone who interferes with it. Am I making myself clear to you all? You can bring the entire active roster in here and watch me put them down one after the other, because I will not stand by and let you do this to him. Do you hear me? I WILL NOT LET YOU."

"Yes," whispered Jamie. "You will."

# 51

# DEADLINE

The sound of her boyfriend's voice swept away the rage that had momentarily overwhelmed Larissa. She turned to the bed, aware that silence had fallen over the infirmary.

Jamie was looking up at her through eyes that were barely open, the ghost of a smile playing across his lips. "I don't want the transfusion," he said, his voice a low croak. "Let it take its course."

"No," she said, her voice wavering. She wanted to punch him, grab him, shake him until he saw sense. "You don't know what you're saying, Jamie."

He lifted his head a few millimetres from his pillow and nodded, incredibly slowly. "I do," he said. "What's in my blood is what we went to Romania for. We all knew this was a possibility, even if we never said it out loud. It was just me that it happened to."

"It's always *just* you," she said, fiercely. "Why can't it be someone else for once?"

"I don't know," he said, and smiled again. "I wouldn't mind. Honest."

Larissa smiled, despite herself. She looked up, and saw Kate and the two senior Operators watching her exchange with her boyfriend with obvious anguish on their faces. Their pain made her feel fractionally better.

She turned back to Jamie. "What do you want me to do?" she asked. "Tell me."

"Stay with me," he said, his voice cracking.

"I will."

"You promise?" he asked.

"I promise," she said, then tried a final time to make him see sense. "You don't have to do this, Jamie. We can go back to the forest, go back with more Operators. We can *make* him help us, make him fight on our side. We can—"

"No," he said. "This is what needs to happen. This is what we do."

"You wanted this," she cried. "You've always wanted this, and now you've got it and I'm not allowed any say in it. Where does this leave me, Jamie? Where does it leave *us*?"

"It doesn't change anything," he whispered. "We'll get through it, like we have everything else. Together."

She couldn't respond; her throat was hot and full as tears finally broke loose and spilled down her cheeks.

"Stay with me," he repeated, his half-open eyes locked on hers.

"I will," she said. "I won't leave this room. Now try and get some sleep. You've got a really shitty morning ahead of you."

Jamie nodded. "I know," he said.

"No," said Larissa, shaking her head. "You don't. But you will." She turned to Cal Holmwood. "You need to get the FTB to send a team to our insertion point at the edge of the forest. The rest of our squad should be there by now. With Tim Albertsson's body."

The Interim Director closed the infirmary doors behind him as quietly as he could and strode away down the Level C corridor.

Kate Randall had decided to stay with her friends, at least until

Jamie fell asleep. Paul Turner had ordered the Surveillance Division to contact the FTB and pass on Larissa's extraction instructions, and was now quietly making arrangements with the medical team to manage Carpenter's hunger when it hit him some time in the next few hours.

As he reached the lift, Holmwood's console beeped on his belt. He lifted it from its loop, saw the name of the Prime Minister glowing up at him, and groaned. He thumbed open first the screen and then the message itself, which was short and to the point.

**Call me immediately. Downing Street number.**

*Great,* thought Cal, as he stepped into the lift and pressed the button marked A. *Absolutely bloody fantastic. Because there's nothing I'd rather do right now than get talked down to by some jumped-up secretary in a school tie.*

Inside his quarters, Holmwood poured himself a large glass of Scotch and settled into the chair behind his desk, the place where he now seemed to spend the vast majority of his time. When half the whisky was gone, he opened a secure communications window and selected the Prime Minister's name from a drop-down menu. There was a long moment of silence as the call was passed through a labyrinth of security connections and layers of encryption, then connected to an office in Downing Street. A second later the leader of the country's voice rang out through speakers set in the walls of the room.

"Colonel Holmwood?"

"I'm here, sir," said Cal. "What can I do for you?"

"Go back in time and not make such a damn mess of all this?" suggested the Prime Minister.

532

Holmwood didn't respond. *Stay calm,* he told himself. *Keep your temper.*

"That was a joke, Colonel," said the Prime Minister, after several uncomfortable seconds had passed.

"Yes, sir," said Cal.

The Prime Minster cleared his throat, obviously embarrassed. "The time has come to go public, Colonel," he said. "Which isn't something I ever thought I would have to say to you, nor something I ever wanted. I hope you know how grateful the Chief of the General Staff and I are for the work that you and your Department do, and for your many years of dedicated service to your country. But the situation has changed, as I'm sure you are aware, and I no longer see another option. That bloody TV show has caused chaos. We have civil unrest in London, Manchester, Birmingham, Bristol, Newcastle and Glasgow, a wave of violence that the police are struggling to contain, let alone do anything to stop. The public are scared, and they have heard no reasons not to be from their government. We need to let them know what we're doing to protect them, which means telling them about Blacklight. I know this won't be what you want to hear, Colonel Holmwood, but I'm afraid it is now necessary."

Cal rolled his eyes, glad the Prime Minister couldn't see the look of contempt on his face.

*You're sorry,* he thought. *Of course you are. You know damn well that taking Blacklight public won't save a single civilian life. If anything, it will make our job even harder, because the vampires who* didn't *know we existed will start looking over their shoulders. But that doesn't matter, does it? Because you need to be seen to be doing something, before the opinion polls fall too far.*

*That's what this is really all about.*

"I need you to wait two more days, sir," he said. "After that, neither my Department nor anyone else is going to be able to keep the public safe. So you can tell them whatever you want."

"You're talking about Zero Hour."

"That's right, sir," said Holmwood.

"Then level with me, Colonel," said the Prime Minister. "Is there anything you can genuinely do to stop it arriving? If you can honestly tell me yes, then I'll give you the two days. Otherwise we're briefing the press in an hour."

"Honestly?" said Holmwood. "I don't know, sir. But if it *can* be stopped, I know that we're the only ones that can do it. And we *have* seen some promising developments in recent days."

"Being?"

"There's very little I can tell you at this point, sir," said Holmwood. He had no intention of giving the Prime Minister any reason to get carried away.

"Then tell me what you can."

"Our research department believe they are closer to a potential cure than at any previous point. And we acquired a new weapon, one that has the potential to be significant, sir." He omitted the fact that the weapon in question was a teenage boy lying unconscious in an infirmary bed.

"A potential cure for vampirism?" asked the Prime Minister.

"Yes, sir."

"Which would work on Dracula?"

"*If* it was perfected and synthesised, *if* we were able to locate him, and *if* it could be introduced into his system, then theoretically yes, sir."

There was a long pause.

"Fine," said the Prime Minister, eventually. "Forty-eight hours,

Colonel. Then you're going to find yourself one of the most famous men in the country."

"I look forward to that, sir," said Cal.

The Prime Minister laughed. "Do whatever you can," he said. "I know you will, but I wanted to say it anyway. Do whatever you can to stop this."

"We will, sir," said Cal.

"I know," said the Prime Minister. "Goodbye, Colonel."

"Goodbye, sir."

A long tone filled the room, signifying that the connection had been cut. Cal closed the comms window, and sat back in his chair.

He had told the Prime Minister the truth; they would do whatever was in their power to stop Zero Hour coming. But as he stared at the Blacklight crest in the centre of his wall screen, the Department's motto emblazoned below it, he was forced to admit to himself that his hopes of success were almost non-existent.

The turning of Jamie Carpenter was a bonus, but was not the giant step forward that the first victim's cooperation would have been. The Browning Theory suggested that Jamie would, in time, become an extremely powerful vampire, and that would certainly be useful. But he was never going to be the equal of the vampire who had bitten him, who had five centuries of power bubbling through his veins.

It was not the only disappointment to come from how DARKWOODS had ended. If the time ever came that it was needed, Jamie would not be able to help them launch PROMETHEUS, the strategic plan that was classified at such a level that Cal would deny it existed if asked by anyone, including the Prime Minister and Paul Turner.

For that, they had needed the first victim himself.

Cal got up from his desk, crossed the room, and unscrewed the cap on the bottle of Scotch. He was about to fill his glass for the second time when the incoming call tone rang through his quarters. He swore heavily, put the bottle down, and turned towards the screen, expecting to see the Prime Minister's name; he had presumably forgotten something he wanted to say, or had changed his mind about the extension he had granted. Instead, the name of the NS9 Director glowed in a new window, above the words ACCEPT and REJECT.

Holmwood strode back to his desk and clicked ACCEPT. The window expanded and General Allen's face appeared; his tanned skin looked pale, and there were bags under his eyes that were almost black. He seemed to have aged ten years since Cal had last spoken to him, barely two days earlier.

"Jesus, Bob," said Cal. "You look like shit. Is everything OK?"

Allen smiled, and shook his head. "Not even close," he said. "You?"

"About the same," said Holmwood. "I've just had to talk the Prime Minister out of going public. The little prick is worried that people are going to be angry with him for not telling them about vamps until now."

"Did you tell him he's going to have bigger problems than that in a couple of days?"

"I tried," said Cal. "He heard me. Whether he listened is another matter."

Allen nodded. "I'm briefing the White House later today," he said. "I'm expecting about the same from them. I should thank you for that, I suppose."

"For what?"

"For letting one of your vamps go on TV and tell the whole world that they're real. That was quality work from your boys, Cal. Great stuff, really."

"Are you kidding me?" asked Cal. "Exactly how was I supposed to stop that from happening? The show is recorded live, in London. Nobody knew what they were going to do until it was happening."

"You couldn't shut it down?" asked Allen. "Once you saw where they were going with it?"

"No, Bob," said Cal. "I can't have a commercial television station taken off the air at a moment's notice. And neither can you, so don't even start with me."

"Fair enough," said Allen. "I suppose it was going to come out somewhere. There was probably no stopping it after McKenna's article."

"Are you going to give me shit for that too?" asked Cal.

Allen rolled his eyes, and smiled. "No, Cal," he said. "I read the reports and I know you did all you could. It's out now, so we just have to deal with it."

"How bad is it over there?" asked Cal.

"Not too bad yet," said Allen. "Your show got picked up and it's running non-stop on the news networks, but we've refuted it as much as possible. We've had some violence in the cities, some reports of hoarding and looting. I've got the National Guard standing by, so we're playing wait and see. But it's going to get worse. I've had half a dozen of my retired Operators get in touch with me today and tell me they've had journalists asking them to go on the record about NS9. Their records are all sealed, classified at the highest level. But the news media tracked them down in less than a day."

"They pay well," said Cal. "For information. Someone will take their money, Bob. Prepare yourself for that."

Allen nodded. "Anyway," he said, "this isn't why I called you, Cal. Can you tell me what happened in Romania?"

"Not much," said Holmwood. "I'm sorry to hear about Tim Albertsson, Bob. But I don't have a report from Larissa yet."

"Why not?" asked Allen. "I had to hear about Albertsson from the Germans. They heard it from their Operator, after the first victim flew them out of the forest. The actual first victim, who they found, Cal. Although I presume you already know that?"

"Larissa got back here half an hour ago," said Cal. "With Lieutenant Carpenter, who was bitten by the first victim. Dealing with that hasn't left me much time to make calls."

Allen frowned. "Jamie was bitten?"

Holmwood nodded.

"Are you transfusing him?"

"No," said Cal. "We're not."

"Jesus," said Allen. "That's cold, Cal. I'm glad I didn't have to make that call."

"Jamie made it," said Cal. "He insisted that we let him turn. He understands what's at stake."

The two men fell silent. Holmwood stared at his American counterpart, refusing to drop his eyes; he would not be made to feel bad about the decision that had been taken in the infirmary, a decision that he and Paul Turner had agreed on their way down to Level C that they would have made for Jamie had he not made it for himself.

*It's for the greater good,* he told himself. *There's no time left for sentiment.*

"How's Larissa taking it?" asked Allen, eventually.

Cal shrugged. "How do you think?"

"I'm honestly surprised she let it happen."

"She made her objections known," said Cal, remembering Larissa's threat to kill everyone on the active roster. "Let's just leave it at that."

"All right," said Allen. "Let's talk about something more cheerful. Did Browning report back to you?"

"Preliminary," said Cal. "He said he'd discovered an anomaly in Adam's blood. And then he told me that one of your Operators tried to kill him."

Allen grimaced. "You heard about that, huh?"

"I did," said Cal. "Have you spoken to Aleksandr?"

"He called me," said Allen. "Is it terrible that I didn't find it hard to believe?"

Cal shook his head. "It was a bad time," he said. "At least he told us. It's not that long since the SPC would have destroyed the files and left the remaining Safeguards in place. Are you cleaning house?"

"We were about to anyway," said Allen. "Our ISAT launches the day after tomorrow. We think that's what set Simmons off. One of my Operators reports having discussed it in his presence, not long before he flipped."

"It wasn't common knowledge?"

Allen shook his head. "Only a few people knew."

"That's it then," said Cal. "It's the same as Brennan. He knew that ISAT would uncover him, so he made a pre-emptive move."

"So it would seem," said Allen. "I can't really process it, Cal. I've known Rich Simmons for fifteen years."

"It's not his fault," said Cal. "You have to remember that. The SPC programmed him."

"So many secrets," said Allen, and sighed deeply. "So many lies."

Cal nodded.

"At least nobody was hurt," continued Allen. "Apart from Simmons, that is. Browning is already asking when he can come home."

"Tell him I'm sending the *Mina II* for him," said Holmwood. "It should be there within eight hours."

"I'll tell him," said Allen. "He's a smart one, Cal. He makes me feel like I should have paid more attention in school."

Holmwood smiled. "I know exactly what you mean, Bob. Put him on the plane for me as soon as she arrives?"

"Of course."

"And don't tell him about Jamie. He doesn't need anything else to worry about."

Cal nodded. "I won't tell—"

The NS9 Director disappeared, his face replaced by the words EMERGENCY COMMUNICATIONS SHUTDOWN. Cal had time to frown before the general alarm, deafeningly loud and horribly familiar, burst out of the speaker above the door of his quarters.

# 52

## PERIMETER BREACH

Paul Turner grabbed the phone from the desk, typed in four numbers, and demanded an immediate report from the Security Division watch commander. He listened carefully, then ordered the general alarm to be stopped. When the screaming two-tone siren fell silent, Turner pulled his radio from his belt, entered his override code, and spoke quickly into the microphone.

"Operators," he said, his voice emerging from every speaker in the Loop. "This is the Security Officer. There has been a perimeter breach, which is being investigated by the Security Division. Carry on with your duties as normal. Out."

He was standing in one of the offices at the rear of the infirmary, waiting for the doctor who had been about to transfuse Jamie Carpenter to return. He had sent him to the Science Division to collect data on the turn, and on the hunger; he did not want Carpenter to suffer any more than was absolutely necessary when his transformation began in earnest. The door to the office flew open and the doctor entered, carrying a stack of files and folders.

"I heard the alarm," he said, breathlessly. "Are we safe?"

"We're fine," said Turner. "I need to go up to Security. I'll be back in fifteen minutes, at which point I'll expect a report and a treatment plan."

The doctor nodded. "Yes, sir."

"Good," said Turner. "Thank you."

He left the man frantically leafing through documents and strode across the infirmary. Kate and Larissa were still huddled round Jamie's bed, chatting softly; as Turner passed, Kate glanced over at him and raised her eyebrows inquiringly. He gave her a tiny shake of his head.

*Nothing for you to worry about.*

Turner walked down the Level C corridor, his radio pressed to the side of his head, the handset tuned to the Security Division frequency.

"Is it the damn protesters again?" he asked, as soon as he heard the Duty Operator's voice.

"We think so, sir. It was a single breach, less than a second. We think they threw something over the fence, or fired something over it, worst case. There's a brief heat signature on the thermal tracking, but no explosion. Perimeter patrol should be onsite now, sir."

"Keep me informed," he said. "I'm going out there."

"Yes, sir," said the Duty Operator. "Out."

Turner cut the connection, placed the radio on his belt, and fought back a momentary urge to scream with frustration. He simply didn't have time to deal with the protesters and their increasingly regular attempts at mischief; there were *so* many more important things that required his attention.

He knew exactly what had happened out at the fence; after the two deaths the previous day, the protesters had mourned their dead, then returned with even greater outrage burning within them, and thrown something over the fence, something designed to shock, to make their point. Turner was expecting to find a burning effigy dressed to look like an Operator, or something equally juvenile.

On a gut level, he respected their right to protest, and would, if pushed, allow that there was merit to some of their arguments. Despite that, what he wanted to do more than anything in the world at this particular moment was drive out to the camp, bang the heads of the leaders of the movement together, and tell them all to go home before they got anybody else hurt. He wanted to explain to them that there were events in motion that were simply beyond their comprehension, and that despite the arguable nobility of their intentions, they were only making things worse.

But of course he couldn't do that.

He stepped into the Level C lift and pressed 0. When the doors opened again, he walked quickly down the corridor and through the double doors that led into the hangar. He scanned the wide semi-circular space, and froze.

Standing in the middle of the hangar, smiling warmly at him, was Valentin Rusmanov.

Turner stared at the vampire, his eyes wide, his entire body reeling with shock. Valentin was wearing a long coat and floating a few centimetres above the concrete floor, an elegant travel bag resting beside his feet. As he slowly began to accept that he wasn't imagining it, the vampire really *was* standing in front of him, his shock gave way first to surprise, then to a profound sense of gratitude.

*He came back,* he thought. *I had honestly given up hope that he would.*

He forced himself to walk towards Valentin. The vampire's smile widened as he approached; when he was within range, the youngest Rusmanov grasped his hand and clapped him hard on the shoulder.

"Major Turner," said Valentin. "Long time no see."

"Valentin," replied Turner, fighting back a smile of his own. He was suddenly almost euphoric at the sight of the ancient vampire. "It's good to see you."

"I wouldn't commit to that sentiment just yet," said Valentin. "Not until you hear what I have to tell you."

Turner nodded. "All right," he said. "Tell me."

Valentin took a deep breath. "I found them," he said. "As I promised I would. Dracula, my brother, their associates. And your former Director."

Ice spilled through Paul Turner's body. "You saw Henry Seward?" he said. "With your own eyes? Is he alive?"

Valentin nodded. "Yes," he said. "For now, at least. But we need to hurry."

Turner frowned. "We?"

"You heard me," said Valentin. "Take me to Cal Holmwood, then get everyone ready. We don't have much time."

# 1 DAY TILL
# ZERO HOUR

# 53

# THE WORLD OF COMMON DAY

Matt Browning walked down the *Mina II*'s ramp on to the familiar tarmac runway of the Loop and paused, rooted to the spot.

He was utterly exhausted; the flight had been barely four hours long, but his body was still running on Nevada time, and was convinced it was barely midnight. That, coupled with the stiff foam collar that was wrapped tightly round his injured neck, the splint and bandage covering his finger, and the emotionally draining experience of the operation in San Francisco, had left him feeling as though he had been hit over the head with a sledgehammer. He wanted nothing more than to climb carefully into his bed and grab at least a couple of hours of desperately needed sleep, before he returned to the Lazarus Project labs and got to work on the data he had brought back from America.

But the sky stopped him in his tracks.

The entire eastern horizon was filled with glorious light, a seemingly endless watercolour vista of pink and purple and orange and yellow, rising from the tops of the trees to a scattered layer of low white clouds, above which the blue-black of the departing night was still visible. It was simply breathtaking; the kind of sky that made even Matt, a man devoted to science and reason, understand why people chose to believe in God. He stared, unable to tear his eyes from the wonder of it all, until a small voice spoke from behind him.

"Oh no," it said. "Your neck."

Matt felt a familiar flutter in his chest and smiled, despite his pain. He turned and found Natalia Lenski looking at him with wide eyes, her blond hair fluttering in the morning breeze.

"It's all right," he said. "Nothing permanent."

She reached out with a trembling hand and gently touched his injured finger. "You are hurt," she said.

"I'll be fine," he said. "Honest. Two or three days of keeping my head still, that's all."

Natalia looked far from convinced, but nodded. She pointed at the sky. "Pretty," she said.

Matt looked directly at her. "Yes," he said.

Natalia blushed, her cheeks colouring a delicate pale pink. Then she darted forward and kissed him, her soft lips pressing urgently against his. Matt frowned, then closed his eyes and kissed her back. The flutter in his stomach turned to heat, spreading up through his chest, until she broke the kiss and stepped back. Matt opened his eyes and saw a look of such profound misery on her face that the fire raging within him was instantly extinguished.

"What's the matter?" he said. "Are you OK?"

"I am sorry," she said. "I wanted you to have something nice before you heard."

Matt frowned again. "Before I heard about what?" he asked.

"About Jamie," said Natalia, and dropped her eyes to the tarmac.

Matt's insides froze. He stared at the Russian teenager, his eyes widening, his legs beginning to shake, then reached out and took hold of her arms. She raised her head and looked at him.

"What about him?" he managed to ask. "What's happened to Jamie?"

Matt walked stiffly along the Level C corridor, his neck throbbing with pain, his heart pounding in his chest, and pushed open the doors to the infirmary.

Jamie was lying in the bed nearest the doors, his eyes closed. On the table beside him stood a glass of water, a pile of files and folders, and two plastic bags full of blood; it was these that drew Matt's gaze.

*This is real,* he thought. *Part of me was hoping Natalia had got it wrong.*

His friend looked peaceful as he slept, but the sight still sent a chill up Matt's spine. It was exactly how Jamie had described *him*, when *he* had been lying in a coma in a guarded room at the back of the infirmary, after Larissa's vampire side had almost killed him. Jamie had come to see him as he lay unconscious, for reasons he had never been able to fully articulate; what had happened to Matt had scared him, he said, and he had felt very alone, in desperate need of someone to talk to. So desperate that he had chosen as his confidant a boy in a coma that he had, at that point, never spoken to.

Matt smiled, even as sorrow filled his heart. This was not how it was supposed to have gone; he was supposed to have found a cure so that Larissa and Jamie's mother could be returned to normal, not find himself standing beside the bed of another innocent person who had been changed forever into something that was both more, and less, than human. As a result, the overriding emotion filling him was guilt.

*You failed him,* he thought. *He believed in you and you let him down. You let them all down.*

Jamie stirred, his long arms rising languidly above his head in a semi-conscious stretch. Then his eyes opened, and for a long moment, the two teenage boys simply stared silently at each other. Then a slow smile rose on to Jamie's face.

"Nice collar," he said. "Shame I haven't got a ball you can fetch."

Matt grinned. "Dick," he said. "How are you, Jamie?"

"I'm not really sure how to answer that," said Jamie.

Matt walked across to the bed and peered down at his friend. "Come on then," he said. "Let's see them."

Jamie smiled, then bared his teeth as though presenting them for inspection at the dentist's. His face contorted and reddened with effort, and after a long moment, two white fangs slid down from above his upper teeth. He ran his tongue across them and shook his head.

"That feels so weird," he said. "I can't even tell you."

"It *looks* weird," said Matt. "What about your eyes?"

"I don't know," said Jamie. "Larissa told me I won't be able to control it for a while. It will just happen."

"I can't believe this," said Matt. "What happened, Jamie? Who did this to you?"

"The first victim," said Jamie. "He bit me."

"The who?"

"Are you kidding me?" asked Jamie. "Don't you ever read your Zero Hour reports?"

Matt shook his head.

"The first man Dracula ever bit," said Jamie. "He's almost as old, maybe almost as powerful. Grey found him in Romania, and we went to see if he would help us fight Dracula."

"Who's we?" asked Matt.

"Me and Larissa," said Jamie. "And four others, from other Departments."

"Jesus," said Matt. "Why didn't you tell me about all this?"

"You were already gone," said Jamie. "We didn't get selected until after you'd gone to Nevada."

"I tried to find you," said Matt, his voice low. "The day before I went. I sent you messages."

"I know," said Jamie. "I'm sorry, mate. I screwed up the night before, screwed up badly. I wasn't up to seeing anyone."

Matt nodded. "So what happened in Romania then? You found this first victim and he attacked you?"

Jamie shrugged. "Sort of," he said. "He refused to help, and Larissa told him he didn't have to, that we could use his blood and what was on his fangs to make vampires powerful enough to fight Dracula. He still refused, so I called him a coward, and he bit me. He said he was giving me what I wanted."

"How did Larissa handle that?" asked Matt.

"Not well," said Jamie. "She screamed and attacked him. I lost consciousness, but she told me that the rest of our squad attacked him as well, and got taken apart. Then he gave me to her and said it was up to her what she did. The next thing I knew she was standing right where you are now, screaming and yelling and saying she'd kill anyone who tried to stop me from being transfused. It was pretty crazy. I managed to talk her out of it, just about."

"Christ," said Matt. "That is crazy."

Jamie shrugged again. "Maybe," he said. "You have to see it from her perspective, though. We've talked about this loads of times, about what would happen if I ever got turned, and she's always made it clear that it would be her worst nightmare. Now it's happened,

551

and to be honest with you, I'm pretty sure that at least part of her thinks I did it on purpose."

"Did you?" asked Matt.

"No," said Jamie, instantly. "I thought about it when we got selected for the op, and I guessed it might be the end result, for at least one of us. But I didn't go looking for it, Matt. It just happened."

Matt nodded. He was sure there was at least a small part of his friend that was going to relish being a vampire, would enjoy the speed and strength that came with being turned, but he didn't think that, given a genuine choice, it would be something Jamie would have volunteered for. With a mother and a girlfriend who were both vampires and both vocally hated the condition, it would have been far more selfish than Matt was willing to believe his friend was capable of being. His turning was going to break his mother's heart, and he was certain that Jamie would never knowingly cause that to happen.

"So what happened to your neck?" asked Jamie. "Did Adam do it?"

"No," said Matt. "It's probably all classified, for now at least, but it wasn't Adam. It was the NS9 squad leader."

Jamie's eyes opened wide. "What the hell?"

Matt shrugged, extremely carefully. "No idea. He put a gun to my head, forced me to take my samples, and dragged me out of the lab. I made him crash the squad's SUV into a wall, and gave myself whiplash in the process."

Jamie's smile had disappeared. "Jesus," he said, softly. "You crashed a car into a wall?"

Matt went to nod, and grimaced as a bolt of pain shot through his neck. "Yeah," he said. "I pressed his foot on the accelerator. He wasn't wearing a seat belt and I was, so it sort of made sense at the time."

Jamie nodded. "You're OK, though?" he asked. "Right?"

"It'll be fine in a few days," said Matt. "Now enough about my neck. I've got a question for you, a big one. I've never asked Larissa, because it felt a bit too personal."

"Go for it," said Jamie.

"What does blood actually taste like?" asked Matt, and smiled widely.

"Honestly?" said Jamie. "It's absolutely disgusting. It takes like metal wire wrapped in raw steak. But the feeling you get when you drink it is indescribable. Literally."

"Did you get the hunger?"

"I think so," said Jamie. "But not like Larissa did, or most other vamps do. When I woke up this morning, there was a painkiller IV in my arm, and one of the doctors gave me blood to drink. So, if I got the hunger at all, it came and went pretty quickly. I reckon getting turned in a state-of-the-art infirmary is the way to go."

Matt grinned. "I'll bear that in mind."

"You should," said Jamie. "So tell me about America, mate. I'm really sorry I didn't know you were going. Did NS9 ask for you?"

"They asked for a scientific observer," said Matt. "Cal picked me to go."

"That's awesome," said Jamie. "And you totally deserve it. So tell me about it."

Matt smiled, and quickly ran through everything that had happened in San Francisco. Jamie's eyes widened as he heard of John Bell's awful final decision, his face screwed up in a grimace of disgust as Matt described recovering the man's blood and flesh from beneath the wheels of the truck, and a look of deep fury settled on to his friend's face as he described the final minutes of Major Simmons' life.

"So what do you make of the results?" asked Jamie, when Matt finished his tale. His eyes were wide and shining. "Is it a cure?"

"Right now?" said Matt. "No. But there's *something* there, something in John Bell's blood that has never been seen anywhere else. The process that cured him is complete, so it's doubtful that the anomaly on its own can be used to cure others. But if we can reverse engineer it to an active state, we might be on to something big."

"It's incredible, mate," said Jamie, softly. "Really, it is. You're going to be the reason I'm not stuck like this forever. And my mum, and Larissa."

"Let's not jump the gun," said Matt. "We don't have a cure yet."

"I know," said Jamie. "Yet."

"We might never have one," said Matt. "There are no guarantees here, Jamie. You need to allow for that. And I didn't really do anything. I was just there."

"That's bullshit," said Jamie. "*You* chased Bell halfway across San Francisco, and *you* got the samples into a lab and found something completely new. Then you crashed a car into a wall, for God's sake. *On purpose.* You have to learn to take some credit, mate. You should be so proud of yourself. And when all this is done, when it's all over and there are no more vampires, people are going to know what you did. I'll make sure of that."

Matt frowned. "Do you really believe that's going to be the future?" he asked.

"Yes," said Jamie. "I do."

He looked at his friend, searching his face for evidence of pretence, for any sign that he was telling him what he thought he wanted to hear, and found none. Jamie's pale blue eyes stared up at him, his jaw set firmly, his mouth curling with the faintest hint of a smile he found deeply reassuring.

*Maybe he's right*, thought Matt. *Maybe there is still hope.*

*Maybe.*

He stood up straight, being careful not to move his neck more than necessary. "I'd better go," he said. "How long are they keeping you down here?"

Jamie shrugged. "I don't know," he said. "I would have thought they'd discharge me today. I'm not ill. I'm just a vampire."

Matt smiled. "I'll come back and see you later if they keep you in," he said.

"No you won't," said Jamie. "But that's OK. Go and do what you have to do. I'll see you soon."

Matt stood awkwardly for a second or two as he tried to think of something else to say, some appropriate, preferably reassuring, way to end his visit, then gave up.

"Bye," he said, and headed for the infirmary doors. He pushed them open, turned along the corridor, and almost walked straight into Kate and Larissa.

"Matt!" cried Kate. "I didn't know you were back."

He grinned. "I just arrived," he said. "Overnight on the *Mina*."

Larissa stepped forward, her eyes locked on his collar, a frown creasing her forehead. "What happened to your neck?" she asked. "Are you OK?"

"I'm fine," said Matt. "Don't worry about it."

Larissa nodded, although he didn't think she looked remotely convinced by his answer. "How did you get on in California?" she asked. "Did you find Adam?"

Matt nodded. "We found him," he said. "There'll be a report, but yeah. We found him."

"And?" asked Kate.

"Nothing definitive," he said. "We'll know more in a couple of days. But it's promising."

"I want to hear all about this," said Larissa. "And I want to know what happened to your neck, Matt. Give us ten minutes while we visit Jamie, then we can go and get breakfast. You can fill us in on your adventure."

Matt shook his head. "I can't," he said. "I'm really sorry, but I have to get to work. Some other time, though?"

"Sure," said Kate, smiling with familiar bemusement. "See you soon, Matt."

He nodded, stepped round the two girls, and walked quickly down the corridor. Behind him, he heard the infirmary doors open and an explosion of raised voices float through them. Then he reached the lift, pressed the button marked F, and was waiting impatiently for the metal doors to slide shut when the console on his belt beeped.

# 54

# EVERYTHING YOU HAVE LEFT

*TWO HOURS LATER*

Cal Holmwood paced back and forth in his quarters, and checked his watch for the hundredth time.

9:58

*Two minutes,* he thought.

Remarkably, Valentin Rusmanov's return was not yet common knowledge. Paul Turner had brought the vampire down to the Interim Director's quarters as midnight approached the previous night, managing to avoid contact with anyone as he did so, and Cal had listened carefully to Valentin's story, a cold sensation gradually spreading throughout his body.

*This is it,* he had instantly realised. *Our chance. The only one we're going to get.*

They had given Cal's bedroom to Valentin, and ordered him not to leave the quarters unless given express permission to do so; his appearance would cause immediate panic. The vampire had agreed and excused himself, leaving Holmwood and Turner to formulate a response to the information he had provided, information upon which, without exaggeration, the fate of the world might very well rest.

The plan they had settled on, which had required a series of video and audio calls, the movement of a number of highly classified satellites, and a complete absence of sleep, was what Cal was about to explain to the men and women of Blacklight, who would by now be waiting for him in the Ops Room.

Holmwood checked his watch again.

10:00

*It's time,* he thought.

He crossed his quarters and stepped out into the corridor, pulling the door shut behind him; Valentin had not yet emerged, which was something of a relief. As soon as he exited the lift on Level 0, Cal could hear a low hum of conversation from inside the Ops Room, the drone of hundreds of lowered voices. He took a deep breath, then turned the door's handle and pushed it open.

Instantly, all conversation stopped.

More than two hundred and fifty pairs of eyes swung towards him, as though synchronised by remote control. Holmwood met them with an even stare, nodded sharply, and walked quickly to the front of the room. He stepped up on to the low stage, positioned himself behind the lectern, and looked out across the massed ranks of the Department he had never wanted to lead, but which he was enormously proud to do.

Paul Turner, Jack Williams and James Van Thal were seated in the front row, looking up at him expectantly. Beyond them, he picked out the faces of Jack's brother Patrick, Angela Darcy, Elizabeth Ellison, and, sitting together at one end of the third row, Lieutenants Carpenter, Browning, Kinley and Randall. Jamie was still pale, the understandable result of the ordeal he had been through, but his blue eyes were clear and focused steadily on Cal's.

"Men and women of Blacklight," he said, trying to keep his voice low and even. "It is, as most of you will be aware, extremely rare for all of us to gather in a single room at the same time. But there are moments when it is necessary, when there is something that involves each and every one of us, something urgent enough to justify calling you all together. This, my friends, is one of those moments."

Cal took a sip from a bottle of water that had been placed on the shelf at the rear of the lectern, and made a mental note to thank whoever had put it there.

"Last night," he continued, "there was a breach at the perimeter of this facility. Following the tragic accident that befell two members of the group that is even now demonstrating beyond our gates, it was widely assumed that this disturbance was the work of the same protesters. That assumption, however, turned out to be false. The perimeter breach was caused by Valentin Rusmanov, who last night kept the promise he made to Major Turner, that he would return when he had information that would prove useful."

There was instant uproar in the Ops Room, as seemingly every member of the Department began speaking at once. Their voices were loud and full of excitement, or fear, or both. Holmwood let the noise build for a few seconds, then brought his hand down on the lectern's top with a sound like a rifle shot.

"Enough!" he shouted. "The information that Valentin brought with him was the precise location of Dracula, Valeri Rusmanov, and Admiral Henry Seward, the Director of this Department. I assume I do not need to explain the importance of this intelligence, nor why I expect nothing less than your complete attention."

He paused, and this time the room remained silent. Cal took a deep breath and was about to continue when Jack Williams got to his feet and raised his hand.

"Yes, Lieutenant?" he said.

"Is Admiral Seward still alive, sir?" asked Jack.

"Yes," said Cal, and saw expressions of shock appear on a number of faces as Jack sat back down. "Valentin saw the Director with his own eyes, along with his brother Valeri, and what he has described to me as a fully recovered Dracula."

He tapped the keys of the lectern's terminal. Behind him, the huge wall screen lit up, displaying a crystal-clear satellite image.

"This is the location in question," he continued. "Château Dauncy, a fortified estate in south-western France, approximately twenty miles south-west of Bordeaux. Investigation of property and land records show that it is owned by a family trust, registered in Geneva and entirely impenetrable. It is, however, the same trust that owns the property in northern Romania that we know was once the Rusmanov family's summer home. Valentin has confirmed these facts and provided an eyewitness account of his visit to the château, a visit that will go on record as having been made at enormous risk to his personal safety."

Holmwood pressed more keys and the screen shifted to an infrared image of the château and its grounds. There was a sharp intake of breath from the watching Operators; moving throughout the image, both within and outside the cold stone walls of the old building, were dozens and dozens of bright yellow and red shapes.

"Jesus," muttered someone near the front. "There are hundreds of them in there."

Holmwood nodded. "This footage was taken at four o'clock this morning. At that time, the Surveillance Division isolated two hundred and ninety-one individual vampire heat signatures in the château and the surrounding grounds, several of which arrived as our satellite was overhead. If Valentin is correct, and we have no reason to doubt his account, two of the vampires you can see behind me are Valeri Rusmanov and Dracula."

The atmosphere in the Ops Room had become so thick it was almost suffocating; excitement and trepidation were palpable, seemingly rising from the pores of the assembled men and women. Their attention was fixed on Holmwood, who waited for several seconds before keying the terminal again. The image on the screen shifted once more, this time to a large digital timer. It read 13:24:17 and was steadily ticking down.

"You all know what this is," said Holmwood. "And you know what it represents. Zero Hour is, and has always been, an approximation, based on the best data available to the Intelligence Division. It may be that we are already too late, that Dracula has regained his full power and stopping him is now already impossible. But I look round this room and I see men and women who could not live with themselves if we accepted defeat without a fight, and allowed terror to spread across this planet unchecked. So, while there remains a chance, no matter how small it may be, we will do what we have always done. We will face the darkness head-on and we will drive it back."

He looked at the hushed ranks of his Department, noting with satisfaction the expressions of determination that had settled on to many of their faces.

"As I'm sure you can imagine," he continued, "we have had an extremely small window in which to prepare a response to Valentin's information. Nevertheless, we have consulted those Departments around the world who are in a position to offer assistance, and a plan has been formulated. The majority of both the active and reserve rosters will be shipping out at 1700 hours, as per briefings and schedules that will be provided after this meeting concludes. A skeleton security force will remain here at the Loop, along with all essential non-active personnel, who will continue their duties as normal. The Operational force will then rendezvous in southern France with Operators from Germany, Russia, South Africa and America, and will move on Château Dauncy at sunset."

A hand shot up on the second row, belonging to Angela Darcy.

"Yes, Lieutenant?" said Cal.

"Why sunset, sir?" she asked, and Holmwood saw a number of Operators nod in obvious agreement. "Why give the vamps the advantage?"

"I understand the question," said Holmwood. "And it *was* a factor in our planning. But there were physical restrictions on how quickly Operators from the other Departments could reach the rendezvous point, and the dark does not wholly favour our enemy. It also allows us to deploy the most powerful weapons in our arsenal, by which I'm referring to Valentin Rusmanov, who has agreed to be part of our Operational force, Lieutenant Larissa Kinley, and Lieutenant Jamie Carpenter."

A shocked silence filled the Ops Room, followed by a low murmur as the Operators digested the news that Cal had given them. He knew exactly where Jamie was sitting, and gave the young Lieutenant an apologetic look.

*I hope he knows why I had to tell them,* he thought. *I hope he understands that they need to hear anything that gives them the slightest hope that I'm not sending them all to their deaths.*

Jamie gave a tiny nod, as though he could read the Interim Director's mind, and kept his gaze steadily focused on the screen, studiously ignoring the many pairs of eyes that had turned towards him. Holmwood nodded in silent thanks, and continued.

"There are almost seven hours until the Operational force

assembles in the hangar," he said. "Each and every one of you will know whether you are going to France within the hour. If you are, study the briefing and prepare yourselves. After which, I suggest that all of you, whether you are going or staying, spend some time talking to the people you love, and reminding yourself of exactly what we are fighting for. This is not a fight with a single life at stake, or a hundred, or even a thousand. This is a fight that will define the very future of the world for every innocent human being and every vampire who means no harm, whether we will live in peace or cower in terror.

"Every one of you knew what you were signing up for when you accepted your invitation to join this Department, and whether or not you ever thought it would come to this, I have absolute faith that you will rise above your own fears and do what needs to be done. We receive no parades, no medals that we could ever wear, no outpouring of thanks from a grateful public, and that is as it should be. We do not need such things, because they have never been why we do what we do. We do it because we are the only ones who can, and we will show that yet again today. We will join our colleagues and we will march together into the darkness. We will destroy Dracula, and Valeri, and every vampire who has allied themselves with them, and we will bring Henry Seward home. Or we will die in the attempt, safe in the knowledge that nobody could have done more, or given more, than the men and women in this room."

The clapping began somewhere near the back of the room, then rolled forward like a tsunami. By the time it reached the front row, most of the Operators were on their feet, cheering and applauding. Paul Turner stood up, clapping steadily, his gaze locked on Holmwood's, the faintest glimmer of a smile on his face.

Cal stared out at the men and women whose lives he had assumed responsibility for; he knew full well that whether or not the attack on Château Dauncy was successful, a significant number of them, perhaps even the majority, would never stand in this room again. The thought hurt his heart, but he pushed the pain away; he knew that the Operators were aware of the risks, and would be going to France with their eyes open. He would tip the odds as far in their favour as he could, and the rest would be up to them.

*This is it,* thought Cal, as the noise reached a deafening crescendo. *One way or the other, it all ends tonight.*

*God help us.*

# 55

# VETERANS' ASSOCIATION

Victor Frankenstein walked quickly down the Level B corridor, eager to return to the sanctuary of his quarters. His stomach was churning at the revelation that Jamie had been turned into a vampire, and his heart was throbbing with a sense of hurt that he knew was absolutely unjustifiable, but which was painful nonetheless; the bitter disappointment that Jamie had not come and told him in person.

*Don't be so damn self-pitying,* he told himself. *Don't you think he had anything more important to do? You don't even know when it happened.*

Cal Holmwood had sent him a message giving him permission not to attend the meeting in the Ops Room – the Interim Director was well aware of what was starting to happen inside Frankenstein's misshapen body, and was entirely sympathetic – but he had thanked his friend and refused. His insides felt like they were on fire, his nerve endings sparking and smouldering, and his skin was so itchy that it was taking all of his resolve not to scratch it away in long, bloody strips. Despite all that, he would not have missed Cal Holmwood's speech for anything. The Interim Director had done a frankly admirable job in Henry Seward's absence, in circumstances as trying as any leader of the Department had ever faced, and he deserved to know that his efforts were appreciated; forcing himself to sit through fifteen minutes of torment had been the very least Frankenstein could do.

He stepped into his quarters and locked the door behind him. He unzipped his uniform down to his waist and shrugged it clear of his arms and torso; there was a moment of glorious relief before the itching returned, relentless and utterly maddening. The strange nature of his birth had denied him a childhood, and his recycled anatomy had left him largely immune to disease; as a result, he had never experienced chickenpox, or measles, and had no frame of reference for the incessant discomfort that accompanied the final hours before each full moon. It would eventually reach the point where he became desperate for the change to come; for all its bone-cracking agony, it was over in less than two minutes, and then he was something else for a little while, something that felt no pain, that ran and hunted and killed.

He had told Cal Holmwood the truth when last they spoke; he had absolutely no control over what happened to him when the full moon rose, and could no more stop the change than he could prevent night following day.

But his condition *was* evolving. He had initially returned to his human form with a black hole in his mind, with little more than the memory of pain. Now that was no longer the case.

The first time he had managed to retain any awareness of himself in his animal state had been in the theatre of La Fraternité de la Nuit, where the combination of his lycanthropy and the reckless bravery of Jamie Carpenter and his friends had saved his life. Through yellow eyes that saw in monochrome and the dizzying, overpowering colours and shapes of his altered nasal spectrum, he had been able to not only recognise Jamie, but also resist the urge to tear out his throat and drink his blood with gusto.

Now his sense of self during the change was pronounced; he didn't have full control, as his animal urges and instincts were often so powerful that they simply could not be ignored, but he was able to remain himself to a far greater extent than previously.

Frankenstein filled his small kettle, and considered Cal Holmwood's instructions as it began to boil.

*Spend some time talking to the people you love. Remind yourself what we're fighting for.*

The number of people to whom the monster would apply that description was extremely small. He *had* loved, on many occasions, throughout the centuries of his life, but those objects of his affection were almost all gone, lost in the mists of time. Now the list would consist of Jamie Carpenter, whom he would definitely see before either or both of them departed for France, Henry Seward, whom he had assumed he would never see again, and the man he was about to try to contact.

The kettle screeched to the boil, billowing steam. Frankenstein made himself a mug of coffee, then opened his locker and looked at the radio handset he had resisted the urge to turn on two days earlier. He lifted it out, held it in his hand for a long time, then pressed its power button. Its screen lit up and a low hum confirmed that it was tuned, sending a flutter of nervous tension dancing up his spine.

*You heard what Cal said,* he told himself. *This might be the last chance you ever get.*

He took a deep breath and held it, trying to shut out the fire burning beneath his skin, trying to slow his racing heart.

"Julian," he said, eventually. "Come in, Julian. Over."

Silence.

Frankenstein released his breath in a low rush. He had sent two heavily encrypted emails to Julian within the last year, despite the obvious risk to them both. The first had informed him of the rescue of his son and disappearance of his wife, the second had detailed Jamie's triumph over Alexandru Rusmanov and the sad fate that had befallen Marie. He had no idea where Julian had been when he sent them, or even whether he was still alive, but he had been unable to live with the thought of not letting his oldest friend know what had happened to his family.

He had not spoken to Julian, however, since the day after his friend had died.

"Come in," he repeated. "Come in, over."

A burst of static sent a spike of pain through his head. In the last hours before the change, his senses became extremely sensitive, and the noise was piercingly unpleasant to his rapidly sharpening ears. Then a voice from the past emerged from the tiny plastic speaker, and Frankenstein felt a lump rise instantly into his throat.

"Frank? Are you there?"

"Yes," he managed. "I'm here, Julian."

"Christ, mate, you have no idea how good it is to hear your voice," said Julian, his own trembling with emotion. "Absolutely no idea."

"You too," said Frankenstein. "I knew you'd be on this frequency. It's like old times."

Julian grunted with laughter. "I tuned on to it yesterday afternoon," he said. "It was pretty much the first thing I did after they left me here. I checked in a few times, but I wasn't holding out much hope, to be honest."

"Cal came to see me," said Frankenstein. "I promised him I would tell him if you tried to contact me, and I meant it when I said it. But after this morning, I'm not sure that promise means very much."

"What happened this morning?" asked Julian.

This was the first of two questions Frankenstein had anticipated, the one that he knew how he was going to answer. For all his iconoclasm, he genuinely believed in Blacklight and what it stood for, and he didn't disobey orders or break rules lightly, regardless of how he knew it must have often seemed. But he also saw little point in hiding from Julian the reality of what was happening, given that there was nothing his old friend could do about it. He wondered, in fact, whether it would be crueller to *tell* Julian, given his position of impotence. Or was it simply always better to know the truth?

"How much do you know?" he asked.

"Bob Allen told me most of it," said Julian. "Or at least I think he did. He told me about Dracula, and about Zero Hour. Cal wouldn't tell me anything, but it was clear that he was scared half to death. Is there something even worse going on that I don't know about?"

Frankenstein smiled. "No," he said. "That's broadly it."

"So what happened this morning?" repeated Julian.

"We've known Dracula was back for several months," said Frankenstein. "We've known Valeri Rusmanov has been protecting him while he recovers, and that they've been holding Henry Seward captive. We just haven't known where. Now we do."

"How?" asked Julian.

"Valentin Rusmanov, of all people," said Frankenstein. "He defected when Dracula was revived, and it was him who found them. He returned last night and gave us the location."

"Valentin *defected*?" asked Julian, his voice full of incredulity. "Are you serious?"

"I'm serious," said Frankenstein. "I didn't believe it for a long time, and I still don't trust him in the slightest, but his information appears to be genuine. The satellites show the location is crawling with vamps."

"A trap?"

"Possibly," said Frankenstein. "But this is Dracula. If there's even a chance of stopping him, we have to take it, regardless of the risk."

"So that's what happened this morning," said Julian. "Cal gave the order was given to go and get him, right?"

"Right," said Frankenstein.

"Who's going?" asked Julian.

Frankenstein laughed. "Everyone," he said. "All of Blacklight, NS9, the SPC, the FTB, the South Africans. Everyone we can get together in time."

"Christ," said Julian. "I wish I could come with you, Frank. I wish that more than anything."

"I wish you could too," said Frankenstein.

"Is Jamie going?" asked Julian. "Don't lie."

"Of course he is," said Frankenstein. "He's an Operator, Julian."

There was a long silence, in which the monster waited for his friend to ask the question he didn't know how he was going to answer; the one that was absolutely inevitable, and had the potential to cause the most harm.

He didn't have to wait long.

"Is he all right?" asked Julian, his voice suddenly hoarse. "My son. Is he OK? This is going to sound crazy, but I saw a vision of him, Frank. When I was in California. I saw something bad. And last night I had a nightmare about him."

Frankenstein made his decision. It was suddenly clear; no good could come from telling Julian what had happened to his son in Romania. Moreover, he simply didn't want to have to be the one to tell him; he had barely begun to process the news himself.

*And in my defence,* he thought, *there's no predicting what Julian would do if he found out, except that it would be extremely unlikely to be considered, or rational. In which case, not telling him could be justified as protecting Jamie.*

"He's fine, Julian," he said. "He's doing well."

There was a long pause.

"He was a vampire, Frank," said Julian, eventually. "In the vision, and in the nightmare. I saw Jamie as a vampire."

A chill barrelled through Frankenstein's body. "What are you talking about?" he asked.

"Did you ever hear the rumours about a vampire who was cured?" asked Julian. "The one people called Adam?"

"I heard them," said Frankenstein.

"Well, I found him," said Julian. "I spent almost a year searching for him, after you told me what had happened to Marie, and I found him. He was living in this cabin in the middle of the California desert. We talked, but he drugged me and I had a vision. I saw Jamie, with red eyes and fangs. He looked at me and told me I was too late. It's why I handed myself in to NS9, Frank. I had to know whether what I'd seen was the truth. And honestly, every minute I spent in a cell was worth it to know he was all right. Do you know what I'm talking about?"

"Yes," said Frankenstein, trying not to let his relief appear in his voice. "I understand."

"Then last night I had a nightmare. The worst I've ever had. I woke up screaming, if you can believe that. I was in our old house, and I could hear Marie singing to Jamie when he was little. And then he was on the ceiling, covered in blood, and his eyes were red."

"It was a dream, Julian," said Frankenstein.

"He told me I was too late," said Julian. "In the dream. He told me again."

"Coincidence," said Frankenstein, hoping he sounded surer

than he felt. "Your brain digging for the worst thing it could find."

"Maybe," said Julian. He didn't sound remotely convinced. "You'll look after him for me, won't you? When you go after Dracula. You'll remember what you swore?"

"Of course I will," said Frankenstein, his voice catching. "I have never forgotten."

"It makes it easier, you know?" said Julian. "Knowing that you're looking out for him. I know how much you care about him."

"I do," said Frankenstein. "And I'll do my best to protect him, like I always have."

"I know you will," said Julian. "That's why you have to promise me something. One last favour, for old times' sake."

Frankenstein drained his coffee and frowned in his empty quarters. "What is it?"

"If you don't stop Dracula," said Julian. "If Zero Hour comes, and the two of you survive, I want you to promise that you'll bring Jamie to see me."

"Julian..."

"I know, Frank, just don't say anything now, OK? Just think about it. Please? We both know what happens if Zero Hour isn't stopped, so what harm could it do? Think about what it really means to protect him, to do what's best for him."

"I *am* thinking about that," said Frankenstein, his voice sharper than he intended. "I always do."

"Promise me," said Julian.

"No," said Frankenstein. "I will not promise. If we fail to stop Zero Hour, I'll consider it. But I'm not giving you any guarantees, Julian. And I suggest you ask yourself whether you genuinely have *his* best interests at heart, or your own."

"Fine," said Julian, his voice suddenly as cold and heavy as a glacier. "I'll do that."

"All right," said Frankenstein. He felt guilty for refusing to promise Julian what he had asked for, and angry with his old friend for putting him in a position where he had to. "I have to go, Julian. It was good to hear your voice."

"Yours too," said Julian, his voice now low and empty. "Good luck out there. Take care of my boy. Out."

Frankenstein turned off the radio. He was overcome with a sudden desire to smash it to pieces against the wall, and found himself gripping it so tightly that the plastic began to creak. When the urge to destroy had passed, he put the radio back into the locker where it had lain dormant for so many months, and got up to make himself more coffee with trembling hands.

# 56

# WHY WE FIGHT

Jamie Carpenter nodded to the Operator behind the desk in the security station and walked quickly down the cellblock on Level H.

He knew from experience that his mother would already be able to hear his footsteps, and would most likely already have identified the smell of him; it was the aspect of vampirism, one that Larissa shared, that had always made him feel most uneasy. Knowing he was coming before they should have been able to felt weirdly like being able to see into the future.

Now, with his head pounding as he struggled to adjust to the sensory overload that came with being a vampire, he was mostly full of admiration at their ability to handle it without going completely crazy. It was as though a two-dimensional world had suddenly been opened up around him; he could hear the breathing of the Operator he had just passed, even though he could no longer see her, could read the printed letters on the notice at the end of the cellblock, even though it was still more than a hundred metres away, and could smell the mingled scents emanating from his mother's cell with a clarity that was disarming.

There was the warm, bitter smell of old tea, the luxurious, pungent aroma of flowers, and the complicated, ethereal aroma of her living, breathing self. Much of it was a mystery to his newly transformed sense of smell, individual scents that seemed redolent of fear and trepidation, of determination and compassion. But shining out of the core of her, filling his nose and head and heart, was a pure, bright pillar of a single unmistakable emotion.

Love.

For him.

It bloomed out of the cell in a cloud so thick it ought to have been visible; it brought tears to Jamie's eyes as he approached the cell, and a hot ball of shame into his chest.

*I always took it for granted that she loved me,* he thought. *I knew, but I never really knew. I never really saw, until now.*

Jamie's heart suddenly blazed with fiery pride at the memory of rescuing his mother from the clutches of Alexandru Rusmanov. But in the same instant, a familiar voice in the back of his head, the one which had been so loud and insistent during the terrible days when she was missing, began to whisper its usual poisonous refrain.

*You don't deserve her love. You never have. You're a bad son.*

Jamie pushed the thought away, as far back and as deep as he could. There was truth in what it said, he knew there was, but he could not afford to dwell on it, not now. The orders for the Château Dauncy operation had beeped on to the screen of his console two minutes earlier, barely ten minutes after he had filed out of the Ops Room. He had read them and walked straight to the lift, even though he was desperate to know which of his friends would be going to France, and to find Frankenstein and explain what had happened to him in Romania.

He wanted his mother to be the first to know what he was about to be part of.

He owed her that much, and more.

Jamie took a deep breath, forced a smile, and stepped out in front of the cell. His mother was standing in the middle of the square room, staring at him with eyes that were wide and damp with tears, her hands over her mouth.

His first thought was, *She knows.*

His second was, *Of course she knows, you idiot. Did you think she wouldn't be able to tell you'd changed?*

"Oh no," said Marie, her voice tiny. "Oh, Jamie. What happened?"

"It's all right, Mum," he said, his voice wavering wildly, then ran his ID card down the sensor on the barrier. The UV wall disappeared and he stepped into the cell. "I'm all right."

"Was it her?" asked Marie. "Did Larissa do this to you?"

Jamie's eyes widened with surprise. "No," he said. "God, no. Of course not. She wouldn't—"

"Tell me the truth, Jamie," said Marie, her eyes narrowing and flickering red.

"I am, Mum," he said. "This is the last thing she ever wanted, honestly it is. She's heartbroken."

He felt tears rise into the corners of his eyes and blinked them away, furiously. But his mother saw them, and the red glow died instantly in her own; she swept forward, her feet above the ground, and wrapped him in a hug so tight he could barely breathe.

"What a mess," she whispered. "What an awful mess this is. What are we going to do?"

Jamie gently prised her arms from around him, and smiled with as much conviction as he could muster. "It'll be OK," he said. "For us, and for everyone else like us. Matt found something in America that's going to make it all OK."

"A cure?" asked Marie, her eyes lighting up with hope.

Jamie shook his head. "Not yet," he said. "But he's hopeful that it will be soon. Then this will all just be a bad memory, Mum."

Marie nodded. He could see in her eyes that she was trying her hardest to believe him.

"Have you thought this through, Jamie?" she asked. "Have you really thought about what it means?"

"I haven't really had a chance to think about anything," he said. "It only happened last night. But I've been dating a vampire for six months, Mum. I know all about it."

"No," said Marie, and shook her head. "You don't. And if Larissa was here she'd tell you the same thing. You can't know unless it happens to you."

"It *has* happened to me," he said, softly.

"You'll never see the sun again," she said, her voice quiet and full of sorrow. "Never again. Never feel it on your skin. Never watch a sunrise, or a sunset."

"I know, Mum."

"And you have to drink blood. Every day, whether you want to or not. You can't imagine how awful that is."

"I know," he repeated. "Why are you telling me all this?"

"Because part of me is worried that you think this is some kind of grand adventure," she said, her tone suddenly deadly serious. "Some exciting game that you can play until your friend comes up with some magic pill and we all go back to normal. But that's not the truth, Jamie. It's a curse, a bloody curse, and there's nothing you or I or anyone else can do about it."

Jamie stared at her for a long moment, his heart beating rapidly in his chest.

"I'm sorry," she said, eventually. "I know how hard this is, and

I didn't mean to shout. But you have to accept that I know what I'm talking about."

"I do," he said, his voice low. "I really do, Mum."

She looked at him and nodded. Then her face crumpled, and she lowered her head as she began to cry.

Jamie stood helplessly for a long moment, staring at his mother as her shoulders trembled and her chest heaved. Then he stepped forward and pulled her tightly against him.

"It's OK,' he whispered. "Don't cry, Mum. It'll be OK."

She didn't respond, but her arms wrapped round his waist.

"Seriously," he said. "You're going to set me off. And I can't cry in my uniform, Mum. Everyone will take the piss."

His mother raised her head and gave him the smallest of sad smiles. "It's just not fair, Jamie," she said, her voice cracking. "Why did this happen to us? What did we do to deserve any of it?"

"Nothing," said Jamie, firmly. "We didn't do anything. None of this is our fault. It's not Dad's fault either. Bad things happen."

"They do," said Marie. "They really do. I'm so proud of you, Jamie. You know that, don't you?"

A huge lump leapt into his throat. "Yeah," he managed. "I know, Mum."

"Do you want tea?"

Jamie smiled. Tea was his mother's first line of defence against whatever the world had to throw at her, an almost automatic response.

"Yes, please," he said. "I'd love a tea."

She let go of him, nodded, and set about laying out cups and saucers. As the kettle began to boil, she looked over at him with a small smile on her face.

"Have you flown yet?" she asked.

Jamie smiled. "Not yet, Mum. I was only turned twelve hours ago."

"There's no point denying what you are," said Marie. "That's what Valentin told me. You might as well enjoy one of the few good things about it. Give it a try."

Jamie's smile widened, then his face furrowed into a mask of concentration.

"It's not like any other kind of movement," said Marie, watching him carefully. "Not like walking or running or jumping. You have to sort of think yourself into the air."

"OK," said Jamie. He focused on the ground beneath his boots, trying to imagine separating from it, trying to force his body to do something impossible. His legs started to tremble with effort, the muscles vibrating beneath his skin. Sweat began to bead on his forehead, and a dull ache settled into his neck and shoulders. He was on the verge of giving up when something clicked in his mind, some switch that had been dormant his entire life; he rose an unsteady few centimetres from the ground and hung there, his arms flailing redundantly for balance at his sides. He felt heat spill into his eyes as they widened with delight, and he grinned at his mother, who was watching him with a mixture of pride and profound sadness. Her expression broke his concentration and he dropped back to the ground.

"I did it," he said. "You saw that, right? I totally did it."

Marie nodded, then spun elegantly through the air, smiling widely at him.

"It's like that, is it?" he asked, grinning up at her.

She shrugged with fake nonchalance, her smile widening even further.

Jamie reached into his mind and found the switch; it was far easier now he knew it was there, knew what to feel for. He bore down on it and this time he shot up into the air, his body flipping forward, out of control. Marie swooped down, took hold of his arms, and righted him; they hung in the air of her cell, mother and son grinning at each other like schoolchildren.

"You're strong," she said. "I couldn't stay up like this for weeks."

"You could have," said Jamie. "You just didn't know you could. Matt came up with a theory that the older the vampire is that bites you, the quicker your power increases, and the stronger you end up being. The vamp who bit me was old, maybe the second oldest there's ever been. But Alexandru bit you, and he's very nearly as ancient."

"Valentin told me I was stronger than most," said Marie. "I thought he was just flattering me."

"He probably was," said Jamie. "But he was also telling you the truth."

Marie removed her hands. Jamie wobbled in the air, then held himself upright, floating steadily a metre above the ground.

"How do you feel?" she asked.

Jamie smiled. "Like I could stay up here all day."

Marie looked at him for a long moment, then descended to the floor of her cell. Jamie followed suit, touching down slightly awkwardly, and smiled at his mother, his eyes wide and glowing red in their corners.

He had always assumed when he saw Larissa flying that it would feel like weightlessness, but he realised now that he had been wrong.

It didn't feel like that at all.

His body still felt like it had weight and mass; what felt different was how it interacted with the air around him, as though the air itself had acquired solidity, which he could now push against and float on top of. It was the most glorious sensation, a feeling of irresistible freedom that he was already yearning to experience again; he wanted to not just float in an underground room, but soar through open skies, swoop and bank and dive, the vast emptiness around him on all sides. Why his girlfriend had not wanted to come home from NS9 was suddenly completely understandable; the empty desert of Nevada must have been like heaven.

"I have to tell you something else, Mum," he said. "Something I'm probably not supposed to."

"Why don't I think this is going to be good?" asked Marie, forcing a tiny smile.

Jamie rolled his eyes. "You're so negative, Mum," he said, and smiled at her. "Anyone would think the world was about to end."

Her smile disappeared. "What are you talking about, Jamie?" she asked.

"Valentin came back," he said. "Last night. He found Dracula, and his brother, and Henry Seward. A team has been put together to go and deal with them once and for all."

"And you're going," said Marie. "Aren't you?"

Jamie nodded.

"Let me come with you," said Marie, instantly. "Let me help."

"I can't, Mum," said Jamie, around the lump that had leapt back into his throat. "You know I don't have that kind of authority."

"I could be useful, though," said Marie, her eyes filling up with tears. "I'm strong now, and fast, and I could look after you, and..."

Jamie felt his heart creak alarmingly; if his mother kept talking, if the concern radiating out of her pores became any sharper and more potent, it would surely break. He reached out and hugged her again, wondering idly when he had last embraced his mother three times in five minutes. She hugged him back fiercely, and Jamie ordered himself to hold it together, to not make this any harder for her than it needed to be.

"I'm coming back," he whispered. "When this is over, I'm coming home."

Marie pulled back and favoured him with a look of immense pride.

"I believe you," she said.

But her eyes told a different story.

Kate Randall knocked on the door of Paul Turner's office and opened it before he had time to shout for her to come in. Anger was bubbling through her like acid, scouring and scalding, and it was taking every iota of her self-control to keep calm. She strode across the office and threw her console down on the Security Officer's desk.

"Can you explain this?" she asked, her voice low and furious.

Turner glanced at the console screen, then looked up at her and frowned.

"Explain what?" he asked.

"I think you know," said Kate. She was breathing hard, almost hyperventilating with anger. "I think you know *exactly* what."

Turner narrowed his eyes, then picked up the console and read the message glowing on its screen.

"You've been ordered to act as Interim Security Officer while the Operational force is in France," he said, and shrugged. "So what?"

"So what?" growled Kate. "Why am I being left here to guard an empty base while everyone else is fighting Dracula? *That's* what."

"Someone from our Division had to stay," said Turner, his voice infuriatingly calm and measured. "And I chose you. You should take it as a compliment, given that you're only a Lieutenant."

"A compliment?" shouted Kate. "Are you actually kidding me? I'm supposed to be pleased that you chose me to twiddle my thumbs on the sidelines while my friends fight for their lives? Really?"

"I didn't say you were supposed to be pleased about it," said Turner. "I expect you to carry out the orders you have been given, the same as everyone else."

Kate stared at her boss, her chest rising and falling rapidly, her face pale. The Security Officer met her gaze, his grey eyes clear and steady.

"What's this really about?" she asked, forcing herself to moderate her tone and volume. "What's going on, Paul? Tell me the truth."

"Nothing's going on," he replied. "I trust you to be in charge in my absence. It's as simple as that."

"I don't believe you," she said. "Are you punishing me? Did I do something wrong?"

"If you had done something wrong, you would know it," said Turner. "You can ask me the same question in as many ways as you like, but the answer isn't going to change. I need you here. It's that simple."

Kate narrowed her eyes. "Is this about Shaun?" she asked.

Turner recoiled, as though she had slapped him rather than simply spoken his son's name. "I'm sorry?" he asked.

"This," she said. "Leaving me here, out of harm's way. Is it about what happened to Shaun?"

"That's beneath you, Kate," he said, his cheeks flushing an angry pink. "It really is."

*Jackpot,* she thought.

"I'm sorry, sir," she said. "If it isn't about him, then tell me the truth. The real truth."

"There is no *real* truth," said Turner, his face darkening, his voice like ice. "There is only *the* truth, which you seem completely unwilling to accept."

"Why don't you want me to go to France, sir?" she asked.

"Because I need you here."

"Why don't you want me to go, sir?"

"I just told you, Lieutenant."

"Why don't you want me to—"

Paul Turner leapt to his feet. His chair shot backwards across the office and crashed into the wall at the same moment he slammed both his hands down on his desk.

"ENOUGH!" he bellowed. "THAT IS ENOUGH OUT OF YOU, LIEUTENANT! ONE MORE WORD AND I'LL—"

"What, sir?" she asked, trying to hold her nerve in the face of his sudden, enormous fury. "What will you do?"

Turner stared at her across the desk; the gaze that had intimidated so many humans and vampires over the years locked directly on her. She met it, hoping he couldn't see her legs begin to shake. After a long moment, he looked down.

"I can't lose you too," he said, his voice barely audible. "I'm sorry, Kate. I just can't."

Kate stared at him. For a long second, she doubted her own ears, believing that the Security Officer's words had been what she wanted to hear rather than what he had actually said. Then he raised his head, and the look on his face told her it was real.

"Hey," she said. "It's all right, sir. It's OK."

He shook his head and produced a fierce smile. "It's not," he said. "It's utterly selfish and I know it is, believe me. But I can't bear the thought of anything happening to you. Not after Shaun."

Kate's heart felt as though it was swelling in her chest, pushing against her sternum and ribs and unleashing a wave of emotion that was almost unbearable. She had seen more in her relatively short life than most: her mother wasting away to nothing; her friends and neighbours slaughtered by Alexandru Rusmanov's followers; her boyfriend dead, his head tilted grotesquely to one side; the look on her father's face when he realised that she was still alive. This moment was not quite the equal of those, but nor was it a million miles away; she fought back tears as she looked at the Security Officer, trying to imagine the enormous strength it must have taken for him to make such a painful admission.

"I understand, sir," she said. "Thank you. For caring."

He shook his head again. "I know it's selfish," he repeated. "But I want to know that you're safe, that you'll *be* safe, no matter what happens to me. I'll rescind the order if you ask me to, although I'm really hoping that you won't."

Kate smiled. The fire that had been raging through her mere minutes earlier was gone, extinguished by the truth of Paul Turner's desperate, panicked desire to protect her.

"I'll stay," she said.

Victor Frankenstein was lying on his bed, his attention focused entirely on trying to ignore the terrible itching beneath his skin, when there was a knock on the door to his quarters. He swung his legs down to the floor, crossed the small room, and pulled the door open.

"Hey," said Jamie Carpenter.

He smiled. "Hey, yourself," he said, and stepped aside. "Come in." The teenager nodded and walked past him. As he did so, Frankenstein saw the red around his eyes, the paleness of his skin.

*He looks like he's been crying,* he thought.

Jamie flopped down into the chair that stood in the corner of the small room. The monster stayed on his feet, looking carefully at the boy he had sworn to protect.

"Are you all right?" he asked.

"Just about," replied Jamie. "I went to visit my mum. It was pretty rough."

"I would imagine it was," said Frankenstein. "I assume she's upset?"

Jamie nodded. "She was," he said. "The first thing she asked me was whether Larissa did it."

Frankenstein grimaced. "I can only imagine how that made you feel," he said. "But you have to remember that she just wants you to be safe. It's hard for her, what you do every day. The dangers you face."

Jamie nodded. "I know that," he said. "And I hate making her worry, I really do. But this is what my life is, and I'm proud of what we do. She's going to have to deal with it eventually."

"She never will," said Frankenstein. "I know that's not what you want to hear, but it's the truth. She will never come to terms with you risking your life every night. She might learn to accept it, but it's never going to be OK. You're the most important thing in the world to her."

"I know," said Jamie. "She wanted to help us, to come to France and fight. Can you believe that?"

"I was friends with your father for a long time, Jamie," said Frankenstein, and smiled. "From everything he told me about her, I'm not remotely surprised."

Jamie nodded and rubbed his eyes. For a moment, silence descended over the small room; it was not uncomfortable, but felt full of things unsaid.

"Do you want to tell me about Romania?" asked Frankenstein. "About what happened?"

Jamie shook his head. "Not right now," he said. "Maybe later. If there *is* a later."

"All right," said Frankenstein. He was keen to know what had taken place in the Teleorman Forest, but he had no desire to press the teenager; he had more than enough to be thinking about right now.

Jamie looked up at him. "Do you miss my dad?" he asked, his voice low and hollow.

For a long moment, Frankenstein didn't respond; his mind was racing with a single, irrational thought.

*Does he know? Can he know that I spoke to Julian less than an hour ago?*

"Yes," he said, eventually. "I miss him. Particularly today."

Jamie nodded. "I do too," he said. "I can't be angry with him any more. It's not worth it. Now I just miss him."

"Your father wasn't perfect," said Frankenstein. "He made mistakes, lots of them. But he loved you and your mother. Never forget that."

Jamie smiled. "I know he did," he said. "And from what people have told me, it sounds like we could have done with him on our side today."

Frankenstein nodded. "We definitely could," he said. "He was one of the finest Operators to ever wear the uniform. I wish he was coming with us."

There was another long silence, as Jamie dropped his eyes to the floor. Frankenstein could almost see the turmoil filling the teenager, the confusion and uncertainty; it was apparent in the hunched arc of his shoulders.

"Do you think he'd be proud of me?" asked Jamie, eventually. "My dad, I mean."

Frankenstein felt a stab of pain in his chest. "He *was* proud of you," he said. "Your mother was the only person on earth who knew him better than I did, so I can tell you that with absolute certainty."

"But now, I mean," said Jamie, looking up. "He never saw me as an Operator. Do you think he would be proud now?"

"Of course he would," said Frankenstein. "And rightly so. If you were mine, I'd be the proudest father in the world."

Jamie smiled. Frankenstein stared at his face as it lit up, seeing him for what he was: a teenage boy who had already endured more than should ever have been asked of him.

*I forget sometimes,* he thought. *He seems so much older, and he's been through so much. But he's just a boy.*

"How are *you* doing?" asked Jamie. "Tonight is the full moon, right?"

Frankenstein nodded. "I'm fine," he said. "Don't worry about me."

"Does it hurt?" asked Jamie. "When it's this close? Can you feel it coming?"

"Yes, it hurts," said Frankenstein. "And yes, I can feel it."

"How can you bear it? Knowing this awful thing is going to happen to you every month?"

Frankenstein grunted with laughter. "What else would you have me do?"

"I don't know," said Jamie.

"What about you?" he asked. "How does it feel to be a vamp?"

Jamie shrugged. "It's hard to explain," he said. "I feel the same, mostly. I mean, I still feel like me. But my senses have gone crazy, like they've all been turbocharged. The world seems totally different to how it did before."

"And the hunger?" asked Frankenstein.

"I don't know," said Jamie, shaking his head. "I was in the infirmary when I turned, and they gave me painkillers and blood as soon as it started. So I really don't know. Larissa has tried to prepare me for it, but she said that you can't really describe it to someone. I guess I'll know when it hits me."

Frankenstein burst out laughing. It was a huge, rumbling sound, like an avalanche on its way to destroy a mountain village.

Jamie narrowed his eyes. "What's so funny?" he asked.

"You and me," said Frankenstein. "A vampire and a werewolf, about to go to war with a creature that most of the world thinks is just a character in a story. How the hell did we get here?"

Jamie grinned. "Fate?" he said. "Destiny? Really, really bad luck?"

"Or karma?" suggested Frankenstein. "Perhaps you and I were terrible people in our previous lives."

Jamie joined in with his laughter, rocking back in his chair and holding his sides, and, for a moment, Frankenstein felt guilty; it seemed unfair that he should be able to laugh while Julian was estranged from the people he loved, while Henry Seward remained in Dracula's clutches, and while the entire Department was preparing for a mission from which many, if not all, of them would not return. But there were times when there was nothing to do but take joy in the simple pleasures of life that were, ultimately, what they were fighting to preserve.

Camaraderie. Friendship. Loyalty.

Love.

Jamie got to his feet, his face pink from the exertion of laughing. "I have to go," he said. "I'll see you in the hangar?"

Frankenstein nodded. "You will."

Jamie walked across the small quarters. Frankenstein stepped back to make room, but the teenager wasn't heading for the door; instead, he wrapped his arms round Frankenstein's chest and gave him a tight, fierce hug.

For a moment, he stood as stiff as a board, unsure of what to do, taken aback by the boy's display of affection. Then slowly, very slowly, he wrapped his arms round Jamie's shoulders.

Kate took a deep breath and pressed the CALL button on her mobile.

At the same time, Matt walked out on to the tarmac beyond the wide hangar doors, his phone pressed to his ear.

"Dad?" they both said.

Cal Holmwood walked down the centre of the Fallen Gallery, past the marble bust of Quincey Harker, and stopped in front of the portraits that filled the wall at the far end. Six men, rendered in careful strokes of oil paint, stared down at him, their eyes clear, their faces stern, their names the stuff of legend.

Jonathan Harker. Abraham Van Helsing. Quincey Morris. John Seward. Henry Carpenter. And his own great-great-grandfather, Arthur Holmwood, whose money had long ago bought the land beneath which Cal now stood. He felt the weight of the past pressing down on him, more so than at any time since his father had come to him on his twenty-first birthday and explained to him that there was another world, one full of darkness and wonder, and that he could be a part of it if he wished. He would have given anything to ask the advice of the founders, even though he doubted they would be able to imagine the scale of the challenge that he was facing; it would nonetheless have eased his restless soul to have someone tell him he was doing the right thing.

Cal lowered his head in a silent moment of respect to his ancestor and his friends, then walked back the way he had come. He reached the most recent portraits, likenesses of George Harker Jr and his brother John, and looked at the remaining space between it and the wooden doors at the end of the gallery. There was enough room for perhaps ten more portraits, the same number on the opposite wall.

*I wonder how much of that room will have been allocated tomorrow,* he thought. *And whether there will be anyone left to see the new pictures hung.*

It had been suggested, on several occasions, that a portrait of Henry Seward be commissioned, but Cal had rejected the idea each time. He was not by nature naive, and as time had passed, he had begun the process of reconciling himself with the idea that the Director was gone. But until he was sure, until the evidence was incontrovertible, he had refused to hang his friend in this place of the dead; it was a stance he was particularly proud of, now that Valentin had confirmed that Seward was still alive.

"You're a real bastard, Henry," he said aloud, staring at the empty space on the wall. "Why did you never tell me how hard this job really was? I was your Deputy for almost five years, and you never gave me the slightest hint of what you must have been going through every day. I could have helped you, if you'd let me."

He tried to imagine what the Director's response would be to this accusation, tried to hear his friend's voice in his head.

*You didn't need to know, Cal. I had no intention of going anywhere, and it was my burden to carry. It came with the job.*

"I thought I understood," he said. "But I didn't really get it. I didn't really know how it felt to have people you saw walking through the corridors the day before, die on an operation you ordered. I didn't understand how much of this basically comes down to doing what you think is best, and hoping you're right."

*It's hard, my old friend. I would never try and tell you otherwise. You mourn every death, and you keep them with you longer than anyone else, because you think on some level they were all down to you. But if that's true, then every Operator that comes back alive is down to you too, down to you sending them out there with the right squad mates and the right training. You can't take it all on your shoulders, Cal. It's too big.*

"We're coming for you, Henry," he said, his voice low. "You just have to hang on a little while longer. You have to promise me you'll do that, because I can't handle what's coming on my own. I'm going to need your help."

*You know me, Cal. I'll hang on as long as I can. You can count on that.*

The Interim Director closed his eyes and nodded in the long, empty room. "I know you will," he said. "I'll see you soon, my friend, and I'll be praying that it's soon enough."

Cal opened his eyes. His head seemed lighter than it had when he entered the Fallen Gallery, and his mind felt sharper; what he had to do seemed clearer, somehow more manageable.

"Thank you, Henry," he said, then strode towards the doors that would take him back out into a base that was full of men and women preparing for war.

Given that she had been mentioned by name in Cal Holmwood's speech, Larissa Kinley was no more surprised than Jamie when the orders for the French operation arrived on her console.

She was pacing in her quarters, waiting impatiently for her boyfriend. After the Interim Director's speech had ended, Jamie had told her he needed some time to himself, time she knew full well he would spend talking to his mother and to Frankenstein. Larissa didn't begrudge him it, even though he knew there was nobody she could talk to, no way for her to follow Cal's instructions. She had briefly considered whether this might finally be the moment to reach out to her family, but had quickly decided against it; it was incredibly unlikely that they would accept a call from her, and even if they did, the amount of lies and tongue-biting self-control that would be required on her part was simply too depressing a prospect. Instead, she paced, and waited, and wondered what the future might hold, for herself and for Jamie.

For them both.

Larissa would never, as long as she lived, forgive the first victim for what he had done to her boyfriend; if the chance ever arose, she intended to make him pay for it in blood. She knew there were people, possibly even amongst those she called her friends, who were sceptical as to how genuine her desire for Jamie never to be turned had truly been. It was understandable; she could see why someone who had never felt their body screaming for fresh blood, threatening madness if it wasn't sated, might consider the idea of a vampire couple and see nothing more than some gooey idea of eternal love. On occasion, she had been sure that even Jamie himself had not believed her position on the matter.

In truth, she had never been more serious about anything in her life.

Vampirism had never felt to her like being anything more than half alive; the condition that many considered a gift had always seemed to her a curse, and there was nothing that Larissa hoped for more in the world than the discovery of a cure. Now, after what had been done to Jamie in Romania, her desire for such a breakthrough was stronger than ever. Because she had been honest the last time they discussed the subject; she wanted to grow old with him, have a real life with him, not some supernatural approximation.

There was a knock on her door. Larissa floated into the air, swept across the small room, and pulled it open to reveal Jamie standing in the corridor. His face was pale, and his eyes were worryingly red, but he smiled instantly at the sight of her, and she felt a familiar rush of panicky love stampede through her. He stepped through the door, kicked it shut behind him, took her face in his hands, and kissed her.

Fire roared through her, and she kissed him back as her vampire side awoke, hungry and full of desire. She forced herself to break the kiss while she was still capable of doing so, and found Jamie staring at her with eyes that glowed the colour of blood. She recoiled as he let go of her face, his smile disappearing.

"What's wrong?" he asked.

"I'm sorry," she said. "I'm just not used to seeing you like that."

He winced. "This is me now, Larissa," he said. "You're going to have to get used to it."

"And I will," she said. "I'm sure I will. It's just going to take a little while."

"OK," said Jamie. He walked across her quarters and let himself flop down on to her bed. Larissa stayed where she was; she was sure he expected her to lie beside him, but she suspected it would probably only make the awkward atmosphere in the room worse.

"How was your mum?" she asked.

Jamie shrugged. "She's fine."

"Frankenstein?" she said. "Is he—"

"I don't want to talk about him," interrupted Jamie. "Or my mum, or anyone else. I want to talk about you and me, Larissa."

"OK," she said, forcing a smile on to her face. "So talk."

"I didn't want this to happen to me," he said, sitting up and looking directly into her eyes. "I know I joked about it too much, and I know at least part of you is wondering whether I'm happy about it. This happened because it needed to, you know that. It was the best we were going to get from the first victim, and it happened to be me that he bit. I didn't do it to hurt you, or spite you, and I need to know that you're going to be OK with it."

*The first victim bit you because you called him a coward, she thought. Let's not forget that part of it. You never asked him if he'd be willing to bite someone, you baited him until he bit you. There's a difference.*

"I know you didn't want this," she said. "And I'll be OK with it. But it's hard for me, Jamie, and I need *you* to understand why."

"OK," he said, and gave her a smile that she was reasonably sure was genuine. "We'll probably both be dead in a few hours anyway."

"That's cheery," said Larissa, and grinned at him. "Thanks a lot."

"My pleasure," said Jamie. He opened his mouth to speak again, but a knock on the door cut his words off in his throat.

Matt Browning stood in the corridor, waiting for his friend to open the door. He heard movement inside the quarters, and as the locks clunked and thudded he allowed his eyes to close for a brief, peaceful moment that he hoped would stave off his tiredness for at least a few more minutes.

After leaving Kate and Larissa outside the infirmary, he had barely had time to say hello to his Lazarus Project colleagues and turn on his computer before the message summoning the entire Department to the Ops Room had arrived. He had hurried back down to the lab as soon as Cal Holmwood finished speaking, and had not been remotely surprised to receive orders to carry on with his work while the Operational force went to confront Dracula; every member of Lazarus had quickly received the same orders, and had responded with clear and obvious relief.

Matt didn't begrudge them it; they were scientists, not soldiers, and, in truth, he had no more desire to face Dracula and Valeri than they did. Where he differed from his colleagues was that his three closest friends in the world *would* be going, with no guarantee that any of them would return.

"Are you OK?" Natalia asked, leaning towards his desk.

"I'm fine," he replied, and gave her what he hoped was a convincing smile.

"You are worried about Jamie and Larissa and Kate?"

"Yeah," he said. "Of course I am."

"You should go and find them," said Natalia. "Before they go."

A hush fell across the lab, as Professor Karlsson got to his feet and asked for everybody's attention.

"You've all had your orders," he said. "So we all know what we're doing. The Interim Director wants us to continue our work, and I expect all of you to follow his orders with your very best effort. I know that it will be hard, that some of you have friends who are about to put themselves in harm's way, but you cannot help them by staring into thin air and worrying about them until they return. The only way you can help is by doing your job. Is that clear?"

There was a murmured chorus of agreement.

"Good," said Karlsson. "On to happier news. Thanks to the efforts of someone in this room, I have returned from Beijing to find that remarkable developments have taken place in my absence.

The preliminary data that I have just finished reviewing is nothing short of astonishing, and I will be handing out new workflows by the end of the day to enable us to best take advantage of it. What I, and I suspect all of you, would like to know, is exactly how we came into possession of this new data. So, Matt, if you'd like to come up here and tell us what happened in San Francisco, I think we'd be very interested to hear it."

Every pair of eyes in the lab turned towards Matt. He blushed, and glanced at Natalia; she was staring at him, her gaze steady, her mouth curled into a small smile of encouragement.

"Matt?" said Professor Karlsson.

He looked at the Lazarus Project Director, then got to his feet.

"I'm sorry, sir," he said. "I'm afraid it'll have to wait."

Matt stepped round his desk, leant down, taking care not to move his neck as he did so, and pressed his lips against Natalia Lenski's. There was an audible intake of breath from his colleagues, and he smiled as he broke the kiss; the Russian girl was looking up at him with eyes that were wide with surprise, but her smile had expanded into a grin that made him feel dizzy.

He had looked into her eyes for a long moment, pregnant with possibility. Then he pushed open the main doors of the lab and stepped out into the corridor, leaving a stunned silence behind him.

The door in front of him opened and Larissa appeared.

"Hey, you," she said, and pulled the door wide. "Come in."

Matt smiled, and stepped past her into her quarters.

"Matt!" exclaimed Jamie. "Good to see you, mate."

"Jamie," he said. "How are you?"

"A creature of the night, by all accounts," said Jamie. "Yourself?"

"I'm fine," said Matt, taking a seat on the edge of Larissa's bed.

"I'm already sick to death of this collar, but I'm fine. Have you guys seen Kate?"

Jamie shook his head. "Not since Cal's speech," he said. "You?"

"No," said Matt. "She must be up in Security. You'll see her in the hangar, I'm sure." He paused. "You are going, right? I mean, I sort of assumed, given what Cal said."

"We're going," said Larissa.

"Are you scared?" he asked.

"I am," she replied. "I don't know about him, but I definitely am."

"I am too," said Jamie. He pushed himself across Larissa's bed until his back was against the wall, the smile gone from his face. "I feel like I'm supposed to say I'm not, but I am."

"You'd be an idiot if you weren't," said Matt. "Being scared means you'll be careful, which means you'll come back."

"Let's hope so," said Larissa.

A horrible silence filled the room.

*This is insane*, thought Matt. *How can we be talking about them dying like it's a genuine possibility? It's ridiculous. They're my age, for Christ's sake, and we're talking about death like it's no big deal.*

"Have you talked to your mum?" he said, eventually. "Does she know what's going on?"

Jamie nodded. "She knows," he said. "She doesn't like it, not in the slightest, but she understands. I thought she was going to ask me not to go, to be honest with you. That's what I was dreading. But she didn't. I don't think she wanted to make it any harder for me."

"That was good of her," said Larissa.

"It was," said Jamie. "She's like that."

Matt stared at his friends, feeling like he was about to either explode or burst into tears. The last few months had been the happiest of his life, the first time he had felt like he truly belonged anywhere. Now it seemed as though it was on the verge of falling apart, and he was utterly furious about it.

"This can't end like this," he said, his voice low and so unlike his usual tone that frowns of surprise appeared on the faces of his friends. "This can't be the last time we're going to sit like this, the three of us together, alive and in one piece. It just can't. Everything we've done, the lives we've saved, and this is what it comes down to? The two of you and everyone else flying off into the night to fight God knows what? It's crazy."

"Matt," said Jamie, gently. "What else are we supposed to do?"

"I don't know," he said, his eyes shining fiercely under the fluorescent light. "OK? All I know is that everything changed for me when I met you. When I met all of you. So you have to promise me that you'll come back. Promise me that you'll make it through this, and that you'll come home."

Larissa winced. "Matt..."

"Just promise," he said, his voice rising alarmingly. "Promise me, right now."

Jamie looked him square in the eye. "I promise to try," he said. "I promise I'll do everything I can to get us home safe. That's going to have to be good enough, mate."

"I promise the same," said Larissa. She was looking at him with obvious concern. "I really do."

Matt breathed out a long, low rush of air, and felt the panic that had been climbing through him abate, ever so slightly. "OK," he said. "I guess that will have to do. And thank you. It means a lot to me."

"It's all right," said Jamie, smiling at him. "It just means that you don't get to leave any details out when we ask you about Natalia."

Matt groaned. "Honestly?" he said. "At a time like this?"

Larissa shrugged. "What better time could there be than right before the end of the world?" she said, and grinned wickedly. "Besides, what else are we supposed to do until we go to the hangar? Spill your guts, my friend, and take your time about it. We want to know *everything*."

# 57

## THE CALM BEFORE

"I don't know about you," said Jamie Carpenter, "but I'm starting to feel a lot better about this."

He was standing on the tarmac of the airport's southern runway, looking towards a pair of huge hangars that stood open to the night air. They were the only centres of light for more than a mile in any direction; the French government had shut down the airport under the cover story of a mercury contamination of the facility's water supply, allowing it to be used as the rallying post for what was now officially known as the Combined Operational Force. With the FTB and the SPC to the north and Blacklight to the west, there had never been a need for a supernatural Department in France, but Jamie was sure that Cal Holmwood and the other Directors were extremely grateful for the French government's assistance; the airport was barely forty minutes' flying time south-east of Château Dauncy.

The hangars that had caught Jamie's attention were part of the complex of buildings that housed SkyBus, the vast aeroplane manufacturer which had been founded in this quiet suburb of southern France. The airport was owned by them, and they in turn were partly owned by the French government, which had made the temporary shutdown relatively straightforward. The buildings were vast, far larger than the maintenance hangars where Blacklight's fleet of helicopters were stored and maintained, bigger even than the main hangar, beneath which the *Mina II* was housed and where Jamie and the rest of the Blacklight Operators had assembled barely an hour earlier. They had been designed to accommodate the most modern passenger planes, but one of them was now home to something even bigger: a Russian An-224 transport.

The plane, one of the largest ever to take to the skies, squatted in the middle of the huge space, its wings almost reaching the distant walls, its nose cone raised, revealing the cavernous space within. The plane had been accompanied on its slow flight down from Polyarny by two Mi-26 transport helicopters. The Russian choppers were parked outside the hangar beside four SA 330 Pumas provided by the French Air Force, surrounded by maintenance crew and security personnel.

The second hangar contained a C-130 Hercules that had lumbered its way up from South Africa, and four CH-53 Sea Stallions that had made the short journey down from the *Schwartzhaus*. In comparison to the huge array of military hardware, the sea of black figures swarming in front of the hangars seemed tiny. But to Jamie, who had been on his way back from Paris when the Loop was attacked by Valeri Rusmanov, it was by far the largest show of Departmental strength he had ever laid eyes on. Including the Blacklight contingent, who were rapidly disembarking from the helicopters that had carried them across the English Channel, there were more than three hundred Operators and support staff waiting to depart for their target location.

"I know what you mean," said Larissa. "It looks like the cavalry has arrived."

"Except for the Americans," said Jamie, peering around at the darkened airport. "I guess they're who we're waiting for?"

As if on cue, a distant rumbling noise became audible to the north. It was too quiet for most of the assembled men and women to hear, but to Larissa and himself it was perfectly clear. They turned towards it, their supernaturally sharp eyes scanning the horizon.

After a minute or so, Larissa raised her arm and pointed with a pale, slender finger. "There," she said.

Jamie followed the line of her outstretched digit and saw nothing. Then three pale yellow dots became visible, moving low over the French countryside, and he reminded himself how much more powerful Larissa was than him; they were both vampires, but there was still a world of difference between them.

The dots grew in size as they approached, until their outlines identified them as cargo planes; they were flying close together, stacked up behind each other like birds in formation. The thunder of their engines was now loud enough to be heard by everyone, and the crowd of Operators and technicians stopped to watch.

The black silhouettes roared towards the runway. When they were almost on top of the airport, three pairs of blinding landing lights burst into life, slicing through the gloom and making every watching Operator shield their eyes. The howl of engines became deafening, and Jamie, who was still adapting to his newly powerful senses, found himself physically vibrating as the scream of the engines poured through him, rooting him to the spot.

The first plane bore down on the runway, passing above the surrounding suburbs at a height that would never have been permitted by any civil aviation authority, then touched down with a screech of rubber and a high-pitched whine that cut through Jamie like a knife. It raced past the hangars, sending a huge wave of air into the watching Operators, causing most of them to take a staggering step back. Fifteen seconds later the second plane touched down, and twenty seconds after that, the third.

As the transports slowed at the distant end of the runway and began to taxi back towards him, Jamie wondered what on earth the men and women who lived in the houses beyond the airport's fence were making of the night's events. The mercury contamination cover story would not explain the deafening convoy of aircraft that had landed at the darkened airport, and anyone watching from their garden would have been treated to a remarkable display of military technology as it skimmed the roof of their house.

With synchronised precision, the pilots rolled the three huge C-17 Globemaster IIIs to a halt with their towering rear cargo doors pointing at the hangars. The deafening engine noise cut out, leaving a silence that was almost unnerving until a cacophony of warning alarms blared out as the ramps began to slowly lower towards the tarmac.

Jamie looked around as the doors yawned wider and wider. Cal Holmwood was standing with Paul Turner, their attention fixed on the new arrivals, and beyond them he could see familiar faces: Ellison, Qiang, Jack and Patrick Williams, Angela Darcy, Dominique Saint-Jacques, and many others he recognised from operations and briefings and the Loop's canteen queue. Beyond the massed ranks of Blacklight stood their helicopters, three of which were now empty, the doors on their sides open. The fourth remained tightly sealed, surrounded by a cordon of Operators; as Jamie watched, it rocked slightly on its wheels, as though something heavy was moving inside it.

The Globemaster ramps thudded to the ground with a series of metallic clangs that echoed across the quiet airport. Jamie looked into the one nearest him and saw the dark, snub-nosed shapes of a pair of AH-64 Apache helicopters, their rotors folded at their sides, their stub wings bristling with weaponry. Out of the other two transports spilled dozens of men and women in black uniforms; they hustled down the ramps with bags over their shoulders and assembled on the tarmac. A tall, broad man walked through the middle of them and approached Cal Holmwood with a thin smile on his face.

"That's General Allen," said Larissa, softly. "The NS9 Director."

Jamie nodded. He recognised the man from video conferences and reports, but had never seen him in the flesh. Allen stopped in front of Holmwood, and the two men shook hands.

"Cutting it fine, Bob," said Holmwood, his voice audible to Jamie and Larissa. "I was starting to think you weren't going to show."

Allen shook his head, his smile widening slightly. "We had a little bit further to come than you," he said, "in case you hadn't noticed. Nine hours to brief a team, load up, and fly halfway round the world. I'd call that pretty good, Cal."

"I suppose so," said Holmwood, and smiled at his friend. "I see you brought me the presents I asked for."

"The Apaches?" said Allen. "Least I could do. I've got another little surprise for you as well."

"What's that?"

"You'll have to wait and see, won't you?"

Holmwood's smile became a grin. "It's good to see you, Bob."

"You too," said Allen. "I'd say it was a pleasure if the circumstances were better, but they never are, are they?"

"No," said Holmwood. "They never are."

"Where do you want my guys?" asked Allen. "This is your show, so give me an order."

"You separated them like I asked you to? Red and Blue Teams?"

The NS9 Director nodded. "I did."

"OK," said Holmwood. "Give them two minutes to shake off the flight, then ask them to form up out here with the others. I'll address everyone at once, and then we can be on our way."

Jamie smiled. The Interim Director sounded like he was trying to get a busload of teenagers ready for a school trip, rather than preparing to launch a classified military operation to confront the most dangerous creature in the world.

"All right," said Allen. "Two minutes."

Holmwood nodded, then turned back to Paul Turner and was quickly deep in conversation. General Allen surveyed the bustling area and stopped, his eyes seeming to come to rest on Jamie. He frowned as the NS9 Director smiled and walked quickly towards him, then realised his mistake; he glanced over at Larissa and saw the wide grin on her face as the American approached.

*Of course*, he thought.

General Allen arrived in front of them, his smile warm and welcoming. Jamie snapped a salute, almost perfectly in time with Larissa, but the NS9 Director waved a hand dismissively.

"At ease," he said, then stepped forward and threw his arms round Larissa. She was lifted off her feet, her eyes flaring pink, and laughed as she demanded to be put down. General Allen did so, then stepped back to look at her.

"It's good to see you, Larissa," he said. "We miss you in Nevada."

She smiled. "That's good to hear. I'd like you to meet Lieutenant Carpenter, sir. Jamie, this is General Allen, Director of NS9."

Allen's eyes widened. "Of course," he said, sticking out a gloved hand. "Damn good to meet you. I've heard a lot about you."

Jamie took the hand, and suppressed a wince of pain as his arm was pumped up and down. "You too, sir. It's an honour."

"I heard about Romania," said Allen. "Way to take one for the team, son."

"Thank you, sir," said Jamie. "It wasn't exactly the plan, I have to say."

"Plans always look great on paper," said Allen. "They don't tend to mean that much in the real world." His smile disappeared, and he turned his attention back to Larissa. "It was hard to hear about Tim Albertsson," he said, his voice suddenly low. "Everything's still pretty sketchy, but I know the two of you were there, so tell me something. Did he make a mistake? Did he do something wrong?"

"No, sir," said Larissa, instantly. "He didn't do anything wrong. He was asleep when the first victim killed him."

Jamie stared at his girlfriend, trying not to let incredulity show on his face.

*Really?* he thought. *You're still defending him, even now?*

Allen nodded again. "I'm glad to hear that," he said. "He leaves a big hole in my Department, and I would hate to think it had been for nothing."

"The first victim had tried to scare us off several times, sir," said Larissa. "We think killing Tim was his final attempt at getting us to turn back."

*Bullshit*, thought Jamie, his incredulity giving way to anger. *You know exactly why Gregor killed him. You're just not saying it.*

"Makes sense," said Allen. "Chop off the head and hope the body falls down. Still hard, though. He volunteered to lead that operation when I was barely two lines into the briefing. Didn't

**607**

even think about it, just jumped right in. You know what he was like."

"I do, sir," said Larissa.

"Yours were the first two names out of his mouth when I asked who he wanted to take with him," said Allen. "I had to pull some strings, as you can probably imagine. There were some people who weren't exactly thrilled about two Blacklight Operators getting the gig. But Tim was adamant that you were who he wanted. It's a damn shame he isn't here to see this."

"I know, sir," said Larissa, softly. "It is."

"Well," said General Allen, straightening himself up and forcing a smile. "There'll be time to mourn him later. I'd better get my team ready. It's going to be a privilege to fight alongside you, both of you. I feel a lot better knowing you're on my side."

Jamie smiled, despite himself; the NS9 Director was so naturally, effortlessly charismatic that he couldn't help it. In that moment, he saw another of the reasons why Larissa had so obviously wanted to stay in Nevada; General Allen's clear affection for her was in direct contrast to how she was viewed at the Loop by the majority of the rank-and-file Operators. The anger that had risen in his chest as she defended Tim Albertsson disappeared, replaced by hot, sickly guilt.

*I don't blame her at all,* he thought. *I wouldn't have blamed her if she'd never come back.*

General Allen strode away across the tarmac. As soon as he was out of earshot, Larissa turned to Jamie, her face creased with worry.

"I know what you must be thinking," she said. "And I'm sorry. I just didn't see any benefit in telling General Allen that his Special Operator was a petty dickhead who couldn't get over himself long enough to do his job. If we survive this, and he asks me about Tim again, I'll tell him the truth, I promise I will. But this wasn't the time."

Jamie smiled. "It's OK," he said. "You're right."

Larissa gave him a smile that almost stopped his heart. Then Paul Turner's amplified voice echoed out of a megaphone, demanding everyone's attention.

The Blacklight Security Officer was standing beside a jeep, in the open back of which stood Cal Holmwood. The Interim Director looked out across the crowd of black-clad men and women and took the megaphone from Turner's hand.

"Welcome to France," he said. "And to the largest Combined Operational Force that has ever been assembled. I'm not going to inspire you with some long-winded speech, because I believe the time for such talk has passed. Every one of you knows what we are here to do, and every one of you understands the potential consequences if we fail. You have all been briefed by your respective Directors, but to reiterate, the plan is straightforward. Those of you who have been designated as Red Team will lead the initial attack on the château."

Jamie glanced over at Larissa, who shot him a narrow smile; they were both Red Team, which now made sense.

"Blue Team will secure the ground perimeter," continued Holmwood. "And will deploy as a second wave. The Apaches will patrol an aerial cordon around the target location, preventing any vamps escaping via the air, while satellite and AWACS overlook will track any attempts at escape through the forest. There is a single Priority Level 1 objective, which is the destruction of the vampire born Vlad Tepes, and most recently known as Dracula. Priority Level 2 is the destruction of the vampire known as Valeri Rusmanov.

Priority Level 3 is the rescue of Admiral Henry Seward, the Director of Blacklight. Everything else is Priority Level neutral. Any questions?"

Silence.

"I want confirmation of Dracula's destruction," he continued. "No ambiguity, no assumptions, no word of mouth. Visual eyewitness confirmation. Get me that, and we can all go home. Good luck to each and every one of you. Dismissed."

There was no cheer, no bugle, no waving of flags; the men and women of the Combined Operational Force simply got to work, loading themselves and their equipment into the transport helicopters. Rotors began to spin and engines cycled up as the pilots worked quickly through their pre-flight checks.

Jamie watched, his stomach twisting slowly with nerves. The downdraught from the rotors swirled the air, forcing him to lean forward against it; he found himself grinning, and felt a heat that was becoming less and less unpleasant spill into the corners of his eyes as he faced Larissa.

"What we were saying before," he shouted, over the rising howl of engines. "It doesn't matter. We can—"

Larissa's hand fastened round his arm. Her eyes were blazing crimson, her fangs wide and gleaming, her face twisted with a huge, hungry grin. She darted forward, so fast he barely saw her move, and kissed him hard on the mouth.

"No more talking," she said. "It's time."

# 58

# THE STORM, PART ONE

## SOUTH-WESTERN FRANCE

The fleet of helicopters roared north-west, keeping their altitude low and their running lights extinguished.

There were seven of them in formation: the two Apache gunships, which had been given the call signs Viper 1 and Viper 2, and five heavy transports, in the bellies of four of which sat just over four hundred Operators, their weapons checked and rechecked, their visors pushed back. Their faces were uniformly pale, but the vast majority were fixed with tight expressions of determination.

Nobody spoke.

There was nothing left to say.

Jamie sat strapped to a bench at the rear of one of the helicopters, next to Larissa and opposite Patrick Williams. The atmosphere in the hold was thick with nervous tension; although nobody said so out loud, everyone was eager for the fighting to start. They trusted themselves, trusted each other, and were as ready as they could be.

All that remained to be seen was whether they would succeed or fail.

\* \* \*

Dracula stood on the balcony that ran round the roof of Château Dauncy, his gaze fixed on the horizon.

His eyes smouldered the colour of lava as the cool evening wind blew his long hair back from his head. For the first time in his unnaturally long life, he stood on the brink of battle without armour, without horses or archers, without any of the weapons he had once deployed with such viciousness. His one concession to the blood-soaked victories of the past hung from his belt, gleaming dully in the light of the full moon.

"They are coming," he said, softly. "I can hear them."

Valeri Rusmanov nodded; he estimated they had five minutes before the helicopters that were rumbling in the distance arrived.

"It is still not too late for you to leave, my lord," he said. "Your followers and I will take care of your enemies."

Dracula smiled at his oldest companion. "Your concern for me is as welcome as always, old friend," he said. "But I will not leave. If I wished to avoid what is coming, I would have killed your brother when he stood before us yesterday. I let him leave because it is time to find out to whose will this world will bend. Ours, or theirs."

"Perhaps a different choice of where to fight, my lord," said Valeri. "The courtyard and grounds do not play to our strengths."

"It matters not," said Dracula. "If I am not all that I would be, then I will die. But if I am ready, as I believe I am, then we will send them to their deaths here as easily as anywhere else."

"Give me an order, my lord," said Valeri. "Tell me what you would have me do."

"Kill them," said Dracula, his smile widening. "Meet them where they land, and kill them all."

\* \* \*

Ten miles from the château, the Apaches accelerated, their noses dipping as they dropped even lower over the forest canopy.

Cal Holmwood watched them from the cockpit of the lead transport with Bob Allen sitting at his side and his heart thumping steadily in his chest. The gunships would circle the château at a distance of five hundred metres, ready to unleash their firepower on any vampire who tried to escape through the air, a prospect that Holmwood was sure would act as a compelling deterrent. He had been aboard an Apache above Kosovo fifteen years earlier, and had watched its pilot open up his helicopter's 30mm chain gun on a barn where a number of turned Serbian soldiers had been hiding; there had been nothing left but smears of blood and splinters of wood.

"Three minutes," said the transport's pilot.

Holmwood nodded, his eyes fixed on the dark expanse of the forest. He told himself to stay calm; in many ways, despite the enormity of the stakes, the operation was one of the most strategically simple he had authorised in his short tenure as Interim Director. Dracula and Valeri had clearly decided to stand and fight, otherwise the château would already have been abandoned, meaning the battle would take place in an enclosed arena. He had organised the largest possible force in the time available, briefed them as fully as possible, and equipped them with every possible weapon and a cordon of heavily armed air support.

It was going to be hand to hand, fast and brutal.

It was going to come down to skill, and experience, and will.

"Two minutes," said the pilot.

Beside him, General Allen lifted his radio to his ear. "SHOWSTOPPER is go," he said. "Repeat, SHOWSTOPPER is go."

Holmwood frowned. "What was that, Bob?" he asked.

"I said I had a surprise for you," said Allen, and smiled widely at his old friend. "Just sit back and watch."

Valeri strode through the château, ordering the massed ranks of vampires to follow him. They did so immediately and without question, their eyes burning red, their faces full of the anticipation of violence.

The eldest of the Rusmanov brothers, who had fought in countless battles over the centuries, felt a familiar calm settle over him as he rounded up his troops. They were not soldiers, not like the trained men that he had once sent into harm's way without a second thought, but they were willing, and that was enough. He had put the word out after his brother's appearance in the château's courtyard, trusting it to spread through the supernatural underground like wildfire and blaze a trail for any vampires with grudges against the men in black to follow. And for the last twenty-four hours they had done so in their dozens, drifting down from Germany and Scandinavia, up from Spain and Italy and Greece. The new arrivals were uniformly awed to be merely standing in the presence of Valeri and his master, and desperate to do harm on their behalf.

In the beautiful, wood-panelled lobby, Valeri turned and faced his army. "Not a single person leaves here alive," he said. "Kill, and keep killing, until vampires are all that breathe. Do so and you will have my master's gratitude."

The vampires hissed and twitched, their eyes blazing. Then the sound of helicopter engines rattled through the thick stone walls of the château, shaking the ground beneath their feet.

"Give no quarter," said Valeri, his eyes darkening until they were almost black. His body felt like a current was being passed through it, humming and sparking and full of power. "If you run, I will tear your heart out myself. Is that clear?"

The vampires grunted and growled their understanding.

Valeri smiled. "There will come a time," he said, "when all of our kind pretend they were here, on this day. Only you will be able to say so honestly. Remember that as the blood begins to spill."

He turned towards the huge double doors of the château, took a deep breath, and threw them open. The thunder of the helicopters roared through them, and Valeri closed his eyes for a long moment, revelling in the imminent prospect of battle.

He frowned. There was something else out there; a distant sound far beyond the helicopters, high-pitched and maddeningly familiar.

Then Valeri's eyes flew open, boiling with black-red fire.

"Downstairs!" he roared. "Into the cellars, all of you!"

The crowd of vampires did as they were told without question, flooding towards the doors that led down to the catacombs beneath the château. Valeri didn't give them a second thought; he was already rocketing up the grand staircase, racing towards his master with all the speed he possessed.

Forty thousand feet above the French coastline, the *Spirit of Nebraska* levelled out and opened her bomb-bay doors.

The B-2 bomber had taken off from Whiteman Air Force Base in Missouri eight hours and almost five thousand miles ago, and had crossed the Atlantic at six hundred and twenty miles an hour. In her cockpit, a wide bubble that rose from the flat surface of her fuselage, Commander Jeff Keller freed the weapons-release control that was set into a panel between him and Flight Lieutenant Will Murray, and nodded as his co-pilot armed their primary ordnance.

"SHOWSTOPPER is go," he said, speaking into the microphone that formed part of his moulded flight helmet. "Time to target fifteen seconds."

"Fifteen seconds," repeated Murray.

The night sky loomed over them, vast and purple-black. They could not see the ground, or their target; the weapon would be guided down to it by the JDAM kit it had been fitted with, a lethally precise navigation system that used an array of live satellite readings to control its descent. At their altitude, they would not even hear the detonation; they would already be more than ten miles to the east, preparing to turn back for the long flight back home.

"Target," said Murray.

"Target," repeated Keller, and pressed a button that glowed green in the darkened cockpit. A shudder ran through the huge aircraft, and the numbers on the targeting computer began to run, showing speed of descent and time since release.

"Weapon free," said Keller. "SHOWSTOPPER is go."

"All stop," shouted General Allen. "Hold station here."

The pilot of their transport hauled back on her stick, raising the helicopter's nose and halting its forward progress. Through the wide windscreen, Cal Holmwood saw the other four transports do likewise, as the two Apaches broke sharply to the left and right, circling around and hovering either side of them.

"What did you do, Bob?" he demanded. "What the hell is going on?"

Allen opened his mouth to respond, but before he could form a single syllable, the night sky lit up as bright as day.

The GBU-32 bunker buster spun down out of the sky at terminal velocity and sliced through the roof of Château Dauncy like a knife through butter.

The bomb was over seven metres long, weighed two and a half

**616**

tons, and carried more than a quarter of a ton of high explosives that was designed to detonate as soon as the bomb reached a complete halt. Which happened when it reached the beautiful, ornate marble floor of the château's lobby.

The explosion ripped through the heart of the old building, blasting up through the roof in a column of fire that was visible for miles in every direction. The east wall, made of heavy grey stone that had stood, unmoving, for centuries, disintegrated completely, blowing up and out in a cloud of dust and a rain of falling rock. The blast wave collapsed the floors of the building, bringing them down on top of each other like a collapsing house of cards, creating a pile of rubble two storeys high within the three remaining walls. The roof was thrown up into the air, and crashed down on the gravel courtyard that surrounded the burning, smoking remains.

"Damn it, Bob!" screamed Holmwood. "Henry is in there, for God's sake! Call it off!"

General Allen rounded on him, his eyes flashing with anger. "Henry Seward is a Blacklight priority," he said. "As far as we're concerned, Dracula is all that matters. And I say that as Henry's friend, because I know he would agree with me."

Holmwood stared at his American counterpart, searching for a way to refute the truth in his friend's words, but coming up empty. Allen returned his gaze for several long seconds, then turned to their pilot.

"Continue," he said.

In the sky to the west of the château, high above the flames rising from the old building, Valeri Rusmanov floated in the air beside his master, his stomach churning with bitter admiration.

*I didn't think they'd bomb us while we had Seward,* he thought. *I obviously underestimated them.*

His master had been so obviously surprised, as he hurtled out on to the balcony, grabbed him by the waist, and launched them both off the roof, that Valeri had been able to carry him clear of the blast zone before his anger had manifested. The first vampire's eyes had flooded black, and he had clearly been about to demand an explanation when the bomb exploded, rendering the question redundant.

"Your followers," said Dracula.

"I sent them to the cellars," said Valeri. "I would imagine the majority have survived."

"Well done, my old friend," said Dracula, and favoured Valeri with a thin smile. "Well done."

"Thank you, my lord," growled Valeri. His relief at having extracted his master was being steadily replaced by a deep, spreading anger. "May I be excused? The battle is upon us."

"You may," said Dracula. "Do what you must."

Paul Turner was out of his seat as soon as the wheels of his helicopter touched down, his T-Bone in hand, his visor down over his face. As Operators from five countries unbuckled themselves around him, he twisted the wide door's handle, and slid it open.

Château Dauncy stood before him, its remaining stone sides surrounding an inferno of orange flame and black smoke that spiralled up into the dark night sky. The helicopters had landed at the edge of the treeline, providing the widest possible space around the building in which to engage the enemy: five hundred metres of gardens and gravel, now studded with broken, burning lumps of the blasted building. Enough room, Turner hoped, for them to make their slight numerical advantage tell, and negate at least part of the speed and agility of their enemy.

He leapt down and surveyed the scene. White light blazed from the Apaches, rendering the courtyard and grounds as bright as day. The smell of the burning building was thick and acrid, and from somewhere inside the remains he could hear screams of pain and terror. There was no sign of movement, in the courtyard or what little of the old building was still standing.

Black figures began to spill out of four of the transports, their boots crunching down on to the gravel, the night air full of the rattle of weapons being made ready to fire. The fifth helicopter, the one nobody was allowed to approach, stood in the centre of the tight line of vehicles, rocking steadily on its wheels.

The howl of the Apache engines was deafening, but Cal Holmwood's voice sounded directly in Turner's earpiece, as clear as a bell.

"As we drew it up, Paul," said the Interim Director. "Good luck."

"What the hell just happened?" Turner asked. "Levelling the château wasn't part of the plan, Cal."

"Ask the bloody Yanks," spat Holmwood. "When this is all over. Go."

Turner allowed himself a brief smile before icy cold settled over him, narrowing his focus to nothing more than the operation and its objectives. He twisted the dial on his belt, then spoke into the ears of every assembled Operator.

"Red Team!" he shouted. "With me."

He walked slowly forward, his mind clear and full of purpose. Almost a hundred and fifty Operators fell quickly into formation behind him, a long, two-deep line of black uniforms and gleaming weaponry. Five metres to his left, three pairs of red eyes glowed in the gloom, and Turner felt his heart swell with confidence at the sight of them.

"Ready One," he shouted. "Go go go!"

The Security Officer ran towards the burning château, his T-Bone raised at his shoulder, a thunder of running footsteps following him across the gravel. The entire eastern wall of the building was gone, replaced by a towering pile of rubble; he could see parts of staircases and walls and floors, all piled together, all open to the night air.

Red Team was still more than three hundred metres from the burning château when Valeri Rusmanov dropped out of the sky in front of them, a wide, angry smile on his face. He stared at them with glowing eyes as they approached, then bellowed something in a language Turner didn't understand.

For a long moment, the crunch of boots on gravel was the only sound. Then a howling, pulsing wave of blackened, smoke-smeared vampires flooded up from the cellars of the old building and raced across the courtyard.

Turner skidded to a halt, twisted the dial on his belt and bellowed, "Now!"

The pilots of the two NS9 Apaches flipped switches on the weapons-control panels in their cockpits.

They were training the two spotlights that hung from their gunships' sidepods on the shattered building, illuminating the crowded mass of vampires rising from the smoking rubble like rats fleeing a fire, their glowing eyes bright scarlet in the powerful beams. With rumbling thuds, ultraviolet filters slid into place over the powerful halogen bulbs, turning the wide beams of light from blinding white to deadly purple.

A millisecond later the screaming started.

The four ultraviolet beams engulfed the vampires as they charged up from the cellars.

There was no chance of avoiding them; the light covered the entire open front of the building, and the vampires burst into flames as soon as they emerged, filling the air with the smell of roasting meat and the high-pitched screams of men and women who were burning alive.

Valeri, who was already advancing towards the black line of Operators, turned back, and howled with fury. A roaring pyre of at least thirty vampires was blazing where the marble lobby of the building had stood, blocking the way in to the cellars and trapping the majority of his followers inside. The burning vampires crawled and screamed and begged for help, as the ones who had been hungriest for violence and bloodshed, the ones who had made it out before the ultraviolet light blazed, stared at their fallen colleagues, their glowing eyes full of sudden panic.

"Attack!" screamed Valeri. "Attack, damn you!"

The vampires who weren't on fire growled in response, then turned towards the advancing line of Operators, and hurled themselves forward. Behind them, the wide ultraviolet beams raked back and forth across the ruined château, engulfing burning vampires who were still trying to crawl away and picking off those who were staring blankly at the carnage that had erupted around them, frozen to the spot.

Valeri looked up at the two Apaches, felt himself pushed back across the gravel by the downdraught of their rotors, and roared with uncontrollable rage; this was not how the battle was supposed to have begun, with his followers burning and trapped inside the shell of what had once been his favourite place in the world.

His howl died away, as he forced himself to think clearly. Then he took a deep breath, and rocketed into the air, as fast and deadly as a cruise missile.

*Didn't see that coming, did you?* thought Cal Holmwood, allowing himself a vicious moment of satisfaction. *That must have been quite a shock.*

The Interim Director of Blacklight was standing at the treeline, where a great cheer had gone up from the men and women of Blue Team as purple light filled the courtyard; the rank and file had been as surprised as the vampires who were now roasting on the château steps. Only he, Paul Turner, and Bob Allen had known; the element of surprise had been absolutely vital.

*And I've got another one for you,* he thought. *A big one.*

Holmwood looked over at the pair of Operators standing beside the only helicopter that had not yet discharged its cargo.

"Be ready," he shouted.

The two figures nodded, and took hold of the handle that would slide open the transport's side door.

"On my go," shouted Holmwood.

*This is going to be something to see,* he thought.

Jamie dropped to one knee as the vampires who had avoided the ultraviolet light surged forward, raised his MP7 to his shoulder, and squeezed the trigger.

Fire licked from the end of the gun's barrel as bullets tore across the courtyard. The vampires at the front of the pack parted like liquid, sliding out of the path of the deadly hail of lead and continuing their charge; the ones behind them were not so lucky. Jamie's bullets punched holes in their knees and thighs and ankles, shattering bone and sending blood spraying into the air. The smell hit his nose instantly; his eyes darkened, his fangs slid down from his gums, and a guttural growl of desire rumbled involuntarily from his throat.

Half a dozen vampires crashed to the ground, screaming in pain, clutching at bullet holes the size of wine corks, their heads thrown back, their eyes flickering red. The air was suddenly full of the smell of cordite and a sound like metallic thunder as Jamie's colleagues opened up on the advancing vampires. For a second, he was momentarily overwhelmed, as something he had never felt before exploded out from his stomach and filled him to the tips of his fingers.

It was bloodlust, pure and simple.

Jamie growled again, and flung himself towards the enemy.

Captain John McDonnell turned his head, sending ultraviolet light sweeping to the left in a sharp arc; Viper 2's spotlights had been slaved to the heads-up display projected on to the windscreen, and responded to the movement of sensors located in his visor. He drifted the helicopter left and craned his head further in the same direction, chasing a staggering vampire and enveloping him in ultraviolet light; he erupted with purple fire and slumped to the gravel, his hands beating weakly at the flames.

McDonnell, who had served as a gunner in Apaches above the snow-capped rises and deep valleys of the Hindu Kush and the oilfields of southern Iraq before being recruited into NS9, and had seen more than his fair share of terrible things through a helicopter windscreen, never ceased to be amazed at the effect the purple light had on vampires; it barely had to touch them before they went up like roman candles.

*Like they've been soaked in jet fuel,* he marvelled.

The Apache swung back and up, angling her nose down as McDonnell searched for movement in the burning château. He was so engrossed in his task that he didn't see the vampire hurtling up from beneath him, as silent and deadly as a shark rising from the depths.

Valeri slammed into the underside of the gunship, his eyes blazing, his head pounding with fury. The helicopter lurched upwards and pitched wildly to the left, its engines screaming as he swooped away, then accelerated towards it again.

He crashed into the windscreen, shattering it, and shoved himself into the cockpit, paying no attention to the strips of skin the broken plexiglass peeled from his arms and shoulders. The gunner cried out, and reached for his sidearm with one hand as the pilot tried desperately to stabilise the Apache; Valeri swung a fist with every ounce of strength he possessed, and hammered it into the man's face. His head burst like a watermelon, gushing out from the shattered plastic of his helmet in a steaming torrent of blood, as his hands grabbed reflexively at nothing. Valeri surged forward, climbing over the gunner's twitching corpse, and sank his fingers into the pilot's throat. He tore it out with a sound like ripping paper, then turned back towards the broken windscreen, leaving the man gurgling out his final breaths.

The Apache bucked and lurched, then spun helplessly towards the ground, its rotors churning futilely, its engines howling. Valeri punched out the remainder of the windscreen as the gravel courtyard rushed up towards him, threw himself through the hole, and pirouetted up and away from the stricken helicopter as it slammed nose first into the ground. There was a millisecond of silence, then the Apache exploded with a hammering thud of noise and heat as its fuel tanks breached, sending a mushroom cloud of orange fire and black smoke billowing into the air.

Valeri was already moving, soaring above the courtyard with the heat of the explosion at his back. Viper 1 pivoted nimbly in the air, its ultraviolet spotlights sweeping towards him; he flung himself beneath them as the second Apache's gunner fired his 30mm chain guns. The noise was simply astonishing, a deafening drumbeat of explosions so loud it felt as though bells were being slammed together inside Valeri's skull. The heavy bullets ripped through the air as fire spat from the barrels of the guns, and Valeri dodged left and right, swooping and diving, flying for his life; he knew that a single one of the bullets could take off his arm or his leg and send him tumbling to the ground, where he would be easy meat for a fortunate Operator. He closed in on the gunship, faster than its targeting systems could follow, then raced between the purple beams and over the top of the squat, ugly helicopter.

The punishing updraught of the rotors sent him tumbling, but he righted himself, and swooped out of the turbulent air before the pilot had time to bring the Apache about. He caught hold of the gunship's long fuselage in front of its vertical tail rotor, and punched a fist through the thin metal housing. The pilot, clearly aware of where Valeri was, spun the Apache in a stomach-churning arc, but the ancient vampire dug in, his knuckles white, the muscles in his arms screaming, and kept his grip. He reached inside the helicopter, grabbed hold of handfuls of wires and cables, and tore them out.

The effect was immediate.

Above Valeri's head, the tail rotors spluttered and whined as sparks leapt from the ragged hole he had made. Where the helicopter had felt immovable, even to him, like something he had to simply hang on to and hope for the best, it suddenly felt like dead weight, as though *he* had become the only thing keeping it in the air. Its nose tipped precariously towards the ground, and Valeri went with it, letting the Apache swing beneath him; as it rose back up, he let go of its tail.

The black gunship flipped end over end, its engines dead, and slammed on to the gravel. It skidded forward, digging a long ditch and throwing up a huge cloud of dust, and crashed into the row of transport helicopters. The first was cracked almost in half by the sliding Apache, its rotor blades breaking and exploding across the courtyard like razor-sharp bullets. Metal shrieked like a wounded animal as the gunship ploughed forward, dragging half of the first transport with it, and came to a halt with its nose stuck through the open door of the second.

Below Valeri, shouts of alarm mingled with screams of pain. He wasted no time waiting to see whether the second Apache would explode as gloriously as the first; he fixed his gaze on the devastated eastern side of the château, and accelerated towards it.

Larissa threw aside the dripping head of a vampire and faced the ruined building.

Behind her, thick black smoke billowed up from the remains of the burning Apache, and she could hear shouted orders and torrents of swearing and cursing from the men and women gathered at the line of transports, one of which now lay in broken pieces. With the ultraviolet beams extinguished, the purple fire covering the vampires quickly died away, leaving a smoking pile of blackened, roasted bodies.

A vampire woman in her fifties leapt towards Larissa as something streaked across the courtyard, so fast it was little more than a blur; it rocketed over the heads of men and women moving and shooting and biting and clawing, the noise of guns and T-Bones mingling with screams of pain and howls of terror. Larissa turned, saw the vampire woman's eyes widen with surprise, and swung a fist with all the power of a wrecking ball. It slammed into the side of the woman's head, shattering her skull and sending her flying through the air, her limbs dangling uselessly, the red glow in her eyes snuffed out. She crashed into a jagged fragment of the château's east wall and crumpled to the ground in an ungainly heap.

Larissa turned back towards the devastated centre of the old building, searching for the source of the blur that had moved overhead. She focused her supernaturally sharp eyes in time to see Valeri Rusmanov plough into the pile of burnt vampires, sending charred limbs and ragged lumps of seared red and black meat into the air. When the pile was cleared, he bellowed at the ground, then turned and threw himself back into the fight.

Instantly, vampires began to once more spill up out of the château's cellars. They spat and hissed as they emerged, their clothes and bodies smeared with dust and blood, their glowing eyes settling on the black-clad figures of Red Team.

High above the courtyard, Dracula watched and smiled as battle was joined in earnest.

He had been surprised and impressed by the initial tactics of his enemy; the bomb that had exploded with such beautiful, devastating force was the attack of an opponent for whom victory was the only thing that mattered, and following it by pinning his forces underground with ultraviolet light had been a masterstroke. It had taken self-restraint not to applaud, even as Valeri's followers screamed and burned below him; their forces had sustained significant casualties by the time his oldest servant made short work of the helicopters and their deadly beams. Dracula was not worried, however; he knew he was watching the early stages of the battle, that it was still taking shape and settling down.

There had been times in his youth when his cause had appeared lost within minutes of the trumpeters falling silent, but on each occasion his forces had eventually triumphed. He knew, better than anyone alive, that battles always came down to will, to who would risk the most for the sake of victory, which was why what was unfolding in the courtyard below was so fascinating; there could be no retreat here, no settlement or negotiated peace. Both sides would fight to their last breath, because what was at stake was not ideology, or religion, or some gilded throne.

At stake was annihilation.

Far below, Valeri cleared the smouldering remains away from the entrances to the cellars, and Dracula watched as a new wave of vampires poured up into the courtyard. He smiled to himself, enjoying the cold air as it floated across his skin, observing the battlefield with expert eyes. His enemy's second force was still gathered at the treeline, close to what remained of the helicopters they had arrived in. The influx of vampires from beneath the château would now surely draw them into the battle, and once reinforcements were no longer a factor, the tide would turn one way or the other.

*And then I will know,* he thought. *Whether I am to remain a mere spectator, or whether I will be required to bloody my hands.*

And as he watched the black figures moving among the trees at the edge of the courtyard, he realised how fervently he hoped it would be the latter.

\* \* \*

Cal Holmwood bellowed for Blue Team to regroup; they had been scattered by the explosion of the first Apache and the crash of the second that had taken out two of their transports. They fell quickly back into line, their faces hidden behind purple visors, as the Interim Director surveyed the battlefield.

The men and women of the Combined Operational Force were fighting with every bit of the skill and courage he had expected, firing and staking and sending blood gushing into the air as they drove the vampires back across the courtyard. But the fighting had already claimed a number of casualties; strewn around the wide space were the dark shapes of fallen Operators, their bodies twisted into unnatural angles, wide pools of crimson spreading beneath them.

Holmwood could not allow himself to think about them.

Not now.

They had pressed their early advantage well, but new vampires were emerging from the burning château in a seemingly endless torrent, and it was vital that he kept momentum moving in their favour.

Cal turned to the Operators stationed outside the sealed transport helicopter; they looked at him expectantly, their gloved hands gripping the handles of the door.

"Go," he said.

# 59

# THE STORM, PART TWO

### CHÂTEAU DAUNCY
### AQUITAINE, SOUTH-WESTERN FRANCE

The huge wolf poked its snout through the helicopter's open door and sniffed the cold night air. There was heat, and violence, and blood, and the sweet, sharp smell of fear, of animals cornered and desperate. A low growl rumbled from its throat, shaking the metal box in which it had been locked for too long.

The wolf's mind was a swirling mixture of anger and frustration, held in check by the tiny part of itself that was still Victor Frankenstein. The memory of the change was fresh, full of the sharp sounds of cracking bones and screams that had become howls as its body was reshaped against its will. The desire to run, to clear away the pain, roared through its head. During its long confinement in the helicopter, it had remained dimly aware of where it was, and what was happening to it; now such almost rational thoughts were gone, driven away by the tantalising scents that filled its nostrils, by the joyful instinct to chase, and hunt.

To kill.

The wolf stepped out of the transport, its huge paws crunching the gravel beneath them, its tail sweeping from side to side, and took a longer, deeper breath. The night air was intoxicating, an almost physical thing that existed far beyond the sensation of mere human beings. Frankenstein's remaining consciousness drank it in, savouring the single thing that he always missed when the moon waned and his body broke back to normal; the air made him feel like he was profoundly connected to the world around him, rather than floating obliviously across the surface.

The wolf's vision began to focus; the pitch darkness of the metal box had dulled the sharpness of its huge yellow eyes, but now they were clearing. Shapes surged back and forth across the curved field, their visible selves mixing with the scents that emanated so clearly from their bodies, creating something that was both less and more than sight. Many of the shapes roared with heat, glowing a colour that was impossible to describe, and Frankenstein's last coherent thought before he began to run was to desperately order himself not to hurt the shapes that were dark and cold.

The wolf took a step forward, its huge head sweeping left and right, its growl deepening and rising in volume, then another, and another. Then it was running, bounding forward on legs that felt as strong as tree trunks, the wind whipping through its fur, the mingled sensation utterly indescribable; an ecstasy of primal physical movement and a profound feeling of fulfilled purpose.

It ran towards the hot, billowing square of the building, racing across the ground, its tongue hanging joyously from the corner of its mouth. The smells of blood and fear intensified as it reached the edge of the battle, triggering sensory explosions inside a mind that was now almost entirely animal, and it accelerated towards a figure at the centre of its vision, a pillar of heat and light and cruel pleasure. The wolf ran forward, relishing the cries of surprise and blooms of terror that accompanied its passing, and leapt gracefully into the air.

For a glorious moment, there was nothing in the entire world except the animal and the cold air rushing over its body. Then it crashed into the glowing figure, its huge front paws sinking their claws into its shoulders and driving it to the ground. The pain that erupted from the pores of the thrashing, squirming vampire was exquisite, and the wolf drove its claws deeper, allowing itself a moment to savour the resulting scream. Then it turned its long snout to the side, opened a mouth full of teeth the length of carving knives, and clamped its jaws round the vampire's throat.

A gout of blood, hot and bittersweet, spurted from the torn jugular, filling the wolf's mouth. The animal reared back, tearing out the meat and muscle of the neck and leaving the vampire's head attached by only the dripping bones of his spine, and swallowed. Blood and flesh tumbled down its gullet and a sensation spread through its body that was far more than just pleasure; it was a deep sense of *happiness*.

The wolf threw back its head and howled, a vast sound that chilled the bones of everyone who heard it. Then it charged across the battlefield, the stricken vampire already forgotten, its mind focused entirely on its next kill.

Valentin Rusmanov watched the massive grey-green wolf stalk a vampire who had to be at least in his early forties, and allowed himself a small smile.

The vampire was backpedalling furiously, his hands raised in a futile gesture of surrender as the animal came for him, its snout low to the ground, a growl that sounded strangely close to laughter rumbling from its blood-soaked muzzle. It was toying with him, swiping its huge paws lazily through the air, until it eventually got bored and leapt forward, pinning the screaming, pleading vampire to the ground. As the jaws snapped shut and the scream was silenced, Valentin found himself empathising with the misshapen creature.

He was bored too.

As he moved forward with the rest of Red Team, he had felt an emotion that he had not been expecting: a strong, strange rush of nostalgia. When he looked back on the life he had led as a human, it was predominantly with a sense of shame; not for the things he had done to men and women who had not deserved them, but for the meek, subservient creature he had once been. He had turned his back on his family after Dracula had been rendered dormant by Van Helsing and his friends, and he had never regretted the decision for a single moment; if anything, he wished he had made it sooner. But as he flew forward, his eyes full of fire, with an enemy before him and comrades at his sides, nostalgia had filled him, if only for a moment. He had fought so many battles, against so many enemies, and there was always a moment when the reasons and the justifications faded away, leaving only the fighting itself, short and violent and thrilling, and the outcome.

Win or lose.

Live or die.

Valentin had destroyed three vampires within the first two minutes of the battle, tearing out their hearts and crushing them before they had time to realise what had befallen them; they had burst with looks of genuine surprise on their faces. His uniform was already coated with steaming blood and strings of exploded flesh, but he paid the mess no attention; his eyes glowed crimson as he slid through the flailing, swinging vampires, as quick and sure-footed as they were panicked and undisciplined. The number of punches and kicks and swipes of clubs and blades aimed at him made it clear that he was a highly sought-after target, the result, no doubt, of orders given by his older brother, or his former master, or both. But Valentin was so much more powerful than the average vampire that he might as well have been a different species, and not a single hand had been laid on him thus far.

He had leapt clear of the flying remains of his third kill, then grabbed a vampire who had been about to sink his fangs into the throat of one of the South African Operators and raised him into the air. He hurled the squirming man to the gravel, heard his bones break with a satisfying series of crunches, and was moving again before the Operator had time to thank him. He scanned the battlefield with his supernatural eyes, searching for bigger game.

Valentin knew that it would ultimately make no difference how many of his brother's followers they destroyed; there would always be more, men and women desperate and unhappy enough to voluntarily enslave themselves to the whims of monsters. If he and the Operators destroyed every single one, but Valeri and Dracula survived, then it would all have been for nothing; the men and women lying dead and dying on the gravel would have given their lives for no reason.

He saw no sign yet of his former master on the battlefield, although this was no surprise; until the last frantic months of his final reign as the Prince of Wallachia, Dracula had overseen his battles from astride his horse, surrounded by his royal guard. Valentin knew that the first vampire would be itching to spill blood, but he also knew that he would resist the urge unless his involvement became necessary; Dracula was a General, not a soldier.

Valeri, on the other hand, had never had any such reservations.

Valentin's eyes darkened and a grin rose on to his face as he saw his brother tear off an Operator's arm and throw it almost casually into the distant trees. Valeri kicked the howling man to the ground and pinned his shoulders with his knees, his hands balled into fists, his huge shoulders hunched, his face a mask of grim determination.

Valentin slid left until he was directly behind his preoccupied brother, then flew silently towards him, his fangs gleaming in the bright light of the full moon.

Jamie leapt into the air, his stake in his hand, and collided with a snarling female vampire; the metal point punctured her torso just below her ribs, and he pushed it up, blood pouring out over his wrist and down his arm, until it pierced her heart. Her eyes flew wide, the red light in them fading away, and then she burst, showering him with steaming blood. Jamie hung in the air, his eyes glowing, his fangs huge and gleaming, and surveyed the carnage being unleashed around him.

The air was thick with the smoke of gunfire and the coppery smell of freshly spilled blood. The fighting had spread out across the wide courtyard, pockets of black-clad Operators standing their ground against a horde of vampires who swooped through the air, growling and snarling and trailing red light.

Screams of pain and fear punctured the heavy rattle of guns and T-Bones, and patches of the gravel were soaked almost black with blood. Frankenstein was charging through the chaos in his wolf form like a missile, tearing and clawing and biting as vampires hurled themselves out of his reach. In the distance, Jamie saw Jack Williams fire his T-Bone, spearing a vamp out of the air and hauling her to the ground, where she popped like a balloon full of blood. He could not, even with his supernatural eyesight, identify any of the fallen Operators; in almost every case, their visors covered their faces.

Jamie looked round and saw Valentin Rusmanov approaching his brother from behind; Valeri seemed oblivious, his attention fixed on the Operator he was pummelling into soup with his huge, pale fists. He was about to fly to Valentin's side, to help him move on the operation's second highest priority, when something incredibly strong grabbed him by the shoulders and spun him round. Jamie reared back, cursing himself for losing focus, for staying still for too long, then saw who had taken hold of him.

"Jesus, Larissa," he said. "You scared me half to death."

His girlfriend grinned, her mouth and chin smeared with blood, her eyes boiling crimson-black. There was no sign of her helmet; she had presumably cast it aside at some point after the fighting had begun.

*She could have shouted,* he thought, as he looked into her eyes. *She could have said my name. But she* wanted *to scare me. Her vampire side is completely in charge.*

"Go and find Henry," said Larissa. "Now, while we've got them on the ropes."

"Find him?" said Jamie, and motioned towards the ruined château. "In there?"

Larissa nodded. "He's still alive," she said. "I can smell him. Can't you?"

Jamie tipped back his head and inhaled deeply. "No," he said. "I can't."

"I can," she growled.

"All right," said Jamie. "Then come with me."

Larissa shook her head. "It doesn't need both of us," she said. "I'm more useful out here."

Jamie glanced down at the gloved hands that were holding him; they looked like they had been painted red.

*If I run into Dracula inside the château, I might need you,* he thought. *But that wasn't what you really meant, was it? You don't want to come with me because you're having too much fun out here.*

"Fine," he said. "Stay here."

She grinned, then rocketed away without another word. Jamie watched her go, wondering how many times already her twisted grin had been the last thing a vampire saw.

"Jamie," shouted a familiar voice from the ground below him. He looked down and saw Angela Darcy looking up at him, her visor pushed back, her face pale.

"Angela," said Jamie. "Are you OK?"

"Surviving," she said. "Are you going for Admiral Seward?"

"Yes," he said. "I am."

Angela smiled, an expression that contained far more anger than humour. "Good," she said. "Then let's go."

Paul Turner threw himself to the ground as the wolf bounded past him, its yellow eyes locked on the shape of a fleeing vampire. The animal, growling with what seemed to Turner like utter delight, swung a huge paw at him as it passed, but he didn't take it personally; he didn't think it wanted to hurt him, but rather that its instinct to chase and hunt was now simply too powerful to overcome.

He scrambled back to his feet, his MP7 in his hands, and sent a volley of fire into a vampire that was flying towards him with a hungry look on her blood-streaked face. The bullets punched a patchwork of holes in her stomach, and her expression changed to one of agony as she turned and fled, trailing blood and purple guts behind her as she broke for the trees. Turner smiled narrowly as she disappeared from view, then surveyed the battle, regaining his bearings.

A single thought was pounding through his mind, no matter how hard he tried to ignore it.

*We might win this. We might actually win this thing.*

Casualties on both sides were already appalling, but crucially, at least as far as he could tell with the naked eye and through the filters of his visor, they were worse for the vamps than for the Combined Operational Force. The release of Frankenstein in his wolf form had caused panic among Valeri's followers, perfectly understandably; they had not expected to be confronted with a wild animal the size of a small car as well as Operators with all their weapons and training. Frankenstein had been the second, and last, of the tricks Cal Holmwood had been able to put up his sleeve at such short notice, and while it had not been as loud or explosive as the surprise that Bob Allen had arranged, it was proving highly effective; now it would come down to the men and women who were fighting so fiercely for each other, and for the future of the world.

Across the courtyard, he saw Cal Holmwood raise an arm, and sweep it forward. The Operators of Blue Team swarmed out from among the transport helicopters and joined the fight, their weapons thundering.

The thought appeared in Turner's mind again, unbidden but even more insistent.

*We might win this. Damn it, we really might.*

Jamie raced towards the ruins of Château Dauncy, Angela Darcy sprinting at his side.

Smoking rubble piled up before them, teetering unsteadily as flames from a hundred small fires licked at it, the smoke and dust almost obscuring the remains of a door frame in the corner of the shattered space, and the stairs that led down from beneath it. Jamie pointed, but Angela was already moving, clambering over fallen stone and shattered wood and descending the stairs, her T-Bone resting easily against her shoulder. He grinned, and followed her.

At the bottom of the stairs stood a stone passage, leading away to the left and right. Pieces of the vampires who had been too close to the entrance when the Apaches turned on their ultraviolet beams were spread across the walls and floor, charred lumps that smoked in the cold air. The smell was nauseating, sweet and rotten.

"Which way?" asked Angela.

Jamie tilted back his head and stretched his newly improved senses, searching past the aroma of burning meat for some sign of Henry Seward: the sound of his voice, a mention of his name, the essential *scent* of the Blacklight Director. He could smell blood, and fire, the sweet heady perfume of wine, and somewhere in the distance he could hear a woman's steady, terrified weeping. He pushed harder, concentrating until his head felt like it was going to burst, and was rewarded; from somewhere in the distance, his nose picked up a familiar smell.

"This way," he said, and flew quickly down the passage to the left. Angela followed him, her feet thudding on the stone floor. They passed a fallen vampire, crushed beneath a section of wall that had collapsed under the impact of the bomb, but still alive. He clawed weakly at them as they passed, his flickering red eyes seeming to focus on nothing; Angela skidded to a halt, and drew her stake from her belt.

"Leave him," said Jamie, his eyes flaring. "He's not what we're here for."

Angela nodded, replaced the stake, and followed him deeper into the cellars. They passed stone archways that opened on to square rooms full of wine racks that would have kept even the most discerning of oenophiles in raptures until their dying day. Several had been tipped over, covering the floors with broken glass and liquid that looked like blood, and smelt almost as sweet.

"Left or right?" asked Angela, as they reached the end of the passage.

Jamie closed his eyes for a long moment, searching for the scent; it was the accumulation of Henry Seward, the smell of his skin and sweat, of his very essence leaking from his pores. He found it, stronger now than before, and pointed down the left-hand corridor.

Angela nodded. Then her eyes widened with warning, and Jamie was moving before she had time to make a sound.

He dropped into a crouch, and felt the air ripple as a huge wooden club was swung through the space where his head had been less than a second earlier. He spun back to his feet and saw a middle-aged vampire struggling for balance with a look of enormous surprise on his face; he had almost swung himself off his feet. Jamie didn't give the man a chance to recover; he launched himself forward, slamming his attacker into the wall with a deafening crash.

The stone cracked under the impact, covering them with dust. Jamie grabbed the vampire by the throat and flew straight upwards, driving the man's head into the ceiling. His eyes rolled and his arms went limp as Jamie spun in the air and threw him to the ground on his back. He had time to let out a single low moan before Angela darted forward and staked him. She leapt back as the vampire exploded, spraying the floor and ceiling with blood, then smiled at Jamie.

"Nice moves," she said. "Vampirism seems to suit you."

Jamie grinned. "Maybe," he said. "It makes some things easier, I'll say that much for it."

"Come on," said Angela. "Let's find Henry."

Jamie nodded, and flew down the corridor. More arches revealed more rooms, but it took only a cursory glance to ascertain that Seward was not in any of them; they were filled with bunk beds and fold-up mattresses, giving them the appearance of dormitories, or barracks.

*Which is exactly what they are*, thought Jamie. *Sleeping quarters for Valeri's army.*

Valeri realised Valentin was behind him a millisecond before the punch landed on the back of his neck.

The impact was devastating; it drove all thought momentarily from his mind as he crashed to the gravel, his vision filled with fireworks of white and red. Acting on nothing more than animal instinct, he threw himself forward across the ground and rolled over in time to see a foot slam down where his head had been. He summoned up reserves of strength, climbed to his feet, and faced his brother.

Valentin was smiling at him, his eyes glowing pale red. He was wearing the all-black uniform of the enemy; the sight of it turned Valeri's stomach, and sent fury boiling through him.

"There are no depths to which you will not sink, are there?" he growled. "No betrayal too great. Mother should have drowned you when you were born."

Valentin rolled his eyes, his smile widening. "Shall we get this over with, brother?" he said. "We both know that you can't beat me, so if you surrender I'll make it quick."

"Surrender?" said Valeri, his eyes narrowing with disgust. "To you? I would die a thousand times first."

"A thousand times seems excessive," said Valentin. "Once will be fine."

The youngest Rusmanov's smile twisted into a snarl of pure violence. He took a quick step to one side, then shot forward, his speed shocking even to Valeri's heightened senses. The elder Rusmanov leapt backwards and swung a haymaker towards where he believed Valentin's face was about to be, but connected with nothing. Valentin ducked the punch as though Valeri had thrown it in slow motion, and slammed a fist into his throat with a sound like breaking crockery.

And suddenly Valeri couldn't breathe.

His eyes bulged as he slid to his knees, his hands clutching at his damaged neck, his body shaking. Valentin circled away with a look of pity on his face, a look that filled Valeri with fear.

*Dear God, he doesn't even intend to finish me. He's just going to watch me choke.*

Valeri ran his fingers over his throat, forcing himself to stay calm. The flesh was already beginning to swell, but he could feel his compacted trachea beneath it, the tube that should be carrying air into lungs that were already screaming for relief. Horror flooded through him as he realised what he needed to do, mixing with the furious shame of having been bested again, so easily, by his brother.

He tipped his head back, pain pulsing through his head and chest, and ripped open a hole in the side of his neck with his bare fingers. Blood gushed down his arm as new agony roared through him, but he ignored it; he pushed his fingers into the hole, past the muscles and tendons, and took hold of his bent and swollen trachea. With panic rising through him, he began to massage the sides of the wounded pipe with his forefinger and thumb, trying to persuade it to reopen.

For a long moment, nothing happened.

Then, with a sound like a newborn's first breath, air whistled down his damaged throat and into his lungs.

Relief flooded through him as he took a deep, rattling breath. He felt some of his strength return, along with a terror beyond anything he had ever experienced. He staggered to his feet, his hand and neck and chest soaked with his own blood, and faced his brother again.

Valentin smiled. "I'm impressed, brother," he said. "Nothing quite like conducting surgery on yourself."

Valeri swayed on unsteady legs. He needed to buy time, to feed and recover; his brother, his hateful, wet little brother who had always been his mother's favourite, was so fast, so unbelievably fast and strong. His terror threatened to overwhelm him as he stared at Valentin. Then he turned and leapt into the air, searching the battlefield with wide, panicked eyes for a way to regroup.

Valentin's hand closed round his ankle.

For a single, seemingly endless moment, Valeri hung stationary in the air, as his power and his brother's cancelled each other out. Then Valentin jerked his arm down, whipping Valeri towards the gravel, his arms flailing helplessly.

He hit the ground face first.

Valeri's nose exploded as his front teeth shattered, sending fresh pain barrelling through his head; it was overwhelming, but he fought against it with all the strength he had left, desperate to keep moving. He crawled forward, staggered to his feet and spun round, lashing out blindly with his fists. As his vision cleared, he found his brother staring at him coldly.

"Men don't run," said Valentin. "You taught me that, brother. Men stand and fight."

Rage thundered through Valeri, momentarily drowning out the pain and fear. He growled, and spread his arms wide. "Come to me then, brother," he said. "Let us finish this."

Valentin smiled. "Your wish is my—"

The words stopped abruptly as Valentin's face changed. His eyes darkened black, and his mouth fell open, as though his power had suddenly been cut. His head rolled slowly backwards, until he was staring up at the sky, his arms hanging limply at his sides.

Valeri wasted no time wondering what was happening. He launched himself forward with everything he had and landed an uppercut on his brother's chin that would have knocked over a building. Valentin hurtled into the air, trailing a torrent of blood, and disappeared over the dark expanse of the forest.

Dracula felt a rush of irritation spread through him as Valeri slumped to the ground, clutching his throat as his brother circled him. The eldest Rusmanov was a disappointment in so many ways, and would likely not survive the night, whatever the outcome of the battle, but removing him from the field at this point would tip the scales in favour of his enemies, and that could not be allowed.

*It's time to end this,* he thought, and felt familiar excitement dance up his spine. *It has gone on long enough.*

He would have readily admitted that Blacklight and its allies had proven themselves worthy opponents; they had been creative, and clever, and thrown themselves into the fight with undoubted bravery and skill. But they were still merely human, with the exception of the wolf and their handful of tame vampires, and no match for what he felt in his bones he had again become.

*A god.*

Dracula drew his sword and descended, like the blade of a guillotine. As the ground rose up towards him, Valentin looked directly at him, his eyes black, his mouth hanging open. Then Valeri swung a punch that connected with a sound like a cannon, and the youngest Rusmanov was gone.

Dracula accelerated, and landed with an impact that echoed across the courtyard. For a long moment, there was silence, as every pair of eyes turned towards him. He stood up straight, and raised his sword as Operators and vampires alike regarded him with stunned horror.

Dracula smiled, and narrowed his eyes.

Then he roared into battle with the force of a hurricane, hacking and rending and growling with the sheer, unadulterated pleasure of violence.

And the surviving Operators, who had begun to tentatively share Paul Turner's belief that they might yet carry the day, understood the reality of their situation.

They had never stood a chance.

# 60

# THE STORM, PART THREE

### CHÂTEAU DAUNCY
### AQUITAINE, SOUTH-WESTERN FRANCE

"So tell me something," said Angela. "If you and Larissa have kids, are they going to come out with fangs and glowing red eyes?"

Jamie stared at her, incredulous. "Are you actually kidding me?" he asked.

Angela smiled. "I'm just making conversation."

"Now, though?" asked Jamie. "Right now? Really?"

Angela's smile widened. "I'm just asking what everyone is wondering," she said. "No need to be so touchy about it."

"Let's talk about it later," said Jamie. "Maybe when the fate of the world isn't resting in our hands?"

"Fine," said Angela, and rolled her eyes theatrically. "Although I'm sure you used to be more fun. Let's get on with it then."

Jamie couldn't help but smile; Angela Darcy was one of the deadliest human beings he had ever met, a woman whose highly classified career was soaked in blood, but she was also one of the most effortlessly charming, and most intelligent. As he reached the end of the passage and stopped in front of a door with a heavy padlock hanging from it, he realised how much calmer he felt, and marvelled at her cleverness.

*I doubt she's ever said a single word without thinking it through first,* he thought. *It sounded like she was fishing for gossip, but she knew it would take my mind off what we're doing. She's never less than two steps ahead of me.*

Henry Seward's scent was stronger than ever as Jamie twisted open the padlock and turned the door's handle. The room beyond it was small, containing only a porcelain sink and a cast-iron bed frame, topped with a bare mattress.

Lying on the thin rectangle of material was Admiral Henry Seward.

Jamie gasped out loud; the sight of the Director was so shocking that he was simply unable to stop himself.

Seward looked as though he had aged ten years in the months since Valeri had stolen him from the Loop. His skin was grey and deeply lined, and hung from his bones like old meat. An eyepatch covered a socket that Jamie presumed was empty, and scars, thick ridges of bright white, criss-crossed his arms and face. His fingertips were wrapped in bloody bandages, and his skin was bruised black and purple.

If he hadn't been able to see the Director's chest rising and falling, Jamie's first assumption would have been that he was looking at a corpse.

"Oh my God," said Angela, her voice tiny beside him.

Seward lifted his head from the mattress and looked at them with a single eye that was filmy and bloodshot. Then something passed across his face, the ghost of an expression of concern.

"Look out..." he croaked.

Jamie's eyes flared red; he spun round and shoved Angela Darcy backwards. She stumbled along the corridor, shouting in protest, but he ignored her; he was turning back into Henry Seward's cell as a vampire woman leapt from behind the door and tore Jamie's throat out with her fingernails.

Cal Holmwood watched Dracula drop from the sky and screamed for the Combined Operational Force to regroup.

It made no difference.

The first vampire was nothing short of a force of nature, a blur of death and mayhem, too fast for the eye to follow. Within thirty seconds of him joining the fight, Holmwood saw four Operators fall at the edge of his sword, limbs hacked clean away, blood pumping into the air in crimson freshets. He bellowed into his helmet's microphone, his words sounding directly in the ears of every Operator still standing, ordering them to fall back and create separation, but for every one who obeyed his order, there was another who was simply frozen to the spot, unable to tear their gaze away from the horror that had been unleashed in their midst.

Cal unholstered his MP7, fired a burst into the air, and ran headlong into the battle. He dodged between Operators and vampires, ducking thrown punches and whistling stakes, heading towards the château, in front of the remains of which Dracula had played his last, most devastating card.

Himself.

A vampire lunged from nowhere and landed a glancing blow on the side of his helmet; he tumbled to the ground, his ears ringing. The MP7 spilled from his grip, and he drew the metal stake from his belt as he rolled on to his back, searching for his attacker. He brought it up as the vampire, who looked barely more than a teenager in his T-shirt and ripped jeans, flung himself down towards him.

The stake slid into the vampire's chest like a knife through butter, stopping the man's fangs centimetres from Holmwood's face. They snapped together, as blood and spit poured on to Holmwood's cheeks and chin, and a pair of red eyes glowered at him; he saw the wide black pupils at the centre of the swirling crimson before the stake worked its way into the vampire's heart, and he exploded across Holmwood's face and body in a vast, steaming deluge.

Cal stifled a cry of disgust, and pushed himself backwards across the ground, his boot heels digging long trenches in the gravel. He felt something hard against his lower back, and turned to see his MP7 lying on the ground. He grabbed it, clambered to his feet, and looked wildly around the battlefield, looking for Paul Turner, looking for—

*Crunch.*

Holmwood rocked forward on the balls of his feet, then looked down at his stomach. The tip of a blade, impossibly wide and wickedly sharp, was sticking out of the black fabric of his uniform. He frowned, confused by what he was seeing, and tried to take a breath.

Nothing happened.

His body seemed to be frozen, locked in some limbo state; he couldn't move, or breathe. Then there was a noise like raw steak being sliced, and the metal tip disappeared. A millisecond later the pain arrived, and he realised what had happened to him.

Cal Holmwood sank to his knees, blood pouring out of a hole in his stomach that seemed almost ridiculous; it was so big, so wide and clean at the edges, that even as his system began to shut down and send him into shock, he wanted to laugh.

Nobody could have a hole that big in their gut and still be alive.

Not for long, at least.

As he pressed his gloved hands to the wound, trying futilely to stem the torrent of steaming blood, he heard the crunch of footsteps on gravel and raised his head. Standing in front of him, with an enormous sword in his hand and an expression on his face that seemed almost benevolent, was Dracula.

"Do not despair," said the ancient vampire, his voice low and gentle. "Your men fought well. They were a credit to you. But you could never have prevailed."

Holmwood tried to speak, but his mouth filled instantly with blood. He gagged, choked down some of the horribly warm liquid, and managed to spit the rest of it out on to the gravel.

"You could be turned," said Dracula, his eyes glowing softly. "Even now there might still be time. But you would not want that, and I would not insult you by insisting. I will give you the dignity of a clean death, one commander of men to another."

Cal Holmwood looked up at the vampire, searching for mercy, for humanity in the monster's face, and finding none.

*I'm sorry,* he thought. *I tried.*

As Dracula swung the sword, he closed his eyes.

To Paul Turner, it seemed to happen in slow motion.

The sword moved through the air as slowly and inevitably as a storm cloud and slid through Cal Holmwood's neck as though it was as insubstantial as smoke. For a terrible moment, one that Turner would relive over and over in his worst nightmares, nothing happened. Then his friend's head slid to one side and tumbled to the ground. Blood spurted up from the stump of his neck in a wide arc as the decapitated body toppled over on to the gravel.

A sound rose through Turner's throat and emerged from his

mouth. It contained nothing recognisable as words; it was a primal scream of shock and misery, a howl of abject despair. He raised his T-Bone and fired it at the distant shape of Dracula, but the first vampire was gone before the stake was halfway to its target. It clattered against a standing piece of château wall, and wound itself back in as Turner scanned the battlefield, searching for the vampire they had come to France to kill. He ran forward, his mind reeling, his only clear thought a simple one.

*If we don't destroy him now, we aren't going to get him. Cal will have died for nothing.*

On the far side of the courtyard, he saw his target.

Dracula was at the edge of the battle, working his way back towards the centre, cutting a bloody swathe through the Combined Operational Force. Black figure after black figure fell beneath his sword, the majority of them not even dead; the huge blade sent them to the ground with terrible, savage wounds, where Valeri's followers fell on them like rabid dogs and finished them off. Turner saw an Operator stand his ground in front of the ancient vampire's onslaught, saw him raise his MP7 and empty it into the vampire's body.

Dracula laughed, and hacked the man almost in half.

As the Operator spun to the ground, his visor flew up, and Turner felt his stomach lurch again. It was Patrick Williams, his eyes rolled white, his torso cleaved open, his blood running out of his body in enormous quantities. Mercy, if there was any left to be had, came in the fact that it was clear, even from a distance, that Williams was dead before he reached the ground.

Turner sprinted forward. He had no idea how to stop the tsunami of death that Dracula had unleashed, or if he even could; he only knew that he had to try, that he had to do something, no matter how futile it might be. He shouldered a vampire out of the way, ducked as the hissing woman swung her razor-sharp nails in his direction, straightened up, and found himself face to face with the first vampire that had ever lived.

Dracula smiled at him, his head cocked to one side, his glowing eyes slightly narrowed, as though he was examining a potentially interesting species of insect. Turner took a deep breath, and was about to raise his T-Bone when a deafening howl filled the air of the courtyard. Dracula had just enough time to frown before the huge grey-green wolf thundered into him from the side, sending them both crashing to the bloodstained gravel.

Jamie staggered backwards, panic surging through him as blood pumped out of his neck in a high-pressure jet. There was no pain, but, as he raised his hands to defend himself against the thrashing, clawing vampire, he noted with horror how heavy they felt; he could already feel himself starting to weaken.

The vampire's whirling fists thudded into his shoulders and face, driving him backwards as his blood gushed against her face and her open, screeching mouth. He reeled, his vision greying at the edges, his legs feeling like they were made of lead, until he heard Angela Darcy say a single word.

"Duck."

Jamie tipped himself back and allowed his weight to pull him to the ground. He hit the stone floor hard; he saw stars, then a metallic blur above him, trailing wire. There was a wet crunch, a howl of pain, then a bang as air rushed into previously occupied space. Blood exploded in the narrow passage, splashing the walls and falling on to him in a thick, sticky rain.

A millisecond later Angela was kneeling at his side.

"Jamie?" she said, her voice low and urgent. "Talk to me, Jamie. What do you need?"

"Blood," he gargled. The word was barely recognisable, but Angela nodded and disappeared. He heard running footsteps, and focused all his attention on the ceiling above him, trying to stay calm, to not go into shock.

*Easy,* he told himself. *Larissa has survived worse than this, more than once. Take it easy.*

He tried. But the sensation of his own blood spilling warmly out over his neck and jaw was so awful that he felt nausea rise up from his stomach, carrying with it the sweet darkness of unconsciousness.

*Crack.*

Angela Darcy's gloved hand connected with his cheek with a sound like a gunshot and his eyes flew open. She was kneeling over him, clutching the vampire who had been lying beneath the collapsed wall, back near the staircase. The man's body had come apart at the waist, so she was technically only holding the upper half of him, but the skin at his neck was still pink, still packed with blood. Angela lowered the man down over Jamie, then took her stake and stabbed a hole in the side of his throat. Blood spilled out – not the hosepipe spray that had erupted from his own severed jugular, more of a thick river – and cascaded into his mouth.

Instantly, Jamie felt his strength return. His eyes flooded red, and a deep growl rose in his throat as he swallowed the still-warm blood. Then he felt something few people on the planet had ever known, a sensation that was almost indescribable.

He felt the gaping wound in his neck repair itself.

It was as though someone had set his spine on fire then soaked his skin in acid; the pain burned and scoured, so vast that all he could do was hang on and hope to ride it out. In the back of his mind, a voice told him to keep drinking, that it would be over soon, so he did.

And it was.

A minute later Jamie sat up and cautiously pressed a gloved finger to his neck. The skin was tender; it felt tight, as though it needed stretching, but the wound was gone. He climbed to his feet and looked at Angela Darcy.

"Thank you," he said.

She smiled. "No problem. You'd do the same for me."

He grinned, then turned back to the room at the end of the corridor. "Come on," he said. "Let's get him out of here."

She nodded and walked into the cell; he followed close behind her.

"Angela?" said Henry Seward, his voice little more than a croak. "Are you real?"

"Yes, sir," she replied. "I'm real, we both are. We're here to get you."

Jamie stared at the Director, his heart racing in his chest, miserable anger flooding him. There could never be enough payback for this, no revenge enough for what Valeri and Dracula had done to one of the finest men he had known.

"Who's that with you?" asked Seward, his voice sounding slightly stronger. "Jamie Carpenter?"

The sound of his name broke Jamie's paralysis. "Yes, sir," he said. "Can you move, sir?"

"I can't walk," said Seward. "My legs won't hold me."

"No problem," said Jamie. He stepped forward, ready to carry the Admiral out of the château and kill any vampire he saw on the way, then stopped; Seward was staring at him with a look of abject horror.

"Oh no," whispered the Director. "Oh, Jamie. What have they done to you?"

"It's a bit of a long story, sir," he said. "Let's save it for another time."

He reached down and scooped Seward up, horrified by how light his body was; it felt as though he was carrying nothing more than a sack of bones. "Angela," he said. "You lead us back the way we came. Anything moves, you shoot first. Got it?"

Angela nodded.

"All right then," said Jamie. "Let's go."

The battle didn't stop when Cal Holmwood died; that would be the thing that Larissa always remembered.

It felt like there should have been a pause, a moment of respect for the Interim Director, but there was nothing; the fighting raged on around her, increasingly feverish and desperate, at least from the perspective of those on the side of humanity. She watched Holmwood fall to the ground as his head rolled away from his body, and felt her vampire side retreat, just for a moment; it did not feel empathy, and was uncomfortable with the concept of loss. With it went the fire that had been burning joyously since the helicopters touched down, what now felt like hours ago, and in its place rose emotions that had been subsumed by her desire to spill blood: grief for Cal Holmwood; pride at the way her friends and colleagues were fighting so valiantly; and a thick wave of guilt at the realisation that she had let Jamie go looking for Henry Seward with only Angela Darcy for company.

Her crimson eyes widened. She turned towards the building, about to go and help her boyfriend, and found herself face to face with Kelly, the NS9 Operator who had been one of her closest friends in Nevada. Her eyes were wide, and her face was pale and blood-spattered beneath a visor that had been pushed up, but she was grinning nonetheless; Larissa smiled involuntarily, taken aback by the sudden appearance of a familiar face.

"Hey," shouted Kelly. "This is pretty wild, huh? Are you OK?"

Larissa nodded. But as she opened her mouth to answer, the hulking shape of Valeri Rusmanov rose up behind her friend, smiling cruelly.

"Look out!" she screamed.

Kelly's face furrowed into a frown. She began to turn, but Valeri's huge hands closed on the sides of her head and lifted her off the ground. Larissa leapt forward, reaching desperately for her friend, as Kelly pounded at the vampire's hands, her legs kicking helplessly at nothing. She was barely five metres away when Valeri twisted Kelly's head sharply; her neck broke with an audible snap that stabbed through Larissa's heart like a knife.

Valeri threw the dead woman aside as though she was nothing, and settled his glowing eyes on Larissa. She skidded to a halt, risked a glance at her fallen friend, who had landed in a tangle of limbs, then focused her attention on the eldest Rusmanov. He was smiling at her, his hands dangling loosely at his sides. Larissa felt the heat in her eyes become almost unbearable as her vampire side returned with a vengeance, bringing with it a rage so great she thought she must surely burst into flames.

"I was hoping you would be here," said Valeri, his smile widening. "You and I have unfinished business, and my brother is not here to rescue you this time."

Larissa's eyes darkened. "I don't need Valentin's help," she hissed.

"I don't need anybody's help. I'm going to tear your heart out with my bare hands."

"Such big words," said Valeri, "from such a little girl."

Larissa smiled, her fangs huge beneath her upper lip. "Are you going to bore me to death?" she asked. "Or are we going to do this?"

Valeri growled, his grin twisting into a mask of anger. He took a step forward, his hands curling into fists. Larissa didn't back down; she stepped off the ground and waited for him to come.

Then a monstrous howl rang out from somewhere across the battlefield, and as Larissa turned towards it, she saw Valeri do the same.

Jamie carried Henry Seward up through the rubble of the château, Angela Darcy at his side, and emerged into a world of chaos.

The smoke from thousands of gunshots hung over the courtyard, and the ground was covered in blood, soaked with it in places. When he had led Angela into the old building, their friends and colleagues had appeared to have the upper hand; now the reverse seemed to be true. Uniformed bodies lay motionless on the ground in appalling numbers, and those still standing seemed on the verge of being routed; vampires swooped and ran and howled with delight as they ripped and tore at the remaining Operators.

Jamie stared across the battlefield, his fangs itching, his eyes blazing. He handed Henry Seward to Angela Darcy, who took him in her arms with a frown on her face.

"Get him to one of the helicopters," he growled. "Then come and find me."

Angela nodded, and raced away across the courtyard, the Blacklight

Director in her arms. Jamie wasted no time watching her go; he scanned the wide space, located the nearest vampire, and threw himself back into the fight.

The wolf skidded across the ground, gravel tearing at its fur and the pale grey-green skin beneath, but didn't even notice the pain; its stomach was full of meat, its mouth was full of blood that wasn't its own, and it was focused entirely on its prey.

The old vampire, the one who, in the distant corner of its mind that was still partly a man, it understood was important, had landed on the ground beside him. The wolf snapped its jaws out, missing the warm outline of the vampire's leg by millimetres; it dug its paws into the gravel, scrambling furiously for purchase, and launched itself forward, intending to tear out the vampire's throat with its teeth.

Another vampire – not as old, but still *old* – slammed into its side, knocking it back to the gravel. A howl of pain burst from its blood-soaked maw as three of its ribs broke, but the wolf was back on its feet immediately. It circled its attacker, the vampire it had been so desperate to kill only seconds earlier now forgotten, then lunged forward, teeth clattering shut on thin air where the vampire's arm had been. It skidded past, stretching out a huge paw as it did so, and felt it connect with the vampire's stomach, drawing an explosion of breath and a grunt of pain.

The wolf lunged again, its claws ripping at the vampire's back, tearing flesh away in long strips, then reared up on its powerful hind legs and bit the back of its prey's neck. Blood spilled into its mouth, energising it, and it pressed forward, trying to force the vampire down to the ground where its advantage would be overwhelming. The vampire resisted, digging his feet into the gravel and pushing back with all his supernatural strength; the wolf felt hands trying to force its jaws open. It bore down, but the vampire possessed strength beyond anything it had ever encountered, and slowly, inevitably, its mouth opened.

The wolf snapped its jaws down towards its prey's head, but the bleeding vampire was too quick; he slid to the left, and caught the wolf by the throat. There was a moment of perfect stillness, as the two monsters brought all their strength to bear. Then the wolf was in the air, the vampire's hands deep in the fur covering its neck and stomach, and found itself flying towards the corner of the ruined stone building.

It hit one of the grey slabs head first, and saw nothing but black.

Larissa paid no attention to Valeri and the Frankenstein wolf, for a simple reason. In front of her, rising to his feet with a sword that was almost as big as him in his hands, was Dracula.

The first vampire glanced over at Valeri as he grappled with the huge wolf, then smiled at her. "You are the one Valeri spoke of," he said. "Blacklight's pet. A traitor to your—"

Larissa blurred across the distance between them and slammed her gloved fist into Dracula's face with all her strength. His words were cut off as he flew backwards, his heels digging long grooves in the gravel, his head rocked back by the force of the blow. She was breathing heavily, almost panting as her vampire side filled her; her skin felt like it was on fire, and her mind contained nothing more than a raging torrent of hatred.

Dracula lowered his head, blood running from his nostrils in two thick streams. He ran the back of his hand under his nose and looked at the smear of red.

"For that," he said, his voice soft, almost friendly, "you will pay a price you cannot imagine."

Larissa smiled. Around her the battle raged, as her friends and colleagues fought with last-ditch courage against odds that were on the verge of becoming overwhelming; she tuned out the noise and the thick smell of blood, forcing herself into the moment, focusing herself entirely on the vampire standing before her.

*Live or die*, she told herself. *Here's where you find out.*

She growled and threw herself at Dracula.

The first vampire was fast, remarkably so, but Larissa realised something within the first second or two of their fight: he was *not* as fast as she had feared. She had fought Valeri Rusmanov, and had seen what the first victim was capable of; Dracula, it appeared, was barely faster than either of them, if at all. As a result, she slipped easily beneath his first punch, a lazy swing that would have nevertheless decapitated most vampires and all humans, and landed a driving punch of her own on his ribs. Dracula grunted, and the slightest flicker of a frown crossed his face as he circled away from her.

*Maybe we overestimated you*, she thought. *We'll see. But I* know *you underestimated me. Didn't see that coming, did you?*

"Quick," he said, almost approvingly. "Perhaps you will be some sport after all."

Larissa wasted no time responding. She feinted left, then darted to her right, a black blur trailing glowing red light, drawing her MP7 as she did so, and unloading it at his stomach from point-blank range. Dracula threw himself into the air, pirouetting gracefully, and the bullets streamed harmlessly beneath him. Her momentum carried her forward, and although she threw herself out of the way as the first vampire dropped from the air like a missile, she wasn't fast enough.

Dracula's foot pistoned out and connected with her chest; Larissa heard something break inside her and screamed in pain as she was flung backwards. She hit the ground on her shoulders, flipped over, and skidded across the gravel on her stomach. She leapt back to her feet, having almost reached the treeline at the edge of the courtyard, and saw Dracula streaking towards her, a wide smile on his pale, narrow face.

*Keep him busy,* she told herself, trying to ignore the sickening waves of pain rolling out from deep within her. *Try and give the others a chance to do something, if nothing else.*

Valeri's back blazed with agony as he strode towards the wolf, intending to tear off its head and throw it as far into the forest as he could manage.

Blood was pouring from where the animal's claws and teeth had gouged his flesh and pooling at his waist; every step sent pain shooting up his spine. The old vampire found himself almost incoherent with rage.

*Wolves and stakes and helicopters and traitors. Animals. Kill them. Tear their hearts out. Rip off their heads. Kill them all.*

He stopped beside the huge wolf. It lay at the foot of a broken piece of château wall, its chest rising and falling, its tongue hanging out of its open mouth. Valeri kicked the animal in its side, feeling hatred pumping through him, then kicked it again, and again. He heard the dry snaps of breaking ribs, but the unconscious wolf gave no response. He leant forward, his hands reaching for the animal's neck, then stopped.

A voice in the back of his mind, the part of himself that was a General first and foremost, was telling him that the wolf was no longer a threat, that loyalty demanded he put his desire for revenge aside. Valeri growled, a low rumble that shook the ground, then straightened up and turned away, looking for his master. He had left him fighting the traitor girl, who was smarter and quicker than he had given her credit. He was not seriously worried that she might actually cause Dracula harm, but it would be good to remove her from the fight as soon as possible; she was a wild card, and such things were unwelcome on a battlefield. Valeri knew they were reaching the final throes of the battle; his brother was gone, Cal Holmwood was dead, the werewolf was unconscious, and once he helped his lord destroy the traitorous vampire brat, he was certain that whatever resistance remained in the ranks of the men and women in black would crumble.

*There.*

His master was near the edge of the courtyard, advancing towards the distant treeline. Beyond him, Valeri could see the black shape of the traitor, her eyes blooming red in the darkness. He growled, and was about to step into the air and speed to his master's side when something hit the back of his head like a bolt of lightning and he slumped to one knee.

The pain thundered through him like the echo of some impossible noise, jarring every single one of his cells and rendering him momentarily blind. A second impact, less powerful than the first but still enough to send him sprawling on to his stomach, landed across his shoulders. He scrambled forward on hands and knees, rolled over, and threw himself backwards. His head was screaming, his limbs slow and heavy, but his survival instinct was still strong, and he escaped the third blow by millimetres. He dragged himself to his feet and faced his attacker.

It was a teenager, barely more than a boy, in the black uniform of the enemy. His eyes glowed the colour of blood, and in his hands he was holding a long piece of one of the rotor blades that had been sheared off when Valeri brought down the Apaches.

Valeri hissed, and staggered backwards.

*How many pets do they have?* he wondered, frantically. *How many more surprises can there be?*

The boy came forward, a look of savage pleasure on his face, and swung the rotor again. Valeri got an arm up to block it, but the force of the blow sent him flying. He scrambled up and was hit again, the heavy length of metal landing agonisingly on his lower back, sending fresh agony through his body and driving him back to the ground. Panic exploded into his system, numbing some, but not all, of the pain, and as he struggled to his feet, an awful thought filled his mind.

*He's going to kill me. He's going to beat me to death with that thing.*

The boy swung the rotor again. Valeri summoned the last of his strength, the very deepest reserves of his resolve, and threw himself to one side, arching his back and throwing his arms out for balance. The chunk of metal skimmed his nose, missed his chest and groin by millimetres, and buried itself in the gravel. The boy frowned, as Valeri moved.

He dropped his shoulder and swung his fists together with everything he had left. They crashed into the boy's stomach; the air left his body with a great bursting sound, and he folded to the ground, his eyes wide, his mouth open, his chest still.

Valeri threw back his head and let out an ungodly shriek of triumph; it echoed around the courtyard like the howl of a banshee. He gritted his teeth against the pain that was coursing through his body and staggered towards the boy, whose face was rapidly turning purple as he struggled to breathe. As Valeri reached him, something clicked inside the boy's body and he dragged in a huge, strangled breath. It made no difference; he pushed weakly at the gravel, trying to retreat, but nothing happened.

The eldest Rusmanov stared down at the teenage vampire with a smile on his face that was nothing short of sadistic. Then something took hold of his wrists, something incredibly strong, and wrenched them up and back, trapping him in place. Valeri surged forward, kicking and squirming, trying to free himself, but whatever had him was as implacable as death.

His eyes began to widen as his shoulders creaked alarmingly, then flew open as his arms broke at the elbows with cracks that rang out across the courtyard.

Valeri screamed. The pain was unbelievable, huge and hot; bile churned in his stomach and he felt his legs give way beneath him as the last of his strength deserted his battered, broken body. He hung limply in the grip of whatever was holding him, utterly powerless to resist.

Jamie Carpenter got up with a narrow smile on his face, despite the pain thumping through him.

For several long seconds after Valeri hit him, he had simply been unable to breathe; his chest had locked tight, no air getting in or out, as pressure built in his head. He suspected that fear, the cold terror that had filled him as the old vampire had approached him, had been what finally overrode his protesting muscles, freeing him from paralysis.

Then something had happened to Valeri. Jamie wasted no time wondering what; he drew the metal stake from his belt, and staggered towards the suspended vampire.

"Look at me," he said, his voice shaky.

Valeri raised his head and Jamie recoiled; the fire in the old vampire's eyes was gone, and he looked so tired, so utterly *exhausted*, that Jamie felt a sickening moment of sympathy for him. He pushed it away and raised the stake in an unsteady hand.

"Say hello to Alexandru for me," he said, and plunged it into the vampire's chest.

Valeri's eyes widened, as a strange expression crossed his face; in the dark nights that followed, when sleep eluded him and his heart was heavy with grief, Jamie would convince himself that it was relief.

Then the second-oldest vampire in the world exploded with a sound like a clap of thunder, spraying steaming blood across Jamie's chest and face. He gagged, wiped his eyes clear with the back of a gloved hand, and felt a smile rise on his face at what he saw.

Standing in front of him, coated in the remains of his brother, was Valentin Rusmanov.

His jaw was horribly broken, his handsome face a mess of unnatural angles and purple-black bruising, and he was coated in a thick crust of dried blood, but his eyes glowed scarlet, and he was smiling lopsidedly at Jamie.

"Come on," he said, his voice mangled by his injuries. "Let's finish this."

# 61

# THE STORM, PART FOUR

Dracula heard a voice say Alexandru's name from across the wide expanse of the courtyard, and turned in time to see a teenage soldier with glowing red eyes thrust a stake into Valeri's heart.

He stared, the vampire girl forgotten entirely, as his oldest comrade died with an explosion that shook the courtyard, the fire in his eyes fading, his mind unable to truly accept what he was seeing. Then he saw Valentin, smiling and covered in his brother's blood, and Dracula's incredulity was replaced with a fury huge enough and hot enough to burn down the entire world. A growl began to rumble deep within him, and his eyes exploded with black fire as he floated into the air, their gaze locked squarely on Valentin and the vampire boy who had ended Valeri's long life.

Then, despite the noise of the dying battle and the fury drowning out everything except the desire to tear out the throats and gorge on the blood of those who had taken his most faithful servant from him, a sound from close by made him move; it was a popping noise, followed by the whir of something unravelling at speed.

Dracula slid to the left, then was thrown forward as a metal stake erupted from the right side of his chest, trailing a metal wire slick with his own blood.

The pain was huge and instantaneous; he threw back his head and howled up at the night sky. The wire was speeding through the hole that had been punched in his body, a feeling so awful that it made his stomach churn. He lowered his head, his eyes roiling with fire, and grabbed hold of it. The metal wire flayed the skin from his hands in sheets, but he barely noticed; his only thought was that he had to get it out of him, whatever it was.

With a roar, he ripped the wire in two and threw it down on to gravel now wet with his blood. He gritted his teeth against the pain. Cold air was whistling through the hole, but he forced himself not to look; no good could come from seeing the severity of his injury. He had undoubtedly seen worse, and blood would fix it, no matter how bad it was.

Dracula turned, his face twisting with hatred, a thick growl rising from his throat, and looked for the vampire girl. *She* had done this to him, he was certain; had shot him in the back like a coward. Before him, the dark expanse of the forest loomed, and even with his remarkable eyesight, he could see nothing moving between the trunks of the trees. Then he spun back round, suddenly aware that he had been still for too long, that he had again presented his back as a target, and caught the vampire girl by the wrist as she thrust a stake towards his chest.

"Not fast enough," he growled. "Not this time."

The girl threw herself backwards, trying to dislodge his grip, her face blazing with anger. Dracula was dragged forward several steps, surprised by her strength and speed. He dug his heels in, then twisted his hand and snapped her wrist with a loud crack.

The colour disappeared from the girl's face as though it had been drained away, and she let out a guttural scream of pain. But even as the noise burst from her mouth, she swung her other hand, connecting solidly with the point of his jaw, sending him staggering backwards. Dracula bore down, and lifted her into the air, keeping himself clear of her swinging fist and kicking feet. He bent her arm behind her back, snarling with pleasure as he felt the bones in her shattered wrist grind together, drawing a scream of even greater pitch from her. Then he grabbed the back of the girl's head with his free hand, and slammed her face first into the gravel with all his strength.

The ground shook with the impact.

The girl went instantly limp.

Dracula released his grip and stood up, a smile of dreadful satisfaction on his blood-smeared face.

*Got you,* he thought.

For a fleeting millisecond that he would never have acknowledged to anybody, a bright pillar of fear had burst into life in his stomach. The treacherous vampire was remarkably powerful, almost as quick and strong as Valeri had been, and Dracula was still reeling from the fate that had befallen his oldest servant when the odds against him had finally become too great. The eldest Rusmanov had fought with honour and courage, and with great dedication to the protection of his master, but he was gone. And if Valeri could be destroyed, then who was to say that same fate could not befall him?

But now the vampire girl lay broken at his feet, and he could turn his attention to Valentin, and to the boy who had wielded the killing stake. Once their spilled blood was added to that of their friends, the battle would finally be over, and the future would belong to him.

\* \* \*

Jamie flew across the courtyard, Valentin Rusmanov at his side, his eyes gleaming in the lights of the transport helicopters and the glow of the full moon.

In the distance, he saw Dracula struggling with an Operator, holding the soldier at arm's length, then grimaced with revulsion as the unfortunate soul was smashed to the ground, and lay still.

*Nobody could have survived that,* he thought. *One more person who gave everything trying to save us all. One more victim to avenge.*

Valentin pulled ahead of him as they approached their target, his damaged face curled into a smile of seemingly vast pleasure. The youngest Rusmanov crashed into Dracula's knees, sending his former master spinning up into the air, a look of surprise on his narrow face. Jamie soared upwards, marvelling at how quickly flying had come to feel almost natural, and met the first vampire in the air, hammering both of his fists down on to the back of his head. Dracula plummeted to the ground like a stone, sending up a cloud of dust as he hit the gravel with an impact that would have killed a normal man. But he was on his feet again instantly, his face a red mask of rage, his eyes the colour of death.

"You dare?" he screamed. "You dare put your hands on me?"

Jamie dropped to the ground beside Valentin and faced him.

"Your time has passed," said Valentin, his voice low and steady. "There is no place for you in this world."

"This world?" bellowed Dracula. "This world is mine, to do with exactly as I please."

"I beg to differ," said Paul Turner, arriving at Jamie's side with his T-Bone at his shoulder, his pale grey eyes as clear as ever.

Jamie felt a surge of pride rush through him. They had come through the fire, his colleagues and friends; they had overcome odds that most would have thought insurmountable, and now they would end what they had started, here and now.

He looked round, and frowned as he saw the Operator that had been slammed to the ground by Dracula peeling themselves up from the gravel. The black-clad figure got to its feet, staggered, then raised its head and looked directly at him.

Jamie gasped.

Larissa looked like she had been run over by a bulldozer.

Her face was a mask of blood, running from dozens of cuts and pooling against ridges of bruising and outcrops of displaced bone. But her eyes glowed fiercely as she flew slowly across the courtyard and stood between him and Valentin.

Jamie turned back to face Dracula, and saw something he had never expected to see on the ancient monster's face.

Fear.

It was fleeting, gone almost as soon as it appeared, but it had been there.

*He's scared*, thought Jamie. *He saw what happened to Valeri and he doesn't know if he can take us all.*

Behind him, heavy footsteps crunched across the gravel, and when hot air blasted across the back of his neck, accompanied by a growl that, under normal circumstances, would have turned his insides to water, Jamie knew exactly who, or rather *what*, had joined them.

"You will pay for what you have done here today," growled Dracula, his black eyes flitting back and forth along the line of Operators and vampires. "They will write stories about the horrors you will suffer. Your deaths will be *legendary*."

Paul Turner was evidently in no mood to listen; without responding, he fired his T-Bone at the ancient vampire's heart.

Dracula leapt out of the way of the projectile, howling with a fury that seemed on the verge of outrage, then was hit from three sides by Jamie, Larissa and Valentin. They bore the screaming, thrashing monster to the ground, shouting for a stake, for someone to bring a stake. Turner rushed forward, drawing one from his belt, and elbowed Larissa aside.

For a glorious moment, Jamie saw Dracula's chest exposed as he and Valentin clung to the first vampire and Turner drew back his arm.

Then the moment was gone.

With strength that, even to Jamie, seemed impossible, Dracula swung his arms together, crunching him against Valentin. His grip failed him as he tumbled to the ground, crying out in pain; it felt like his back had been broken. He rolled over in time to see Dracula leap into the air, narrowly avoiding the huge wolf form of Frankenstein as it lunged for his ankles, and hover above the courtyard, his arms outstretched.

"Loyal subjects!" he shouted, his voice echoing across the battlefield. "To me!"

Then he shot up into the night sky like a bullet, followed by the remainder of Valeri's army, and was gone.

For a long moment, nobody moved, or spoke.

Silence descended over the courtyard, as the surviving Operators processed the reality that the battle was over. Larissa stared up at the sky, her ruined face momentarily forgotten, her heart pounding in her chest.

*Missed him,* she thought. *One chance, and we missed it.*

"No," said Valentin, as though he could read her mind. "This ends now, one way or the other." He shot into the sky and vanished in the direction his former master had fled.

"I have to go too," she said. "I have to help him."

"No," said Paul Turner, regarding her with his usual cold expression. "It's over, Larissa. We have men and women here who need our help."

"To hell with them," she said, far more callously than she intended. "If Dracula gets away, then every dead Operator gave their life for nothing. You have to see that!"

"It's over," repeated Turner.

Larissa looked desperately to Jamie for help, her eyes glowing crimson, her hands trembling; she felt as though she was on the verge of tears.

*So close*, she thought. *Damn it, we were so close.*

"Larissa's right, sir," said Jamie. "She could help. Between her and Valentin, it might be enough. There might still be a chance."

"How many times must I repeat myself, Lieutenant?" asked Turner, his voice low and full of danger. "I'm telling you this is finished."

"Where's the Director?" asked Jamie. "Where's Cal?"

"He's gone," said Turner, his face momentarily creasing with pain.

Jamie stared at the Security Officer. "What do you mean, gone?" he asked.

"I mean he's dead, Jamie," said Turner. "Which makes me Interim Director of Blacklight, and I am telling you, *both of you*, that we have wounded Operators who need our help. I want you to find the most seriously injured, fly them back to the Loop, then return here as quickly as you can. Is that clear?"

Larissa felt anger sweep up through her. "I can't do that, sir," she said. "I'm sorry."

Turner turned the full weight of his icy stare on her. "You will follow my order, Lieutenant Kinley, or you will be court-martialled," he said. "There are good men and women lying out there, men and women who are our friends, and who fought with everything they had. You will not abandon them now, when they need you the most."

"Yes," said a voice. "She will."

Larissa turned towards it, and felt her heart break in her chest.

Henry Seward was standing in front of her, holding tightly to Angela Darcy. He was horribly thin, his skin a ruin of scars and bruises, his hair white and lank, a black patch covering one of his eye sockets. But his visible eye was clear, and his mouth was set in a firm line of determination that she knew all too well.

"Henry," said Turner, his eyes widening with obvious concern. "You should be—"

"I should be here, Paul," said Seward, his voice a rasp of effort. "I am still the Director of our Department, as far as I am aware."

Turner winced, and nodded.

"Lieutenant Carpenter," he said. "Do as Major Turner ordered. Quickly now."

"Yes, sir," said Jamie, and raced away across the battlefield. Seward watched him go, then turned to Larissa, and smiled.

"Go after Dracula," he said. "Now. While there is still time."

Larissa smiled back at the Director, and hurled herself into the air.

# 62

# LEAVE IT ALL ON THE FIELD

## *SOMEWHERE OVER SOUTHERN FRANCE*

Dracula flew south-east, burning with the shame of having been forced to retreat.

His mouth was full of fresh blood; as soon as he was clear of the château, he had taken hold of the nearest of Valeri's followers, ripped out the man's throat with his teeth, and drunk until he was sated. The new skin that had filled the hole in his chest fizzed and itched, and as he felt the blood revive him, felt his strength return, the shame grew hotter and sharper.

Part of his brain was whispering that he had nobody but himself to blame, that he had underestimated his enemy and been too confident, but he pushed the thought away with an audible snarl. If it had not been for Valentin's sickening act of fratricide, the battle would surely now be won, and all of vampire-kind would be looking towards a future in which they were the dominant species on the planet, with him as their ruler. Instead, he had been undone by something that could not have been predicted: that Valeri would die at his brother's hand, leaving his master to fight alone.

Dracula forced his mind towards happier thoughts, of the horrors he would inflict on Valentin and the vampire girl and boy when the time came. He plumbed the depths of his memory for the unholiest tortures of his youth, for the punishments that even *he* had considered too savage, too unnatural; for the three vampires who had cost him so dearly, he would revive them all.

Flying behind him in a ragged V were the remnants of Valeri's followers. There were maybe twenty-five of them; the rest had sprayed their insides out across the courtyard of Château Dauncy, giving their lives in the service of their master. The ones who had survived were soaked with blood that wasn't theirs, which pleased Dracula. It was never difficult to recruit new meat, desperate acolytes useful for little more than cannon fodder. But these men and women had fought a highly trained enemy and survived; perhaps he would be able to draw some servants who were actually useful from their ranks. The simple fact of their survival suggested either resourcefulness or an aptitude for violence, both qualities that he admired.

The cold night air whistled over his skin as he led the vampires away from the site of their defeat. He had no idea where they would go, not yet; there were places that Valeri had told him about that would be safe, but for now, he was thinking no further than somewhere to lay low, somewhere he could lick his wounds and plot his vengeance. He glanced back over his shoulder, and frowned.

There seemed to be fewer vampires following him.

Dracula rolled in the air, so that he was flying with his back to the ground, and counted.

*Sixteen,* he thought. *Where the hell have the rest of them gone?*

Then, by the light of the full moon, he saw.

Behind the ragged formation of men and women, two black shapes rose up from the darkness, as quick and silent as birds of prey. They grabbed the two vampires flying at the back, wrapped hands round their mouths and throats, and bore them away towards the distant ground in complete silence, the attacks unnoticed by the rest of the exhausted, defeated vampires.

Rage burst through Dracula. He opened his mouth to scream at his followers, to warn them that they were being picked off, but before the first word was formed, something crashed into him with such force that his first thought was that a meteor had hit him.

He spun through the air, the sky and ground revolving wildly as he fought to steady himself, cries of alarm and shrieks of terror ringing out above him. As he arrested his spin and slowed, he saw Valentin – cursed, treacherous Valentin – smile down at him before rocketing into the remnants of his brother's army, scattering them in every direction. Dracula righted himself, and was about to pursue the vile traitor who had done so much to undo him when he was hit on the back of the neck by what could only have been a planet, such was the weight of the blow. His eyes spun in his head, his vision greying to nothing, and he dropped towards the distant ground like a dead weight.

Consciousness returned to Dracula as the dark ground rushed up to meet him, alarmingly close. His head was pounding, and his neck felt like it had swollen to twice its usual size; had he been anything less than he was, the blow would surely have broken it. He flailed his arms, engaging the strange, supernatural instinct that controlled his ability to fly, and managed to slow his descent. In the distance, he saw the yellow lights of a cluster of houses, but below him all was dark.

He hit the ground with a sickening crunch; he howled in pain, but rolled over and forced himself to his feet. Valentin and the vampire girl – it was her, he knew it was, it had to be – would be on him quickly, trying to finish him off before he recovered from the fall. He lifted the arm he had landed on and felt the bones grind agonisingly together as a terrible thought filled his head.

*I should be stronger than this. Much stronger, and faster. My God, could they actually beat me? Is it truly possible?*

The followers he had inherited from Valeri began to land beside him, their eyes wide and full of panic. There were eight of them now, only eight, and no sign of the two traitors who had wrought such chaos. Dracula looked up and searched the sky for them, trying to anticipate their next attack, then leapt out of the way as something fell towards him. He stared at it, his mind churning with revulsion and sudden, awful admiration.

Lying on the ground was a vampire torso. The limbs were all gone, the arms torn out at the shoulders, the legs at mid-thigh, and above the neck was nothing but a ragged, spouting stump.

*Thud.*

Dracula looked around, his supernaturally sharp eyes searching for the source of the noise.

*Thud.*

*Thud thud.*

One of the vampires cried out, her eyes flaring red, her hands scrabbling at her hair. Out of the brown curls flew a severed hand; it fell wetly to the ground, the fingers pale and curled like claws, a ruby ring gleaming brightly on one of them. Then the thuds of falling objects became a drumbeat, as pieces of the vampires they had been flying alongside only minutes earlier poured out of the sky like gruesome rain: legs, hands, faces, ears, fingers, kneecaps, eyeballs, noses, livers, lungs, long strings of intestines, still-beating hearts.

The vampires howled and hissed, rushing back and forth, trying to avoid the falling horror. Dracula merely stared, his eyes wide.

*This is what I would have done*, he marvelled. *If I were them. Exactly what I would have done.*

Valentin Rusmanov hurled the severed head of a vampire towards the field below and wiped his blood-soaked hands on his uniform. He looked over at Larissa Kinley, floating alongside him, and grinned.

"I think we have their attention," he said. "What say we put an end to this?"

Larissa growled, her eyes blazing in the darkness.

It was all the answer Valentin needed.

His grin widened, then he rolled elegantly in the air and rocketed towards the ground; he landed in the centre of the wide meadow, barely a second later, and regarded his former master. Dracula was standing with his huge sword in his hands, a look of what almost appeared to be grudging respect on his face. The last of Valeri's followers – he quickly counted eight of them – were huddled behind the first vampire, their faces contorted with fear. As Larissa touched down beside him, Valentin called to them.

"You vampires who followed my brother," he said. "Leave now and your lives will be spared. This is your only chance to avoid destruction."

Dracula growled, and glanced over his shoulder. None of the cowering group of men and women moved, although Valentin could see the desperate desire to do so on several of their faces.

"Fine," he said, and shrugged. "Have it your way."

He launched himself towards his former master, his mind pulsing with the pleasure of violence and a feeling he had experienced incredibly rarely over the course of his long life: the satisfaction of being on the side of good, of doing the right thing for once.

Dracula reared back, and swung his sword in a huge killing

sweep. Valentin slid beneath it without slowing, and tore into his brother's followers like a whirlwind. Behind him, he heard a heavy crunch, and a cry of pain from Larissa, but didn't turn back; he had complete confidence in her ability to handle herself, even against Dracula.

The vampires tried to flee as he barrelled into them, but were far too slow. He decapitated one with a flick of his wrist, sending the man's head spinning away across the field, leaving his body clutching at nothing. It took two faltering, headless steps before it crashed to the ground, pumping blood. Valentin spun to his left, and swung his fist in a rising backhand that caught a female vampire beneath her chin. She flew into the air as though she had been launched from a catapult, spinning over and over, and disappeared into the darkness.

Two of the vampires leapt into the air and flew for their lives. Valentin let them go; these men and women were a sideshow, and he had no intention of letting them distract him from his real target for a moment longer than necessary. The four remaining vampires fled towards Dracula, presumably hoping for his protection, but as Valentin turned to follow them, he saw that his former master didn't afford them so much as a glance; he was concentrating wholly on his fight with Larissa.

Fresh blood poured from her nose, and she had been driven back by the blur of Dracula's sword. She was dodging the heavy swings, darting to her left and right, but there was clear concern on her face; if a single hack or slash connected, the damage would be catastrophic.

*Hold on,* thought Valentin. *I'm coming.*

He thundered across the bare field and slammed into Dracula's lower back with the force of a runaway train. The first vampire howled and sank to his knees, the cords in his neck standing out as his head was thrown back. Valentin spun gracefully over him, and landed neatly beside Larissa.

"Are you all right?" he asked.

"I'm fine," she growled. "Let's put him out of his misery."

Valentin nodded, and looked at Dracula. The first vampire had regained his feet, and was staring at them with a hatred that burned like molten lava. Pain was etched on his face, in the hunch of his shoulders, and Valentin suddenly understood that his former master had realised the truth.

*He's going to die,* he thought. *Right now, in this place. And he knows it.*

Dracula raised his sword.

"To the last," he spat. "I grapple with thee."

Valentin leapt forward, ready to pull the beating heart from the ancient monster's chest and show it to him before he died. Larissa leapt too, her arms outstretched, her face a savage mask of pleasure. One of Valeri's followers threw himself in front of Dracula, his hands raised, perhaps hoping to make some final sacrifice to a master to whom he meant less than nothing. Valentin sped round him as though he wasn't there, his attention fixed solely on Dracula.

Then Larissa cried out, and he turned back.

The vampire follower had thrust out a hand as she flew past him, and one of his razor-sharp fingernails had sliced a neat, straight line across the vampire girl's throat. She tumbled from the air, and as Valentin watched, the cut opened up like a widely smiling mouth, blood erupting from it in a high-pressure jet. His eyes widened and he changed course, rotating his body, his feet touching the ground briefly, as he prepared to fly to her assistance.

Then there was movement behind him; a rush of air, a glint of metal. A millisecond later Valentin felt pain, then knew no more.

Larissa cried out as the fingernail slid through her skin.

Her balance was fatally compromised, and she crashed to the ground as blood spurted out of her neck, bright scarlet and steaming hot. She clamped a gloved hand over the wound, felt the heat in her eyes boil up to a temperature that was almost unbearable, and was about to reach for the vampire who had done this to her when she saw Dracula move.

Valentin had arrested his advance and was clearly about to throw himself in her direction when Dracula's sword rose up between his legs and cut him in half.

The huge blade exited the top of Valentin's head with a noise like shattering glass, trailing a shocking quantity of blood behind it. The exertion of the blow clearly took it out of Dracula, who staggered backwards, his sword dragging along the ground as though it was suddenly too heavy to lift, but Larissa barely noticed. Her crimson eyes were fixed entirely on Valentin.

The youngest Rusmanov swayed for a long, terrible moment, then collapsed to the ground in two pieces; the huge sword had split him from groin to skull. Steaming organs spilled out of his body, writhing gently in the cold air, as more blood than Larissa had ever seen gushed out on to the ground. One of Valentin's eyes winked grotesquely as his fingers drummed involuntarily against his legs.

Everyone stopped.

Dracula had sunk down to one knee, his face etched with agony, as the four remaining members of Valeri's army stared at Valentin, their faces fixed with expressions of horror.

Larissa forced herself to move, to ignore the panic bubbling up inside her. She staggered to her feet, blood pumping out between her gloved fingers, and, with her free hand tore off the head of the vampire who had injured her. His attention was focused on Valentin's gruesome remains, and she was on him before he even knew she had moved. His head came loose with an awful pop; she threw it aside and buried her face in the stump of his neck, and drank as quickly as she could. She felt the skin beneath her fingers knit back together as she circled away from the remaining vampires, suddenly aware that she was outnumbered.

She was on her own.

Dracula got back to his feet and smiled at her. "A battle has many movements," he said. "Many changes of momentum. But all that matters is who stands at the end. And you and I still stand."

The last three vampire acolytes stared at her, their eyes glowing, the terror that had so openly gripped them as she and Valentin descended from the night sky replaced by anger, now that the odds were again in their favour. She met their master's gaze, then glanced down at where the pieces of Valentin lay steaming and trembling.

And realised something.

*He didn't explode. Why didn't he explode like all the others? Like his brother?*

Larissa circled slowly to her left, keeping her eyes fixed on Dracula and his followers, then glanced downwards again, and saw it. In the left half of Valentin's rapidly draining chest cavity, in a soup of blood and bile, lay his motionless heart.

Still intact.

"Shall we finish this?" asked Dracula. "Or has your appetite for the fight diminished now you stand alone?"

Larissa growled. She took a step forward, bringing her feet next to Valentin's remains, and stared at the first vampire. His pale face was full of pain and exhaustion, and she wondered, for a fleeting moment, whether she could take him on her own, whether she could bring an end to the horror, right there and then.

*It's possible*, she thought. *Not likely, not likely at all, but possible.*

She took another step, and felt her foot slide through something wet. Revulsion shuddered through her; it cleared her mind, pushed back her vampire side, and the right thing to do, the *only* thing, was suddenly clear. Blacklight had already taken losses she doubted it could withstand; if *she* died now, if she tried to kill Dracula and failed, then Valentin would be destroyed as well, and two of the only reasons to believe they might get another chance to end the first vampire would be gone.

*But what if you don't fail?* hissed her retreating vampire self. *You can end this now.*

Larissa growled. "Your day will come," she said, looking directly into the first vampire's eyes. "And I will be there when it does. You can count on that."

"I shall be looking forward to it," said Dracula, and smiled.

"I wouldn't be," said Larissa. "If I were you."

Then she moved, fast enough to make one of Valeri's vampires gasp out loud. Without taking her eyes from Dracula's, she reached down, scooped up the limp, sodden halves of Valentin Rusmanov, and disappeared into the sky.

# 63

# TIME WAITS FOR NO MAN

Jamie opened his eyes as the helicopter touched down outside the Loop's hangar, and rubbed them roughly with the palms of his hands.

He had slept through most of his second journey back from Château Dauncy; not through choice, but from complete exhaustion. After Henry Seward's intervention on the battlefield, he had done as Paul Turner ordered and searched the wide gravel courtyard for injured survivors. At the base of the high northern wall, one of the three that were still standing more or less intact, he had found an Operator he recognised, but whose name he didn't know; one of the hundreds of semi-familiar men and women that passed him in the grey corridors of the Loop. The man's barely conscious face was pale, sweat stood out on his forehead and upper lip, and his mouth was twisted with a tight grimace of pain. The cause of his expression was horribly apparent: his stomach had been opened from belt to sternum, and his gloved hands were the only things keeping his guts inside his body.

Jamie scooped him up as gently as he was able, and flew him back to the Loop as fast as his supernatural muscles would carry him, his heart racing with concern for Larissa. He was sure that

Valentin would look after her, but he had no idea whether that would be enough, for either of them. Dracula had unquestionably been on the ropes, beginning to wear down before their eyes, but chasing after him was nonetheless remarkably dangerous, even for two vampires as powerful as Valentin and his girlfriend.

Somewhere over the English Channel, the Operator began to scream. The high-pitched shrieks of pain hurt Jamie's ears, and continued all the way to the Loop, where he delivered the stricken man into the care of two of the Department's doctors.

As they rushed the Operator away on a stretcher, Jamie threw himself back into the air, pushing his tired body as hard as he dared towards the devastated château. When he arrived, the courtyard was quiet and almost empty. The remainder of the injured survivors were on their way to the Loop in one of the transport helicopters, accompanied by the Tiger gunships that had been summoned from Toulouse-Blagnac to escort them. That left two intact helicopters sitting on the gravel, into one of which the bodies of the dead were being loaded.

With no one left to carry back to the Loop, Jamie joined the men and women who had chosen to stay and carry out this most miserable of tasks. He was not remotely surprised to see Angela Darcy and Lizzy Ellison among their number; he was certain that Paul Turner would have been there too, had he not been needed back at the headquarters of the Department he was now in charge of.

*Or is he?* Jamie wondered. *Maybe Henry Seward is still Director? I don't know how that works.*

As the helicopter rumbled north-west, the news had come through the speakers in Jamie's helmet that Larissa had arrived safely at the Loop, and he had lowered his head and silently wept.

The scale of what had happened in the grounds of the château was so huge that he was struggling not to let it overwhelm him.

Cal Holmwood was dead.

Patrick Williams was dead.

Operators who had fought with everything they had were dead.

Valeri Rusmanov was dead.

And Dracula had survived.

As the tears rolled down his cheeks, fully aware that the other Operators sitting in the helicopter's hold were doing him the courtesy of pretending not to notice them, Jamie tried to find a way to convince himself that so much death had been worth it.

The roar of the helicopter's engine began to subside as Angela Darcy slid open its long door. He stood up and made his way across to it; Angela gave him a small smile as he approached her, which he returned as he leapt down on to the tarmac. His feet had barely touched the ground when Larissa thundered into him, almost sending him flying; only her arms, which were crushing him against her, kept him upright. For a long moment, he merely hung in her grip, unable to persuade his aching limbs to do anything. Then, slowly, he wrapped his arms round her waist and buried his face against her neck. When he finally drew away, noticing with a pang of teenage shame the wet patches his tears had left on her uniform, the helicopter was empty, and they were alone in the landing area.

"What happened?" he asked, his voice low and thick. "With Dracula."

Larissa shook her head. "Later," she said.

"Valentin?"

She nodded. "He's here," she said. "He's going to be all right."

Jamie grimaced, and felt tears appear in the corners of his eyes again. "Cal," he said. "And Jack's brother. So many people."

"I know," said Larissa.

There was nothing else to say; it was all too big, too raw, too hard to be solved or improved by words. Jamie knew better than anyone that time was the only thing that would heal the Department's broken heart.

Larissa put her arm round his shoulders as they walked slowly into the hangar. The floor was smeared with blood and covered in torn strips of gauze and bandaging, and the double doors at the rear were wedged open with a pair of black helmets, presumably because the flow of stretchers had been so heavy. Jamie walked through them, not sure of where they should go now, or what they should do, and saw Matt Browning and Kate Randall hurrying along the corridor towards them. He carefully removed Larissa's arm from around his shoulders, and smiled as his friends started to run, their boots thudding on the grey floor.

They crashed into him, shouting and yelling and asking a hundred questions at once, and despite it all, despite the pain in his chest and the tiredness in his limbs, he started to laugh. Larissa joined in, throwing her arms round them all and holding them tightly.

"It's so good to see you," said Matt, his eyes wet with tears. "Larissa told us you were OK, that you'd made it out, but until I saw for myself..."

"You got Valeri, Jamie," said Kate, her eyes wide. "I can't believe it. You got him."

"*We* got him," said Jamie. "Me and Valentin. Then him and Larissa chased after Dracula. Can you believe that? They *chased* him, on their own."

Kate nodded. "She told us. It's unbelievable."

"It isn't," said Jamie, and gave his girlfriend a long look. "I saw it with my own eyes. Turner tried to stop her until Henry Seward overruled him. But she was going anyway."

Larissa blushed, her cheeks turning a beautiful pale pink, and smiled at him.

"We saw Admiral Seward," said Matt. "We came up to help when everyone started arriving. I never really thought I'd see him again."

"Neither did I," said Jamie. "I don't think anyone did."

There was a loud crackle from the speakers set at intervals along the corridor, followed by Paul Turner's amplified voice. The Security Officer, or Interim Director, or whatever he now was, sounded more exhausted than Jamie had ever heard him, but his voice still contained its usual streak of steel.

"Attention everyone currently hearing my voice," he said. "With the exception of medical personnel, please gather at once in the Ops Room on Level 0. Those of you who do not call the Loop home, please find a member of Blacklight to show you the way. Thank you."

Jamie looked round at his friends. "Come on," he said. "We'll go together."


Nobody sat down in the Ops Room.

The chairs were still there, the plastic seats that had last been occupied as Cal Holmwood gave what would now stand as his final briefing, but they had been pushed to the sides of the room, leaving a wide space that was now full of men and women. Jamie noted the subtle differences in uniform that identified Operators from Russia, Germany, America and South Africa, saw the white coats of the Science Division, the pale, shocked faces of the Blacklight Operators who had manned the Loop while their friends and colleagues fought for their lives. Standing near the back, his face pale, his eyes clear, was Aleksandr Ovechkin, talking quietly to Bob Allen. The two Directors seemed to be struggling to stay upright; it looked like a strong gust of wind would have blown them over. Notably missing from the assembly, along with the men and women working furiously in the infirmary, was Frankenstein. The monster was still in his wolf form, and had been sealed into one of the maintenance hangars out by the runway; it had been deemed too dangerous to try and get him down to his usual cell on Level H.

The room fell silent as Paul Turner stepped through the door and made his way up to the lectern at the front. For a long moment, he didn't speak, just looked out over the bloodied ranks of men and women who had fought and survived.

"Nothing I say," he said, eventually, "will lessen the pain of this moment. Nothing will bring back those we have lost. Investigations are under way, reports are being prepared, and briefings will begin tomorrow. But for now I would ask nothing more from you than a minute's silence."

Turner typed briefly on the lectern's terminal and the wall screen behind him bloomed into life. What it showed, in plain white letters on a black background, was a list of names, a list that was horribly long. He turned to face it, then lowered his head. As one, the crowd of men and women behind him did the same.

Jamie stared at the floor. He felt Larissa's hand slowly move into his, and held it gratefully. The names made real the horror they had endured in the courtyard of Château Dauncy; by necessity, he had made himself numb to the real cost of their actions. The operation, its priorities and its success, had been all he had allowed himself to think about. As people fell around him, Jamie had forced himself not to really see them.

Now he would.

He raised his head and looked at the names, feeling the truth of what each one truly meant. They represented parents who had lost their children, boys and girls who had lost fathers and mothers, brothers and friends who had left holes in the lives of their loved ones that nothing would ever fill.

He saw Cal Holmwood's name halfway down the first column. Patrick Williams was near the bottom of the second.

On the low stage at the front of the room, Paul Turner raised his head and turned back to the lectern, his face shockingly pale. He tapped the terminal a second time, then faced the screen as everyone in the Ops Room lifted their heads. Jamie could see tears on many of the faces, men and women holding each other up, arms round shoulders, hands clasped in hands.

The screen changed, the list of the dead replaced by a large digital clock. It read 00:00:00:53 and was counting steadily down.

Jamie watched, his hand still entwined with Larissa's. Beside him, he heard Matt breathing deeply, and out of the corner of his eye he saw Kate's face set in a tight expression of determination.

*00:00:00:45*
*00:00:00:44*
*00:00:00:43*

He glanced around the silent Ops Room. Every pair of eyes was fixed on the screen. He saw Jack Williams standing near the front, Angela Darcy and Dominique Saint-Jacques holding him up by his shoulders, and his heart went out to his friend.

*00:00:00:31*
*00:00:00:30*
*00:00:00:29*

Jamie looked up at Paul Turner, standing alone on the stage, and wondered how the man had even been able to step on to another battlefield, given what had happened to his son. In truth, he could not begin to imagine how the brilliant, glacial Major even managed to get out of bed every morning.

*00:00:00:17*

*00:00:00:16*

*00:00:00:15*

Valentin Rusmanov was standing by the door, watching the countdown with an unreadable expression on his narrow face, a face that was still covered with the dried blood of his brother.

*00:00:00:10*

*00:00:00:09*

*00:00:00:08*

Jamie squeezed Larissa's hand. It felt as though every single person in the Ops Room was holding their breath.

*00:00:00:02*

*00:00:00:01*

*00:00:00:00*

"Time's up," he whispered.

# ZERO HOUR

# EPILOGUE
# HAPPILY EVER AFTER

### TWO DAYS LATER

Larissa Kinley took a deep breath and knocked on her boyfriend's door.

The process of repairing the reeling, battered Department was ongoing in every corner of the Loop, and she had done her part, and more; she had patrolled, and fought, and done everything asked of her by Paul Turner, who was adjusting as quickly as humanly possible to his new role as Director. Henry Seward had been given a mandatory leave of absence, to recover from the ravages of his captivity, and the Security Officer had shouldered the burden that had so worn down Cal Holmwood with typical cold precision. Broken bones were healing, cuts and bruises were beginning to fade, and recruitment to fill the gaps left by those lost in France was already under way; physically, at least, Blacklight was recovering. But lurking in the background, more poisonous and dangerous than any wound, was the conviction that had settled deeply into the ranks of Operators and staff: the belief that it was all now utterly pointless.

The consensus of opinion was that they had missed their one chance to destroy Dracula. Nobody was being blamed, out loud at least, but it had been adopted as fact by an ever-increasing number of the men and women who populated the Loop. The first vampire's rise was complete, and Zero Hour had come and gone. They were still standing, but for how much longer?

Larissa refused to surrender to this line of thinking. She believed there was a chance, no matter how small or how rapidly diminishing it might be, that they could still prevail. She had seen Dracula up close, closer than anyone else apart from Valentin Rusmanov, and had seen the fear on his face as the Battle of Château Dauncy neared its conclusion, when he had been confronted by men and women who were not afraid of him, and who were powerful enough to hurt him, even destroy him.

She knew she would spend the rest of her life second-guessing her decision to take what remained of Valentin and flee, rather than fight. But she also had no doubt that the chance to test herself against Dracula would come again, a prospect her vampire side, which had become louder and more insistent than ever, was positively relishing.

*One shot*, she thought. *Just one more shot at him. That's all I ask.*

The events of Zero Hour had made one thing abundantly clear to her, solidifying something she had always known, deep down. Although she could still not be one hundred per cent certain that it was Julian Carpenter whom Cal Holmwood had greeted in the hangar, she no longer cared; she was going to tell Jamie what she had heard, and let him decide for himself what he wanted to do. If the frightened masses within the Department were correct, and the end of the world was truly nigh, she had no intention of taking something so potentially important to her grave with her. She was going to tell her boyfriend and to hell with the consequences.

If Paul Turner had her court-martialled, so be it.

If Jamie never wanted to speak to her again, so be it.

She would tell him what she knew, and if he still cared to know the truth about herself and Tim Albertsson, she would tell him that too.

*No more secrets,* she told herself. *Like we promised, but never really delivered. Time for a clean slate.*

She knocked on the door again, listening for sounds of movement from inside her boyfriend's quarters; Jamie could usually be relied upon for a low volley of swearing and grumbling whenever anyone knocked on his door.

But there was nothing.

Larissa frowned and pulled her console from her belt. She opened the messaging function, entered Jamie's name, and tapped out a short message.

### Where are you?

She replaced the console on her belt and flew towards the lift at the end of the Level B corridor, trying to ignore the tiny knot of worry that had risen into her stomach.

"Where are we going?" asked Jamie, as the double doors swung shut behind them. "And what's so important that we have to go right this minute?"

Frankenstein shook his head. "You're going to have to trust me, Jamie."

He rolled his eyes. Operational Squad J-5, which had mercifully survived the Battle of Château Dauncy intact, had been stood down for the night, and Jamie had been looking forward to the possibility of sleeping for longer than four hours. He had been intending to drag Larissa and his friends to the officers' mess for a drink when Frankenstein had approached him outside the Level 0 lift, and told him there was somewhere he needed to take him. Jamie had sighed, but followed the monster back along the corridor towards the hangar; if Frankenstein said it was important, then it most likely was.

The two men walked quickly through the hangar and pulled open the doors of one of the black SUVs parked against the wall. Jamie slid into the passenger seat as the monster climbed behind the wheel and keyed the ignition. The big engine growled, then settled, as the car sped out across the base, the artificial canopy shimmering above them in the dark gloom of the evening, the huge ultraviolet bombs standing silently at regular intervals across the grounds; having them permanently armed and ready had been one of Paul Turner's first orders upon taking charge of the Department.

They passed through the authorisation tunnel, roared past the protesters' encampment without slowing, and out on to civilian roads.

"You're really not going to tell me anything?" asked Jamie.

"I'm sorry," said Frankenstein, his eyes fixed on the road. "I made a promise."

"To who?" asked Jamie.

"I can't tell you that," said Frankenstein.

Jamie frowned at the monster for a long moment, then shrugged and sat back in his seat. "This better be worth it," he said. "This was probably going to be my only night off before the world ends."

Frankenstein smiled, but didn't reply.

The steady rumbling of the engine and the comfortable seat beneath him sent tiredness flooding through Jamie, and he felt his eyelids begin to flutter. He forced them open, and saw Frankenstein glance over at him. The monster had an expression on his grey-green face that was almost kind.

"Get some sleep," said Frankenstein. "I'll wake you when we get there."

Jamie nodded, leant his head against the window, and closed his eyes.

When he opened them again, Frankenstein was shaking him gently.

They were parked outside a small cottage at the end of a gravel track; Jamie craned round in his seat and saw no other houses. Beyond the small row of trees that stood on his side of the car, Jamie could see a huge expanse of flat countryside, a landscape of browns and greens that seemed to go on forever.

"They're the Norfolk Broads," said Frankenstein, as though reading his mind.

He pushed open the door and stepped down on to the track, his limbs stiff and aching. Frankenstein didn't move, and Jamie stuck his head back into the car.

"Aren't you coming?" he asked.

Frankenstein shook his head.

Jamie frowned, and pushed the door shut. He walked round the front of the vehicle and stopped before a small garden gate; it opened on to a short path that led to the cottage's front door.

The house was low, built of white stone with a red tiled roof. Smoke curled slowly from a chimney, billowing up into the darkening sky. Jamie took a deep breath, lifted the latch, and pushed the gate open.

His boots crunched on gravel as he approached the door, his eyes fixed on the brass knocker that hung in the centre of red panels of wood. There was nothing obviously threatening about this place, but for some reason he was nervous; his heart was beating hard in his chest, and adrenaline was dripping slowly into his limbs, causing them to tremble slightly. He could feel heat behind his eyes, and pushed it back, preventing it from bursting into the glowing red light that he was still far from used to.

Jamie stopped on the stone front step and reached out with a gloved hand. He gripped the knocker, rapped it twice against the door, then stood back, and waited.

The door swung open with a long creak and Jamie staggered backwards, his eyes wide, his heart stopped in his chest, as he stared at something impossible.

His father was standing in the doorway.

# TO BE
# CONCLUDED...

# ACKNOWLEDGEMENTS

As ever, my gratitude is due first to my agent Charlie Campbell and my editor Nick Lake, the former for making sure this book got written, the latter for making it as good as it could be.

My girlfriend Sarah put up with the long writing process, and even longer edit, with seemingly endless patience. This was a hard book, one that took its toll on me and the people around me, but she braved the worst of the storm without complaint. Her support humbles me.

Sam Swinnerton, Hannah Bourne, and everyone at HarperCollins Children's Books, for their endless enthusiasm and creativity.

Mum, Peter, Sue, Ken, Kay, Tony, Kevin, Jo. For always managing to keep the fear out of your eyes when you asked 'how's the book going?'

My friends, who helped in ways far too numerous to list. Joe Donaldson, Mick Watson, Janie and Jon Thorn, James Smythe, Jared Shurin, Anne Perry, Lou Morgan, Patrick Ness, Jon Oliver, James Dawson, Tom Pollock, Kim Curran, Amy McCulloch.

And lastly, and most importantly, my endless thanks to everyone who has read the series so far, especially those of you who have taken the time to send me Tweets and messages and emails. Without you I would just be shouting into a void.

Will Hill
London, February 2014

# DEPARTMENT 19

# DARKEST NIGHT

## THE BLOOD-POUNDING CONCLUSION

# EPIC

## IN THE

## DEPARTMENT 19 SERIES.

The brave men and women of Department 19 have fought Dracula at every turn, but now Zero Hour has passed and the ancient vampire is at full strength.

Inside Department 19, the Operators are exhausted and fractured. Jamie, Larissa, Matt and Kate are each struggling with their own demons. When the friends need each other most, they are further apart than ever.

Outside the Department, the world reels from the revelation that vampires are real. Violence and paranoia spread around the globe and, when it finally comes, Dracula's opening move is more vicious than anyone could have imagined.

A final battle looms between the forces of darkness and the last, massed ranks of those who stand against it. A battle that will define the future of humanity. A battle that simply cannot be lost...

# COMING JUNE 2015